About the Author

Henry Mill Phillips is a pen name. The author spent his formative years and working life in Birmingham and the Black Country before retiring to South Wales. Married, he is a lifelong martial artist with an interest in military history and a passion for nature and all of her creatures.

Dedicated to the spirit and people of the Black Country and to Holly Lodge, my alma mater.

Henry Mill Phillips

Black Hearts and
Blue Devils

AUSTIN MACAULEY PUBLISHERS™

LONDON * CAMBRIDGE * NEW YORK * SHARJAH

A CIP catalogue record for this title is available from the British Library.

ISBN 9781398404847 (Paperback)
ISBN 9781398404854 (Hardback)
ISBN 9781398404861 (ePub e-book)

www.austinmacauley.com

First Published 2022
Austin Macauley Publishers Ltd®
1 Canada Square
Canary Wharf
London
E14 5AA

For information and inspiration, I am indebted to the Black Country Living Museum, Dudley Castle and Zoo, and the Black Country Bugle weekly publication, as well as to many publications and websites, chief of which have been the following:

Black Country Bugle (website).
Black Country Muse, particularly its section on Blackheath.
Britain in Old Photographs Series.
British History On-Line.
Hitchmough's Black Country Pubs.
Made in Oldbury.
Rowley Village.

For Background to the places and stories in this book please visit the Facebook page entitled "Black Hearts and Blue Devils" and/or visit the website at https://henrymillphillips.ampbk.com/

Preface

The first thing I wish to impart to you, the prospective reader, is that this is a story from the late 1880s about the Black Country. Or at least certain parts of the Black Country. And, being Smethwick born and Black Country by inclination, I will state here and now that I include my town of birth as being part of the Black Country. There are those who disagree with this designation, I know. All I can say is that I would in turn disagree with them: no letters or emails please!

But seriously now, the second thing which you need to know, which should be soon apparent, but which I ask you to bear in mind when reading, is that this is a work of fiction, albeit centred around areas, stories and events which will be well known to serious Black Country aficionados. If you are one of these, I would at the outset ask for your patience and indulgence whenever you find that, in the interests of a good yarn, or in my ignorance, I have altered facts, or embroidered upon, or diminished any other version of that same Black Country anecdote, with which you yourself are familiar. That goes for my taking certain liberties with geography and timescale too. Having granted me that concession, I hope that you will find this book entertaining.

Of course, if you are someone who knows little of the Black Country and its traditions already, all that I need to say to you at this point is, enjoy!

Thirdly, the characters. Needless to say, these, with one or two exceptions, are just as fictional as the rest of the story, there as vehicles of the plot, not as historical figures to be hunted down on the internet. Having said that I have endeavoured to mostly use names, surnames at least, that I know exist or existed in the various locations depicted, primarily Blackheath, Rowley Regis and Smethwick. And I would be giving nothing away if I were to here mention the Lively family. So I will.

The Lively's, certain of them, are some of the main characters in the story. In contrast to some of the other names and characters, they are, all of them, complete figments of my imagination. The name itself came across my desk by chance while I happened to be looking for one. Random enough, so I took it.

Fourthly, perhaps the biggest bone of contention: Dialect and Accent. Now, I was not around in the 1880s and who knows how the spoken 'spake' has changed since? One thing that I do know is that there would have been a very noticeable difference between the use of the second person singular and the second person plural. Coward that I am, I have not attempted to illustrate that difference, sticking mostly to the plural. But the changes go beyond that: I know that I have seen, and heard, huge changes in my own time. As a young man living in Oldbury in the late seventies or early eighties I met some young ladies from either Cradley or Cradley Heath (apologies, I now know that not distinguishing between the two is tantamount to sacrilege) and had great trouble understanding them. I knew what they meant of course, but could I make out the words? No. Then again, when I met my wife's paternal grandmother, who was from Blackheath, she had so many odd turns of phrase (more to do with dialect and a unique lost grammar than accent) that my wife would have to translate. Those were the days, but they are fast disappearing. My point is that accents (and let us for the sake of simplicity restrict ourselves to just those), they do change with the generations, with the geographic area (very tight ones in the past), and with the particular mood of the particular individual at any particular time, and the company he or she happens to be keeping. Therefore, what I have done in these pages is to have certain characters speak in my best written approximation of what I believe a person of that description or area sounds like, or would have sounded like. And the furthest I can go back, in terms of authenticity, is my own lifetime, basing the characters' delivery on my own experience and that of family, particularly that of my wife, who is undeniably a Black Country wench. Of course, there is the added complication that every listener hears the same sounds in their own unique way: I have expressed what I hear, as well as the written word can convey it. Now, having said that, it would be quite a strain on any reader to have to interpret my interpretation of an accent right through the book, so I have limited these 'interpretations' to certain characters and situations, switching also to the occasional non-standard words mid-sentence or paragraph, just to remind the reader where we are and just who any particular character is. The character of Jack Cutler is a good example. Again, I know there will be purists who will not be entirely happy with various renditions, and I do acknowledge in advance that they may have a point! Nevertheless, to the 'outsiders' among you, I hope that my efforts in this regard give you a genuine feeling for the different accents. It all adds to the atmosphere!

Finally, the plot. We have heroes and villains (I invite you to choose your own favourite), and not unexpectedly much of the action revolves around the interaction of those two archetypal categories. Plot and sub plots meander to expose the reader to a sprinkling of the traditions and yarns, those legends and tall tales, of which the fabric of the Black Country is made. As well as to give pause to contemplate the heroic stoicism of all those working men and women who made this country great.

The Black Country has its fair share of myth and legend, its ghosts and ghouls and witches, and, to give the supernatural its due, I have taken two mythical entities and given them parts to play, these being the well-known Spring Heeled Jack, and the lesser-known Blue Devil(s) of Rowley. Another legend, about a certain lodger at a certain canal-side pub, I have taken the liberty of marrying to a related myth and have then pursued that combination to its logical conclusion, very much a fictional one.

But, I am saying too much; so I will stop. Except to again express my sincere hope that you enjoy reading this book.

A word of warning though. Life in the Black Country of the 1880s was no picnic. I have not imagined it so.

Chapter 1

1879

It started to rain. The misty evening dampness was changing to fine drizzle as gravity claimed the specks of silver coalescence. The two mares would appreciate a cooling rest, and Abe asked them to stop as the waggon reached a flattening out of the land near the top of the hill.

He pulled in the brake and looked into the back. There was his precious living cargo: sister and four brothers. All tired, and all depending on him; trusting him. Abraham Lively, at seventeen years of age was head of the family now. His sister Miriam was eighteen months older, but this was a man's world after all. She was sitting between the youngest, arms holding them to her: Frank and Wilf were twins and just coming up to twelve. They weren't sleeping – too uncomfortable for that – but sitting eyes closed with their heads down enveloped by an oilskin. They looked dead beat. Behind them a lump in a blanket on the floor told Abe that brother John was with them, in body at least. He had bagged the best spot when they had started out and had spent a lot of time kipping under his blanket. Though at fifteen John was not the youngest of the brothers, by a count of three, he always seemed to have gotten out of chores which the rest took for granted. Abe knew that John had always been mother's especial favourite. Well, all things pass…

"Where are we then?" The soft voice of Josh, the middle brother, brought Abe back to the here and now.

"Still in Halesowen I think."

"I thought that was Halesowen down there?" A question, not a statement. Josh was looking into his eyes with that honesty and innocence of expression which made everyone love him. Except father that is. Their dad had never taken to Josh. Perhaps that was on account of Josh's fair skin and hair. It made him the odd man out: the other siblings were dark haired with darker skin than Josh, though not as swarthy as their father had been.

"That's the main part of it. This is just the outskirts. Look, there's a farm here. Remind you of home?"

"Home never had all this clattering," returned Josh. "Anyway, it's not home any more, is it? Home's just this waggon now. That's all that's left, and the horses." His voice was steady and even, but there was a sadness there, a fear, which he could not conceal from Abe. Because Abe felt the same.

The farm did remind Josh of home though. It was a little hill farm, just a small steep smallholding in truth, clinging on in the midst of smoke and the soot. In the gathering gloom he could make out two or three pale blobs which were sheep, wandering unconcerned by the ceaseless background din; chewing on the grass and growing fat. A green link to sanity amongst the bricks and noise and dirt of the streets they had passed through since arriving in Halesowen. Josh didn't like Halesowen.

Wilf and Frank were moving around now.

"Are we nearly there then?" said Wilf to nobody in particular.

"No. We're in Halesowen," said Josh.

"You said we would be there before it was dark!" Wilf now directed the accusation at Abe.

"It's not far now," said Abe to them all. He was reasonably sure of that.

"I want a piddle," said Frank as he skipped to the ground, suddenly alive again.

"All right. Just go as far as the bushes over there. There's nobody around. Anybody else?"

As it happened, all of the boys availed themselves of the stop to relieve themselves and stretch their legs, including John, who said nothing to anyone. Miriam stayed put and watched the mares: they weren't used to these sounds and needed reassurance. They all did.

By the time they had all finished poking around the dusk was giving way to night. Abe was last back up on the waggon and he paused to survey the surrounding country. The open fields at the top of the hill afforded a more or less uninterrupted view down onto the land below.

He looked out over an alien world. Not an hour since, they had been driving through bright fields neatly ordered by lines of hedgerows and overlooked by darker patches of woodland on the hills, and all of it bursting with the pressure of life which was welling up through the earth and the roots and the leaves to kiss the sun. Spring had most definitely sprung. But not here. Here Nature was in thrall to something else. Here she was a victim. The short journey through the clickety clack and tapping of the huddled workshops crowding the street below, and the low sighing of the bellows – like the gaspings of an old man with consumption – was as but a dulcet prelude to the vision of brutality now revealed.

In a dark amphitheatre of herculean span a great glow from ten thousand angry red fires mocked the stars in heaven. White mouthed caverns spewed globules of radiance to the rhythmic strokes of falling metal – devils' hammers striking monstrous anvils. Smaller conflagrations burned with an orange glow, sparks scattered from the blows. The canals and waterways running criss-cross hither and thither stood out in patches of reflection like bleeding veins. And the sounds of violence mesmerised him as blow after blow bit into the black body of the beast which lay coiled before him, chained in iron and steel. The hammers fell and the blades carved into that flesh and the beast roared in pain and whimpered and endured. And the smoke trickled as black blood spilling from the black flesh and it swelled the bloated purple pall which clung with crimson edges to far off indigo ridges while the white moon sailed impotent and aloof, like a disenfranchised angel of mercy.

And the demons would never stop, for they were immune to pity.

Abe had heard tales of this 'black country.' But he had not expected this.

"Good God. What have I done?"

Chapter 2

The Royal Oak, 1887

It was a beautiful spring afternoon, as long as you discounted the smoggy haze. To the creakings of springs and leather and the smiting of cobbles with iron, the wedding coach halted outside the Royal Oak. Without delay, the bride and groom descended and entered the lounge of that venerable establishment. It seemed dark inside; the big room shut out much of the sunlight at that time of day, and a couple of gas lamps were fizzling away on low. The woman looked around with a critical eye, but was pleased by what she saw: in front of her and facing the street the well-stocked bar was all gleaming brass and polished oak; the floorboards had been sanded clean; and tables were set out – neatly and without causing a clutter. At each end of the bar, and at some of the tables, blue glass vases contained flowers collected or grown by well-wishers, or so she supposed. There were daffodils and orange chrysanthemums and carnations of various shades of red. To her right a small makeshift stage was already occupied by Ian Smith and the two Fays, setting out their instruments. To her left a low fire glowed in the immaculately blackened grate: the cloudless sky presaged a nip in the air when the sun went down. She saw that the old-fashioned candle chandelier had been dusted down and the light from a score of candles chinked off the crystal and played shapes on the yellowed ceiling. And the smell of the tallow mixed with the whiff of burning coal, and was subsumed within the comforting backdrop of malt and hops. Yes, this would do. This would certainly do.

"Back in a tick," she said to the staff and, "won't be long," to her new husband as, kissing his cheek, she strode upstairs.

She went straight to her room and looked in the mirror. Miriam Beckett, for that's who she was now, was still a damned attractive woman, if she said so herself. Not that other people didn't tell her so, not least her new husband Jack. She was five feet nine, which was almost unheard of tall for a woman of Blackheath. But then again, she was no native: her home had been the sheep-cropped fields and green hills of Shropshire where fresh clean air and clean living engendered sturdier stock. She thought of her brothers. All of them, even the twins now, stood taller than most of the locals, many of whom were regular customers here at the Oak. By and large she found the local men courteous and polite – at least in her presence – and imbued with a resilience which belied their almost universally slight statures. But, raised in the smoke, and driven by the insatiable hunger of the machines, many died young nevertheless: she had heard of men crushed and mangled and burned; some she had seen waste away almost before her eyes. Dr Wharton would call it consumption or pleurisy or polio. She called it hopelessness.

With a shiver, and counting her blessings, she looked back into the mirror, at her dark good looks. No matter what her name, nobody could ever doubt that she was a Lively. And she wanted out of this dress! She had not worn her very best dress for the ceremony: her very best dress was an extravagant claret-red number with velvet panelling. It was a gift from John Henry, God bless him, and she had married him in it – as many locals could no doubt recall. It would not have been a proper choice for today. Instead, she had chosen a dress nearly ten years old, one that had been the prized possession of the young country girl who had left country life behind a lifetime – eight years – ago. It was of good quality – the Livelys had been of the gentry once – and was made of taffeta and cotton in browns and green. The fabric was less heavy than the current fashion, but she had been glad of that as she stood in St. Paul's Church with the sun beating through the stained glass and directly onto the bride and groom. In terms of style, she was pleased with the effect she had achieved by means of the perspicacious purchase and remodelling of a second-hand crinolette which, except to those whose business it was to know such things, made it look quite fashionable. She knew that certain people might 'tut-tut' over the green, unlucky colour to get married in you know. That was a superstition to which Miriam did not subscribe.

There's precious little green around here anyway. It makes a change to see some, she said to herself, persuading herself. And she looked out at the ash-stained street, where the soot sought out any virgin vegetable life, and, for the presumption of staking a claim in its realm of coal and coke and molten metal, choked it to a lingering death…

No, the only downside had been that her shape was no longer that of a girl, but that of a woman. The answer had been to lace up her corset extra tightly. Very tightly. A situation she would now rectify – she intended to do some dancing tonight.

Through the window, she saw her guests, sauntering happily up from Long Lane, the vicar among them. The reverend Ebenezer Hodgetts had removed his dog-collar though that had not improved his florid countenance. No doubt he would be looking forward to sampling her finest ales. Full of life and curly of hair, he was not exactly abstemious for a religious man! It always made her smile.

Hurrying now, she hung up her 'wedding dress', loosened off the whalebone and slipped on a plain black skirt and a white lace blouse, and comfortable shoes. Almost out, she paused. And looked at the barren bed. The bed in which she had slept alone for two years, ever since John Henry had left her. Then she shut the door and skipped downstairs.

#

16

After the service, Abe Lively had shared a ride with the doc., Doctor Wharton, and so had arrived before the foot bound elements. He was half way through his first pint when he saw his sister waltz down and take the arm of her husband of half an hour. Abe was pleased for her. Jack Beckett was a handsome man in his mid-thirties who held down a responsible, and presumably well-paid, job at the brickworks in Old Hill. Like his predecessor, he was an incomer, but in his case only from as far away as Wolverhampton. She needed the support of a man, her brother thought. Not that she was not a strong character in her own right – Abe could testify to that – but she had been lonely. Ever since the death of John Henry in the typhoid outbreak. He knew it, if she wouldn't admit it. Abe had moved into a room at the Oak, she had asked him; would feel more secure with a man on the premises, she had said. He had been happy to agree, even though she would not hear of any rent. He knew she was not exactly rolling in money, however, so he had made up his mind that this would be a temporary arrangement. Temporary had over-stretched its definition by now however, and with the change in circumstances he would have to be thinking about it…

"How are you then, Sis?" he said as he walked over. "Why the change of clothes? I think you can allow yourself a day off!"

"When do I ever get a day off running this place? And I'm very well, thank you for asking. That is, we're very well. Aren't we Jack?" She took Jack's arm and planted a big kiss on his full red lips, her brother in the corner of her eye. Abe was almost embarrassed. He had been the one watching over his sister since John Henry had been gone. He had always been there to keep her safe. He would take a step back now.

"Congratulations again." The round yet solid bulk of Doctor Wharton inserted itself into the scene.

"Why, thank you very much my good doctor," replied the bride whimsically.

"I hope that the two of us can equal your own marital record in due course. How long is it now? 20 years?"

"20 come August."

"And will Mrs Wharton not be joining you this afternoon?"

"Unfortunately no. She went home after the service. As you know, she does a lot of work on behalf of the temperance movement, and it probably wouldn't look proper for her to be seen in this, er, in a public house. No offence meant."

"And none taken, I'm sure. Happily you don't share her convictions in that direction, and luckily for me there's plenty of others of your persuasion. Otherwise I'd be in queer street."

"Well I'm very glad you're not! This is my favourite watering hole in town, you know?"

"Naturally!" beamed Miriam, then turned to Abe. "Abe, little rabbit, don't get too drunk. What would the magistrates say about our fine upstanding police sergeant turning up sloshed for duty tomorrow and a Sunday too?"

17

"Don't know, I'll ask one," said Abe as he turned to the doctor.

"Speaking for the bench," rejoined the balding bulk that was Grayson Wharton, "I'm sure that we would all be prepared to stretch a point – given the occasion!"

The latter remark was for the ears of Abe alone, as the happy couple had already turned away and were busy mingling as the place filled with guests, conversation and the clinking of glasses.

"But if I could just talk shop for a couple of minutes?" continued the magistrate.

"Fire away," said the sergeant.

"Let's sit then." Wharton gestured to a two-man alcove sheltered from the hubbub. "Now," said the older man as they sat, "how's the investigation into the sheep rustling incident going? I know it's not really my place to ask but I'm being pestered by a certain member of the parish council, and…"

"A certain member that happens to double as a sheep farmer?" interrupted the policeman, though he wasn't sure that a few disconnected bits of barely adequate grazing and a handful of scrawny animals could be called any kind of farm.

"A certain member who shall remain nameless Sergeant."

"All right. What does this nameless person expect me to do? We're stretched a bit thin you know. What with all the incomers, this town is growing all the time, and it's not only attracting law abiding folk looking for honest work. Blackheath and Rowley covers more of an area than you might think: we're patrolling almost into Dudley and overlapping with our colleagues in Old Hill, and to the edges of Langley and Halesowen. That's twenty-four hours a day, and that's a lot of ground to cover for a sergeant and four constables."

"Well I'm afraid that you're the victim of your own success. You know how highly the council regards your skills – your arrest and conviction rate is second to none. Big improvement on your predecessor."

My predecessor was a lazy sod who was too soft or too scared to enforce the letter of the law. Of course it's a bloody improvement!

"And," pressed home the doctor, "don't forget that there were just the three of you last year. It's thanks to the goodwill and influence of the council that the force was persuaded to up your number. How's brother Josh liking his new job by the way?"

Trust you to play that card.

"He's adapting well. Safer than working in the mine I think, even if he wasn't actually digging and hauling like most of the other poor bleeders. His height's now an advantage rather than a hindrance."

Men were killed in the mines on a regular basis, that was true, and it meant that the Livelys were obligated to Wharton. Abe said: "All right, look. There are no clues about these sheep. I've asked, but as usual nobody has seen anything. But if they were taken by a gang – and didn't just wander off – then they had to go somewhere for disposal."

"Which brings us to the 'Shoulder Of Mutton' then," said Wharton.

"I suppose it does," said Abe, "and my uncle."

"Glad you said that. There's some might think that you haven't been down that rather obvious avenue for, er, personal reasons," said the magistrate, "though I wouldn't be one of them of course," he added sheepishly as Abe's expression hardened.

"It's my job to enforce the law and bring criminals to justice, without fear or favour. I like to think I have always done that…"

"Granted, granted," agreed Wharton. "No complaints there. No complaints at all."

"Good, wouldn't want to miss out on that, what was it? Exchequer grant, yes. Comes in useful I dare say."

"Yes, yes. You know it does, and we're all jolly grateful I'm sure," the doctor assured him.

"Well then," continued the sergeant, "as long as there's criminals out there, I'll keep arresting them. That's what I signed up to, but, as I say, we are stretched and there is a limit: we could double our number and still have barely enough time to just move on tramps and deal with the day-to-day street rogues and vagrants. A no nonsense, hard line, was what I was told. That's how they run it, we run it, out of Old Hill and I'm obliged to follow that. I'm only a lowly sergeant remember," added Abe pointedly. "Unless the Chief Constable himself has had a change of heart?"

"I think I can confidently say that he has not," replied the doctor, "about the policy I mean."

"So. It's a question of how to efficiently use our time," continued the sergeant, "we don't generally get the luxury of having time to ask pointless questions. However…"

"You will endeavour to find the time now?" anticipated the doctor.

"As it seems to be bothering you so much, yes. Supposed to be a day off tomorrow, morning at least, but I'll go and see my uncle instead."

"Good. As long as you are seen to go through the motions I think that will be enough."

"Even if it gets us nowhere?"

"Even if it gets us nowhere. Another pint?"

"Certainly." Abe finished his dregs and handed his tankard over. "Cheers."

#

Daylight was ebbing away when John Lively stepped in. He had not attended the church service but had worked his scheduled Saturday shift. He hadn't tried for a swap with anyone on a different rota. Too much trouble. His choice, and he needed the money. In any case, unlike his brothers, and his sister presumably, he didn't believe in all this Jesus stuff, much as it had been stuffed down his throat as a boy. So, after a hard day puddling and hammering viscous steel he was ready for a drink. You couldn't count the three pints consumed on shift out of his allowance – that was just necessary rehydration.

So, clocking off and leaving the foundry, he had stepped out with a purpose, past the Brades Works, past excavations and hillocks of spoil, until, quite soon, he reached Blackheath proper. Crossing Long Lane to a small row of shops he went down a narrow entry and let himself in by the back door to his lodging house behind the bakers. He had topped up his wash jug from the supply left for him by his landlady, the baker's wife, in the scullery and had gone back to his room for a wash-down. It was just a single room, but there was only him and it was of a decent size. John considered himself lucky – at least he was free. In the winter, it had had the advantage of being if not warm then not cold to come home to, having the benefit of the ovens next door warming his walls. It was not cold tonight and he did not anticipate lighting a fire. So, he had shook and folded his work clothes and placed them in a small trunk which doubled as a chair. He had thrown his underwear, vest and pants, into an old basket and donned the clean set which he had left folded on the bed. Feeling much refreshed, he pulled a smaller trunk, of cedar, from under the bed, clanging it against the chamber pot as he did so. This box needed a key, which John retrieved from a hiding place in the bedstead. He set the trunk upon the bed and opened it. On top, wrapped in clean sacking was a heavy cold lump. He put this to one side and took out his best clothes: white shirt and sky-blue neckerchief, dark blue waistcoat, navy flannel trousers, and his pride and joy, a heavy and elaborate cavalry tunic. The man he had won it from, in a game of cards, had said that it was an officer's jacket, hussars. Be that as it may, it was certainly eye-catching, if obviously faded. And it set off his waistcoat and trousers beautifully, it being blue with gold gimp loops (which however John was not in the habit of fastening) and edged with gold braid. At some point the sleeve brading denoting rank had been picked off, but it was still the best jacket that anyone had around here, in his opinion. And it suited him down to the ground!

Now, standing in the doorway of the Royal Oak, all eyes were drawn to the powerful looking man in the blue jacket. He could tell. So, he would let them look; let them take it all in: his physique, that tunic, his shiny greased black hair and a dark skin made even darker – exotic looking – by months of tanning in the furnace rooms. Unlike his big brother, John did not cover his good looks with facial hair and was fastidious about shaving. He liked to think he looked dangerous…

"John! Where have you been?"

The scene was spoiled by the appearance of brother Abe. One of the few men John considered could rival him. A man who had always overshadowed him.

"I've had to work, haven't I? I told you about it."

"So you did. How about a drink then?"

"You buying?"

"I'm buying."

"Lead on then!"

As they neared the bar Ian Smith struck up a suitably jolly tune on his squeeze box accompanied by the two ladies on fiddle. Immediately, enthused dancers appeared, to

20

glide through the horizontal seams of tobacco smoke, scattering them into blue wisps which spiralled around like phantom revellers, and were gone.

Drinks secured Abe asked "Have you seen Miriam yet?"

"I've just got here."

"You ought to pay your respects. We missed you in church."

"No helping it. I had to work, didn't I? I'll see her in a minute."

On cue, their sister materialised, put down her pint and hugged the two men to her.

"Hello again Bunny Rabbit. Hello John. You enjoying yourself my darling?"

John kissed his sister's cheek. *He was always bunny, or little rabbit. I'm always just John.*

"Hello Sis," said brother John and looked her up and down. "You look lovely," then, "you didn't get married in that did you?"

"Of course not," said Miriam.

"Which you would know if you'd been there," added Abe.

"I've already told you. I had to work. Some of us haven't got such a cushy life as others."

"It's all right. I know. I know," said Miriam, "and I know it's been a bit rough for you lately. Have you seen Josie? I thought she might come…"

"No. She's avoiding me, and I'm avoiding her. She's back with her dad," returned John sourly.

"Any chance of you two reconciling?" asked Abe.

"Joking en't ya?"

"And what of little Royston?" asked Miriam.

"Still with Josie's aunt in Dudley. It's for the best. They're childless now and I think they need him as much as he needs them. He needs a woman looking after him and Josie can't squeeze him in at her dad's. No, he's better off where he is."

Leaving you unfettered and fancy free, thought Abe.

"Do you go to see him?" enquired Miriam.

"Look. This is a celebration isn't it? Let's not talk about my problems," sidestepped John.

Jack Beckett appeared and insisted on shaking hands with the brothers. Looking at John he said:

"Oy up John. Got that coot on agen? Yoh'll wear it 'aht! Anyroad, nice to see ya. Ow bist?"

"Cor complain. Ow am yoh?" returned the man wearing 'that coot.'

Abe was always fascinated by the way his younger brothers, especially this one, could switch to the local 'spake' when it suited. Abe himself didn't notice the dialect when speaking to strangers, but it did sound odd coming from family. As he enjoyed his beer, half listening to the rhythm of the words being exchanged, he realised that they no longer consisted merely of pleasantries.

"An' mek sure yoh look after 'er, or you'll have me to answer to," said John who, observed Abe, had switched back to his usual mode of speech in mid-sentence. Probably a sign that drink was taking over. It had seemed to really have taken a hold of late. His father's weakness…

"I'm sure that Miriam can look after herself John. Be a good lad. And smile please!" said Abe in a cross between his big brother's and his policeman's voice. Then, before Jack could react, he whisked the newly-weds away to meet a fictitious well-wisher.

John let them go with a shrug and lent back, a little too nonchalantly, onto the bar. During his conversation with his siblings he had been half watching a particularly attractive auburn-haired girl, sitting chatting with two friends, much plainer friends, at a table at a window. The last of the sunlight was penetrating the square panes and played on the silky chestnut of her hair and made her skin glow so that she shimmered within an aura that touched him from twenty feet away. He found himself breathing it in, swallowing it. It smelled of lavender and tasted of sex.

He knew who she was. He had spoken to her before, in passing. But he had been with Josie then. Not that that need have stopped him, but it did make for complications. This girl though, she was a cut above his usual conquests, and he was little unsure of his charms with someone like this. Gwendoline, her name was, Gwendoline Cavenny. He would get another pint and amble over…

The barman handed over a fresh foaming jug of dark mild ale and John turned back into the room. But he couldn't see Gwendoline. Then he did. She was dancing. With Abe! Well, thanks for that! Talk about brotherly love, you bastard! He sank his pint and ordered another.

Abe returned the young lady to her friends. They had all worked together as order and invoice clerks in the offices of a dry goods warehouse and Abe had made their acquaintance when he had investigated, then arrested, their supervisor, Bernard Docker, for petty embezzlement. Gwen had succeeded him as supervisor, which had been quite a coup for a woman. Docker was still in Stafford gaol – would be for five years – doing hard labour. Not a young man, he might not survive it. Wife and kids had given up the struggle and now resided in the workhouse, or rather, separate workhouses. It was a genuine pity, but Abe could not let pity sway him. His duty had to override pity. Without law and order there would be a lot more suffering in the world. The law ensured the greatest good for the greatest number. Docker had betrayed his employer, his family, and society when he had done what he had done. And that's how Abraham Lively saw it….

He kissed Gwen's hand and took his leave of the three girls. She was a pretty thing and he felt she was attracted to him. But Abe's heart was elsewhere, fickle as it was.

#

The night was wearing on and the twins were enjoying the warmth that came from a good fire, good beer, and the company of a couple of girls. As the beer went down the girls, it seemed to the boys, got prettier. The girls pretended not to notice the effect; they just let the twins keep buying them drinks. Sissy and Dora were proper working wenches, brought up on hard graft and ale, and could match the two 'chaps' pint for pint. They were sisters and earned a living as chain-makers. Dora was the elder, only by three to four years, but three or four years was a long time here. At twenty-four she had already been widowed, and, perforce, was looking for a husband and father for her two boys. Her man had worked in the deafening confines of the pressing shop at Messrs. B&B Price, a fact which had contributed – with a belly-full of beer – to his precipitate death by runaway omnibus, as he hadn't heard it coming. Years of long hard graft had begun to nibble away at Dora's delicate youthful features. Little sister Sissy, who actually stood half a foot taller, seemed as yet unscathed. Both welcomed a night out with two young chaps even though, and probably because, it was 'just a bit of fun.' These two Livelys had determined to live off brains, not brawn. The twins were now nineteen years of age, and had made the most of the one thing their father's creditors had been unable to take from them, that is to say their education. That, and the respect which the community had for their big brother and sister, had enabled Wilf to land a job four years ago at the local apothecary's on High Street. The establishment was a not immodest concern whose owner, Jonathan Hingley, was a widower, getting on in years, suffering from gout and a partial paralysis of his left arm courtesy of a brush with polio as a youngster. Given these handicaps the old man had come to rely more and more upon Wilf who in consequence was doing all right, thank you very much. Frank had taken longer to settle, and had seen his share of the insides of forges and factories, a fact which ensured that he would be forever grateful to the Reverend Smith. The Methodist minister had provided the introduction which meant that Frank the schoolmaster now spent his days wrestling with nothing more taxing than the odd truant, rather than with hurtling lengths of murderous steel. Glancing around, the schoolmaster was just thinking that he ought to say hello to his benefactor, perhaps buy him a drink, when he was recalled to the moment by a blue shape lurching out of the periphery. It plonked itself down between Wilf and his girl, prising them apart.

"All right lads?" said John. "Good do en't it? Is this your girlfriend then Wilfy? A big 'un en't she?"

Sissy was not the kind of girl to take this kind of thing lying down. She was indeed a big girl, as girls went in Blackheath. She was twenty-one years old and at her physical peak: five-feet-eight of anvil-conditioned bone and sinew with an attractive, almost feral, face. One of the first things you noticed about her was that she had well-built forearms and strong hands dotted with red flecks where errant sparks had burnt them. The scars might have looked incongruous on a girl dressed for a night out, but not here. Around here working with hammer and anvil and hot metal was women's work as well as men's...

But tough as Sissy might be, she hesitated to respond to John's insensitive comment. She knew that this man in the fancy coat was Wilf's brother, and she knew of his reputation. In the interval, sensing through the alcoholic haze that he had gone too far, John continued,

"No offence, love. I like a big strong woman. I think they can be most attractive."

"Sissy, this is my brother John," said Wilf.

"Pleased to meet you Sissy." John offered a calloused hand, which, after a pause, was met by another calloused hand. Each squeezed and tested the mettle of the other before disengaging.

"Hello John." Sissy decided to humour him. He was obviously as pissed as a rat.

"Wilf's tode me a lot about ya." Not that Wilf had told her anything about John at all, but she hoped that the cliché would act as a mild put-down.

It worked. Mistake. John decided to blow it up out of all proportion.

"Have you now you little rake? Been talking behind my back have you?"

Frank knew the signs. Unlike Wilf he drank with men like this regularly, old factory mates. But this one was bigger. He liked John – a lot – but when he was like this he was just a different person: a living vessel for the Demon Drink. Frank tried to distract him:

"John. What you drinking?"

"Get me another…no, tell you what, get me a whisky."

Shit – he was at the whisky stage. What's more, he was coming over to Frank and Dora now. Frank saw Wilf breathe a sigh of relief; couldn't blame him, he had always been the delicate one of the pair. Still, this version of John was really too much for either of them to handle.

Addressing Dora now, John said, "Hello my darling. I'm John."

"John. Come to the bar with me," attempted Frank.

"I'm sure you can manage little brother. I'll just sit here and keep your girlfriend company. Matter of fact, you go with him Wilf, and I'll keep both of them company. Go on, I'll give you the money for mine when you come back."

Sissy was getting tired of this. "We doh need your company and we day ask for it."

"Ar, that's right. And yoh've 'ad enough to drink a'ready," said Dora.

"Ah bay gooin' anyweer," said John, now mocking their speech in a slow high-pitched musical tone.

"Except home. With me." Rescued by the long arm of the law! Which reached over and gently pulled John away from the threatened affray. "Come on John, I'm going your way," said Abe. "We can have a night cap at yours."

John scowled then shrugged. "Good idea. I could do with some fresh air." And they left.

When that 'fresh' air did hit him John realised how drunk he was. And was actually glad that Abe had pulled him out when he did. How many times had he embarrassed himself in his cups? Besides, he wouldn't want to throw up on his tunic. All at once, he was back at his place, with Abe.

Abe watched as John pottered around the small but neatly arranged lodgings. Having taken off his precious jacket he dug out two metal cups and half a bottle of what looked like gin. He poured out a couple of measures and handed one to Abe, who was sitting on a chest. John sat on the bed.

"What's this then?" said Abe.

"Just a drop of gin."

"Not moonshine then?"

"No. It's proper stuff – officer! No, honestly. Drink up, it'll put hairs on your chest."

Abe thought of asking to see the label before he put the stuff to his lips. But it smelt like proper gin and he had no wish to agitate his brother who had grown quite affable. So he drank.

"Remember when we got here? Didn't have many hairs on our chests then," reminisced Abe.

"I certainly didn't," said John, "I was only a kid. Now it feels like I was never a kid. Where's the time gone? This place has driven us apart you know. I wish we had never come here. I wish everything was back how it was when we were all back home. With mom and dad."

Abe said: "Except that mom and dad are dead and going back's not an option. You know that. There's no home, no family, and no work for us back there. It's all gone… Jesus, you can remember what it was like – even people with work to do were slowly starving to death."

"That wouldn't happen to us," muttered John.

"Why not? Without the wealth and privileges of our family, without our inheritance, we would be reduced to manual labour – amongst people the Lively's had traditionally lorded it over. There would have been no swanning about and drinking for you. You would have been too busy thinking about food! At least here we eat."

John thought about that. "Don't exaggerate. This is the eighties."

Abe took another sip of gin and looked at his young brother. Their lives as sons of the flamboyant Gabriel Lively had indeed seemed charmed. But the young John that had raced them to the pond, and climbed trees, and just rambled over the clean green hills, through endless summer days, he could see no trace of. There was just a man with sad eyes.

"Maybe it's a bit of an exaggeration," said Abe. "But we've done all right here, haven't we?"

"You and Miriam have dropped on your feet, and Josh with you I suppose. But some of us are only really surviving. Look at this." John gestured around the room. "What have I got to look forward to?"

"You've got your family."

"What – a wife who hates me and a son I may never even see again?"

"What about us. Your brothers. And Miriam?"

"That's what I say! We're not close any more. We've drifted apart." John finished his gin.

"That's just what happens when people grow up! They start new families and their lives take different paths. But there's no need to lose the old family ties. They're still there."

"I don't think so. Coming here changed everything. We've swapped green fields and happiness for smoke and hopelessness. If I were a religious man in any way, I would say that God had forsaken this place along with the people in it. All the churches they've erected round here make no difference – in fact they prove my point. I'll tell you one thing I believe in though. The Devil. He exists. He owns factories, and mines."

"Bloody hell John," said Abe, "stop feeling so bloody sorry for yourself. There's plenty in the workhouse worse off."

"Yeah, and we'll all be joining them sooner or later."

"Don't be so daft. It's the booze talking."

"Yes it is! And it's right. Funny thing, eh? Drinking takes away the pain, but when that's gone you can get clarity: you can stop and think about what it is you're running from; so the pain starts again. There's no hope for us you know."

"What do you mean no hope? We've all heard about your gallivanting. You seem to enjoy yourself well enough."

"You think you know me?"

"'Course I do. You're my little brother."

"You knew the kid from Nash. I'm not him."

"We all change. It's called growing up."

"It's not that. It's this place. It's black and depressing."

"You could leave."

"It's a big decision," said John, "I'd be on my own. I've got friends here at least. And everybody I can call family's here. Even if they don't want to see me."

"That's not true." Abe found himself suddenly intrigued by the grain of the wooden chest and looked down to feel it. He needn't have bothered – John was contemplating the bottom of his empty cup.

"You can be an awkward bugger," continued Abe.

"Is that what I am?"

"Yes. But that's just you. Always has been. It's part of your charm. If ever there was any trouble around, it always found you."

"That's me, a picture of bad luck."

"Nah. Nothing serious ever happens."

"Yet!" corrected John.

"Nor will it. Remember when we first got here and the three of us went to the fair at the bottom of Powke Lane?"

"Yes, I do," said John, a jovial aspect stealing onto his saturnine features despite himself, "could have been very nasty that."

"Stay on for your free ride!" intoned Abe, rather loudly. And they saw the scene again. Abe and Miriam and John had paid their money and got on a particularly fast merry-go round. They played a hurdy-gurdy tune and spun you around for a good three minutes. On this occasion however, the 'John jinx' had struck and the rough looking machine operator stationed at the centre of the ride – like a vicious spider in a web according afterwards to John – had decided to treat everybody to a 'free ride.' No problem there you might say. Except that during the initial ride and for reasons possibly unknown even to himself, John had managed to detach himself from the trusty steed to which he had been clinging and for a full half-minute at least had been reduced to a desperate scrabble, on the decking, with half of his cramping body hanging over the outer edge of the speeding ride, only clinging on with one leg hooked around a rail and his fingertips inserted between the boards.

"That bastard," said John. "I was so relieved when we started to slow down, then he did that! It was like torture."

"I don't think he even saw you down there," Abe chuckled, "I think he did it to impress Miriam."

"He must have known!" protested John, a sparkle back in his eye, "you two saw me!"

"I know, but there was nothing we could do. We were laughing too much."

"Bastards!"

"What the hell were you thinking? What were you doing on the floor?"

"I was thinking, I hope I don't get my head squashed by a wooden horse, or get catapulted off into the crowd. That would have shown 'em though…"

"And all us bastards could do was laugh!"

"Yes. Bastards!"

Both were laughing heartily now. Brothers in booze, and blood.

When the laughter ebbed, the mood changed.

"Those were the days," said John.

"Certainly were. And there are plenty more to come."

"Can't wait," said John. "I'm going to have some water. Want some?"

"No. About time I was going," said Abe. He went to take out their father's watch, but thought better of it.

27

So, they shook hands on the step and through the small window facing the back-alley John watched Abe's silhouette till it disappeared. When he was out of sight he listened for his footsteps and imagined he could hear them taking his big brother all the way back to the Royal Oak; to the room provided for him by a loving sister. Then, despite being the worse for wear, he carefully brushed his best clothes and hung them from a picture rail to air. He extinguished the paraffin lamp and opened the window before tucking himself into bed. Then he stared up into the darkness before finally falling to sleep to dream the old dream of a home to which he would never return.

Chapter 3

The Shoulder of Mutton

The next morning, Sunday morning, Abe was not on duty, had made sure of it, and slept in till seven. He got out of bed, dipped his whale bone toothbrush into the tooth powder, and began to part the night from his teeth. Mouth unfurred and refreshed, he proceeded to his vigorous morning exercise programme, to get the blood flowing. Afterwards, warmed up and loose, he took his time over his toilet, splashing water from the ewer to the bowl, washing himself down from head to toe, and saving just enough water to shave with. He was always fastidious about his beard, it being essential for a man in his position to impart an air of authority and responsibility: to his way of thinking a beard was a must. But not a wild straggly specimen the like of which there were plenty adorning, or rather obscuring, the faces of some of the male population. No. Such unkempt specimens betokened recklessness and lack of discipline. Abe's style of choice was a neatly husbanded rim-beard stretching from each ear and meeting on the point of his chin to form a continuous but narrow band of frizzy dark brown hair. His fingertips made enquiries of the contours either side of the divide, and found evidence of trespassing sprouts of bristle which had overstepped their bounds; the mirror corroborated it.

His razor lay awaiting the call to duty, tortoiseshell handle enfolding the delicate steel. Abe took it from its allotted space in the top drawer of the wash-table, released the blade from the protecting grips, and inspected it. It was unblemished and keen, the more so after he had worked it along the strop half a dozen times and wiped it clean. He set it aside, almost reverentially, lathered up his brush and face, and set about arresting all of the new growth which had ventured beyond the pale. The hollow ground steel, expertly honed, so delicate and yet so blood-lettingly sharp made this easy, even with cold water and thin lather. After washing off the last of the soap and drying his face, it only remained to rub some bay rum into his hands and apply to the newly-shaved face: it stung but smelled good. In the mirror Abe fancied he saw a young Abraham Lincoln, or a Brunel. Only better looking! He didn't always reach for the bay rum –it was more of an occasional treat – but today was special. Today he was going to see Alice! Before then he had a couple of calls to make. But first, breakfast.

Downstairs in the kitchen Mary had the stove going. Sometimes, it got oppressively hot in here, but at this hour and at this time of year the warmth was still welcome.

"Good morning Mary."

"Good morning Mr Abraham. You look smart today." Which indeed he did, in full collar and tie and a bowler under his arm.

"Well, it is Sunday," ventured Abe.

"So that smell-nice is for the benefit of the vicar then, is it?" continued Mary. The bay rum couldn't be missed, even over the smell of the coals and breakfast.

"Yes, all right, I'm going up to Haden Hill House later."

"Thought you had a bit of a twinkle in your eye," said Mary.

"You've still got quite the twinkle yourself," Abe flattered.

"Bit old though," sighed Mary.

That's an understatement, thought Abe. He had known Mary ever since he had moved into this place, which was ever since Miriam had lost John Henry. And she had seemed ancient then. The old girl was excruciatingly thin and shuffled about the place as if in leaden boots, the result of an obvious stiffness, of pain, in her lower limbs: arthritis Doc Wharton had called it; nothing to be done. Apart from when she slept, under the stairs, Abe believed that she spent her whole life in this kitchen, which to her credit she kept clean and tidy. Here she was at least always warm, once having lit the fire. Her frail constitution effectively imprisoned her, like a canary in a cage. Like a canary, she could never fly free…

Abe feared that one day soon her simple duties would be too much for her. He liked to think that Miriam would not let her go to the workhouse when that happened. Loyalty was one of his guiding principles and, it also pleased him to think, a virtue shared by his family. But loyalty did not pay bills…

"You'll be wanting some breakfast, I suppose?" interjected the old bird.

"Yes please, Mary. What is there?"

As it turned out Abe ate a satisfying Sunday breakfast of oatmeal, followed by toast and dripping with fried eggs and a couple of rashers of bacon. More bacon had been cooked and was being kept warm on a hot plate, ready for when the happy couple surfaced. Abe had no desire to be drawn into awkward conversation involving the night before, therefore he quickly downed his mug of tea, bade farewell to old Mary, and made his escape into the street.

Although it was Sunday, a dingy yellow man-made miasma pervaded the place. The air today was very still, and without a breeze it would take all day for the week's fumes to diffuse away. But by then the whole production cycle would start again. A whiff of sulphur started his nose watering again. Smut and noxious vapours were almost universally present, their concentrations only dependent on the strength and direction of the air currents. It was always every citizen's hope that the Oldbury chemical works stayed forever downwind: wishful thinking; more often than not the stink of rotten eggs and sharp, throat grabbing almonds, or toxic pear drops added to the already miserable concoction of fire born pollutants and the all-pervading animal aroma of horse piss and horse shit. For all his size and strength he was particularly susceptible to the various components of the Black Country air. He was not alone in this of course; lots of people complained of coughs and sore throats on an intermittent basis, but it seemed to Abe that his own symptoms hardly ever went away. Handkerchiefs were the order of the day, every day, and as Abe crossed the street, deftly skipping over a particularly large pile of horse muck, he whisked out today's patch of white linen and wiped away the excess nasal fluid. Another reason that he didn't cultivate a moustache with his beard…

#

In no more than sixty paces he was outside Cyril's place. Viewed from the street, 'The Shoulder of Mutton' was a less impressive looking establishment than 'The Royal Oak.' Only two floors, squatter looking, Abe remembered that it stretched back a long way behind the façade. To the rear of the premises, across a cobbled yard, was an abattoir, a slaughter-house as the locals would always have it. The butchery service it provided accounted for the pub's name, at least that was Abe's supposition. And it brought him to the business in hand. Abe was a reluctant visitor. Apart from a couple of official visits to sort out drunken affrays, he had not set foot in this place for…what? Five, six years? Nor had he exchanged more than half a dozen words with his uncle. *Which is a shame*, he thought, *in one way*. Uncle Cyril was the reason the displaced children had settled here eight years ago. For reasons unknown, Cyril had left the green expanses they had called home to set himself up here, in this pub. This was when Abe was still a young lad, and his father forbade any questions about Cyril's departure. But it didn't seem to him to have been an amicable one: Abe remembered his father had seemed to drink a lot more from then on. Cyril had taken off one day, severing ties, with all the money he had in the world. This he had invested in a pub – this pub. Once, and much later, it had been their sanctuary: after their parents' deaths, after they had lost everything, uncle Cyril had welcomed them with open arms.

Wonder what kind of welcome I'll get today? Abe thumped on the thick oak door. Then again. A man's voice floated through the panels.

"Who is it?"

"It's Abraham Lively. I've come to see Cyril." Nothing. "I'm his nephew. Tell him I'm here."

Abe heard retreating footsteps and muffled shouting. In fact, Cyril was not a blood relation. He had married Abe's aunt Lucy who, like her sister, was now long dead. Of her he only remembered voluminous dresses, sparkling jewellery and – most of all – ringlets framing a face forever out of focus. The only other thing he remembered was the

31

word 'eccentric.' It had cropped up regularly when his aunt was the topic of conversation…

The clunks of bolts being withdrawn was followed by the door opening. Abe was confronted by a slightly built young man. He had big brown eyes and what might have been the beginnings of a smile, or perhaps a smirk.

"Come in," said the young man. He was in his shirtsleeves but his clothes looked clean, pressed even. As the door closed it wafted the smell of eau de cologne. "That way." He pointed to a door at the end of the dim corridor and gestured to Abe to go first. Abe started along the hallway. He felt uncomfortable, whether nervous about meeting uncle Cyril again, or having this stranger following him in the dark, he couldn't decide…

He pushed open the door and was greeted by the warmth of the fire burning in the grate immediately opposite. Also by a growl from a huge black dog lying next to it. Abe was always wary of unfamiliar dogs – no telling what tricks they had been taught. The beast began to rise, along with Abe's heart-rate: he was sandwiched between an unfriendly dog and the unsettling character behind him.

"Sabre, down!" Uncle Cyril's voice, unmistakable. He was a good dog and lay back down without a sound, pausing only to turn two and a half times around a tight circle to tamp down his invisible grass. He settled with his back to the interloper, one ear cocked, and the little man closed the door. Looking around, the first thing Abe saw was a large round table, at which were seated four men: all young, all neatly moustached, four flat caps deposited on an old coat rack, typical workers headgear these days – only old men still clung to the old felt hats now. But they were not working, they were playing cards – though not for money by all appearances – and drinking from tankards. Admittedly it was a Sunday, a day of rest, but they looked like they had not a care in the world. *Such is the arrogance of youth.* They all gave him the hard stare until the door-opener sat back down with them – his name was Jack apparently.

Uncle Cyril sat at a separate table with what looked like his ledger. He met Abe's eyes, shut the book, stood and held out his hand.

"Young Abraham. It's good to see you son," said the publican as Abe strode across the distance to grasp the proffered token of greeting. Cyril Crane had a firm candid grip and the intelligent grey eyes that Abe remembered. His fair hair had become as grey as those eyes though it was still luxuriantly thick, and tied back in a pony tail. Like his young adherents (*guests, employees, what were they?*) he had adopted the new trend of going beardless, but in contrast to the young men, his moustache was rampant and lavish, as if to signal that he was the boss of this herd, the dominant stag. Not as tall as his visitor, Cyril's broad, almost squat, frame had put on a few pounds in the wrong places these last few years, and his limestone slab of a face with the broken nose, souvenir of underestimating a too lively gelding without a martingale, had been softened by a creeping pale pudginess. But he still looked the sort of character you would not want to get into an argument with. His voice though sounded as if plucked from another's throat,

32

for unlike his physique it was light and soft as silk, and delivered from between his trademark gapped front teeth, it flirted with a lisp. Years before, contemplating this dichotomy, Abe had been struck by the phrase 'an iron fist in a velvet glove.' It still resonated.

"It's good to see you too uncle," said the policeman.

"What brings you here this bright Sunday morning – please, sit down – business or pleasure?" Cyril gestured to the wooden chair opposite his own.

"Thanks. Well, a bit of both really…" *But mostly business.*

"Let's put the business to one side for a bit then. Jack. Could you get Abe a pint please? What's your poison?"

"Just a small one – bitter – I've got to nip in the station later."

"The station? You don't look like you're on duty. Who's the lucky girl?"

Abe pretended not to hear. *I'm not about to tell you mate.*

Cyril didn't push it. "Nice hat," he said.

"Thanks." Abe transferred his attention to the bowler on the table, brushing away a questionable speck of dust with a casual third finger.

"How's the law enforcement business going then? I hear you're doing well. They'll be making you inspector next."

Yes, I'm working on that aren't I? "I doubt that's on the cards," said Abe. And that may have been true, but he hoped it wasn't. "Uphill struggle most of the time, but I've had some good successes true enough."

"But you're enjoying it are you?"

"Yes. There's a certain satisfaction to be had."

"Good. You don't have to go through life miserable. If ever that job turns sour, or if you don't get that promotion, you know you can always come to me."

Abe was searching for words.

"You do know that don't you?" continued Cyril. "Blood's thicker than water; water under the bridge, and all that. There's no hard feelings here."

Abe was not so sure about the hard feelings. Uncle Cyril was expert at getting you to let your guard down. Abe well remembered how this softly spoken picture of affability had been the personification of incandescent rage, six years ago; when Miriam had taken up with, then married Cyril's arch-rival, the hated J. H. Hughes, esq., licensed to purvey beers, wines, spirits, etc., etc…Abe suspected that not all of the water had passed under Cyril's bridge; that the row with Miriam had had dimensions other than business rivalry. Cyril would not admit that, and Miriam chose not to discuss it.

So Abe merely said, "That's good to know Cyril. I will always be in your debt for taking us in when we needed a home. We all respect you for that, you should know that." *But that doesn't mean I have to trust you.*

"That's what family's for," said Cyril.

At which point Jack returned, set down a jug in front of the visitor, and turned.

33

"Thank you, Jack." Cyril called Jack back. "Jack, do you know the sergeant? He's a good man."

"Hello Jack," said Abe. Jack nodded and returned to his card game.

"So, how's your sister? How did it go yesterday?" enquired Cyril.

"It went well. Shame you couldn't be there."

"Yes. I thought it would be better if I stayed away."

So much for water under the bridge.

"I did send a present," continued Cyril.

"Really? What?"

"Did you enjoy the roasted pig?"

"I didn't try it."

"I had it butchered for the occasion. Should have been plenty to go round, she was a fine big sow. Why didn't you have any?"

"I intended to, but family business intervened."

"Oh?"

"John. John had drunk too much, and was beginning to make a nuisance of himself…"

"You mean he was enjoying himself. Nothing wrong with that, surely. At least he's got a bit of life in him!"

"And he'll burn all that life up very quickly if he carries on like it. Anyway, he was disturbing the guests, so I took him home."

"Shame. I always liked John. Lot like me when I was younger. I used to be a bit of a loner, you know. What's he doing now?"

"Working in an iron works out towards Brades Village. I worry about him. He gets really depressed."

"Tell you what, I'll go and see him. See if I can cheer him up. He might like a job working for me. Beats working your roe out in a factory."

That depends on what you get him into. "Working for you doing what?" Abe enquired innocently.

"Just odd jobs, you know. This and that."

And a bit of the other no doubt. Abe had lived with Cyril and knew that his income derived from various sources, not all of them above board. Cyril was the main instigator and controller of gambling – be it involving cards, dogs, horses, or bare-knuckled men – from here to Dudley. And lots of other places. He abhorred blood sports however, and would not countenance setting beast against beast; men were a different matter. Gambling was not illegal in itself, but a labyrinth of law and regulation meant that most avenues for wagering were, or could be interpreted as such. Certainly the law's refusal to recognise the enforceability of gambling debts encouraged a sort of free for all which inevitably, and quickly, escalated into a certain species of criminality. But there were enough cracks and grey areas for a clever operator to duck and dive, and hopefully avoid

34

prosecution, if not detection. Cyril was certainly clever, and too clever to ever admit that he was any such 'operator.' Abe could live with that: illegal gaming dens would never be stamped out, and it was suspected that his uncle had at least a couple on the go at all times. But of course, suspicion and rumour were not admissible in a court, and at least with a single man or gang controlling them, incidents of a more serious nature, of violence, were attenuated. Thus, the copper in him rationalised turning a blind eye, by and large, to Cyril's business interests. Moreover, it was true, he was in Cyril's debt. *Let sleeping dogs lie.*

They chatted away and Abe finished his drink. He knew that Cyril was very well informed and that he was just giving Abe the time to come to the point. Abe did so.

"So, uncle, speaking as both policeman and family, can I ask your advice on an incident which I am investigating…"

"You want to know if I had anything to do with the disappearance of Parkes' sheep two weeks ago. That is to say, you and that fat quack Wharton want to know."

Yes, very well informed, and sharp.

"No, I wanted to ask if you knew anything about it, not whether you were involved. Big difference. There's not much goes on around here you don't know about."

"That's very flattering, I'm sure. Unfortunately, in this case I know absolutely nothing at all. Which disappoints me. Must be losing my touch."

Abe doubted that. Cyril must have at least heard a whisper, but as for being directly involved, rustling was not his style, reasoned Abe. At least he could report back that he had investigated this avenue of enquiry.

"So you've not been approached about any unusual slaughter work lately? Or an employee?" Abe couldn't help but glance toward Jack.

"None whatsoever. I'm sure Mick would have mentioned it."

"Mick?"

"My slaughter man. You remember him?"

"No, I don't."

"You don't remember mad Mick? Been with me years."

"Why do you call him that?"

"It's his name," said Cyril drily.

"The 'mad' bit. I'm sure his mother didn't christen him that."

"Well no. I doubt whether our Mick was ever christened at all. It's Mick O'Rourke. The 'mad' is a recent sobriquet."

"Glad we've sorted that out. So, same question, why do you call him mad?"

"Oh, I don't," replied Cyril, enjoying himself tremendously. "Don't know whether I'd dare. Some do, some call him that. There's some that think he enjoys his work a little too much."

"Does he?"

"I wouldn't know. What's the definition of too much?" Cyril's flippant delivery changed as he continued:

"What I do know, young Abraham, is that death comes to all of us, sooner or later. And for the poor sods that are herded into the drop-forges and factories every day, and the rolling mills or the mines, it very often comes sooner; it comes from crushing and cutting and burning and choking. The dead are the lucky ones; the maimed have to enter a lower level of hell; you've seen them. And if they survive all that, they are just burnt up by the constant grind, and chucked away like so many lumps of slag…That's why I'm so glad that you have risen above all that—"

Abe cut in. "What's that got to do with this Mick?"

"Oh yes, Mick. The point is that what we have here is a case of the pot calling the kettle black. How mad is mad Mick compared to your typical working man? To date, he's never been crushed by a falling sheep, impaled by a runaway pig, nor indeed had his neck broken by a chicken. Just the opposite in fact. Yep. So, who's mad here?"

"I think I might need to talk to this paragon of common sense."

"Not possible. He's off for a few days, to see his mother. But there's no need anyway. Mr Cutler oversees that part of the business, don't you Jack?"

The little man with the big eyes had been following every word.

"That's right Mr Crane," he said, without looking up from the cards.

"And can you vouch for the fact that we haven't handled any potentially stolen livestock, in the last two to three weeks say."

"I certainly can Mr Crane." Cutler threw in his hand and stood. "As soon as news of the missing sheep reached me I went straight into Mick to make sure that we hadn't processed any animals without receiving and issuing the appropriate paperwork. He assured me that we had not."

"This mad Mick sounds well educated for a slaughter-man," said Abe "seeing how he deals with all the paperwork. When did you say he was back?"

"We only trust him to kill things efficiently and turn them into meat, interjected Cyril. Mr Cutler looks after all the paperwork."

Why am I not surprised?

"The books record all livestock received, who the legal owners are, and how much money was exchanged. Sometimes we just cut up the animals into saleable chunks for the owners, and sometimes we agree a price to purchase the whole shipment and sell the meat on ourselves. But it's all there in black and white, and red," explained Cutler.

"So, your meat sales are presumably recorded in a sales ledger," began Abe, eyeing the book that Cyril had closed earlier. "They can all be traced back to these books that you keep?"

"Yes. More or less. The weights in my books don't usually tally exactly, it's the nature of the product, isn't it? But they're accurate enough to prove the point."

"The point?"

36

"That everything's above board," said Cutler pointedly.

Of course, stolen animals wouldn't go through any books at all, would they?

"What do you do with the waste?"

"There's very little waste, Abraham," cut in Cyril. "People round here can't afford to waste food. All the innards are turned into something – tripe, sausages, faggots, black pudding. The only thing that doesn't get used is the shit in the tubes, Mick says. That gets washed down the soak-aways with any spilled blood. It's a very efficient operation. The locals have an appropriate saying about pigs, which you may have heard. No? Everything eaten except the squeal! Now, would you like Mr Cutler to run you through the paperwork?"

"That won't be necessary thanks." *Talk about a forlorn hope.* "I'll just have to trust you," said Abe switching off the policeman.

"Yes, you will, won't you," said Cutler coldly.

"Well that's about it then. I really need to get going now. Thank you for your time, uncle."

"Right," said Cyril, "it really was good to see you Abraham." He held out his hand which Abe shook rather formally.

"Jack will show you out," said Cyril as he returned to his ledger.

"This way," said Cutler and pointed down the corridor with a walking cane which was topped with a brass facsimile of what looked to be a dog's head, or a wolf's. This time Abe was having none of it.

"Lead the way he ordered."

#

When Cutler had shut the door to the street and shot the bolts he trotted back to Cyril.

"He's gone."

"Good. I hope you were polite."

"Do you think he suspected anything?"

"Your attitude and demeanour didn't help, but yes, of course he did. He's too intelligent to believe he could ever prove anything though."

"But he'll keep snooping?"

"Probably not. The police are too busy to indulge in wild goose chases. He only came at the behest of Wharton. And don't forget – don't ever forget – he's family. If we don't push our luck he won't bother us. That means no more forays into, shall we say, new business opportunities. You got that Jack?"

"Yes. Got it."

"Good. Now go and make sure Mick's not got anything incriminating hanging around."

37

"Doing it now," said Cutler as he exited the room. As he made his way out back he thought about that copper. He determined to keep a very close eye on sergeant Abraham Lively in future. Stuff what Cyril said, any threat to the well-being of Jack Cutler esq. he was not going to tolerate.

Chapter 4

The Station

Whilst his brother was enjoying his tete a tete at the Shoulder Of Mutton, constable Joshua Lively was a few hundred yards up the road at "the station." The police HQ for the district was actually in nearby Old Hill, close to the magistrates' courts, where petty criminals were tried at the Petty Sessions. At present, reason obscure, Old Hill police station boasted both a permanent uniformed and a detective inspector. The Blackheath police station on the other hand was a very modest affair, being no more than a converted coaching house, a small one, which had not so long ago stood in verdant countryside. Now, it marked an invisible border between the old Rowley village and the burgeoning town of Blackheath. From the frontage, the houses and shops going uphill in the direction of St. Giles Church were traditionally counted as being of 'the village', whilst those going oppositely and down were part of Blackheath. At least, this was so in common parlance, a habit of speech founded on handed down memories of times past. For, in truth, the distinction to an untutored eye was impossible to discern. The huddled dwellings and diverse retail premises which ribboned along the road from the very bottom to the very top all had the same well-worn look about them, whichever side of the mental divide they were planted.

Josh Lively was sat exactly astride this fictitious border as he updated the station log. Being on duty he would miss church today. That is to say, he was unable to attend. Although a regular Sunday church-goer, it was the social contact which drew him there, rather than a burning Christian imperative. He would miss catching up with his brothers – except John of course, who never went to church – but he didn't think that God would hold his non-attendance against him. Josh believed, like a non-conformist, that God lived not in a building but in your heart, if indeed anywhere.

With the doors – one to the street and two leading 'out the back' – shut, it was unusually quiet. The ticking of the old clock and the scratching of pen on paper gradually became the only sounds of which he was aware, as the world faded away. The warmth of the sun benumbed his senses as he paused to dip his pen and round up his thoughts. Yellow light beamed through high window panes which dissected it into individual shafts of brightness in which, impelled by unseen forces, swirled a universe of shiny specks of dust. Josh lost himself, imagining each speck to be a little life in itself, or a lost soul, each moved around randomly at the whim of unseen powers, of tiny gods…

Bang!

Josh jumped out of his reverie, and his skin, dropping the pen and blobbing ink onto the desk in the process. The door swung open.

"Oy oy chap," said constable Clark as he entered.

"Bloody hell Gordon, don't do that," replied Josh.

"Do what?"

"Creep up and bang the door like that. You nearly scared me to death!"

"What do you mean 'creep up'? I just came up the steps and walked in, as you do. I do work here you know…What? Did I wake you up?"

"No, I was just writing up the log and enjoying a bit of peace and quiet," protested Josh. "What brings you back so early?"

"It's not that early," said Clark, ostentatiously taking out his prized pocket watch and comparing it with the office clock. "You're nearly seven minutes slow."

"Still makes you early."

Clark merely shrugged. "It's a bit slow out there today. Everybody in church and out of mischief I suppose."

"Not the bad 'uns," opined Josh.

"You'd be surprised. Even hardened crooks get an attack of conscience now and then, come Sunday."

"Which can't be a bad thing," said Josh.

"Not when it leaves me time for a nice cup of tea," said P.C. Clark as he entered another room, "it's like an insurance policy for them. They may not believe but there's no harm in hedging your bets…the stoves a bit low, you sure you haven't been asleep?"

"Throw a bit more coal on, water's already hot. It'll boil in no time."

No time turned out to be a good ten minutes, following which constable Clark produced two mugs of strong hot tea. He deposited one of the steaming beverages on the leather topped desk at which Josh sat. The desk had seen better days – rather like Gordon Clark thought Josh, he must be forty if he's a day – and the brown which might once have been red leather was worn and scuffed, and covered with overlapping roundels speaking of countless cuppas set down on the long-suffering desk by a succession of long-suffering public servants.

"Good do last night?" ventured Clark. "Jack's a lucky man."

Josh thought that statement suggestively salacious, or had he imagined it? *Best not talk like that in front of Abe.* "How did the match go?" Clark had been otherwise engaged on the day of the wedding, officiating as a football match referee.

"I'm trying to forget it."

"Why, what happened?"

"I ended up sending half the clerks' team off, and two of the miners. Clerks and miners has always been a grudge match."

"Got a bit scrappy did it?"

"All of the matches round here are a bit scrappy. This one was downright violent! The only reason it didn't turn into a full-blown riot was because I threatened to arrest the ringleaders – fat chance of me getting that lot into custody though. I threatened to arrest some of the spectators an' all; some of them young hard-knocks from the 'Shoulder' was egging them on; you know, thin moustaches and fat caps and no respect for their elders."

"So how bad was it? Broken legs time?"

"No. Bad cuts and black eyes. Miraculously. The clerks started it, raving mad."

"Too much time spent sat on their backsides perhaps?"

"Probably. Certainly had energy to burn yesterday. Do you know what one of them called me?"

"Something to do with being blind?"

"How did you guess? A blind effing donkey he said. He thought I didn't hear, but I've got his number."

Josh stifled a smile. If the grumbling clerk had been had up for slander he would probably have got off: P.C. Clark was famously short sighted and on patrol had a permanent squint, complementing a splendid, if yellowing, set of buck teeth. No, fair's fair, blind donkey was a not inaccurate description. Not sure about the effing bit…

"So who won?"

"It was 10 – 7 to the miners when I had to abandon the game. There was only ten minutes to go, but I couldn't risk them occupying the same pitch any longer."

"Bet you're looking forward to the rematch then."

"Not likely. Either the result stands, or they can get another referee."

"If you'd known you could have ducked out before and covered for me. I had to turn up to the service in uniform."

"Well, you can thank your brother for that, even-handed to a fault that man."

"Yes, he's something to aspire to."

"I didn't mean it as a compliment – to a fault I said."

At that moment a pitiful howling was heard from the direction of the cells. Both men decided that the best course of action was to do nothing. So that's what they did. That is to say, that neither offered to venture toward the source of the disturbance. Instead, constable Clark decided to synchronise the office clock so that it displayed the correct time according to his own trusted timepiece, Josh concentrated on finishing his tea. Gordon's unfinished liquid sat upon the desk, gathering to itself the glittering airborne particles, lustres extinguishing one by one on contact, as by a grim reaper at the threshold of a miniature Hades.

Clark knocked back the rest of his tea and the wailing stopped. Both men waited for it to resume. As it did not, they relaxed, and Clark went out to pour himself a second helping. He was coming back in when it started back up, accompanied this time by a rhythmic thumping.

"A copper's work is never done," said constable Clark. Josh assumed he was referring to the racket in the cells, but he may merely have been making a general observation, because he sat back down with every sign that he heard nothing of that sort at all.

"Sounds like it's coming from number one," Josh suggested. "But isn't everything bolted down?"

"Should be," said a reclining Clark.

"God, I hope it's not the slops bucket."

"Who's in there?" enquired Clark laconically.

"A young lady called Daisy," Josh consulted the log. The relevant entry had been completed by P.C. Payne that morning as he finished his shift. It said that the woman had been arrested for being drunk and disorderly, and that he suspected her of soliciting. "Daisy Hackett," continued Josh.

"Right," said Clark, barely suppressing a grin. "What's she in for?"

"Just a D&D."

"Right," said the older man again. It was apparent to him that Josh had never come across Miss Hackett before, although in point of fact a more careful review of the book would have told him that she had more than a passing familiarity with the insides of the cells.

"She seems a bit distressed," said Clark with all the sympathy that a cat has for a cornered mouse. "You had better go and check on her." Josh was the officer in charge of custody today, thus responsible for the two ramshackle examples of humanity currently detained, although Clark had seniority. "Or shall I go?" continued the short-sighted donkey, casually.

Quick to infer an implication of non-competence, Josh got to his feet: "No. I'll go. I'm on the desk today."

"Better go now then, she'll be waking the night shift in a minute." The night shift, in the persons this day of constables Payne and the appositely named P.C. Stride – beat coppers were expected to patrol with an adequate gait to cover two and a half miles in an hour – were usually dead to the world at this hour, buried under blankets in small rooms upstairs. But this racket threatened to stir even the blessed departed to indignant complaint.

Wasting no further time, Josh gathered up the keys from a desk drawer and went through the door to the cells, leaving Clark to his tea. It was louder out here, and he could hear something banging against the iron-clad door of cell number one. He could make out that the voice was pleading, demanding, to be let out. Thankfully, the detainee next door was not joining in. Josh slid back the grille covering to check on him. God knows how, but he slept on – his chest was very noticeably moving up and down – as he had slept since Josh took over. He must be both drunk and deaf. Or perhaps pretending to be asleep to avoid the street. Whatever, he was no problem at present. *Right then me lass, let's see what you're up to.* As Josh looked in on cell number one, the noise abruptly ceased. Through the grille he could make out the empty cot, affixed to the far wall beneath a small barred window, unglazed to aid ventilation. There was no sunlight on this side, and hardly ever was, thanks to the claustrophobic press of neighbouring buildings. Therefore, inmates spent their time in a disorientating eight by ten crepuscular world, which whether by accident or by design encouraged sleep rather than rowdiness. More often than not. The small corridor outside though had a skylight and daylight illuminated a cell whenever the door was opened, or when a curious officer opened the observation hatch, as Josh had. But he could not see the incarcerated Daisy, just the cot, the slops bucket (thankfully upright) and the whitewashed walls, continuously depositing white flakes onto the red quarry-tiled floor. *She must be standing to one side of the door.* Josh put his face as close to the grille as his nose dared.

"Daisy? Are you all right in there?" A grunt, then words, muffled and low:

"Can I go now?"

"If you're sober we'll see about it in an hour or so."

"I want to go now! You've got no right keeping me here." And the thuds resumed. *She's sitting against the door. Good God, I hope that's not her head.*

"Daisy, I'm coming in." Josh unlocked the door and pulled it open whereupon the inebriate spilled out and sprawled at his feet. She was clutching a brown knee-length boot with which she had obviously been striking the door. Josh bent to sit her upright and only quick reflexes saved his head from taking over from the door; the return swipe he avoided by lifting his ankles sharply.

"Don't touch me," shouted Daisy. Josh was ready for the next blow, which admittedly was now half hearted at best, and he caught the boot and pulled it from its owner's rather grimy hand. It all went through his head very quickly – the unexpected weight, the solidity, and the attached greasy leather straps – and just as quickly he dropped it as if it were a viper. Not a boot at all. Well, yes, a boot, but one with a leg still in it! A false leg at any rate. *A false leg!* Recovering his wits, he gingerly moved the weapon out of reach with his size elevens. He realised that the boot was an integral part of the prosthetic, quite a clever design. The girl was watching him.

"Didn't expect that, did you?" she laughed.

By now Josh had regained his composure. "No, I didn't young lady." For she was young, if not a lady in the strictest sense. Underneath a wild bunch of dark hair, she looked no more than sixteen or seventeen; and she may have been younger, aged prematurely, for it was safe to assume that life had not been kind to her. "I certainly didn't. You know that assaulting a police officer is a serious matter, don't you?"

"Sorry, I thought you were going to hit me. You know, for shouting. I'm sorry I shouted, but I get these nightmares."

43

"No, I came in because I thought you might have hurt yourself…Has anyone else hit you?"

Daisy changed the subject. "I haven't met you before. You new?"

"Not that new. You've obviously been a guest here before," said Josh. "Look, you can't crawl about like that, that floor's cold. If I help you to the cot and give you back your, er, leg, can you promise me to put it back on and behave? Then, if you look presentable and sober, I think you can go."

"All right, I promise. Help me up?"

Josh took the offered hand and lifted her upright. She was pathetically light, and he suddenly felt very protective of her. Gently, he helped her to the little bed and sat her down. "Do you need any help with this?" he said as he handed her the erstwhile weapon. Thankfully, she did not. "If you like, I can bring you some water to wash with before you go. Make yourself more presentable?"

"Thank you, that would be nice."

"And I'll leave the hatch open so you can see better, and not get scared." With that he turned to go. He had already lingered for too long, just like the smell: the cells were impregnated with a distinctive odour that no amount of carbolic could ever remove or disguise. Or perhaps it could, physically. But once experienced never forgotten, and even a brief visit to the cells was enough to bring it all back: a nauseating but complex blend of notes, the cutting smell of stale urine is first to assail the nostrils, then sour sick and old sweat layers itself over the top until, finally, the overloaded senses register only the distinctly unsubtle fragrance of human excrement.

But as he strode away she called out to him. "Thank you, constable. You've been kinder than I deserve. What's your name?"

"It's P.C. Lively, Miss."

"Lively? Any relation to the sergeant?"

"My brother."

"That explains it."

"Explains what?"

"What you're doing here."

Josh was standing in the doorway now. "I'll be back soon." As he spoke Daisy had begun to reaffix her lower leg. Fascinated, Josh watched, as much as decency allowed. The real leg wore a boot which didn't match, he noticed. Still, you wouldn't normally be able to see that…

She realised he was staring and, affecting a modesty which her record might suggest she did not possess, pulled her skirts down to her ankles.

"I'm sorry. I didn't mean to stare."

"It's understandable. Thank you again for your kindness."

"It's nothing." It really had been nothing at all; common courtesy.

Before he could lock her in, she added: "You know, you really have got a gentle way about you. A goodness. Not like a copper at all. I know, I've met plenty. You're not one of them. Look after yourself."

And with that dubious compliment, P.C. Lively closed the door.

On his return, he discovered that Clark had helped himself to some biscuits that Josh had secreted in a desk drawer.

"Nice biscuits," commented the pilferer.

"Glad you like them," said Josh. "You'll never guess what just happened."

"She hit you with a wooden leg."

"You knew?"

"Yes, but I didn't want to spoil the surprise. I hope you gave her what for."

"Not exactly. She didn't mean anything, and she didn't hit me."

"That was lucky. Confiscate it, did you?"

"On the contrary. I'll be releasing her soon."

"You're a big softy you are. You want to watch out for that."

"It's not a question of being soft, it's a question of being fair."

Clark rolled his eyes and shook his head.

"Look.," persisted the younger man, "that's just a young girl out there. She couldn't be any more than sixteen. She's obviously had a hard life, what with her leg and all…"

"You mean what without her leg an' all…"

"And but for the grace of God, that could be a sister of mine in there, or yours."

"Yes, but she's neither, is she? And we've got a job to do, haven't we? Criminals are criminals; it's not our job to analyse why they're bent, or what bent 'em. Where would that get us?"

"Oh, I agree. It's our job to keep law and order. But what's the point of law and order, eh?" He didn't give Clark chance to respond and continued. "The point of it, surely, is to help maintain a happy and harmonious society. Do you think we can do that by locking up unfortunates whose only crime is that they've drunk too much?"

"They don't pay me to think, nor you. The fact is D&D is a crime, and that little vixen is lucky we don't charge her. Matter of fact, I think we should rethink that policy in her case. She's becoming a pest."

"You know Gordon, you're a hard-hearted bastard."

"No. Just practical."

"What's practical about wasting our time, and the cell space, on poor drunks who mean nobody any harm? There are real criminals out there!"

"You just wait till you've been doing the job as long as I have. Them poor drunks aren't always harmless buffoons. In fact they almost never are. Just the opposite. A lot of serious violence and vandalism starts with a drink or two. Come on, you must have learned this by now. At least a night locked away protects the public for a few hours. And it makes them think twice about doing it again."

"I don't know whether it does. You can't tar everyone with the same brush."

"You bloody well can. If I could, I'd have them all up before the beak. But as I say, I'm a practical man."

"Even if you sent every one of them to court, and the court had resources to deal with them, you'd not get rid of the problem. Drunkenness is never going to go away until the lives of working men and women are dramatically improved. So they don't have to retreat into a bottle."

"Yeah, yeah, and pigs might fly. You'll be wanting to start a bloody trade union next. Go on then, let her off with a nice friendly pat on the head, and ask her not to do it again. See what you get, apart from scabies. She'll be back, maybe not tomorrow or the next day – she's itinerant – but she'll be back, exactly the same except older. Mark my words. Tell you what, I'll do you a prediction." Clark's face invited the question.

"What?"

"I guarantee that wherever she is tomorrow night, she'll be legless!"

"Very funny."

And so it went on, until there was a knock at the door.

Chapter 5

Rowley Hills

When Abe left the Royal Oak the morning after the wedding, Miriam was already up. She had left Jack in bed, snoring, and crossed the corridor to her small dressing room. She hadn't planned on getting up so early but she was restless. She thought she had heard Abe moving about on the floor above, and then heard light footsteps on the stairs as Marlene, her housekeeper come barmaid, returned from making up fires downstairs. Marlene would now be waiting for bedchambers to be vacated so that she could make up beds and remove chamber pots. Servants might be a luxury these days, but Miriam would not do without Marlene.

Although up and about sooner than expected, Miriam had no intention of going to church. She wanted another kind of communion today. A private one.

She still dressed in her Sunday best, except for her shoes. This morning she put on her old pair of comfortable walking boots; they wouldn't be noticed under her skirts. Then, as she plucked up a well-worn shawl from a hook, her mind was drawn to something in the street below. A figure. Unmistakable. It was Abe, just crossing the road and making his way toward the junction. A big man, her brother looked so small from here. *Little Rabbit*. She guessed that he was on his way to the station, conscientious as he was, before going to meet the Haden Hill girl.

I'm going that way. We could have walked together.

It was another fine spring morning and Miriam had resolved to get away from the town and spend an hour in the hills, no more than twenty minutes' brisk walking away. In this geography the people of Blackheath and Rowley were more fortunate than some. They were living in effect in conurbations in between larger conurbations, and, in the in between spaces, there was a surprising amount of greenery, notably to the North and East, before Dudley was reached or the sprawls of Oldbury and Smethwick, and indeed, following the compass, the huge mass of Birmingham itself. Immediately westwards there was less green open space. Apart from vestige populations along canal towpaths and railway lines, the vegetable kingdom here was limited to ever decreasing remnants as the greedy industries of the Black Country strove to make Netherton and Cradley contiguous with the towns of Blackheath and Rowley, encroachments which forever threatened to expand and join with the other black lands until the whole natural world was gone.

But that hadn't happened yet, and Miriam would take full advantage of the fact. Before she set out she stopped off for some breakfast, which meant running the gauntlet of questions from her erstwhile housekeeper, and now breakfast cook, Mary the canary…

#

Behind schedule now, Miriam exited twenty-five minutes later. Abe was long gone of course, and the sky was now overcast. But she was confident of it staying dry and stepped out with a purpose. It took no time to reach the junction, where she turned right towards Rowley. The streets were not quite yet Sunday quiet. Most adults were indoors, togging themselves out in their Sunday best so that they could pay a proper homage, via their chosen brand of Christianity, to whichever subtle reflection of Godhead their denomination might espouse. Children were not exempt and would be spending a considerable portion of their afternoon at Sunday school. But it was dimensionally intolerable to coop up the young ones, Sunday or no. Every working household was perpetually and irredeemably overcrowded and parents had little choice but to shoo the swarming offspring onto the streets. Hence, at regular intervals, each narrow doorway disgorged a horde of diminutive creatures into the grown-up less and traffic-less Sunday street, like gangs of cockroaches disturbed by the light, but in reverse. Very pretty cockroaches they were, pressed and scrubbed for the Sabbath. They milled around chaotically, though less rumbustiously than they would otherwise – woe betide them that spoiled their best clothes or clean shoes – until, quite suddenly, all would disperse and the street would become truly Sunday quiet. Many that Miriam passed knew her name and polite 'good mornings' went to and fro' until she reached the cop shop.

She had caught up with Abe. Perhaps, he would like to walk with her.

Taking the half a dozen steps to the station door two at a time, she knocked and entered.

Her little brother Josh was sitting at a desk facing her. Facing him, and with his back to the door was another constable who turned round as she entered.

"Morning Sis!" said Josh enthusiastically, "Didn't expect to see you today."

"Good morning Josh. Morning Gordon."

"Please sit down here," said P.C. Clark, vacating his seat.

"Thank you." Miriam sat.

"So, no crooks to arrest then?" She looked from one to the other.

"I just stopped off for a quick cup of tea," said Clark, "and a philosophical chat with my colleague here."

"I wouldn't describe it as philosophical," observed Josh.

"What were you talking about?"

"Josh was just telling me about a book he's reading by some German bloke. Mark something, wasn't it."

"That's Marx. Karl Marx," corrected Josh.

"Oh yes, I've heard of him," said Miriam.

"It's all about London, isn't it, Josh?" said Clark disingenuously.

"Eh?"

"You know. You said…You said the short title was Das Capital," straight-faced Clark went on. "I suppose it must be Berlin then?"

The penny dropped. "Get out of it," said Josh. "You know Marx then?"

"Never had the pleasure."

"You know what I mean…"

Miriam joined in at that: "P.C. Clark, you really are an awful man. Stop it I say." A jovial command, with an uncompromising undercurrent.

Bowing, Clark said, "If you say so Mrs Hughes, Beckett…Anyway, I was just going. Got to see a man about a dog. I'll see you later Josh. Cheerio both." And he put on his helmet and disappeared.

She turned to Josh. "Where's Abe? I thought he would be here."

"No, haven't seen him."

"And you're not expecting him?"

"No, but you never know with Abe."

"I know. I saw him heading this way and I just assumed…You look a bit pale. Are you eating enough?"

Josh thought about his purloined biscuit stocks. "I eat plenty, don't worry. I've always been pale; goes with the hair, and the light in here doesn't help. But I'm as fit as a fiddle. You look great as usual."

"Thanks, I don't feel it."

"Why ever not? You should be on top of the world. It was a great day yesterday."

"That's probably it. It must have taken a lot out of me. I'm going for a walk to clear the cobwebs."

"Where to?"

"Just the usual, as far as the old oaks."

"Good. It's a nice day for it." And so it seemed, for as they had been talking the sun had broken through again. The office was warming up to the extent that further ventilation was called for.

"Yes," she agreed.

"It was a good night last night. I got there at about 9.30. But you already know that of course. What I didn't mention is that, as I arrived, Abe left, with John."

"Oh no! How bad was he?"

"Didn't look too bad at all actually. But apparently he had upset Frank and Wilf, or rather their girls. Precautionary measure – for his own protection as we coppers say."

"They didn't mention it either. I wondered where Abe had got to so early."

"Well, no harm done I think."

A voice from the cells: "Constable Lively, can you hear me?"

"Sounds like you are wanted. I'd better let you get on." Miriam stood and kissed Josh's forehead before he got up.

As she made her way to the door Josh asked, "Shall I tell him you were looking for him?"

"Yes, no, it's nothing."

"Constable. Constable? I'm ready to go now. You said." The voice was getting louder.

"Right. I'll leave you to it then." Miriam made the break and left.

"Right you are," said Josh to the closing door. He picked up the keys. "I'm coming Daisy."

#

Miriam stepped out into the sunshine. The police station smelled like cabbage, though she doubted that they were cooking any. Out here, the breeze was blowing what could almost be described as fresh air. Slinging her bag over her shoulder she saw that the children had all disappeared, shepherded off to various outlets of spiritual enlightenment, or at least of moral improvement.

A pregnant stillness pervaded, as if the earth were about to exhale. Miriam stepped out again, heading uphill toward the church. From this point on she was in Rowley, with its eight hundred years of history, and leaving behind the upstart yet vigorous scion that was Blackheath. But you would not know it unless you knew it: tightly bunched terraces, occupied in the main by mining families, were randomly squashed amongst shop fronts and all manner of outlets for liquid refreshment. The shops catered for the simple requisites of the largely sedentary population: she passed the butcher shop owned by Fred Levett, who was even now no doubt enthusiastically singing the praises of one slaughtered lamb as a prelude to chopping up probably a half a dozen more with equal enthusiasm, come the working week; across the way, Peggy Oakley's little grocer's shop was locked up, but through the window could be made out the wooden boxes which served as extra display space, outside on the pavement, during business hours. Many a hapless youngster had received a clip round the ear from the constables, or indeed from Peggy before the rheumatism got her, for lingering just a little too long and a little too suspiciously in the vicinity of her celebrated lardy cakes. A few doors up, and Betsy Mallin's premises were open. Betsy was known for being more than a little 'saft', and had reputedly never set foot in church, over an argument with a minister about a hymn, for thirty years. She was no doubt sitting in the cramped space behind the counters, low down at the back, doing nothing in particular as usual. She would sit on guard for hours at a stretch, unable to see much, surely, beyond the untidy counters on which shiny tins rubbed shoulders with rusty tins of diverse brands of tobacco and snuff; in front of the tinned merchandise, cardboard cigarette cartons, young and old, manned the frontlines, regimented in colourful lines or squares by maker and name. There were offerings from messrs. Players and Wills, from Philip Morris and Benson and Hedges, from Taddy and Carreras; there were Turkish cigarettes and Egyptian cigarettes, and English cigarettes, like Capstan, Craven A, Gold Flake, Black Cat, and Navy Cut. And they bore all manner of designs from cats to robins, from castles to warships, painted clowns to painted oriental ladies. But the most popular was always Players Navy Cut with the familiar bearded sailor. The sweet emanations from all that tobacco at Betsy's was only outdone by the smell of confectionery, for Betsy also purveyed boiled sweets in all the colours of the rainbow. In jars lining the walls could be found pear drops and wine gums and brandy balls, a selection of toffees, coconut ice, and chocolate limes. Chocolate limes were Miriam's favourite, and she would often pop in to buy a couple of ounces, and a ginger beer if it was hot; and she would linger to soak up the pleasurable aromas, perhaps buying Abe one of the little paper parcels of snuff that Betsy made up herself and sold at a ha'penny a throw. *Or should that be a sniff?* The stock didn't seem to turn around at all quickly, even the sweets, and even the kids' favourite, kayli, cascading in crystallised waves of impossibly bright sedimentary colours, still lay virtually unexcavated. Perhaps that could be accounted for by poor old Betsy having acquired the reputation amongst the children of being a witch! Luckily, most of her stock was mostly non-perishable, or at least long-lived. But Betsy would not be expecting any customers today, you understand, it being Sunday and all.

Moving on, Miriam passed the premises of Edward Parkes, a coal merchant, whose client base must have been somewhat restricted given that miners made up so much of the population and that miners were entitled to a weekly ration of coal as part of their wages. She had never fathomed it. What she did know, was that Mr Parkes' long-suffering dapple-grey mare, Rose her name was, hauled not only coal, but also milk from the small herd – the appellation flattered – belonging to his brother, councillor Parkes. It was councillor Parkes that had lodged the recent complaint with the police about missing sheep. The Parkes were a family of some significance locally, boasting a lineage which stretched back to the reign of King Henry the Eighth at least, as they would have it, and the councillor rejoiced in the name of Azariah: Azariah Melzar Parkes was ancient crooked and bald. But sharp as a tack when he needed to be. In addition to a double fronted shop selling crockery and hardware on the one side and drapery on the other, he owned a motley collection of sheep, pigs, and moth-eaten cattle which eked out a meagre existence on the blighted black fields dotted around between the rivet works and the ever-expanding mines. For the owners sank the shafts wherever their surveys took them, and followed the thick seam wherever it led, destroying green spaces, undermining property and, occasionally, swallowing homes. It was their legal right you see. Subsidence was

51

evidenced here and there by the strange lopsided attitude of houses and shops, like drunkards frozen in mid-stagger. Even the handsome mock-gothic structure that was St. Giles Church, built on the site of the mediaeval church only some fifty years ago, was slowly sinking into the ground, its worshippers, an understandably diminishing bunch, taking their lives in their hands, and those of God of course, each and every time they bared their heads and entered. In comparison to the parlous state of the house of God, Absalom Bennett's, the cobbler's shop which Miriam now passed opposite, had got off lightly: the only evidence of the insidious excavations of the human moles on his property was to be found in the fact that his door had sealed tight against the jamb, which necessitated him serving his customers these days through an open window which also served him as his principal means of egress and exit. For there was no escaping the mining. The mines were everywhere. There was no plan, no order. Wherever the thick seam was easily accessible a pit was born. And wherever there was a pit there were miners. Invariably, their cheap and mean messuages were thrown up in a hurry, higgledy-piggledy, and as close to the workings as possible, so that the colliers could roll straight out of bed in the morning and straight into work. It was no surprise that these were the houses which suffered most from undermining, most risk of being engulfed by the blackness below…

Just for a footstep, Miriam paused beside the saddler's. This was Thomas Clayton's shop now. Now that his partner was dead; her partner; her husband. John Henry Hughes had been a man of many talents. He had to be; you couldn't expect to thrive by just running a pub. Even one as large and well-established as the Royal Oak. When John Henry had been alive Miriam had helped with brewing and cooking and generally acting the landlady. During the day, John Henry had plied his trade as a saddler. They had made a good team, and earned enough not merely to survive, but to prosper, even putting some savings away. But, he was dead now, and the savings were shrinking. Hence the new alliance, with Jack. Life had to go on…

She knew better than to linger for long, so she carried on, although she did pause for a moment whilst looking in Mr Parkes' window, where a new dress was on display. Perhaps she would treat herself when the dust had settled.

When she reached St. Giles and the crossroads on the brow of the hill, she rested against the church yard wall for a moment, and looked to the other side of the street where still stood the little house which had been Mary's home when they had first met. An old nailer's cottage, it was a tiny two up two down with an earth privy shared by four families. An insubstantial ragged figure passed before a window: it may have been no more than a stray memory…Nailers were a dying breed now, their pathetic incomes squeezed more and more by mechanisation and foreign competition. Most of the men had been forced to find other employment, leaving only women and children at home to continue the tradition, providing a much-needed secondary income. These benighted souls were on a treadmill of longer and longer hours for less and less return. Soon, like Mary's family, they would all be gone.

There were two substantial pubs here, within spitting distance of the church. The Ward Arms, named for the Earl Of Dudley, Lord Ward, and the Ring Of Bells, opposite, were a cut above most of the local drinking establishments, and rivalled the success of the Oak. But there were many more pubs and beer houses, all competing to attract customers away from Miriam, to take the bread from her table. *Counting the Ward Arms and the Ring Of Bells, there were, what? Half a dozen?* Since heading up from the station she had passed The Britannia, The Vine, The Malt Shovel, The King's Arms and the Swan. *That's seven, and that's only pubs. Not counting the more immediate threats in Blackheath.* All of the Landlords had other strings to their bow. *Uncle Cyril has his abattoir –along with less transparent earnings – and I, I have Jack.*

Thoughts of business were left hanging in the graveyard air as she continued her way, leaving Rowley behind. Soon, the land to her right became free of buildings or holes dug by men, and she stepped off the road to climb Rough Hill. Further off, someone had tethered a couple of ponies, no doubt without permission, but they would be enjoying the new vegetation nonetheless. Amidst clumps of dried grasses and woody stems of last year's crop of what would soon reveal themselves again to be St. John's Wort, or Wormwood, Willowherb or Cow Parsley or Cockscomb, new grass and spring flowers were pushing through in praise of the returning sun. Here and there between bramble tangles and exposed patches of browny-blue rock – the famous Rowley Rag – were scattered bundles of pale-yellow daffodils, their faces shyly tilted downwards, blushing bridesmaids at the marriage of sky and earth. More numerous were the ragamuffin heads of gangs of cheeky dandelions, clamouring for attention, brash and profligate. And looking on from their alder-sapling enclave, the primroses were aloof and beautiful. *It's strange how the first flowers of spring seem to be yellow, as if they were Mother Nature's sun-charm. But if so, the Blackthorn aren't part of it.* Indeed, the Blackthorn very definitely were not part of it: the scattered bushes stood out with exuberant creamy white displays, stealing a march on the sleeping hawthorn, the dominant tree in the summer scrubland of the hill.

Miriam picked her way upwards on a familiar path, taking care to crush no blooms, and in return left unmolested by the clinging thorns of the blackberry patches. She took her time, respectful of the power and bounty of Nature which transformed this place at this time of the year, in spite of the poison and destruction being visited on the earth just over the hill, and on the other side of the road. In those places, Nature had little power and spring meant only that less money had to be spent on coal or candles or on gaslight. There, men knew only darkness, perpetual winter of the soul. But here, even so close to the mines and factories, the seasons turned as they always had. Miriam looked forward to the summer when the yellow flowers would be joined and replaced by those of differing hues. She thought of the Ox-Eye Daisies and Bee Orchids, Scabious and Self-

Heal, Forget-Me-Not and Speedwell, Clover and Dead-Nettle and Vetches. With these came her favourite distractions, the butterflies, flittering from flower to flower and dancing the days away. In the very hottest of years the butterflies were swamped by unnatural numbers of day-flying Burnett moths. Last year had been one such. For some reason, these small creatures, in so many numbers, disturbed Miriam. *Perhaps it's the way they fly. Different to the butterflies.* For they flew in straight lines with no butterfly flourish, heavy not light. And their metallic wing casings were the colours of the furnace, black as soot and flaming red. *It's as if they were made in a forge and fitted with tiny clockwork engines, then sent here as tiny ambassadors for another world. To negotiate what?*

Her dark musings ceased as she reached her destination. She called them the three wise men. They were old specimens, relics of ancient days; repositories of who knows what memories. Their trunks had long since been hollowed by time and truncated by wounding and weather. Not quite as old as the hills, they looked dead. But every year, by some immortal and inexorable magic, these dead shells brought forth green life in tribute to the summer sun. Now though, the twigs were bare. Miriam took her shawl from her bag and lay it on the ground. She knelt on it and put her palms to the earth, onto a slab of cold rock where it stood proud of the surrounding grass. If she closed her eyes she could feel the vital power of that magic, throbbing. And eternal. So, eyes closed, she breathed deeply and let it enter her. When she was full, she sat back and reached out with her eyes. The oaks were near the brow of the hill and from here she could look out and see the undulating green shades which were the Clent Hills, bounding a valley variously pitted and scarred black by the industrious activity of human beings. She was not inclined to dwell on that and let her mind focus on the horizon, scanning right. And there it was. Home – as had been – a long purple and indigo wave against the blue-grey sky; the Clee Hills. The restless bumblebees droned on, a soothing sound that belied the urgency of the little creatures' peregrinations. Somewhere, a skylark was singing his heart out. At the speed of thought Miriam reached out and was there, thirty-five miles away amongst the people of the past. Back to the old days, to her favourite day ever. A magical day…

The lark was singing and hooves pounded the turf. The riders in red sashes came a-whooping, swords bouncing from their waists. The horses were straining sinew and pumping their hearts for joy. Because it was spring. A big bay gelding was in the lead, his blood fired by the shouts of the crowd and the heels of his rider; the chestnut mare was next, but wouldn't make it. An obviously aged strawberry roan was way back, a diminutive figure perched atop its broad sway back, saddle-less. In fact, the entire field rode bareback. That was the rule, their tradition.

The onlookers cheered afresh as the bay got there first. The queen was smiling. As if there had been any doubt. When it came to a flat-out race Abraham Lively, barely fifteen years of age, was one of the best riders between here and Ludlow. Having circled the maypole, he dismounted to claim his prize. The straw man was bound to the maytree. Abe freed him from his bonds and thence a triumphant procession proceeded toward the mill where to rowdy cheers Abe held aloft the wooden sword and struck off the straw man's head. The body he threw into the flatness of the millpond. Abe was king now. The death mask was retrieved and presented to the regicide. But now it was decorated with green shoots and flowers, as was the cloak which the villagers threw around him. Then, the King Of The Wood went to meet his Queen Of The May. Miriam would always remember this moment. Until death and beyond. For on that day, she was sure, the whole village had been transported to another realm, where time and death were meaningless. It was as if the fairies had loaned her the eyes of a hawk and the ears and nose of a hound: colours were impossibly vivid, every detail picked out in light, every sound mingling to an unearthly melody, every smell a sweet bouquet. And the sunlight on her skin was the gentle caress of a lover.

The mask could not disguise Abe's infectious smile as they all proceeded from house to house, collecting the tithe: offerings of sweets or beer or painted eggs. As they went they chanted:

> "Death swims in the water,
> The Old Man gone for slaughter,
> A new King for the May,
> And all the flowers gay."

They were at the door of the inn. A man came out with an egg in each hand. Miriam could not see his face, the sun was in her eyes. She blessed him for the gift, but as Miriam took the eggs they slipped through her fingers and hit the ground. They were addled. Two pathetic yolk-wet chicks spilled dead from the shells. No, not dead. One started chirping weakly, then louder. Then, it was the cry of a human infant. John Henry stamped on it and blood spurted from under his boot.

And she woke up. The skylark was still singing, accompanied by an enthusiastic hedge-sparrow from the top of a hawthorn. But they sang in vain, the mood was broken. Back to reality. As Miriam made her way back down she no longer looked to the far away hills. Before her lay the factories and furnaces and chain shops and mines of Netherton and Cradley, and beyond. All, or nearly all, paused for breath before the frenzy of fire of a new week. There were a myriad towers: squat blast-furnaces, chimneys tall, upturned titanic bottles at the Doulton works, delicate seeming wheeled contraptions over the shafts, and a mighty conglomeration of erections signifying that veritable city of hard slog and hard steel that was the domain of Messrs. Noah Hingley & Sons. This rag-tag army of mismatched monuments to man-made gods were waiting for the dawn; to recommence their war of attrition against Mother Nature...

Nearer at hand was the canal, at Windmill End, where the barges took on coal and iron and the stone from Hailstone quarry. There was no blasting today and the trams from the quarry were not running. Mines were closed on the Sabbath, but they still needed to be pumped out and so the engine house pumps were running today as always. But the sound from that solitary source was nothing compared to what was to come. Because tomorrow a cacophony from horses and men and machines would assault the ears of the angels themselves as the miners, smelters, iron workers, brick and pipe makers, great drop hammers and saw mills rolled back into action. But today it was quiet; and still, apart from a few wisps of smoke rising from the slag heaps. Which is probably why she noticed something in a pepper pot.

From this point at Windmill End the Dudley number two canal runs through the hillside by way of the Netherton tunnel, a three-thousand-yard semicircle of dank dripping brickwork enclosing a chill blackness punctuated at long intervals by pools of light from above – from the pepper pots. They are round shafts cutting upwards from the roof of the tunnel through the hill and into the daylight, where they emerge as small round towers with round tops of meshed metalwork. So, they look like very large pepper pots. Which let in light and let out stale air.

It was a bird. A bird fluttering at the top of the pot. Trapped behind the mesh. Miriam struggled between a heap of scrap metal and a random pile of slag on the verge and made her way to within half a dozen yards of the shaft. A starling. The poor thing was desperately throwing itself against the metal, trying to get out.

How did he get there? Surely he couldn't have flown along hundreds of yards of tunnel? No, there's a gap all round the bottom. He must have got in that way. So, if he got himself in, why doesn't he get himself out the same way? Instead of wasting energy in futile struggle? Where are your friends then Mr Starling? I'm sorry, I can't help you. Look down, look, you can get out down there. I can't help you. You've got to do it yourself.

If anything, her presence only agitated the bird, and Miriam made her way back to the road. There, she turned. The bird had gone. Perhaps he had remembered the way out after all. Unless, exhausted, he had dropped into murky death.

Miriam hurried back to town. She had work to do. And it was raining.

Chapter 6

The California

In the working-class households of Rowley and Blackheath, Monday was always a particularly busy day. Or at least that was so for the women folk. For Monday was wash day and wash day was a long steaming slippery drudge of mending and heavy lifting and pounding with the dolly and boiling and wringing and soaking and wringing again and…And all done in the sticky wash day heat inside impossibly oppressive confines of kitchen or scullery or brew house: families were large – survival rates for children having improved by leaps and bounds within the space of a very few years – but houses were as small as ever. Which all challenged the staying power of even the most equable of housewives, amongst whom Nora Biddulph could not be counted; the equable ones that is. Nora had always been prone to impatience, and ten years of marriage and six children had only transformed an already cutting tongue into an instrument of the most extreme mental torture. Or at least that's what her husband thought, privately you understand. But then again her paramour, Stephen Biddulph – Steve to his mates at the pub and the pit – was not only slight of stature but remarkably easy going. Saftness his wife called it, letting himself get put on…

It was perhaps unsurprising then, that on Mondays Mr Biddulph always conspired to get home after work as late as possible, eat his tea, necessarily cold, and sneak into bed without bestirring his exhausted better half. Or the dragon as he affectionately liked to think of her, never letting it get as far as his lips. His was a policy of letting sleeping dogs lie. Trouble with sleeping dogs was that they woke up and started barking…

Thus, inevitably, Monday night was an important drinking night, there being precious little alternative for those wishing to hide away for a few hours than to pass the time in an establishment which purveyed alcohol. And that many men had the same Monday-phobia was testified to by the fact that, on the first working day of the week, the numerous pubs were always more packed than usual for a work day, crowded out with large numbers of beardless men who quite obviously had not been home yet. In those days, extravagant facial hair had really had its day, at least amongst the labouring classes, though still almost a badge of self-perceived rank amongst office wallahs, and figures in authority such as magistrates, business owners and the police. On that Monday in 1887

Steve Biddulph and his mate William Westwood had elected to drink at the 'California' on Halesowen Street. Only miners and railway workers usually drank there. The clothes told you that. But if you had been loitering outside, as did many a youngster, and were only just tall enough to see over the occluded section of window glass, and could only see faces, you would have known that this was a working man's pub, a working-class pub. For each face, apart from the odd renegade moustache, was clean shaven. But not in the interests of fashion, not primarily. No. Keeping your face clear of hair was just a sensible thing to do when you worked in hot and dirty or dusty conditions. A quick swill of the face at the pit-head and Steve and Bill had been ready for a nice relaxing night boozing. They deserved it. They were hewers, spending their life at the coalface, often undermining the Thick, and risking their lives routinely. The pair's latest drinking companion was young John Till who had been a part of their gang for a couple of years now. They had all been doing very well and the butty had decided to promote John, from hurrier, pulling tubs of coal from the face to the horse ways, to working with Biddulph and Westwood as hewer. John had never been in the California and so they decided to celebrate his change in status there. The pub was really no different to many of the others within spitting distance. It did have a few unusual ornamental fittings on the inside, but that was all really. Plus the unusual name of course. The name was a hangover from a previous owner who had emigrated to the west coast of America in the thirties or forties and had struck it lucky in the gold rush of forty-nine. Eminently sensibly, said adventurer, one Benjamin Gadd, had not pushed his luck and had returned home, investing his money in a sure-fire business venture, namely a pub. Given the source of his funds, the name, 'California', was an understandable choice. Unfortunately, both his luck and his judgement lacked stamina: the varnish was hardly dry when the incautious Mr Gadd lost the whole kit and caboodle gambling with a brewer from Lichfield.

Be that as it may, the provenance of the place was the last thing on the minds of Messrs. Biddulph, Westwood and Till that night. They were out to celebrate! And why not? So it was that when the bull sounded at six the three pals repaired straight to the front door of the California, ducking out of one kind of fog into another. They nabbed a table in the corner, and let the beer flow.

It was sometime after ten when the newly-promoted hewer found himself outside in the street, bent forward with both hands planted against a cold brick wall, substitute for his truant sense of balance. The other two stood with him and now, instead of exhorting him to 'ger it down ya' they were advising him to 'ger it up,' together with the assurance that, "yoh'll feel much better."

But young Till couldn't get it up, at least no more of it. The retching had tied his guts in knots. He just wanted to be home. He tried a few steps but only fell back, heavily, against the wall, before sliding slowly down it. He was a well-built young chap but after much huffing and puffing, not to mention effing and blinding, his companions, somewhat the worse for wear themselves, succeeded in getting him to his feet. Once upright, the

58

two older men supporting the young man, and each other, they set off. It all went well for all of half a dozen steps, when they were all pulled down by the unmanageable weight. Despite what awaited him at home, or perhaps because of it, collier Biddulph was the least inebriated of the three.

"'old up. Doh yoh move, ah've gorran idea," he announced. Then disappeared. Over the hubbub from the pub Bill Westwood could make out the banging of a yard door and some squeaking and clanging. A large wheelbarrow came wobbling out of the fog, propelled by Biddulph.

"That's bostin'," said Bill. "Where did yoh ger et?"

"It's out o' Doreen Pickering's fowd. Her woh mind. Ah'll tek et back tomorra."

With teamwork and little more grunting young Till was wedged into the barrow, problem solved. The propelling pair made their way toward the Oldbury Road, purposefully striding out, in their own minds, but in reality, describing a very inefficient zigzag line all over the road. But for one random factor, which after all might not immediately suggest itself to minds less than sober and otherwise occupied, the only result of failing to maintain a straight course might have been that the half-conscious body of John Till would have arrived at his mother's doorstep about ten minutes later than the drivers of his improvised cab had planned. However, on that particular night the random factor loomed rather large, for out of the wet fog came clattering a huge black horse pulling an enclosed cart which, devoid of any cargo, provided only minimal resistance for a fizzy animal anxious to get back to its hay net. Thus it was that the drunks in charge of the wheel barrow had very little time to react. And reacting in haste, not to say terror, they caused the inert mass that was the oldest son of widow Till to spill out of the overturning receptacle, into the road, and under the iron hooves of the horse, which, suspecting a sneak attack from a predator, did what equines are prone to do, and panicked. In the resultant rearing and neighing and flailing of hooves, young John was struck a mortal blow. Reprieved, in its own mind, the horse bolted for it. Presumably, the driver eventually got things under control. Strangely however, he never returned to the scene.

#

Tuesday morning, and sergeant Lively and his brother were at the scene.

"Right then Josh. This is where it happened. Is that correct?"

"Yes, just in line with that bit of broken kerb, under the Colman's Starch sign. I think you can still make out some blood spots."

Abe took a few paces and squatted to take a look. "Yes, I think it is blood." He stood. "So, let's get this straight, these two miners, what were their names?"

Josh took out his pocket book, "William Josiah Westwood and Stephen Biddulph, no middle name. Both work at the Bell End pit and live in the owner's cottages opposite, toward Siviter Street."

"And this Westwood and Biddulph were pushing this unconscious kid up the road in a wheelbarrow, were they? In the middle of the road. Drunk. In the dark. What did they have to say for themselves?"

"Well," began John, scanning his notes for inspiration, "story is that they got so drunk last night that young Till couldn't stand and they couldn't support him. So they put him in the wheelbarrow to get him home. Good idea really, except for that horse bolting. Tragic. Absolutely tragic."

"So, just another unfortunate accident then?"

"Seems so, yes. Doctor Wharton confirms that the blow to the head that killed him is consistent with being clobbered by a hoof."

"Did you consider that it might not have been an accident?"

"What, murder? Seems unlikely. I shouldn't think a young lad like that would have any serious enemies. Never been in trouble as far as we know."

"Did you ask? About enemies?"

Josh faltered. "Well no...but, I mean..."

"Relax. I agree with you. I don't think he was deliberately targeted. But that doesn't mean there's no blame attached. Get hold of Payne and Stride. I want a full report on the circumstances leading up to the lad's death. They can start in the pub, see if he was a completely voluntary participant in this piss up. These two older blokes were reckless, and the drink's no excuse. What do you think? Drag them in on suspicion of manslaughter?"

"Manslaughter? But that's serious."

"So's death. And what about the horse and driver?"

"He never came back. All they can say is that it was a big black horse, pulling a cart, that came from that direction." Josh pointed up the road, "and hit them from behind. I don't think it was their fault at all you know. It was ever so foggy last night."

Abe ignored the last comment. "So where were they going, I wonder?" He looked back up the road, toward the Shoulder Of Mutton. *Uncle Cyril has a black horse, and two or three carts...Getting into deep water here. Let's get rid of Josh.*

"Josh. Where's the wheelbarrow?"

"Doctor Wharton said he didn't need it. It didn't provide any clues, so I returned it from where they borrowed it."

"And that was in another person's yard wasn't it?"

"Yes. The owner is a Mrs Pickering."

"And they asked if they could take it did they?"

"Well, I don't suppose it was appropriate..."

"It wasn't appropriate, no. So, they just appropriated it. That's larceny then is it? What are you going to do P.C. Lively?"

"What do you want me to do?"

"I think you should interview Mrs Pickering. If she's not happy about them 'borrowing' her property, then you can arrest these two twits on suspicion of thieving. Right, off you go then."

"Will do, Sarge." Josh turned away and headed off toward the Pickering residence. In his own mind he had no doubt that nothing would come of it. Neighbours borrowed things all the time, that was the way it was…

As usual Cyril Crane was on the ball and had done a little investigating of his own. Jack Cutler was getting cocky, running schemes on the side. This was both risky, and disrespectful. Cyril was in the outbuildings at the far end of his yard, where was housed his two draught horses, a grey and a big black, together with a trap and a waggon and waggonette which were all used for his legitimate businesses. Smoke, the grey, would pull small loads, generally odd barrels to and from the brewers. Heavier loads and paid haulage jobs involved the bigger waggon, and Jingles, his black mare. That Tuesday morning, suspicions aroused, he had been checking on his animals and vehicles. He had immediately seen that things were not as he had left them, and Jingles looked like she had been sweating. Given the news of last night and Jack's increasingly wilful streak, it didn't need a great leap of imagination to link the dead kid, Jingles, and Jack Cutler.

Crane knew that he could expect a visit from the police. First order of business then was to make sure that there was nothing on the premises which might prove incriminating. He would give Jingles a quick wisp down with a handful of hay. It would remove the sweat marks and calm her down: she was edgy, unusually head shy; but only Cyril could spot that. After the rub-down Cyril expertly ran his hands over the smooth black coat and searched for any wounds, particularly around the hooves, which he picked and oiled. He moved hurriedly out of the stall then, for a choking bile threatened to overcome him, his spleen venting a living anger which threatened his usual self-control. Stupid! A young man dead for no good reason, Jingle's life put in danger, and unwelcome attention drawn to the whole operation. He went back to the Shoulder and almost kicked a stubborn back door off its hinges. He would have words with Jack. But he would calm down first.

Josh had enjoyed a nice cup of tea with the widow Pickering and was feeling pleased with himself: there was more to policing than just arresting all and sundry. His statement would confirm that the old dear knew Biddulph very well and that of course she didn't mind him borrowing her wheelbarrow. She was only glad that neither Stephen nor Mr Westwood had been hurt. It was the waggon-driver they needed to find, speeding around at night like a lunatic.

As he walked back onto the street Abe saw him.

"Payne and Stride here yet?" enquired the sergeant.

"No. I sent for them but they were off-duty, so it might take them a while."

"We haven't got time to wait on their pleasure. Have you got your statement from the wheelbarrow owner?"

"Yes. Seems she's quite pally with Biddulph, who's a popular character as far as I can make out. Wouldn't dream of pressing charges."

"Lucky for him. I still think we'll get them both in for a roasting though. A man's dead after all."

"Is that really necessary? They must feel so bad about it already."

"They don't feel as bad about it as John Till, or his mother. Anyway, it sends a message to all the other drunken louts."

"I suppose that's true," conceded Josh.

"No sense in hanging about for that dozy pair. Come with me to the California, they'll be open by now. We can talk to the landlord."

#

A small smoky fire fuelled by a pile of drying-out slack, the soft murmur of conversation and the smell of beer slops combined to create a strangely comforting atmosphere. It reminded Abe of home, of course, his new home. A wood panelled wall was decorated with faded mementos of a fake Wild West: an Indian tomahawk, a peace pipe and two crossed lances were adorned with the tatty remains of what were once, putatively, eagle feathers. Perhaps not sensible implements, with the exception of the pipe of peace perhaps, to leave in a public bar within the reach of hard drinking men. Fortunately, stout screws with chewed up heads affixed the potential instruments of foreseeable violence securely to the walls and had withstood the tests of time.

Against the panelling sat three men and an old woman, each nursing a half pint of a brown beverage, barely enough sipped to remove the frothy heads, and talking in tired, low tones, conspirators in indolence. Above their heads, eavesdropping, a moth-eaten buffalo's head stared across at the coal fire, feigning indifference through coal black eyes.

The owner of the establishment stood at the bar, looking at a bit of a loose end. Still, he would have no doubt preferred that status quo to the appearance of two uniformed police officers on the threshold.

"I'll take the landlord Josh, you try the customers," said Abe nodding in the direction of the quartet. "Morning Reg," he continued.

A small and slight figure under a billycock hat and wearing the distinctively striped workhouse pattern shirt and waistcoat beneath an equally give-away fearnought cloth jacket had been perched at the other end of the bar guarding a lonely pint. At the sound of Abe's voice, this dapper old gentleman jumped down from the bar stool with alacrity, a ready albeit toothless smile and a sharp, left-handed, military salute announcing, "Corporal Reginald Phillips, 38th. Of Foot, reporting for duty sergeant."

Practised in the routine, Abe responded. "At ease corporal."

"Thank you, sergeant."

Abe approached the landlord and Josh drew the short straw.

"Good morning constable. What's your name lad?"

"Hello Reg. We've met before, haven't we?"

"No. I don't think so. Never forget a face me."

In fact, these days Reg did occasionally forget a face. He had forgotten Josh's face, as well as his name.

"It's constable Lively Reg. Josh."

"Pleased to meet you Josh." Reg. stuck out his good hand which Josh dutifully shook.

"Sorry about the left hand, but as you can see, the right one's missing." As per usual, ex corporal Reginald Phillips, late of the South Staffs, had neatly tucked and folded his right sleeve at elbow level – where his right arm terminated – and pinned it to his upper arm.

"It's an honour to shake an old soldier's hand, either one," said Josh.

"Old soldier? Yes, that's me. I'm fifty-four you know!"

And you look it Reg, you poor old bugger.

"It's been thirty-four years since I lost me arm you know. Bet you can't guess where?"

In the Crimea by any chance?

"In the Crimean War. You're too young to remember that of course. It was the Russian Bear against the British Lion, and the Frogs. And some Turks an' all. Turks was on our side, but they didn't amount to much. Foreign Johnnies; can't trust 'em. Look, that's where I got this." Reg gestured to his chest whereto was affixed the still bright sky blue and yellow ribbon threaded through his shining campaign medal. Josh knew, because he had been told before, that the two oak leaf clasps signified that Reg had seen action in two battles during the campaign.

"These two bars," went on the old man, "mean that I was at Inkerman and Sebastopol…"

Yes, I think you might have mentioned that.

"Did you ever hear about the siege of Sebastopol?"

"I heard it was a living hell." *From you!* "A freezing hell with cholera and snipers ready to put you out of your misery. Trench warfare, wretched business."

"Yes. Wretched business, trench warfare. You took the words right out of my mouth."

"Were you in here last night Reg.?"

"No. Can't afford to drink all the time. And it's not always that easy to get out of the workhouse. Depends on what's cooking," continued Reg with a knowing wink which escaped the young policeman entirely.

"Right then. I just need to go and…"

But the old soldier's timing was impeccable and Josh never stood a chance. "There was a group of us," he said as he grasped the young man's forearm and looked earnestly into his eyes.

"There was fifteen or twenty of us, sent to storm the Russian rifle pits. We showed 'em. The ones that ran was lucky. Only I got shot, in the hand. Surgeon took the hand; gangrene took the rest."

Oh. He's missed out the captain. Forgotten him no doubt.

"Captain Vam, he was our captain. Dutch he was, originally; I think. Foreign anyway. But more than a match for them poncy public school English officers. He was a good man, and a damn good C.O. Yes, I'll always remember what he said…"

At this point Reg was staring into space, a momentary time traveller, retrieving memories. Josh would have not made a good military officer, though, for instead of seizing this opportunity and making a tactical withdrawal, he found himself drawn back into the skirmish.

Decisive.

"Decisive he said it was. Clearing them Russkis out. Decisive."

As Reg took a self-congratulatory, but expertly timed, swig of beer, Josh was looking round with what felt absurdly like a growing panic. Abe had finished with the man behind the bar and was talking to the buffalo party. May as well stay put.

"Buy you a half Reg?"

"That's very kind of you son. What did you say your name was?"

"It's Josh."

"But I only drink pints Josh," said Reg as he produced as if by magic a now empty pint pot. "Bitter please Josh."

When Reg's refill had arrived, he attacked another favourite theme. "You've heard of Florence Nightingale? Yes of course you have. Well I met her, in hospital. Scutari…"

Saved your life, she did. An angel she was.

"She saved my life you know. They called her the Lady With The Lamp. I called her an angel."

"Well she did a good job. You're still here."

"Yes, cleanliness and fresh air. That's the secret to health and long life."

64

Sure it's not hot air?

But Josh had to admit that, on the cleanliness front, you couldn't fault this old man. He kept his hair and beard in trim, or somebody did; his clothes were unsoiled; and he kept his old boots bulled to a mirror shine which put Josh's efforts to shame.

During the ensuing continuation of the trip down Memory Lane, another customer came in and ordered a pint. Josh clocked him. He had a pretty good idea that the able bodied and sober young man along the bar did not hold down what you might call a regular job. He was pretty sure that he was one of Cyril's crew. Abe saw it too, and signalled Josh to stay where he was, with Reg. Abe went over to ask the new comer the question of the hour – had he been in last night? One ear on that conversation and the other under siege from Reg, Josh gathered that the young man had not been in last night, had popped in at random today, no particular reason. Abe was not quite prepared to believe him, and Derek Woolley did not care that he wasn't. For Woolley had come for a reason, which was to glean information: had the police identified the killer horse? And what did they know of the driver? Woolley had a full freckled still boyish face which belied his criminal mentality. He also had big ears, literally and figuratively. Like Josh he was employing each ear independently, and it paid off. Swiftly downing his drink, he made off in haste, eager to report back to Jack.

The corporal was still rambling, about the comings and goings at the workhouse now, as Josh finally broke away to turn to Abe.

"Anything?"

"Not really. We'll get Payne and Stride to do some more digging when the miners knock off tonight. Interesting that one of uncle Cyril's hangers-on chose this moment to show up though."

"Yes, I know. Cyril's got a big black horse. What did he say?"

#

Abe had caught Cyril alone this time.

"Come in and sit down. I won't offer you a drink. I can see you're on duty. What can I help you with?"

"There was an unfortunate incident yesterday involving some drunks and a horse and cart. A young man was killed."

"I heard that. It's the gossip of the hour. If you want to know if anybody's dropped any hint of who was responsible, I can't help. Nobody knows anything."

"Except that the horse was a large black one and the driver was heading in this direction, before the fog swallowed them."

"And I've got a large black horse. Well, I'm not the only one. Anyway, lots of horses look black at night. And the road doesn't magically stop here does it? Could have been heading for Oldbury and beyond."

"I know, but I have to start somewhere. Process of elimination. Can you vouch for the whereabouts of your horses and, er, employees last night?"

"No," said Cyril flatly.

"Ah…"

"Not the lads anyway. They have personal lives as well you know. I don't keep them on a leash."

Perhaps I ought to.

"I see," *perhaps you should,* "And the horses?"

"Look, I knew you or your men would be around, and I've already checked. They haven't been out since I put them away yesterday, about seven that was. One's a grey anyway, so you can eliminate him. Carts and harness all present and correct. Satisfactory?"

Not really. "Yes, thank you uncle. That's helpful. What about your 'Mad Mick'? He lives in I believe. Did he see or hear anything?"

"Actually, he's away again," *he really is this time,* "but, as I say, there's no way that Jingles – that's the black mare – was out without me knowing. If there was anybody messing around back there the dog would have told me. Will that be all then?"

"Yes, thank you again uncle." Abe offered his hand which was readily grasped by the older man. His heart wanted to trust his uncle, or at least believe him, but the lawman in his head got in the way. Doing the job was a point of honour for him, but so was family loyalty. And he owed his uncle much, even if the debt was an old one…

"Not at all," said Cyril. "I just feel sorry for the boy's mother. It's ironic, isn't it?"

"What is?"

"How many times do you think his mother had told him about playing in the 'oss road? Only for two grown-up clowns to dump him in a barrow and throw him under a horse?"

"Throw him?"

"Figure of speech."

"Right. Well thanks for your time…"

"Next time, come out of uniform and have a drink. I'm sure John will come. We can have a family reunion."

"I'll think about it. You will remember to speak to your men, won't you?"

"Oh yes, I intend to."

And he meant it.

Chapter 7

Hackett Street

The Wesleyan Methodist Church in Hackett Street had a regular Sunday congregation of forty or fifty devout souls drawn from a dozen local families. Like many such local institutions it had an austere brick façade broken with regular slit like glazed gaps, arched and unstained, where the light was allowed in. The ascetic effect in this case was softened as the builders had chosen a buff brick over the more common red, with detailing over door and window arches complementing in engineering-brick blue. Still – ugly some might call it. But if beauty be in the eye of the beholder, and the beholder a worshipper, there was no doubt that it was a thing of beauty whenever the faithful were in attendance, seeing it as they always did, clad in a patina of praise and prayer of their own making.

On this particular Sunday, there was a latecomer. A latecomer and a newcomer, and, to tell truth, he found the building wholly unattractive; more like a prison than a church. The scales would fall from his eyes when he came to appreciate that grace in which the whole holy edifice was steeped. At least some might tell him that, if they could read his mind. But as the Holy Spirit had not gifted any of today's gathering the power to read minds, the issue would never arise...

The shepherd and flock here prided themselves on their gusto and hymns, unaccompanied though they were by any musical instrument. And on this Sunday, it was at the end of the last verse of an exuberant and suitably rousing 'Onward Christian Soldiers' that the interloper sneaked in and ensconced himself, as if as a disguise, next to two particularly large ladies already squashed on a pew, packed even though at the back. Had he walked in and sat without such an obvious effort to be unobtrusive, he would not have been so obtrusive. As it was, every head took its moment to turn and satisfy its owner's curiosity. This was a stranger to these hallowed halls. But not a stranger, if only through reputation, to some in the congregation. For these, surprise, tinged with a vague sense of desecration, was the predominant feeling. And yet for one certain individual, there was a genuine pleasure, born of a sure and certain hope that he was here for her.

For his part, John Lively, spruced up and smart, would have freely admitted, if anyone had cared to ask, that, despite a good C. of E. upbringing, he was not of the religious persuasion. But it was not religion that had persuaded him to come here. No, this operation had a more worldly objective. He had made his reconnaissance yesterday. The church had been empty, the quiet transfixed by the cutting and dusty-sweet smell of bluebells and honesty. Unlike the Anglican churches he had once been used to, this place was unpretentious, even Spartan. It reminded him of her. He had made up his mind to sit at the back and time his exit as she passed. And so here he was. Since meeting Sissy Flavell at his sister's wedding, she had simply grown on him. He remembered her firmness of grip and spirit and imagined the firmness of her forge-conditioned body. Was she his type? Begrudgingly, John would admit that he had never had a particular 'type' when it came to the ladies: as long as it was female, clean, and with all of the bits still attached, that was all the qualification he had needed. Mind you, that did restrict the field somewhat in this God forsaken town. *Christ,* John remembered where he was, *sorry, I mean, blimey, I've seen some real shit since I got here. What kind of God plans things to turn out like this? Surely not an omnipotent one? Perhaps He can't think straight because of all the noise being hurled at him from all these different Churches, and all the arguing? Who knows? He does move in mysterious ways apparently…*

But perhaps there came a time to grow and sober up. Sissy was different. A different girl for a different John? He had been impressed by the way she stood up to him, fixing him with strong hand and eye. Nobody did that, but she had. In a matter of days he had elevated her to 'must have' status, but in a good and wholesome way. A few passing nods led to a few passing hellos or good mornings, then to longer exchanges, when the passing was slower. Eventually she had disclosed that this was her church.

"I might see you there next week," he had said.

"It would be good to see you there. Everyone's welcome." *There is more joy in heaven, and all that.*

And he took that as his invitation.

From where he sat he only caught glimpses of her, but *she's here all right.* So, he leant back to listen to the service. The really rather portly preacher had the unfortunate knack of projecting a monotone drone of a voice which was no doubt intended to imbue the listener with a sense of solemnity, or holiness perhaps. Not known for his holiness in any case, John Lively proceeded to solemnly nod off. He was awakened with a nudge and everyone standing for the next hymn. But he didn't know this one, which was a pity because he had a good singing voice and felt obliged to join in.

"And am I only born to die?
And must I suddenly comply
With Nature's stern decree?
What after death for me remains?
Celestial joy or hellish pains…"

Well, this is a barrel of fucking laughs.

After an eternity of standing and mumbling, the Lord allowed John to sit back down. By the time the preacher was on his sermon, though, John's head was getting heavy again. *Don't fall asleep. Pay attention.*

The round cleric was looking right at him, or so it seemed through disobedient eyelids.

"Cease from anger and forsake wrath: Fret not thyself in any wise to do evil."

What are you picking on me for? Not very Christian of you.

Drone, drone…

"A little that a righteous man hath is better than the riches of many wicked."

But then again, it's hard to be righteous when your kids are starving.

"And the Lord shall help them, and deliver them. He shall deliver them from the wicked, and save them, because they trust in him."

I'll drink to that.

Half an hour later, in the bar of the George and Dragon, he was doing just that. Sissy was with him. Maybe it was the Lord's doing?

"So," she said, "how long have you been a Methodist then?"

"About an hour, I suppose."

"It shows. I heard you struggling with the last hymn."

"You heard then? In my defence, it was a completely new one on me. Couldn't get the tune at all. And when I did think I might have it I was dragged right off by some old gal singing pitch perfect in front and several octaves beyond me."

"That explains it then."

"What?"

"I thought somebody was strangling a cat."

"Which is why I gave up and shut up."

"Wise decision. So, if it wasn't for the singing, what brought you to our church today?"

"I think you know said John," watching her blush.

"What do you think of it?"

"I was brought up C. of E., so it looks a bit bare and bleak to me…"

"Ah, but that shouldn't matter should it? It's the feel of the place, surely. You can feel the presence of God as soon as you walk in. You know what I mean. Have you ever walked into an empty church? There's a stillness there. A peace. I always feel closer to God there."

John didn't tell her that he had been there the day before, alone, and had felt only the quiet; a relative quiet at least. Stillness can sometimes bring peace. A chance to think things through. Thoughts sometimes changed into prayers, and answers sometimes came, but John was not sure that it was God who sent them. He was no longer convinced, as the child had been, that there was any God. But he wasn't sure of his ground and would not deny Him out loud, saying to her, "I've been in empty churches and empty halls and empty factories. They all feel similar, which is empty and unusually quiet. I think it's the unaccustomed silence that makes you think of…" He was struggling for a word, but there was only one, "God, I suppose. He doesn't have to actually be there, in that place, but that's not to say that in that quietness you can't find God, inside yourself. He's everywhere anyway, isn't He?" He was thinking it through as he spoke now, "And you can hear him in such places precisely because you have found somewhere quiet and shut out the world. That's why people close their eyes to pray. But this world of ours, this world of toil and pain and noise and smoke… this stops us seeing Him and hearing Him. And there's no getting back till we can leave such lives behind. This place just doesn't allow us the peace of mind to really contact God. And I think He knows it. He's probably written us off as a lost cause." *And everyone attending church each Sunday morning could better spend their time.*

She felt his passion, and his confusion and she wanted to take him in her arms to feel that passion, to banish that confusion and bring him the comfort of faith. But she merely said, "We're not on our own, Jesus taught us that. You just have to trust in him." She left it at that and asked,

"But did you enjoy the service?"

"Truth?"

"Yes, of course."

"To be honest, I found it a bit boring. I mean, I was looking forward to blasting out a few good hymns – haven't had a good sing in ages – but, as I say, I didn't even know the tunes, apart from 'Onward Christian Soldiers' but that was finishing as I got there. Just my luck!"

Sissy looked disappointed. John had to retrieve the situation. "Not that there wasn't a lot of food for thought, of course. Usually is. But I think it was the preacher, or minister, or whatever he was."

"He's a local preacher. The minister we only see about once a month. Anyway, what about him?"

"It's just that voice. How can anyone sound so boring?"

She laughed then. "He's known for it is our Septimus. Better than the rest of the pompous bunch."

"What? The preachers?"

"No. I'm talking about his snotty family, the Siviters."

"I've heard the name but I'm not familiar with them."

"I don't think anybody is. Don't want to be. Got a couple of shops and a bit of land and they think they're above folk like us. They were nail-masters twenty or thirty years ago selling rod to the nailers and buying the finished product. You're not from around here but the masters were always unpopular and the Siviters were worst of all, rigging the weights and buying cheap. Real blood money."

"So that's one lot for everlasting hellfire then?"

70

"You'd think so, wouldn't you? Seem to be thriving well enough on this earth."

"Ah, but don't forget – the wicked shall perish and the enemies of the Lord shall be as the fat of lambs consumed in the smoke, or fire…"

"You were listening well considering you were bored!"

"It's not the first time I've been in church."

"Anyway," continued the girl, "today's Siviters aren't the same ones that bled the nailers. You can't blame them for inheriting money and being stuck up. I think."

"I thought pride was one of the seven deadly sins?" He left the question hanging and took a swig of his pint before continuing. "That's the danger of wealth. Having money encourages the sin of pride, just has having none encourages the sin of envy. At the very least. So, as far as I can make out, we're all buggered. Excuse my French!"

"That's why we go to church and at least try to follow the bible's teachings." It was Sissy's turn to take a pull on her pint. "Wouldn't you say?"

"I don't know whether I would. Seems to me the powers that be, the government, the employers, gaffers, call 'em what you will, they've stolen real religion and feed it back to us in some perverted form to keep us under control…"

"Oh come on. I've heard this kind of rubbish before. No offence."

"None taken. I know what you mean. But think about it. Just think about the psalm what's his name was on about today."

"It's Siviter. What about it?"

"Well, it's typical of the way they try to get you to see things. There's an implication that there's 'righteousness' in being poor – and presumably honest, that's a joke – and that the troubles of the world are down to a load of 'wicked' people who are wicked because they are not poor, clinging to worldly things."

"I think the righteous are those that remain honest and hardworking despite being poor."

"And you've hit the nail on the head! Hardworking is it? To what end? To make the rich richer, in the process presumably making them more wicked."

"John, that's saft. We all need to work, don't we?"

"But ideally, we should all be paid more for our labour. Even things up a bit. Perish the thought though. So we are told to be good and our reward will be in heaven. And we believe it. But do the rich believe it?"

"Some of them do. Most of them I'd say."

"Yes but it's all show. If they were at all worried they'd be giving away their money and estates like there was no tomorrow."

"But somebody has to be in charge. It's just the way of things."

"Perhaps it doesn't have to be that way at all. Look at that fat preacher today, spouting on about the rewards waiting for us in heaven. He's getting his reward here judging by the state of him. It's downright typical."

Sissy thought this one over and finished her drink. "I don't know whether I can agree with you but I understand your argument. Even in Methodism the preachers and ministers are mostly from, shall I say, non-working backgrounds. Even in this day and age. But I think that's because really poor people – and I don't count myself amongst them, thank God – really poor people have enough to think about putting food on the table. You're right there. It's a poverty trap, that's what it is." She was rather pleased with this turn of phrase, so she repeated: "A poverty trap."

"That's exactly what it is. Things are designed to extract our last drops of sweat so that the rich get richer, which makes the nation richer. And powerful…Hence the empire, which I'm not criticising by the way."

"This is getting to be a rather deep conversation isn't it?"

"I'm sorry. I don't usually go on like this, except to my brother sometimes."

"Don't apologise. I'm enjoying it."

"I'm sure you didn't come here to talk politics."

"I thought we were talking religion?"

"Same thing arguably. But I don't want to argue with you; you might 'smosh me over the yed with yer omma.' Another drink?"

She laughed now. "Yes I bloody well might. Look, you've got me swearing on a Sunday now."

"I'm sure He'll forgive you. Drink?"

"No thanks. My sister's cooking Sunday dinner and I don't want to turn up smelling like I've been in the boozer, even if I have. You have one though."

"No, I think I'll take a leaf out of your book. I might have one later though, to celebrate my new job."

"What new job's this?"

"With my uncle Cyril. He owns the Shoulder Of Mutton. Haven't told him I'll accept yet, but I think I will."

"I know him. Or of him. What will you be doing?"

"Mainly driving. He runs a little haulage business on the side."

"That's not the only business he has on the side, I heard."

"Yes, well there's the butchery as well of course."

"That's not exactly what I meant."

"I know. People like to talk, don't they? He's not the villain he's made out to be. And he's family."

"And it won't be awkward, your brother being a copper?"

"Two brothers actually. But no, not at all. If my uncle was the crook everybody says he is, wouldn't Abe – that's Sergeant Lively – wouldn't he have locked him up by now?"

Sissy didn't care to answer that, and merely shrugged.

"Besides," John went on, "what's a few risks running the gauntlet with the local constabulary compared to an early and horrible death?"

"What do you mean?"

"I mean that we're all like lambs to the slaughter in that bloody ironworks. Shall I tell you what decided me?"

"If you want to."

"Well then," John pursed his lips and let the breath escape before going on. "Last Tuesday. Last Tuesday it was. At work. One of my workmates was loading ore into the furnace. It's fed in at the top. Anyway, he was tipping a load in, same as he did most days, when he disappeared. He just fell in. God knows why: lost his balance; overcome by the heat; perhaps he just wanted to end it all. Whatever. So in he goes and gets melted down with the iron. Nothing left. Nothing to bury. Nothing to mourn over. No more Alf. Just like that. One minute he was with us, then he was gone. Without a trace. As if he never existed in the first place. He might have been someone we just imagined, except there was still a pie he was keeping warm next to one of the ovens, for his dinner; and that was gone next day when a guard dog ate it."

Was this a joke? Sissy looked into his eyes and decided that it was not.

"John. I'm ever so sorry. It must have been really horrible. Were you good friends?"

"Not really. But something like that gets you thinking about life. Your own."

"I suppose accidents happen. I've seen some pretty bad burns in my time, but nothing like that."

"Well, you're lucky. But the point is, and this harks back to what we were talking about earlier, that a lot of these so-called accidents shouldn't happen. It's all down to greed. A lot are caused purely by the fact that people are over-worked. And the people exploiting them, the owners, are the people the bible is banging on about, or should be. The wicked oppressing the righteous if you like. And I don't care if they do go to church, it doesn't change what they are. And what they are is wrong and cruel and callous."

"You're very passionate about this aren't you? You care don't you? That's a very Christian trait you know."

"I wouldn't necessarily say that. Don't get me wrong, I've come across some very unsavoury characters in this town, amongst the working classes I mean. There's some real bad 'uns about. But I don't think anyone can put their hand on heart and say they were born that way. It's the system that does for them, the life they inherit."

"So how do you explain the decent folk? The people that are straight and true even if they haven't got everything. Me for instance?"

"I can't. Unless you assume that Man is basically good and has to be turned to evil, and not the other way around."

"I would agree with that."

"That's it then. Everybody's good, till there's a chance to earn money out of your neighbour. You know, I really can't understand why every working man isn't pushing to be a member of a trade union."

"Are you in a union?"

"That's the point. Not enough willing to support one where I worked. Not surprising

73

really. The last man trying to organise one was sacked and had to leave town to find work. Troublemaker see."

"And I don't suppose there's such a thing as a union for nephews?"

"I never heard of one."

It went quiet between them then and Sissy started making moves to leave.

"Hold on," said John, "I haven't told you the best bit yet."

"And what's the best bit?"

"After Alf's accident, after the metal had been run off into the moulds, they got the vicar in to bless them! Last rites for some slabs of metal! Would you bloody well believe it?"

Sissy wasn't sure she could take this seriously. She threw incredulity back at his earnest expression, and, pensively, he batted back, "Perhaps his parents should have called him Shadrach." And they both collapsed in giggles.

After dinner, when she had had time to digest the day, Sissy came to suspect that she was falling in love.

Chapter 8

Of Dogs and Devils

The warming summer ushered in a season of silliness and tall tales. Lighter nights and clement weather encouraged folk to drink more, to hang around in the street, and to generally chew the fat. Occasionally, a particular topic of conversation would take hold, assuming a life of its own and spreading like wildfire. Sometimes, a story turned to speculation; speculation spawned titillation; titillation turned to hysteria; hysteria, fear. Fear threatened law and order, and hence the peace of mind of Sergeant Abraham Lively.

It happened that in 1887 a drunken encounter, memories of a past bogey man, and irresponsible reporting, so inflamed the human propensity for myth making and self-delusion that it sparked a conflagration that threatened to burn away rational thought, seeding in its stead the germs of a sort of infectious voluntary panic.

It began on a muggy Saturday night, in the Springfield district, with thunder clouds gathering. It was already past closing when an old quarry hand left the Hailstone public house. According to his own statement later he had 'had a few' (it was Saturday after all) but nevertheless, and to his credit, was able to make his way home under his own steam. At any rate, that had been the intention. He had bidden farewell to the rump of diehard, and illegal, drinkers in his chosen watering hole, and, door sealed behind him, he had begun to stagger his happy way towards Tippity Green and home. But in no more than fifty paces a pleasant meandering through a comforting stupefaction and familiar streets abruptly became a sleep-walk into hell. For, all of a sudden, with a whoosh and a flapping of devilish wings, a huge figure dropped out of the sky to confront him, just outside the barbers. It was ten feet tall, but only six away, with eyes like saucers, cloven hooves and horns which could clearly be seen, where the trousers ended and under his hat. At least, that was the tale as told by the Blackheath Weekly Advertiser two days later, and it was the article in that worthy and eminent publication that prompted the almost immediate dispatch of P.C. John Payne to investigate.

Contrary to the constable's expectations, the alleged victim stubbornly stuck to the preposterous version of events related by the aforementioned rag, with the exception of the clothes: the monster he said was in fact hat-less and trouser-less, but appeared to be wearing some sort of flowing blue garment to cover his modesty! But yes, the wings were there, with little quills, like new feathers sprouting, or the hair that appears if you don't shave for several mornings; huge eyes; and short curly horns under a shaggy topping of coarse hairs. And claws! Scary claws. The constable was understandably sceptical.

"If you were that scared how come you had time to notice all this detail?" he asked.

"Norabaht to ever ferger et. Ah bay sleepin' yoh know, norra wink. Keep seein' et," averred the witness and victim, one Davy Dimmock.

Payne had interviewed the drinkers in the Hailstone, to whom the unfortunate had fled after encountering the apparition, and all accounts confirmed that he had seemed very frightened indeed,' 'scared to jeff' as one put it, whilst a less refined soul added, "shittin' 'isself." Enquiries as to the state of Dimmock's sobriety indicated that he had had no more than 'normal' and was by no means drunk, an assertion vigorously affirmed by the principal player. Payne of course, took this with a pinch of salt, man of the world as he was. He had another card to play, and asked how Dimmock could make out fine details on what had been a dark and alcohol-befogged night.

Got you there you drunken old git!

"That's part on it though ay it? That's part o' the 'orror. The 'orror, ah sed. Ah wish to God ah couldn' see 'im. But that wor on was et? No, yoh couldn't miss 'im, cuz he was a glowin'. Glowin' blue 'e was. It was flowin' rahnd 'im, all swirly. Ah con see et now. 'Orrible, 'orrible…"

So, according to dozy Davy – dozy Davy Dimmock – as Payne had secretly labelled him, the thing exuded a cold blue light which enveloped him, like an overcoat he had said. One thing you could say about this monster was that he had an extensive wardrobe. Payne reflected that details of the creature's sartorial preferences were in no wise the least bizarre aspect of the case: the silly old bugger was convinced that if this blueness touched him, then he would die, and he would be taken to hell by this demon. This Blue Devil as Dimmock would have it…

So, the thing was just standing there, looking at him. It held out its hand, or claw, and his heart lurched. He couldn't get past it and fleeing meant turning his back. But although forty-odd now, he was still a good runner, and so, after an eternity of seconds, his baffled brain finally decided that he should make his way swiftly back to the pub. Thus, he turned and ran to the Hailstone as smartly as jellied legs would allow. Too scared to look back, yet he knew it followed him; his eyes fixed on the pub door, so far away, and a clop-clop filling his ears as it hopped along behind. Too late he realised his mistake: by the time the door was unlocked and opened it would be on him. But no! Suddenly it leapt over him onto the roof of the pub, off into the road where it jigged along until it turned an abrupt ninety degrees and over the fence into the quarry, when the blue light vanished like a snuffed candle. And he was banging and shouting like a madman till the door swung open.

Payne had taken his statements a week since. But by now, fuelled by another frivolous piece in the Advertiser, the situation had descended into farce. The provocative, now front page, headline read 'Lock Up Your Daughters – Jack's Back!' The journalistic theory had been that the terrible 'apparition' which had 'terrorised' regulars at the Hailstone had been none other than the infamous Spring Heeled Jack, last seen in these parts in 1855. That week's issue had gone to town on the Spring Heeled Jack legend. Apart from the front-page report which included statements from 'eye witnesses' at the Hailstone, there was an article inside summarising the known history of Jack, and possibly some hitherto unknown history, together with alleged testimony of past victims. There was even reproduced a really quite disturbing drawing of the fiend, portrayed as a chimera of man's body, goat's feet and donkey's head (but with short horns and human ears), spewing smoke and fire and holding outstretched with scaly hands a black cloak which might have been wings. And wearing evening dress!

Payne's report had concluded that this was simply a case of the D.T.s. The blue devil had as well have been a pink elephant. Another one down to the booze.

Except that the paper hadn't let things lie, and Jack suddenly leapt off the pages and, by way of human credulity, into the streets. Reports of Jack proliferated. He was seen jumping back and forth over the cut in Tividale, standing on the remains of the Hail Stone in the midnight moonlight, running up and down Portway Road rattling doors and scaring the children, sneaking into brew-houses and spoiling the beer. Then, a young lady was followed in Netherton in broad daylight, and as dusk fell nearer to home, a woman was accosted on her own doorstep.

Sergeant Lively already had his hands full, as usual. He had not seen Alice for nearly a month and it grieved him. And now this Spring Heeled Jack nonsense had gone too far. Excepting the blue devil incident, all of the subsequent actual sightings had been by women. This led Abe to suspect, siding with Payne's opinion, that the natural emotional turbulence of the feminine spirit, excited by irresponsible journalism and front yard gossip, was, to put it bluntly, causing these women to see things that just weren't there. He couldn't be sure of course. He couldn't rule out some local prankster with a mask and a particularly athletic physique. Whatever. He needed to put it to bed. He blew out the lamp and tried to get some sleep.

#

Saturday. Abe anticipated an evening of incident. Last weekend had seen boozed up bands of locals on the prowl, looking for Jack and a break from the banal; and breaching the peace. He intended to get to the bottom of all the prattle and put a stop to it. Friday night's miscreants had been processed by early afternoon, leaving him time to speak to the alleged victims personally. The two incidents which stood out, owing to the proximity of the witnesses to the creature, were, firstly, the case of Mrs Edna Webb, a lady residing in Church Road, Rowley, who had answered a knock on the door to be confronted by the fiend and, secondly that of Davy Dimmock, the first victim of a 'blue devil' which had spawned the reports of similar, but interestingly not identical, creatures all over the parish, and beyond.

Mrs Webb's front door was open, and there was a veritable swarm of Church Road natives milling around outside it, like workers around a queen bee. The commotion only intensified when an officer of the law turned up, and he was funnelled toward the doorstep and Edna Webb by her new found court. All of this of course only served to confirm the sergeant's prejudice that this was a case of attention-seeking. His judgement was backed by the fact that the woman's statement about her ordeal and the description of 'Jack' tallied very closely, too closely, with the 1850s case reported in the newspaper and with the illustration accompanying it. And then there was the poor victim herself: she didn't look poor, unless in the financial sense, and she didn't much look like a victim. As he introduced himself she puffed herself up with self-importance and ushered him ostentatiously into the parlour, shutting the noise out and the rabble. It was a small room and the musty smell whispered to him in embarrassed tone that it was used only on special occasions. There were a couple of well-worn armchairs in shades of green, lighter where the sunlight had caught them over the years; what must once have been a good quality card table from a better quality home than this, cards long since a mere memory and supplanted by a blue glazed vase, bereft of flowers at present; a small but sturdy oak dresser upon which was perched, somewhat precariously in parts, what was obviously the best, never used, china; and a framed wedding portrait of two impossibly young looking figures masquerading as bride and groom. The whole was enclosed by claustrophobic paisley patterned wallpaper, rusty brown on cream, and rested on an attractive floral rug which had seen very little traffic.

Mrs Webb motioned him to one of the chairs, the one facing the window.

"Please, tek a seat officer."

Abe had read Payne's report. He was more interested in the witness than the story. So after politely declining tea, he had her walk him through the events and locations of the evening in question.

The children were in bed and her husband was 'up the bloody boozer as usual' – The Ring Of Bells was his favourite, which seemed to be a choice dictated not only by the beer but by the presence of certain 'mates an' floosies'. She was settled in the kitchen darning her husband's socks and her son's green pullover. As Abe looked around said kitchen he found it unexceptional, apart, perhaps, from a half-finished bottle of gin tucked away on a high shelf, out of the reach of any child. Not Mr Webb's bottle he surmised, the faint whiff of gin he had noticed when the lady of the house had let him in confirmed it for him. The light was gone and the table lamp lit when she thought she had heard a knock on the door. No she didn't go straight to the door because she was not sure she had heard it. No she wasn't worried about Spring Heeled Jack; yes she had heard of

78

him of course, but hadn't expected him to come calling. So, no, the door was not locked. Then the knocking did start. Loud knocking. Yes of course she asked who was there. But there was no reply. Probably her drunken husband, home early and acting yampy. So she put the darning down, on the table there, strode to the door and yanked it open to confront him. What a fright! What a terrible, awful fright. Standing there in this long black cloak, touching the floor it was…No, couldn't comment on any other clothes because of the cloak wrapped round him. But it was awful. It had a long face like a donkey, and horns. He might have had a hat but she can't remember. Oh, and hooves. No, the cloak only covered one foot, you could see the other. Smoke was coming out of his nose and then, all of a sudden he reached forward and grabbed the front of her dress and pulled it down over her…well, you know. She screamed of course, and then she must have fainted. Anyway, that scared him because he jumped up and disappeared. No, sorry, this was before she fainted, or as she was falling she supposes. Anyway he was gone, then Ben was here. He saved her you know, picked her up and took her in. No, he carried her into the parlour (Abe was willing to bet that that was where the husband found them), she had asked him to, proper chair to recover in. Mr Webb? He came home two hours later. Ben lives next door, with his parents. He's a builder. She's known him since he was a nipper…

Abe found young Benjamin Key in the street as he left. He could corroborate only the fact that he had responded to Mrs Webb' scream. No, he couldn't explain why he was the only person in the street to hear. Abe had his own theory. No, there was no sign of 'Jack', but he could jump over buildings, couldn't he? And, no, Mrs Webb hadn't wanted to call the police, at first. Too embarrassed. Abe knew that much.

He could do them for wasting police time, but he couldn't really prove it. Besides, it wasn't as if they were real criminals, like thieves or robbers. Stickler as he was, he didn't believe in overkill. No time for it. Therefore, today, he merely attempted to take the heat out of the situation by politely, but firmly, suggesting that if the Jack sightings did not die a natural death, the circumstances of the two of them being alone in the house, without calling for the police, would necessitate a much more intrusive investigation involving the questioning of Mrs Webb and the neighbours…and Mr Webb.

Quarter past four and he was done with the indiscreet lovers. A warm afternoon, he took a pleasant stroll down towards Tippity Green and Springfield, stopping briefly to give an obvious tramp his marching orders. Marching orders: that was a good one. These itinerant ex-soldiers were a nuisance; no home, no family, and no reason to abide by the rules…

When he reached the Hailstone pub it was still closed, as he expected. But, also as expected, the barber's was open. He planned to treat himself to a haircut and a proper hot-towel shave. The barber's shop door was open and the red and white stripes of the barber's pole appeared to be luring in more than paying customers, for above the paper screen running along the bottom edge of the shop windows, a couple of wasps and a clutch of bluebottles – probably a dead horse somewhere – together with a few smaller winged relatives were alternately crawling upwards then flying away on a short circuit before instinct and ignorance returned them again and again to the glass and futile crawling. Like prisoners on a treadmill, with headaches. Except that they had committed no crime. Nevertheless, there would be no release from their self-imposed sentence other than through an exhausted death, delivering them to the insect charnel house of dried-up corpses which crunched and creaked underfoot and littered the dusty skirting-line under the window. Until deftly swept into the street by barber Rock to blow away with the latest batch of assorted hair clippings. Gone forever.

Through the panes and above the screen could be discerned the upper body and big square head of Harold Rock. Barber Rock as he was referred to, even by family members. The figure shuffled and bent and stood and bent and shuffled again all within a defined space where, unseen, Abe knew that a customer was benefitting from the professional ministrations of the big man. Abe removed his helmet and duty band and walked in. The place was full of people. That is to say, the man himself, three customers including the one in the chair, his assistant – a little runt of an eleven-year-old with rickets who was also the barber's nephew – and now Abe.

Eyes turned and tongues paused when a uniform came in. But then the barber stopped snipping and gave the sergeant a smile:

"Worrow Sarge. 'Ow bin ya?"

"Bay three bad Haitch," said Abe, not entirely comfortable with his own rendition of colloquial repartie. *Best forget it…*

"Won't be long," said Rock, "just finishing with Jake here and then there's only the three of you."

Jake's short back and sides was perfect for the heat of summer and the mine. As Abe sat the barber was applying a flame from a greasy taper to the newly shaven hairs at the back of the sitter's head and neck. To seal the open ends you see; stop chills getting in. Then he was dextrously swinging a hand-held mirror at angles to the big mirror and the customer's head and without waiting for sign of approval swiftly swept away the sheet, gave it a practised shake and hung it up with one hand, whilst retrieving Jake's cap with the other. A furtive passing of chinking coin, a smart handshake, and another satisfied customer was on his way.

"Now, who's next?" said the barber.

"Ben was fust," said a pock marked midget of a man with watery eyes, nodding toward the younger man to his left.

"Cheers Chap," said the bloke at the front of the queue, in a distinctly different accent. "But perhaps we'd better let the Sergeant go first." He turned to Abe. "You're probably in a hurry."

Abe grinned. But only inside. Benjamin Fuller was trying too hard. No doubt he felt uncomfortable in the presence of the man who had been responsible for detaining him overnight on three occasions in the last six months. Routine stuff though, so Abe just said, "Good to see you Ben. I trust that you are in fine fettle. You haven't been in to see me for a while."

"Er, no. No I haven't," said an embarrassed Fuller, who, despite his surname, was actually one of the cohorts of miners living and working in the immediate vicinity. "It's nice to see you again. Do you want to go first?" he continued.

"Not at all. Not at all. I'm in no hurry. Off duty you know. Please." Abe gestured to the chair where the big man was waiting to cocoon his next victim in white linen and caress his skin with shining steel.

"Thanks," muttered Fuller as the Rock pounced.

The barber set to. Abe looked at the old man sitting at right angles to him, but he had buried his face in a paper and did not deign to make eye contact. Abe hoped that there was nothing in it about Jack or the blue devil; all he could see was some back page football articles which meant nothing to him. Rock was discussing some arcane aspect of hair cutting with Fuller as Abe's senses were distracted by other aural and olfactory input. Underlying the intermittent talk, the snip of scissors and the occasional buzz as a fly veered off course, there was a continual bubble and hiss and the smell of soap and camphor, or it may have been eucalyptus, as the hot water for the shaving brushes simmered on the little stove and the damp towels, infused with soothing oils (camphor or eucalyptus today, but otherwise witch hazel, or sandalwood, or lavender) stewed away in a copper pot, lid chinking whenever the pressure built up enough to release a wisp of steam. In front of the barber's chair was a big mirror, handy when you were carrying on a conversation from behind someone's head, and, arranged below and alongside, all the paraphernalia that went with the business of the house. Prominent were a selection of razors of differing shapes and sizes hanging in a row, with blades exposed. None were as fancy as Abe's, mostly being bone-handled, but he had no doubt that the steel was of the best and keenest, and would certainly do the job, whatever that job may be; nasty things razors, in the wrong hands…

Rock was talking to him now: "How have you been then Abraham? What do you reckon to this Spring Heeled Jack stuff?"

The barber always called him Abraham or Sarge. Never the formality of 'sergeant', nor the familiarity of 'Abe.' The two big men had hit it off as soon as they met. They had discussed the finer points of wrestling and boxing over a trim, and continued it over a drink. There was a lot to admire, and respect about Barber Rock. And like a rock he was, albeit something not quite as hard as granite or the rag these days. Years do that to a man. A good business man, he had turned his back on a potential career in pugilism; had seen too many boxers broken down before their time. Once, a younger man, and his claim to fame, he went three rounds with world champion William Perry, the Tipton Slasher. A slasher past his prime and no longer a world champion, and in a demonstration

81

bout, admittedly. But given the ferocity of fights in those days, even 'demonstration' ones, impressive enough.

"It's just that: stuff – and nonsense. Bored people always have to jump on the bandwaggon. And this one's driven by an imaginary devil in a dinner suit and loaded with beer."

"You're probably right."

"Probably?"

"Folk around here have seen some queer things over the years. I mean right here, in Springfield. In and around the quarry to be exact."

"What kind of things?"

Barber Rock looked at the other two men, listening raptly to the conversation. "We don't talk too much about it. The older ones amongst us were brought up to think it's unlucky, might bring the Blue Devil back. That's what we've always called it. The youngsters, now, that's different, they only laugh about it: somebody as drinks too much and sees things has got a case of 'the Blue Devils' they say. But they won't go near the Hail Stone after dark. That's the standing stone, what's left of it, not the pub."

"What's special about it? It's just a piece of rock that's jutting out because it hasn't been blasted yet isn't it?"

"Nobody ever told you?"

"No, what?"

"Yoh listen to 'im mate. Doh goo pokin' abaht there at night," intervened the clapped-out midget.

"He's right," continued Rock. "There's something unholy about it. Correction, that should be holy. But not Jesus Christ and the Holy Ghost holy. Ghost yes, probably. An unholy one. And God of course. But not our God. Not your Sunday morning sing a few hymns, listen to the vicar spouting, leave him in the church God…"

"What are you telling me Haitch?" said Abe.

"That stone's been there longer than Christianity. The druids lived here, and they prayed to it and they probably did human sacrifices. They say it raised a power which lives in the rock, and you can still feel it at certain times. When there's a full moon. If you're brave enough to try it."

"Have you tried it?"

"I did once. Not about to do it again."

"Why?" Abe saw a cloud pass over the countenance of the big man. It looked suspiciously like fear; and the barber seemed momentarily frozen; his hands had ceased their mechanical time-conditioned snipping and combing. "Oh come on," continued Abe, "druids have been gone for centuries, if they ever existed at all. What can they possibly have to do with giant bloody grasshoppers jumping about in this day and age? It's just a silly drunken superstition."

"Tell 'im about the witches Barber Rock," cut in the ugly runt again.

"There are no witches, not anymore," said the barber composure and snipping resumed. "Abraham's right. Just a load of drunken talk, in all probability."

"Just because they don't fly about on brooms with pointy 'ats don't mean there's none about. Even today," persisted the little man, "there's still them that follow the old ways."

"So how many witches do you know then?" contributed Fuller sarcastically from the chair.

"Well, I don't know any by name do I? Not for certain."

"I'll bet you don't," said the half-shorn smirking miner.

"What about Dotty Dunn?" continued the short-arse.

"Who's that?" asked Abe.

"Just a saft old woman that thinks she can heal you with a few spells and some plants. It's only the plants that do any good, if anything," explained Barber Rock.

"A herbalist then?"

"If you like, but certainly no witch. And you should be careful what you say Eric. You might get someone into trouble, including yourself. Isn't that right sergeant Lively?" The Barber emphasised the formal title.

"That's right, Eric." *So that's his name is it?* "Wouldn't want to run you in for provoking a breach of the peace." And Abe winked conspiratorially at young Peter, the bandy-legged nephew, who was not sure what to make of the threatening way the conversation seemed to have suddenly turned.

Ben's haircut finished, Rock's attention turned to the shaving. The live blade dissuaded the young miner from unnecessary movement, and the conversation died for an instant. All that was heard was the steaming and bubbling of the soap and towels, and what sounded like snoring…Where was it? Coming from under a bench in the corner Abe decided. Looking into the shadow, he could make out something that looked like an old coat lying on the floor under a fuzzy brown piece of, what? It wasn't another item of discarded apparel because, on closer inspection, it could be discerned that whatever it was moved with the rhythm of sleep; breath in, a pause, breath out, a pause, breath in, and so on. Just then, a customer came in and spoke, and an ear flicked. *A dog then, or cat.*

"Worrow Aitch," said the newcomer whose dusty pale work clothes and tanned face distinguished the quarry man from the miner in the chair, more of whose fleshly paleness was being revealed by the barber's blade by the second, and whose boots, yet visible beneath the cover, were anthracite black. As he spoke, and even before he had time to say, "Where's the babby?" the 'babby' rushed out to meet him with all the vigour it could muster. Which is to say, not much. It was a dog. Or had been once. And hardly much bigger than a cat. If Abe had been asked to hazard a guess as to its age he would probably have said extremely old indeed, for a dog. Though in spritely condition for a walking corpse. Well, walking on three legs anyway, the fourth being carried clear and never

83

touching the ground. It was of the terrier type with a short coat of curly ginger hair which must have known better days, clinging to a carcass mutilated by time. The little creature approached the man with obvious happiness, the kind of unconditional emotion which only dogs and small children display. The man for his part stooped to greet and fuss this ancient shop denizen, and treated her – for a bitch she was – with soft words and strokings and pattings; and scratchings, pork scratchings. Excitement over and treats consumed, the babby, or Mitzi to use her given name, dutifully, and Abe suspected gratefully, returned to her makeshift bed under the overhang to get on with sleeping away what was left of her allotted span.

The tall thin man took off his hat and sat next to old Eric and as far away from the police officer as space, comfort and manners allowed.

"Woh be long Norman," said Rock without turning.

"Righto," said the lanky quarryman, and nodding an acknowledgement to the sergeant, clapped Eric gently on the back "'Ow am ya Eric? Yoh fit and well?" To which Eric replied in more of the vernacular, but not much more. "Ahr," is all he said, but Norman seemed to read volumes into it, "that's bostin'," he said, with all the appearance of a genuine pleasure in it.

The newcomer turned out to be very talkative, "Eh, but 'er's grand ay 'er?" he remarked in reference to the sleeping scrap of old fur and bones. And Abe, with nothing else to do (Eric was still possessively clutching the newspaper and laboriously scouring every square inch from close range) found himself tuning in.

"It's a shame to see her like this though. But she is getting on isn't she? What is she, fourteen?" asked Norman.

"Only just thirteen," replied the barber who was just finishing up with the miner, "plenty of life yet."

For the life of him, Abe couldn't see it. But it was Rock's dog and he knew her best. Or perhaps it was just wishful thinking.

"I like a proper dog. A big dog," enjoined the newly smartened-up miner as he vacated the chair, "that one's just a rat."

Rock turned on him sharply and Fuller shrank away. "You mind what you say about my little girl. She's got as much spirit as any of your bull terriers, more than most."

"Sorry," continued the cowed collier, "it was only a figure of…"

Rock was on a roll now. "You should have seen her when she was younger. Champion ratter she was. You ask the pigeon fanciers that drink in the Cock. She's won us enough money off them over the years. Fastest little killer in the business. You probably remember her when she was still ratting, don't you Peter?"

"I think so," said Peter, "but I was only a kid. But they remember Mitzi all right. Still ask me about her. Don't ask about you uncle, but they ask about Mitzi. Little miss rag o' nothin' they call her."

"That's it, yes," said Rock almost sentimentally, seeing again the ratting ring, hearing the purposeful growls and the squeaks of fear and death as they floated up to feed the greedy excitement of the surrounding gamblers, wreathed in smoke and sound. And coming back to the moment he added, "Peter still catches rats for them don't you my boy? Earns us a bit extra."

"How does that work Peter?" enquired Abe of the boy.

"When they want rats I sell them some. I've got a ferret named Maude– she's a gill, a girl, a boy might not be able to get down all the holes – she chases them out and I catch them in a cage or a net and put them into cages, or buckets with lids on, then I deliver them. I get tuppence ha'penny for a dozen. But it's not very often…"

"You know," said Abe, winking at the barber, "I might have to confiscate this ferret. Maude you say? Against the law, gambling, you see."

The poor lad didn't know what to say, and, despite the wink, Rock realised that here was an officer of the law who actually had a valid legal point. So he was quick to come to the boy's defence.

"It's not really gambling though is it? Maybe a few coppers change hands but it's all about entertainment really. In any case, the rats are vermin; spread disease, pissing in the pigeon feed; kills 'em you know, the pigeons. And if they get into a loft they'll take the young uns right out from underneath the parents and eat them. It's a public service really. Parish ought to pay us."

"Possibly," agreed Abe. "But there are proper rat-catchers to do that."

"Yes and the rats die a slow death in their traps and on their poison. A dog's much quicker. And the rats get a chance to go down fighting," said Rock.

"Not much of a sporting chance to come out alive," observed Abe.

"Well, no, not in that respect. Some put up more of a struggle than others though. Some just seem to give up, some bite back. All different, like people really I suppose. But they all die at the end of it yes. That's the way it is. They're only rats."

"Is that why she limps, rat bite? Or just old age?"

Norman laughed. "It would have to be a bloody big rat to do that much damage, wouldn't it Barber Rock? No, that particular rat was a badger."

Abe raised his eyebrows. "A badger you say?"

At which the barber came back hurriedly, "Yes, at least that's what I thought it must have been," said the big man with a pointed glance at the tall man, which Abe was not intended to see. "We were out for a walk in the woods and she ran off. Couldn't find her. Shouted her for ages. When she did come back something had obviously had her. It was a midsummer evening and old Brock's sometimes out while it's still light at that time of year…"

But Abe hadn't missed the glance. The uniform had that effect; and Abe was used to it. It was right that people respected it; could be downright scary when they didn't. He looked at the little bundle of fur with a new respect.

"Have you always kept dogs Haitch?" enquired the sergeant, passing the time.

"I've always kept at least one. Terriers mostly, Jack Russells."

"Ar,'e on'y pleyze ot it doh yoh 'Aitch? Not lahrk we fum Crerdly Eeth." The almost incomprehensible Cradley Heath dialect of Fuller announced that he had not left yet.

"I'll give you playing at it," said Rock with what might have been humour, or what might have been just the opposite.

Fuller was taking no chances. "Only kidding," he said as he took his hat and his leave. "Buy you a pint later," was heard as the door slammed and Eric took his turn.

"All got one on 'em that lot from Cradley Heath," said Eric as he sat. He offered nothing more, so Abe asked, "I always thought his accent was a bit different. He's from Cradley you say? What brings him here then?"

"He lives just down the road, followed the work," replied Barber Rock. "Him and his wife and five kids and three bull terriers."

Abe had broken up enough dog-fights to know that bull terriers were bred for one thing in the black country. "They're fighting dogs aren't they? I hope he keeps them under better control than he does himself on a Saturday night."

"He's a Cradley Heath man," said Rock, "and it's Cradley Heath, not Cradley by the way, so you won't see his dogs off the lead in public unless it's for a fight. Very proud of them they are. They all aspire to the best-bred animals. The better the dog you've got, the better the man you are. That's the way they are."

"But of course our man Fuller doesn't fight his dogs does he? Not on my patch. It's illegal you know."

"Perish the thought," said the barber. "We're all law-abiding citizens round here aren't we chaps?"

"Of course we are," said Norman joining in what he supposed was a joke.

"Not like them buggers in Cradley Heath," added old Eric, "it's like the bleeding Wild West it is, full of hairy chain-makers with nasty tempers – and that's just the women. Ugly as sin and hard as nails them women."

The little fellow was getting quite animated about it. Abe couldn't but wonder whether the old man had loved and lost a Cradley wench. *Correction, Cradley Heath.*

"You're not fond of the place I gather?" asked Abe.

"Place is all right. Just the people. Don't like them." And he couldn't be persuaded to say more on the matter.

"I don't agree with the way they treat the dogs," said the tall quarryman. "I know they breed them to fight but the injuries are so bad they end up having to put half of them down. I wouldn't trust one around my kids, they make them too vicious."

"Yes, well, we all know you're a big softie Norm," said the barber over his shoulder, "and you're talking about something you don't know enough about. You ask anybody with bull terriers and they'll tell you that they're daft as a bottle of pop round people, especially kids. Just have to watch them round small animals."

"What like babbies you mean? I don't think you can trust any animal brought up on blood and killing."

"Well I won't argue with you," said Rock – the quarryman was a customer after all – "but I'm not sure I would agree either. What do you say Sarge?"

"I'm not that familiar with the breed. All I can say, in my official capacity, is that it seems to me these dogs are bred only for fighting, or most of them at least. It follows that the practice is only serving to perpetuate the pernicious practice of illegal gambling which it is my duty to stamp out, not to mention my duty under the Cruelty To Animals Act of course." Rather a stuffy statement, Abe realised, so he continued, "but that's a copper's view. Personally, I've got nothing against dogs, bull terriers included."

"No, you're right, and so's Eric," rejoined the tall quarryman. "The dogs are just dogs; it's the people what ruin 'em."

"But they're not just dogs are they?" observed Abe. "I mean, if the urge to fight is bred into them already, they're something different to something that's grown out of an ordinary puppy, if I can put it like that."

"That's true of all breeds though," said Rock. "We breed from the fastest in the case of whippets, and the best ratters in the case of Russells. We do it for all our animals."

"Pity we don't stop crooks breeding then and only let good church-goers have children. Make my life easier," mused the copper in him.

"Or we could stop all the ugly short-arses in Cradley Heath breeding," said Eric, coming back to life.

Rich coming from you, grinned Abe.

"Geld the lot," concluded Eric.

"I'll tell you what Barber Rock," said Norman "you wouldn't be so keen on 'em if they swiped old Mitzi there and used her as training bait."

That hit a nerve, and the barber was moved to raise his voice. "No I bloody well wouldn't. Let the fuckers try it, that's all. I'll wrap their own fucking chains round their necks and drop 'em in the cut."

"Well, you look after her then. It still goes on you know."

"Yes I did know. But not so much round here. Whippets and Russells. They only kill rats and catch dinner which, as I said, does society a service."

"But fights do happen around here," said the sergeant, "I know from professional experience."

"Yes but most of the dog-owners are from out of the area…" said Rock.

"Bloody Cradley Heath," piped up Eric.

"They might be from outside the area, but if they can come in to have fights, they can come in and nick a few little terriers like yours," Norman pointed out.

"I've heard of this baiting with small dogs business, but I thought it was just a myth. Or at least not something that happened very often," ventured Abe.

"Well you'd be wrong then," began the quarryman.

"Not entirely," said Rock, interrupting him. "It happens, yes, but it's not like it was. Perhaps if there's a particularly big meeting coming up."

"A big fight you mean? Lot of money changing hands?" asked Abe.

"That's it," agreed the barber.

"So, how's it work then? Is the idea to stir up the dogs' blood by tossing them some stray small furry creature to rip up?"

"Yes and no," butted in Norman.

"Which is to say," continued Rock, "yes they let them rip up little animals, a cat say, but not on the day of the fight, not usually, that would just be needless cruelty, blood for the sake of it. No, all this takes place as part of the training, you see."

"A cat though? Surely it would just jump out of the ring, wouldn't it?" said the policeman.

"Not if it's tied by the tail to a lump of pig iron in a cellar," said Norman in suspicious detail.

"They use all sorts of tricks," continued Rock, "or so I'm told. As I think I said, I don't agree with it. It's true there's not a lot of it round these parts, but that's just here. Unfortunately it's alive and well elsewhere."

"Bloody Cradley Heath," came a voice from the chair.

"What I can tell you," said Norman looking the copper in the eye "is that not so long ago three or four pubs on your beat used to hold meets regular. My dad remembers the way the old 'uns used to train their dogs. First thing is, they would always give 'em raw meat. Some days they would get just a bowl of blood, and that would continue till they were half starved. That's when they would throw in a cat, or a little old dog, to get them used to killing. Not that they would be allowed to eat what they killed, unless it was a rabbit, and especially not the dogs, problem controlling them in a real fight otherwise, but they would only get fed once they had killed…"

"Sounds a bit brutal," said Abe. "Wouldn't they fight anyway?"

"Probably would," said the barber. "But some people have to just go that bit further. A hard life makes hard men."

"But that's only so the dogs can keep their hand in, so to speak." Norman seemed to know a lot about the subject. *Or is it just bullshit?* "Coming up to a big fight," continued Norman, "what they used to do is pit their dogs against other dogs, but small ones. Little aggressive terriers are ideal. I've heard it said that the really serious owners would let their dog kill a little ratter every day for a week before the actual fight proper."

"That's a lot of dead dogs though," observed the policeman. "Where did they come from? More to the point, what happened to the bodies?"

"Easy," replied the quarryman. "They nick 'em and then throw 'em down a disused pit, or just incinerate 'em."

Charming. And I thought the hunt could be ruthless. At least it doesn't betray its own; doesn't betray the human-canine bond. Just kills foxes…

The conversation had taken a turn which sucked it into the degenerate depths of a fractured working-class psyche: Abe was grateful when they started talking about the weather…

Chapter 9

A Visit to the Workhouse

There was a workhouse which lay just off the main road from Blackheath to Dudley, on the borders of what the locals would call Tippity Green and Cock Green, not far from Barber Rock's establishment. Like all edifices erected for the good of the poor, it had more of the appearance of a place of correction than a place of salvation: heavy square lines of uniform brickwork punctured by sharp ordered rows of small bare windows and an imposing grand entrance which somehow recalled something from Dante. The theme of control, if not of incarceration, was emphasised by the surrounding curtain wall, broken only to allow for a covered gatehouse, garrisoned by a stern gatekeeper. And the effect was by no means accidental, for it was well-known that the indolent poor needed discipline, constant discipline – handed down by those that knew about these things – if they were to be saved from a sordid descent into crime and anarchy.

Dressed in his accustomed shades of brown and pallid skinned, the workhouse master bore the weight of his enormous responsibility with commendable stoicism. He was congratulating himself on the fact, as he sat, waiting. At his big brown desk, in his big white-washed office: for all the world an outsized garden spider at the centre of a web; one of bricks and mortar and dutiful humanity; a hub from which radiated along the four points of the compass, the scrupulously scrubbed corridors which opened into the tangle of rooms and wards and other spaces wherein the indigent residents worked, and ate, and slept, and generally spent their time going about the business of survival.

Of course, he did not see himself as anything as mundane as that familiar arachnid. For, as all roads once led to Rome, it is said, so those corridors conducted all of the staff of that worthy establishment to and from the focal point that was the master's desk, whence the latter-day imperator dispensed instruction, and judgement. You see, he was like a Roman Emperor of old, holding in the balance the well-being, if not to say the very lives, of his subjects. At least, in his fondest reveries, that his how he liked to think of himself.

But to tell the truth, Gideon Gross would have made but a very seedy Emperor. He was thirty-eight years of age with still a rather child-like and attractive countenance. Or so it was until he parted his lips to smile, which he often did, though whether occasioned by natural jollity or an affectation disguising something else, was hard to say. When he opened his mouth it could be observed, without too much perspicacity, that his teeth were in a bad way: the uneven rows of yellow and black were redolent of old and decayed picket fencing; paint gone, parts broken, loose, or missing; beyond redemption. The corollary of master Gideon's inadequate oral hygiene, was an unfortunate and unpleasant reek which his speech was apt to disseminate on the fungal warmth of his breath. Unfortunately for his social aspirations, the smell was easily detectable by the average human nose at hand-shaking range. Further, his once beautiful blonde barnet was thinning now, and it would not be many years before ineffectual attempts at disguise by way of judicious sticking and combing would have to be abandoned to inevitable baldness. As it was, it was long, thin, and lank, more for want of care than due to any dietary insufficiency: a conclusion that could be supported by two simple observations. Firstly, in contrast with the pristine cleanliness of his office and the punctilious neatness of the rest of the building, courtesy of his employees, Mr Gross' sartorial style could at best be described as drab, and more realistically as shabby, his apparel appearing constantly in need of pressing if not of washing; his size nine shoes in need of a shine. His hair went along with the general theme. Also, and secondly, he was rather a large man. Not tall, but still a large man. 'Stiff' as the locals had it. But it went beyond that. To make no bones about it, the man was fat – unlikely therefore to be suffering from any serious nutritional shortcomings. To be fair to him neither the demands of his role nor his extra-mural activities called for much in the way of physical exertion, and neither afforded the opportunity for physical recreation. So: fat he was, and fat he would stay. Perhaps after all then, in so far as their vices are conceived in the popular imagination, his corpulence at least justified a comparison with the imperial potentates of ancient Italy.

Today, the Emperor, this epitome of pulchritude, was expecting a visitor. As he glanced at his watch there was a soft distinctive knock on the door. *Bang on time* he thought as he returned the timepiece, secreting it beneath generous folds of cloth around his generous middle. At the command, the porter opened the door, ushered in the visitor – respectfully – and hurried off to resume guard duty at the gates. A slight dark man, neatly dressed (someone had once described him as 'dapper', which earned a bloody nose), with attractive features and an easy gait glided through the space between the door and the desk. The two men met across that substantial item of furniture, the newcomer smiling cheerfully and the other nodding back. The contrast was striking. A Julius Caesar before a Nero.

The visitor took in, not for the first time, the functional simplicity of the office, and the apparent lack of concern with personal vanity evidenced by the master's appearance. At their first meeting he had been tempted to attribute these facts to Mr Gross having something of the Spartan in his make-up. But he had soon abandoned that premise in favour of an alternative explanation: that the man was simply of parsimonious habits. A miser some would say. Not to mention a lazy sod.

"A'do Gideon," said the thin man to the fat man with a wink and slid into the spare chair near the desk.

"Worroh Jack. Si' dahn why doh ya?"

"Thanks," said Jack Cutler, ignoring the mild sarcasm. Perhaps it had been justified. "Cup of tea by any chance?"

"Of course," the master replied and rose to pull a bell chord by the side of the fire place. Jack noticed that a fire was made up but had not been lit and although it was summer there was a chill to the big bare room. *Not that he would feel it under all that blubber.*

When the master was again seated Jack asked, "Everything all right?"

"Yes. All good," said Gross.

"No problems then? Everybody keeping their mouths shut?"

"Yes, yes. Everything's, normal. No problems," the master assured him, then added, "unless you know something I don't."

It may have been that at that moment Jack Cutler was about to divulge that he did indeed know something that the fat man did not. However, at that very same moment a sudden and harassed looking female member of staff, whose youth had long ago deserted her, but not evidently a cantankerous propensity, honed no doubt by years of practice, entered and asked altogether too sarcastically in Cutler's opinion, "You rang, M'lord?"

"Yes, thank you Fanny. Thank you. I know how busy you must be. Could you just get one of the girls to make a pot of tea for two?"

"All right. Will that be all? I've got things to do."

"Yes, thank you Fanny. Much appreciated. Oh, no…and some muffins please, with jam. Send one of the girls with it." The redoubtable Fanny was already turning to go when the master added: "Send Muriel…that's lovely. Really appreciate it. Lovely." He raised his voice as the door slammed shut. "Thank you, Fanny." And she was gone, without so much a glance at the master's visitor, which suited Mr Cutler, thank you very much. Not that he could be sure of what she had looked at, you understand, on account of him having taken care to keep his back to the unruly woman, and his face averted.

"I thought you were the boss in here," said an amused Cutler. Irony was doing the rounds today.

"That?" queried Gross. "It doesn't pay to antagonise people for no reason, I've found. You need allies in our position. Why make enemies? You must have found this out for yourself, a man in your…" Gross was conscious that he might be trespassing into a dangerous area here, "position," he finished hurriedly.

"No, you're right," admitted Cutler, "we don't want malcontents getting their heads together and manufacturing grievances. Somebody might start to listen." *You're not so green as you are cabbage-looking are you, Fat Bloke.*

"That's exactly it," said a gratified Gross. "So what did you mean earlier?"

"What do you mean, what did I mean?" teased Cutler.

"You know. About people keeping their mouths shut. Do you know something?"

"Oh, I know a lot of things," said a nonchalant Cutler, and enigmatically he hoped, "but we'll come to that by and by. Let's discuss the state of the business first shall we, partner?"

"Where shall we start?"

"We shall start by going through the books. You can talk me through the items of income and expenditure, as you like to call them." Cutler's voice was business-like, they might have been two bankers discussing an account over luncheon and a glass of wine. But what he said next, expressed in a soft predatory growl completely at odds with his previous tone, betokened an entirely different manner of business operation, and it made the master squirm, "And if there's something in there that I don't like, you are not going to like the consequences." Cutler emphasised the 'you' and the 'not' And as he said it, by way of illustration of said consequences, young Jack Cutler smote his palm with the silver-topped head of his cane after a fashion which inevitably suggested itself to the sole onlooker, that the hand was a mere substitute target. Certainly not as good as, say, a fat head with thinning hair atop a corpulent torso…Conscience clean though, at least on this occasion, the master held Cutler's gaze and said, "I'll get the books then…"

As it happened, there was nothing for the visitor to gripe about. The unlikely partners had an essentially simple and ordinary business model, in so far as, as in all commerce, there was a source, or sources, of funds, and there were certain expenditures. Offsetting one element against another left a surplus for distribution amongst the proprietors, though you may have guessed that in their case the split was by no means '50:50'. But the most difficult part of the operation lay in keeping its existence a secret, confined to the select and requisite few, and above all in keeping the authorities, and especially the officers of the law, completely in the dark. For to be sure, the operation in question was an entirely illegal, not to say immoral, one. The conspirators' bread and butter was that portion of parish funds –funds allocated in good faith and charity for upkeep of the workhouse, for its running and the maintenance of its destitute and desolate denizens – as they could reasonably annex without raising suspicion. A few crumbs could be made by skimping on rations, but the safer option, and one which, purely as a side effect, had a less deleterious effect on the health of the inmates, was simply to submit false invoices: Cutlers' patronage ensured chosen suppliers had access to a regular and reliable market to dispose of both honest and questionably obtained materials. Quid pro quo, they would inflate prices or quantities by a margin dictated by Cutler, a margin skimmed off by the partners. In the case of stolen goods, there was often an apparent discount against expected market prices, and as this tended to have the effect of balancing out the whole budget, it helped to conceal the overcharges; in fact the whole racket. The beauty of it was that these were genuine traders, although perforce from outside the immediate area, and, by dint of their connivance, outside the law, who submitted 'genuine' paperwork, and whose complicity ensured solidarity should the police come snooping. It only remained for Gross to work his magic in the double-entry system, in whose mysteries he was a dark adept.

But it was not until it became possible to manipulate, on paper, the actual number of mouths to feed and souls to shelter, and to keep that particular pot boiling, that serious remuneration had been achieved. The idea had started not with any claim on the living however, but against the dead; when master Gideon had the idea of forging death certificates, by-passing the parish clerks. He reckoned that by forging the right bits of paper, and by keeping any interfering relatives away from the corpse, that he could get the undertakers to dispose of a body to the university in Birmingham, and pocket the finder's fee. There was still very much a thriving market for fresh bodies. In fact there was far less opprobrium attached to that macabre business these days, since the setting up of the Anatomy Inspectorate, than there had been in the days of audacious grave-robbers and dashing highwaymen of forty odd years ago, when, paradoxically, men's sensibilities had actually been far rougher. A clear case of the law of the land leading morals, Gideon had thought. He had heard that undertakers and medical schools alike were by no means fussy about paperwork. But, how to make the requisite contacts? Despite his natural predilection for paper crime, Gross had never mixed, at least not by deliberate choice, with any element of the criminal fraternity. But, yes, a share of the sale proceeds of such 'medical items', plus an income from the funds allotted by the parish for the continued maintenance of any corpse that was not a corpse, as far as they knew, would certainly boost his old-age fund. And the dead man, or woman, would conveniently be found to have discharged themselves should questions be asked. But he needed to be put in touch with the right people, people prepared to turn a blind eye to 'irregularities.' Old man Gaunt, the local undertaker, was far too good for that, stuck up bugger: polished his shoes and his halo religiously every morning. Well, more fool him…

So, through a modestly paid but highly deniable third party, he had cast his hook into the ever-shifting muddy waters of the local underworld. And the fish that took the line was nothing like the master could have imagined: it was small but tenacious, and strong enough to pull him down into the depths; and the bank was far too slippery steep for him to jump back out now, Cutler had seen to that.

Under Cutler, the high-risk, and outdated, body selling idea was sunk and set aside. Their criminal enterprise still depended on bodies of course, but living ones as opposed to dead, fictitious as opposed to real, sold to the parish on paper as opposed to shady undertakers in coffins. Now, new inmates were created by a simple alchemy of ink and paper, the Relieving Officer's child-like script and signature no impediment to the talented counterfeiter that Gideon Gross had become. Cutler's powers of persuasion, not to mention intimidation, was insurance against detection, and his network of colleagues – to talk plainly, his gang – could be depended upon, on the evidence of at least one trial occasion, to provide actual living and breathing individuals to act the part in case of an inspection of the premises. And it was working. The young entrepreneur had taken

Gross' ramshackle opportunistic and irregular filching and, with a little sound investment on security, had transformed it from a business going nowhere into a thriving commercial operation, complete even with its own set of books and figures albeit ones which no self-respecting accountant would deign to sign off, unless it were possible for an accountant to be self-respecting and dishonest at one and the same time.

The fat man was thinking to himself how lucky he was that he had fallen in with Mr Cutler. Yes, he could be moody, but he probably had things on his mind to make him moody. Things like protecting the business, and his partner. Cutler was very definitely an acquired taste, but having come to know him over the past six months, he had come to respect him – the money helped with that of course – and to trust him. Which was a remarkable and ironic coincidence, for at that precise instant the respected and trusted Mr Cutler was just reminding himself that you couldn't trust a fat man: flabby mind makes a flabby body, and Cutler could evaluate this man's mind by the betrayal that was his swollen belly. No steel to the man. He would crack at the slightest pressure. *No doubt spilling pusillanimous green puss all over the floor like a rotten egg.* Shutting out that not at all pleasant image, Cutler moved swiftly on.

"Right then, Gideon. Two special items on the agenda today."

"Agenda? What agenda?" queried a bemused Gideon Gross.

"My agenda, Mr Gross. All right?" The tone was friendly; polite.

"Well, yes, certainly. What, em, items?"

"Number one, and it's a big number one, is security," said Cutler, "but we'll leave that till last."

Gideon was tempted, but only tempted, to come back with, "Wouldn't that make it number two then?" Discretion is after all the better part of valour according to the oft quoted trite shorthand. Instead, our fat friend found himself contemplating the ramifications of that word. Security. Somehow, he found Cutler's use of it, his emphasis, disturbing, threatening. *What have I done? What does he know? Not the girl, nobody knows about that…*

"I know what you're thinking," said Cutler.

A low sound issued from the suddenly dry throat of the master. "What?"

"You're thinking I'm just on my hobby-horse again. That there's nothing to worry about."

Gideon started to relax, but Cutler hadn't finished yet. "Well, don't you be too sure about that."

Uncomfortably, the master opened his mouth to speak, but Cutler cut across him. "So, item two. Tell me about the Tipton meeting last week."

At last Gideon felt himself on firmer ground. "Well, as you know, these things are usually only poorly attended. If they meet in Dudley, there's usually six or seven Guardians turn up, but Tipton's out of the way for most of them and they mostly struggle to get a quorum, which is three, not counting the clerk." With no obvious reaction from his partner, the fat one added another, gratuitous and hurried, "As you know."

Then, Cutler did react, with mild impatience. "Any problems? Yes or no?"

"No."

"You're sure?"

"Yes. It's just a routine little ritual they go through every other week. I can't remember the last time they interviewed any new admissions. Why should they? They've got my word for it, which means that they've also got Lilly's word for it – that's the Receiving Officer – because I forge his words, and the clerk vouches for everything because that's what I tell him to do. It's all done and dusted in half an hour, then they get down to the important business, which is eating and swilling port. The current batch of Guardians are all old and gullible, even the elected ones have been at it for years, and they basically get elected by default. They *think* they've seen it all, and that's to our advantage."

"But that would change if they picked up on any untoward rumours, wouldn't it?" observed the senior partner.

"I suppose so," agreed the master.

"You suppose so! Complacency killed the cat you know, to coin a phrase."

"No, no. I agree."

"Good. And you've still got that clerk firmly in your pocket?"

"Most definitely. No fear of that. He'd never dare say anything…"

Rash and complacent. Dear oh dear…

"He just endorses anything I enter. I could make us treble what we make now," continued the fat man, now in full swing.

"And that's where I come in," said Cutler cutting him off short and sternly. "If complacency killed the cat, greed will most surely kill the pig." And he let those black shark eyes bore into the master's skull, all the while conveying the image of a dead swine: one in shabby clothes and scuffed shoes, and sat not a million miles away. And then abruptly, the psychotic glaze was gone and the little man continued in an almost cordial fashion. "Gideon, I don't care what you have on the clerk…"

As a matter of fact, this was true. Jack Cutler did not care to think too deeply on what this fat goon had on the clerk. For Mr Cutler, an avowed criminal and self-confessed rogue, had his own ideas about what was right and wrong, what was within the pale and what outside, who could be harmed in pursuit of profit and who was off limits. He did not associate his mind-set in terms of morality, but he had his own code nonetheless, the basis for which was perhaps something of a mystery in a man who married an ascetic streak of atheism with a total disrespect for the law. So, no, he did not dwell on what the master 'had' on the clerk, because he suspected, only suspected mind you, that it had something to do with inappropriate activity with young inmates…

"If you get greedy," he continued, "it won't matter if the clerk remains quiet and compliant, because them questions that ain't being asked now will start to be asked. And then it's the end! At least it will be for you!" The thought of such an outcome was apparently a challenge to Cutler's equanimity for he was losing his outward poise and slipping into a more aggressive mode, demonstrating his points with sharp raps on the floor with his stick, which he had not set down since his arrival.

Gross preferred not to contemplate the exact nature of the 'end' that Cutler had in mind. He only saw that his sometime affable business associate was conjuring a tantrum out of nothing at all. Hurriedly then, he offered his apology, "Look, I didn't say I was going to up the stakes like that. I was just saying how I've got the clerk under control. I'm totally guided by you in all this, you're the boss." It was the first time it had been said in so many words. Cutler was indubitably 'the boss' in this relationship. "You give me the figures you want to see and I'll tie up the paperwork. You can rely on me Jack. I hope you know that by now."

Whether it was the display of subservience, or whether the mood had passed in any case, or indeed whether Cutler had merely been shamming for effect, but his demeanour switched from stormy to clear in the space of the few seconds it took for Gross to utter his last words. "Good. Reliable is good. Loose cannon bad. Understood?"

The master assured the young man that he had.

Tea and muffins at this juncture arrived, by way of a pretty little girl wearing a shy smile and a blue gingham dress and who seemed quite overwhelmed in their presence. This was perhaps understandable as the whole delivery and setting out of the tea things was conducted in an unsettling almost total silence, the two men having nothing to say to each other save that which was secret, and little to say to the girl. The big door having been closed behind her as she left, the business continued as they ate and drank.

"Right now, Gideon, do you know when this place is due its next inspection?"

With some trepidation the master had to explain that unfortunately he did not know. "Not for sure. Not yet. But that, on the positive side, it was probably at least a month away."

"Contingency plans then?" It was only half a question.

"Same as before. With your permission of course," said Gross, "We'll use casuals to get the numbers of adults to match the ones created, or resurrected, in the books. That's never going to be a problem. But we don't want to be seen to be top heavy on adults so it may be an idea if you could borrow a few youngsters again, four or five would do it. If that's not a problem?"

"It could be a problem. You can have three. I'll use the Adams kids again, nobody will notice. I'm not going to risk bringing anybody else in. This way we're not taking any chances."

"I'm sure there's them out there that would lend you a couple more for a mere pittance…" ventured the fat man. He had forgotten already that you should not prod at a wasps' nest.

"This ain't a bleedin' charity you know," said the smaller man, not at all ironically. "And you're forgetting point one aren't you?"

"Point one?"

"Point one," repeated Cutler, again emphasizing with a rap of his stick before continuing, "security," rap, "security," rap, "security!" rap. Each word and each rap was delivered with increasing vehemence, surging to a crescendo before breaking on the rocks of self-control and ebbing into seemingly rational discourse. "It's time to discuss security," he said equably.

"But I thought…" blustered the master before being cut off by a raised finger.

"Security, Mr Gross. Do you know the meaning of the word? I'm not about to extend the circle of participants to new people. For reasons you don't need to know, I can trust Mr and Mrs Adams, but that's just a bonus. I'm not involving anybody new. We've already got a problem we shouldn't have."

"What do you mean?" asked an increasingly rattled Gideon Gross, "We've been careful. Who's been asking questions?"

"At this point, I'm not so much worried about questions as statements," said Jack Cutler, waiting, as if the distinction would provide some kind of revelation to his partner. But it went over Gross' head. He didn't have a clue (and why should he?) He looked at Cutler vacuously and then around the austere enclosure as if beseeching the intervention of some invisible interpreter from the other side.

After a moment of mild amusement tinged with exasperation, the man with the silver-topped cane continued, "What I mean Mr Peabrain is that somebody has been talking."

The fat man's fat belly lurched, and it had nothing to do with the surfeit of sticky muffins he had consumed. Visions of the police knocking at the door made the airy white room seem suddenly suffocating. Sheet-white himself now he heard himself ask, "What do you mean? Who?"

The other ignored the question. "How tight a ship do you run? Who have you let in?"

"Nobody. Nobody. It's still you and me, and my good lady wife of course, and the porter, but he's your man of course."

A ghost of a smirk from young Jack. Fat bloke was really sweating it, and the description of the equally fat matron as his 'good lady wife' just tickled him somehow. "And the clerk of course. Thomas is it." A prompt not a question.

"Yes, Thomas," agreed the master "but he doesn't get a share of the profits of course…"

"Of course," rejoined Cutler, "but perhaps I might make a suggestion? He already knows more than is good for him, and it's only blackmail, your blackmail, that's keeping him from talking. Now, blackmail can be most efficacious, I know, but it's arguably not the best basis for an on-going productive relationship."

"And?" queried an uneasy junior partner. He could guess what was coming.

"And," returned Cutler smoothly, "I think it might be time to cut him in. Just a token you understand. Carrot and stick; stick and carrot. With me?"

"Well, it's a thought," conceded Gross, though reluctantly, for he well knew that any 'cut' for the clerk would not be funded in the minutest percentage from the share of the man sat in front of him.

"Think about it then," commanded the boss. "Give him a carrot, and you've also got a bigger stick. He can hardly go to the coppers and say he's being blackmailed, but by the way the blackmailer's also paying him! That's you by the way. I trust my name's been left out of it?"

"Of course, I'm not saft."

"Didn't say you were." *Might have thought it.* "So, if it's not a question of any, shall we say operational, changes, then who's been careless enough to attract wagging ears?"

Gross let out a short puff of pent-up apprehension. "I really don't know," he said, "I mean, we take all precautions, as you've taught us. The business is only ever discussed in this very room, and as you can see the walls are thick and solid and the door is heavy and stout. As for the windows, they're too high to even see in from the garden, unless you climb a tree. And there are no trees."

Cutler looked around the room and he looked at Gross. He believed him, in this. But Woolley had proved himself more than reliable, and he believed Woolley more. And Woolley had said that the police could easily have been alerted by the conversation he had overheard. So he asked more directly. "What about the inmates?"

"No. They know nothing," said their master dismissively, "The way we operate nobody would even suspect."

Cutler took the last with a pinch of salt. Gross evidently had a low opinion of the deductive capabilities of his charges. *Snobbish arrogance that is. A hard life is just as likely to sharpen the wits as dull them.* And that's how Jack Cutler had survived his harsh childhood, through the application of a blend of intelligence with amoral pragmatism. He wondered what the fat man would think of his partner if he knew that he had been born, and abandoned, in a place just like this, and to the revelation that, hardly twelve years of age, he had run away after beating the overbearing master to within an inch of his life, with a cricket bat. As Cutler had once put it, the master had been out for a duck, and he had ducked out. Of course, he was not called Cutler then…

"And what can you tell me about an old man by the name of Reginald Phillips?"

"Reg? Reg Phillips?"

"Yes," coaxed Cutler. "That's what I said."

"He's been in and out of here for years. Before my time. Only got one arm, well one and a half really, but he gets the odd job for short spells. Last one was night watchman at the scrap yard behind Lench's."

"So, he just comes and goes as he pleases," enquired Cutler?

"More or less. Signs himself out and gets himself let back in on the nod. Everybody knows him you see."

"And you don't think it's a bit risky, for us I mean. Letting him wander back and forth?"

"Well, no. He can't possibly know anything. He's just an old man; likes to talk a lot…" Gideon wished he hadn't just said that.

"Well he knows *something*," said Cutler. "And that and a propensity to jaw – thanks for that by the way – makes him a threat. I don't like threats. I like to sleep easy."

"What's he said then?" asked the master. He was starting to get anxious about the direction that the conversation was going.

In truth, Jack was not entirely sure what the old soldier had said. Not the details that is. But the point was that he had been heard spilling his guts in his cups about this place, and to a copper of all people. All right, the copper obviously hadn't cottoned on. This time. But they had seemed very pally, and who's to say the copper wouldn't pay more attention to his blather next time? *Perhaps there should be no next time.* In answer to the master's question he summed up all this in one word, "Enough," he said, and left his partner to speculate on what that might encompass.

"What are we going to do?" said the fat man with a stammer. "Shall I bar him out? Or keep him locked in?"

"Neither," said Cutler. "*You* won't be doing anything *You've* done enough. But he'll have to be dealt with one way or another. Have you got any more that treat the place like a bloody hotel?"

"No. Generally, people are here for the duration. If they *are* discharged, they tend to stay away. Except casuals of course, they're only in for…"

"Well, you'd better think twice about how you control the comings and goings. You've got Duberley, use him."

Gross thought about the tough-looking porter provided courtesy of Cutler. They would have to be desperate to try to get through the gate if he was barring it, unless they came mob-handed. Anthony Duberley was every inch a ruffian and no amount of careful grooming could ever disguise it. You only had to look into his eyes, not that you would want to. There was a void there, not the blackness Cutler sometimes let slip, but simply an emptiness of emotion, of spirit, as if he were merely some kind of clever machine, going about the bidding of its maker; with a purpose perhaps, but with no conscience. Not that the master had not seen his share of empty husks of humanity: the factories and furnaces and mines sucked men dry and cut them loose all the time, and many ended their days in such a place as this. But some, like Duberley, for some reason lost their

100

souls very early in the game, leaving a strong body untenanted by any concern for compassion or sympathy and conscious only of the most basic, primary passions. Such bodies were dangerous, but sometimes useful, as when stationed at the gate of this very establishment. Gross wondered how many other Duberleys were in with Cutler.

"What's going to happen to Reg?" he said, "You're not going to hurt him, are you?"

"No," assured Cutler firmly. *Though somebody else might.* "We just need to find out what he knows and who he's spoken to," *and then shut his trap for good,* "and then ask him to desist," he substituted.

"Do you want me to talk to him?" offered Gross.

"No. Thank you but I think it's best if you stay out of it. Keep your hands clean. I'll do this at arm's length, don't want anything coming back on you. That wouldn't be good." *Because I might have to shut you up an' all.* "Don't worry. Forget about it."

"If you say so," said Gross, grateful for an excuse not to follow where his suspicions had been leading. He was seeing Cutler in a new light, that of a protector who would take care of all problems as long as he trusted in him. And he made up his mind to do just that, no matter what. He would trust his partner's judgement without question and follow his lead. And he would do nothing to mar that trust which Jack Cutler undoubtedly placed in him...

"I do say so," rejoined Cutler. "Now, was there any other business?"

Glad to see daylight from the nefarious thicket into which the discussion had steered him, the fat man brightened. "The matron sends her compliments and asks when we can expect our next special consignment of meat. That mutton was much appreciated. Damn good quality."

A smile flickered across lean dark features, *as farmer Parkes would no doubt testify, if he had me in court,* "Thank your wife for her compliments and tell her I reciprocate. Unfortunately, the meat situation is a bit up in the air at the moment." *Thanks to that bloody sergeant and his ungrateful uncle.* Cutler could see his relationship with Cyril coming to an end in the near future. Cyril's trust had gone, he could feel as much. Besides, it was not in Cutler's nature to play second fiddle... "Anything else?" he asked briskly.

"I don't think so."

"Good. Then I'll take my leave." Cutler rose and held out his hand. It was met by a clammy insipid clumsy clasp from the other man. From an early age Jack had laid great store in the quality of a handshake. To those with sharpened perception, such as himself, it told you almost everything you needed to know about a man. Unfortunately for him, Gross' handshake only ever confirmed Cutler's existing opinion of his partner, that he was weak and unresilient. He could see that this particular partnership having a short shelf life. *Nothing like making hay while the sun shines.* Still, he shook the master's hand with every outward sign of trust and cordiality. The man had said so himself, it doesn't pay to antagonise people for no reason. *Not when you might need to get close enough to kill them.*

As the visitor was stepping out of the office the young girl came back to timidly collect the tea things.

"Thank you, Muriel," said Gross, "but don't run away just yet, I've got something to talk to you about."

As he walked away Jack heard the key turn. He explained to himself, unsuccessfully, that it was not his business. He took a half a dozen steps, turned and went back to the office, banging on the door noisily. It was opened a crack to reveal one side of Gross' pudgy white face; one watery eye focussed on the returned shape of Jack Cutler, and the brain yet to suggest an explanation. Taking care not to stand too close to that fetid maw, Cutler pushed the door and barged in. The girl and the tea things were revealed in momentary still life till the girl took the opportunity to start gathering the crocks together. "Thank you my dear. Got everything? Good. You can go." Which she did, sharply. Then he gave the fat man a piece of his mind, another one.

On the way out, he stopped to pick up his girl. Duberley was ready for him and let him in. A hunk of muscle and love rushed him. Jack Cutler stooped to meet the wet kisses, returning his own.

"How's me little girl then? Did you miss me?" The dog whined and grunted, for all the world confirming that yes, she had missed him, but that now he was back all was right with the world. "Has uncle Tony been looking after you? He's a good 'un ain't he?"

'Uncle Tony' was hardly ever referred to in affectionate terms. And people could just not bring themselves to address him so; and that suited Duberley. He did not care for useless prattle or false sentimentality. He liked to keep himself to himself, and called no man friend, except perhaps this one.

"She's been no trouble," offered Duberley, "lay down as good as gold waiting for you."

"No, she's a good girl," confirmed Cutler, "anything else to report?"

"No sign of that old soldier since he took himself off last night. And nothing unusual, no, nothing to report."

"Right," said Jack Cutler. "Let me know if you get bored and we will give somebody else a turn."

"That's all right. I like the quiet…"

"Good. So, keep your eye on that fat twerp and his wife. I want to know if he leaves, follow if you can. Let me know about any unusual visitors, the usual."

"Will do," replied the dour man. And that was a promise Cutler knew he could rely on.

He left in a good mood, satisfied with the state of play. Perhaps he would visit the old chaps at the Gosty tunnel, Cyril's charity cases as he called them. Crane seemed genuinely to have a soft spot for the motley half dozen adopted down and outs whom he had charged with helping boats through the tunnel. The outlay of a few coppers for the needy no doubt gave him an excuse to feel good about himself. All the beneficiaries had to do was turn up, assist those crews that needed it, make friends, on behalf of their benefactor, and keep their ears open – the water gypsies were a fertile source of information. The extra cash on top of the pittance of parish relief kept them happy, and willing enough: at least when the weather was mild, when it was a pleasant way to spend the day; there was even a pub situated most conveniently close. It did require the occasional surprise visit however to ensure that the men kept to their side of the deal, and Jack had decided that it was a good day for a walk. He was never happier than when he was with his dog. Boadicea, he had named her, but that was soon substituted with Bo; they had been together for four years, a lifetime for her…

He was just about to start whistling a tune as he turned onto the main road – stifling the urge and ducking back around the corner as he caught sight of a familiar figure: the sergeant was in uniform but helmetless; off duty perhaps. Cutler and Bo followed at a safe distance and saw him enter the Hailstone. Couldn't blame him. Nothing like a pint or two on a warm day. But it had been a close shave. Here he was preaching to that fat slug about being careful, and he had almost allowed the law to see him coming out of the workhouse. Well, he would have to take extra precautions in future. Perhaps a disguise was in order? He could pretend to be respectable!

But it was no laughing matter. That copper was not stupid, and he was a big bugger. Not to mention the Shoulder connection. *Could end up turning into a proper bluebottle in the ointment.*

Chapter 10

On the Trail of Spring Heeled Jack

Abe felt renewed after his haircut and shave. The conversations from the barber's chair had piqued his curiosity, which was now having a lively discussion of its own with his innate distrust of any story connected with Spring Heeled Jack. He was sure that the sightings were all the product of alcohol-befuddled panic, or attention-seeking. But something else had interested him in the barber-shop banter, and it was calling to something in him long buried, as the flame draws the moth from the safety of the darkness into alien and perilous territory.

He had been surprised to learn that the sightings of a large blue unidentifiable creature with prodigious and unearthly leaping abilities were nothing new. And in particular he had been struck by the fact that the stories seemed to originate in this very small area around the quarries hereabouts. Judging by the anecdotes of Rock's clientele, the apparitions were well known here, almost a part of the culture. But it was an extremely local kind of culture if it was confined to Springfield: perhaps it was just that the conversation had never turned to it, but back in Blackheath, he had never heard any mention of a 'blue devil' and was sure that had he asked, nobody would have had an inkling of what he was rambling on about. He hadn't taken Rock for the superstitious type, yet even he had lent credence to the stories. More than that, something in the quarry had once frightened him badly, he was sure of that.

Fascinated by the mythical quality of the tales, he let his mind wander. If barber Rock's revelations were to be believed, what was the link between the appearances? Was there a timetable, with a measurable number of months or years between the events? Perhaps there was no timetable; perhaps the thing manifested itself to individuals under some kind of emotional stress. If that were the case though, did it mean that the spring-heeled fiend was simply a figment of a disturbed brain? Abe would have liked to think this, but the locals, some of them, would not subscribe to that theory. To them, the testimony of eye witnesses, reported regularly over the course of many years, generations as they had it, outweighed the 'common sense' arguments of the disbelievers. Believers were castigated as superstitious and gullible by the scoffers, who pitied their ignorance;

unbelievers were accused of narrow-mindedness and fear by the myth followers, who pitied their lack of imagination.

The same opposing forces were working in Abe's brain as he walked. Mysterious jumping creatures unknown to science in Rowley? Preposterous, wasn't it? Where was the physical evidence? What was the experience of an 'eye witness' worth? Abe reflected that he had never seen a giraffe, or an elephant. But he had no doubt that they existed.

All right then, if the monsters were 'real' what were they, and when would they appear next? Was he wrong about Spring Heeled Jack?

Abe shook himself awake. *What am I thinking? It's just a superstition. The biggest devil at work here is the demon drink.*

But even as he sought refuge in the rational mind, something long locked away was rattling the shutters…

As he walked, the relaxed invigoration he had felt from the haircut and hot shave and fragrant oils was being eroded by his disorderly cogitations upon the blue denizens of the rocks, who had begun to take on a small measure of life, of sorts, in his mind's eye. He was approaching the doorway of the Hailstone, the very spot where not three weeks ago, a victim had been almost cornered. Abe suddenly had the distinct feeling that eyes, unfriendly eyes, were watching him. Alert now, he stopped abruptly and swiftly turned, as if to stop someone pouncing! And he felt an idiot: looking back there was nobody in sight, save for half a dozen short-trousered kids he had passed earlier playing tip-cat. He laughed at himself for winding himself up. He needed a drink!

The open entrance was leaking Saturday afternoon smoke and geniality; the beery smell and hubbub of contented conversation greeted him like an old friend, and escorted him to the bar. Abe noticed only the barest ripple from his passage through that amiable status quo, a sign perhaps, he surmised, that, for the weekend at least, this particular little community of imbibers was at peace with the world. Abe had set foot in this place only once before and some years ago; and to be sure, judging by his officers' reports, or rather by the lack of them, this was about the most peaceable and law abiding of pubs under his official purview. And perhaps this explained the scant attention paid to him, both stranger and police officer: no guilty consciences!

The landlady wore the regulation high-buttoned blouse, long dark skirt, and apron (which latter item of apparel usually came in a choice of varying shades and permutations of white and spotted, depending on when last washed. In this case, it must be said, it was near the clean end of the spectrum, being as close to gleaming white as soaking and dollying would allow, and with not so much as the smallest observable beery blemish. Still, the day was young). Business-like, she had pinned up her long auburn hair and rolled back her sleeves, ready for him. A slender willowy woman, still attractive, in her forties, no, late thirties, Abe would say; she caught his eye in a second and held it as she reduced the distance between them. Now, Abe was with her in a small sphere of sudden intimacy, hop scented and lavender oil; he was her sole object of attention, her only concern in the world; and she spoke as a long-lost friend, found again. All of a sudden, she was gone, bestowing favours on the next thirsty source of income.

Abe automatically eyed the warm change in his hand, half seeing it – head of Victoria, a wren – and unconsciously verified the landlady's arithmetic, and honesty, before closing his fist around it and slipping it into his trouser pocket. He picked up his pint. The room was not over-large and it was standing room only by now, so he edged up about four feet to stand in the crook of a right angle formed where the bar was transected by a brick pier supporting the main ceiling timbers. From this position, protected on two fronts from the constant jostling of the paying public, he could rest his drink on the counter and look around the room and out into the street at the same time. Whilst the clientele inside was predominantly male, the opposite sex, and minors, dominated the comings and goings in the street: the outdoor was doing a thriving trade serving housewives who hurried and wandered by (depending on the location and proclivities of their husbands) clutching bottles and crocks either to be filled with the brown stuff, or, already filled, to be delivered safely home. A couple of the young chaps who had earlier been playing tip-cat had evidently got bored with it, or the sticks had been broken into unusable pieces, because they appeared as he watched and proceeded to make a nuisance of themselves by obstructing the progress of a group of younger girls' perfectly innocent game of hop-scotch, firstly by sitting on the course and then, by means of a sly manoeuvre, obtaining possession of the hop-scotch glass which they threw back and forth to one-another, taunting the young ones. Abe's instinct for what was right was affronted by this horseplay, and so it was with some satisfaction that it was confirmed to him, in short order, that the principles of fair play seemed alive and well here: for no sooner had the boys started their game of catch with their illicit booty than a diminutive but fierce looking lady, well past the first blush of spring, in a blue shawl, began to chastise them roundly. The nearest offender, no doubt expecting only a verbal attack, stood his ground, though more probably for want of sense than want of fear, and was taken by surprise when the redoubtable lady got close enough to clip him round the ear in a most unlady-like fashion and with such irresistible vehemence that he actually stumbled forward, dropping the glass. Slow wits translated to slow movement, and he made the mistake of tarrying, which earned him a sharp kick up the backside from a well-aimed boot. That message did get his full attention and, calling to his companion, he was off down the road like lightning, his comrade in crime at his heels...

Abe was gratified to see justice served. It was never too early to instil respect for the law, be it in the shape of a copper or, as for this particular incipient jail-bird, one's elders. He felt strangely at ease here, the more so as the beer went down. The mood was friendly but people weren't pushy, and he was left to his own devices. On his second pint he was telling himself that he really must find a witness or two connected with the purpose of his visit, when a grey whiskered old chap with thin features, apart from a fine fat cauliflower ear, and a long brown great-coat walked in from the street and made his way through the foggy press. Nodding to Abe he stood next to him and waited for the landlady's soft grey eyes to latch onto him, which they did very shortly: she knew her trade. While the newcomer was being served Abe found himself staring at the crusty brown scab which described where the top of the man's head had been lacerated and abraded, evidently quite recently. Given the wound and the locality Abe deduced that this was one of the local 'rock smashers.' He could imagine the culprit being a stray chunk of sharp Rowley Rag, exacting retribution even as it was dislodged from the ages by the pernicious application of a stick of dynamite. Absorbed in his thoughts, Abe was unconscious of the fact that the object of his attention was now very much aware of it, and returning it. Abe came to and realised the old gent was smiling up at him in some amusement.

"Yoh lookin' at mahr war wound?" asked the cauliflower ear.

"Sorry, day-dreaming," said the visitor.

"Ah've 'ad wuss," confided the brown coat, and added, "Sergeant Lively is it?"

Now, said Sergeant Lively was not one so proud as to assume that his reputation preceded him, and so, despite the obvious clue, which he wore, it came as at least a mild surprise that a total stranger should have his name (if not his rank) at the tip of his tongue. He remarked as much to the grey whiskers, who turned out indeed to have been an old quarry hand who, christened Thomas, went by the name of Tom; Tom Pickerill. Also as it turned out, Abraham was not the only Lively brother who had drunk in this establishment, for old Tom seemed to know brother John very well. At the mention of his brother's name Abe immediately jumped to his brother's defence, and the wrong conclusion. "Yes, he likes his drink, does John. Too much sometimes. There's no real bad in him, just that when he's had a drink he can lose his temper; and control of his fists."

"What do you mean?" said the old chap.

"Well, just that…"

"Because there's never been any trouble with John here. Just the opposite; he's stepped in a calmed thing down a couple of times. He's a big 'un and folk tend to pay attention."

Abe was pleasantly shocked, almost stunned. This sounded more like the brother he thought he had lost for good; not like the morose and disillusioned drinker that had been gradually banishing him these last couple of years. "Does he come here often?" he began. Then, realising how banal that sounded said, "I mean, when was the last time you saw him?" which now made him sound like a police officer taking a statement…

But such subtleties of language escaped old Tom. Or perhaps he let them go. "Hasn't been in as often as he used to, lately."

"He's got a new girlfriend." Abe offered one fact as if it accounted for the other…

"Oh," said Tom as if that explained nothing, "he ought to bring her in then. Anyway, at least he's sent his brother. Cheers, Sergeant," at which he raised his glass and drank.

Abe followed suit. He almost said, "Call me Abe, I'm off duty," but thought better of it; diminishing respect for the office and all that. So he simply said, "Cheers," then broke off to take in the room. The largely male crowd exuded an atmosphere of peace and contentment. Maybe that would change as consumption of the brown stuff rose…

Turning back to Tom, he asked, "You live locally, unless I'm mistaken. What do you make of these Spring Heeled Jack stories?"

The older man paused, put down his pint, and following a bout of puffing and tutting said, "Born and bred. No, you're not mistaken. And it's all blown up into something it never was…" He said no more, but continued to sigh and to shake his head at what Abe supposed was a subject he considered unworthy of further comment. Or perhaps, there was too much to know where to begin…

So Abe prompted. "You reckon it's all made up nonsense then? All the sightings? Just hysteria, or booze?"

"That's what you think is it?"

"It's the most sensible explanation. But I haven't entirely made up my mind. That's why I'm asking."

"Have you spoken to Davy?"

"Dimmock? Not personally. I was hoping to have a chat to him today; buy him a drink."

"Yes, he'd like that. The drink I mean, though I haven't seen him since that night. You might find he won't want to talk though."

"You were here that night? At the end?"

"Certainly was. There's a regular bunch of us stops over for a few after time. One fewer now I suspect, at least when it's dark out…I shouldn't be telling you this, should I?"

"I'm off duty, relax." Abe wondered who had just said that. "About this Davy character, did you mean that he doesn't like to talk to the police, or just won't talk about Jack?"

"Look," said Tom sharply, then lowered his voice, "forget this so-called Jack. Spring Heeled Jack's just a story; made up. But," he continued "like a lot of stories it's probably based on something; something else."

"Based on what then?" enquired Abe.

The man in the brown coat suddenly realised that he still had it on, or at least made a great play of suddenly being unbearably hot under its oppressive folds. He almost tore it off, in a practised action which perhaps explained the lack of at least three buttons. Once off, the surplus layer was rolled up and deposited at its owner's feet, for safe keeping until its insulating properties were needed again. Following his short-lived exertions old Tom was naturally consumed by an overwhelming desire to quench his thirst: he settled the remains of his pint, only sipped hitherto, with one swift gulp. Cooled and refreshed, at least momentarily, he met Abe's gaze with raised eyebrows and a

108

knowing nod. "There is a creature out there, I don't doubt it. Some might call it a monster, like your newspaper stories. But I don't call it a monster. A monster kills folk don't it? Even your Spring Heeled Jack hasn't killed anybody. Anyway, this creature as I call it, it's no use you hunting it, 'cause it only appears when it chooses. And it can't be killed, 'cause it's not a living thing like a dog or a horse or a man."

That didn't make sense to Abe, and it was starting to sound more like an ignorant superstition; myth making on the hoof. Nevertheless he politely asked, "What makes you say that?"

"Because Sergeant, I'm one of the few as have seen it. For real. This was a long time ago, when I was just starting out at work. And I wasn't drunk neither."

"What happened?" encouraged Abe.

But at that moment, like an actor coming out of character, old Tom abruptly changed the mood. "Just a minute," he said, "what was you saying about buying a drink?" The face took on a mock quizzical come innocent expression as the quarryman's gaze flitted around the room, as if he were a chicken, deciding what to peck at next. Taking the hint, Abe diligently searched his pockets and called in another two pints. The beer swiftly dispelled the sham distraction…

"Where were we?" said Tom.

"You were telling me about when you saw Spring Heeled Jack," replied Abe.

"I never saw anything of the sort," the old man asserted, straight faced.

Abe had the uncomfortable feeling that he had been taken for a ride, or at least for a drink. And him a police sergeant! "Are you standing there telling me that you just obtained that pint by deception. That's fraud that is," expostulated the copper.

"No. Calm down. You just got your, erm, wording wrong, that's all." At this point Tom edged closer and lowered his voice, "Listen, like I said, I never saw this Spring Heeled Jack character, but…you ever heard of the blue devils?" Tom seemed to be nervous of being overheard, but as far as Abe could see nobody was taking a blind bit of notice. Nevertheless, he took his cue from the old man and moderated his own volume.

"Yes. It was in Dimmock's statement."

"Yes. And that's what he saw. It's the paper that mentioned your Spring Heeled Jack, not Davy I'll bet. Everything fits you see, the quarry, the blueness – and horns even. This Jack thing's just a twisted memory of the devils. The blue devils, go back much further than your jumping Jack thing."

"How far?" prompted Abe.

"My grandfather told me about the legends. Except as far as the folks round here in them days was concerned, they were more than legends."

"I've been living here eight years," said Abe. "And until this summer, I hadn't heard of this Blue Devil."

"No," corrected Tom, "you haven't. Lived round here that is. You live in Blackheath. That's a new town remember, with lots of newcomers, from all over. The blue devils belong to us, just us at this end of Rowley. Even here most people don't believe any more. That's this science for you. Where was science when old Davy nearly got scared to death then, eh?"

Assuming this was a rhetorical question, Abe waited for Tom to carry on.

"People saw the devils more often in them days, not so much these days. And they only come out of two places, far as I know: that's this quarry here, Hailstone quarry, and over at Blue Rock quarry. But until this year, nothing for ten years at least. That was when they blew up most of the old Hail Stone: what you see now is just the remains. It killed two of the blokes as blasted it though, too much dynamite they said…But no, they don't come out as often these days. Perhaps they've been educated out of people; perhaps they're dying out, like that bird the sailors ate. What was it?"

"The dodo," said Abe.

"Ahr, that's it."

"And you say you've seen this Blue Devil?"

"Ahr, me an' Davy now. The pair on us."

"Can you tell me about it?" coaxed Abe.

Tom Pickerell looked down into his half-finished pint and swirled the liquid around, staring into it as if for inspiration. He was taking his time. Perhaps he looked to the pattern of froth left on the glass to transport him into the past; perhaps he sought out miniature blue devils etched in fleeting foam, as the old women read the patterns in tea leaves to steal into the future. He looked up and his face said, "All right then, if you insist." Then he said, "I was fifteen and I'm 52 now. So it was, what? You work it out."

Thirty-seven years thought Abe. About 1850 then.

"I remember it was very cold. We had all knocked off. Saturday it was, late afternoon. We had been doing a lot of blasting that day. On a fresh section, closer to the Hail Stone than they had done for years, by all accounts. Some of the older blokes was a bit rattled, but us young chaps just laughed. We didn't believe in ghosts and goblins. The Hail Stone was just another piece of rock to us. They said anybody damaging it would be dead in a year. Well, men were killed in the quarry all the time, still are, and I for one took no notice of the stories – it was usually carelessness that killed folk – their own or the masters' – not ghosts, blue or any other colour…. I remember I went back for something in my dinner box. So I was alone there and the light was fading rapid…"

"And it felt scary, unnerving?" asked the policeman.

Tom shook his head. "Not at all. I was young and strong and trusted in God. Anybody coming at me would wish he hadn't bothered. But then I saw something, and I changed my mind. I was never the same after. Went to church after church looking for answers. And you know what? There aren't any. Just so-called holy men telling you that you imagined it because God never made any such things, or that the devil was after you 'cause you were as sinner. Well I know what I saw, and I know I was no sinner. And if Satan was after me you'd think he'd try harder. Because, I tell you, I saw this thing just the once. And sometimes I wish I never saw it at all, and sometimes I wish I could see it again, just to see if it would let me understand, something. But no, all I ever got, from most folk, was laughed at. And these vicars: they preach this and they preach that, but they're like them parrots, they don't really know bugger all; just talk. I laugh at them now, haven't been inside a church in years. Next time I do it will be in a box…"

At this juncture Abe deemed it appropriate to turn the conversation, or rather the old fellow's increasingly aggressive diatribe, back to the day of the sighting. As the old man went off on one and further off the subject, he interrupted, "But Tom. Tom. Tell me, what was it you actually saw?"

"Oh, right. Yes. Well, I was heading back to the gate when I thought I saw a flash of light out of the corner of my eye, to the right. Then it was gone. I turned around and there it was again, just a glow behind a pile of rock. I thought it was my imagination, because it seemed to be from a blue light of some kind. Well, we had no lamps with a blue flame, but I thought, perhaps somebody had left a lamp out, and it's picking up colour from the rock."

"But it wasn't a lamp, was it?" said Abe, drawn in by the earnest telling of the tale.

"Hold up, I was getting to it," said Tom, "no, it wasn't no lamp. I went to check, but when I got within twenty feet it went out. Or rather whatever it was vanished, 'cause there was no lamp on the spot, lit or otherwise. Anyway, I thought, stuff this, I'm out here freezing and me mates are nice and warm and cosy in the pub. So I turned smartly about – and there he was. In front of me; his back to a forty-foot rock face, and his feet planted on a big jumble of shot rocks waiting to go in the tubs for the gravel crusher." Here, the old man froze, retrieving images.

"How far away was it Tom?" asked Abe. Receiving no response he touched the old man's arm, "Tom?"

The contact thawed the old man back into the here and now. "Sorry," he said, "I was just thinking…"

"Describe it for me, Tom."

Tom chose to take a good slug of beer before going on, "It just looked like a man, but a bloody big 'un. Seven or eight feet? Hard to say…"

"A shadow perhaps?" suggested Abe.

"No chance. Not mine nor any other bugger's, because there was no other bugger there except one saft sod. And I told you it was blue. Not just the colour, like in a blue coat or blue paint 'cause like I said it was getting dark and you couldn't have made it out. But it was tinged with a blueness that just seemed to leak out; a sort of weak light wrapped round him; enough to make you able to see him, but not enough to light up the surroundings. And I could see these, like lumps, on his head. Horns really, you know. Little horns, on the side of his head, not the front."

"Some kind of headgear?" interposed the policeman, "like my helmet?"

"No, I don't think so."

"What was he wearing, Tom?"

"That's the queer thing about it. I remember it really well, but, I couldn't tell you if he had any clothes on. I remember the face, and the blue. Just an ordinary face, but big and blue, with horns. I think he just wanted me to know he was there. I was scared stiff, just from the look of him I suppose, but I didn't think he was going to attack me. I just knew he wasn't. Curiosity more than anything I think. I think he just wanted to look…"

"Could it have been someone having you on? One of your mates?"

"Not unless any of 'em could jump straight up, thirty feet up a sheer rock face, and then disappear like a snuffed candle in the dark – which is what this thing did. Never saw it again, and that suited me. He only appears to the same person once, or so the stories go."

"So how long did you have him in sight?"

"Must have been all of five seconds, beginning to end. Now, does that earn me another pint?"

While Abe was doing the honours, his new-found friend wandered to the far end of the bar to accost a tall and round-faced man with a mass of curly brown hair, turning grey beneath an oddly old-fashioned hat, and sparkly green eyes to match his flamboyantly arranged green neck-scarf. After a short conversation, during which the aforesaid green eyes were flashed in Abe's direction more than once, Tom and the green scarf advanced on Abe's position. "This is the gaffer," said Tom, "he'll tell you all about the devils."

The curly-haired man thrust out his hand, "Sergeant Lively, I presume. I'm Charlie, Charlie Spragg." He took the Sergeant's hand with a warm and firm grip and with a countenance expressing such good humour that Abe responded immediately with a smile and, "Please, call me Abe."

The increasing volume of human voices in the bar made it difficult to hold a conversation, particularly for those with older and cauliflowered ears, and therefore 'the gaffer' suggested that they cede their place at the bar to fresh customers and retire to the quieter confines of the snug. Before the move, they stocked up on fresh drinks, the gaffer having volunteered a round. If Abe had been paying more attention, if his wits weren't already dampened from the transfusion of John Barleycorn's spirit, he may have noticed that the normally attentive landlady did not seem to notice him, and that it was left to a little barmaid to do the honours. Then, beers in hand, the trio made their way over to the open doorway – always open because there was no actual door on the hinges – which led into a narrow yellow-tiled corridor from where could be accessed to the right the busy little outdoor, retailing beers and ciders through the open shutters, and a snug to the left: their destination. The gaffer had ensured there was a free table in an alcove corner. And that's where they headed.

The trio sat down and made themselves comfortable. It was quieter in here, the smaller room being dominated by the arguably more genteel presence of, mainly, supervisors from the Doulton works, whereas the main bar had evidently been the territory of the working quarryman and factory or warehouse hand.

"I gather this is not entirely a social visit?" said Charlie.

"Well, I'm not here on duty, if that's what you mean, although I was hoping for some background information pertinent to one particular investigation."

"Which Tom has mentioned," interjected Spragg.

"Yes, and he's been very helpful. So much so in fact that this is turning out to be much more of a social occasion than I had anticipated," said Abe, warming in the glow of hospitality and a few pints of splendid beer, "you keep a nice pint."

"We do try," said the gaffer. "Another drink? It's on the house."

"Well, I'm already on my third, but yes, why not? One more for the road. You're a gentleman."

"Perish the thought," said Spragg, motioning to a boy in the corridor, and giving him their drinks order.

After some apparent confusion as to who was paying for that round, a pleasant half-hour ensued, during which Abe finished his third pint and all but polished off the fourth. The meantime, the gaffer, an avid believer, expanded upon what Rock had said about the devils, or devil, singular, possibly, for in his opinion the sightings were too infrequent to posit the existence of a whole colony or swarm of them; a small family perchance. Like Barber Rock's, the Spragg family roots went back generations into this ground so he said. And like Barber Rock, he linked the appearances of the Blue Devil with the ancient Hail Stone, from which the pub derived its name.

"What I'm saying is," explained an emotional Charlie, "is that there's something abroad hereabouts that shouldn't be. Or maybe it's us, the people, that shouldn't be here."

"What do you mean?" said Abe.

"He means that this is the Blue Devil's land and he objects to us blowing the shit out of it," piped in Tom.

"Look," continued the gaffer, "I'm not sure what this Blue Devil is, but I firmly believe he exists. It's not too far-fetched is it? Science is making discoveries about things all the time. What about electricity?"

"Electricity?" repeated Abe vacantly, "you've lost me."

"Well, who's to say that these things are creatures, but not like us. Not of blood and flesh and bone, but made up of electricity, or something like it. It would explain the blue glow."

"Anything's possible," conceded Abe, "but why here, and why aren't they seen all the time?"

"I wouldn't know," said Charlie, "could be that conditions have to be just right, like the years some butterflies are everywhere, and the next there's not a one…but I don't think they like the blasting." At this point Charlie broke off to study Abe's face, and seemed to make a decision, "I'll tell you what I think. I think these creatures live in the ground. I think they've been there, here, for thousands of years, and I know that they don't like us disturbing them. We had one of them spiritualist women do an investigation about ten years ago, and that's what she reckoned."

"So, what? We damage their home, or disturb their sleep and they come out to warn us off, like ants when a kid pokes a stick in the nest? If so…" began Abe.

"That's exactly what it's like," interrupted Tom, "except that they aren't warning us off anything, just warning us. For our own good."

"Warning us?" queried Abe.

"Yes, that's what we reckon," continued the gaffer. "In my grandfather's time most of the land round here was trees and woods and farms. Not much in the way of what you might call industry. But look at it now. It's a bleeding mess, excuse my French. Just slag heaps and smoke and coal dust and dirt, and huge black holes torn into the soft green of the fields, or dynamite blasted. Mother Nature they call it. Well, if it is our mother, she's ageing bad. We're killing her, and it will do us no good. People are too blind to see, but I will tell you this: there's a reckoning coming; and we'll all have to pay, blood for blood."

Abe thought that this was all getting a bit melodramatic. Furthermore, Spraggs' description was not entirely accurate, for he well knew that in this neck of the woods there was still plenty of untouched nature to find, like on the hills, away from the quarries. Sergeant Lively began to suspect that Charles Spragg esquire was losing his marbles. But, he went along with it. "Do you think Davy Dimmock will be in then?"

"I shouldn't think so, not now," said the gaffer. "It's getting on and he's too scared to be out of doors around here after dark."

"He really was that frightened?" queried Abe.

"White as a sheet he was, and lost for words, which isn't like our Davy at all, not by a long chalk. Oh yes, he saw our devil all right. It changed him."

"Like me," remarked Tom. "Laughed at for years I was. Nobody believed me see? Not none of my mates any road. And I don't think you believe me do you?" he said, looking at a spot somewhere on Abe's forehead.

The policeman thought about it, looking at Tom then Charlie, then back. Souls bared, they awaited his judgement with eager apprehension.

Abe was not about to answer directly. Instead, he had decided to tell them a story of his own. It had been floating up from somewhere dark as the beer went down, and he told it like this:

"I'll make a deal with you. If you are prepared to believe what I'm about to tell you, I'm prepared to give credence to your blue devil yarn."

The two looked at him quizzically, but said nothing. Then Charlie Spragg pursed his lips and nodded an assent.

"Right. Well, as you are probably aware, I'm not from these parts," began Abe.

"Tell by the way you speak," observed Tom.

"Indeed," continued Abe, "I've often been accused of not 'spakin proper.' I'm originally from a little place called Nash." In response to interrogative raised eyebrows he added, "it's in the Shropshire hills." The Shropshire hills may as well have been on the moon for all the hint of recognition he got from the pair. Moving on he explained: "Nash is a very different place to Rowley or Blackheath. It's still very much a small village in the middle of nowhere, very much still attached to old rural traditions, or at least it was when I left." He paused to check they were still with him. They were.

"I'll give you an example. Life there still revolves around the seasons, around natural cycles. Timeless cycles, it used to be thought. It's important for planting and harvesting of course. Without planting there is no harvest; without a harvest there is no life, only starvation. Living in towns and cities it's easy to forget these things."

"What's this got to do with the Blue Devil?" said Tom, cutting in to the flow.

"Coming to it," replied Abe patiently. "Because the life or death of the crops meant the life or death of the people, over the years, centuries even, rituals grew up to help ensure that crops did not fail. That's how I imagine it started anyway."

"How what started?" asked Charlie.

"These rituals, or customs, or superstitions if you will. The main thing is that in Nash, which I don't suppose is any different from any other rural village or hamlet up and down the country, it's still considered unlucky, if not downright foolhardy, not to propitiate the, what? The gods if you like, or…"

Abe noticed that old Tom was seemingly searching the ceiling for something, and soundlessly trying to get his mouth around some sound. "You all right Tom?" he asked.

"Ah would be if ah knowed what yoh was on abaht. Wot was that big werd, propertate or summat?"

The question reminded Abe, as the black country dialect should have, that not everybody had had the start that he had benefitted from.

"I'm sorry Tom. What I meant to say was that people in these villages still think that if they don't keep the gods, or goddesses, happy they might decide to take away the power that makes the crops grow. Because that power, they think, comes from these gods, or spirits. And it's the same power that causes the animals to reproduce, and the people."

"But that's just an old superstition," said Charlie. "We know better than that now."

Abe held up a cautionary finger, "I might say the same thing about blue devils."

Charlie swallowed this argument and asked, "But folk don't really believe that there are gods that watch over the crops, and might cause them not to grow if they didn't like what they were doing. Do they?"

"We're getting into murky waters here aren't we?" continued Abe. He was about to point out that the majority of the inhabitants of the entire region, if not the entire nation, were Christians who believed that God had a direct hand in making the harvest happen, hence harvest festivals. But the conversation was getting deep enough as it was. And so he decided not to. "No, I don't think people think about it in such stark terms anymore. Generations ago, perhaps they did, but now I think it's a case of people going through the motions. Better safe than sorry as they say."

"But folk have actually seen the blue devils, like Tom here, and my grandmother for another," protested the gaffer, "we don't know what they are yet, but they've been seen!"

"Which brings us back to the point," said Abe. "You know about the May-pole celebrations?"

"Yes. The little 'uns dance around them, and there's saft games and such. It's a holiday. Don't see as much of it these days though, it's dying."

"I agree," said Abe. "I went to a May day fete in Dudley, in the castle grounds, a couple of years back, but it wasn't the same."

"In what way?" asked Spragg.

"As you can imagine, from what I've said, in Nash we – they – take it all pretty seriously. I want to tell you about the tradition we have of killing the May King."

"Not the Queen?" asked Tom.

"No, a man's more important when it comes to fertility. His seed – his power – impregnates the many you see."

Looking at the pair of them, it was not entirely clear that they did see. Perhaps they were embarrassed. He ploughed on. "So, the way it goes is, each winter the green things of the earth – trees and crops – are killed by the dark and cold, or cut down by the people; and each spring the Old Man Of The Woods, who is the father of all the green things, has to breathe life and power back into them, so that they can start to grow. The Old Man Of The Woods is also known as the King Of The Woods, or the Green Man. Be that as it may, there's a problem: the Old Man Of The Woods is just that, an old man. Old men are weak and feeble, and you can't trust a weak King Of The Woods – or King Of The May – to have enough in him to get things going, so to speak. So, we kill him. And crown a new king."

"Kill him how?" said Charlie suspiciously.

"In mime. Only in mime. A new king is crowned each year, or it's the old king with a new face. That way the Green Man comes each year and makes the leaves sprout, flowers to bloom, and corn to grow and ripen. But – we don't know if he would if we didn't go through the show of killing the old king. Yes, I know, we live in enlightened times, but the way it's thought of in the country is 'why tempt fate?' Besides, it makes for a smashing celebration, with music and dancing and drinking. Not to be missed…"

"Sounds a real giggle," said the gaffer unconvincingly. "So how exactly do you kill this woody old bloke then? In your play-acting? Chop him up and stick him on a bonfire, is it?"

"Just the opposite. He's drowned. A dummy made out of sticks and straw is thrown into the mill-pond; the corn brook on occasion, but more usually the mill pond. Sometimes its head is chopped off first, just to make sure I think, but not always. The

116

village lads compete for the honour of committing murder by racing each other on horseback. The winner becomes the King Of The May. That year's Green Man."

"I still don't see what this has got to do with our Blue Devil," chipped in old Tom.

"Yes, what are you trying to say?" said Charlie.

"Sorry, yes. I think the point is that the people of Nash and…round here…"

"Springfield," prompted Tom.

"Thank you," said Abe. "They both believe in creatures, or powers, that not everybody can see. Things that live just beyond our senses. Like in our dreams."

"I didn't dream it!" protested Tom.

"No, I'm not saying you did…"

"So you believe us then?" said Charlie.

"I'm certainly prepared to believe," said Abe, "and I'll tell you why: I've been to that place that not everybody sees, and I've seen something that lives there; something that nobody else in Nash ever saw."

"What was it you saw?" said Tom, now all ears.

"I saw the Green Man."

If Abe expected this revelation to stun his audience into silence and disbelief, he was mistaken. Perhaps they had too much invested in their own credence to question another's; an inevitable quid pro quo. Whatever, Tom merely asked matter-of-factly, "And I bet nobody believed you did they? They laughed at you like they laughed at me."

"No Tom. Nobody laughed, because I told nobody. Not about the Green Man anyway."

"Will you tell us then? Now?" asked Charlie.

Abe had already decided that he would. There was something about this day, this place, that encouraged him to share. So…

"I was fifteen, same age as you Tom when you had your experience, and it was a week since the May Day festival, so the Green Man was still very fresh in our minds, which may have had something to do with it. We were out on the horses, Miriam – that's my sister – and I, and my brother John on a little safe pony: he was never a good rider. It was a Sunday, and we met up with a couple of village lads, no, three in fact, out on an assortment of nags. We had a little jumping competition, over a few logs and old barrels. Against their mounts, it was too easy for me. So I gave myself a handicap, riding without a saddle, then without saddle or bridle, holding only fistfuls of mane and tightly with my legs on the mare's greasy flanks. The four of us lads, not John, were showing off. But I had to push it that bit too far didn't I? Miriam said that that was enough now, that I would hurt myself…" Abe was reliving the whole thing in his head, and the pub had faded into a blur of sound and shadows.

"But yoh day tek no nowtice." Tom's black country cadence brought the place and time back into focus.

"No Tom. I knew better, as young men always do, and yes indeed, I took no notice, as you say."

"Pride comes before a fall," observed Charlie.

"Just so. One more go, I insisted. True to form, the horse sailed over smoothly and was cantering out on the other side to the hoots and cheers of my adolescent companions. Then, for no good reason, which is good enough reason for a silly mare, she jinked to one side, and I was off."

Tom's frustration slipped free of the grip of his self-control again, lubricated by the beer. "What's that got to do with the Blue Devil though? Or the bloody Green Man for that matter?"

"I'll tell you directly!" Abe had raised his voice. It was his story and he would tell it his way. *Silly old duffer.* "Don't interrupt and I'll get to it quicker. All right?"

A shrug. Abe carried on. "Anyway I was out cold, must have hit my head. When I woke up I was at the top of the field, by the woods, looking back to where I had come from. I could see Miriam and John and the others huddled around, looking at something between their legs. Great, I thought. Let me wander off in a daze why don't you. I remember thinking, 'what are you looking at?' As soon as I thought it I was there. I mean right there, back with them. But above them, looking down. And I saw what they were looking at. It was me, lying there, out cold, pale as death."

"What did you do?" asked Tom.

"Do? What could I do? I was knocked out. Anyway, when they couldn't wake me they started to panic; I saw it all. They propped me up on John's pony and, bodies each side, they held me in place. John and a village lad named Tench held onto the other horses, then they all traipsed off with my body and left me there!"

"But…what happened?" said Tom.

"Well you obviously didn't die," added Charlie, "because you're no ghost."

"Well, I wanted to follow them, but now I seemed rooted to the spot. Then, something made me look back to the woods. That's when I saw the Green Man. He was huge and green and covered in what might have been clothes made up of lots of bits of green cloth, or they might have been leaves; like one of the dummies we used to make, but bigger. And he had a black face and horns like a stag."

Tom seemed to be having something of a eureka moment: "Like the Blue Devil. A big bugger with horns. I reckon they'm the same thing but different kinds. Like sparrows and robins – both birds but different."

"That's a reasonable working theory," said Abe. "Like I said, I never told anybody about the Green Man before. Miriam knows about me leaving my body, and I think she believes that, but giant green monsters watching us? Bit of a stretch, or at least it was till I started learning about the blue devils, and now I'm thinking twice: these things may actually exist. I mean, I think they can be seen, sometimes, but they can't be here most of the time, or there would be lots and lots of sightings. Perhaps they pop into our world

118

only occasionally and then…pop out again. I don't know…" And he really didn't know. He was losing himself in wheels within wheels and the close atmosphere of the snug and the booze was making his head spin. He faltered, unable to hang onto a reliable thought, much less utter a comprehensible sentence.

He was brought round by a buzz of insistent questioning and nudges. "But where do they come from then? Out of the rocks? The sky? Where?" badgered the old man.

Abe had no answer that made any sense. And that made him have second thoughts and feel foolish, no better than any drunken clown holding forth after too much booze. And it angered him. "How the bloody hell should I know? It's a mystery – that means nobody knows! May as well be from the bloody moon, for all I care."

"All right, all right," said Tom, "only making a few suggestions."

"Sorry," said Abe. "The point is; all I'm trying to say is, we don't know everything, science that is. I mean, look at me. I saw them put me on that pony, and I could hear what they were saying, and I didn't imagine it."

"And you saw the Green Man," said Tom.

"I think I did, yes. I felt like a ghost. Perhaps that's what he was. I felt as if I should go to him, but then something snapped like a spring and I felt myself travelling along the ground at great speed, like on a raft on a fast-flowing river, just pushed along. I saw the back of my own head in the minutest of detail, even though I was a long way off, like looking through a telescope with one eye, but with the other one open. I went faster and faster toward that spot until I thought there must be an almighty collision. But then I was behind my eyes, my real eyes, and I opened them and spoke."

"What did you say?"

"Can't remember. But I saw that Miriam was crying, I remember that. She was convinced I was dead, they all were. We all promised to keep quiet about my lucky escape. The next day at home I told Miriam about my strange experience, omitting the part about the Green Man. She kissed me on the head and put her finger to my lips. I haven't spoken of it since except to strangers, to you."

It was finished, the story and his strength. Fortunately, he was seated, for he felt his legs to have no more substance than two mere ribbons of boneless flesh. Breathing a sigh he waited for more questions.

"That's grand," said Tom. "I knew there was something different about you. Like me. I believe you, but take it from me, just be careful who else you tell; might land you up in the loony bin. They tried to get me you know; don't you let them."

This sounded rather less than comforting. Abe took a look at the gaffer, who said, "You certainly know how to tell a good yarn, Sergeant; and it's been a pleasure but it's time for me to go. Errands to run; got to see a man about a dog…" With that he stood, shook Abe's hand heartily, and went out.

Abe had been so wrapped up in the past that he almost failed to recognise his surroundings. As his full complement of senses and wits returned, he felt a sudden and irrepressible urge to flee the close confines of the little room and get out into the evening air.

"Right, I'd better make a move too," he announced, extending his hand and best wishes to Tom, and his stride, as he made swiftly for the exit.

But Tom was not finished with Sergeant Lively yet. As Abe got to the street and started breathing cooler air, the old man, now enclosed once more by his brown great coat with half the buttons AWOL, tugged at his sleeve.

"If you step forward a pace, you can see two patches of damaged tiles. That's where the Blue Devil landed. Look."

Curious, Abe stepped further away from the threshold. As he did so half a tile, no doubt dislodged by the strong winds that had been building, smashed onto the pavement beside him. Instinctively, Abe looked up: just in time to see another tile, or at least a large section of tile, just parting company with the roof at the gutter line, on a trajectory with Abe's face. He just had time to quickly look down before being rendered unconscious by a sharp blow to the top of the cranium. His inert body hit the floor a split second after the transgressing tile.

Chapter 11

Tipping Points

John had always liked dogs, the bigger the better. The combination of undemanding companionship and selfless loyalty to clan was one which most men could only aspire to. A dog will put his life on the line for you even as human friends fade away. John liked dogs, and they liked him.

Cyril Crane's huge black hound come mastiff had accepted him because Cyril had demonstrated that John Lively was a friend, and because he knew the man liked him. And so the big dog had been content, happy even, to accept John's robust attentions: the wagging tail did not know how to lie. John was close enough to discern the little light flecks in the animal's brown eyes and, this close to, scratching the solid as rock head, the darkness of the coat was revealed to be a stratum of coal black overlaid with rusty brown brindling. But, he guessed, not many people got close enough to appreciate it, for they well knew that the placid creature which they were accustomed to see, lying mostly inert in its accustomed corner, was liable to transform itself into a rushing hundred and twenty pounds – or so – onslaught of bristling hackles and slashing teeth if it perceived a threat, real or otherwise, to its master. And that was only be expected. John respected that. Fortunately, tonight the big dog was in a good mood, taking his cue from the fact that Cyril and the big young man were getting on like a house on fire, as they sat at a private table in the long bar-room of the Shoulder Of Mutton, no slouches in getting through a belly-burning bottle of port of uncertain provenance.

"Old Sabre's taken to you; doesn't like most. He knows you're family," observed Cyril.

John looked down at the black lump of muscle, parked like an anvil at his feet. Sabre. Perhaps named for the sharp white teeth, weapons which John had seen flashed only in noisy greeting. Still, a good name that, Sabre. And a worthy companion for a Lively, even if Cyril was not a Lively by blood...

Topping up the glasses, the uncle continued, "So, you've been thinking about my offer. What's the verdict? Like to come and work for me?"

True to his word, uncle Cyril had paid John a visit on the very same day that he had intimated to John's big brother, sergeant Lively, that he would do so. He had appeared at John's door that night, in the dark, illuminated but softly by the saffron glow which escaped as the door was opened, and shrouded in the oilskin he was wont to throw around himself, no matter what the weather, and a wide brimmed hat throwing his face into shadow. Like a wraith he had appeared, like some antique footpad, disgorged by the gibbet and resurrected in flesh. To be frank, Cyril Crane had a flair for the dramatic, and often found business dealings benefitted from the exercise of a little of the actor's stock in trade, be that along the lines of either tragedy or comedy; for it had been apparent to him from a young age that we are all acting out parts all the time, and happy are those that are honest enough to recognise it. But the object of this particular visitation was not a man to be easily affrighted or intimidated, which in retrospect Cyril had considered fortunate, for a more nervous character might have lashed out in shock – and you would not enjoy being lashed out at by someone built like a brick...out-house. Paradoxically, it was not until Cyril had removed the hat and stepped properly into the light that John's poise had been disturbed. Apart from glimpses across the street he had not seen his uncle, not spoken to him, for a couple of years. John had been just stepping out himself, and, somehow with Cyril ashamed of his meagre dwelling, he persuaded the older man to accompany him and reconvene the reunion around the corner, in the California.

That had been last month. John had listened and promised to consider what had been said; which he had done, contemplating with the silverfish and the little moths in the little room, pressing in ever smaller as the days passed, until the smell of baking bread threatened to entomb him forever. And then the incident at work with Alf and the furnace...and so, finally, he had rolled up at the Shoulder and asked to see the boss.

"I must admit; working in the factory is not what you might call conducive to good health. It's just a means to an end, which is to earn enough to keep body and soul together. But no way to earn a living really, not for me. A way to earn a ticket to useless old age and decrepitude more like..." John had reflected out loud.

"If you live that long," rejoined his uncle.

"That's a point," conceded John, remembering again poor old melted down Alf, "but, with the utmost respect, a career choice involving spending time locked up at her majesty's pleasure in Stafford gaol, would also seem to be less than ideal."

"John! Whatever do you mean son?" said Cyril, openly disingenuous, and then, leaning forward confiding more seriously, "look, I run a diverse little operation here. Some of it's perfectly legal and above board, like the haulage business; respectable you might say. But, I will admit, in response to your unasked questions – questions to which you know the answers anyway – that there are certain aspects of certain dealings that might well fall on the other side of the legal fence."

John disengaged and looked around to make sure that potential ear-wiggers were out of range before continuing, "Like your illegal gambling operations?"

"Gambling operations," repeated Cyril. "Yes, indeed. Given the current state of the law, which as you know is really but a plaything of politicians sitting in ivory towers, they are illegal, as you say. But that's what makes them so very lucrative. If you play your cards right as they say. Silly though really, isn't it? I mean we all like a little bet now and again, most of us anyway. It's part of our nature I think: the flip of a coin, the turn of a card, a whippet's turn of speed, how much of a beating a man take for money; we just like to speculate. But the so-called law knows better. Still, it's not for me to bite the hand that feeds me – so to speak…"

"But you say that I needn't get involved in any of the, er, dodgy stuff, not if I didn't want to?"

"That's right. Start you on as a driver, and you could be useful in the pub, keeping a lid on any trouble – and keeping your ears open. Then there's my properties in Darby End, I bought them a few months ago; you could drive down and collect the rent for me…There won't be set hours, like you're tied to now, and I'll more than match your existing wages. Can't say fairer than that, can I?"

"It certainly sounds attractive," said John. "What's the catch?"

"No catch. You're my nephew, remember. And it's about time this family started sticking together."

"And what about Abe? There's no mistaking what side of the legal fence he's on is there?"

"That's one way of putting it, though I wouldn't be too sure about that. Your brother's too intelligent not to appreciate what the lawyers might call the grey areas," opined Cyril.

"That doesn't mean he won't act to uphold the law. He can be a real stickler, believe me."

"Oh, I've heard the tales," said the uncle. "But Abe and I have an understanding; a tacit one I'll admit, but we understand each other. That is to say, he knows that I control certain nominally illicit operations."

"Gambling, you mean?"

"Basically, yes," said Cyril.

"Run for you by your gang of hard men?"

"That sounds as if I only employ them for that quality. But the truth is that someone has to help me with organising events, controlling crowds, looking after stakes, and watching out for the law. It's not a one-man operation. It just so happens that some of our customers are sometimes inclined to cut up rough, so the people that do work for me do need to be able to look after themselves, as I'm sure you will appreciate."

"Well, that certainly puts my mind at ease on that point," said John ironically but with good humour, "and what kind of area, geographic area, are these 'employees' expected to cover?"

"Well," said Cyril, "we're based in Blackheath, as you know, and we operate from here to the Buffery, to Whiteheath, to Quinton and to the edges of Halesowen, just up the road here. That, as it so happens is all on Abe's patch, or mostly so. And because

Abe's patch is also my patch, he knows that certain rules apply. My rules. Without me there would be a free-for-all, and much more violence."

"Better the devil you know," mused John.

"Exactly. Though I do actually consider myself to be one of the good 'uns," said Cyril. "Also, of course, I'm organised, and that makes it difficult for the police to prove anything," he added confidently.

"So things just settle into a pattern, a stand-off?" said John.

"That's how it works," confirmed the older man. "It can get quite cosy, unless someone sticks a spoke in the wheel." An image of a sly young man named Cutler flashed in Cyril's head.

"What do you mean?" asked John.

"I mean, like I said, there are rules, parameters if you will. Break the unwritten rules or cross the line, then the truce don't necessarily have to be upheld. With me?"

John was not entirely sure that he was. "Abe might be content to let sleeping dogs lie, as you say, but what if he finds out I'm working for you?"

"Oh, he will. But, so what if he does? You're not doing anything illegal. I'll bet he'd be pleased to see you out of that smelting works," said Cyril, and offered as further inducement, "he was quick enough to get Josh away from that mine."

"That's right, he was," agreed John. "All right uncle, I accept."

"It's Cyril," said the man with the flat nose, "one more for the road?"

As they shook on it, the big dog caught the change and stood to celebrate with enthusiastic barks.

"All right Sabre. Down boy. Down now, it's all right. Good boy. That's it, it's all right."

And Cyril knew that it would be. He had an ally on board who would prove more than a match for Jack Cutler if push came to shove. As for John sticking to 'legitimate' duties, well, the borderline was a blurry one; one innocuous trip over the line would lead to another until the line had disappeared. But what did that matter? Cyril would look out for him.

#

Sissy had been seeing John regularly for a month or more during which time physical attraction and a mutual admiration of qualities entirely distinct from the physical had begun to resolve itself into a realisation that both wanted more: John's decision to work for Cyril was greatly influenced by that consideration; a potentially high-reward move if he were prepared to involve himself in his uncle's more questionable dealings; and in his guts he knew that he would involve himself, probably even enjoy it. For her part, Sissy was looking for opportunities to leave the family forge, dreaming of a fresh start with John. But fresh starts were a rare commodity in her world: money, it always came down

124

to money. And then there was John's marital status. He still had a wife, though both of them would expunge this from conversation, and as far as possible, from memory. It was however no use crying over sour milk as Miriam's old kitchen help was fond of misquoting, and the meantime Sissy concentrated on cultivating relationships with John's siblings. Opportunity for interaction with the boys was rare, but Miriam was a different matter. After an initial awkwardness, no doubt engendered by John's matrimonial and paternal ties (his Baggage as the owner sometimes unkindly referred to them), the two women found that they got on well. Miriam saw a strong character who would stand no nonsense and provide the kind of firm hand her potentially wayward brother needed. Anything that benefitted her brothers would always get Miriam's vote. For Siss, getting on with the family matriarch she considered a prerequisite. Fortunately, that had been an easy task: the two women were firm friends and completely comfortable in each other's company in no time at all, Miriam admiring the powerful physical presence and industriousness of her brother's girl, who reciprocated with an appreciation of the business acumen and elegance of John's striking-looking sister.

Before going off to see Cyril, John had imposed on Miriam to 'look after Siss' while he 'just nipped out' on 'some urgent business.' Glad to be so imposed upon, Miriam took the opportunity for a break, delegating duties to her dutiful new husband and to her barmaid Marlene, and sat with Sissy at the very same table, at that same window, where, on the day of Miriam's wedding, had sat a different female object of John Lively's affection, albeit a very transient one. So much remained the same yet so much had changed in such a very short time. Be that as it may, the window seat, you see, had the advantage that it was away from the main press and clamour, sufficiently so for two ladies to be able to enjoy a pleasant exchange without raising their voices. For forty minutes, the aforementioned ladies discussed everything from ingredients for the best cold creams, to the ingredients for the best sausages, to the ingredients for the best men.

Sissy was bemoaning the fashion for skin-whiteners and it was approaching nine when Miriam, who always kept one landlady's eye on the door, noticed the arrival of two unaccompanied females. It was of course no longer unheard of for women to frequent licensed premises absent the accompaniment of a male member of family. In this case however, Miriam's experienced scrutiny confirmed immediately that these two weren't here for a sociable drink. Besides, she knew one of the pair: Hetty Arblaster was a dumpy, big-bosomed woman of, what? Thirty? It was hard to say as she had a plump round face, the type of face which could smooth out the normal wrinkles of time, at least for a while, and, to boot, it was invariably tastelessly obscured with rouge; like it was going out of fashion. It was a jolly, almost a comic, face. Until you got close enough to pick up in the slightly piggy eyes a faint gleam, which Miriam would have described as malicious, or at least lunatic, had anyone asked directly. The landlady suspected that both the glint and the rouge were connected by a common cause, to wit an unfortunate addiction to strong spirit, with gin being the culprit of choice, for it is well-known that over-indulgence in such spirituous liquor degrades the complexion, as well as being deleterious for a person's proper mind.

Hetty was scanning the room, armed with a large and dangerous looking black hand-bag. Miriam could see that there was trouble afoot. Hetty's companion she did not recognise, but that lady's pugnacious demeanour coupled with a tight-lipped sour and bony countenance did nothing to reassure. The second woman was not tall, only as tall as Hetty, who herself in the height stakes could in all fairness be described as short at best, and she did not have the benefit of such an implement as the portly woman's blunderbuss of a hand-bag; rather, she sported a neat little purse of soft cloth suspended from a strap over her shoulder. To compensate, however, she was carrying an accessory altogether more suited to her general soma-type, this being a rolled up red umbrella with a noticeably long metal tip, which she handled in a familiar manner which suggested that its utility went beyond defending the bearer from the assaults of mere raindrops.

Hetty's eyes locked onto the object of her search, standing at the bar, where he had been drinking and minding his own business for half an hour. It was a black headed man, whose build, whether by dint of natural propensity, or by the details of his existence so far, or a combination of both, could only be defined as fragile. His bearing and movement were nothing if not twitchy, clothing just on the shabby side of respectable. Valiant, it was his habit to seek to off-set the defects in his vesture and physical constitution by way of a modest investment in perfumed hair unguent, thus sprucing up the whole ensemble. A worthy course of action you would think, would you not? Alas, coupled with the inadequate garb already alluded to, and the unprofessionally styled lank black mane, parted and combed to one side and stuck to the skull as if with glue, the effect achieved was the exact opposite of its objective, creating in fact an undeserved impression of the utmost greasy seediness: too liberal an application of the magic balm suggested nothing as much as the fact that the poor chap was so down at heel that his finances only allowed for a spoonful of lard massaged into his locks. General lack of discrimination, of good taste, in the facial hair department only served to exacerbate the self-inflicted problem, for he sported – although one might deem that word wholly inappropriate – a horizontally truncated moustache, a 'snot-brake' as the model has been referred to. Worse, his facial fuzz was thick with a tendency to spikiness so that the impression given by this supralabial cultivation was of a man who had affixed a small blacking brush beneath his nose. Had he had a circle of male friends, or any friends, his nickname might indeed have been 'Blacking Brush.' Sadly, such is mere speculation, for Samson Arblaster's appearance and nervous disposition, the very antithesis of what the Christian name selected by his parents had presumably meant to prefigure, resulted quite simply in an inability to make new friends. As for old friends, they had disappeared quite soon after his marriage…

The net result was an individual uncommonly susceptible to the ravages of a rapacious woman, hence his regular retreat to the familiar bar at the Royal Oak, where he had just called in another half. Exhibiting more prescience than his luckless progenitors, Samson this night felt the pernicious pressure of Hetty's gaze at the nape of his neck. Without turning around, he hunkered down and froze, like a frightened rabbit. But within seconds the juby trap that was Mrs Arblaster was within range to launch a verbal assault. Poor Samson shied like an ill-treated horse. "Hetty," he said, as if pleasantly surprised to see her, "what am yoh doin' 'ere?" and did his best to raise a disarming smile whilst glancing between Hetty and her companion, who remained on guard near the door.

Miriam gestured to Sissy. "Look. Something's going to kick off."

As people stopped talking to take in this new source of entertainment, Sissy could plainly hear what was going on.

"Never mind what ah'm a doin' 'ere, what am yoh doin' 'ere?"

"Ah was just…"

"Doh interrupt. Why ay yoh bin um today?"

Why indeed, pondered Sissy.

"I have been," protested the husband.

"Don't come that. You knocked off and went straight out with your mates to get drunk."

Samson kept to himself the thoughts that he did not have the coin nor the inclination to get drunk, nor thanks to her any 'mates.' But he hadn't given up on his defence yet.

"I did come home. Look, I put my best scarf on. You weren't there: I looked in the oven but there was no dinner. I mean," he continued bravely, "I'm out at work all day; surely the least that a man can expect is for his wife to have his dinner waiting," *even if she's not there herself, which would be no bad thing.*

Now, if he had voiced this observation in private, she would have given him what for. But, as the not altogether guileless iron-monger's clerk had made his stand in public, in a bastion of the working man, of which class individual members there present were already mumbling sympathy with the husband's perspective, the attacker deemed it prudent to protect her flank.

"But Samson, my love," she returned in what she imagined were affectionate tones, "I was only next door with Mrs Evans."

"I thought you were out…" he started.

"Out Samson? Out? Out where? When do I ever get to go out?"

Whenever you and your cronies in your so-called gin-tasting committee feel like going out and getting rat-arsed, on my money.

"I told you," and she went on the attack. "I was borrowing some bread and sausages from next door so that I could put you something on the table when you got in. The kids ate the last of the bread and dripping before I sent them out to play…"

Out of your way you mean. Samson had his own explanation for why there was no food in the house.

"Instead of complaining you should stop drinking us out of house and home…"

Pot calling the kettle black.

"…and give me proper housekeeping money to get a decent shop in. Anyway, now that I'm here you can give me this week's, before you drink it all. I've got to pay Mrs Evans straight back, wouldn't be right not to."

"I'll come back and see her."

"No, No," she said rather hurriedly, "you don't need to. Just give me the money. You finish your drink, have another one if you like. Sausages are in the oven."

The man reached into his jacket pocket, took out a small bag of coins, and emptied it into his wife's hand. Then, summoning a morsel of pride, he said loudly, but not unambiguously, "There you are then my dearest. Take it and go, it's all I've got on me. I'll be home for my dinner when I'm ready."

Hetty Arblaster stood immobile, considering what she had heard, and what she had received. Presently, she decided that he had given her too little and said too much, which conclusion caused her red face to redden all the more as she launched herself at her husband, with every sign of conducting a non-consensual search of his person.

By this time, however, Miriam had seen enough and intervened. The Royal Oak had always been a cut above other licensed premises in the area, at least in her mind. John Henry had worked hard to keep it so and so did she. In other establishments, fights were a regular feature, their frequency proportional to the strength of the liquor dispensed, and inversely proportional to the physical and moral strengths of the landlords. But, at least since it became the home of the sergeant of police, the Oak had always attracted the less boisterous element, such as the innocuous Mr Arblaster…

Before Hetty Arblaster could come to grips with her husband, a tall and athletic woman stepped between them. "Excuse me madam, but I'm going to ask you to leave."

"This is my husband, stay out of it," said Hetty and the gin, none too cautiously.

"And this is my pub, so mind your tone," came back the resonating voice with just the hint of a growl, "and I'm asking you to leave. Now, please."

At this point the big landlady was joined by the muscular chain-maker. Faced with that formidable female alliance, Mrs Arblaster felt immediately inclined to accept the invitation to vacate the premises. And she would have done so there and then if not for a well-meaning intervention.

It so happened, that a small group of men, in transit to or from the bar, had gathered at the scene, curious as to the outcome of this matrimonial encounter. It also so happened that amongst these was a short-sighted and bald-headed miner by the name of Stanley Gethin. Not unusually, Stan had recently suffered an injury down the pit, when, extending his stride to avoid a puddle, he had placed his foot atop a skittish piece of anthracite, which promised support only mischievously to remove that support as soon as his foot touched it. The result was a badly torn knee which the owner was nursing slowly back to pain-free strength, but which as yet, being only some forty-eight hours old, was still extremely tender. As Mrs Arblaster was just withdrawing, and as the miner was taking a pace or two backwards to afford egress to her above average girth, the hatchet faced one, umbrella in hand, was just arriving on the scene, presumably to lend moral support and register her two-penny worth. Now, there was a point in the room, some eighteen to twenty inches above the floor boards towards which converged both the miner's delicate joint and the tip of the woman's brolly. The two objects collided in excruciating coincidence, producing a high-pitched wail of agony totally at odds with the rugged masculinity of Stan, 'the man', Gethin, who in short order had collapsed to one knee in front of the hatchet faced one, like a suitor proposing marriage. But loving caresses were the last thing on Stanley's pain-befogged mind: in a flash he was up and towering over his assailant, clapping furious eyes on her and grabbing her instrument of torture with both hands with a view to disarming her.

"Give me that blood..." he began but bit his tongue. He was a proper black countryman and knew better than to swear in front of a woman, let alone strike one, no matter what the provocation. Nevertheless, he wanted that umbrella. But Mrs Tromans (to give the lady who looked like she was constantly sucking a lemon her proper name) had other ideas. A tugging match ensued, in which the miner, conscious of his dignity, and that of the lady, or perhaps simply wary of hurting his leg, after only a couple of unsuccessful yanks gave up and relinquished his grip. Unfortunately, this gallant surrender had unintended results, for poor Mrs Tromans had thrown all her weight into the effort of protecting her property, so that when Stan's resistance was suddenly removed, she catapulted herself backwards, landing embarrassingly on her derrière and loosing her handbag whose monetary contents spilled onto the floor as she struck her head, although very lightly, against the side of the bar. A brief pandemonium ensued, with Hetty Arblaster railing against the cruel assault and trying unsuccessfully to cuff the much taller Mr Gethin around the ears. But the strategic positioning of Miriam and Sissy reduced the affray to a verbal one almost instantaneously, whereafter attention switched to the downed combatant.

Jack Beckett had been prompt in coming to Mrs Tromans' aid, gathering up her coins whilst she gathered her wits. On her feet now, she joined with her companion in insisting that the police be called to address this crime. Rather than have them march off to find a constable, or Abe, and telling only one half of the story, Miriam sequestered the pair in a corner, gave them a complimentary port and lemon and waited for them to calm down.

As luck would have it, the law dropped in some ten minutes later, in the form of P.C. Joshua Lively. With some difficulty Miriam kept the two women – troublemakers in her book – seated, and escorted Josh over to them to take particulars. Josh had always had a way with animals, a gentleness which most of them seemed to trust (there had been one family hound which took advantage of it!), and Miriam now saw that same engaging and kind manner put to use against the anger and bruised pride which had been emanating from the two friends like a bad smell.

As she saw the mood change, Miriam approached the table. "Everything all right?" she enquired of none in particular, but more of her brother than the others.

Josh turned and smiled. "Yes, we're just having a nice chat, aren't we ladies?" Without waiting for a reply he continued, "I was just saying to Mrs Tromans that I'm going to have stern words with Mr Gethin. He doesn't know his own strength, and he should. But you're looking much better Mrs T., the colour's coming back into your cheeks. You look quite radiant in fact. And you Mrs Arblaster, I trust that your spirits have settled?"

"I still think that man should be arrested for assault," replied the round woman.

"Ah, but that cuts both ways, doesn't it? From what I've learned from my sister, you Mrs T. struck the first blow as it were."

"But it was just an accident protested that lady. I thought we agreed on that?"

"And indeed we did," said the policeman, closing the trap, "and that unfortunate accident led to another, to wit, your little tumble Mrs T. As I said, I will be having words with Mr Gethin – and I suggest that you are gone before then – but nevertheless and after all this whole misadventure was clearly unintended. Case closed."

Hetty Arblaster did not look persuaded, so the constable continued in more serious vein. "Of course, as to the causes of this evening's events, my experience leads me to suspect the incriminating influence of alcohol. I could insist that the parties involved submit to a sobriety test, back at the station…"

"I'm sure that won't be necessary cut in Mrs Tromans. As you say, accidents do happen. And there's no harm done," she continued whilst standing and adjusting her dress. "Come on Hetty, it's time we were going. Good evening constable."

The constable rose and with the utmost civility bade the two friends a good night and courteously escorted them to the threshold, holding open the door, before closing it on the matter.

Miriam had been amazed at the transformation of the prickly pair under Josh's emollient influence. Perhaps they would have responded so to any handsome man, but she doubted it. Josh was something special, but that was only to be expected. He was a Lively.

#

Josh had already left by the time John returned. Miriam gave him a potted version of the umbrella affair.

"If it had been Abe, they might not have got off so lightly," observed John.

"I don't know," replied his sister, "he can be tactful and charming when he wants to be."

"Which isn't that often," said John.

"When did you last see him?" asked Miriam.

"Two or three weeks ago. Why?"

"I don't know. Maybe he's mellowing with age or something, but he doesn't seem half so enthusiastic about what you might call the letter of the law."

"No, he gets his constables to do it," said John, "or perhaps he's realised that if you locked all the drunks up you'd need a station as big as Dudley castle."

"No, it's not that. He's definitely getting more remote since…" she was going to say since she had remarried, but thought better of it, "he just seems distracted."

"Well, he is trying to catch the Devil. That ought to distract anybody," said John.

"Be serious…"

"It's love then," joked her brother.

"Hmh, I hope not. That jumped up little Haden Hill girl's not for him. It can only end in tears."

John had been thinking. "You don't think he's going back, you know, to how he was? Do you?" he said, suddenly serious.

"God. I really hope not. But he's definitely changed these last few weeks."

"But he's not having blackouts is he?"

"Not that I know of. No. Somebody would have said. Don't mention them. They used to really scare me you know. I mean really."

"I know. You and me both."

"But it was me that covered them up, and kept it a secret."

"I was as guilty," offered John.

"You were a kid. It was down to me. He should have been seen by a doctor."

"We weren't to know. He just fell off a horse. Happens all the time. You get knocked out and then wake up again. It's happened to me a couple of times, though not at the hands of a horse. Anyway, he got over it."

"Yes he did. I'm just saying he doesn't seem himself. Overwork probably."

"Probably," agreed John, "he's a delicate soul, isn't he?" *Don't know how he'd cope with a week of my job.*

"Do me a favour though John? Keep an eye on him."

"I will, we both will." *And no doubt he will be keeping a closer eye on me in future.*

It was closing time by now. John rescued Siss from yet another allegedly entertaining anecdote about Jack Beckett's childhood on the cut.

"No Abe yet?" she asked of Miriam.

"No. It's rare for him not to be in by ten," said Miriam and shot a glance at John which said *see, I told you. Not like him.* "He'll be home any minute now," she added.

"We'll hang on for a few minutes then," said Sissy.

"There's no need," the landlady assured them.

But brother John decided that yes, they would wait on Abe's return. Over another drink.

There was only blackness. A void spanning a handful of brief minutes, or an eternity. He became the blackness, then, he was in the blackness, a speck of light alone. Then, other things moved in the blackness: colours flitting, shapes indistinct, and vague sounds with no points of origin. The sounds resolved themselves first. They were words, and the words reached into the black and pulled him into the light. He could not see clearly at first, but there was a source of light and blurred bodies moving in front of it. And the words brought focus, words formed by black country voices.

"There you are. Back in the land of the living. How are you Sergeant? How do you feel?"

A hand rested gently on his shoulder, soft but firm imperative staying his urge to get up. He recognised the grey-green eyes of the landlady, now expressing concern as easily as they had shone earlier with vocational coquetry.

"I'm good, I think," said Abe. "Bit of a headache. What happened?"

"An argument with a loose tile it seems. Fell on you off the roof. Tom here found you."

Abe looked past the ministering angel and saw his recent drinking companion, embarrassed grin accompanying an apologetic little wave.

Abe waved back from…Where? Where was he? On a bed, in what was evidently a woman's bedroom. "Where am I?" he asked as he sat upright.

"Don't get up," said the woman, all business-like now, "You're in my bedroom, at the Hailstone."

"Your bedroom?" repeated Abe. "But why?"

"Saft question," she said. "You were knocked out cold. We needed somewhere to lie you down, and this is it. You wouldn't fit on the kitchen table."

"Oh, thank you," said Abe, after that information had sunk in, "How long…"

"Only a few minutes, but your head's cut." And she showed him a folded tea-towel stained red. "You should have put your helmet on."

Now that he was upright she enlisted the help of old Tom and the pair applied some absorbent gamgee to the top of his head and somehow kept it in place by profuse swathing of the same. There was a mirror on the dresser and the patient took a look at himself. *I look like a bloody Indian fakir.* His head dressing did indeed recall some indigenous inhabitant of the subcontinent, but his skin betrayed the illusion: it was uncharacteristically white, as pale as marling clay. Nevertheless, apart from the aforementioned 'bit of a headache' he averred that he was as right as rain and announced his intention to be off.

"Off where?" asked his nurse.

"Home of course."

"And where's that? Royal Oak is it?"

"That's right. Just up the road. Only five minutes."

"More like ten, if you step out sharp, and I don't believe you should in your condition; you could fall over."

"Madam, I assure you…"

"Don't call me madam. What's this, a whorehouse?"

"Sorry, I didn't…" began a still groggy Abe.

"It's Sarah. Call me Sarah."

"Sorry – Sarah. I appreciate your help."

"Good, so you should. And you can thank me by letting me drive you home."

She was not in the mood to be argued with, and he was in no state to push it.

"All right," he said, "but it will be dark soon, perhaps your husband…"

"I'm a widow," she said.

"But I thought…Who's the gaffer then?" said Abe looking to Tom who had shrunk into an unlit corner.

His use of the expression obviously amused her, as she laughed, with her eyes too, and brought her face to within a foot of his and said, "I'm the gaffer, and you will do what I say." With that, she took his arm, helped him to his feet and led him from the room. "Come on," she said, "I can find a quiet spot for you to sit till the transport's ready. Can't keep you in here, people might talk."

Old Tom shut the door behind them, locked it and gave Sarah the key before nodding a brief farewell to the injured man and his escort, and making himself scarce.

A little later, she sat him on a stool in the street for a few minutes and to get some air. He was conscious of pressing faces, jaundiced against yellowing panes as nosey drinkers slaked their curiosity. It was dark, and he felt the urge to just go now, on foot, back into Blackheath. Then he heard the clopping of a trotting horse, it seemed to be coming up the lane, but the sound was echoing, possibly bouncing against the adjacent huge blue brick façade of the sanitary works of Doulton & Co., possibly against the sides of his own skull. He took a few deep breaths, which only served to fuel his headache, and then a young lad came around the bend driving a 'one-hoss cart', the hoss in question being a piebald cob of something just over fourteen hands, and being blessed with the wholly incongruous name of Comanche, after the celebrated seventh cavalry mount…*How long have I been sitting here? Doesn't seem to have taken long to tack up and harness.*

The pony drew level, a contented looking well fed animal with a kind yet nevertheless an indifferent eye. The lad jumped down and held the pony's head.

"All right missus?" he said to Sarah who had appeared behind Abe's left shoulder without him being aware of it.

"Yes, thank you young Frederick. Just wait a second while we get on board."

The boy nodded in acknowledgement.

Ten minutes later the landlady of the Hailstone was thumping against the closed doors of the landlady of the Royal Oak with one hand and keeping hold of her brother with the other.

The door opened; it was John. He stood there with a puzzled expression, then it was the woman to whom he spoke.

"Sarah, what happened?"

Before Sarah could respond, she was confronted by Miriam Beckett, and the same question. Miriam didn't wait for explanation, but forthwith relieved the Springfield woman of her charge and sat her brother straight down.

"Are you all right Rabbit? What have you done?"

"I'm good. Just a scratch on the head."

"It looks more than that," said Miriam, eyeing the abundant dressing and Abe's lady-friend with suspicion.

"It's not as bad as it looks; just an awkward spot to bandage," offered Sarah.

"Did you do this?"

"Yes, a tile fell off the roof. Your brother was unlucky enough to be under it."

"Your roof was it then?" pressed Miriam. "What was he doing there?"

John could see that the line of questioning was leading to nothing pleasant: "Sarah is the landlady of the Hailstone, Miriam. I expect that Abe was just having a drink, wasn't he?" he suggested, hopefully.

"Yes," confirmed Sarah, "he had a few pints. Seemed to be enjoying himself."

"Was he now?" Miriam's tone was sarcastic.

"Will you all stop talking about me as if I wasn't here. What am I, dead?" said Abe.

She turned to him, and stood behind him in a proprietary fashion, hands on his shoulders, before leaning closer. "Sorry Rabbit. How are you feeling? You don't look good, and there's blood on your collar. Why don't I help you to your room? You need to lie down, and I can take your collar and soak it."

By this time the invalid was the sole object of attention of five pairs of eyes: the dark browns of the Lively clan (Jack Beckett being a member by marriage), and the green and grey of Sissy and Sarah.

"That's a job for the men," interjected Miriam's husband, "John, some help please."

"Right you are Jack," said John, "and thank you Sarah for helping him back. Much appreciated."

"Looks like I'm outnumbered and surrounded," said Abe, "now I know how General Custer felt. Sarah, thank you, I'll see you again. Thank you, for everything. See you soon."

This last produced just the hint of a scowl on the handsome features of Miriam Beckett. It was gone in an instant, as she kissed Abe good night and made sure he was herded away with no further contact with his erstwhile nurse.

The men having left, the triad of females was at first silent. Then, Miriam said stiffly, "Well, thank you for helping my brother – Mrs?"

"Bates," said Sarah. "Sarah Bates."

"Well, thank you, Mrs Bates. Have you been acquainted with Abraham for long?"

"No, not at all. I only met him tonight because of that loose tile."

"Quite so," said Miriam.

"But you do know John?" asked Sissy.

Sarah Bates was not about to be intimidated, even by these two imposing-looking women: she may have been but slight but considered herself by no means inferior in terms of character. Besides, she had years on this pair, and that ought to count for something.

"Oh yes, I know John," she said at length, then added provocatively, "Only in a, professional, capacity you understand."

It took Sissy a few beats to satisfy herself that the still good-looking older woman was referring only to the profession of landlady, and that she was teasing. By then, the visitor had announced that the takings didn't count themselves, that she must be going, and had let herself out, leaving the door wide open. Even as Miriam was closing it, the clatter off horse shoes and iron-clad wheels could be heard heading off into the dark.

When she turned around John was back, now wearing his fancy military jacket, and Siss in her shawl. It was way past time Siss was home, but John had something to say to Miriam before they left.

"He was knocked out," he said, only to her.

"How do you know? Did he say?"

"Not exactly, but I pieced it together. They had to lay him on…they laid him down. He was unconscious, though perhaps only for a minute."

She grasped his blue sleeve then, and he felt her unease through it.

"Look, I'll watch out for him; best I can," reassured brother John. "If you need me, send somebody to the Shoulder to tell Cyril, and I'll be here directly. Don't worry, it's nothing."

He hugged her, took Sissy's arm, and was gone.

Cyril? What's he doing with Cyril?

Chapter 12

One Sunday in Smethwick

The single bell tolled out the happy message: it's Sunday; the sun is shining, and God is waiting for you. Come in. Come in and be saved!

The little group of people who were yet to enter on that early summer's day in 1887 began to file in dutifully, the men removing their headgear out of respect for the Lord, and for the ladies to whom they gave way, as they had been taught. Augustus Algernon Wellings held himself back though. He was enjoying the sun, absorbing its warmth and the antics of a family of robins – a mother and three well grown chicks – as they flitted from grave to grave. He knew this mother, or thought he did: there was a nest in a holed and discarded kettle in a dog-rose near to the boundary wall on the north side. Her timing must have been impeccable for it was well known that the young Reverend Astbury, energetic and keen after a mere three years in post, was very fastidious about keeping the church and church yard spick and span, and certainly free of casually tossed rubbish, such as an old holed kettle. However, the redbreast's God-given skills of self-propagation, combining serendipitously with a passion for natural history which the vicar had inherited from his earthly father, had elevated an act of ignorant desecration to the realms of divinely inspired art, at least to the reverend's mind. And so the squatters had received his blessing. Augustus knew that the mother had already raised one brood this year, or hoped she had, for he had watched them as eggs, then as floppy bald nestlings gaping up yellow at him on impossibly scrawny necks, then, as little feathery balls, but proper birds now, spilling out into the roses and the thorns, jostling for the next airborne mouthful. Then, the bush was empty, and the damp graves bereft of those small sparks of life. He liked to think they had flown away, and not that they had been ended by some predator, or taken captive by a capricious child.

These three however were demonstrably alive and thriving. Just now, the fluffy babies were alighting on the gravestone of Master Edward Henry, who, if he had lived, would be forty-five years of age today. But he had given up the ghost forty years ago, a mere baby himself, and he now lay alone. As if acknowledging that begging atop a child's grave were inappropriate, as if they could read, or as if possessed of some psychic power of intuition, they immediately vacated that stone and perched themselves comfortably on its neighbour, a monument marking the last resting place of Ann Hughes, a lady who had departed this life as a young woman in 1836, and also of her husband John, who, to judge by the fifty years chiselled between them, had been in no hurry to join her. Whilst he watched the mother bird busily hunting up small red worms from the grave mounds, he wondered if the occupants of those mounds, food for worms, would be glad that the worms were in turn food for new life, or whether, bitter in death's shackles, they cursed the little thieves, and all the living. No, of course not! The dead were just dead. The three chubby chicks were very much full of life, bullying their frail looking mother – he had decided that no father could be so selfless – into ever greater exertions to feed insatiable appetites.

Kids. No respect for their elders these days. Augustus was in a good mood, and looking forward to the service, which was not always the case. Thanks to the generosity a century and a half ago, and the strict stipulation, of Miss Dorothy Parkes, Smethwick Church – the old chapel as it was known – had a proper vicar; a man of letters; a proper Church of England vicar; always had had. And in its present incarnation, this paradigm of pastoral virtue was enclosed within the diminutive and always very neat form of the youthful George Astbury, in his own mind at least, a cut above the travelling parsons, or whatever they were called, which seemed to be the norm in the Methodist chapels.

At length the little family flew away and Augustus turned to engage with the small group of stragglers who were waiting on him. "Come on then," he said, taking his wife's hand and ushering his young son and daughter along in front. But the Wellings clan present that day was not confined to this couple and their offspring. Today, not unusually, brother Gus was at the head of a larger family party. His mother Gladys was in her mid-fifties now, and very spritely considering a hard life of child-bearing which had, to her way of thinking, amply rewarded her by blessing her with thirteen surviving children and of whom, at thirty-five years, Augustus was senior. Of that thirteen no less than half a dozen had congregated at the church today: there was Augustus of course (Gus to all but his mother), second brother Jonathan, as yet unattached, and brothers Phillip and Christopher, the one wed to a plain and plump girl and the other with no strong affiliations, other than to his mother and siblings – and to the bottle. The female representative was Irene, voice as rough as gravel, but soft hearted to a fault, married to a local carpenter and doing quite well, thank you very much. Today, Irene was in charge of her young sister Catherine, who at ten was excited at the prospect of attending church with the grown-ups.

Inside, the party secured their usual spot near the back, to the left of the single aisle, under the balcony. It was cooler in here, and the eyes took but little time to adjust to the lack of direct sunlight, for there was plenty of light entering, though bent and refracted through large areas of stained glass, paling the gas lamps into insignificance. Augustus sat quiet, listening to the strains of the pipe organ, going nowhere in anticipation of something else. It might have been his imagination, but he always felt that the sense of

137

calm that he got in this place was virtually tangible. Decades – more – of devotion and prayer and incense and music, had embedded it into the plaster and the walls, and the dead wood of the pews and the choir and the pulpit: the fabric was so saturated that this feeling, power, whatever it was, was wont to leak out, latching onto the resident fusty smell of polish and smoke-infused vestments and candle fat. It settled over him and penetrated into his chest where, if he were very quiet, he could detect it, like the wing beats of a sparrow, trapped far off in a high chimney. It made him feel calm and excited at the same time, and he closed his eyes to say his silent prayers.

He prayed, as he always prayed, for his father and mother; the one dead and buried, though not here, these last three years, the other still very much alive and kicking. For his mother, he prayed for health and long life; his father, he hoped was at peace. He used to pray for revenge. A just revenge had been the object of his very first real prayers, as an adult at least, projected upon the managers of Henry Mitchell and Co.'s Cape Hill brewery: monsters who had cheated his father of his rights and worried him into a hole in the ground. Starting out, he hadn't really believed in the power of prayer, but it had made him feel better. Then, a short month later, the principal culprits were both dead themselves. He had been glad of the deaths, and then began to ask himself whether they were not entirely coincidental. *Perhaps not,* came the answer, *who knows?* And so now it was his habit on Sunday to say prayers, the good kind, just in case. And God? That was an even knottier question. He was not sure he believed in His existence, but the alternative was horrible to think on. So, he came here every Sunday, with as much of the family as cared or were free to come, prayed and listened to a droning sermon, and sang, and walked out past the grave markers and tried not to think about death.

Today, the reverend Astbury was in typical form in as much as his subject, based upon Proverbs chapter three verse five – "Trust in the Lord with all your heart, and do not rely on your own insight..." – he had reinterpreted and summarised under the title: 'The Ignorance of Man.' And that was the extent of the summarising, for the rest of the sermon went in exactly the other direction, expanding itself outwards in increasingly dubious circular logic. It started off on a fairly intelligible, if debatable and lengthy, premise: that Man's knowledge of the world, his science, is necessarily limited by the very nature of that physical existence which science seeks to measure, existence as we know it being merely a physical manifestation, a shadow, of the spiritual essence of life which emanates from behind a veil forever impervious to science, but not to God. Food for thought perhaps, had it been left there. However, appetites were rather spoiled as the reverend George insisted on leading the congregation out of the light of concise clarity into a stumbling tour of a dark maze of circuitous reasoning and repetition, lit only by the artificial glow of his own hubris, and peppered with obscure references, scriptural and secular, designed, at best guess, to demonstrate that faith was superior to knowledge...and in the process, to break down the critical faculties of any brighter than average parishioners, who might get the dangerous idea that the more knowledge they

138

had, the less faith they needed, or that all the suffering in their world was random and pointless.

Whatever the intent, half way through, half the Wellings family were daydreaming, and the other half were actually dozing (such was the advantage of sitting near the back!) Each attended on Sundays for diverse reasons, their own reasons. But being bored by a twenty-minute speech that could say what it needed in two, and from the lips of someone looking down his nose at you from an ivory tower – or the big oak pulpit in his case – was not in the ranks of the more popular motivators.

Observances fulfilled for another week, Augustus led his charges quickly out past the vicar, absorbed in ingratiating himself with the Sankeys – one of the posh families that rented seats in the balcony – then smartly through the churchyard onto the street, whence the whole gaggle trailed the few hundred yards downhill then up onto Wellington Road towards the large three story property that housed three generations of Wellings: mother, four of her sons, three wives, daughter Catherine, along with older teenagers Nancy and Joyce, and half a dozen assorted grandchildren.

#

The big rented house was a legacy of his father's time, the family focal point, where, on Sunday at least, most of the clan would gather. To Gladys Wellings, the big house was a blessing, with the capacity to home more than half of her children, keeping them close – with all the advantages that mutual support: physical, psychological, and above all financial, could offer. It was not a bad neighbourhood they lived in, sat on the leading edge of urbanisation, with open fields and even some woodland within walking distance. But urbanisation was progress, and progress would not be progress if it did not progress; and this fleeting frontier would soon be overrun by armies of navvies with their waggons and their tractors, always pushing, breaking boundaries as the huge appetites of the burgeoning industries of Birmingham and West Bromwich and North Smethwick ate into virgin territory, raising its standard of black and white and silver – of smut and steam and steel – over conquered greenery, briefly, before moving on. And, spawned in the waves of progress, in their wake, thousands of human drones to occupy the gobbled-up spaces, infecting Gaia's emerald epidermis – breaking out into eruptions of concrete and brick and tarmacadam.

But for now, the inhabitants of number eighteen Wellington Road heard the approaching clamour but dimly, and got on with their lives: the rental on the property was by no measurement cheap, and with the death of father Wellings, a commercial artist and draftsman, it required the contribution of all resident wage earners to keep the wolf, if not from the door, then at least beyond the garden gate. In one sense, the apprehension of adversity was a good thing, for it served to bind them all together all the stronger, as did the family and state-sponsored rituals of Sunday.

Today, the gathering was a particularly full one, all of the brothers being present, with the exception of Victor whose family resided with frail Aunt Vera in Soho, in the thick of the industrial revolution, in a tiny terraced house wedged between railway tracks and the sprawling and huge cluster of buildings that was James Watt and Co.'s Soho Foundry. And all of the daughters were present today, again save one, this being sister Dorothy, the sixth child born into this generation, who never came now owing to the fact that she had married a young miner from Merthyr Tydfil, a short and restless Celt with a pinched hook of a nose that made him look like an over-sized raptor; he had swooped over the border like a one-man raiding party and in the course of six short months had wooed her, wed her, and made off to the Valleys with his booty…

Numbers today dictated that the meal, prepared by the teenage girls under their mother's supervision, was taken in two locations, with the boys and their wives settled around an extendable table in the front sitting room, and the rest confined to the kitchen and scullery. The front room was of generous proportions: light came in and the gaze was drawn out through a large bay window, with decorated glass surrounds depicting tree branches populated by representations of an indeterminate passerine species; the wallpaper continued the ornithological theme in a stylized oriental fashion; the sashes were open, and as Augustus finished his breast of lamb he heard a real bird burst into song, a blackbird enjoying Sunday afternoon from the middle of the magnolia tree in the front garden. As he looked out he saw an equally hearty creature, in the form of an eager-looking chestnut gelding being ridden out by a gent in a topper who looked like he was having trouble containing his mount's energy. Augustus did not envy him: he himself had never learned to ride, none of them had, and he knew very little about horses. But he took the time to appreciate the horse's fluid power, because today he had that time. Tomorrow, the bird would still be singing in the tree, carefree as today – as for the people, and the young horse probably, Monday meant a return to the grudge of long hours to earn their keep. Gladys Wellings' boys had not inherited their father's artistic bent and all were moulded into the working-class tradition, which meant, around this area, employment in the various 'metal-bashing' concerns for which Smethwick, scion of the vast black conglomeration of clamourous factories that was Birmingham, was famous. Mostly, it was back breaking work; and the boys? None of them were particularly tall, but all, relatively young, were fit and strong, although with a tendency to stockiness which presaged a running to fat in middle age. Except for Douglas. Douglas had always been of particularly light build, which had been to his advantage in his army days: it made long marches a breeze, and he had quickly taken to the life and been promoted to lance corporal. And it was the promotion which had invalided him out, disabled by a bullet wound to the shoulder which had failed to kill him, but which had succeeded in killing nerves to his left arm, leaving it to wither these last three years. In fact, he had been lucky to keep the arm, the .45 round could easily have taken it off, but he had been lucky, the doctors reckoned. But Dougie Wellings didn't feel lucky, unless you counted bad luck: the misfortune to be on a firing range on the same day as a particularly incompetent recruit still coming to terms, as it transpired, with the intricacies of a Martini-Henry Mark 2 and the notion of due respect for its lethal potential.

If Douglas was always the thinnest of the bunch, Christopher sitting next to Dougie, was always likely to be the chubbiest. He was temporarily jobless after a drunken altercation during which, it was alleged, a fellow-worker's head had been pressed recklessly close to the business end of a steam stamper. But, there are always two sides to an argument, and Chris Wellings maintained that his had never been heard. Augustus worried about Chris and his drinking habits, as he worried about Doug. But there was nothing Gus could do for a dead arm.

His thoughts were interrupted by his youngest, five-year-old Patrick James. "What's for pudding Mommy?"

Mommy, a sharp featured black haired pale skinned person with warm glittering green eyes and a quick Irish tongue replied in time-honoured fashion. "You can't have any pudding till you've eaten your dinner. Eat your belly draught."

Patrick James did not want to eat his meat, not when, he knew, there was rice pudding to come. He could smell the nutmeg. Sweet rice pudding with nutmeg was his favourite, today at any rate, as far as he was concerned. He stalled. "There's too much rind on it, I can't eat it, it's gristle. Daddy doesn't eat gristle."

"Don't bring me into it," said his father, "listen to your mother and eat your meat."

The youngster was not finished yet. "I can't. It's a very fatty meat," he opined, aping some overheard conversation.

"It's good for you," insisted his mother, "do you want me to cut it up for you?"

This was an insult to inchoate manhood. He sulked.

"Look," continued the mother, "some poor animal has died to put that meat on your plate. Don't waste it."

This seemed to get through and he started pushing the bits of dead pig around with his fork and picked up a knife. "What's belly draught then?"

"It's from a pig," said his mother.

"A pig?"

"Yes, it's part of a pig. It's a pig's belly."

"So, it's a pig's belly," reasoned the young man, "but why's it draughty then?"

A good-natured laugh sounded from a pale and bony faced man down the table, "Because somebody left the sty door open," it said.

The boy seized upon the diversion. "Did they uncle Jon?"

Augustus intervened. "Eat your meat. Shall I cut it up for you?"

"No," the boy squirmed, "will you cut it up for me uncle Jon?"

"O' course I will, son. With your permission Bridget."

The mother was still nodding assent as uncle Jon Wellings was on his feet. He leaned over and started slicing the meat into tiny pieces.

141

The parents eyed each other. Patrick and Jon got on well. The boy liked all of his uncles, but uncle Jon was his favourite. It was uncle Jon who was always first to whisk him up and spin him around until he was dizzy, or sit him on his shoulders and charge up and down the garden at what seemed to a child breakneck speed.

"You've got your odour clown on," observed young Pat.

"Yes, it's Sunday. Can't be gooin' to church all dirty and smelly."

"It smells nice. Is it a lot of money?" enquired Patrick.

Jonathan could sense another diversionary tactic. "There you are," he said, "all cut up nice." With that he picked up a piece of the meat, in truth more fat than anything, and popped it, cold and soft, into his own mouth. "It's nice," he lied, "mek ya grow up big an' strong. You'll be buying me a drink round the pub before long – if you eat your dinners."

That was enough for the young man. He set to with a vengeance, though not necessarily with gusto. Jon went back to his place to wipe a greasy paw and to await the advent of the rice pudding. Wendy, in her mid-twenties with thin hair and a rosy Sunday-scrubbed face and whose Sunday smell was reliably that of carbolic soap and mothballs, leant into her brother-in-law. "You're very good with kids aren't you? Isn't it about time you settled down and had some of your own?"

"Plenty of time for that," said Jonathan simply.

"He ain't met the perfect woman yet, have you Jon?" said brother Phil, Wendy's spouse, who trailed Jon in years, by a count of three, but was way ahead in the fatherhood stakes, by the same margin, despite the carbolic and mothballs.

This exchange prompted their mother to contribute. "Wendy's right our Jon. You're thirty-three now. They'll all be married off before you get round to it."

"Yes mom," said Jon, "I'm thirty-three – nearly – and old enough to mek up me own mind. Anyway, if I got married I would have to get somewhere bigger. Move in here can I?"

"Son, I'd love to have you, but…"

"But there's no room at the inn, I know. You can't help that. And I can't help…not being married."

There was a pause then. Chris Wellings, who had obviously found something alcoholic to drink between church and dinner interjected none too quietly. "Tek no notice Jon. You'm better off without 'em, women: they'm trouble. Love 'em and leave 'em that's my motto – bring the kids up the same way!" He followed this wise saw with a suggestive guffaw and looked around the table with bright pleased with myself eyes.

But if he was looking for approval he was disappointed. His mother spoke. "Christopher! Don't be so rude. Now behave yourself! You'll be eating in the scullery next week."

"Sorry mom," said the offender, "only 'aving a bit of fun."

"Ladies and children present," Augustus reminded him.

"You'm right. Got a bit carried away. Sorry Gus, girls."

"All right. Time and a place, you know that," admonished big brother.

"Yes, the pub," agreed Chris, "who's coming tonight?"

"Count on me," said Jon.

"Where are you going?" asked Donald, "it's Sunday."

"Blue Gates will be open. Shall we make it a lads' night?"

"I'll be there when the kids are in bed then," said Don, "Gus?"

"Yeah. I suppose I'll have to come and keep an eye on you."

"Phil?" queried Chris.

"I don't know," replied the ginger–headed one, "I've got things to do. And it's work tomorrow," he said glancing sideways at his wife.

"I thought you were going to say you had a prior engagement. Tea with the Queen was it?"

"No," replied Phil, "she's busy this week. But she sent me a letter to say I could visit her at Buckingham Palace next weekend."

"Yeah, probably wants you to clean out the privies. You'd mek a good night soil man."

"They've got sewers you nitwit."

"All right, perhaps she wants you to clean out the sewers. Must be getting full by now," Chris came back.

"I don't think they ever need cleaning do they?" intervened Don, "it all just flows away. Ends up in the sea, I think."

"What about ours?" enquired Phil. "We're nowhere near the sea."

Before this inappropriate dinner time conjecture could be explored further, young James interrupted it, "Do you really know the Queen then, uncle Phil?"

"Gin hall queens, more like," said Chris, under his breath.

"No Jimmy, they're just playing me up. I have seen her though. In Birmingham. Last March."

"Granny says you could have bin blowed up," piped up Jimmy's ten-year-old sister, Mary.

"Yes, you could have," agreed her grandmother, "and then where would your wife be with three children to look after?"

"I told you Mom. There was no danger of that. The roads were all lined with police, and they had pistols and rifles. Any Irishman with any sense would be miles away."

"Don't you be too sure of that Phillip. Cunning as foxes those Fenians, and nasty with it." When Bridget pronounced on this subject, everyone paid heed: being a Derry girl she ought to know what she was talking about.

"Well, I'm still here," was all that Phillip said.

"I hardly think we're in any danger if we stick to our own area, and don't go gallivanting into Brum for some big event or such. And don't forget, we've had no bombings in England for, what? Two or three years," said Gus, "the papers said their organisation had been disrupted, that's the way they put it. Anyway, that kind of pressure might have worked on Gladstone, but the Conservatives will have none of it, you can be sure." He looked at his wife and covered her hand with his, "and that's why I voted for them."

"Let's not get onto politics at the dinner table boys," said Wendy, "you can bore each other with it later."

In actual fact, Bridget was dying to talk politics, an obsession she shared with all of the citizens of her native soil. That she would never vote only served to whet her appetite. But, for the sake of cordial dinner relations, she changed the subject.

#

Shortly afterwards, six of the seven boys were in the back garden, in and around the small strip of lawn bounded by cabbage and onion patches and the tall criss-cross canes tied with twine, up which strove slowly but surely with unalterable green instinct the next runner bean crop. The regular back and forth flitter of half a dozen white butterflies portended a threat to that green life, a threat to be dealt with harshly. But not today. Today, the insects were welcome comrades, emblems of the light-hearted Sabbath-day mood, mirroring the darting energy of the children who filled the place with running and skipping and laughing and shouting.

As usual, uncle Jon was most in demand. Today apparently, he was a wicked witch seeking out fat little children to roast and eat. Needless to say, the prospective menu items were exciting themselves to distraction, daring their pursuer to come closer before, nerves failing, they scattered away on paroxysms of panic and enfeebling laughter. There was always a price to pay, and such feverish agitation must sooner or later lead to a collision involving soft young bodies and tender young heads; and it would end in tears. But for now, they were enjoying themselves…

The other brothers were content to drink from their glasses of watery dark beer, and to draw off strong cigarettes which cut through snot and assaulted the lungs, pleasing deceitfully. It was not unusual for Doug to be the odd one out on these occasions, and so it was today, for he stood slightly detached, apart from the crowd, parking his cheeks against the curving bull nosed copings of the low garden wall, smoking and watching. He loved his family, and especially his brothers. But he had come home from the army after an absence, with a wound that would never heal, and no permanent job. He didn't feel like one of them anymore, not like when they were kids, when their father was alive. But he would do anything for them, even Chris, who could be hurtful with too much booze in him. Nevertheless, it was Dougie more often than any other who had carried his drunken sibling home from whatever watering hole it had happened to be.

144

At three o'clock they had a visitor. From his perch on the wall Doug saw coming out from along the side of the house the lumbering out-size form and square close-cropped head that belonged to his old school friend Stephen Vyle. To be fair to him the lumbering, most of it, was accounted for by his 'gammy leg', his left knee having suffered permanent insult as a result of an argument with an iron shod wheel when he was eight. The argument was settled in favour of the wheel, both in terms of the result – a dislocated knee – and in terms of justification: the boy should not have ignored the warnings of his mother and run into the horse road just as a speeding cab was approaching. His recklessness caused him extreme pain, a visit to the hospital (after a home-made splint and a week on laudanum produced no improvement), and a twelve-month period of virtual immobilisation which estranged him from what little education had been available to him. Doug liked Stephen, nonetheless he had to admit that he was not over-blessed with sharp wits, though whether for want of schooling or through an inherited deficiency – the same deficiency perhaps that had caused him to step into a flying wheel – Doug was unsure. What he was sure of, however, was that there was no malice in the big man, which was fortunate considering the size of him, that he had been a loyal friend, and that he had been good to his mother.

Doug sauntered over to meet him and thrust out his good right hand, "Ado Steve, how the hell are you? Haven't seen you in ages. What you doing here?"

"Ado mate," replied big Steve with a gappy smile, "I've bin to see me mom. How you doing? How's Chris, and the rest?"

"You can ask 'em, come on."

There followed a typically masculine ritual of handshakes and back-slapping as the brothers renewed their various acquaintances, some casual, some less so, with the visitor.

Children banished for now, Doug, Chris and Jon retired with their guest to the cool of the large windowed cellar where the beer was kept. Sitting and lounging, as the mood took them, the conversation turned to what Mr Vyle had been up to this last year.

"Bin workin' away ain't I?" he said with a wink.

"Away where?" they asked.

"Do you know Jack Cutler? He used to live round here."

"No, never heard of him," said Doug.

"Is he a little thin bloke?" asked Chris, although, relatively speaking, he, in common with his brothers, was not exactly what might be described as big-boned.

"Yes, he's little, but wiry, not thin, and bloody hard with it. Black hair, big eyes?"

"I think I have come across him," said Chris, suddenly more interested.

"That sounds like John Cutler, I know him; heard he went away. Calling himself Jack is he?" said Jon. "What about him?"

"I'm working for him," said Vyle.

"You ain't?" said Chris.

"Why, who is he?" asked Doug, trying to catch up.

"Tell y' later," said Jon.

"Where are you working then?" asked Doug, "you ain't bin round 'ere 'ave ya?"

"Nah, I told ya. I've come to see me Mom. I work in Black'eath."

"I've heard of it, but wouldn't know how to get there. Where is it?" enquired Doug.

Vyle was visibly engaged in mental combat, struggling to marshal description of a geography he knew well enough but found difficult to impart in words. Jon came to his rescue: "It's by Oldbury, towards Dudley. Got some nice little boozers ain' it Chris?"

"Oh, not bad, you know, not bad – if you don't mind ugly women," came the reply.

"I thought you said there was no such thing after a couple of pints?" Jon reminded him.

"Depends on how good the beer is and how bad the women are," explained Chris, *or men in your case* he suspected.

"So, what's happening in Blackheath these days then, Steve?" asked Doug, "anything exciting?"

"Well," said Steve, "funny you should ask that."

#

After he had gone Doug said, "Do you believe him about this Spring Heeled Jack thing then Jon?"

"Well, not being funny or anything, I don't think he's got the imagination to mek it up. That don't mean there's any such thing though, except in people's 'eads."

"I've just 'ad an idea," said Chris. "It's bin weeks since we all went out together, all the lads. And it's last year since we went on one of our jaunts, proper like. So why don't we all g'to Black'eath next weekend and see if we can hunt down this Jumping Jack thingy, or at least get pissed?"

"That might be a laugh," agreed his brothers.

Chapter 13

A New Recruit

The morning after the night before hit Abe's eyelids, coaxing them open; a call to shake off the night and switch to daytime mode. He had decided in a fog before passing out that he would rise with the sun, get himself ready, breakfast on whatever he could find downstairs, and be off before encountering another human being or any questions. But morning had frustrated him, for the more she let fall her light the more Abe felt the weight of it pinning his eyes shut. If he let it in, the heavy and thick feeling in his skull would only absorb it and grow like a toxic weed. He waited, and thought about sitting up, but knew that he would have to take his time in case he was still groggy. Something in him was glad of the excuse, so he arranged with himself that he would stay put, just for five minutes. Five minutes or so later and he stirred again, and finally prised apart his eyelids. So much for plans: the alarm clock informed him that he had left it for much longer than five minutes, and pointed its fingers reproachfully at ten to eight as it tut-tutted away. He sat up. Not bad. He stood. Good. Everything appeared to be in working order. His head was stinging, but just a bit; just the scalp really. The headache was gone. There was a scabby patch matting some of his hair, but removing it risked liberating more bloodflow. So he left it and combed around it: he would be removing his bowler today only when absolutely necessary. Looked like his pillowcase would be getting an early wash though. Behind schedule and not in the mood now, he didn't bother with any morning exercise, but did take great care with the rest of his toilet. After drying off his trusty razor, he had a decision to make: eau de cologne or bay rum? Two bottles vied for attention, but as usual it was the bay room that was chosen, an old friend that he relied on. Profligate, he swamped his face with it.

#

He was surprised in the kitchen by his sister. Not that he should have been surprised – a landlady's work is never done – but she did come up behind him very quietly whilst he was rifling through the contents of the pantry, hoping not to be heard.

"What are you doing skulking about?"

He jumped, letting slip a carving knife with which he had been threatening the remains of a loaf. "Oh, morning Miriam. Just getting something to keep me going. Didn't want to disturb anyone."

"Keep you going where? Off to see your girlfriend are you?"

"Later, yes. I was going to pop in the station first. They'll be expecting me."

"Well then. You're the boss, no need to rush. Sit down and let me get Mary to do you some eggs. You'll want that toasted, it's stale," she said, surveying the ragged chunks that her brother had hacked at.

He knew that his chance for an anonymous exit had gone, so he surrendered with a show of goodwill. "If you could, that would be marvellous," he said, then added, "you might need to help her though. I haven't got all day."

"That's all right. Just sit down and let me look at that head."

He obeyed.

"Ooh, Rabbit. That looks nasty. Does it hurt?"

"Not really, no. Bit sore, that's all. Be gone this time next week…Don't touch!" he nearly shouted at the end.

"I thought you said it didn't hurt?"

"It doesn't, but I don't want you starting it bleeding again. I've got to go out after this."

"All right. I'll bathe it for you tonight. Stay there and I'll get us something to eat." It was an order.

She came back with two plates of eggs and buttered toast – not dripping, butter – then briefly disappeared again for coffee and cutlery.

"This is nice," she opined, "it's been ages since I've been able to sit down to breakfast with my brother. Get that down you – you need it after last night."

"Why? I wasn't drunk."

"Maybe not drunk exactly, but you'd certainly had more than enough. Not like you."

"Had I? Is it not? Who's to say? You're not my mother you know." He hadn't meant to sound unkind, but he could see that that was the way she took it. "Sorry," he said, "perhaps I was in a bit of a state, but I had had a bit of a bang on the bonce," he said, using local vocabulary to refer to the injured portion of his person, "it was lucky that Sarah was there to help."

"Ooh, Ooh, Sarah is it? If the silly cow bothered to keep her roof in a decent state of repair, you wouldn't have ended up with your head split open. She could have killed you for God's sake. Silly tart."

"Miriam, don't call her that. She helped me out of the goodness of her heart," protested Abe.

The temperature in the kitchen was rising, and it had nothing to do with how much coal was in the stove. Old Mary diplomatically decided that she needed something from somewhere else.

"I don't think it was her heart that prompted it. Might have been another part of her anatomy."

"Miriam, you're being ridiculous," said her brother, although somewhere secretly flattered by her inference.

"Oh, I'm ridiculous am I?"

"No, I didn't say that. I said you're being ridiculous."

"Am I though? I'm not the one cavorting with a…I've heard about her; the way she flirts with all the men. Does more than flirt. I'll be bound, a woman like that."

"A woman like what? A woman who runs a pub, who lost her husband? Sounds like somebody else I know."

"Me? I'm nothing like her! And Thanks. Thanks for bringing that up again. Just what I needed."

Abe could have sworn that his sister was hiding tears, but he knew that she never cried.

"Sis, I'm sorry," he said as he captured her hand in both of his across the table and pressed it to his cheek. "I'm sorry," he repeated, "I know what you've lost."

"No you don't."

"Perhaps I don't. But try not to get bitter."

"I'm not bitter! Why am I bitter? I'm not bitter."

"Why are you being so disagreeable about Sarah then? There's nothing to be jealous about."

Miriam flushed. "Jealous? Now who's being ridiculous? I'm just trying to look after my baby brother. Always have. That's what sisters do."

"Well, if that's the case, thank you big sister. Appreciated. But I'm not a kid any more either don't forget."

"I don't think men ever grow up. You watch that woman. Only after one thing."

And she can have it, thought her brother flippantly. "Yes, well I'm sure she was just concerned about a customer. Even if it was more than that, we're both free agents aren't we?"

"She's married."

"She told me she was a widow."

"That as well. She's got another man now."

Even more like you then.

"So she remarried?"

"Common law husband as they say."

"Oh. Who? Who says?"

"I don't know, it's just what I've been told."

"And you believe everything you're told?"

"That doesn't matter. It's obvious to me what she's like, but if you want to go and get involved with her…"

"I don't. I only met her last night."

"Well, if you did you've been warned. Don't come crying to me when it all goes wrong."

"I won't. It won't come to it. I'm seeing Alice, remember."

A big sigh of exasperation from Miriam.

"What? I can't do anything right can I? You don't like Sarah because she's too common, living in sin, and you don't like Alice because she's living the high life – too posh! You're always criticising these days. It never used to be like this between us. What's got into you?"

Miriam could hardly tell him that she felt betrayed by his affection for other women. Women who would hurt him. It disappointed her. And yes, she supposed that she was jealous, as a sister. She couldn't say so; she merely replied, "Nothing."

Abe took the plunge: "Miriam, there is. I don't think you're happy, are you? Is it Jack? Has he done something? You can tell me; anything. You can always tell me. Come on mommy bunny."

She looked at him, and smiled in spite of herself. "You haven't called me that in a long time. Since you were ten."

"Is it that long? Maybe I ought to get back into the habit: it's nice to see you smile. So what is it? Jack not pulling his weight?"

"No. Well yes, a bit. But it's not Jack. I'm just feeling under the weather. It's not…it's probably John Henry – I miss him."

"But you've got Jack. He's a good man, isn't he?"

"It's not the same."

"Not the same? What are you saying? You must love him though. Don't you?"

"Do I? Must I? Why?"

"But why?"

"Why marry him you mean? Because a woman needs a husband, financially at least. And a woman – a young woman – on her own is never looked on as respectable. Just look at your…forget it."

"Are you saying that you only married for money?"

"There you go again. Grow up! The facts of life aren't all about sex you know. Certainly not about love. Love is a luxury I can't afford."

Abe was stunned. His sister was living a sham, and he never knew it. He wanted to hold her close and tell her it would all be all right. But he didn't. Instead he took her hand again and squeezed it and looked into her eyes. "I'm here," he said, "I'll be here for you whenever you need me. Just call and I'll come."

Miriam was retreating back behind the big sister façade now. "Thank you, Rabbit. Don't look so upset, I'm just being silly; as I said, under the weather." She withdrew her hand and stood to clear her plate away although she hadn't eaten much. "You stay there and finish your breakfast."

As he ate they carried on talking. "Thank Jack for putting me to bed last night," said Abe, "and John as well when you see him."

"I will," she replied. "I think he's been seeing a lot of Cyril."

"What, our uncle Cyril? Who told you this?"

"Yes, our uncle Cyril. And Siss told me. Met with him for a drink in the Cali, and he was with him last night."

"Was he now? That's interesting. I'll bet he's offered him a job."

"Is that a problem for you?"

"It remains to be seen. I hope not."

"Will you keep an eye on him then? Look after him I mean."

"Of course I will. He's our brother isn't he?"

"Yes," said the sister, "yes he is."

On finishing his food and drink Abe bade goodbye to his sister with the usual hug and the usual kiss, except that the usual kiss was on the cheek. On this occasion it strayed and lips met lips. Both naturally understood that it been accidental.

#

The cop shop was busy. Irrespective of the dregs of last night's drinking deposited in overfull cells, there were three policemen in the front office, two of whom were particularly animated, generating quiet amusement in the third, who masked it in a show of checking over the charge sheets. Josh Lively's attention was split between paperwork and listening to P.C. Gordon Clark as he gave a new recruit the benefit of his vast experience.

"Well, you do look smart, I'll give you that. Lose the kepi though. We don't do caps and kepis out of here."

"But I thought," began the new man.

"You thought what?" challenged Clark.

"Kepi for daytime duties, helmet for nights and inclement weather."

"Ooh, inclement weather is it? We get lots of that round here – rains rocks and bottles sometimes. And a helmet gives you more protection in that kind of shower than a crappy kepi. Got it?"

"I understand what you're saying."

"Good, but yes, otherwise well turned out, yes. It's important to be well turned out," he preached, "the public look up to us and they respect us. So you don't go around looking scruffy. Ruins the image, see. Now you might have seen some constables, let's say in – where was it you come from? Halesowen is it? Yes, Halesowen. In Halesowen it's Worcestershire Constabulary of course; funny lot…" There was a pause as Clark evidently reviewed some hidden memory, not unpleasant judging by the vacant grin that suffused his features and exposed an even greater expanse of equine-like off-white gnashers. "Where was I?" he continued, setting his face straight after a brief interval of blessed silence, "Oh yes, as I was saying, you might not be used to seeing the smart turnout what's called for round here. You might have been used to seeing police constables who don't really make an effort: they might not bull their boots every day, for instance, and think that's perfectly acceptable; I knew one who only did it if they got scuffed or muddy. Not on though, is it? No self-discipline; wouldn't last five minutes in the army. Or perhaps they might not feel like changing their collar every day, if it looks clean, and they think that's perfectly acceptable; after all, who's to know? I'll tell ya who's to know, you do. Like I said, self-discipline. If you can't discipline yourself, how can you be trusted to discipline others? Jesus, that's what this job's all about isn't it?" Not giving the new lad a chance to express an opinion, the offensive continued, "I've come across others who undo their top buttons if it's warm out, or take off their helmets – or other headgear," he said with a nod toward the offending kepi, "just for a while, you see; and they think that's perfectly acceptable. Wrong. What kind of message does it send to the crooks, eh? 'Can't cope with a bit of sunshine? No chance of apprehending me then.' Don't you agree? I mean, do such failings make for a good copper? What do you say? You must have an opinion. Or do you? Well, what is it then?"

The donkey-faced one finally stopped for breath. The recruit did have his own ideas of course, but whatever they were he was sure that P.C. Clark would twist them into something perfectly unacceptable. He shot a hopeless glance towards Josh, but Josh kept his head down. He had undergone his own rites of passage, and learning to side-step the bullshit from this particular quarter was one of them. He saw no reason to spare the new bloke the same pleasures.

"Don't look at him," continued Clark, "when you're out there on your own, nobody's going to help you. So, what's your view on all this then, Mr Salt?"

P.C. Samuel Salt decided to play it safe. "You're right of course. We should always try to look well turned out and smart. It gives people confidence in us if we have confidence, and pride, in ourselves, and the uniform. That makes for a copper who can be trusted to uphold the law without fear or favour."

Well put, thought Josh, *Abe's going to love you.*

"That's fine as far as it goes young Salt. But, will a smart uniform and shiny buttons impress the hardened criminal as much as the law-abiding member of the public? Hardly –it stands to reason don't it? I mean, they might take one look at you with your nice clean boots and polished buttons and think, 'hello, this bloke looks like a bit of a powder puff. All done up and scared to get his hands dirty, or his shoes.' You could be inviting trouble."

Josh could see that 'young Salt' was anything but a 'powder puff.' His buttoned tunic (fastened all the way to the top with meticulously buffed buttonry of course) was pulled snugly smooth over a powerful looking chest and back which, he had no doubt, enclosed a powerful set of lungs. Coupled with large reddened knuckles and less than symmetrical facial features – in the nose region – that torso told him that this was a man more than passingly acquainted with the not so gentle arts of self-defence. He wondered that Gordon could not see that, because, the way the conversation was going, Josh could see what was coming next; and what was coming next was not going to go the way his older colleague had in mind: P.C. Clark stood two or three inches taller than the new man, and that and age was what he appeared to be relying on; short-sighted in more ways than one.

"I suppose there is a danger of that," admitted the recruit in his deceptively soft but precise manner, "if any particular hardened criminal was too dense to know what he was looking at."

If that was a barb aimed at his present interlocutor, it found no purchase in the thick hide of the donkey, who was already continuing afresh.

"Oh, trust me, me boy, they are dense, the lot of 'em. Thick as two short puddings. Most of 'em would do you in if they thought they could get away with it, but the rope's a sure and certain disincentive. I always like to compare them to dogs you know – vicious dogs; untrained. And you have to train 'em, like a dog. Learn 'em. What do you think then? Could you learn 'em? Eh? Are you up to it?"

"I think so."

"Good to hear it. So, a practical example." He picked up a spoon reclining in an empty mug after tea duty. "Let's say this spoon is a knife," he said as he slipped it into his pocket, "and I'm a suspicious looking bruiser trying to force open a shop door. So, you go over to question him – come on then, come over – when all of a sudden he's got this kni…" But all of a sudden, he hadn't got this kni, nor any other masquerading piece of cutlery, nor control of the situation. Even as the hand left the pocket a sharp chopping action had knocked the pretend weapon to the floor, and the man in front of the pretend villain was behind him and securing him with the classic collar and seat of pants landlords' chucking out grip.

That move gave Josh a pretty good idea of where Samuel Salt had come by his combat training, or to be more accurate, the type of establishment that had nurtured it. His private smirk turned into an open grin as a red-faced P.C. Clark was steered a few paces towards the door before being gently released. "He had you there Gordon," he chuckled.

"I wasn't ready though," protested the crestfallen tutor.

"No, you weren't. Sorry for that," said the young man, "but that's the whole point, isn't it? That's what you've been trying to tell me, haven't you? That you've got to be ready for anything. I was listening."

"Well, I'm glad you've been paying attention," said Clark, playing for time while he sorted out his emotions. "That's very good. But you wouldn't catch me again."

"I'm sure I wouldn't, a man with your experience. I certainly wouldn't want to try that trick on you again. Shake?" The new boy offered his hand. After the slightest of

153

pauses Gordon Clark took it, having decided to salve his bruised pride with Salt's flattery – diplomacy as Josh saw it – and the swift gesture of reconciliation.

In an instant he had also come to the conclusion that this was a man to be respected. "Welcome aboard P.C. Salt," he said, "I think you're going to do all right."

This companionable exchange was interrupted by the opening of the front door. Against the light was outlined a large figure wearing civilian clothes and a bowler hat. Another step and the door closed and their tentative individual identifications were confirmed. It was the boss, Sergeant Lively. Another step and he stopped, looked down and carefully lifted his right foot, then stooped to retrieve a now misshapen spoon.

"What's this doing on the floor?" The question was addressed pointedly at Clark.

"Sorry Sergeant, I dropped it just as you were coming in. I was just about to pick it up."

"Make sure you wash it," was the only acknowledgement.

The sergeant took in the new recruit appraisingly. "Uniform fits well. It suits you. Lose the kepi though, special occasions and parade only. Have these two been showing you the ropes?"

"Yes sergeant, they've both been really helpful."

"Good. What's the plan for Mr Salt today Josh?"

"Gordon, P.C. Clark, is going to man the desk, and I thought I'd take P.C. Salt round one of my regular routes, down into Springfield then up and back down Portway Hill."

"Right, I'm coming with you. Let's go."

And so they went. Leaving Clark to sort out paperwork and his feelings in solitude.

#

Where the route reached its greatest elevation, Abe left his two uniformed colleagues and headed along a track at the top of Turner's Hill. Above, a pitiless sun assaulted the brave remnants of vegetation, wilting them, desiccating them, last vestiges of life retreating to the roots. After a hundred and fifty yards, give or take, he stopped beneath a wrinkled old Hawthorn on the dry and dusty ground. It was certainly turning out to be an exceptionally hot year: pity the poor blighters in the factories slaving before a myriad man-made suns. Everyone you met, the greeting was universal: 'Ay et 'ot?' or, in less refined, male dominated environs it might be more forcibly expressed as 'Ay et bloody 'ot?' or 'Bloody 'ot ay et?' Or permutations involving assorted imprecations. But the general consensus was that, yes, it was indeed exceptionally hot...

He spread an outsize handkerchief, parked his backside and leaned against the trunk. He was looking out over a short expanse of grass which stretched away fairly flat for forty yards before sloping down out of sight. Between the drop off and the far hills, and closer than the canals around Bumble Hole, there was a big hole with a big lump of rock sticking up like an island. There were no figures moving in the hole, not like there would

154

be tomorrow when they would be scurrying around, brief insects, dwarfed by rock and the ancient Hail Stone, or what was left of it. It seemed to him that it was not a natural lump of rock, not carved by nature, but the sad violated ruins of some solemn edifice built by some primeval race. To serve as a monument perhaps, or as a last bastion of a dying breed, a fortress disguised under accretions of time. But that was just fanciful.

The sun had been attracted by the blackness of his hat, and under it sweat had steamed his carefully arranged hair into a soggy mat. Removing his headgear, he allowed the vapours to escape and allowed in a cooling breeze to soothe the inflamed patch of skin around his wound. From his perch beneath the pinched but still green hawthorn leaves he looked across into the blue-grey of the quarry. It was the Sabbath, and the usual thundering and clanging in the quarry and the sounds of fire and steam from farther away was muted in respect. Today, the machines merely whispered in idle anticipation – the odd thud and tinkling of chains somewhere, the soft hiss of power held in reserve. Abe imagined that all men had mysteriously vanished from the earth, killed by some potent new plague perhaps, or just swallowed up. Only he was safe, on high, protected by the Hail Stone, and the Blue Devil. And he imagined his little patch of green expanding and covering the holes and the ugly black scars and eating into the mine-works and warehouses and factories and the squalid squashed up houses, like green mould spreading on bread. Until it was all gone, all the works of men, entombed by Nature. He could see it levelling everything but the Hail Stone...He didn't know how long he had been staring at it, but he was suddenly conscious of a bird calling. What kind of bird Miriam would know, or John, or Josh. Abe had never really understood their fascination with our feathered friends. He was more interested in bigger beasts – horses. You could have some fun on a horse: horsemanship had been his passion, that and wrestling. *Oh, it was you was it? You didn't sound much like a robin.* A bold redbreast, an unusually red breast, had crept up from behind him and alighted on an overhanging twig. The little bird fixed the big man straight in the eye.

"What do you want? I've got nothing for you," said the man.

Apparently satisfied with this admission the bird flitted down to the withered grass before him. The fire of the sun was citrining the green stalks and forcing an eruption of fine seed-bearing spikes, a transmutation of dying into the spores of new beginnings. He watched as the creature became lost in the tufts: they were blowing in the wind, creating a shimmering gauze of out of focus purpled browns. Woven into its fabric, white glints betrayed ox eye daisies and the white ran with the breeze and mixed with yellow dots of hawks beard and dabs of poppy red, as if swirled on an artist's palette, back and forth. And the sad grass sighed forlorn in the breeze. It was hypnotic; Abe felt a migraine coming on. He fell back within himself, eyes open but unseeing. A stab of poppy red, and he closed them. His lips mouthed unheard words.

"Where are you?"

"I'm here. You can't see me."

"It's the grass. You're small, and it's bigger than you."

"I can be bigger if I please. I don't please. I'm here to tell you something Abraham."

"How do you know my name?"

"You told me. Remember? We're friends. Aren't we?"

"I don't know. Who are you?"

"I said. A friend."

"Is it you then robin?"

"It can be. Call me Robin if you like. Or Jack, I like Jack. Make up your mind between the red and the blue."

"Show yourself."

"I won't. Not yet. But if you really want to see me, all you have to do is turn around."

But Abe could not turn around. And was not sure that he wanted to. Then, as if this were an everyday encounter with one of the dubious characters which his profession brought him into contact with, he began: "I'm a police officer…"

"I know who you are," said the voice, "I know exactly who you are. Don't worry. I'm your friend. Just remember that. I'm your friend."

"All right, if you say so. You said you wanted to tell me something."

"Yes. To warn you. Something bad is coming."

"What?"

"You'll know. You need to be strong."

"I am strong."

"Good. But if you find you're not strong enough, you have me. The policeman isn't real."

"And you are?"

"Something bad is coming."

"You said. But what?"

"Something bad is coming. Look, another friend…" and the voice was fading.

The spell and his stare was broken by the busy movements of the robin – just an ordinary robin now – visible again and much closer. He hopped onto Abe's boot, and for some reason it caused the big man to start, scaring his visitor into cover.

Unsettled, the man got to his feet, dusted himself off, and at a rapid pace put himself out of eyeshot of the quarry. It was only on checking his watch that he realised that a five-minute break in the shade of a friendly tree had turned into an hour beneath a cloud of unknowing.

It was time that he was moving. He had planned a leisurely stroll to Haden Hill House to keep his appointment with Alice. As it was, he would have to step out, and he cursed falling asleep – which is all that had happened – and the fact that he would now arrive somewhat less cool, calm and collected than he had planned.

156

Chapter 14

The Big House

George Alfred Haden Haden-Best was troubled. He was troubled by that self-same sense of moral rectitude which had prompted him, a bachelor and every intention of staying that way, to display his sense of Christian charity by adopting two local working-class girls and bestowing on them all of the privileges natural daughters would have received. Alice Cocklin and Emily Bryant had both been taken in six years ago when Alice was nearly twelve and Emily just gone thirteen. Both remembered their old lives, not bad lives by the standards of their former peers, but promising nothing but unrelenting toil and an early grave nonetheless. Both had much to be grateful for, and they were, their father was sure of that. But it was Alice. Alice was the problem. He should have seen it coming; in fact he had seen it coming but had put off doing anything about it, hoping it would fizzle out of its own accord. If he had acted sooner it would have been kinder, certainly easier for him. The Lord Jesus had enjoined us to 'judge not', but Mr Haden-Best knew he must do just that. However, he was confident that any court in this world or the next would acquit him on the grounds of achieving a greater good. Alice would soon get over it, and he was sure that the handsome young police sergeant had plenty of other female admirers. He did like the sergeant, but that was not important; he couldn't allow this infant friendship to grow, not let it turn into something else. No, best stifle it now.

A knock on the door. "Come in, Alice."

Alice duly entered. A girl in her late teens, she looked older. She was neither tall nor short and her hair, not fair but not strikingly dark was tied back informally to hang like a horse tail. She was slight of figure without being thin, and with a subtle elegance accentuated by her light green box-pleated skirt incorporating the most up to date apron drape styling. Complementing the lines, her simple, but expensive, blouse was tight sleeved and buttoned at the cuffs and along a high crocheted collar. Dressed for walking out, observed her papa. He also noted that she had gone to the trouble of disguising small imperfections of complexion with powder, and had accentuated her eyebrows, her most expressive and, to him, endearing feature. This was going to be difficult.

"Ah, Alice," he said, as if he had been expecting anyone else. "Please sit down." Alice hesitated. It was not usual for her adopted father to summon her to the library, which was very much his private place. Briefly she was anxious, but the shadow was banished by the light of her affection for this man, whom she trusted above all others. So she sat herself down in the red armchair. Mr Best rose from his immaculately polished walnut writing desk and stood with his back to the fireplace, out of habit for the weather was clement and there had been no call to light a fire today as yet.

"And how are you today?" he opened.

"I'm very well Papa. Are you?"

"Yes, yes. I'm in excellent health. Er, no more fainting fits then?"

"No, no. That's all behind me."

"Good. Still following Dr Shaw's advice on your diet, and doing the exercises he prescribed?"

"Yes. Well, when I remember."

"He's a good man is Dr Shaw. From a good family too."

"I've no doubt that he is, but he's so stuffy with it!"

The conversation was getting into awkward territory. Best changed direction.

"You haven't shown me any of your drawings for a while. Bored with it are you?"

"No, not at all; not really. I've been doing more photography of late, Em's teaching me. But I dare say I will return to my drawings in good time."

"Good. That's good. You're very talented you know."

"In your eyes perhaps…"

"No, you are. So, er, you've plenty to occupy yourself with then? Not getting bored with…anything?"

"Papa. How could I be bored? I have the most wonderful home, and I have you and I have Emily. Every day I count my blessings. Who could want more?"

I'm glad you put it that way. He needed the right words to get to the point. The room contained a fine collection of books on diverse subjects: botany and zoology figured largely, and there was a particularly valuable exquisitely bound set of volumes containing the works of the excellent Mr Dickens. Somewhere in all these books were the words he needed. But they were useless there…Mr Best felt that the room was far too small and far too hot: it was not a small room, far from it, but the shelves and the dark panelling and the ornate carved woodwork ate up space; the furniture and cabinets full of examples of the taxidermist's art took up more, so that now, he realised, it was far too small and far too hot.

Alice noted the flushed cheeks. "Papa, what is it? You've turned very red."

"I'm feeling hot. Would you be good enough to lift the sash a couple of inches?"

"Of course," she said getting up.

Best was glad of the opportunity to retreat behind his desk. It was a little further away from the red armchair than the fireplace, and he felt protected by its solidity. So much so that as soon as Alice was seated again he grasped the nettle.

"So, this Sergeant Lively…" and he let it hang there. It gave him chance to observe, and what he observed made him sigh: Alice's head came up and her eyes smiled as she said, "Abraham you mean? He'll be here in an hour. What about him?"

"What about him," repeated her father, possibly to himself. "Now, I want you to be honest with me, you know you can be. What is he to you?"

"What? You know what he is. He's my friend, a good friend. Good company."

"Nothing more?"

"No. At least not yet."

Which for the concerned father was both good and bad news. His timing had not been so far awry, he would split the 'No' from the 'not yet.'

"And that's the point Alice. To be blunt, I can't afford for that friendship to become something else. Do you see?"

It was her turn to colour. "No, what is there to see? Perhaps you could explain?" she said, raising her eyebrows, and challenging him with her stare.

"Well then, without meaning to sound crass, he's not good enough for you."

"Papa, with respect," said the daughter, for she did respect him, love him even, and that restrained her natural propensity to petulance when crossed, "you have taught me, me and Emily both, that humble origins or a mean station in life are not proper yardsticks for measuring individual worth. You proved that when you adopted us."

"Let me rephrase myself. This has nothing to do with the personal qualities of the sergeant, which by all accounts are exceptional. But it has everything to do with my love for you – and Emily – and the fact that having raised you up, I will not stand idly by to see my good works reversed, and you return to a life of care and want."

"But Papa, I'm sure…"

"There will be no buts Alice. Remember your place. I am asking you to obey me in this; to see the world as it is and to see sense. But, make no mistake, if you will not, I will compel you. You are a minor and I will compel you, make no mistake at all." He stared back at her. "Now," he continued, raising an admonitory finger, "please, for me, just go away and think about it. You will see that I am right." With that, he rang for the butler, who, being stood directly outside the library door, entered instantaneously. For the benefit of both the master now proceeded: "I think it best – having made the decision – if we make a clean break today. I will tell sergeant Lively when he arrives. In the meantime, and until he has come and gone, Smart will escort you to your room."

Alice could feel tears welling, whether from anger, frustration or remorse she did not know, but she would not let them see, so she went along with Smart. Deep down though – and on second thoughts not that deep at all really – she knew which side her bread was buttered.

The master flopped down in the armchair his daughter had recently vacated. One down, one to go. But the worst was over.

#

"Tasty pint that. Another?"

"It's your round, what do you think?"

"One for the road then," said Jack Cutler, trying to attract the barmaid's attention. But either she was too busy with esoteric bar staff tasks, or she chose to ignore Cutler's peremptory gesticulations. Jack was in a good mood, enjoying a midday drink with his new-found friend, and so he chose to believe it was the former. Shaking his head slowly in a sort of grudging acceptance of the inevitability of the coming ordeal and glancing toward his new mate, as much to say, "Can't get the staff these days," he rose from his perch on the stool and marched two glasses in hand to the small counter which straddled strategically two smoky rooms and which had rather ambitiously appropriated to itself the title of 'bar.'

"Two more Connie," his voice said cheerfully. Said Connie, a short and scrawny woman of mature years with a pronounced limp and a stoop, and, apparently, no comb (her hair looked as if it had not seen one since Adam was a lad, and she at school with him) moved to collect the glasses. And it was evident that Jack's cheeriness was not reciprocated, even in sham. She grunted something back, but it took Jack a few beats to decipher what it was that she was attempting to communicate. Whenever he interacted with Connie it was always the same; it reminded him of trying to hold a conversation with a goose, not that he had ever held a conversation with a goose, or any other type of wild or domestic fowl; it was just that she spoke with a sort of sibilant honk – not her fault, he supposed, but not his either, the fact that she had been born with a cleft palate. Not exactly a siren, to lure in the male clientele in their droves, but Cyril trusted her, and the Shoulder did as brisk a business as most other pubs, with less trouble than most. As he stood there re-running her lines in his head and trying to make sense of them, he was mesmerised by the sight of the single remaining incisor in her upper jaw which moved like something with a life of its own. Being neighbour-less, it had spread itself out, growing to preposterous proportions and, curiously, occupying the very centre of the gum line, so that it at least maintained a symmetry with the rest of her very wrinkled but otherwise unremarkable physiognomy. Pickled onion tooth, that's what the kids called her, God alone knew why.

He was still getting his ear in when the crotchety bar tender delivered two beers with a less than tender thump. As he was paying he could hear her battering at his defences, berating him about being too lazy to get off his arse and walk to the bar.

"You might think you're something special round here, but you're not. And I'm not a bleeding waitress – you'll wear your bleeding fingers out with all that clicking. Or somebody will snap 'em off."

"Yes, I'm sure you're right. Thank you Connie, and keep the change." And he sipped the tops off both pints preparatory to making himself scarce sharpish.

Arriving safely back, "There you go," he said placing the drinks down.

"What's this, short measures?" said the new friend.

"Sorry. I spilt a bit. Cheers."

"Cheers," said John Lively.

"You know, I never thought I would get on this well with a Lively."

"Why?"

"Well, two of you are coppers, aren't you? And from what I've seen of your big brother he's a right stick in the mud. Walks round like he's got a poker down his back (*or up his arse*). No offence."

John only smiled to himself, "None taken. He does give that impression – and that's mainly because that's mainly the way he is, at least at work. He's always had a thing about the rules and what's fair."

Jack felt bound to point out what to him had always been bleeding obvious, that, "The two aren't always the same thing. In fact, in this world of Haves and Have-Nots the rules of the Haves are designed to ensure that the Have-Nots remain Have-Nots, and vice versa. And that's no way fair is it?"

"I know what you mean," admitted the Lively, "but not all rules are bad; all laws."

Jack looked dubious, and made sure John saw it. "Well, let's not fall out over it," he said, changing to levity and giving one of his reliably winning winks.

"I won't," said John.

"But now that you're one of us," continued Cutler, "what would you do if it came to it; to deciding between your family and us?"

"You forget. Cyril is family, and Cyril's the boss."

"But your brother is the law. What about his choices? Would he put the law and duty before family? Before his brother, let's say? Stickler for rules as he is?"

John was ready for this. "Well, first off, it won't come to it. Second, Abe will always do right by his family; that's the big unwritten rule. He believes in the job because he thinks enforcing the law makes for an ordered and stable society: and that is what preserves his family, enables them to thrive, and that's why he's like he is. He's always felt responsible for us."

"He's told you this, has he?"

"Not in so many words."

"Right. Well, I'm glad to hear it. Sorry for bringing it up."

"No, it's best to clear the air. If you hadn't been thinking about it, I would have thought I had misjudged you."

"Lovely." Jack downed his beer. "I'll see you tomorrow at nine, sharp."

"Nine? I could get used to this."

"Oh, you will Johnno me boy, you will."

He stuck out his bony hand which was engulfed by the meaty mitt of the Lively lad whose warm flesh met a cool hard hand which refused to be subordinated despite its small size. Instead, that cold hardness drew upon the big man's body heat, as if feeding on his vitality. Then, tipping his hat with his handsome walking stick, Cutler left. John watched him go. He walked straight to the door and despite the room being well populated, he did not have to squeeze by or beg pardon of anyone – people just made way for the little man as he moved. Well, it was his patch after all.

Within thirty seconds of Cutler vacating the premises, out of nowhere Cyril appeared and sat down.

"You seem to be getting on well with Jack," he commented.

"Yes. Not quite as I had imagined. He can be very entertaining. Likeable."

"You like him then? Does he like you?"

"Wait a minute. I didn't say I liked him. He's likeable, I said; in a general sort of way. I can see why people would like him; follow him."

"Exactly. Good lad, you've seen it, as I said you would. He's clever is Jack, and that combined with his, what? Likeability? That makes him dangerous. Because he's not content to play second fiddle to anyone. Only a matter of time…"

"I know. He was asking questions about Abe and Josh. That put my guard up straight away, not that it was down in the first place. But, aside from that, we do genuinely get on. I should be able to keep him pretty close."

"That's good. But try not to upset him, I hear he's got an unforgiving nature and a nasty temper, though he's hidden it from me of course. He's getting too big for his boots, and if we don't take him down a peg, I don't know where it will end."

"So, what do you want me to do?" asked John.

"How much do you know about dog fighting?" asked his uncle.

#

With no more than half a dozen oar strokes Abe had powered the rowing boat to the little island. After tying it securely and steadying the rocking with one foot, he extended a hand to Alice; she took it gracefully and stepped over the side. The little ornamental mound was hardly terra firma, but that was the fun of it. Disembarked, the lady supervised the unloading of a blanket on which they were to sit. Crucially, the boat contained a stiff broom for sweeping away the dry duck droppings – the wet ones demanded another technique…From the nearest bank, some twenty-five yards away, they were supervised by an additional pair of female eyes, those of Alice's tutor, Miss Finch, who had strict instructions from the master of the house not to let Alice out of her sight. Abe accepted this – if in sight, at least they were out of earshot for a while, as long as they kept their speech moderated.

As Abe unpacked lemonade and sandwiches he glanced up to admire his companion. Her hair had been pulled back, braided and curled into a bun at the back, leaving a short tail dangling and tied with a small white ribbon, so that it reminded him of the braids which had hung from gentlemen's wigs in the last century, a fashion derived, somewhat implausibly he had heard, to help protect the neck against sword cuts. But there was nobody about to be wielding sabres today…he took in her delicate little ears, if anything just a shade too small, and the strong jaw: with the sun behind her he could make out the very fine blonde down which covered her pale cheeks, like the peaches they grew in the glasshouses. Most of all it was her eyes that drew him; she caught his staring. "What?" she asked.

"You'll burn. Where's your hat?" he replied.

She answered with a smile, retrieved a rustic chic straw hat from the boat, and balanced it on her head.

"Better?" she enquired.

"Yes. Got to look after you."

"Have you? I thought that's what my father was for," she teased.

"Figure of speech," he replied.

"Not that I object to your attentions of course," she continued in the same playful vein.

"Good. I wouldn't like to be a nuisance."

"You're not a nuisance Abe, you're a welcome distraction. I don't see you enough for you to become a nuisance. It's three weeks since you last came to see us."

"It's four. I know, it's the job. People depend on me. I can't always get away. Officially, I mostly shouldn't."

"It's nice to know you take your position seriously, and that you are happy in your work."

"Happy? I don't know about that. Contented though. Yes, contented in my work, that fits better. Doing a good job is satisfying. But it's not just that: I need to make a good impression; I want to progress. Next step, inspector. I'm not going to be a sergeant all my life. I come from better stock than that."

"Yes, you told me…" and then changing the subject and the mood she said, "so tell me about some interesting cases then."

"Well, did I tell you about the lock-keeper's wife who lay in wait for her drunken husband with a frying pan and knocked him into the canal?"

"Sounds like an everyday story of black-country folk. What's so special about this one, did she kill him and get herself hanged?"

"No, nothing more serious than a good soaking. Thing is though, she'd had a few herself; didn't realise it wasn't her husband coming down the towpath, it was the vicar!"

"Oops – tell me more…"

#

They spent an hour passing the time, he talking about incidents he had attended, but only the tame ones, you understand, those suitable for the ears of a lady, and with actual names withheld or altered of course. And in a voice totally devoid of the common accent, she spoke of her world, the world that had opened up to her in the big house, and she avoided any reference to the old life she had been plucked from by her benefactor. Abe guessed that the girls had been adopted when they were ten or eleven, so Alice had had about eight years to eradicate that verbal give-away. Abe assumed, quite erroneously as it happened, that she was ashamed of her origins. She was not, and had kept in touch with her blood. But that was a private matter and besides, she owed it to her new father to fit into this new world; and so she sat and chatted away like a real lady, without a care in the world, about art and photography and travel to places far and wide, most of which her visitor could never aspire to see. But Abe did aspire – to her world – because, if only in a strictly rural way, he had once been part of it. Alice had been raised up from humble beginnings; Abraham and his family had travelled in exactly the opposite direction; there was a kind of symmetry about them, as if fate had brought them together. *But if you believe in fate, what's so special about that?* This was part of Alice's appeal, most of it had he cared to admit it: her existence held out the promise of a way back.

When the wind started to chill, he rowed back. Miss Finch was waiting, two increasingly animated fleecy bundles, one white, one black, straining against her in an effort to confer their noisy greetings on the landing party.

"Let them go. Let them go Miss Finch!" cried Alice rapturously, "they will be fine."

Miss Finch obliged and Floss and Fluff, the girls' new toy poodle puppies spilled over the grass at a pace which their immature sense of balance only just kept up with, yipping and yapping in unrestrained joy.

"Hello darlings! Have you missed me then? Good boy Fluff, good girl Floss," said Alice with more affection than he had ever seen her display.

The pair made their way back to the house, each holding a canine mascot. They walked leisurely on a gravelled path between ornamental trees from across the globe and out onto the grass and through the small flock of stocky black faced sheep, presently employed keeping the turf short and springy but ultimately destined for the table (Abe was familiar with Suffolks – they were good eating). The livestock were prevented from reaching the more formally planted area nearer the house by the ha-ha, a shallow ditch and low gated wall. Passing through, the boating couple, Miss Finch and the dogs carried on past the dove cote and the old hall, until finally reaching the doors of the main house, where Abe would take his leave. They paused; he wanted to say something; to tell her, something; to ask if she felt, the same? But the time was gone. Quickly, the admirable

164

Miss Finch had closed with them and taken charge of the dogs. But she removed them only a few paces and well within eavesdropping range. So they parted with a brief handshake; she had called him Sergeant Lively, for the benefit of the chaperone, he supposed, and thanked him for his company. She said that she would write to him and invite him again. Write to him? He could see her sitting in an elegant room at an elegant desk in her elegant clothes and penning a polite perfumed note. And he saw a neat, too good for this place messenger arrive with it at his home, a pub where the great Sergeant Abraham Lively occupied a single pathetic little room. And he saw the elegant perfume swiftly overwhelmed and dragged down by beer fumes, as a lark in bird lime, and the crisp white paper become crumpled and smudged, doing the rounds of speculation before being presented to the legitimate addressee. How much of a fool was he? Things would have to change!

#

She had taken her time writing, but when the letter came, Abe realised that, in actual fact, he had been too busy to notice the delay. He could not believe how events queued up, just to fill his days: a breach of the peace here, an affray there, theft, robbery, soliciting, assault, and more, and every combination of same. But every arrest and conviction enhanced his standing in the eyes of those that mattered – he hoped. There hadn't been a good murder for a couple of years: that would be something to get his teeth into! He imagined tracking down the heinous killer of some poor innocent, or better still, of someone of some stature in society; and he imagined bringing the perpetrator to a swift justice at the end of a precisely measured drop, and being rewarded with his well-deserved promotion...

She had taken her time but today was the day. As he walked along Waterfall Lane towards Beauty Bank he remembered the day he had first been called to the big house. He was there at the request of inspector Millership from Old Hill and together they had tracked down (not very difficult in the February snow) an intruder whose presence had caused an unwelcome panic in the two young ladies of the house, in response to which Mr Haden-Best had demanded action. And action there had been: the intruder had turned out to be a hungry vagrant, an unemployed and homeless farm labourer, who had tried to force the doors of the old hall in the hope only, he averred, of getting into the warm. But it was obvious that if he was trying to break in for that, he was trying to steal food. Now burglary is a serious offence, and particularly so when committed by the lower social orders against their betters. This criminal was apprehended in short order and was even now keeping himself warm operating a treadmill with fellow reprobates. That was the law. Following that success the inspector suggested – insisted – that the sergeant keep in touch with the family, a tangible police presence to reassure them that they were safe – and that the local constabulary knew where their priorities lay!

Another two minutes and he was nodding to the old man in the little wooden gatehouse, installed since the incident with the itinerant, and was striding through the gates of the main driveway; it swept up west of the house at a distance of two hundred yards before sweeping back south in an arc, allowing coaches to approach from the front, emerging from between hedgerows into a wide cobbled circle where they could turn for the journey back. Sergeant Lively was not travelling in such style today– perhaps he would treat himself when he came to announce himself as inspector Lively – but Shanks' pony did have the advantage that it enabled him to take a short cut along a footpath that led past an ornamental pond. In the winter, when he had first seen it, it had been populated by an exquisite selection of impossibly pretty diminutive ducks. His favourites were what Alice told him were the Japanese Mandarin Ducks; the little male, resplendent in blues and white and purple and oranges, with upturned orange feathers, like a set of sails complete with small white spinnakers, or like something on a high-society lady's hat, and an extravagant display of russet neck plumes veiling each side of the little neck, was sculpted so precisely he looked as if he had been carved and painted in a toy-maker's shop and set upon the water for the amusement of the children – which in a sense he had. Unlike the larger body of water beyond the ha-ha – a funny name he always thought, who said he had no sense of humour? – the pond had no island, hence it was protected by a small fence designed to keep out hungry foxes. What it did have was a little bronze fountain with some kind of mermaid like creature, a water angel, who sat above a shallow bowl of water which overflowed continuously, a life-giving blessing to the doves from the cote, pigeons really, living on borrowed time, who visited to imbibe delicately and to bathe boisterously. And below, dimly seen through the falling water, cast in metal and in permanent combat, a scaled down gigantic snake wrapped itself around an open-mouthed crocodilian, death locked. Abe didn't like it, and he did not like what had happened to his Mandarin friend, in such a short season. He could pick the bird out because he was the only one, of a reduced population, with the russet neck feathers – or what remained of them, just a few straggly remnants on an unremarkable spotty grey-brown bird which seemed to know him; perhaps he remembered? The poor thing looked very much the worse for wear, hard to believe the seasons would one day restore his glory. In fact, they never could, for as the little duck turned Abe saw that he had lost an eye. He turned again and again regarded him through the one good eye with what Abe imagined to be sadness. The sergeant was not in the mood for sadness, and moved on.

He cut to the front of the house, leaving the dejected ducks and the neglected pond behind. He was now back on part of the coach track, in the turning area. Inside that large circle was an immaculately kept lawn whose green smoothness had been broken into by the dirt brown of geometrically arranged flower beds of various sizes, and stocked tightly with, at present, hundreds of chrysanthemums in a tumultuous cacophony of colour. When the wind turned, their perfume almost overwhelmed. He reached the main door of the house. It was an impressive red brick building inset with large creamy stone blocks on the front elevation and stone detailing around windows and door frames. It was new, perhaps ten years old, with numerous tall chimneys. Strangely, set immediately adjoining, if not actually conjoining, was another impressive building, also of red brick, thinner bricks than the modern ones, and of a gentler, paler shade of red, as if time had washed away the colour: this was the old Jacobean hall, of three stories compared to the new house's two; nevertheless they were matched in height; past and present statements of wealth. Alice had said that her father intended to demolish the old and extend the new in due course, but that he must wait until old aunty Barr had left, presumably by way of the bone yard. He had never seen the mysterious old lady, and he gathered that few people had. He looked across at the old-fashioned leaded windows and tried to see in. Had he seen a face looking back? Probably not. He knocked on the door. After a minute, the butler opened it.

"Sergeant Lively," he observed flatly, "just one moment please." And he shut the door. Which was peculiar. He was expected, and was normally shown straight into the hallway, to sit and wait till Alice and a chaperone appeared. He turned and took in the scenery. Past the formal gardens with the blooms of the moment and a few trees of some foreign origin the ha-ha marked the boundary with the rest of the grounds, not formally laid out but still with the unmistakable stamp of human intervention, an improvement on nature. This side of the little wall was planted with more flowers, tall flowers. What were they? Delphiniums, or gladioli – he never remembered the difference. Perhaps neither...He felt as if he was being watched from the house, but it would have been impolite to allow his gaze to penetrate past the exterior, and so, uncomfortable now, he feigned interest in the cobbles beneath his feet. Then he took to pacing a few yards from the door and back again, before repeating the process. After some lengthy minutes, the door opened again and the butler caught his eye.

"Thank you for waiting sergeant. The master will see you now."

The master? Haden-Best he presumed. He had met him only once to speak to, aside from a passing 'good day', when he had first attended with the inspector. The butler led him as far as what he knew to be the library. Peculiar again. Having knocked and received acknowledgement he swung the door open and gestured the visitor enter, and with a nod expressive of some secret message that Abe could not decipher, for good or ill, he shut him in. In front of Abe, standing back to the fireplace as earlier, stood the – today – stern figure of George Alfred Haden Haden-Best. The master. A glance at him was the key to understanding the butler's nod, and it was nothing good. But hadn't he known that? Really? Nothing good, no. Something bad in fact. He had been warned – something bad was coming.

The library was Best's sanctuary and stronghold, and in it and through it he was endeavouring to project an image of authority and power, although his faith enjoined him to humility and mercy. The library spoke on his behalf, of wealth and intellect, hallmarks of an elite club, members only: the whole room was oak-panelled, even the ceiling, a long way up even to Abe, and from which hung a sophisticated cluster of lamps powered by electricity, adding their artificial illumination to the daylight admitted by the big sash window. Over the marble fireplace, recesses and shelves of oak displayed expensive objects of cut glass and porcelain, and a silver carriage clock, while on the top shelf, flanked by two matching heart shaped Royal Worcester pedestal vases, pride of place was given to a fine specimen of the taxidermist's craft, a large bird of prey of a type unfamiliar to the sergeant. Like the vases it was cream and brown; she had traded open skies for immortality of a sort, depending on the preservative power of whatever chemicals bird-stuffers used. Not the bird's choice though, rather one forced upon her. Like the one Abe feared was now to be forced on him…He had never understood the passion amongst some types for displaying corpses around the home: you could appreciate an animal best in life; displaying it in premature death seemed to him perverse. He suspected, no, he knew that the practice had more to do with demonstrating power, a kind of hubristic cleverness to demonstrate mankind's mastery over nature, or to hide a man's inadequacy. That bird had company in this room. As he entered, Abe had been unable to avoid seeing a large glass cabinet set in the wall near the window. It contained more innocent sacrifices to the god of smug self-importance and idle curiosity: in an implausible montage, half a dozen kingfishers were fixed in flights to nowhere, or sitting, waiting for the oblivion of disintegration by time and mites; and all in impossible proximity with as many again long-billed waders – he tentatively identified a woodcock and a redshank – and smack in the middle, a lone red-headed duck, a pochard. Feathers gleamed as the light hit them, colours still bright in death, and their little eyes sparkled – not with the spark of life within, merely electric light bouncing off glass. And in the bottom right, a feast of avian delights before her, a lone polecat on the hunt, fated forever to go hungry. Abe could smell the decay, hear ten thousand tiny scavengers chewing and crawling through feather and fur. If it took them a hundred years, they would consume that brief immortality and heap scorn on the arrogance that fabricated it. And, he had seen other specimens, captured on silver chloride and constrained within gilded frames – Emily, and Alice. They belonged to him. He saw all this and realised it in a flash.

"Beautiful, isn't she?" The master's voice cut the brief dusty stillness and made him start.

"What?"

"My Saker. I saw you looking. Magnificent creature, don't you think?"

Abe was not sure that honesty would be the best policy here, so he merely said, 'yes.' As he did so their eyes met in earnest.

"Thank you for coming, sergeant. Please sit down."

#

The front door shut to with an unfriendly finality. Black clouds swirled around him so that he hardly saw where he was. But he knew where he was, and he knew he must leave the place and his humiliation behind. To calm himself he took some deep breaths; the sickly stench of chrysanthemum made him retch. He made his way back the way he had come. The scruffy one-eyed duck was still there waiting, watching him.

"Don't know what you're looking so bloody smug about you little bastard. You want to watch you don't end up in a glass case; no, too fucking shabby for that aren't you? Not up to standard, don't you know; you and me both. If I were you I'd fuck off before I ended up in the pot. Good luck you little bugger. Won't see me again this side of hell."

He passed on, fulminating against the injustice of the world, the proud and the privileged, and chopping off a dozen chrysanthemum heads as he passed. The scruffy little duck didn't understand. He watched the noisy figure till it disappeared.

The first pub that he came to was the Crown and it was open for the midday influx, the landlord being a respectable former bailiff well qualified for a Sunday licence; so he stepped in for a drink; in fact several. For some reason, and he couldn't remember how, he found himself some hours later knocking on that same door which, at what seemed to him now an age ago, had been opened to the desperate rapping of a drunken quarryman, ushering in the Spring Heeled Jack hysteria; and with almost as much urgency.

"Well, this is a surprise," said the landlady. "You'd better come in before someone tells your sister on you." So he did.

Chapter 15

Old Soldiers, and All That

The room was warm, and so was his mood, the warm beer having its looked-for effect. Although done up like a dog's dinner, complete with necktie which only added to the throttling tightness of a properly buttoned up collar, Derek Woolley felt very relaxed, and, thanks to a little bonus from Jack Cutler, esquire, he had money to burn, or should that be to drown? Like a toff, that's how he felt.

He had taken an omnibus to Oldbury today, ostensibly on business, but mostly so that he could indulge himself in another little treat: a proper soak at the public baths. So, what better way to end a pleasant day than to enjoy a convivial drink in civilised surroundings? As far as drinking establishments went, the Handel Hotel was about as civilised as Blackheath got. A cut above the rest, it boasted its own ballroom to cater for four hundred, and, if not hosting an actual, formal, ball – a rare thing in these parts – it did put on entertainment several times per week. Like tonight. For him, the place had the dubious advantage of being situated a mere stone's throw from the Shoulder Of Mutton, so that if any of his – for want of a fuller, perhaps more incriminating expression – employers needed him, he could make himself immediately available. He hoped that they would not need him. He was at the bar, seated, not standing like a lout, and was on his third over-priced pint – civilisation comes at a premium – since finishing his previously over-priced drink which, contrary to the barman's assurances had failed to impress, or to last. The 'gin sling' had been nothing to write home about, and he was in no hurry to sling another back. Hence, he was back on a more familiar libation: 'looking the part' had its limits!

He sat swivelled on his stool looking down the big room. It had been partitioned off tonight, a Tuesday: tonight's act was not well-known and in any case big events were rare; Saturday jobs usually. The entertainment this evening was courtesy of a twenty-something female singer with a half way decent voice and a whole way decent figure. Face was nothing exceptional, but, as he always said, though never in mixed company of course, "Who looks at the mantel shelf when he's poking the fire?" Not that his poker had seen much action, more's the pity…She was accompanied by an antique long-haired grizzled specimen slouching over an ancient and gnarled upright piano. As he watched, and being alone, he wrapped himself within a cosy little bubble, a temporary world in which he was a visiting VIP, perhaps a millionaire from America to whom Suzy – that was the entertainer's name, probably not her real one, Suzy Love – to whom she had immediately been attracted. Indeed, as the night wore on her eyes met his, he thought, more times than was coincidence.

In between songs the universal pub murmuration reasserted itself, and Derek became increasingly annoyed by the inane chatter emanating from a particular table of what he gathered were drapers' assistants, or at least two of them were. They had been already installed when he arrived, and he had been struck by their volume then, although it was not on account of them being big drinkers; that type never were. It irked him that they seemed at home here. How could they afford to frequent a place like this? Jumped up little squirts. And the squirts were disrespectful too, it seemed to him, sometimes still talking in what seemed to him deliberately loud voices and chortling stridently over some vacuous remark, even when the lovely Suzy had broken into the first bars of a fresh offering. They still hadn't settled down now, but, he made up his mind to ignore them and sipped his pint, politely.

She was singing what she claimed was an old favourite, entitled, "All Around My Hat." Derek was unfamiliar with it, but it turned out to be about a lost love who had got himself transported for seven years for stealing something or other. More fool him for getting caught, said Woolley's professional pride. *Never mind him love, I'll look after you.* He drank up and called in another. During this song, and to Woolley's further vexation, three young girls, evidently shop girls and known to the existing source of interference with his pleasure, arrived to much incontinent braying from the drapery quartet. To be fair, they settled down swiftly and were not heard all the way through 'Beautiful Dreamer', the rendition of which for reasons known only to himself almost had him in tears. There was an interlude then, and he went to answer a call of nature, leaving strict instruction that his seat should be saved, also reserving it with a tactical positioning of about a quarter of a pint of unfinished ale, to secure his base.

When he came back, he saw that more people had arrived, but that his seat had not been requisitioned. However, possibly to counter the increased volume, or perhaps to get themselves noticed, the shop boys had become even more raucous. One of them, a tall and gangly youth with a pronounced Adam's apple, ripe for punching, and obsequiously over polished oversized feet stretched out into the gangway to the peril of incautious passers-by, was recounting – again – presumably for the benefit of the lately arrived female contingent, a story about some unfortunate customer of advancing years who did not have the best grasp, evidently, of language, and had had the bad luck to cross the threshold of whatever piddling little retail outlet the bean-pole worked at. So, for the third time, Woolley was about to be bored by the same story. To make matters worse, the teller was making every effort to ensure that his audience's attention did not waver, as it clearly must, by effectively suspending the discourse, prolonging the agony, till the listeners bowed to his will and gave him their full attention. He did so by, every time he noticed a head turning away or someone trying to get a word in edgeways, repeating, again and again, "so ah sed..." before continuing...

"So ah sed to the ode bat, ah cor 'elp ya if yoh doh gimme sum ahdea 'o the saze yoh wannt." At this point, somebody must have shown an impolite lack of interest because the annoying git raised his annoying voice: "En 'er sed, en 'er sed, 'er sed, well ah doh really know, 'er seys. So ah sed, well 'ow big is y'son, ah sed. En 'er seys, 'es abaht normal for 'is airge, 'er seys – which is fifteen ah fahnd aht after ten minutes o' ewseless chat. So ah sed, well that's no ewse to me Madam, ah sed, is it? So, ah tek a coupla sherts off the shelf an' 'old 'em up for 'er an' ask 'er which uns closest to 'is saze. Well, by this time, ah'm gerrin' peeved, what with other customers waitin' yoh understond. So 'er seys, 'er seys, well ah doh know," and here he slowed down for dramatic effect, "ah doh know. 'Es very deceasive." And then the punch line: "So ah sed, ah sed, in that case Madam, in that case, p'raps yoh oughta gerrim a shroud!" It wasn't as funny as the bean-pole imagined, but he was rewarded with some polite tittering, although that was obviously not enough for him because he started to roar with laughter as if he had told the funniest joke in the world, and never heard it before. And with Miss Love about to restart, this was the straw that broke the back of Derek Woolley's temporary tolerance. He went over.

"Excuse me, er, gentlemen, I really think that you should have some consideration, and keep the noise down. And you," he said to the gawky bean-pole with the tempting Adam's apple, 'Arse Head' and he articulated the words very clearly, not even dropping his 'H', "If I have to listen to that stupid story about the shirts again, it will be you needing the shroud. Got it, Arse Head?"

One of his mates was obviously made of sterner stuff than the bean-pole. "We're doing no harm. It's not a bloody wake is it? Is it Colin?" Colin the beanpole did not reply.

"You heard what I said," said Woolley.

"And who are you to tell us what to do?" asked the sterner stuff shop assistant.

"Just watch it."

"No," continued the shop assistant and the drink, "you just watch it," he said, checking on the locations, if not the attitudes of his colleagues, "there's four of us. Who do you think you are?"

Woolley's blood pressure was rising and taking his temper with it. Much of the red stuff was congregating in his distinctive aural apparatus, his distinguishing feature. And perhaps it was this that saved the four shop lads from a beating, if not then, then later. Because, whilst in this place a member of Cutler's gang would not be the first character into whom you would expect to bump, and to be sure Mr Woolley was not usually quite so fastidious about his attire, his big red ears suddenly rang a bell for one of the girls, and she knew exactly 'who he thought he was.' A swiftly whispered phrase involving the words Jack Cutler, and a glance in Woolley's direction...

Meanwhile, Woolley had picked up on the misplaced arithmetical threat: "Yes, you can count. I can count an' all. Marvellous, ain't it, education?"

By then the message had done its rounds, and the tall one took the lead in appeasement. "Yes it is. Education, yes. You're quite right; we'll keep it down. Didn't realise we were getting so loud. You know what it's like when you're enjoying yourself."

"Yes. I'd appreciate it."

He returned to his perch at the bar, but the mood had been spoiled. And when the lovely Suzy began a little ditty entitled 'Father's A Drunkard And Mother Is Dead' he was not displeased to receive a note to say that he was wanted in the public bar.

#

"What is it Steve?"

Big Stephen Vyle had taken the opportunity to avail himself of a pint. "Oh, Derek," he said and swallowing the last of it, "it's Reg Phillips."

Surrounded by the fug of tobacco smoke and the oppressive local dialect, his friend's voice was like a desert oasis. "What about him?"

"He's in the California."

"Is he though?" It was not a question.

"Yes. And I heard him talking. Looks like he's signed himself out again; probably got a night watchman job on, though I don't know what use he would be if there was any real trouble…"

"He wouldn't. Some of the owners do it out of charity, salves their consciences as they say. Him being an old soldier, especially."

"Like you, you mean?"

"Not so much of the old mate! What else was he saying?"

"Well, I couldn't hear properly, it was noisy, but I know he mentioned the workhouse and that fatso boss of the place. The master is it?"

"That's it, the master they call him; Gross, Gideon Gross. What a fat bastard…So what did you make out?"

"Something about him being onto a good thing with one of the young girls. I know Mr Cutler wasn't pleased about him forcing his attentions…"

"Who would be! No, you're not wrong there Steve. Jack doesn't want him rocking any boats, so to speak," and he tapped his nose conspiratorially as if his big companion had the first clue as to what the gesture was meant to allude, "and he's got his eye on old Reg; he wasn't supposed to be let out, I think; too dangerous with that mouth on him. Look, wherever he plans on going, he can't leave it too late, not long till kicking out. Tell you what, you take a stroll past to check he's still there, though I'm sure he won't leave till he has to. I'm going to find Jack."

173

Ten minutes later he found Vyle in the shadows in Halesowen Street. Amongst the drinkers coming and going the two were inconspicuous except in all likelihood to a sober observer; so, safe enough.

"What did Mr Cutler say?" asked Vyle.

"He's not about. We'll have to deal with it."

And right on time, an unmistakable one-armed figure emerged onto the street, seemingly none the worse for whatever he had been tipping down his throat. It made a sharp left with commendable precision and started to march off purposefully. The pair lying in wait merely had to cross the street to intercept.

"Hello Reginald," said Woolley.

Ex Corporal Phillips stopped abruptly, startled by the stealthy approach of the two men, one large, and the other very large. "Er, 'ello. Uhm, do ah know ya?"

"What? You don't remember me? We had a drink together, oh, I don't know when now, but recently. It's Dan, Dan Smith."

For the life of him, Reg couldn't remember: his memory wasn't what it was; so he resorted to an accustomed ploy, and bluffed it. "Oh ar. Day see ya proper at first. 'Ow bin ya Dan?"

"I'm very well Reg. How's yourself?"

"Cor complern."

"Good, good. This is my friend Stan." Steve nodded and Reg nodded back. "Have you got five minutes? We need to talk."

"Worrabaht? Ah gorra job on tonight."

"The master sent us, Mr Gross."

"Oh."

"Yes, we've got a message for you, but you need to come with us first."

"But ah gorra be at Lench's…"

"Only take ten minutes."

"I thought yoh said fahve minutes?"

Woolley leaned in, conversationally but with a threatening undertone, "Reg mate, five minutes, ten minutes, what's a few minutes between friends Reg. Eh?"

The Sebastopol spirit was buried, but not dead. "Ah doh know…" began the old soldier.

"Look Reg, this is important," and the threat became overt, "come with us or I'll get me mate here to sling you over his shoulder and carry you."

Big Steve took a pace forward. Reg was suitably persuaded.

"All right. Ten minutes yoh say?"

"Probably less than that. Come on," said Woolley, taking him by the good arm, "let's cross over." *Where there's no light.*

They made their way through the gloom and patches of fog, which aided and abetted their manoeuvres as if they had a stake in proceedings, making their way towards St.

Paul's. They would stop before they reached holy ground; where the railway line passed beneath the road, adjacent to the churchyard. The cold grey iron of the bridge detached itself from the cold grey blanket of fog as they approached. This patch of road was overreached by the boughs of a large elm growing in the corner of the graveyard, its massive proportions fed by dead townsfolk, the most recent of which being one James Mason, sleeping under green boughs forever, or at least that had been the expectation. A straggling elder, clinging onto the tiny strip of land behind the bridge, added its own restless colluding shadows, rustling in the erratic puffs of night air.

Woolley stopped them on the footway on the bridge.

"Worris it yoh've gorra tell me then?" asked a now frightened old man, "yoh sed the master wannted me."

"No, I said we had a message. Sit him up on the bridge Steve, he must be worn out."

Before he knew it, Reg felt himself floating up lightly before coming back down with a bump on the dusty rusting iron of the bridge. Only then did he find time to react. He reacted because he found himself sat on cold hard metal straddling a swirling blackness at the bottom of which lay more cold hard metal. At the mercy of balance and gravity; of these two. Anybody would have reacted as Reg did, which is to say not calmly. He began to scrabble in an effort to get down. Finding this impossible whilst pinned in place by a strong long arm, he grabbed it and held on for dear life.

"Stop it Reg, stop it," said Woolley. But Reg would not stop it, so the ginger one prised loose the fingers of the old soldier's only hand, but as soon as he did he flailed and grabbed again. So he gave him a sharp slap to the back of the head. "Now stop it, I've told you. Calm down, we just want to talk. Now, loose my friend's arm or you'll get another clout." Woolley lifted his hand in warning, and Reg loosed his grip and waited.

"Now, when I said that the master had a message," continued Woolley, "I really meant that someone else had." That started Reg's mind racing, suspicion fuelling panic, and he started to fidget, dangerously.

"Careful Reg, you don't want to fall do you?" admonished his captor.

"Yes, be careful Reg," repeated Vyle with somewhat more compassion, as he moved closer so as to be able to catch him should he fall. The old man relaxed, a little.

"Now," said Woolley, "this message is from a friend of mine, a Mr Cutler."

A vacant look from the old man. "You do know Mr Cutler, don't you Reg?" prompted Woolley, glancing up and down the street for tell-tale warnings progressing through the murk.

"Ay sure," said Reg, who genuinely was not sure, though, truth be known he had never clapped eyes on Jack Cutler, at least not in the incriminating environs that Woolley had in mind, let alone met the man.

Woolley had not given up. "You know, Mr Cutler. Jack Cutler. A friend of the master's. You've seen him at the workhouse."

The old man felt scared. It made him sick, and confused. His old brain sought a way out, so it decided that it would be best if old Reg bluffed again. The sooner he had heard them out, the sooner he would be on his way. "Oh ahr, 'course. Mr Cutler, ah've sid 'im with the master," he agreed and for good measure, seeing that this Mr Cutler was a friend of his abductors, added, "seems a nice bloke."

Down the track and in Woolley's head, wheels were turning. He arrived at a decision before the train: slipping one hand furtively beneath the old chap's foot – he must have weighed all of seven stone wringing wet – he flipped the insubstantial object of suspicion over and backwards with ease; over the bridge and backwards out of sight, to plunge down onto the iron rails and the iron hard sleepers and the unkind rough stones hewn and crushed in the devil's quarry itself. So fell the hero of Sebastopol.

Woolley watched him disappear, first his face, then his torso, and his legs. He had a clear memory of the worn and holey soles of a pair of well-polished boots before everything disappeared into black. It was not a long way down, but easily enough to kill. Had the murderer wished to reassure himself that the body had indeed hit bottom, by listening for a thud, that some magic had not transformed poor old Reg into a bird to fly away, or that some strange breeze had not picked up that feather of a man and wafted him to safety, he would have found the task even beyond his big ears – for by then the train out of Blackheath station was on them, all hiss and thunder, a man-made dragon belching sparks and steam. When the noise and the obfuscation had dissipated, Woolley looked at the face of his unwitting partner in crime – this crime at least. And he saw the blank bleached pallor of shock. He shook him: "Stevie, come on. Look lively now," he said and tried to drag him away. But it was like trying to move an anvil with your little finger.

"What happened?" said the big man after an age.

"He fell, Stevie, he fell. It was an accident. He just fell."

"But why?"

"Because he was a silly old fool."

"But they'll blame us."

"Possibly, if they catch us. We don't want to be seen standing here like spare pricks at a wedding. We need to move. All right?"

"Yes."

"Follow me then. Come on!"

They retreated for sanctuary into the churchyard, where Woolley outlined a cover story, should they be questioned.

"So you've got it?" he asked his slower companion.

"Yes. After I met you in the hotel we had one drink and went back to your room for some gin."

"That's right, and that's just what we're going to do now. We'll say we had too much and passed out. You can sleep on the floor; can't be helped, and it's only for one night."

"Why don't we just tell the police we were talking to him and he lost his balance and fell?"

"Are you stupid? Don't you think they'll want to know what we are all doing there, together, in the first place?"

"Oh, yeah…I was just thinking, what if somebody saw us with him?"

"I don't think they did, and even if they did I doubt whether they'd remember, at least not enough to identify us."

"But, what if…"

"Look, stop worrying. What's done is done. If anybody asks you anything, you know nothing. Right?"

"But what if somebody saw us? They'd know we were lying."

"A witness? We'll cross that bridge when we come to it – or push 'em over it! No, listen, one more thing: you'd better get down there and make sure he's dead. Or we will be for it!"

If short on wits, at least of the quick variety, Stephen Vyle was not short on guts, nor was he tickle-stomached. Derek Woolley had heard it said, half in jest usually, that his mate was too stupid to be scared. Well, Woolley doubted that that was the source of his friend's pluck, and he was grateful that poking around a mangled corpse was not going to be a problem for Vyle. No sooner had Woolley given the assurance that he would keep watch than he was watching a large shape, blurred by the night and the fog, heaving itself over the low church boundary and fading onto the embankment: interspersed rustles and cracks, boots on gravel, boots thudding and skidding back up and bringing with him, attached to his person, the curiously pungent odours of crushed greenery; wormwood and pineapple weed, detectable even through the toxic night smog.

"Well?"

"He's dead all right," confirmed Vyle. "Not as messy as I thought though; he missed the track and the train missed him, mostly. Probably just clipped him; finished him off."

"Just as well, you don't want blood all over you."

"No. There was some on my hands but I wiped it off on the way up."

"I know. You smell of the embankment. Come on."

They worked their way to the churchyard gate. The fog had dispersed and so they took extra care stepping back out onto the street. Vyle was tempted to look over to see if the body could be seen now, but caution and Woolley prevailed and so they crossed over, just two anonymous friends on their way home after a night out. As they passed they both looked down the track in the direction that the train had gone. It was quiet as the grave, and in the hollow the last wisps of fog were roaming along behind in a leisurely pursuit.

On the way to the rat hole that Woolley called home, temporarily, he saw, quite oblivious of them, the annoying draper from earlier – from another world. He was alone and an easy target, but enough excitement for one day…

Your lucky night mate.

#

The young man stood even as Reg fell, and passed within a yard of him, reaching up for his old black leather bag and a dark ulster coat. He put them on the seat beside him and placed alongside them his top hat. This was the last train of the day, of the night, and at this hour he had the compartment to himself. It was a rather beaten-up compartment in an old and beat-up third-class carriage; a dull blend of brown and cream illuminated but insipidly by the sickly yellow diffusion from a struggling gas lamp. The light lacked the strength to penetrate the soot-stained glass and made of it a mirror. So, instead of a view of the outside to distract him from his dull surroundings, he could only see a paler reflection of his little cell, and himself. Not unnaturally then, he looked at himself. If the train had been morning-full, he wondered what the locals, the regular inhabitants of the carriage, would make of him: no doubt the unfamiliar figure would have stood out as better dressed than the average citizen, wearing a dark blue, almost black, woollen suit of good quality, though shiny with age in places, set off by a blue and orange tie, and complemented by waistcoat of contrasting white and navy diamonds, whereupon, suspended from the topmost button but one, could be seen a thick silver watch chain which snaked down and disappeared into a left hand pocket. Perhaps, to them, his clothes would betoken if not a gentleman (for the frayed cuffs and worn shoes told of hard times), then a tradesman of some kind; perhaps an apothecary; or a solicitor's clerk…

He pulled his other bag from under the seat. A recently acquired, not altogether honestly, small suitcase enclosing toilet accessories and sundry spare items of clothing, which were not a perfect fit owing to the fact that they had been purloined from a slightly larger specimen. He was not proud of this acquisition, partly because it pained him to think that he had been forced to resort to petty larceny, but mainly because the stolen items, being a less than ideal fit, didn't do him justice. What of the morality of it? His victim had not even been a Christian soul, let alone a Catholic, so it didn't count.

The train was already slowing for the next stop and by the time the end of it had cleared Reginald Phillip's body, the young man was all set to alight.

He wondered if his nefarious dealings in London had been linked to him. Was he on a police watch list? He doubted it, he wasn't stupid. Still, he wondered what his wanted poster might look like, whether the likeness would be true: 'Wanted', no that was a bit too wild west. Perhaps something like 'Information Required As To The Whereabouts Of Francis Thompson, Mid-Twenties, Brown Haired And Of Medium Build Last Known To Be Living In The Whitechapel District And Working As A General Labourer…' etc., etc. *Labourer be damned. Poetic genius more like. Still, they'll never find me here.*

As soon as his feet touched the platform at the grimy little station, Old Hill it was called, he was pounced on by a porter with an eye for fresh meat and relieved of his bags.

178

It was dark, and a low clinging mist clutched at his legs and swirled around his feet and moved as if populated by some fast moving but occult fog-dwelling fauna. Through an opaque ochre curtain the disc of a moon just on the wane was trying to dispel its shade, but it was futile; the occlusion crowded in and made the night its own. And the fog dampened out the sounds, and the night heightened the smells. This night in this place had its own peculiar tang: the steam and smoke from the engine; the whiff of burning, similar to a London smog but with its own signature, more metallic somehow and less watery but, rather, dry like some exotic spice; certainly unlike his home. Home. He was half way back but having second thoughts. London had been cold, callous, but the further he got from it, the less he remembered it bothering him. Running out of cash, he had been determined to go home and throw himself on the mercy of his father, but the closer he got to it, the more he remembered why he had left. Birmingham had seemed a good compromise. A big city offering scope for employment, and perhaps even the opportunity to frequent whatever artistic circuits there were, and promulgate his work. He dreamed of finding a rich sponsor. But, he was to be disappointed. As far as he could ascertain, Birmingham was a city of artisans, not of artists; eminently practical people, but with little imagination, in his opinion. And then in a local newspaper he had come across an article about a small town in the black country where according to reports the, no doubt benighted and ignorant, locals were being 'terrorised' by some fantastical leaping creature reputed to be not entirely human. It caught his imagination; fine inspiration for a new poem. "Why not?" he thought.

And here he was. By making him speak slowly, and repeat himself as necessary Francis Thompson deciphered the sounds emanating from the porter and made a decision. He would stay in Old Hill, or Ode 'ill as the porter had it (apparently the letter 'l' was silent in their pronunciation of it, as was the ''aitch') because, by his account, Blackheath itself could get very rowdy at night, and on balance, he preferred to have at least the choice of peace and quiet. Besides he was a poet and this after all was 'Ode Hill' and you couldn't get a clearer omen than that could you he reasoned flippantly.

The porter was a small man, but made up for his lack of height or brawn with a sort of irrepressible and bustling inner energy which expressed itself in his quick actions and an apparent strength which belied the size; and perhaps it was this that kept him small. Francis recognised it: he had seen it amongst the lowest and poorest on the docksides of London. It would not last long, that vitality and perhaps God had never intended it to. But he was still a young man, this porter, and an engaging character; and Francis took to him and his peculiar way of talking straight away. It turned out that the man's aunt ran a small inn which catered for one or two guests, and, fortuitously, it was not far from this very station. Happily, again, the best room happened to be unoccupied just at present, and which, by dint of Lenny's (such was the man's name) good offices could be secured today at a discount. Well, it so happened that a lodging off the beaten track suited

Thompson perfectly; also he was not so flush that he could refuse the discount so kindly offered. Indeed he would need to be making plans to secure more funds before too long.

The little man carried his bags to the street, slippery and stinking with horse piss and the decaying leaves of cabbages spilt from the cart of some diurnal street vendor. The choice of transportation was between a rather beaten up four-wheeler to which was attached an unmatched pair of tired and sad-looking coloured equines, and a relatively tidy hansom cab standing within the dim aura of an inadequate gas lamp, with a more alert looking dark horse: bay, black, or even dark chestnut – the pathetic light from the lamp did not allow more specific identification in these conditions. He guessed that the owner of the four-wheeler was down on his luck, at least more so than the owner of the modern vehicle. So, that should make him cheaper, and a fare would do him a favour. But would it do his poor beasts a favour? His destination might be at the top of a steep hill, for all he knew, and he doubted that the fare would be translated into better rations for the pair. So, what to do? As he stood there, a cold breeze blew in from the platform and whined around his ears as if it had something to say – which it did, which was 'put your coat on.' So he did, and he made up his mind. He was going to like it here, and he would arrive in style, in the hansom. He wouldn't worry about money, his muse would provide.

Tipping young Lenny secured a destination and a means to the discounted price. He stepped into the cab and made sure that he was fully ensconced before mentioning an address: he had no intention of being banged about by a flighty horse jolting off at the command of an over-eager cabbie; and he took off his hat as a precaution against rutted roads squashing it against the roof. Then: "To the Navigation," he said.

Chapter 16

Opinions

Cyril Crane crossed the street and stood with a cobbler's to his right and a haberdashery to his left. In front of him and between them ran a narrow darkly bricked passageway which led to – as proclaimed by the intervening stone lintel above – 'Market Chambers.' The name was a blind: it conjured up images of an august and dignified premises bustling with barristers and QCs with white wigs and black gowns, designing eloquent and balanced speeches to sway gullible jurors without upsetting the judge, and rushing out to order cabs to hurtle post haste, but with dignity of course, to the local seats of justice; and short sighted spectacled solicitors diligently dredging scores of tomes of dusty cases to support some arcane argument on codicils or conveyancing; and clerks scribbling and scratching from dawn till dusk; dipping and blotting and scratching and scratting…And all in the noble cause of justice.

Of course, the reality was very different. Market Chambers were a squashed and cramped row of some four single roomed premises – hence 'Chambers' – served by a single privy along a gravel path which terminated behind the California public house. They were not even in the town's market, although close to it. *'All a bit of a charade really – but that's life,'* thought 'uncle' Cyril, as he stepped through the portal, to leave behind the everyday world and retail premises and enter into another domain; of an alternative commerce where the commodities for sale were very much the fruits of men's learning and cunning rather than men's labour and sinews; esoteric fruits of long hours of study distilled into words for the benefit of a purchaser for value. Non-perishable and intangible, but not in their effect. No, certainly not: the law was a powerful ally; or enemy.

His destination was the second of premises along, past the red painted door of the accountants, Tibbetts and Company: another ambitious, or perhaps merely pathetically hopeful title, old man Tibbetts being reduced these days to running his shrinking business alone except for the help of a not so young and incorrigible 'trainee' with unruly hair and a reputation for rowdiness quite unbecoming in an aspiring professional. The second door was a solid looking one with a good lock, the top half being split into rectangular glazed segments; the glass bevelled so that it allowed in light and allowed the occupant to detect via his shadow an approaching visitor or customer; whilst presenting only a distorted image to a passing nosey-parker. A no fuss brass plaque announced quite simply: "A. Griesbach. Solicitor."

Before he could knock a voice summoned, "Do come in, Mr Crane. You're exactly on time." Cyril Crane duly turned the brass knob and stepped inside. The hinges were well oiled and the door swung smoothly and soundlessly, until, having travelled almost exactly ninety degrees, it grated to a halt where it rubbed against the floorboards. Alan Griesbach was standing to greet him. This solicitor was neither bespectacled nor, as far as his visitor knew, short-sighted. His desk was large but plain, with a separate stand for ink and pens and sealing wax. He worked alone in a little valley in the middle of the desk, between mountains of paper to his right and to his left. Cyril noticed that, as usual on his visits, the right-hand mountain – completed work – was the higher. The office, for such it was, exuded an air of methodical competence. Here was no swarming of precipitate legal practitioners, the room was far too small for that; here was no vast library of antique and contradictory precedents, the room was likewise far too small for that, and Alan Griesbach needed no such embellishments; and there were certainly no frantic quill pushers scrawling away at reams of thick yellow paper, they would have disturbed the tranquillity of the room, which again would have been too small for the paper let alone the quill pushers – moreover, was there not a firm of copyists located conveniently in this very row of businesses?

The absence of a supporting cast worried Cyril Crane not one scrap. He much preferred the real thing to the scene suggested by the imagination. In this world, apart from the piled-up papers on the desk, the room was neat and uncluttered: a reflection, he supposed of the sharp mind inhabiting it. There was the desk and the lawyer's own comfortable swivel chair of course, there were a couple of functional chairs for visiting clients, there was a small Georgian cabinet upon which sat a lockable glass fronted case containing perhaps half a dozen old books. These were possibly law books, but probably, Cyril guessed, not consulted very often, for the most used and most useful books the solicitor kept near to him, conveniently positioned on a shelf at arm's length from his accustomed seat at the desk. These consisted of a small collection of slimmer volumes including bound copies of parish ordinances and Acts Of Parliament, prominent among which was the Offences Against The Person Act of 1861. Leather tooled copies of Blackstone's commentaries – two volumes – served as a utilitarian book-end.

Cyril Crane tugged the door away from the abrasive patch of floor and closed it. "You've got a sticking door there," he remarked redundantly.

"Same as last time you were in. It's been like it since the winter. Come in Cyril, and take a pew," urged the lawyer.

Cyril removed his big hat and took the offered hand. Not for the first time he looked into the shorter man's ash grey eyes and wondered that they were not literally flashing with sparks from the cogitations which he knew from experience were always whirring behind them. The man had a charm of his own, albeit an acquired taste; an innate ability to instil confidence in his professional abilities. He would have liked to have known the younger man, for in truth the redoubtable solicitor was well into middle age, if not past. Traces in his accent had persuaded Cyril that there was some Irish in his ancestry, and Cyril could imagine the balding and greying, but still trim, old lawyer in his youth, with a mass of black curls and a mass of energy whose almost magical remnants could still be felt today. Living on his wits, the years had not filled out his frame like manual labour might have done, and he had never been a large man to begin with, but there was no doubting his mental strength. Cyril liked the man. In a moment of fancy completely at odds with his normal character, he saw the lawyer as an old leprechaun, trapped in the world of men, his own purgatory, till the curse that sent him here was broken...

"I'll send a lad over to trim the bottom for you...the door. Tomorrow afternoon about four suit you?"

"That's very kind of you, my friend."

As Cyril sat, closer, the illusion faded, for the signs of human mortality in the face opposite were plain: the sagging and hollow cheeks, the little thread veins invading the same and encroaching on the nose, the one grey eye a little too grey...

The lawyer distracted him from his distractions. "Right then, Cyril, me old mucker, as some of my clients would say, how the devil are you then?"

"I'm good," said the old mucker.

"Glad to hear it. I'm good too. In fact I feel on top of the world today. Would you like a drink? I have whisky."

This was not shaping up like a typical interview. "What's the occasion," enquired the visitor.

"The occasion? The occasion is I'm celebrating."

"Celebrating what?"

"A case. Life, if you like. I've had an entertaining day. I'll tell you of it. Whisky then?"

"Aren't you on duty or whatever you call it?"

"Lord, I'm not a policeman. Besides, you are my last appointment."

"In that case, yes please."

The cabinet beneath the stray old books revealed its purpose when the solicitor unlocked it to retrieve a couple from a collection of good quality cut glasses, which he examined with circumspection before applying a quick wipe to remove any dust, with a piece of lint which he no doubt kept for that very purpose. From the same secure cache he produced an almost full bottle of single malt – not Irish but Blair Atholl Scotch – and poured.

"Cheers," they said.

"So, before we get down to business, do you want to tell me what's got you in such a good mood then?"

"I'm always in a good mood," protested the lawyer.

"Most of the time," conceded Cyril diplomatically.

"I only sulk when I lose, and that's a rare occurrence."

Cyril knew that for a fact. "So, you had a good morning in court I presume?"

"I did. The last case was particularly entertaining. Might interest you; concerns that Haden-Best fellow."

"Why should that particularly interest me?"

"Well, what with your nephew being sweet on his daughter…"

"Who, John?"

"That's the police sergeant is it?"

"No. That's Abraham."

"Then, it's Abraham that's sweet on her. Didn't you know?"

"I didn't know he was 'sweet' on anyone. I always thought he was too busy; but, we're not as close as I'd like."

"I see. What happened?"

"It's a long story. Come on, tell me about your day."

"Well, do you know Haden Hill House at all? That's old Haden-Best's pile if you didn't know."

"Yes I know, and can't say that I do. Why?"

"Right then. Well it's a big place. Plenty of servants, including a gardener to keep the grounds in trim. Local chap. And our story is about him. Now, as you know, I've lived in these parts a good long while now, estranged from my native soil, just like you…" at this point Cyril thought of enquiring as to the whereabouts of the Griesbach native soil, but the lawyer was in full flow.

"And don't misunderstand me," continued the little man, "I've always admired the locals. I must confess, they're a hard-working breed, by and large. So what if they overindulge in liquid pleasures now and then, or even regularly? I for one don't blame them. It's a damned hard life, and a man deserves some respite, doesn't he? God knows they won't have a comfortable old age to look forward to. Best to get your pleasures when you can, 'for tomorrow we die.' Thank God for an education, eh? But for all their admirable qualities, you can't help but wonder where this particular species was in the queue when the brains were being dished out, can you?"

"That's what you might call a sweeping generalisation, I think," opined the publican.

"Your objection is noted and the point taken," rejoined the lawyer, "but let me draw your attention to the case of the Queen and Michael Nicholas, an apposite precedent I feel, to rebut your presumption of prejudice by generalisation."

"You've lost me," admitted Cyril.

"Here, have another drink; help you concentrate," said the lawyer as he carefully poured.

"So, this Michael Nicholls case," continued Cyril.

"Nicholas," corrected the honed intellect of the professional advocate without hesitation, "Michael Nicholas."

"Anyway," persevered the visitor, "what about it? Is it a famous case?"

"It is now. With me at least. Michael Nicholas is the name of Haden-Best's gardener – former gardener I should say. He was in court this morning. I was prosecuting."

"Big case was it?"

"Petty larceny."

"Oh, dear. Hardly a great test of your skills then. Or was it?"

"No, you're right. A trivial matter, but the client not so. And a fellow has to make a living you understand."

"I do, I do," said the gambling boss with feeling. "So what did this gardener do?"

"Stole oranges and such from the hothouses."

"Scrumping you mean?" queried Cyril, incredulous, "You mean you did somebody for scrumping. Hold on, I'm sure I can rustle you up some good defendants…"

"Accuseds," corrected Griesbach grumpily.

"Yes," continued Crane, "do six-year-olds count?"

"Yes, yes very funny. There was more to it than that. The man was making a business of it, boxing it up and selling it off to as yet unidentified itinerant costermongers. I believe it was your nephew who put Haden-Best onto it; some comment he made to the daughter."

"Oh yes, he's quite the detective. But surely, if so much was going missing it would have been obvious in any case?"

"Not necessarily. As you know – perhaps you don't – the master is proud of his Christian faith…"

"Which is why I'm surprised he took action for such a paltry matter; could have just sacked him," interrupted Cyril.

"You're not wrong. I believe it was the butler who pushed for a prosecution, and, as it transpired, the man was robbing not just his master, a gross breach of trust by the way, but also the church."

"The church?"

"Yes, and one particular church. The one in Old Hill founded by Best's brother-in-law, Holy Trinity; the one with the Sunday school under Best's patronage. The purloined perishables were intended as charitable packages to be sent to the church for onward distribution to the poorest of the congregation. The gardener controlled the whole supply chain, no questions asked. Except that, eventually, questions were asked, and answered."

"I see," said Cyril. "He bit the hand that fed him. I can see ingratitude there, and disloyalty, but why do you call him stupid? It seems to me he had a nice little racket going. Probably, he was only found out because he got too greedy."

"You may well be right," said the lawyer. He had seen enough in his years of prosecuting and defending to concede as much, and to realise that Cyril spoke from a similar experience, but on the other side of the fence – putatively.

"So, ungrateful, disloyal and greedy then. But not stupid."

"Quite the contrary. I haven't finished the tale yet."

"Well then, do go on."

"Well, he decided to plead guilty at the last minute, no doubt assuming that would help him; a dubious tactic I might add. He was fined three pounds ten with ten shillings costs – on the spot."

"And?" enquired Cyril's raised eyebrow, which query the solicitor forestalled with a raised finger...

"The point is, if he couldn't come up with the money there and then he was going to be taken straight down to do three months hard labour. The magistrate was a bit of an old ditherer, so to speed up proceedings I asked the prisoner directly, 'Do you have the wherewithal to pay?' Now, obviously, nobody expected the accused to have that kind of money about his person, so we all confidently anticipated seeing him carted off to the appropriate house of correction. Magistrates quite often give the option of a fine, even though there's little chance of the money being found; it probably helps them sleep a little easier; really, if you want my opinion, justice should be made of sterner stuff. Be that as it may, this particular offender wasn't done yet. Unsurprisingly, he did not have four pounds immediately available. But what he did next astounded the whole court. 'I do,' he said, 'I do have the wherewithal as you call it, only not in cash.' And with that he produced from inside his old and tatty jacket, a smart and shiny pocket watch and chain completely out of character with that item of clothing, and its wearer. By this time the magistrate had woken up and he deduced, almost as quickly as the rest of the court had, that this item was most likely ill-gotten. He had the man immediately rearrested right there."

"And the watch? Where had it come from?"

"The butler was sent for and he recognised it immediately. One of Haden-Best's guests mislaid it six months ago. Unlike the gardener you see, the butler had both a good brain and a good memory. So my old friend, how's that for stupidity? The man was as thick as pig shit, and I rest my case."

"Hmh. Speaking of cases," said Cyril, "have you thought on the situation I mentioned?"

"You mean about the 'dying declaration' principle and your friend awaiting execution in Shrewsbury gaol?"

"Acquaintance," corrected Crane, "ex acquaintance rather."

"Soon to be..."

"No, I meant that I only met him once or twice, briefly."

"I know what you meant."

"I know you did. But there's always time to get in touch."

"Why now?" enquired the solicitor.

"Because he can help me right a wrong before he meets his end. His lawyer is a talented young lad, and is still pushing an appeal, but it's likely to be refused, luckily. Which leaves me with a very short period of opportunity."

"Opportunity to obtain from him some form of written statement or deposition of past transgressions? That's what you meant, yes? But nothing to do with the crime for which he now awaits the hangman? Yes, that was it. But a 'dying declaration' doesn't fit the bill, I'm afraid. So, essentially, you're after something to be used in some dubious scheme of your own, some document, which you do not see fit to explain to your legal adviser. Who also happens to be an old friend, I might add."

"As I said, I'd rather not say what I want this, er, document, for but you can rest assured that it will be used to serve the ends of justice. Just not necessarily the kind of justice that goes through a court."

"Very well, but you must realise that without all of the facts any advice I offer will have to be vague at best; that's your choice. Therefore, reading between the lines as I must, I believe I can summarise as follows: you are seeking to use some written admission about something which occurred in the not so recent past to influence a person or persons unknown, almost certainly concerning a crime committed by such person or persons in partnership with the poor fool waiting to be hanged. This crime would probably be of a serious nature, otherwise it would not be worth your while going to all this trouble, I'm thinking. Either that, or it's the result, the potential result, that makes it worth your while; or it's both. And whatever you are up to, success depends on using this document as a threat to get what you want. If the proper authorities get involved you miss your objective. Right?"

"More or less."

"In that case I must caution that if the condemned man hasn't already given up this old partner, any sort of document which might come to light, shall we say from a concerned private citizen at a later date, after the execution I mean, is always going to have credibility issues, not to say admissibility issues, if it came to court. Corroboration is key here, but you can't corroborate something that's either inadmissible, or discredited you see? No? That is to say, any competent defence lawyer is immediately going to attempt to discredit a document signed by a now dead person, say on the grounds of forgery or of some undue influence or bribery – let's say for instance that the prisoner's family suddenly came into some unusual good fortune…

"Now, given all that, any last-minute confession or similar statement taken down by any police officer, or by any officer of the court – such a myself – is required to be referred to the authorities if it divulge any actionable crime. So, unless I am much mistaken, your witness to this, deposition let's call it, would have to be a professional man, or men, unconnected with the legal profession. A doctor or a priest perhaps, both of which might have occasion to visit an incarcerated villain."

"You're too bloody clever you are. That's why I don't want to tell you too much, you know too much already."

"You're quite right. The more I know, the less I should be helping you. So, let's do it this way: two old friends were having a drink; one of them happened to be a solicitor, the other a publican; whilst swapping stories, the publican brought up a hypothetical situation, based on a conversation he had heard in a pub, something about what was called a dying declaration, or some such. Wasn't it?"

"That's exactly right," said Cyril. "No, I mean it. That's what actually happened."

"Well that's all right then isn't it? But let's dispose of this dying declaration thing to start with shall we? It's a red herring: it can only be used as evidence to support a charge of causing the death of the person making the declaration, made whilst that person was expecting certain and proximate death, at least in criminal matters it seems. Technically, a dying declaration is an exception to the hearsay evidence rule, but we needn't be bothered with that because, as I say, it's a red herring here. Now, what could prove useful on the other hand is the naïve logic behind the outrageous fiction that the rule is based on, to wit that anybody about to meet their maker is very likely to be telling the truth. I know, laughable isn't it? But that bloke in the pub –let's say he was an articled clerk discussing a case – wasn't so far off the mark, in as much as any signed declaration witnessed by a person of reputable character immediately prior to the declarant's death – any churchman let's say – might carry some weight, provided you can persuade a court that the same sort of reasoning is to be applied. Possibly. Because as I say the hearsay rules…"

"Let me stop you there," said Cyril. "Possibly, you said?"

"Well of course possibly," continued the lawyer. "The obvious disadvantage is that the person making the statement cannot be called to be examined further, if he's dead, and can't answer any trenchant awkward questions or rebut any other accusation. In conclusion, my advice, as a friend that is, would be get yourself some sort of corroborating evidence. Clear enough?"

"I think so," said Cyril with a sigh. "Let me see, we've got a possibly, we've got a might – I'm sure I heard a might – we've got a red herring and all based on, what was it you said? A naïve fiction."

"An outrageous fiction," corrected his friend.

"Whatever. It's never straightforward is it?" said the dispirited client.

"There's no fun in straightforward and certainly no profit. This is the legal profession we're talking about," pointed out the solicitor.

"So this document may or not have the power to convict somebody?"

"That's about the size of it. And that's if it came to court through the usual channels, the police that is."

"I don't intend it coming before any court."

"I never thought otherwise. But ponder this, and think hard on it: once your man is dead, he's dead, and you can't cross examine a dead man; no cross examination, no fair trial, and the dying deposition, to use the correct terminology, is just a useless scrap of paper. So whatever your threat, be it criminal or civil proceedings, just make sure that your source is alive when you make it. And if you were to use it without going to the magistrates, which is the correct route, presenting the case to them I mean, and if your, er, target, went to the authorities himself, to report somebody using something privately obtained for some personal advantage with the law as a bargaining chip, not only would its evidential strength be compromised, but the police might start casting around to come up with other charges. Blackmail for instance. Which is no trivial matter..."

Fifteen minutes later Cyril Crane was back on the street. The fresh air reminded him that he had drunk almost half a bottle of whisky. His head was still spinning from the alcohol and typically equivocal legal advice. Around him, normality had replaced an earlier excitement. He made his way home. Not for the first time he reminded himself that the law was an ass. Well, if it was that much of an ass, he would harness it to a cart of his own design.

#

A public death always manifests itself in a kind of excitement, waves of fascination spreading out to the remaining members of the herd; an excitement born of relief; that it was not their turn this time; that death had come prowling and picked on another. It meant that they were safe, somehow. For today.

On this particular morning their scapegoat had been that sacrificial scrap of battered humanity which had been Corporal Reginald Phillips, late of the South Staffordshire Regiment, the bloody and pestilent fields of the Crimea, the tender care of the Tippity Green Workhouse and a young thug by the name of Woolley. By the time that Cyril Crane had set out to visit his friend and lawyer that day, the police had been, investigated, had the late Mr Phillips removed, and dispersed the gawping crowd. All done and dusted.

Except that Sergeant Abraham Lively was not convinced that it was all done, or dusted. He was telling inspector Thomas Oakden as much, but the inspector – Tommy to his friends, including close colleagues when it suited – was having none of it. The sergeant was concerned about something, that being the matter, trivial possibly, or possibly significant, of the deceased's treasured campaign medal: it was nowhere to be found. To Abe Lively this said that someone had, at the very least, interfered with the body and its possessions before the death had been reported. At worst that the old man's death had not been accidental, and not a suicide as the inspector seemed to think.

Abe tried again. "But what about the missing medal, sir?"

"Fuck me, there must be a dozen explanations. Maybe, it's been carried up the track by a train, might be miles. Maybe, it's in some shitty little Blackheath pissing pawn shop: if he was living in the workhouse he couldn't have been exactly rolling in it, unless you're talking shit. Or maybe it's in the pocket of one o' them as found him – get one of your constables off his arse to check if you're that bothered. Fuck me drunk."

In defence of his mouth, it must be said that Tommy Oakden had been cursed at birth with a belligerent nature, only exacerbated by a particularly harsh upbringing. This had produced an aggressive youth to whom problem solving automatically included physical violence, but that, to his credit, and after a close call which had nearly killed his best friend, he had taught himself to relinquish his old ways and find his salvation by way of a career in the police, ironically. The remnants of his old life were now only glimpsed in what was usually referred to as his 'colourful language' which he had long ago created as a sort of coping mechanism, a sublimation of physical violence. In short, instead of hitting people, he had learnt to swear at them. In fact, the inspector had developed quite a penchant for it. His everyday colleagues hardly noticed his imprecations any more, but they certainly did not endear him to sergeant Lively. And whilst not 'toning down' his language as he was frequently asked to do – such requests were guaranteed to produce the opposite result – the inspector was aware of the sergeant's reputation as a law enforcer, and was well aware of his size. That called for a modicum of respect he reckoned. Not that Oakden himself was a small man; never had been. He liked to think of himself as 'beefy', although in fact the last half dozen years and the booze had altered the balance of his subordinates' opinion to 'porky'. But that was something they kept to themselves, naturally.

The balding inspector was never slow to point out that he had seen it all in his time, and prided himself on being able to sum up a situation instantly. Such was the great depth of his experience, that he would interpret a scene intuitively, even without reference to any actual evidence. And then he would hold forth with relish, emphasising his points with generous helpings of cursing.

And so today, hearing of the old man's parlous physical and economic condition, and looking up from the line to the bridge, he was quick and confident in declaring a verdict of suicide. Abe tried to introduce other elements into the frame, but the inspector's mind's eye was focused irrevocably on suicide.

"What do you think is the explanation then sir?" persevered the sergeant with forced politeness.

"Bollocks! Do I have to fucking well spell it out? Again? Fuck me I'm surrounded by it."

He didn't elaborate on which 'it' that it was he was surrounded by. Which was probably a good thing given the state of the sergeant's temper, running a little hot since the encounter at Haden Hill House, even allowing for the softening and cooling effect of the touch of his new lady friend at the Hailstone. The inspector seemed to sense it; at any rate his attitude became pally rather than dictatorial.

"Look," continued Oakden, "I'd probably kill myself if I had to resort to that workhouse for support. From what I'm told the master's a right fat tosser."

He's not the only one. And you my tubby friend are foul-mouthed to boot. And that's what you need – up the backside...

"This poor old bugger had probably had enough, what with being old and destitute and only having one arm an' all; and he decided to end it all. I've seen it before. Fished one out of the cut last week with bricks in his pockets. At least that twat had the decency to leave a note. Not like this old git. This pratt's got you all in a lather about foul play. Take my word, he killed himself, that's the logic of it. I mean, what's the alternative? Murder? Who'd have anything against this docile old sod?"

"Could have been a robbery gone wrong, sir," ventured Abe.

"Not fucking likely. What self-respecting robber would bother with this destitute old bastard?"

There's no such thing as a self-respecting robber. Just robbing scum.

"Besides, if he was robbed, how come there was still tuppence on him?"

"The medal..."

"Oh yes, the bleeding medal. Cheap tat. You can't spend a medal, unless you pawned it first – for coppers. And what silly pillock would be saft enough to leave that kind of trail, eh? Tell you what I think. I think he pawned it himself, or sold it, for one last drink before he killed himself. The tuppence in his pocket is his change. Makes sense to me. Tell you what, if it still bothers you – though I think it will be a waste of fucking time – find out if he was drinking locally last night. And why that fat fucker at the workhouse let him out to cause this fucking nuisance. All right? It's in your hands."

"Thank you inspector, I'll check."

"Do that. I want a report on my desk by tomorrow evening, six o'clock." Sensing some reluctance, the detective added, "And Inspector Millership will happily confirm that if you feel like bothering him with such shit."

"No, that won't be necessary," said the sergeant. The rumour was that Oakden and Millership – Abe's direct superior – went back a long way. He wished he were dealing with Millership now. He could be hard but at least he wasn't blinkered, and he certainly had a cleaner mouth. Blackheath and Old Hill district boasted two inspectors, but both Millership and Oakden were currently based at the main station in Court Street. Very cosy for them. Cosy enough to wear on Millership's nerves. Hence Oakden had been given, with no choice in the matter, a roving commission, even allowed to wear civilian clothes on duty, as he was today. This was justified, if anyone asked, as being an experiment into the benefits of employing plain clothed officers, of detectives: in which role Oakden naturally felt God-gifted. He took to it like a duck to water, but didn't swim as well, referring to himself as 'detective inspector' and eschewing the uniform whenever he could get away with it. Letting him get away with it was a small price to pay to keep him out of your hair and at arm's length.

"Right," said the mouth, "I'm pissing off back to Old Hill. You've got today and tomorrow, then I want this case closed. Fair enough?"

"Fair enough, inspector."

Without more ado Oakden began to make his way back up the embankment, a more difficult task for a big man than the descent. The gradient and the fullness of his mud-stained figure elicited not only breathless huffs and puffs but a stream of choice words wheezed out in the gaps between, and, notwithstanding his cardio-vascular exertions, a couple of stumbles persuaded him to plumb the depths of his lurid lexicon, reaching the top in a vivid crescendo of red-faced invective which could still be detected, fading away, after the man himself had, mercifully, disappeared.

"What a c**t," said Abe to himself. Not language he would normally dream of deploying – but he felt curiously better for it. He called over P.C. Clark, who, having been watching the inspector's indecorous departure, was still grinning like a Cheshire cat.

"He's a card that one," offered the constable.

"Not the word I would have chosen." *But the first letter's the same.* "Now Clark, you knew the deceased didn't you?"

"Yes sergeant," affirmed the constable, glancing toward the muddy blooded blanket covering the little immobile mound that pulled at the eyes. He didn't notice the little bird that had landed on it and seemed to be taking great interest in it; only Abe did. "I don't know of anybody that didn't like him. Oh, I know he could go on sometimes, but that's what old men do, and there's no harm in it…"

"So you subscribe to the suicide theory then?" enquired the sergeant.

"It's one explanation."

"Ah! And you think there's another?" said the sergeant, anxious to have an ally against the inspector's narrow-minded position, "what?"

"Well," began Clark, less sure of himself under the spotlight, "trains are dangerous things. Could have been an accident."

"An accident? He accidentally threw himself off the bridge?"

"No. He might have been taking a shortcut and been struck. It doesn't look like he landed right in front of the train, otherwise all that's left would have been a trail of strawberry jam between here and Old Hill station. It's possible."

Abe had to admit to himself that the position of the body did fit with the glancing blow scenario. What that told of the circumstances leading to the death he was not so sure. As he mulled it over P.C. Clark continued.

"Did I tell you my cousin used to work on the rail tracks? Maintenance?"

"No," said the sergeant, "is it relevant?"

"Well, only in as much as he died on them. Same as that old bugger."

Abe took a peep in the direction of the blanket. The bird was still there, and he was sure it was looking straight at him. He didn't feel well…

Clark was in the middle of some reminiscence: "…Yes, that's how they found him; next to the track, lying flat, staring up, with the top of his head sliced clean off; clean as a whistle; took it off like topping a boiled egg it did."

"What did? Who?"

"Like I've just told you, the brake shoe."

"Brake shoe?"

"Yes, that's what they call them, I think. He was just unlucky, wrong place at the wrong time; must have been faulty…"

"Stop!" demanded the sergeant. "Start again. Who's dead and how?"

"My cousin, last year. He was checking on the state of the rails – that was his job – when a train came past and braked. One of the brakes broke off and sliced the top of his head off. Terrible accident."

"So what's that got to do with this? Are you suggesting some kind of connection?"

"Well, no, not at all. It's just an interesting story about the railway."

"Not that interesting. Fatal accidents do happen you know."

"But I haven't told you the best bit yet."

"Go on then," indulged the sergeant.

"Well, when they got there they noticed some little birds in the trees eating the berries…"

"So?"

"So, there were no berries. It was only just March. When they got closer they could see it was bits of brain. Lots of little globs of brain sprouting like fruit on the twigs. Fancy finding that eh?"

"Close were you? You and your cousin?"

"Nah. Hardly knew him."

The sergeant felt himself compelled to ask, "These birds, were they robins?"

"Oh no. There was a load of 'em. Sparrows they were."

"Right," said the sergeant briskly, "any other theories constable? About Mr Phillips I mean."

"Erm, no. On second thoughts, I think an accident's unlikely. Yes, suicide. You and the inspector are probably right."

"I haven't made my mind up."

"Oh."

"Let me ask you something. You knew the deceased. You saw him with that medal. You heard the stories. Now, do you believe that he would ever have parted with it, voluntarily that is?"

A light went on. "You're right. His pride and joy that was. But the inspector got one thing right: he only had that medal; that was the only thing of any possible value he ever had on him. He had his pride, and he had that medal. But they were the same thing. It was everything to him. He had nothing else. He'd die before parting with it."

"Exactly. That's why we need to find it. I want you and Josh to get right on it, as soon as we finish here."

"Right you are sarge."

"And Clark."

"Yes sergeant."

"I want you and Josh to drop everything else today. Find that medal and we find ourselves a murderer."

"You're convinced it was foul play then, sarge?"

"I am." *A little bird told me.*

Chapter 17

More About Jack

It had been a quiet Monday shift for Josh. The real trouble generally kicked off at weekends. The formally charged offenders had already been carted off to Old Hill by the time he got back from the beat. The tally for his own patrol that day had been a couple warnings to move on, issued to two separate shifty looking individuals – incorrigible rogues if ever he'd seen one – a clip round the ear for an obnoxious kid who should not have been on the street at that time, plus his one arrest: the traditional and obligatory disorderly drunk, currently sleeping it off out the back in a cell. Detective Inspector Oakden's deadline had come and gone before he had started his beat, and despite Josh's best efforts, assisted (though not exactly ably, he thought) by Gordon Clark, the fate and location of Reg Phillips' campaign medal remained a matter of conjecture if not debate. Abe would have put in his report by now; case closed, presumably. Josh did not know for sure since he had not seen his brother since the discovery of the old man's body. He had left Clark to find the sergeant and report the negative findings. It was getting difficult to keep track of his brother's movements, which was very much uncharacteristic as far as Josh was concerned. And it was obvious that the old hands – Clark, Payne, Stride – had noticed, but any mutterings they kept sotto voce when the sergeant's brother was around. Putting it plainly – to himself – Josh had to admit that Abe was neglecting his duties, and it coincided with him taking up with that woman from the Hailstone. He knew the men would cover for the sergeant, and had been, for they all owed him something, but only to a point. So, while he sat in the station sipping tea and cogitating, he made a decision. He would go and see Miriam about it.

As he sat back, mulling over what to say to her, P.C. Salt stepped in with a pursuing patch of night, and P.C. Clark with the air of someone who had something important to impart. In fact he couldn't wait. No sooner was he over the threshold than he had to blurt it out, "Ah've sid it! Ah've bloody well sid it!"

"Seen what?" asked Josh.

"It. Him. You know…"

"I don't think I do," said Josh, although in truth he did.

"He means Spring Heeled Jack," said Salt impatiently. "There, I've said it, and I haven't been struck by lightning."

"Not yet," replied Clark under his breath.

But Josh heard. "Oh, come on! Not you two as well!"

"Don't count me with him," urged Salt.

"I thought we'd heard the last of this nonsense," continued Josh. "Abe's tried really hard to make it go away. What will he say when he hears a police officer is stoking the flames again?"

"Don't condemn me without hearing me out," said Clark, and added, ostensibly innocently, "where is your brother anyway? Shouldn't he be here?"

Josh ignored Clark. "Did you see this thing as well Sam?"

"Well, I saw something, but I don't know whether it was Spring Heeled Jack. Now, it might have been Spring Heeled Jack, but from where we were there was no way of knowing if it was him – Spring Heeled Jack I mean. Oh no! I've said it three times. I'm doomed, damned to the fiery pit. God help us all!"

"Give it a bloody rest," said Clark testily.

"What do you mean?" said Salt, wide eyed and innocent.

"You're taking the piss again. All I said was…"

"All you said was 'oh no, don't mention his name. It will summon him up. It's a known fact; don't mention his name.' I think that's what you said anyway, 'cause you were too scared to talk in a normal voice."

"I wasn't, I just didn't want him to get away, and I didn't say it…"

"Yeah, all right. If you say so." Salt turned to an amused Josh and pretended that he could not see the unsubtle rude hand gestures being made behind his back by P.C. Clark. "I'm with the sergeant on this. There's been too much of this superstitious tripe already. It's even got to our fine upstanding colleague here."

"No sense in taking chances. You get to live longer that way," said the fine upstanding colleague. A statement of the obvious which merited no response.

"Right then Gordon, you'd better start from the beginning," said Josh.

"Right. Well, we were patrolling along the Dudley Road, down by the posh bog factory."

"You mean the Doulton works?" queried Josh.

"Yes, the piss-ware works…"

"I only saw pipes, hundreds of 'em," began P.C. Salt.

"Well, anyway," resumed Clark, "we saw a couple of blokes coming towards us; one of them had a bag; and we thought 'hello', most honest working men are in the pub at this time of night – this was gone nine and it was getting a bit dark and foggy – so what were they up to then? So they were, oh, about a hundred yards away, give or take; but we were in the shadows like, and when we…"

"To cut a long story short," intervened Salt, "we saw a couple of dodgy characters, chased 'em to the cut and lost 'em. Looking out for them, we saw a strange light bobbing around and we advanced to investigate."

"A train passing through?" mused Josh, "perspective can get a bit warped in the dark."

"No. No chance of that," said Sam Salt with certainty.

Josh pursued another angle, "couldn't have been a lamp could it? Somebody lighting their way home?"

"That's what we thought," interjected Clark excitedly, "but if it was a lamp, it was being held by a ruddy great giant grasshopper – or something – 'cause it was jumping over the cut, backwards and forwards it went. Up and down and backwards and forwards, and flitting along the towpath…"

"And then it disappeared," commented Salt flatly.

"What do you mean disappeared?"

"It was a good way away when we first noticed it; couple of hundred yards maybe, it's hard to tell in the dark. At first we just watched, not sure what we were seeing; then we began our approach," said P.C Salt, "exercising all due caution of course," he added with a sidelong glance at his fellow adventurer.

"And then it just vanished into thin air," added Clark, "leapt away probably. We must have scared it off."

"No doubt," said Josh just a little dubiously.

"No doubt," repeated Salt drily.

"So you've nothing to show for it. No evidence," observed Josh.

"Not as such," said Clark, secretly relieved.

"We had a good look around, but nothing," explained Salt.

"And what do you think Sam?" enquired Josh, "did you see something supernatural tonight? A ghoul from the grave? A fiend from hell? One of those blue devils perhaps? Or," – he couldn't resist it – "perhaps it was Spring Heeled Jack himself!"

"To be fair," replied Salt glancing at Clark, "it can get a bit creepy down there in the dark. What with that mist that comes off the water; gives you a chill like somebody walking over your grave sometimes. And it's dangerous – you got the spoil heaps shutting out what bit of light there is, so you can't see too well and there's piles of discarded lumps of metal, big old blown boilers and huge old cog wheels and tangled lumps of rusty scrap: all bristling with sharp points and edges ready to jab you like a cutthroat in the night, and leave you bleeding like a slaughtered sheep…"

"I know. I have been along a canal you know," interjected Josh.

"Yes, sorry. So that's why you can't just go rushing blind and headlong into that lot, Gordon's right there."

"Not to mention falling into that filthy water in the dark," Clark reminded him.

"Well exactly," said Salt. "That said however, I do think it's most likely some local prankster having us on."

"Seems a bit speculative," said Josh, "I mean, you'd never have seen him unless you'd followed those two suspects…"

"Could have been in on it," countered Salt.

"Still, if you're going for effect, why not do it somewhere more obvious, with more people?"

"More chance of getting caught," ventured Salt.

"Or, it really was some kind of monster, and he was actually doing his best to keep a low profile," suggested Clark, "unlikely though," he admitted in the face of disapproving looks. "Where's Abe? He'll know what to do."

"The sergeant will be in in the morning," Josh assured him on a wing and a prayer. "I imagine he'll want to investigate in the daylight. Gordon, do you want to do your stint in here now? I'll carry on with Samuel."

"Righto. Yes, will do, good idea," said P.C. Clark with unbecoming alacrity.

#

From Windmill End, where Clark's giant grasshopper had capered and disappeared, the man-made watercourse that was Dudley number two canal flowed (because there was a flow, ever so tiny, barely perceptible, but still a flow), through the colliery, past the 'bog works' in Springfield, on towards Blackheath and thence Old Hill. And it was at Old Hill, not far from the railway station and close to the Navigation that it found in the dawn that was breaking up the dark night before, stood in the middle of a bridge, a young man of poetic inclination. It was a little iron bridge, steel really; a new one set on dark blue bricks patched with mauve, steel panelled and grey painted, and it spanned the canal here. The cut as the locals invariably, and descriptively, labelled it.

On the left bank, sixty or seventy yards back, stood his lodgings, the inn, little more than a pub with a spare room, the Navigation, whence that cab had transported him on the smoggy night of his arrival in this town; this hiding place. He was coatless, and cold now, for 'that mist that comes off the water' was only just finally dissipating, tenuous remnants haunting the surface, always their last refuge, before the onslaught of daylight and the warmth of a renewed sun. To his right lay the road to the station. A week, almost. A week since he had caught that cab, or rather, that cab had caught him, for, had he but known, he could very easily have walked the distance to his lodgings. Still, nothing like arriving in style. Might yet pay him; buy him some much-needed credence and credit.

He had a sensitive nature, that's why he was a poet. But, he knew, that did not make him soft. Quite the opposite probably. He was tough, and rough surroundings were grist to his artistic ambitions, and coarse companions his muses. Like a chameleon, therefore, he could fit in anywhere. And he had. He would soon have his landlady eating out of his hand, while at the same time he had infiltrated the nearby infamous and squalid Terrace Street, squeezed, near the top of 'Heartfail Hill' between canal and 'sleck' heaps and respectability; whose inhabitants had abandoned the law, as God had so evidently abandoned them. Intractable and indifferent to either threat or entreaty, the police interfered in their lives only when absolutely necessary to prevent wider contagion. Thus, over a period of years, in Terrace Street there were oscillations between action and containment: a cleansing operation would remove all the more experienced troublemakers from the equation by ensuring that they were locked away, and left to rot; but then, a new generation would arise, Scarretts and Crumps and Whitmores, with the arrogance of youth and a desire to hit back. Abraham Lively had sealed his reputation when he had sorted out their fathers with the fist and the boot and the truncheon, but he was in no hurry to repeat the experience. It was towards this den of iniquity that the young poet had gravitated, almost naturally. He even found a place to smoke opium, for inspiration should he need it. But he didn't need it. So, one sample and he had not returned; proud of his self-control. Day to day, gin and beer sufficed. Or a small bottle of laudanum, like the one he had just finished, the bottle now lying under a good green fathom, he shouldn't wonder; the one that had turned his latest dreams into monstrous distortions of human impulse and human action. Intoxicated intoxications. But they had gone as soon as he had opened his eyes that morning, opening into a dark and suffocating little room inside a dark and suffocating world, masquerading as reality, sucking him through. He had dressed hurriedly and incomplete, and had let himself out, treading bare-foot on the still closed daisies that lived in the cracks in the paving, as they awaited the day's unfolding.

So there he stood on the bridge, between night and day, straddling the water. The light was winning now, blotting out the last sickly shadows of his dreams. They were gone again. One day, he would find a way to drag them into this realm, and his art would become divine. Sleep and drugs served as but impermanent bridges, he knew, always reduced to useless charred skeletons by Apollo's first arrows. He must build a new bridge, one impervious to the flames, like this little iron bridge, and shed the light of truth onto this veil of tears. So how?

He stood, navigating his thoughts, as a narrow boat passed between his legs with a load of coal from Bumble Hole. The towing horse was tough and long-suffering and pale as a ghost. The towpath stopped at the tunnel. He supposed that to continue it through it would have been too expensive, or else that horses were expected to panic in the dark, for the tunnel was indeed very long – a third of a mile according to the landlady – and black as midnight. As he had observed previously, a young crew member, a lad of about ten in this instance, was designated to unhitch the animal, turn it around, and walk it along the road, over the hill, to meet up on the other side. The lad with the horse was quite obviously part of a family which crewed this boat: that he could see, there was a mother and father and five small children of various ages but all with the same stick-thin physiques which were inherited from circumstance rather than genetics, and certainly not a by-product of a healthy outdoor life in the fresh air. On the contrary, the life was one of hard labour which paid not enough for the family to eat well; and the industrialised air could hardly be described as fresh, unless in relative terms. The difficulties were aggravated by the cabin space in which these itinerants were obliged to cook, eat and sleep. With the overriding objective of maximising cargo, the crew quarters on these boats could hardly be described as roomy. He could imagine the family wedged in in the winter, shut off from the cold but roasting and coughing on blown back smoke from the stove. It would make the black hole of Calcutta seem light and airy; at any rate, he wouldn't fancy it. To be fair to Fellows, Morton & Co. the boats had not been designed as family homes: time was when a man and his mate could earn enough to maintain proper land-based abodes; but not now, for the railways had come. The railways meant competition, and competition meant less profit; less profit meant cut backs, and the first thing to cut back on was always wages. True, the railways meant more jobs, but the working population was also growing so…Plus, the water gypsies abhorred being tied to one spot. So they clung on doggedly, proud at least of their superficial independence and of the narrow boats, whose cabins were invariably spick and span, brightly painted and adorned with polished brassware. From what Thompson had so far seen, was seeing now, they must get used to the graft and deprivations, for they seemed to manage, and typically, as this family, seemed stubbornly cheerful on it.

Whilst mother and father were using poles and hooks to manoeuvre into the mouth of the tunnel, there appeared, as before and as if by magic, a group of men, three this time, who accosted the travellers. These were greeted with amiable familiarity by Mr and Mrs Navigator and, after some brief chewing of the fat, two of them boarded. With somewhat less agility than a three-legged donkey it must be admitted, but then they were very clearly getting on a bit. However, once lying on the bows on overhanging planks their old legs got to work, with a seasoned strength no doubt conditioned by this very exercise, which is to say walking the walls of the tunnel hauling the boat along with them. Legging they called it. He watched as they all disappeared, slowly, into the artificial night of Gosty Hill. At first, he listened to the voices, magnified and reverberating up and down the long tube of brickwork, the grunts of exertion answered by echoes, as if earlier souls who had undergone the journey were giving encouragement, or warning. Life was hard, he reflected; indifferent rather. The echoes faded to nothing.

He had stood here yesterday, between meals, facing the tunnel and playing a game: he was reaching out with his senses, as if out of his body, to detect at extreme range the plod of the approaching horse, and then the more subtle and irregular sounds of a boat pushing through the dusty water, or bumping against the blue bricked canal banks. It was amazing how this simple little exercise heightened the senses and quickened the spirit. But it was human voices he had heard first, obvious from far away. They spoiled the game. People always did. Usually, he gave only a passing thought to the insignificant creatures passing beneath him: once swallowed by the black they were out of sight and out of mind. But not today, today was different. As the last visible vestige of the small smudgy coal boat disappeared into darkness, he allowed his mind to pursue it, and to overtake it. What happened to all these busy little men, their free will propelling them to the next pay day, and the next, until there were no more? Wrapped up in their own little worlds, the unrelenting daily drudge in fact a welcome distraction. As the rich man had the distractions of wealth and luxury, politicians and kings their power, and the poets had their dreams, so the poor man had his toil. All distraction, all of it. From the only certainty. Death. From the moment of birth he was on your trail, sniffing you down. Sportingly, he gave most a head start. But no matter how fast you ran or how far, he always caught you and gave you back to God. The game was rigged. We had the serpent to thank for that.

Pulling back, he noticed, in procession, on the iron before him, at right angles to the humans' direction of travel, that small black ants were going about their own business in their own world. In one direction, a stream of individuals faithfully followed one another, for that was all that their existence allowed. Many were transporting goods, some recognisably edible and some not. In the other direction a returning column, cargo gone. All busily contributing to their female dominated society for the greater good; very like the men in the boats.

Randomly, reaper-like, he selected a victim. One carrying a tiny twig; to what purpose she probably did not know. He had picked up a sliver of sharp metal from amongst the wind-blown tussocks of swarf collecting on the bridge here, and then, with discrimination and exquisite delicacy, as he had once been taught to cut human flesh, he sliced the creature in two. In its death throes he watched as a fellow worker stopped, little antennae questioning delicately, gently, as if with real concern. But briefly. Soon, she was gone, depriving the dying one of her wooden prize, and burden. Back in the throng, back with the living, and hurrying on. Two more anonymous ants made cursory enquiry of the corpse, as such she now was. And then she was ignored. Forgotten.

The others marched on with such single-minded purpose, reaching out with their tiny consciousness to their destination, that it seemed reasonable to assume that the minds and the purpose had existences of their own. So he took his thumb and obliterated a dozen sisters. He liked the idea of being Death.

"So, where are you now? Where have you gone? So fixed on your goal. How can that intensity of intention just cease to be?" After a while he answers his own question: "It cannot. Intangible it was and intangible it remains. It cannot! It is merely transmuted beyond human sense. Alchemy, not murder…"

Squashing another dozen, he is suddenly hungry and strides back to find out what's for breakfast.

#

At five fifty-five in the morning, and half an hour before expected, Sergeant Abraham Lively arrived, apparently refreshed and relaxed; more relaxed, on duty, than they were accustomed to experiencing him in fact. By this time, Clark had already taken himself off to an unofficial early bed, having tired himself out writing up a report to describe the events of the night before. He had jotted laboriously with pen and ink, his gift for spelling and composition little better than his eleven-year-old self etching his letters into slate. At least pencil and slate did not smudge and scruffy the finished article irrevocably, nor leave dirty dark blue stains on the hands which faded too slow, ingrained accusers of shabby ineptitude. He had read it three times over, anxious that he may have missed some vital clue necessitating a post-script. But, at last, he was satisfied and signed it off, rewarding himself by knocking off ten minutes early. He deserved it, and the sergeant would never know: he ran a tighter ship than Captain Bligh, they joked. Clark was no Fletcher Christian, but the sergeant wouldn't know.

But the sergeant did know. He surprised Josh and the rest however by carrying on as if he had not noticed. P.C.s Payne and Stride reported then, and the customary roundup of the events of the last shift ensued. Josh left the Spring Heeled Jack item till last. Abe listened and looked at the mess of blots and misspellings that was Clark's report. He cleared off a chair and sat with a sigh.

"I thought we had heard the last of this," he complained to nobody in particular.

"That's what I said," volunteered Josh.

"And that's why Clark's nipped off early is it?"

"He was in a bit of…"

"No excuses required Josh," intervened his brother, "he's not exactly over-endowed when it comes to courage, I know that. But he's a good man, you all are…"

Josh was surprised. It sounded like he had just paid them all a compliment. And he had called him Josh, not constable. He waited for Abe to continue. It sounded like he had more to say in the same vein. But no.

"Nevertheless, I'll be having words with him about not pulling his weight," promised the sergeant. "Now Salt, what's your interpretation of this account?" he asked, tapping the report book and giving nothing away.

"Well sergeant, I think it's open to interpretation."

"In what way?"

"It was dark; we only saw this thing from a distance."

"This thing? Are you agreeing that there was a thing?"

"No sergeant, not as such. I mean, it was a 'thing' only in so far as we couldn't make out what it was. So, yes, it was an unidentified 'thing', of some kind. Not a monster, necessarily. There might be a perfectly ordinary explanation."

"Josh," continued the sergeant, "this, er, phenomenon shall we call it, was seen next to the pit workings at Windmill End. You've worked in a pit, anything you can think of

202

that might cause this effect? This illusion? Don't miners wear lamps? Could it have just been a miner going about his business with his lamp on?"

"Well, the lights do look funny in the dark, from a distance they bob about like glow-worms. You can't always see the men. But this was in the middle of a shift, and nobody would have been wandering around the canals for the fun of it. Besides, it's the huge jumps that make this so odd. That's what frightened Clark."

"I can vouch for that," intervened constable Salt, "and I hesitate to say this, but the way it moved, it didn't seem like anything human."

Abe chose to ignore this. "So, Josh, you have no explanation?"

"Not really, not if we're taking Clark's story literally."

"And that's just it," said Abe, "it's a story, that's all. A story based on an impression from a distance. Now then Salt, you were there. What's the verdict? Man or monster?"

Salt thought for a second. "I'm not the superstitious sort sergeant. I know that there must be some logical explanation. In the cold light of day I'm not even sure that my memory isn't playing tricks. But in the dark, with an unknown threat and in the company of an, erm, excitable, colleague…it's different. But it must have been a man. Of course it must. No such thing as monsters, except the human ones."

The sergeant grinned, "Now I'm very glad you said that. We've had too much hysteria already, haven't we? Wouldn't want police officers of all people joining the madness. Josh, I want you to collar P.C. Clark, now, and warn him that if he breathes a syllable of this to man or beast I'll chop off his balls and let the kids have 'em for marlies. Constable Salt, you're going to be putting some extra hours in. Consider it part of the training."

"Yes sergeant. What do you want me to do?" asked an eager Samuel Salt.

"You are familiar with the miners' cottages at Windmill end, yes?"

"Yes, sergeant, reasonably familiar."

"Good. Go and see if you can find any witnesses to our phenomenon. Do it now."

P.C.s Salt and Lively duly took their leave. Sergeant Lively turned to the fresh shift members, Stride and Payne. "Right, you two. Carry on as normal. Oh, and P.C. Payne."

"Yes sergeant?"

"Get rid of that drunk from the cells unless you're going to waste time charging him. He's been stinking the place out long enough."

"Yes sergeant. Where will you be?" he enquired and hurriedly added, "should you be needed I mean?"

"You won't need me, I'm sure. I'll see you later."

He turned and left. In his pocket he had the list of enterprises, legitimate and not so much, which Clark and his brother had visited in their fruitless attempt to locate Reg Phillips' missing medal. To his credit, Clark had been like a dog with a bone with it, judging by his own account. Doggedness was a useful trait in a policeman and Clark was a good policeman; maybe a bit short in the old-fashioned guts department, but nobody was perfect. Abe would not go too hard on him. But it was frustrating. If he could prove Oakden wrong – bombastic bugger – and solve what Abe suspected was a murder, well, that would certainly be one in the eye for Inspector Porky. Not to mention showing that Haden-Best idiot what kind of man he had cast off!

#

Sergeant Lively had not really expected young constable Salt to gain much in Windmill End, except experience. To start with, it was an insular little community within a community, with a tradition for keeping to themselves and sorting out their own problems. The trait was mostly influenced by the fact that all of Windmill End's able-bodied men were gainfully employed within a short walk of their dwellings, whether in the mine or on the wharf-side, and the pub. As a result, the indigenous adults never wandered far, and became obsessively attached to their own little patch. In extremis only they spoke to the police. That's not to say that they were therefore lawless, you understand, for their moral and social mores were in no way inferior to those of any of their close God-loving neighbours. They just preferred to police them themselves. Furthermore, any hard-working Windmill Ender would either have been working a night shift or in full on drinking mode in the pub, probably drunk, at just before ten when Clark and Salt were poking around. The women would have been at home of course, probably already lying abed exhausted from the ordeal of the weekly wash, and even if they had seen anything, they would be wary of talking to a copper.

The sergeant had turned out to be right, mostly. One person did speak to him. In fact she took no persuading at all: Maureen Thompson was a widow; husband and eldest son lost to the mines, another son emigrated, and three daughters in service in Wolverhampton and Stafford. And so she had been left alone. A proud and once strong woman turned hard and mean by impotent bitterness honed by a never-ending grief. Of course, she had a working community around her, but the more she saw of women with living families, men with loving and attentive wives, the more her own loss ate into her, maggot like. In the end, instead of her crutch as she grew older, she made of that community a burden. And so she abandoned it, surviving figuratively and literally on its fringe.

When, eventually, the cracked and creaky door opened to P.C. Salt that morning, his impression was of a once stout woman creaking and cracked by time herself. A flicker in those old dry eyes. Of what? Recognition? Annoyance?

"What?" was all she croaked.

The constable removed his helmet and began in his very politest policeman manner.

"Excuse the intrusion, Madam. I'm sure that you must be very busy, but I wonder if you would spare a minute to answer a few questions."

"About what?" said she suspicious.

"Well, there have been reports of strange lights around the area. Up yonder on the canal."

He nearly missed it, but for a split second the years dropped away, a light came on in the old lady's eyes, and was gone. But her attitude changed.

"You should have said. Please step in. Thank God you've come," she said, almost enthusiastically, "I've been out of my mind with worry. Come inside, step in…"

#

In the late afternoon, Francis Thompson donned collar and tie, took up his newly acquired walking stick, and perambulated at pace toward the middle of Blackheath where by all accounts the best entertainment was to be had.

But it was early yet, and there was little to do but drink. No sign even of any street girls, unless the whores in this vicinity were of such refinement that they were not recognisable as such at all, which he supposed would counter the whole purpose. More likely the local bobbies were too sharp for them to venture out in daylight. Good for them. Good show…

Having sampled the same beery offerings from the same brewer at a couple of pubs, he moved on to a third. It was his intention to explore several, but not so many as to render him incapable. He was sure that most of the locals were inoffensive enough, at least sober, but if not he was more than confident in his one-on-one skills as long as he was possessed of his stick: not so much walking aid as much as weapon; a very useful weapon, with a heavy metal knob of a handle and its potentially lethal iron clad tip. Push came to shove, he could keep an aggressor at arms' length and a stick away. As he walked he imagined it: prod prodding with the tip for distance – not letting him grab it mind – and then swivelling it round to deliver a crippler with the heavy end. Best thing next to a keen blade…

He was at his next stop. It looked an inviting place. A double wooden slatted door was propped back on both sides, opening into what looked like the main room: a long room with a polished floor – no sawdust – and a clean looking bar where light glanced off the brass fittings of a row of pumps. He took a few steps. The seating was mostly standard pub stuff: wooden tables with plain wooden chairs or stools; but there were a few upholstered seats in cosy alcoves set out to one side. It looked and smelled clean, cleaner than his lodgings, whose homespun marketing slogans – including 'we haven't got no fleas,' or unintelligible words to that effect – were definitely in need of some professional tweaking. It smelt of polish and beer and fresh pipe smoke. The smokers were old-timers, near the end of the line; exclusively male they puffed out clouds of spent nicotine and time between parsimonious sips of beer and the laying down of dominoes. That was the predominant sound in here, the intermittent click clack as the miniature tombstones were laid down, and the occasional grunts of satisfaction or frustration at the turn of events. The place was not exactly packed; it had just turned five and the working population had yet to be 'loosed out' to quench its thirst. 'Knocking off' was an hour away, then no doubt this place would be thrumming. All good for the publican of course, but he preferred it like this: you could sit and think and drink in peace. Yes, this was a nice place, he decided. So he made his way, in no hurry, to the bar. Two women were engrossed in talk, one either side of the bar. As he approached he paid attention to their voices. One had the – already to him – unmistakable rhythm of this part of the world; almost musical he thought, and unlike the twangy annoyance of Birmingham speech. He had soon come to realise that there was a divide between 'Brummagem' and that part of South Staffordshire that some would refer to as the Black Country. Nowadays that divide manifested as a rivalry, more or less friendly, between the two, but it had not always been so: in 1643 Prince Rupert had sacked Birmingham, the city being for Parliament, and Birmingham's racial memory had not forgotten, nor that this Black Country had been for the King. The poet suspected that the divide went back further than that, but that was beyond his scholarship...

The other voice, that of the taller woman, the one behind the bar, spoke altogether differently. Slowly, yes, he doubted she had grown up in a city, but elegantly and clear. Not from around here, and educated, he would say. They were talking about somebody by the name of John –

Miriam broke off as a smartly dressed stranger drew near.

"Yes, Sir. What can I do for you?"

Francis Thomas fixed her eye directly, then said, "That depends; beer I think. What would you recommend?"

"I've just put on a new barrel of mild ale. All the way from Lichfield. It's a favourite with the regulars."

"Who am I to argue with such august aficionados? A pint please."

He installed himself in a window seat where he could keep an eye on the comings and goings, and also on the two women. He had taken a shine to the barmaid – no, landlady, she must be, married too. Not that her friend was bad looking: her apparel designated her a hard-working individual, that was true, but with a decent dress, a proper hair-do and a dab of make-up, she could be quite a beauty. They both could. He was pleased with his choice of place and position, but the drink disappointed. A little weak and not to his taste. Still, that would make it last longer...

"He's not exactly your usual sort of customer. Seen him before?" Sissy was asking.

"No, can't say that I have," said Miriam, "he's certainly not from hereabouts. And he's not a working man, is he? You can see that. Still, his money's as good as the next man's I dare say."

"So what's he doing here I wonder?" rejoined Sissy.

"Perhaps he's here on business," suggested Miriam.

Sissy shook her head. "He doesn't strike me as a businessman, not a very successful one in any case. He talks posh, but he's fallen on hard times if he's any sort of gentleman, judging by the wear and tear on his cuffs and shoes. Mind you I'm one to talk. Look at the state of me."

"But you've been working."

"I know. What's his excuse?"

"Does he need one?" returned Miriam. "You seem to have taken a dislike to a total stranger Siss. What's wrong?"

"You know me; fine one for snap judgements – look at me and your John! No, I mean, yes, I don't like him; I think he was a bit cheeky."

"He only asked for a drink!"

"I don't like the way he asked!"

The landlady leaned closer. "Keep your voice down, he'll hear you. He is a paying customer you know."

"Sorry. Speaking of which, fill her up," said her friend, handing her glass over, "I'm not going home just yet. My sister will expect help with the washing. No chance. I'm shattered, and it's not often I can finish early. I'll stay and chat a while if that's all right with you."

"Of course, it is. I'm glad of the company, Siss."

"I'll go when the men start to come in. What time does Marlene come on?"

"When she's finished her chores, but no later than six. Then it will be just the two of us till Jack gets back."

"What time's that?"

Miriam shook her head and bit her lip. "Who knows? When he's finished. I never know what time to expect him. You know how busy it gets. We need him, but he thinks he can roll in when he likes. I don't think…" and she stopped.

"What? What don't you think?"

"I don't think he always comes straight home."

"Oh. Surely not. Have you spoken to him about it?" solicited her friend.

"I've tried. He just tells me that he's busy at work; that he loves me; then he kisses me as if that's the end of it. I don't push it, it wouldn't be fair."

"Not fair? Why?"

"I'm not be the woman he thinks I am…"

"What do you mean?"

"Nothing. It doesn't matter. He works hard and brings in good money, but when he gets home, it's my home; one that I used to share with someone else. I think, he thinks I'm always comparing him…"

"And are you. Are you love?"

"Yes. I'm afraid I am. And I'm ashamed to say I find him wanting."

"Oh Miriam, don't say that. Don't be ashamed. John Henry was your first love, wasn't he? You're not going to forget him overnight. Not at all I hope. But, perhaps the memories will fade. Bound to aren't they? That's what time's for, to take away the pain. And you'll create new memories, brighter ones, with Jack. It will just take time, I think. I hope so. Don't be sad Miriam."

"It's not sadness. I'm not sad. Like you say, I'm just adjusting. I dwell in the past too much, I know. I'll get over it."

"O' course you will. In a few years, with a couple of kids running you ragged, you won't have time to dwell on anything."

Miriam stood back. Her friend saw that she was turning something over in her head. "Jack wants children," she said.

"Well, that's bostin'. When are you…" And now Sissy pulled herself up: Miriam wore a miles away expression and her eyes had swollen. A single tear broke, and broke whatever spell had her. She brushed it quickly away and leaned closer.

"Siss, that's just it. Can I trust you?"

"That's a saft question," she returned without thinking, and then, more gently said, "yes, of course you can. You know that. I'm your friend. What's wrong?"

But if Miriam had been about to reveal something, she had changed her mind. "No, not here," she said, looking around the room, "later. Now, what were you saying about John and Cyril?"

Sissy deemed it prudent to accept the change of tack.

"Well, taking up with your uncle seems to have actually been good for him. I know I've not known him long, but I do know he could be a bit gloomy at times. Like he had nothing to look forward to. But now, I don't know. He's just happier; hopeful somehow. Optimistic, that's the word, yes. Optimistic."

"You give Cyril too much credit," said Miriam, "don't you think the new found spring in his step has anything to do with you?"

"Well, I'd like to think so."

"Good. Because I know so. I'm his big sister remember. He was never the life and soul of the party, even when he was drunk, when he became quite the opposite in fact, come to think of it. But mostly, he seemed to prefer his own company. Aloof, if you like. Taciturn. Alone with his dark thoughts probably. But he didn't mean to offend, it was just the way he was made. And he got worse after our mother died. After that there was only ever Abe who seemed to be able to reach him – but now there's you. No, you've done him the world of good."

"I'm glad you think so, thank you," said Sissy.

"And," continued Miriam, "he will need your good influence to temper the temptations coming his way."

"Temptations?"

"Yes. Little brother says he is only doing honest work, albeit for an employer who, shall we say, cannot always say the same. But if he's not careful, he will get sucked into more questionable activities."

"I know, and we've spoken about that. A full and frank discussion as they say."

"With John?" exclaimed the landlady, before lowering her voice, "you are doing well!"

"Yes well, be that as it may, he's a grown man, as he pointed out, and he'll make his own decisions…"

"Even if they're bad ones," observed Miriam.

"He promised to be careful," Sissy assured her, "and that's all I can ask. Mind you there is something going on which he's keeping close to his chest. A project of your uncle's is all he's said about it."

"Any idea what?"

"No, but I think Jack Cutler's involved."

"Jack Cutler? Who's he?"

"You've not heard of him? Works for your uncle, like John. But not like John: he's a bad 'un is Mr Cutler, even if half the rumours are to be believed. I think John gets on with him though…"

Miriam cut her off with a look and a finger.

"Gets on with who?" said a familiar male voice.

"Sissy's father. How are you Josh," said Miriam as her brother reached the counter.

"I'm great, thanks for asking. Sissy, good to see you. How's that big bad brother of mine?"

"John's great an' all," said she, "but o' course I'm biased."

"Well, give him my regards. We see far too little of him. How's yourself? You're looking well."

"I'm well enough," she conceded.

"Are you having a drink?" queried Miriam, "or are you on duty?"

"When am I not? We're all on special duty today, like it or not. Little project of Abe's; can't say too much…"

"You Lively chaps seem to like your secret projects," said Sissy to the floor.

Josh did not bite on it. Instead he said to Miriam, "Anyway I can see you're busy. We can catch up tomorrow."

"I would hardly call this busy," said his sister with a nod toward the empty floor space. "Siss and I were just chatting, you know; indulging in idle gossip as women do. Isn't that right, Siss?"

"That's right, just passing the time, as you do," said Siss. And if she said it a little too eagerly, Josh did not know her well enough to notice.

"No, no," continued Josh to Miriam, "I'll catch you some time tomorrow. Where's Marlene?"

"She'll be back soon, if you want to drop by later?"

"No," said Josh, "I'll be busy later. I'll come back tomorrow; when you're not manning the bar. We can…catch up."

"On what?" asked his sister, detecting an ulterior motive.

"This and that," he said, before confiding quietly and closer, "I want to ask your opinion about Abe. I don't think he's…"

Again Miriam cautioned with a gesture. Looking over Josh's shoulder she said, "What's this a raid?"

In the instant before he had a chance to turn around Josh was momentarily perplexed. But as he turned, he heard Miriam say, "To what do we owe the pleasure of this visitation Sergeant?" and he knew what to expect. He saw his brother coming toward them. The sergeant slowed as the cast of characters huddled at the bar registered, but then he came on again. But not without looking long and hard at the stranger lounging in the window.

Francis Thompson saw a second copper come in not two minutes behind the first, and this one a sergeant no less. What was this, a bloody policeman's ball? He instinctively distrusted coppers, and he leaned back, nonchalantly, to dispel any outward sign of tension.

"Josh, what are you doing here?" was Abe's first question, and then, "hello Sis, on your own?"

"Only till six," replied Miriam, "then Marlene will be on."

"Good. You put in enough hours. How's John then, Sissy; have you seen him, Sis?"

"Not recently," and, "he's good," came back from the two women.

"Cyril treating him well?"

"Yes. He certainly seems to be," replied Sissy.

"Good, good. He deserves it."

"And how are you? We've been worrying about you," began the sergeant's sister, "you know, with that nasty knock you took…"

"We?" rounded Abe suspiciously, "who have you been talking to?" he asked, eyes boring into the constable.

"Not me," squeaked Josh involuntarily.

"Nobody," continued Miriam, "I mean me. I've been worried about you. But you knew that."

"I've told you, don't be. If I want your help, or your concern, you'll be the first to know. Now…"

"The first?" interjected Miriam, "not your new…"

"The first," confirmed her brother, softening, "always. Now P.C. Lively, if you haven't caught up with Clark, I suggest you do so immediately, and then get yourself back to the station, I expect you could do with a kip. We're starting at 7.30 remember. Well? Off you go then."

Josh was glad of an excuse to leave. "Right, I'm going. See you later then." And he went.

"So what can we do for you?" enquired the landlady, "you never come in when you're on duty. Not without there being a fight."

"Well, perhaps I'm not on duty at this precise moment," said Abe Lively affably as he removed his duty arm-band. "I'll have a swift half please. That is to say a pint – of my usual."

If Miriam had been surprised at this she did not show it. She was just glad to see her brother in a good mood, and before she knew it she had pulled a pint and set it before him. He paid, took a swallow, and glanced over his shoulder as he quaffed again. "Who's the bloke at the window?" he queried.

"Not a clue. He's not been in here before," replied his sister.

Abe caught the man's eye across the room. Like most, he didn't hold the policeman's gaze for long, looking to his drink as a cop-out. But in the split second that their eyes held, Abe knew that he did not like this interloper. "Watch him. There's something off about him."

Miriam ignored Sissy's 'told you so' look. "What? You know that at first glance do you? He doesn't look like much of a villain to me."

"All I'm saying is, there's something, off…Like this beer; ugh, what's in it? It tastes funny."

"Funny? What do you mean funny?" repeated Miriam. She picked up the glass and sipped. "It's fine," she declared, "Siss, what do you think?"

Sissy sipped and agreed with the landlady: "No, tastes normal to me." She handed it back to Abe. Tentatively, he took it and sniffed.

"No, it's off that is," he averred, "it tastes like…If I didn't know better, I'd say there was blood in it."

"Don't talk such bloody rubbish. What kind of place do you think I'm running here? It's your mouth that's off," concluded the indignant landlady, pouring the disputatious drink into the slops, "there, it's gone. Shall I pour you another one?"

Abashed now, Abe spoke softly, "I shouldn't be drinking really. I just thought…Besides, I feel sick all of a sudden." The sergeant put out his hand to his eyes, as if to block out the light.

"Are you all right?" asked Sissy.

"Headache," muttered Abe, and he headed towards a chair. He didn't make it, for he could not relinquish the support of the counter, so unsteady were his feet. Sissy rushed to support him and Miriam was round the bar like a shot. "Let's get him into the back," she said, "come on."

As the big tough copper was carried out between two members of the weaker sex, the newcomer smiled. *That will teach him to stare at me.*

211

In the big Royal Oak kitchen they walked him in like a cripple to a table and propped him up at it.

"There," said Miriam. "Just rest a while. How are you feeling now?"

Reply there was none, so she sat opposite and clasped his cold hands. "Abe, I said how are you now? Are you all right Rabbit?"

He stared straight through her, eyes disconnected from the world; or in another. Miriam sent old Mary to find Marlene, then tried again. Gently tapping his hands she was coaxing him back, but he was deaf and blind to her. To everything.

Concerned, Sissy began to shake his shoulder.

"Don't!" cautioned Miriam.

"What's wrong with him?"

"I don't know."

"Shall I fetch the doctor?"

"No. I've seen it before, a while ago, but I've seen it. Just wait, it's temporary, I'm sure. Do you know if John is over the road?"

"I can check."

"If you would. But can you be quick?"

"Of course I will. Be back in two shakes."

"And Siss."

"What?"

"Only John. Not a word to another soul about this. They could take Abe's job away. You understand?"

"Yes. Yes I do. Don't worry."

As she left the building she felt his eyes on her. The sergeant was right: there was something off about that one. Quickly establishing that John was not around, she re-entered the bar room just as the stranger was leaving, with a smirk. She ignored him and went straight through to the kitchen.

"How is he?" she asked.

"Still out of it," said Miriam between biting her lip, "no John then?"

"No, sorry. Does John know about his condition then?"

"It's not a condition. It's a delayed concussion – that knock on the head. John and I have been keeping an eye on him, that's all. It's that bloody woman's fault."

"What bloody woman? What are you talking about?"

They both looked at him. He seemed perfectly compos mentis, and was looking at them both. "What woman?" he asked again.

"Oh, there you are Rabbit. Where have you been?"

"What do you mean where have I been? You know where I've been. I was in the bar and I've just sat down here."

"You haven't just sat down," began Sissy.

"No, because we sat you down," interposed Miriam.

"Well, yes, I know, thank you. Felt a bit dickey. Actually, come to think of it, it's gone; gone as quickly as it came on. Strange. I'm feeling as right as rain now."

"No headache?"

"No. How about a cup of tea then?"

#

The sergeant addressed his full complement that evening.

"Now, I've called you all here because constable Salt has uncovered a lead in this Spring Heeled Jack affair. Constable, would you please summarise the result of your investigation to your comrades."

"Yes, sergeant. At approximately 8.30 a.m. today I interviewed one Mrs Maureen Alice Thompson, a widow, who lives near to the canal side at Windmill End. In response to questions about the mysterious lights seen in and around the canal the previous evening – as so cogently described in constable Clark's report – she was, after she got her wits together, very forthcoming. She says the lights have been a regular occurrence for the past week. Living alone, she has been naturally very fearful and has taken to locking herself indoors and drawing the curtains well before dusk. When questioned further, she confessed that she had never heard of Spring Heeled Jack as she keeps herself to herself. Therefore, I do not believe that we have a case of a copy-cat retelling, which is all that most accounts amount to. Nevertheless, the poor old wench has clearly been terrified by what she describes as…" and here Salt consulted his notebook, "a dark figure with flames coming out of his mouth, jumping the cut. When asked about what the figure might be wearing she replied 'nothing but shadders!' What's more," he said, looking straight at Clark, "she said that it actually landed on the middle of the cut, on the water, and took off again." This revelation started a murmur which moved around the room. He waited for effect, in particular for Clark's pallor to turn seven shades paler (leaving his prominent teeth looking all the yellower) before adding "But you do have to put this down to an old lady's poor eyesight at night."

"However," cut in their sergeant, "I am satisfied that like Clark and Salt, this witness did see something strange last night, or at least something that she could not make out or recognise, and it's been going on these past several evenings. Your sighting seems to have been corroborated Clark."

"Yes sergeant," was all that Clark could say. He didn't particularly like where he thought this was going.

"Thank you constable," continued Abe Lively, dismissing Salt, "now bear in mind all of you that this is only a single witness, and a lonely old woman whose mind might well have been playing tricks on her, or who might well have made the whole thing up for attention. However, her account seems, and I say seems, to agree with what Clark and Salt have described, which is, basically a light which appears to skip or jump over the water."

"So, are we saying that it's Spring Heeled Jack?" enquired Payne.

"No constable, we're not. I'm working on the theory that we have a prankster at large. A prankster who started off this whole ludicrous chain of events. Someone having a laff as they say around here. Well, I intend to catch our happy little joker and see how much he laughs when he's in the clink for breach of the peace, or nuisance, or assault. He'll be laughing on the other side of his face! Now did you all bring a change of clothes

as I asked? Not you Clark. You're staying here."

P.C. Clark manfully resisted the urge to protest.

Chapter 18

It's Joe, Not Jack

Joseph Darby had high hopes for himself. He knew that he was getting fitter and stronger, and had every expectation of maintaining the trend. At twenty-six years of age he had not yet reached the peak of either his ability or ambition.

In his sights now was W.G. Hamlington's title. He was due to meet the American in December and had every intention of depriving him of his world championship belt. That would make him seriously famous, and rich. Not bad for a lowly Netherton chap, a Windmill Ender. Yes, he was well known enough as it was, but only in certain circles, and strictly locally. He wanted more than that. When he was old and feeble he wanted to look back at his name in the history books. But that was only the icing on the cake. Fame after all was a means to an end. His end was wealth, money. Comfort and security he wanted; want and drudgery he did not. He dreamed that he would have enough to set himself up, before an ageing body let him down, and an athlete of fresh renown stepped into his shoes. A pub, yes. That was reliable way of earning a living. He would buy one and staff it with pretty young girls and live on its proceeds and his memories to a grand old age. Until the Lord called him away.

But that was putting the cart before the horse. He had to beat Hamlington first, and that called for practice, practice, and more practice. Fortuitously, being a skilled blacksmith, he was not beholden to any one employer, and not bound by the typical work routine, which gradually enfeebled the less fortunate. Rather, his relative independence he used to strengthen his mind and body. Although he did have to work for a living – just now – he was able to plan his days and his energy expenditure around his, mostly crepuscular and nocturnal, 'training.' The intelligent combination of said training, work in the smithy, and rest and the good food which his various exertions enabled him to afford, had produced a young man who if not unusually tall, was noticeably muscular and athletic looking. And it was not just for show, as anyone who had attended one of his bouts would know. But perhaps bouts is not the right word, for his public appearances did not necessarily include any opponent, in the usual sense. Demonstration perhaps? Or performance. Performances which caused money to change hands: the bigger the stakes, the bigger Joe's cut. This was where Joe's heart lay, making money for indulging in the sport he loved. As a school kid, he had always displayed a natural athletic ability, particularly in jumping. He was like a little goat, continually jumping up onto things: chairs and tables at first, but as he grew he was showing off on and over horses and carts, and man-made structures of all kinds, sure footed as any mountain ungulate, and wider and wider bodies of cold water or hot slag heaps, never getting wet, or burned, and easily outdistancing pursuing comrades who inevitably chickened out and had to make detours. Young Josey Darby was always king of the castle, and there came a point when it seemed that his skills were almost supernatural:

"Yoh'll never jump that. It ay 'umanly possible," was the frequently voiced conventional wisdom, to which the answer came back:

"Wanna bet?"

And things just took off. To the point when he had to be very careful about his training, particularly when practising a new trick to confound the paying public, or when there was a bet to be won. And especially in the latter eventuality: losers were not always good losers and Joe had soon learned that he must have a protector to guarantee he kept his earnings, not to mention two unbroken legs. And so he had obtained a sponsor who had expressed great interest in his talent and ambitions and whose influence – a palpably physical thing embodied in some no nonsense and tough-looking personal adherents – ensured without fail that when Joe won a bet or a competition fair and square, he was able to enforce access to his winnings, and enjoy their peaceful possession; which was more than the law was necessarily prepared to do for him. He was grateful to the owner of the Shoulder Of Mutton for that. Cyril Crane had even provided an escort to a match in Yorkshire some months ago, where the prize money was well worth fighting over and where a man without friends might well have found himself at the mercy of unkind strangers. But Mr Crane was not supporting him merely out of the goodness of his heart, he knew; he had a business to run – insurance he called it – and would not be pleased if he tipped his hand to rivals. So, today, he would train here, where he would not be disturbed, either by spies, or by school kids: these latter were a real nuisance, usually cheeky and always in the way. Privacy and peace and quiet, that's all he asked for. And at this time of day this stretch of canal was as private as he was going to get, and peaceful in a sort of exhausted way: tired men in the pubs, kids under the weather eyes of their worn-out mums, burning up their bread and dripping in narrow streets and uneven fodes on scratch games of footer, with bundles of tied up paper in place of a leather ball as like as not; or improvised games of two or three a side cricket. Or, for the girls, skipping, or...whatever – it did not matter. As long as they were not bothering him, that was grand.

As anticipated, the towpath was quiet. A stray gust briefly pushed a fluffy white feather along the water, before it was braked by surface tension and the skimming of soot. Where had that come from? Odds were on a passing pigeon; there were certainly no swans around here, not even a desperate lonely duck. The dirty canals were certainly not like the country rivers, not like the Severn and the Stour which he remembered vividly from infrequent trips as a boy. The canals were rivers tamed, dark veins of commerce, filled with a viscous and turbid black blood which brooked no trespass from the wild green world. Only Man and his creatures allowed here...

He was taking his time this evening. He realised he had been day-dreaming and shook himself out of it. He was at his chosen spot, where the banks beyond the towing path were kept relatively clear of the ubiquitous metallic junk, near to the thin strip of brickwork that sat in the middle of the canal here, a baked clay island where the toll masters detained boats to measure their draughts: draughts correlated with tonnage, tonnage determined their toll. Hanging his ruck sack on the hooks on the side of the toll hut, locked up and left for the night, he began to strip for action; down to breeches, short sleeved shirt and a very light pair of short leather boots with only a few carefully positioned studs – he needed grip but not weight – and which laced up as far as the ankle to give comforting support. Inevitably, as he began his limbering up, his knees, calves and palms accumulated patches of soot and bits of clinker which pricked him and attached themselves to his bare skin, before being brushed off to leave tiny temporary craters. Yes, when he had made his money his little pub would be beside a river with grassy tracks, not cinders; and lined with trees and rushes, not smoke stacks and rubbish; and the only thing laying on the water would be leaves or petals, or pollen perhaps, not soot; and the water would be clean and alive and flowing and full of silver fish, and herons in the reeds – instead of dank and stagnant and littered with rubbish and murdered puppies rotting because someone could not afford a licence...

To those who made their living from and around the cut, to those who aspired to nothing better, to nothing purer, Joe would say, "Good luck to you." If it suited them – and most learned to live happily with their lot at least on the surface – then who was he to judge? On the other hand, he knew chaps who were filled with the fire of trade unionism, who wanted to change the world for the benefit of the working poor – which was most people that Joe knew. Cloud cuckoo-land, that's where they were living. Theirs was an impossible dream. All that a man could hope for was to change a single life, his own life. That alone was in his gift. And that's the philosophy Joe was following. Not a dream.

But this woh get the babby washd. Werke yer ahdeas up Joseph!

With the change of mind-set, Joe decided, chirpy chap that he was, that it was a wonderful evening full of promise, as was his life. Cheerfully then, he set to. First, he ran slowly along the towpath. After a couple of hundred yards, he sprinted for fifty, but on a curving course dictated by the usual obstacles. But he did not go full pelt. Both the track and his pace undulated: he was not training for speed, no kind of running for that matter, and had no wish to pull a calf muscle or hamstring, or worse, trip into the water. That would put him back; the object was to go forwards. He turned and ran the other way, then repeated the pattern three times. Back at his point of origin and his belongings, he was ready for a few warm up jumps. Static jumps, no run ups, not in this session, not

217

tonight. So, moving away from the canal side to the other side of the towpath he practised over various familiar pieces of ruined masonry and machinery for height, or over damp depressions in the ground for length; all from the feet together bent knee position. Then he was ready for his weights which he retrieved from a waterproofed canvas bag which also contained his supper, his reward, of 'grey payse' in a jar and a meat pie carefully wrapped in newspaper. The dumb bells immediately snuggled into their accustomed position in his hands. He had made them himself to precise tolerances and weights and they were part of him now, of his body and mind, as soon as he touched them. As precious as gold almost.

Thus equipped and in a fine sweat, he walked to the good flat piece of ground along the towing path which he had measured out over previous sessions and knew to be thirty-eight yards long. Starting at one end he crouched down – but gently. He needed to make sure his muscles and tendons, potentially too tight after an afternoon at the anvil, were properly ready. He began to swing his arms, slowly at first, but getting higher with each repetition as the momentum of his torso transferred itself along them and gave the dumb bells life and motion. Higher they went, and higher. And faster. And deeper he bent and deeper each time that the weights came down. And he stopped; laid the warm metal down. Time to stretch again. Now. He was ready. A few warm up swings, then – Crouch. Stretch. Jump!

The dumb bells flew with a life of their own, summoning the supple but hard little human body to follow. His first leap cleared ten feet and as the weights came back down his locust legs cushioned the landing and flexed, energy stored as in springs, before, aided by the flying iron, they exploded power once more – another eleven feet. And the action was repeated, smooth as a well-oiled piston, till he ran out of piste. Eight continuous jumps. He took a deep breath, shook himself loose, and measured to his final landing spot. Then he went again, and would keep on going till he could not improve on any of the three previous runs. It would be time for a rest then; some water and a couple of biscuits before getting onto the water jumps, over the cut.

#

Although delving into a potentially supernatural phenomenon, the plain clothes patrol under Sergeant Lively's command that evening consisted, necessarily, of ordinary men: the redoubtable constables of Blackheath police. Mere mortals, and very much so, none had been initiated – unsurprisingly – into any sort of esoteric brotherhood, and therefore none had been instructed in secret arts of divination, nor had any been gifted with any form of clairvoyance or precognition. In short, they had no idea what the hell they would encounter tonight.

The sergeant and P.C. Salt were in civvies, warrant cards at the ready but truncheonless: those dead give aways had been left at the station. However, if they were prevented from looking forward, there was nothing to stop them looking back; back on experience. And what experience told them was that a good whack with a truncheon could salvage the most desperate of situations. So, truncheonless as they were, they had prudently substituted freshly fashioned 'walking' sticks – for self-defence, or offence depending on circumstances. Stout enough to subdue a monster. Probably.

Salt and the sergeant had made their way up the same stretch of canal as had Salt and Clark the night before, heading toward the interchange at Windmill End. As the path straightened out, near the bridge at Springfield Lane, they saw movement ahead. At a nod from the sergeant they both climbed off the towpath, onto the road and up onto the bridge. The parapet was capped with large half-round coping bricks, convenient for a pedestrian to lean upon unless that pedestrian were a police officer looking for a modicum of concealment, for the tops of the copings stood but a few inches below the four-foot mark, and Salt and Lively were of course considerably taller than that. But the bridge gave them a good view along the next stretch of canal: they could make out the next bridge, at the junction where, hopefully well-concealed, lurked Stride and Payne, also in plain clothes, and constable Joshua Lively who was in uniform (upon reflection it had been deemed prudent to leave at least one member of the party in a state of dress which immediately informed any nosey local that this was police business). The object of their attention, a man carrying a hold-all and wearing a rucksack, had stopped perhaps a couple of hundred yards away, perhaps a touch less. He had laid down the bag, evidently intending to dally there, at least for a while. The sergeant beckoned his colleague to crouch down so as not to attract the man's attention. From their vantage point they settled down to watch. Lacking the benefit of an accompanying uniform, an officious passer-by might conceivably have conjectured that this pair were up to no good, might have demanded to know what they were damn well about. But there was no passer-by, officious or otherwise, and even if there had appeared an individual with a particularly pushy propensity, it would have to have been developed to the point of the psychotic, or else at least been supported by superior numbers, to approach these two. And so our hypothetical passer-by would in all likelihood have walked quietly on, keeping his suspicions to himself, never to know the truth.

As they watched the young man – for such the spring of his gait suggested – began to disrobe, perhaps preparatory to taking a rather unpleasant dip.

"Hello," said Abe softly, "what have we here?"

"What's he taking his clothes off for?" returned Salt. "Is it a suicide?"

"They usually leave their clothes on – more weight you see. Except for shoes. I don't know why but for some reason most of 'em take them off and place them neatly somewhere nearby…No, let's just wait and see."

So they waited. At first bemused, they came to realise that they were watching an individual of considerable athletic ability going through his paces. Apart from this, they had seen nothing remarkable or unusual on their evening stalk. This was the last stretch of canal before the junction with the Netherton branch canal, a newer section of waterway which would take boats off to Stourbridge in one direction and in the other as far as Dudley port, via a splendid gas-lit feat of engineering known simply as the Netherton tunnel: twenty-seven feet across with a towpath on each side, and one mile and almost six furlongs in length, straight through the Rowley Hills to Tividale. It was almost certainly in this area, along this last stretch, that Salt and his colleague had seen the elusive bouncing light. Both onlookers were sure in their minds that they were watching the person responsible. It was too much of a coincidence that this man was here, tonight, in this spot, and, well, jumping around like he had springs in his heels. Admittedly, this diminutive terror was not clearing houses or, as the widow would have it, the width of the canal, but nevertheless, it was too much of a coincidence.

P.C. Salt interrupted his thoughts. "What do you think then sergeant? Is this our Spring Heeled Jack?"

"It seems a good bet. He's not spitting fire and jumping onto roofs, but people do exaggerate, don't they?"

"Even when they're sober, which isn't all that regular an occurrence," added the constable. "And what's the chances of coming across someone like this when we're looking for a something hopping about…Too much of a coincidence."

"Exactly my thoughts. Let's just wait a bit though. I'm quite enjoying the show," said his superior.

At length, the man finished his exertions, spread a sack on the ground, and delved into a bag. He laid out items on the ground, amongst them something which the sergeant thought he recognised. He stared hard, nudging the constable.

"What do you reckon that is P.C. Salt?"

"Looks like a biscuit, sergeant. Or a sandwich."

"Not what he's eating. Look, what's that he's put down to his left? It looks to me like…"

"A miner's helmet, complete with a teapot lamp," confirmed Salt.

"Correct me if I'm wrong but those things burn oil don't they?"

"Yes, or fat."

"And it's a wick, yes? So you can adjust the flame?"

The constable did not bother to answer, nor had he been expected to. Instead, he exclaimed. "Breathing fire! Bloody hell. It was just a lamp after all. Breathing bloody fire!"

"Language constable, you are on duty," admonished his sergeant; then added, "but you're bloody well right. If this isn't our Spring Heeled Jack, I'll eat my hat."

"Shall we go and get him then?"

"No rush," the sergeant assured him, "look, he's starting again."

He was right. This time the human flea hopped from the canal side onto the toll island, and then with no pause and a flamboyant swing of the dumb bells cleared the water on the other side, to land on a little wooden jetty that protruded somewhat into the flat black liquid. It was a big jump, that second leg, certainly from a standstill. But the most remarkable thing about it was that as the muscular little legs flailed the air, as if seeking some secret and invisible but not insubstantial purchase, it looked as if he must surely fall short, must end up in the murky solution of dirt and dust and dross, and end up swimming for it. But no: as his right foot reached the surface, as it landed on it, he pushed himself off with barely a ripple and propelled himself forward. Or seemed to. As if the water were solid…

"Did you see that?" exclaimed the dumbfounded constable. Only in a whisper so as not to give them away, a soft but awestruck whisper that came out more like a wheeze.

"I did, I did. Or I think I did," replied the sergeant.

"How's that humanly possible," said Salt, more of an observation than a question.

"I don't know," admitted Abe Lively, pulling himself together, "but he's definitely just a man, not some kind of creature new to science. Must be some kind of trick; an optical illusion. Let's see if he does it again."

#

Joe Darby did do it again, several times. The illusion of taking off from water was one he had mastered long ago, and it was an old favourite at some of his regular venues. He was always looking to improve on it, however. But the technique was no good in a real competition, where entertainment value was of no consequence, only straight length. Or height, as the case may be. But it was a bit of fun, and in demonstration events it was a real show stopper. It would be all the more impressive next time he did it because he planned to do it in the dark, with flame, perhaps over a large tank. He had thought of modifying his weights with little torches which would illuminate his passage across the watery void with an eerie streak. But he had quickly discounted that for personal safety reasons, and had instead been experimenting with a leather miner's hat and lamp, tied on securely, but had not been pleased with the look of it, nor the risk of setting his head alight.

#

Joe's acrobatics over the canal along with the incriminating waiting headgear was enough for the sergeant. "That's it. There's your monster. Doesn't look so scary now does he?" he opined.

"Things seldom do when you understand them," replied the constable. Sagely, he thought. Then he was given his orders.

"I want you to take the right-hand bank here, and I'll take the left. Walk normally, don't rush, and stay four or five yards behind me. Don't want to scare him."

"Scare him? Serve him right," said Salt.

"Yes, well we don't want him running," cautioned the sergeant, "judging by what we've seen I doubt we could catch him. And we'll leave the sticks. He doesn't look like he could best either of us in a fight. And as I say, we don't want to scare him."

#

Jumping Joe was not scared, yet. He saw the man approaching, looking decidedly casual – suspicious – and was apprehensive. Not scared, but definitely apprehensive. It might well be perfectly innocent, somebody taking a shortcut. Or possibly one of Mr Crane's men sent to check on him. He would wait and see. Hardly a matter of life and death. But even if it became so – a matter of life and death – he could always scarper; nobody would be able to catch him. He was not about to abandon his belongings lightly, any of them. Then he detected another man approaching on the opposite bank. Why? To cut off his escape? They did not know him. He was not about to run yet, but his apprehension had increased. Now he was on the verge of scared. How to play this?

#

But he needed no answer to the question, for at that point it was forestalled by a hail from the man on his side of the water.

"Hello sir. I'm sorry for disturbing you. I'm a police officer and I'd like to ask you a few questions if I may."

He sounded polite enough, but what did that count for? He also had the tone and bearing of a typical copper, but that could have been an act. And if he was what he said he was, why was he sneaking round down here, with a comrade but no uniform? And Joe had met some coppers, proper policemen to all appearances, whose uniforms were nothing more than the proverbial sheep's clothing. You couldn't be too careful…

He saw no need to run yet. He could see both of them clearly now and he was well within escape distance. Both were big and powerful, he could tell that, and that was to their disadvantage in a chase with someone small and powerful, and light. Plenty of time yet…

"Who are you?" he shot back.

"It's the police, sir. I'm Sergeant Lively, and this is my colleague P.C. Salt, P.C. Samuel Salt. We saw you doing your exercises. We just need to talk to you for five minutes," the man assured him.

They felt like coppers; and they looked like bruisers, but the two were not contradictory, quite the opposite in fact. But why no uniforms?

"Where are your uniforms then?"

"Special orders tonight. My orders," returned the man glibly, "plain clothes duty. I have a warrant card if you would like to see it," he said, reaching into his jacket and striding forward.

"Wait!" snapped Joe. The man obeyed. "How do I know you've not been sent to harm me?"

"Harm you sir? We're the police, we're not your enemy. Do you have enemies, sir? Or are you hiding something, from the law that is?"

That sounded like another copper question to Joe. He looked tough, but not beat up. Not like a hired thug. And he had heard that name, Lively.

"Show me the card then," said Joe, "but stay there." Both strangers halted and the nearer one held up a piece of paper or card enclosed in some kind wallet, held open. Too far away to make out detail though.

#

Abe could see that the young man was twitchy. He wondered why that might be; who a law-abiding citizen might be afeared of. He also knew he could not read the card from this distance, but he had to slow him down; make him think twice. This was his prime Spring Heeled Jack suspect, and he was not about to lose him. And if it turned out that this person was not after all responsible for the recent panic, Abe was nevertheless fomenting a plan to ensure that he ended it.

"I know you can't read it from there," said the policeman slipping the card back into his pocket. "We don't have to come any closer, but I can prove we're the police if you let me. Agreed? Or do you have something to hide?"

"How?" answered the acrobat, "and no, I've got nothing to hide from the law."

"That's all good then," said Abe, reassuringly he hoped. "You stay there then, and look, here's my police whistle. I'm going to summon my colleagues who have concealed themselves a bit further on."

"Go on then," said the young man.

Abe gave two short blasts and a long one. Nothing happened. His quarry started edging back. "I'll try again."

He did. This time running feet could be heard; approaching.

#

Joe spotted two men coming as fast as they dared. Unfortunately for them they were on the opposite bank and therefore out of the game, because Joe would not cross. Not when he would be outnumbered three to one. No, he preferred the odds this side, and he fancied his chances of showing this chap a clean pair of heels; well, a sooty pair of heels anyway. As he had feared, somebody was out to get him. But who? Why? But these were questions for another time: scooping up only his trousers, he ran. And as he ran he was

223

aware of the fake sergeant Lively chasing after him. He would soon lose him between familiar obstacles and the gathering gloom. As he raced round an old blown boiler he ran into something solid which hadn't been there yesterday. It caught him on the top of the chest and, thanks to the momentum imparted by those powerful springs of legs, the bottom part of his body carried on whilst the top half remained blocked. The result? As to be expected his body went from vertical to horizontal, seemingly suspended at neck height for an impossible interval, before, gravity asserting itself, it plummeted down to hit the hard rough ground. Joe just had time to wonder why he hadn't noticed a beam there before, when the breath and sense was momentarily knocked out of him by his not so soft landing. After he managed to persuade his lungs that they really must continue with their allotted task, after the pain in his head had registered on a scale below unbearable, after he realised that nothing was broken and when, finally his eyes were able to focus, he bade them look up to identify what had brought him down. He was shaken, bruised and cut probably, but perhaps all was not lost. Perhaps he was not going to get an 'ommerin' – or worse. For what he saw was the distinctive silhouette of a young uniformed police constable. And as it sank in he heard the footsteps and then the voice he had recently become acquainted with.

"Well done Josh. What kept you?"

The uniform moved slightly to talk to the voice. Joe realised that the beam that had laid him low had been the one attached to this copper's shoulder. The uniform was talking now. A soft voice, young but firm.

"Sorry about that Abe – sergeant. Stride and Payne had an argument about the signal. Payne thought that it had meant 'come urgently, support required' – or words to that effect – while Stride insisted that it meant 'suspect coming your way.' Your second whistle decided us!"

"Well, P.C. Stride almost mucked things up. As well as getting our friend here a clobbering."

"I didn't clobber him," protested Josh, "I merely put out my arm to stop him, he was getting a good head of steam up and I just thought…"

"Josh. Josh! No need to apologise. I know you weren't trying to hurt him. Relax, you've done a good job here. Good work…Now who have we here?" said Abe, offering his hand to the recumbent jumper.

By the time Abe had caught up with the still dazed runner and his brother, P.C.s Stride and Payne had met up with constable Salt and were now separated from the scene of the recent action by some twenty feet of water.

"Do you need any assistance?" enquired Stride blithely.

"Does it look like?" replied the sergeant testily, "Are you looking to take on the mantle of station buffoon? Because you're well on the way today. Get yourself round here sharpish. All of you, we're done."

Ah'd 'ave to be gooin sum to compete wi' Clark, was Stride's grumpy observation – which of course he kept to himself whilst moving himself to the nearest bridge, sharpish, as ordered. He had to admit though that it had been a totally inapt and extraneous question: with the man floored and so firmly in the brothers' grasp they all saw that the answer to the question was an emphatic no. Why had he opened his mouth? Misplaced politeness perhaps? Now the sergeant was in a mood, and he was in the firing line. *Keep a low profile Stevie…*

It had been a silly question. Abe and Josh had a firm grip on their much smaller and still half stunned suspect as Stride had shouted over. The sergeant was already put out by Stride's spoke in the operational wheel, arguing the toss about the signal. He was losing patience with ineptitude. *Silly bleeder…*

After his head had cleared their captive sat up, and they helped him to his feet. Immediately they took his wrists and cuffed them. "What's this for?" complained the prisoner gesturing, as best he could, to the hand cuffs which pinned his arms behind his back.

"Just a precaution," said the big man mechanically as he gave them an unpleasant yank, presumably to check that the constable had applied them correctly. Joe had by now concluded that this was not the fake sergeant Lively, as he had earlier inaccurately surmised, but in fact a genuine policeman, the real sergeant Lively. And now that he was caught and immobilised he noticed that he had dropped the 'sir.'

"All right then, Sergeant Lively is it?" began Joe, "What's all this about?"

"We've had a complaint about suspicious goings on along the canal hereabouts. It's raised concerns amongst local citizens."

"What citizens?" asked the jumper with suspicion, as the three from the other side arrived. "Look sergeant, if you're implying that I'm the cause of this 'concern' I have to tell you that I come down here precisely to avoid my fellow citizens. I'm trying to get some serious training in here."

"Training for what?"

"You must have seen me."

"Just answer the question."

"All right. You've never heard of Josey Darby? Even in passing?"

"Can't say that I have. And that's you is it? Josey Derby?"

"Yes, well, Joseph Darby to use my proper Christian name. And Darby as in the end."

"Don't come the clever son. So that's Joseph Darby, Darby spelt with an 'A'?"

"That's correct sergeant."

"Glad we sorted that out. Are you keeping a note of this Stride?"

In a self-induced protective cocoon, the mention of his name shocked the out of favour constable into a stammer: "What? Notes you say?"

"That's right. I hope you're keeping notes."

"Yes, yes. Certainly. Notes, yes."

"So what have you got so far?"

Stride might have been keeping a low profile but there was nothing wrong with his ears. Years of experience enabled him to cover and to slip straight into what the sergeant wanted to hear: "Suspect apprehended at approximately 9.15 p.m. on the canal bank adjacent to Windmill End; suspect had been attempting to flee but was detained by constable Lively pending the imminent arrival on the scene of sergeant Lively who had given chase; suspect described as of medium height, slim but muscular build, dark haired and aged between twenty and thirty; suspect gave his name as Joseph Darby – with an 'A' – and was wearing…"

The said sergeant Lively interrupted him. "Yes, that will do Stride. Now Mr Darby, you were saying?"

"Why is he calling me a suspect? Suspected of what?"

"Never mind about that, it's just the way we report things. Back to business: you were about to tell me about your training. Please be specific."

"All right, I jump things. For money sometimes. I'm good at it. I'm so good that I'm challenging for the world title later this year. That's what I'm training for."

"Didn't know there was such a thing," commented Josh.

"Nor I," said his brother, "sounds impressive doesn't it?" He may have sounded a little sceptical.

"And it's true!" interjected an animated Joe Darby, "what's more I intend to win. What's more again, folk around here know me, it's my home patch. That's partly why I chose this place: I try not to attract attention, but if anybody did happen to see me these last few nights they would know who I was and what I was doing, or should have."

"Nevertheless," continued the sergeant, "we have a witness to your crepuscular activities. One you have very nearly frightened out of her wits."

"Her wits?" repeated the detainee. "Who are you talking about? Come on, don't I have a right to know?"

"I suppose you do. Very well, we have received a complaint from a Mrs Maureen Thompson, a widow…"

"That explains it!" exclaimed young Joe. "That old bat. She's an evil old cow, she is. She's having you on. She knows me very well, and what I do – and she doesn't like me."

"Oh? And why is that?" questioned sergeant Lively.

"I was at school with her son. Best mates we were, and after. She's jealous that's all."

"Jealous? What, of your, er, career?"

"There is that. But she's mostly jealous just 'cause I'm alive."

"Doesn't sound like much of a motive," said Lively.

"Ah, but it is you see. Because he's dead. Chewed up by a winding engine. And here's me his happy pal still breathing in and out and getting on with life."

"So she's got it in for you has she?"

"Yes. But for anybody really. Only pleasure she gets. She must be laughing her socks off about this. What exactly did she say about me?"

At this point, constable Salt stepped in, squinting at his note book in the fading light. "She said that she had seen a monster – that would be you sir – clothed in shadows and breathing fire and leaping over the canal."

"That's a load of oss muck that is," opined the captive.

"I don't know so much," said the sergeant. "We saw you doing your so-called training. Quite remarkable really. So tell me, just how far can you jump?"

But young Joe was angry about the calumny which had been perpetrated by the perfidious widow, and he was still thinking about it. "And what the bloody 'ell does that mean, 'clothed in shadows'? I mean, I ask ya. You can see what I'm wearing. As for breathing fire, there's this lamp o' course, but, I don't know. Breathing fire? Really?"

Abe was starting to sympathise. He found that he liked this man; liked his straightforward manner and his obvious dedication to bettering himself.

"In any case," continued the young athlete, "I know where moaning Mo lives, and there's no way she can see this bit of the cut from her house, and this bit of the cut's where I've been coming, not up by the basin where she looks out."

"He's right Sarge," confirmed Salt, "this bit's not visible from where the widow says she looks out."

"There you are then," said Joe triumphantly.

But Abe had not finished with him yet. "So you deny do you Mr Darby, practising your acrobatics over Mrs Thompson's bit of cut, as you describe it?"

"I do indeed, sergeant. So am I free to go then?"

"So Mrs Thompson was lying then?" prompted the sergeant.

"Let's just say that she was mistaken," said Joe in charitable vein.

"And you've never tried your jumping up there?"

"Not at all. It's not private enough. And I can't practise water jumping up there, the cut's far too wide. I can only do it here because of these narrow stretches."

"That reminds me," said the sergeant, "you didn't answer the question."

"What question?"

"How far can you jump?"

"In a single bound, from a static position, what we call a spring jump, with weights, I can do fourteen foot six and a half, but I'm improving all the time. Without my weights it's less but I can do a bit more with a run up of course, but not round cluttered places like this and definitely not enough to clear the width of the cut up there. Besides it's spring jumping I'm training for…"

227

"If that's the case, then it would seem put you in the clear, because I think, from memory, the width up there is considerably more than fourteen or fifteen feet. Would you agree Josh?"

"Certainly," replied his brother. "At least twenty feet, I would have thought."

"And the rest. That's what I was…" began Joe Darby

"Which," continued the sergeant, "gets you off the hook. Unless of course you were lying about your abilities."

"Don't be saft. I'm good, but I'm not that good. Who do you think I am, Spring Heeled Jack?"

Abe could not resist. "Now, it's funny you should say that sir," he returned, key to the handcuffs poised. The young jumper did not take the bait, so he continued, "Look, you're not under arrest, but I would deem it a great favour if you would accompany me back to the station for a chat."

"How could I refuse?"

Chapter 19

Cutler and Crane

The day after the night of the detention of the pseudo Spring Heeled Jack, aka Jumping Joe Darby, Cyril Crane was having a business meeting – more of an interview really – with his foreman. This foreman presided over a shadowy group of men; a group of men upon whom Cyril Crane relied, but over whom immediate control had been delegated to said trusted foreman. If you could describe Jack Cutler as Crane's foreman, then these 'shadow–men' were his employees. Unofficial ones of course, and by no means upright rate paying citizens; lawless types in fact. Jack as middleman suited Cyril: he was an effective buffer against any allegation of impropriety, not to say criminality. Whilst Cyril kept his hands clean, any mud would, hopefully, only be thrown as far as, and stick to, Mr Cutler. And that had a value, and Jack Cutler knew his worth, and Cyril Crane therefore paid him handsomely, although not quite, in Jack's opinion, commensurate to the responsibility he bore and the risks he took. Cyril knew, or rather suspected (for Jack was good at keeping secrets) that his lieutenant had other irons in other fires, but had always been prepared to ignore them as long as Jack did his job and as long as he did not engage with any enterprise which brought suspicion sniffing round Cyril's door, such as that farcical sheep rustling incident. But if the third party shield provided by Cutler, Cyril's safety fence as it were, was advantageous, it also came with one major and decidedly detrimental corollary: the more contact that Cutler had with 'the men' the less they came into contact with Crane, naturally promoting the former's influence at the expense of the latter's. In fact, of late, Cyril had come to suspect that there was very little that was natural about that process of divorce; the fact that most of his old and trusted minions had faded away, to be replaced by young bloods noticeably friendly with Cutler, he now regarded as fishy to say the least. Yes, there was a natural turnover of staff in any trade, and it was by no means a rare occurrence in his business for an operative to be present and correct one minute, only, for excellent reasons connected with life and liberty, to have disappeared abruptly from the face of the earth by the next. But this? This was too convenient, and a trend not in his favour. Where did the fresh faces look for leadership? As far as Cutler he thought. He could guess at his motives, and it made him uncomfortable.

Cyril looked across the table at the sharp dressed young man sitting opposite. The outward nattiness distracted from the ordered and sharp mind behind the façade. For Cutler was adept at concealing his intellect when it suited him. A dark little fox, whose handsome features and genial front one could easily take to – unless it was your chicken coop he was raiding. *Are you Jack? Are you after my chickens?* The animated dark eyes quickly revised the last of the written notes in front of him, and then Mr Cutler began his summary.

"So, after allowing for expenses, we should be on for another good month. Perhaps not as lucrative as the month previous, but not far off. Not at all bad," he concluded.

"I think you're being a little financially prudent, if I may say so. That bare knuckle do at The Tavern almost doubled the average week's takings on stakes. At least that's what it says here," rejoined Cyril, tapping a ledger.

"I know. But, as you say, it was an extraordinary event, in more ways than one. That's why the expenses were so high."

"And there we have it. The expenses. Some of these entries are a bit vague."

"Vague?"

"Yes, vague. The income and expenditure is all laid out clearly, but what that expenditure is, particularly when it comes down to 'miscellaneous' expenses is none too clear to me."

"I'm sorry. I don't like to go into too much detail. I mean, if I put down something like 'bribe for Inspector Oakden to turn a blind eye' or 'cost of two whores for the night to keep the customers coming' how would it look if it fell into the wrong hands?"

"If any of this fell into the wrong hands as you put it, such sordid little details would make not one jot of difference. But to me, here…To me they are important. Is that clear?"

"Crystal," said Cutler coldly, and his soft brown eyes went as hard and black and cold as flakes of obsidian in snow.

Cyril could not make his mind up if Cutler's cooling was because he resented being caught out, or because he resented the slur on his professional ethics; nor could he be sure that Cutler had not allowed him to see the change, to make him wonder just that. He decided to set a little test.

"All right, still at The Tavern, what's this £3?"

"Where about is that?"

Cyril took his book and pointed to the entry. "It just says 'additional fee, BR.' Why should I accept that? Right off the bottom line that is. That kind of thing is open to abuse, you must know that."

"Boss, you know I do. And like I said, the entries are cryptic for our own protection. But you see that little tick below it? That means there's a separate note about it."

"Where?" queried Cyril.

"In here." Cutler fished out a well-worn note book from his back pocket and placed it on the desk. "Now, let's look at the page number on the ledger, yes, and…" as he spoke he was rustling through pencil-filled dog-eared leaves of thin paper, "it was £3 you said. £3 exactly it was. I know it was because I remember what it was for. There you are." He tossed the open book to Cyril. "There's only one tick per page, and the ledger page number corresponds to this page in the notes. There's the tick in the notes look; there's the reference to the page in that ledger; and there's the note. Shall I read it for you? My writing's not exactly copper plate."

"Please," said Cyril simply.

"Right – 'additional £3 paid to the landlord of The Tavern for use of premises, Saturday 16th July, 1887. Paid to Roy Bastable Friday 15th July, 1887.' That's the BR referred to in the ledger, only the initials inverted for security."

"Hold on," said Cyril, "I thought we paid him his agreed fee a week before this."

"We did. But he had the coppers sniffing round on the Thursday. It was that Oakden on a fishing expedition. Unnerved him. Didn't let on but the inspector made all sorts of threats about what would happen if and when. So, he got cold feet at the last minute."

"But he should have stuck to the deal. Rather than paying him you should have roughed him up."

"I considered it, but it was a bit close to the event, with everybody laid on. Didn't want anybody questioning black eyes and broken fingers. And I certainly didn't want to make an enemy of him, we've worked together profitably in the past as you know."

"So you decided to throw my money at him instead."

"I thought it best. It was with the proviso that if Oakden found out, he would have to use it to buy him off. And that if he didn't – get rid of the nosey git that is – then he would get a clobbering. But, as you know, that's not good for business, generally. A last resort…"

"I'm still three quid down."

"I know, and I'll make sure we get it back next time."

Cyril was not prepared to let it go at that. He was still testing. "I think I want it back now. We can find somewhere else for the next event as you call it. Sounds to me like our Mr Bastable's losing his bottle in any case. I want you to go and get the money back."

Jack paused before replying. "You're the boss," he said.

Glad you remember. "This note book Jack?"

"Yes?"

"Why do you keep it on you?"

"For convenience really. And security again. You can't be too careful. Wouldn't do to keep all the pieces of the jigsaw in one place, would it?"

"Quite," said Cyril, not really meaning it, "tell me, I suppose you get receipts for such payments?"

"Only rarely, and they're coded. But most people, the last thing they want is any kind of record, coded or not."

"So how…" began Cyril.

"How are the entries verified?" suggested Jack, "they're all witnessed. Look, there's my signature on this one, and there's the signature, or rather the mark, of the witness."

"Who is?" enquired Cyril.

"A Mr Derek Woolley, of our acquaintance."

More yours than mine. "But of course," replied Cyril.

Jack reacted to sarcasm when it suited him. "Look Boss, if you don't trust me, please tell me. And if you don't, anymore, what have I done? Give me a chance to defend myself."

"Who said I don't trust you?"

"All these questions did."

"Routine business practice."

"You never used to ask so many. What's changed?"

"I suppose I've got more time on my hands these days."

"Well, that's partly down to me, I like to think. So, you're saying that I'm the victim of my own success? Because we have been successful together, haven't we?"

Cyril could not deny it. And he began to doubt his doubts. But then he remembered how cunning his opponent was. No, their past relationship was no guarantee of future events. And no, he was sure that Jack would not be satisfied with the status quo. But when would he make his move? If Cyril just sacked him, he could take most of the workforce with him. *Play along for now.*

"You're right of course," said Crane, "things are on the up and up, and I'm grateful."

"As am I," said Cutler, "your trust buys a lot of loyalty."

"Yes, I'm sure it does," agreed the boss. *As well as my cash.* "We do make a good team."

"I'm glad we agree," said the little man. *Good team be damned. Why are you bringing your nephew in to spy on me then? And it's not a team when there's one on top.*

"Nevertheless," continued Crane, asserting his position, "I want that three quid back. See what you can do will you?"

"I'll get the dog then," said Cutler, retrieving Boadicea's lead from the floor. At that, there was a knocking at the door. The dogs, Boadicea and Sabre, who had lain quiet until now, both took notice and stood. Bo was suspicious, but Sabre knew that knock, and his tail wagged. "Who's that, we're closed," intoned Jack Cutler automatically.

"That will be our John…" said Cyril.

Our John? He's no family of mine.

"Let him in on the way out would you?"

"I'll do that," came the short reply. The little man turned to leave, his rescued dog and a three quid debt in tow.

From the passage, muffled greetings. "A'do John."

"Jack. How you doing?"

"Can't complain. Even if it is raining."

"And how's Bo?"

"She's great."

"Yes she's a lovely dog, aren't you girl? Right then, see you later."

"Right you are."

A slam and footsteps. John came in brushing little drops of dewy drizzle from his jacket. He took off his hat and shook it. "Sabre! Come on boy."

The big dog ran to him and they wrestled playfully. With difficulty, John Lively side-stepped the rambunctious beast to make the table, signalling a truce.

"Is the door locked?" his uncle enquired?

"Yes. I slid the bolt."

"Good, sit down then." John did so.

"So," continued the uncle, business-like, "anything unusual to report?"

"About Jack you mean?"

"That's right. Anything?"

"It's early days of course, but as far as I can tell he runs the lads fairly and efficiently. Like a well-oiled machine as they say. And they only involve themselves in your business, as you've explained it to me, nothing else. Seems to be above board. He keeps records of any money changing hands, as I think you know."

"Books can be fiddled," remarked Cyril.

"I don't suppose it's unusual in this line of work to run into characters out to skim a bit off the top," offered John.

"No, but it's where it might lead that worries me. I told you about that sheep stealing incident didn't I? The one that got your brother calling?"

"Yes you did. He was wrong to involve you of course, but apart from that, what's the deal? I mean, do you expect exclusive rights to his time and activities?"

"No, I don't. But that sheep stealing stuff was just too reckless. As you say, it nearly incriminated me. And a boy was killed too."

"Killed?"

"Fell in front of my horse drunk. But the bloody horse should never have been out."

"I didn't know that. I mean, not that it was your horse."

"No, our Jack wouldn't mention that would he? Borrowed without permission. And the trouble with him going off and running little scams on his own is that he won't keep it small. He's too ambitious and too confident. Sooner or later, I'll be in the way."

"So you suspect his loyalty?"

"I suspect his disloyalty. What do you think?"

"Well, he does strike me as a bit of a bastard. But a straight bastard. Good company too."

"You just watch it. He's as changeable as the weather. And he's got an ugly side."

"If you say so. But, as I say, he seems to be doing a straight job. Hard to tell whether money's going missing of course, given that records can be falsified. I suppose you're the best judge of that."

Cyril changed tack. "What about friends. Seen anybody you didn't know?"

"No. Just the usual gang. And the dog of course. He's like you in that; loves that dog."

"The dog's not an issue, but the gang is. You wouldn't know this but since Jack's been with me he's replaced all my old stalwarts with new people loyal to him. I don't have to spell out to you that that's dangerous."

John let this sink in before replying. "Look. Like I said, I find him good company; always gets his round in, never stingy; polite to women and patient with kids. A good loff as they say. But. But you're family and I work for you, that's the first thing. The second is that if Jack has replaced all your people with his own, then you have to question his motive. If you say he's a threat, if you need to move against him, then I'm with you."

"Thanks, son. That makes three of us then."

"Three?"

"You, me and mad Mick O'Rourke."

John shook his head. "Lord help us then. Come to think of it though, with Mick on our side, Lord help them."

"So you see, he can't whittle us down any more. If I'm right about him – and I can't afford not to assume I am – then he could make his move any time," explained Cyril.

"So what do we do?" asked John.

Well, it just so happens that that nasty bag of washing Solomon Mallen is looking for a favour.

"That's the bloke from Cradley Heath, the dog fighter?"

"Yes, together with his entourage of so-called trainers and bookies, and toughs."

"How does that help us? I thought you said you don't like dog fighters, and Solomon Mallen even less."

"I'm glad you remember. So that when I tell you that I will be facilitating a meet for him here on our patch, you will guess, I hope, that I have a hidden agenda."

"Well, if I hadn't guessed, you've told me now. What's the plan?"

"The plan, such as it's clear to me at present, involves you and your brother, the eminent Sergeant Lively."

"How?"

"Let's just say that – just supposing – that the law got wind of a big illegal event, well in advance you understand, so that they had ample time to prepare. What would they do?"

"Lie in wait probably," surmised John Lively, "and what would be the source of this ill wind, or who?" he asked, knowing the answer.

"I'm looking at him," smirked Cyril.

John pursed his lips dubious, and shook his head. "I know I've not been in the business for long, but I do know what everybody thinks of informants, and what can happen to them."

"But that's the beauty of it," declared his uncle, "you won't be informing. Not on me, and not on your workmates, except one."

"Cutler you mean?"

"Cutler I mean."

"I don't know about this."

"But you just said you would help."

"That was before you mentioned bringing Abe in on anything."

"We're not bringing him in," his uncle assured him, "he will just be acting on information received. Should be quite a feather in his cap. He'll love you for it."

"You think so? Why don't you tell him then?"

"Because he doesn't trust me for one. For another, he might be tempted to name me as his source."

But John disagreed. "No, you're wrong. He wouldn't wish to harm you."

"Nevertheless," cautioned the old man, "let's make it cast iron shall we? You will have to be the one. It will have to be presented as if I know nothing about it; a genuine inside tip."

"Lie to him you mean?"

"It's not a lie. It will be true what you tell him. Don't mention me at all; he will make the assumption for you."

"So what's your end objective?"

"To kill two birds with one stone, Cutler and Mallen, together with as many of his cronies – Mallen's – as get swept up with him. Unlike the birds, they won't be dead of course, unfortunately, just locked away at her majesty's pleasure."

"I need time to think about it."

"Don't take too long. I'll make it worth your while. How's that young lady of yours by the way?"

"She's fine and dandy," said big John.

"That's nice. I'm pleased for you. They tell me you're planning on moving in together."

John had no clue who 'they' might be but was not surprised at Cyril's accurate summation of his intentions. "That's right," he said, "she wants to set up in her own shop. But that takes money of course."

"Exactly," pronounced his uncle. "As I say, don't take too long to decide."

#

Sergeant Lively was on his beat in Cock Green and intending to call in at the offices of the Blackheath Advertiser. As he was turning over in his mind what he would say when he got there, he rounded the corner into Tippity Green, half paying attention, and came face to face with a man walking a dog. At first intending to make room, he realised he knew this man.

"Good day," said the policeman, "it's Mr Cutler isn't it?"

"That's correct sergeant. We met at your uncle's."

"That's right. What are you doing in this neck of the woods?" He was just making conversation, but, after all, he was on duty and in uniform. No surprise then that Jack Cutler did not take it that way. And particularly unsurprising given the shock to his system, bumping into the law, when he had only just stepped out of the workhouse within which, as the sergeant would know well enough, Mr Cutler could not possibly have any business. Not of the legitimate kind at any rate.

"I'm just walking my dog, as you can see. It's important to exercise them. Nothing illegal in that is there?"

"Good Lord, no. I was just surprised to see you."

And I you. "Same here," said Jack.

"So, what's his name?"

"She. It's Boadicea."

"Nice dog," said Abe. He moved to pat her on the head, but whether because conscious of this man interrupting her walk, or of the fact that he was not entirely comfortable around dogs, or for some other reason, this animal was not about to be petted. As the policeman switched his attention from owner to companion, he was persuaded to change his mind about physical contact. Persuaded by a curled lip, red gums, white teeth, and a soft growl.

"She doesn't take to strangers," her owner explained. *Well, not you anyway.*

And then Jack Cutler split his face in a burst of genuine amusement.

"It's no laughing matter…" began the sergeant, taking a step back and looking at the dog again.

"No, it wasn't that it was the bird."

"What bird?"

"Didn't you just see that?"

"What?"

"Your little friend. I saw him following you up the street."

Abe turned and checked behind him. Nothing. He turned and faced Cutler with a question.

"It landed right on your shoulder," explained Jack, "you saw him, surely? Or felt him."

"I don't know what you're talking about," said Abe. But he suspected. He could feel it.

"You're joking," returned Jack.

"No, I'm not. What?"

"A bird. It was a little bird. A robin. It looked like it was talking to you."

"A robin you say. I didn't see it."

"It's gone now. You were distracted by Bo I think. Perhaps that's what upset her. Strange."

"As you say, strange," said Abe. He did not feel like discussing his 'little friend' with Cutler.

But Jack was not ready to drop it. "Mind you, I've heard tell of robins becoming very tame, even eating out of people's hands. So perhaps it's understandable. It just looked a bit comical. Sorry."

"I'm sure it did," replied sergeant Lively. He didn't feel like laughing though. Something had been bothering him, haunting him almost, since he had dozed off under that tree over the Hailstone. A robin, or something, had landed on him then too. And while it had been all in his own head, while nobody else had seen it, as Clark had failed to notice it hopping up and down on Reg Phillips' body like it wanted to draw attention, he could persuade himself that it was all imagination, brought on no doubt by that crack on the skull. But now that excuse was gone. For now someone else had seen it. Perhaps also a dog. Or was it all coincidence, just a friendly robin somebody had been feeding? But why growl at a little bird? It hadn't really been a bird, he knew that. He had tried to think back, and he didn't think robins moved quite like that, not with such exaggerated hops, like miniature…

But good. Cutler had seen it. Good, he wasn't going mad. Nevertheless all this was unsettling, to say the least. What did it want? Was it really trying to tell him something? Perhaps if it succeeded it would go away. They went away before, when he was a boy. And then it struck him. It had appeared on Reg's corpse, and it had appeared now, whilst he was talking to Cutler. Perhaps bumping into him was not an accident. After all he knew that Jack Cutler walked the shady side of the streets. So he asked him.

"Joking aside, I'm glad I've met you today: I'm conducting an investigation and I'm getting nowhere. You know a lot of the local characters, and I was wondering if you'd heard anything."

"What kind of investigation is it?"

Abe weighed the word carefully, tone and pitch, then with a poker expression, let it drop. 'Murder.'

If he was expecting shock to register, it didn't. Neither did guilt.

"Murder?" repeated Cutler, apparently with nothing more than passing curiosity, "whose murder?"

"Did you know old Reginald Phillips?"

Just a flicker, then "That's the old bloke who threw himself off the bridge, isn't it? Suicide, I heard."

"Well, that verdict's still open," said the copper.

"So what makes you suspect murder?" asked Cutler.

A little too casually?

"That's information that has to remain confidential for now."

"I understand," said Jack. He understood only too well. *Bloody hell Woolley boy, what trail have you left? It better be a dead end.*

"So you've not heard any whispers," prompted the copper.

More than whispers, but you're not to know.

"I hardly knew the old fellah," said Jack. "I think I've seen him pottering around once or twice, but I never really took much notice. Just another poor old nobody to be frank. The most fame he got was by killing himself – dying," he corrected.

"Well, I'd be grateful if you would keep your ears open."

"You can count on it. May I?" he asked, nodding in his direction of travel.

"Yes of course. I shan't detain you. Good day."

"Good day," rejoined Jack Cutler, and lost no time in continuing his peregrinations.

As Abe continued on his way, he got to thinking again. He instinctively distrusted that man and was not entirely convinced by his avowal of ignorance. He decided that he would compile a list of his known associates and see if any links revealed themselves. Links to what he was not quite sure yet, but one thing he was sure of: bumping into Cutler was not pure chance. He would trust his little friend in that.

#

Some time later, Jack found himself in Blackheath. It was approaching midday now and he found himself at a bit of a loose end. A pint? Why not? He happened to be looking straight at the Royal Oak. He had been in there precisely once since arriving in these parts. Not that it wasn't a nice enough pub, it was; a cut above. But it was his pub, the sergeant's, or at least he lived there. With his sister, withal. Enemy territory really. And so, although so close to the Shoulder, he avoided it. Usually. But today? Why not? What the hell. If Lively could stop him in the street and poke his nose into Jack's business, Jack could stop for a drink at Lively's pub and poke around in his. In a manner of speaking.

"Come on Darling," he said to his faithful companion, who dutifully followed.

The room was just as he remembered it, polished wood and polished brass and varnished walls all catching variously-hued reflections from the small fire. There was invariably a daytime fire in these establishments, everybody was drawn to the life of fire. Comforting, to be sure, good for business. Besides, it was quite a big room and noticeably cooler than outdoors. There was another room, the obligatory 'snug'; filled with smoke and claustrophobic warmth, where the old and decrepit tended to gather, probably, he surmised idly, to keep the life force from oozing from their cold thin bones. Jack did not like snugs. Just the word gave him the collywobbles, reminded him of cockroaches in

238

crevices. Passing the time with dull pastimes until the release of a dull death. If they were lucky.

Jack took to few people, unless to use them. As a rule. But old ones downright depressed him. He would never get that old. He would never be a snug dweller. There were plenty of places around whose layout consisted of a central pouring point serving a jungle of such small rooms, all potential 'snugs.' Jack avoided them like the plague, although that was not difficult: unlike most working men (and Jack was proud of his origins, if not a manual worker himself these days) he was not overly dependent on the comfort of alcohol. Perhaps, having found a way to avoid a life of debilitating physical toil, he had never developed a need for that particular crutch. Or perhaps Jack was just different. He certainly felt that he was. However, he did appreciate a well-kept pint, but would usually make two or three last all night. Neither did he smoke. And women? Complications. If he did have a vice it was that he resolutely looked after number one, but then again, some would call that a virtue. Ten years he reckoned. Ten years and he would have enough. He was a young man and didn't want to age and fatten here. Ten good years and he was gone, retired, living the life of Reilly. Might even call himself Reilly. Or Rooney; he could get away with an Irish accent...

He bought a pint from a middle-aged ginger-haired woman whose eyelashes reminded him of a pig, and he retired to a chair with its back to the wall and giving him a good view of both the bar and the doors. It was quiet yet. Besides himself and Bo, there were two quiet but hard looking women with their heads together over what looked like glasses of gin. Squandering their housekeeping and cooking up trouble for some poor bloke or other. Also, there was an unwelcome leak of the inevitable oldies from their inner snug sanctum: four trespassers; only four as yet for it was early to start drinking, particularly when you were virtually penniless. Fortunately, they confined themselves to a discrete little alcove, studying cards before laying them down silently and sucking beer not quite so but sparingly. There was just an irregular soft flutter of sound at the end of each hand, a release of minor tension, then back to their mute manoeuvrings.

And then there was someone else. Sticking out like a sore thumb with his smart jacket and fancy waistcoat. Jack noticed that he was in a possession of a cane, like his own. But probably not that much like his. New to town, without a doubt, he was holding a handsome lady captive, bound by a loop of incessant chatter. He knew her – Miriam Lively, as was. Jack could not make out what the fancy waistcoat was saying; whatever it was, the sergeant's sister did not look bored exactly. In fact, she seemed to be enjoying herself. Interesting, her being only a few months' wed, or re-wed. What would her husband think? Or the sergeant?

Presently, she broke away and disappeared through a door, presumably into a private part of the building. With nothing to look at behind the bar, the stranger turned on his elbow and surveyed the room. Not much to look at there, so it was not a complete surprise when the garrulous stranger's eyes alighted on and fixed Jack's table. Jack looked back.

He was struck by the man's features: they were much like his own; a bystander might assume they were brothers. But a bystander of discrimination would of course notice the difference, for whereas Jack was olive-skinned, this man was unhealthily swarthy; where Cutler was lean faced, the other verged on the gaunt; and where young Jack's luxuriant jet black hair hung shining and free to his collar, this person's dark mop was blackened with excess oil, as if he had been attacked with a grease-gun, and swept back, clinging to his skull before hanging in a wedge behind and curling up like a duck's tail, and just as waterproof no doubt. In short, decided Jack with satisfaction, an inferior specimen. Except, perhaps, for his eyes. He had the same black eyes as Cutler, but different. If he had not known any better he might have described them as…But he had taken too long to take it all in: he was coming over. The last thing Jack wanted was a bloody nuisance assailing him with inconsequential chit-chat, but it looked like that's what he was about to get.

"Good morrow to you, sir," the suddenly adjacent voice cutting through his thoughts.

"It's past noon," Jack pointed out.

The stranger made an extravagant show of consulting his pocket watch. "So it is, so it is. My apologies; and Good day to you sir. And what a pleasant day it is if I may make so bold, to be imbibing of the juice of the barley and soaking up the bonhomie of good company."

It was pleasant enough till you came along. So bugger off.

If the stranger were a mind reader, it was a thick-skinned one. Persisting with the idea of making friendly contact, he thrust out his hand. "The name's Smith. Francis Smith." Thompson had decided on the subterfuge at the last minute. Couldn't be too careful.

Jack couldn't place the accent, and decided it was affected, like his manner. He couldn't say he liked the man, but then again there were few that he did like. Nevertheless, Jack's own convention dictated that he take any hand offered openly, whether in friendship, promise, apology, or whatever other motive as long as it was honest. He had no reason to suspect that this character had any devious design, therefore he took it. His firm hand did not meet a twin, for it met a soft and sweaty counterpart. Somehow, Jack felt infected, as if the weak flaccidity were a symptom of some debilitating illness. A disease transmitted by touch. Jack was not used to feeling like this – uneasy he felt. And he wanted nothing so much as to take his hand back, but he was held as if in soft sucking quicksand.

It was Bo who rescued him. She had been curled up half asleep before the Smith character came over. Now, she was up, pushing between them possessively, hackles raised. A growl turned to frantic wet barks. Unsurprisingly, Thompson quickly disengaged and backed off. Jack stopped his dog barking, but she was distressed now and would not lie down again. She was normally a placid beast. But this was the second time today that she had taken against someone. The copper first, now this. He hoped that she was not sickening. Rabies? But you don't get rabies in Blackheath; not in this day and age. No, nothing was wrong with her. It's just this bloke. The copper, he could understand, a traditional adversary, she had picked up on that. But she was worse now, really upset.

Jack looked to Thomson. How to describe that expression? Secretly smug? Or did he always look like that?

"You're upsetting her. Go away."

Thompson obliged by putting his now empty glass down on an adjoining table and taking himself back to the bar where he retrieved his propped-up stick. The landlady had returned to investigate the commotion: he bade her a rather old fashioned and flowery adieu, turned, and made his way to the door by a circuitous route. Safely there, he span round sharply before pointing with ire and his stick: "You ought to keep that animal under control," he advised.

"Thanks for the tip mate," said Cutler apparently quite calmly, "mind how you go, won't you?"

Thompson was gone; Miriam saw the situation defused and carried on with her business. But Jack Cutler had not finished with Mr Smith. Nobody spoke about his dog like that. First off, he would have a word with his new friend John about the bounder's conduct toward his sister, see if he couldn't get him roughed up by proxy. Shouldn't be too difficult if he told it right, which is to say, wrong. Give the other one something to think about an' all.

#

Following an interesting conversation with the editor of the Advertiser, Abraham Lively was leaving its premises even as the poet was vacating the Royal Oak. But whereas Thompson had taken his leave on a sour note, the sergeant was well pleased with himself. Moses Munn had promised to be a tough nut to crack being at one and the same time both a cynic and a noser out of good stories. A sceptical disposition well suited his journalistic career, although in all fairness it had to be allowed that the scepticism would probably never have come into being had it not been for his choice of said career; no spring-chicken, he had a gut feel for the truth of things, although he often disregarded it in the pursuit of sales. Thus, he had bent the facts, even invented a few, to fuel his Spring Heeled Jack articles. But, the story was already old news, and he was unsure how much mileage was left in it in any case. So when the sergeant came knocking with a suggestion for another article, ostensibly to 'put the record straight' it did not take too much police pressure for him to agree to run it, despite one or two basic flaws that suggested themselves.

The policeman left the shop and strapped on his helmet. Old Moses knew what side his bread was buttered. There was no way he would want to get on the wrong side of the police, that would be cutting off your nose to spite your face. He looked forward to Thursday's edition.

A fog was blowing in, quite unexpectedly and bringing the damp. But Abe was content with the day's work. It would draw the Spring Heeled Jack chapter to a close. He could forget it.

If he really believed that, he was nonetheless mistaken.

Chapter 20

Sloggers

The man propping himself up at the bar of the George And Dragon was being very patient. At least, in his inebriated state and given his high opinion of himself, reinforced as usual today by the presence of his pals, occupying the far end of the room, variously huddled and sprawled as the mood, conversation and the alcohol took them, that's the way he saw it. The others had only just started on fresh pints, but Kevin Percival, all of eighteen years of age with the rashness of youth considered himself an accomplished drinker, his proficiency born of dubious experience – which he advertised by eschewing the house pots or glasses, and insisted on presenting his own pewter tankard. He had proved his ability and his manhood by knocking back his fourth pint at an accelerated rate, even as the others were slowing down. His mate Chris could generally be relied upon, but that stalwart guzzler had pleaded a heavy night the night before. The young Percival was inclined to believe him, or perhaps he was just feeling his age: he must have had at least half a dozen years on him and they proclaimed themselves, and their nature, in his encroaching podginess. But still a hard man. Hadn't he tried to crush a man's head under a die stamper? No, not a man to cross, particularly when the rest of the Wellings clan would always back him. There were three of his brothers with him today; four of them; four Wellings and two Percivals.

He realised that, thinking of the others, he had half turned to face them. In that interval, the silly barmaid had picked on somebody else to serve. A podger!

"Hello John," she was saying in her silly half-soaked voice, "the usual is it?"

Before the big man named John could reply, young Percival piped up.

"Hold on. I was first," he complained feelingly, though whether out of a genuine sense of fair play, or whether he was merely piqued by the fact that a pretty girl –well, not unattractive at least – had overlooked him in favour of a handsome and taller man, he was not honest enough with himself to decide. A bit of both perhaps. He hated it when that happened. Why couldn't they just use their eyes and what little brains they had to clock who was next and remember it? It didn't take a bloody genius did it?

"I'm sure you were," said John Lively, "but you were looking the other way, so you can't blame Jenny. She's a busy girl."

Percival was obliged to look up to meet the other man's eyes. A big bloke, he obviously thought a lot of himself. *Bigheaded twat. Somebody ought to kick your arse; teach you a lesson.* Street-wise, he realised that he was not up to the job. Not alone. Not face to face. So he just said, "Well, I was still here first, and fair's fair."

"I can't argue with that," said the big man, annoyingly magnanimous, and gesturing for the smaller man to proceed.

Like he's doing me a big favour. Bigheaded bastard. Holding that thought, the younger Percival, for he was with older brother Paul today, got his drink and made his way through the mainly standing clientele back to his own group.

With two beers in hand, John Lively was just turning to make his way to the little back room which was their favoured drinking spot, when Sissy appeared.

"Is there anywhere to sit in here?" she asked, "the other room's full."

"No. Most of the furniture's been appropriated by the crowd at the back. I suggest that we stand at the bar and drink these, then adjourn to the Oak."

"Good idea. Miriam will find us somewhere to sit down. Are you comfortable with spending the night there though?"

"Why shouldn't I be?"

"Well, you know. She'll have questions."

"About what I'm up to with Cyril you mean? No, it's not a problem. She's my sister and has a right to ask. But I'm not obliged to answer. I'll tell her some things of course, but probably not everything. Depends what she asks. She might well be too busy to spend more than two minutes with us anyway, especially if Jack's not there. And if he is, I might be having words with him, about what you told me."

"I wish I hadn't told you now."

"You had to. Look, if he's there and everything seems like married bliss, I'll just leave it. All right?"

"I wish you would. It can be awkward enough batting off her questions about you. Promise me, let's keep off the sensitive personal stuff, eh?" And she took his chin gently so that he had to look straight into her insistent green eyes.

"I promise," he said, "we're supposed to be out to enjoy ourselves after all." And he kissed her forehead.

"Thank you," she replied before turning to the buxom wench behind the bar. "It's very busy this evening Jen. Who's them at the back?"

Jenny seemed glad to share. "I don't know, but Mr Hackett thinks they might be trouble. He's sent a boy to the police station."

'Them at the back' appeared to be behaving themselves now and John, who had often been castigated himself for the crime of liking a drink and becoming a bit too noisy on it, didn't see why the landlord, who had seen all sorts and everything in his time, should be particularly concerned. "I think they're just a group of friends out for a friendly drink. Can't say I've seen 'em before, but that's nothing untoward."

Nevertheless, he edged down the bar to where stood the proprietor. Sissy followed.

"Evening Fred," said John.

"John, Siss, 'ow bin ya?"

"Good," replied John for the both of them.

"Hello Fred," added Sissy.

"Jenny says you think these boys might be trouble," remarked John to the landlord, gesturing behind him without turning. The group was now in direct line of sight, had he been looking through the back of his head.

Behind the bar, Fred Hackett had no such handicap. "Why d' yo think I'm stonding 'ere?" he said.

John assumed the question required no answer, and waited for him to go on, which after a pause for inhalation, he did: "You ever heard of the Smethwick sloggers, John?"

"No, is it a cricket team? Or football?"

"Might be. They like kickin' things arahnd. 'Eads though, not footballs."

"Go on."

"Ah used to run a little plerce in Langley. That's nearer to Smethwick than we am 'ere o' course. That's probly why Ah know 'em and yoh doh. Plus, yoh Livelys 'em newcummers still."

"So, you're going back a bit? Before my time. Some of them don't look very old…"

"I've heard of the Birmingham sloggers," interjected Sissy, "though I've never seen them. But they were vicious thugs. This lot don't seem so bad, and there's only, what? Six of them. Hardly a rampaging mob…"

But the landlord was not having it rationalised away. He knew what he knew. "Appearances can lie," he asserted, "it ay 'ow they look, it's 'ow they act. An' jus' cuz they'm mainly sober, or look it, thar ay alwiz a good thing. A sober mon determined to cause trouble, is more derngerous than a drunk."

"If that's the case," said John, "there's nothing to worry about. That chap I met at the bar seemed well bladdered. You sure about them?"

"Ah ay sure who he was. A new member, p'raps. But a couple 'o th'others look familiar."

"That would hardly hold up in a court of law. Why don't you just leave them to drink up and move on. Why look for trouble? If they're who you say they are, they've got to get home tonight."

"Forewarned is forearmed," replied the landlord, "an' it ay that far, even if yoh miss the last buz – more's the pity."

"All right, so they've got a reputation – if it is them. For what exactly?"

"Fighting an' rampagin.' They cum in, get drunk, smosh the plerce up, an' piss off."

"We see fights all the time," protested John Lively.

"Not like this. They'm planned, and they cum equipped. Did yoh notice they all got belts wi' big buckles, but brerces an' all."

"I did. Concealed weapons you're saying?"

"That's it. No'r an obvious, actual weapon; nuthin' a copper could object to, but wropped arahnd the fist or swung at the ferce…"

"I get the picture," said big John, imagining a glittering buckle swung sharply against a bare head, "yes, I had noticed the belts and the big boots; also that they're all wearing red polka-dot scarves."

"Ahh!" exclaimed Hackett in triumph, "that's 'ow ah know 'em. Them scarves, they'm like a uniform they am, the sloggers alwiz wears the serme scarves. Used to be plerne red, but they doh fool me."

Half joking John said, "Are you sure they're not just a group of lads out for a drink, who happen to like polka-dot?"

"Bollocks," said Fred Hackett with finality.

#

Of course, all this talk engendered surreptitious or unconscious glances toward the suspect six. And they noticed. Certainly, Kevin Percival noticed, and it prompted a question.

"Are you looking at me?"

Now, given that the volume of the aggregated conversations in a room full of half drunk people, many of whom were half deaf as a consequence of years of labouring in proximity to the casual disabling din of clanking metals and machines, is always going to be high, then it was no wonder that to make himself heard Percival's question was posed at great amplitude. Which caused all the other voices to falter as ears were set to wagging. They all knew that particular tone, and in particular that classic question. They all knew what it meant. It meant trouble. It meant a fight.

John Lively may have been a reformed character, but he was still a proud one. To tell the truth, it had usually been pride that got him into trouble – this kind of trouble – but he had learned not to respond to trivial slights with violence; well, not with disproportionate violence in any case. He still had a reputation amongst many as a drunken troublemaker too prone to use his fists to extricate himself from that same self-made trouble. But in his own eyes, and in the eyes of Sissy he hoped, he was a strong and fair man who was prepared to defend his woman and his friends, his family and his honour. Sometimes, his old reputation was useful – locals out for mischief knew better than to antagonise him, just on word of mouth alone. That was good, particularly given his new job…But this challenger was no local, and ignorant of the tales.

John Lively turned to face Kevin Percival. He looked very young, with a swagger which may have been the booze talking, or working, or may have been one born of confidence in the back up of his five friends. Or perhaps he was just a tough individual. He looked tough, or rather, he had a roughness that suggested toughness. He was by no means huge, not as big as John, but with a big broad head that seemed to have stretched his nose across, flattening it. The eyes also, they were drawn out into slits through which he peered with an almost evil mien, or perhaps he could not afford spectacles? Mongoloid looking, or Chinese, except for the thin blonde moustache and blonde stubble matching the shaved blonde of his head. An ugly looking customer to be sure.

John Lively stared back at the slits. Without now having to raise his voice he said, "As a matter of fact, I was. We've not seen you and your friends in here before, and we were just curious about where you were from."

"Curiosity killed the cat," came back the taunt. Some of the others thought this witty no doubt, for sniggers were exchanged, inexpertly concealed into half-finished pots.

"It's nice to know who you are drinking with, that's all. My name's John."

"Is it, and what's your friend's name?" asked Percival, eyeing Sissy through his slits. It was a challenge.

"None of your damned business," replied John, losing his patience.

"There you are then," came back Percival spitefully, "and mine's no business of yours. And our business is our business, not yours. And if we want to come in here for a drink, we can. It's an Englishman's right. We don't answer to you…"

The slits became even narrower. Perhaps that's why he advanced a little closer, because he couldn't see so well. Or perhaps he was going to throw a punch – he was getting worked up enough. John was taking no chances: he rushed the man and pushed him in mid-flow. The force had been carefully measured: he staggered back before tripping himself up and landing at his friends' feet.

Like a nest of ants confronted with fire, the crowd receded as one, clearing the floor, leaving a circle of bare board; a ring in fact, should the would-be combatants care to indulge. And it had gone very quiet.

"You bastard," spat Percival, "you've had it now."

As he got up a clear calm voice stopped him in his tracks.

"Sit down Kevin," ordered Augustus Wellings. But Percival was loathe to back down. "You tell him Paul," continued Wellings, "he's your brother."

Paul Percival was as ugly as his younger brother, but in a different way. Bullet-headed to the point of freakishness with crater ridden acne'd skin further violated by a red scar along his left cheek, memento of a disagreement with a Welsh pitman over the spilling of a few dregs of best bitter. And the Welshman had had the worst of it, hospitalised by his own blade. Paul's reedy voice commanded: "Sit down Kev, we've not come here to fight," he said, then winking at the crowd adding, "not today."

The younger brother obeyed and both turned their backs to the bar and continued their conversations with the Wellings: Chris was getting back into his stride – hair of the dog and all that – and Dougie was taking slow drags and alternating with swigs with his good arm. And there was Jon Wellings, life and soul of the party, and Augustus Alexander, repository of group common sense. Four handsome brothers, in company with two decidedly unlovely ones.

Altercation or no, John and Sissy both were not about to waste the drinks that had already been poured. They stood at the bar to finish them. Quietly, a figure joined them.

"Hello sir, miss," said Augustus Wellings, "thank you for your restraint there. Please accept my apologies for my companion."

John looked. The man seemed genuine. "Thank you, but there's no need to apologise: it's Saturday at the pub; it's normal. I think we did well not coming to blows."

"Yes, well I know who would have had the worst of it. Again, thank you for your restraint. He was about to punch you, you know…" said Wellings, then, changing tone and offering his hand, "It's Augustus, Augustus Wellings. But people call me Gus."

John looked again. There didn't appear to be any guile, any slyness, in him – and he was getting practice at spotting it lately. So he took the hand, small and warm but bumped with callouses at the finger roots.

"I'm John Lively, and this," he said, drawing Sissy close, "is Siss. My fiancée." He felt that he could not, in front of a stranger, demean Sissy by describing her as – what? Friend? Girlfriend? Companion? No, in the present context any such description lent itself to misinterpretation. He would not have that, and so fiancée it was. Sissy was blushing at this confirmation of status.

"Hello Miss," said Gus Wellings.

"Hello Gus," said she.

"What brings you to Blackheath?" enquired John. "Looking for work?"

"God, no. We're just out on a little jaunt; change of scene. My brothers and their friends like to visit somewhere different on occasion. I'm not usually included, but this time I thought 'what the hell.'"

"As Blackheath is so alluring…" prompted Sissy.

"Well, yes, as a matter of fact. Intriguing at least. We've had an enjoyable afternoon looking for this Spring Heeled Jack that's been terrorising the neighbourhood."

"And?"

"And all we found was that we were working up a thirst. So, here we are."

"Might be your best chance of seeing him," confided the Lively boy, "it's strange, but it's only the blind drunk as see him…it's all a load of rubbish, but it makes a good story to keep the kids quiet. It all started with some piss-head scaring himself when he saw somebody running along the canal with a lantern –so my brother tells me, he's the police sergeant here. Mad isn't it?"

"I suppose it enlivens a boring existence," said Gus.

Not just a handsome face thought John. "That's true. Anyway, what's with these matching scarves?"

"Oh, it's just a little tradition of theirs. Not of mine though, you will notice," said Gus, indicating his plain neck-wear. Red, no spots.

The landlord had been listening to the exchange.

"So, you're not a gang then?"

Wellings turned. "Gang? What's your definition of a gang?"

"Well, I'll tell you," continued Fred Hackett, "where are you from all of you, exactly."

"Smethwick. But if you had had your ears open you would have picked up on that."

"I did wonder," admitted Hackett. "I also wondered about your connection with the sloggers."

Wellings paused before replying, looked the landlord in the eye. "That's a term I've heard used, but not in a good way. If you want to use it about us, that's your prerogative. But, make no mistake. We're not hear to do any 'slogging' as you call it, unless by that you mean going out for an enjoyable drink with mates." And looking to John as a kindred spirit, he added, "The way I heard it, the sloggers retired long ago; there comes a time to cast off the rash folly of youth; you grow up; I know I did."

"So I was right," interjected the landlord.

"As I said, think what you like, but I repeat, we're not out to cause any trouble. My young friend apart that is…" He nodded in the direction of the Percivals, "And that was just that youthful folly I was talking about; exuberance and good beer spilling over. But he's learned from it, thanks to our friend here…"

"All right," agreed the landlord, "I see that and I take your word on it. All the same, I'd appreciate it if you would finish your drinks and leave."

"Suit yourself. I'm sure there's plenty of other places would welcome the custom." Gus turned to John Lively. "Apologies again John. No hard feelings."

John took the hand again. "Of course not."

By now, John and Siss were ready to leave. If they had done so directly then the Livelys' troubles with the so-called sloggers may have ended there and then. But as fate opted, their exit was delayed when Sissy was importuned by an inquisitive neighbour asking after her sister's well-being. So it was that their feet had taken less than half a dozen steps down the street when the pub disgorged its unwelcome party of monster hunters. As bad luck would have it, the young Percival was in the van and seething indignant at the landlord's disrespect. A lungful of fresh air, and alcohol charged blood rushed to his already debilitated brain, stimulating only the most primitive parts. He then made out his late opponent walking away scot-free. And with his back to him. A god-sent chance! Without further thought or ado, he ran up to the pair and punched his enemy on the back of the skull. To his credit, and unnervingly, the victim of this covert and cowardly act, who had remained rock solid throughout, merely turned and asked, "Is that as hard as you can hit?" At the same time, he was watching the doors of the 'Dragon' where the expellees were exiting one by one. As each appeared, the sequence of opening and closing of inner and outer leaf doors caused a small cloud of pub smoke to be disgorged with him, as if a real dragon had swallowed them but, choking on tough meat, was coughing them up. In vain, he searched for Gus Wellings, but he would no doubt be

249

last out, making sure that all of his straying flock was accounted for. And it was while he was scanning for the one person who could defuse what was otherwise coming that the pusillanimous Percival made his second underhand move. Still close enough, he leant back and, taking the weight off the front leg, lashed out with it in a sweeping action. The heavy boot caught John Lively just above the knee cap – lucky, because contacting lower it would have had enough power to dislocate or break the joint. As it was, it succeeded in bringing the big man down on one knee, down hard on the awkward hard cobbles. The stupid lad had done it now. No matter what the squirt tried next, John Lively was angry, and not so injured as not to be able to utterly crush the little ruffian. He was going to get up and give him a real battering. He deserved it.

Before he could act, however, somebody else intervened. Somebody tough, unafraid, and female. Standing over her man, she pushed at Percival's chest.

The words were calm and cold, "Get away from him if you know what's good for you."

"Piss off!" was the reply. He tried to push past her as John Lively was getting up – and ended up in a wrestling match against a strength he had not expected in a woman.

Touching a woman like that; fighting with a woman, his fiancée, now brought big John to a new plateau of wrath and determination. It is probable that the visitor would have been killed if, there and then, another voice had not boomed out, freezing the scene.

"Oi! What do you think you're doing?"

The sergeant's uniform, and that of Joshua Lively brought an end to the physical hostilities.

The rest of the sloggers had all emerged from the pub as if moths from a cocoon whose wings of comprehension and action had yet to harden. By the time they had, the law had arrived…

"Take your hands off her," ordered the sergeant. The culprit did so, holding both up in submission.

"Sissy, come away," said the policeman, "John, what's going on?"

"I met this one in the pub," replied his brother, "had words but nothing serious. Still, we decided to leave them to it; we were walking down to the Oak when he ran up behind me and punched and kicked me."

"Is that what happened, Siss?" checked Sergeant Lively.

"Yes, Abe, he's a madman."

"Liar," shouted Percival. Abe wondered which part of Sissy's answer he disagreed with. He wasn't about to believe anything he said anyway. "Right then, I'm arresting you on a charge of common assault. Anything you say will be taken down and used in evidence. Do you have anything to say?"

"No, but my friends might," replied the assailant with a nod up the road.

Abe looked at five men, strangers to him, standing outside the pub and looking on. Counting the one who had started the trouble, the police were outnumbered three to one, but only two to one if you counted John, which you could count on. The Livelys had coped with much worse and so Abe had no qualms about taking this man into custody.

Before he could act, however, Gus Wellings stepped forward. "Look sergeant," he said, showing open hands, "if we agree to leave immediately will you let us go? Leave town I mean. Believe me, this one will get a thumping both from me and his brother there. Might get a few bruises, but at least his old mother will see him home safe."

"And you are?" asked Abe Lively.

"Augustus Wellings, visiting from Smethwick."

"You're a long way off the beaten track aren't you?"

"I know. We came to see your Spring Heeled Jack."

"For fuck's sake," exclaimed the copper, mimicking the bad example of inspector Oakden: from him being rather prudish about swearing he had found it slipping out of him with a mind of its own recently. He had heard enough of Jack and all the old demons it summoned. Best get shot of this lot as soon as possible.

"John?" he enquired.

"Just clear 'em off and be done," replied his civilian brother.

Josh confidently predicted that John's attacker would not get off so lightly. He was due an appearance before the justices, and get what was coming. But Abe surprised him by saying, "Right you are. And you," he continued, turning to Percival, "clear off and don't think about coming back. Ever."

With that, he delivered an almighty kick with a large shiny boot to the offender's bony behind. In the heat of the moment, the pain overriding good sense, and not realising how fortunate he had been, on more than one count, the young aggressor turned around and threw a foolhardy left cross. The policeman was ready for it, expected it even, wanted it. A small swift arc of dense ironwood intercepted the transgressing wrist from above, converting momentum to a shock wave which attacked the nerves and paralysed the offending limb. And more. Kevin Percival's forearm was hard and knotty from habitually hauling and carrying chunks of wrought iron, but not meaty enough to stop the crushing power of the truncheon from penetrating to bone, and breaking it. Percival whelped like a whipped dog, dancing on the spot in agony. Impulsively, his comrades pitched forward, in unconscious protest, though not necessarily to attack. But Josh Lively was taking no chances, and not altogether self-possessed, he swung wildly with his own truncheon to maintain a safe interval. Four of them appreciated the danger and held back. The fifth, in the shape of poor crippled Dougie Wellings was just too slow to shy and was laid low by a glancing blow to the temple which drew blood.

That changed things. The sloggers may not have come looking for trouble but now that it had found them they were minded to react with force. But they were down to four now, against three big men, two of whom were armed with truncheons and legal authority. Not to mention a hard as nails woman. Thus, they squared off tensely, standing protectively around Gus Wellings who was kneeling to aid his stricken brother. He looked up.

"What kind of man picks on an old soldier with a bad arm?" he asked.

"I'm sorry," replied Josh, "it was an accident."

"What? You accidentally drew your truncheon and hit him round the head?"

"What do you think is going to happen if you rush us like that?" said Abe in his brother's defence.

Whatever response might have been made, or whatever may have transpired without the arrival of reinforcements it is difficult to say. Perhaps nothing more would have been said; perhaps there would not have been any more violence. We shall never know, for at that moment P.C.s Salt and Clark arrived and the sloggers were now well and truly outmatched.

The sergeant now stepped forward to close matters. "I should arrest you all for affray. That's the lot of you. All crowded together in a stinking cell for the night. For two nights – until your trip to court on Monday. And don't think we couldn't take you all by force. If we needed to."

The Percivals and Wellings looked at the cast of characters now fanned around them, and had no doubt of that.

"If we needed to?" Gus had latched onto the implication, "but you're not going to?"

"No, I'm not."

"May I ask why not?"

"Look around you. I think justice has been served. It only remains for you to give me your word."

"My word?"

"That you'll leave here immediately, like you said. And not come back."

"Then you have it."

"Good," said Abe as he helped Dougie to his feet, "are you all right?"

"I'll live," said the bloodied man.

"Salt."

"Sergeant?" enquired P.C. Salt.

"Bandage please."

Salt handed over a roll of lint from his tunic pocket. Always a useful item in that line of work.

Abraham Lively gave it to Augustus Wellings. "Thank You," said the Smethwick man.

"What about me?" bleated a white-faced Kevin Percival, gingerly clasping his left arm as if it were about to fall off.

"You!" said the sergeant rounding on the pathetic kid, "you deserved it. So stop snivelling before I change my mind." And looking at Gus continued, "Get him out of here will you?"

Gus exchanged nods with Abe. "Straight away," he said, "come on, let's go."

The last the sergeant saw of them, they were wandering down the road past St. Paul's. The church marked a boundary – they were the responsibility of Halesowen constabulary now…

"We could have taken them," said Salt to nobody in particular.

"Yes," agreed Josh absently.

"I thought you said that there was more to policing than throwing people in cells and totting up arrests?" came back Salt.

"Yes, but," began Josh but shut up when he realised Abe's ears were within range. But, then, he was surprised when his brother answered for him, "That's right, there is. They've learned their lesson so let's not waste any more time and effort on them. They won't be back. Think of all the paperwork; the slopping out, traipsing down to Old Hill to sit done up like a dog's dinner in a hot court room, listening to the pompous old magistrates droning on about protecting society – protecting their own interests more like, and their jumped-up friends'. They look down on all of us you know…"

It had sounded to Josh that his brother had plenty more to say, and with increasing emotion. However, the sergeant stopped abruptly, seemed to think twice. Nevertheless it had been a revelation: the equivalent of the Archbishop Of Canterbury letting on that he had never been all that keen on God.

It was P.C. Clark who brought them all down to earth. "Yes sergeant, and it's a good thing too. We'll need the cells for proper criminals tonight. There's been a proper crime. That's what we came to tell you. A murder!"

#

Francis Thompson, with impeccable timing, had taken leave of his drinking companions just before they had taken leave of their senses, and the trouble started. In the Three Furnaces, he had been drinking with three Irishmen – great drinking companions he always found, until a certain saturation point had been reached. He admired the Irish: a race of poetic disposition – having much in common with himself therefore – and as far as he could tell the Irish character was indomitably devil-may-care and the Irishman's tongue practised in the art of witty persuasion. The blarney they called it. And it was all very entertaining, and Thompson had been enjoying the company. Your average Irishman, sober, in the appreciation of culture and finer things, he found a cut above the average Englishman – certainly an Englishman born and raised in this present insular community – but drunk, that is to say past that crucial saturation point, he turned into the worst kind of Dark Age Celtic savage: violent and unpredictable.

He had felt the saturation point approaching, the musical rhythm of their speech, and its softness, drowned out by alcohol and converted to a loud garble totally unworthy of the tongue of Swift and Goldsmith. It got worse. Beer-soaked testiness turned to open challenge. The atmosphere was balanced on a knife edge, and there was no way to take it off without getting cut. He knew he must leave. It displeased him; the night had started so well but was ruined. He was angry with them. And disappointed. He despised himself for that; after all, what were they really? Animals who just happened to be wearing clothes and talking; and drinking of course. Not worth bothering with really. He got up and ran a gauntlet of grubby hands which he pressed briefly. He left them then to get on with it. They would get to fighting soon; that's what they did the Irish; been killing each other for donkeys'. This lot were supposed to be Catholics too, but they wouldn't let a little thing like faith get in the way of a good brawl.

He stepped onto the street. Immediately, he was immersed in a warren of mean slums and back alleys and blind alleys and reeking rubbish-strewn yards, juxtapositioned illogically and nightmarish; where downtrodden men asserted their right to brief life by way of violence and insemination of their downtrodden women, who, like the stray cats and dogs, dropped kids continuously, and dropped more to replace the ones who died in infancy from everything from whooping cough to crushing hooves, although in truth the root of it was always the same, and that was ignorant poverty. Many of the inhabitants of that area were so poor that they did not visit the pub, even on a Saturday. Rather, they lolled around stinking of cheap gut rot on the way to insensibility. It was still warm at that time of year, and some of the human wreckage had found its way to the front of the houses, catching the sun in the street. He was surprised to note that most of these still held themselves in a more or less vertical posture, leaning territorially against door jambs or sat in what might have been their one and only kitchen chair. And many were decidedly underdressed to be seen in public: one decrepit chap sporting only his beer-stained under-vest, braces let down to swing from the waist band of his scruffy moleskins. He would cop it if the police came round; although, they did tend to avoid this barbarous quarter unless in force.

He took all of this in as he stood outside the Three Furnaces, carefully positioning his hat and pulling on his tight black gloves. He started to vaguely wander then, in the direction of his lodgings, no clear plan in mind. Curiously, he felt at home here. The raw animal struggle stared you in the face. In its own way it was inspiring: in the midst of death we are in life. He had no fear, he was a giant amongst Lilliputians; his wits and his stick unbeatable allies against at least half a dozen local yahoos.

Then, when he was gone not fifty yards, an almighty crashing and shouting erupted in the room which he had just left.

#

Henry Higgins had known Michael Hickey for years. They had come over on the boat together. And in – to them – a foreign land, it made them cleave to each other; developed a bond of sorts. But not necessarily of friendship. What then? Comradeship? They worked together, enjoying the same rewards, suffering the same privations.

Companionship then? They were drinking partners when there were no closer friends to hand; or, more to the nub of it, no lady friends.

And, as usual, it was a female that was at the heart of the latest disagreement between the two. As Hickey would come to contemplate later, if briefly, if love of money was the root of all evil, then booze and women, either or both, came a damn close second. And who was she? This siren, this Delilah, this Jezebel? We shall never know, for it is a fact that come nightfall, no matter how he dredged it, his thick head would not give up the answer. But he had time to think now, and he knew what he must do.

#

All the hollering had stopped the young poet in his tracks. Turning around, he saw one of his Gaelic drinking acquaintances, blood pouring down from his scalp onto his face emphasising the red rage which evidently possessed him. Profaning, almost unintelligibly, he made a bee line for a dishevelled shop which in small faded lettering coyly announced itself a butcher's. He ran straight in and then out again, pursued slowly by a fat and forty-odd individual wearing a striped apron whose appearance thus immediately suggested that here was the eponymous proprietor of the premises. For those in any doubt, he was brandishing that clichéd epitome of the trade, a meat cleaver; and was in turn followed by a yapping little white terrier. Whether the animal offered support, or was merely in pursuit of the chance of a sausage, is not germane to the present story…

#

George Hobley was behind his counter wiping off his mincing machine prior to getting on with cutting up a side of beef which was waiting patiently for his attention on the scarred block at the back of the shop. He wasn't a young man, and wasn't a fit man, in fact quite a fat man; and his bones ached these days – he dreaded the winter. Not then, a man of action, particularly of swift action, which is what you need when a thief runs into your shop.

#

Michael Hickey knew exactly where he was going. He had often passed the shop and seen the butcher at work. Where there was a butcher, there were knives. And a knife just now would be perfect: he would settle Higgins' hash this time. Higgins was not a big lad, but neither was Hickey, and Higgins usually got the better of their altercations. Usually; not this time. It was Higgins that had started with the weapons, in the shape of a heavy two-handled metal spit-pot; Mick would finish it with an altogether more efficient one. He ran in, but the knives were behind the counter where, not unexpectedly, stood the butcher. He had his back to the Irishman; Mick's eyes darted around the room; it was a long one. Away in the back, a glint summoned him. Hardly stopping he rushed on. There was a wooden bench here, with a thick top. On it lay the aged remains of a small and mean cow, or half a cow at any rate. As he got there a collection of flies who had found their way in from the street, possibly fresh from another decayed ungulate, arose in a small cloud of complaint. But Mick was not interested in them, nor in their meal, so they settled down quickly when he left. He left with his prize: a long and sharp and pointed beef boning knife. A proper stabbing blade it was and he clutched it with a mad determination as he rushed past the butcher out into the street almost before the fat man had registered that he was there. Almost. The shopkeeper flew out after him, meat cleaver in hand, as fast as his legs would allow. Which is to say not very. He would certainly not catch the thief unless he could speed up his old limbs, which he could not; and would not, considering what the younger man had armed himself with. Pausing for thought, he slowed down, and watched the scene play out.

#

Francis Thompson saw Henry Higgins emerge from the pub, drunk enough that he had to be supported by another pal known to the watcher only as Pat –there was always a Pat in these gatherings. No sooner had the Irishman taken his first breath of outside air, he spotted Hickey approaching with a cold stare and cold steel. His eyes widened with fear and understanding: the man whom he had just walloped with that pot had well and truly upped the ante in the shape of a viciously sharp thin knife. A split second – and if anything Higgins' eyes then opened even wider, but now mostly in horror, and a little bit of pain. There was a visceral aggression behind the blow. Indifferent, the knife cut through warm flesh as dutifully as cold. When Hickey pulled it out his friend Henry was as good as dead.

It just depended on how fast the blood flowed. There was a lot of it finding its way out of the victim already, soaking his clothes mauve and beginning to drip, then stream, down onto the paving. Higgins put a hand to his belly and looked at the blood as if he had never seen this red stuff before. He stared down at the speckles on the ground, then dropped, one knee then the other. Then he pitched forward, right hand still pressed to his belly. He landed flat on his face, with one arm under him. Those of a morbidly inquisitive disposition might have noticed that there was still sufficient circulating fluids for the uncontrolled contact with the ground to have produced a small amount of blood from the nose. But a nose bleed was the least of his worries. In fact, at that point, though technically still a living and sentient being, his traumatised brain was not allowing him to worry, nor think of anything in fact. Which was a blessing, you would have thought.

Knife still in hand, Michael Hickey became aware of the gathering crowd, encroaching cautiously. He looked from face to face, turning toward each in turn, as if challenging them, threatening them; or bewildered. This produced a reciprocating ripple effect as onlookers backed away and then edged forward as the knifeman turned away. He had run his course; now from predator he had become prey, as the fox at bay is encircled by the hounds. But one dog stood alone, still and placid. Their eyes met and the red mist of rage and the blackness were taken away, absorbed by the poet's own black eyes. Thompson looked calmly at the killer, with an air of detachment that took any fight out of him. Fascinated, he watched as Hickey returned the knife to its owner.

"You had better have this now," he said, handing over the crimsoned blade, handle first.

Disarmed, he was at the mercy of the pack, who lost no time descending on him, dispensing a little natural justice of their own before bundling him up and securing him with a roll of strong string supplied courtesy of Hobley's butchers. Fun over, the attention switched to the by now dead body. Blood was spreading thickly to form a tepid soupy puddle. The body's head lay lower than the rip in his belly, and his life juices soon swamped his face; would have drowned on it had he been alive.

Francis stood inches away from the creeping crimson fluid. He could smell it. He could even see, he thought, little wisps of steam rising up as the air claimed the blood's heat: bits of soul abandoning the mortal body. It excited him, and breathing it all in, he realised something: he had known this would happen; had been waiting for something bad; expected it. That was the thing about his God-given sensibilities, he thought, refined to the point of veritable clairvoyance…

You did not need to be psychic to anticipate the arrival of the police. They arrived in force – four of them – and Thompson stepped back to observe.

They were led, he noticed, by the disagreeable sergeant from the pub with the agreeable landlady. They moved the crowd back and the sergeant crouched close to the dead man.

Abe Lively stood. The man was dead all right. "Josh, go and fetch Dr Wharton please, and something to move the body."

"Will do," replied the constable, "though I don't think there's much he can do for the patient is there?" he added with a grin.

"Get on with you," replied his brother.

Josh started on his way back to Rowley and the doctor's house, as P.C.s Salt and Clark presented the prisoner, now more securely held with iron. Clark had retrieved the murder weapon and set it down on the ground near the corpse. They moved the crowd back, then, a semblance of order achieved, the sergeant asked, "Now, who saw what happened?"

There was no shortage of witnesses and the salient points were quickly established: Henry Higgins, the deceased, had been in the Three Furnaces with a friend and fellow Irishman, Michael Hickey, the prisoner. According to an acquaintance, and main witness, Patrick O'Connell, the three labourers had sat together perfectly amicably, in company with a young Englishman they had recently met, but who had left before the trouble started. O'Connell was still under the influence and could recall an argument, but not what it was about. The next thing, Henry had hit Michael over the head with a heavy brass pot, which Michael, a tobacco-chewer, had been spitting into. Dazed, Hickey had nevertheless been able to stand and he ran out. Curious, O'Connell followed, supporting a worse for wear Higgins. As they stood in the street, O'Connell had seen Hickey rush up with a knife like a man possessed, and plunge it deep into Higgins' guts. And that was it for old Henry. Other witnesses, including George Hobley, were able to provide details of where the knife came from. It seemed a clear case of murder: the decision to exit the pub, steal a knife, and return to inflict a savage blow was sure evidence of malice aforethought…

After cautioning, the killer said nothing. He seemed not at all sure where he was; however, a heavy blow to the cranium could do that. Salt and Clark escorted their prize – the arrest of a murderer was by no means commonplace – to the station, where in due course the dead consequence of his loss of control joined him, in the wooden shack out the back, on a handcart, under a tarpaulin and some inquisitive bluebottles. It was summer and still warm, and so in due course the corpse would have to be manhandled into the relative cool of the cellar beneath the station. But not by Josh Lively, who planned on making himself unavailable for that particular task.

#

Doctor Wharton watched the corpse go. As soon as it was loaded and covered, the crowd had abruptly lost interest, switching off like a hooded hawk.

"Excitement over," he observed, "never ceases to amaze me how they just take it in their stride; get used to it I suppose. Typical Saturday evening thuggery."

"It's not often it turns to murder though," said the sergeant. "We get lots of fights of course, we've all got bruises to testify to that, but murder? Not had one since somebody beat that boatmen and threw him in the cut at Darby End. But that must have been eighteen months ago."

"As I recall, that case was never closed," said the doc.

"No. No it wasn't. It's tricky with boating people. They don't trust the law, and most don't respect it either. Water gypsies we call 'em."

"Yes," agreed the doctor, although he had no personal experience of such people, "still, this should be an easy one. Solves itself, eh what? Another scalp for you."

"Hardly a difficult investigation…"

"Still," continued the doctor, "the figures…"

"Oh, stuff the figures. I'm getting tired of making other people look good, and getting nothing for it," muttered the policeman.

"I hope that's not aimed at me," protested the good doctor.

"Oh – no. No, it's not. You've been a good friend…"

"I'm glad you agree. But you know the game."

"Yes I do," the sergeant concurred. "But that doesn't mean I have to play it all the time. What about a half-time respite?"

"Perhaps you can relax more when you make inspector. But the when of it depends on your record of course," counselled Wharton.

"That bait's been dangling a while. Meantime, we've been arresting and charging all and sundry, including some poor buggers who just needed a cell for the night…"

"Oh dear, you do sound depressed. Look, your promotion will come, trust me, because you're a good public servant. And I see it like this, any extra funds that we may come into goes back into helping the community," argued the doctor.

And bolsters your standing as a JP thought Abe.

"Hasn't helped Mr Higgins has it?" pointed out the disenchanted copper.

"Who?"

"The dead bloke," said Abe with a nod.

"Oh. No. He's beyond help now. Depending on your religious beliefs of course."

"And I'm willing to bet his dying won't get me anywhere either. Old Hill will probably take the credit. After all, as I said, it's not my investigation; it just fell into my lap, poor uncouth plodder as I am."

"You're too modest."

"I've never been accused of that before."

"Well, I'm accusing you of it now. Cheer up! I count you as a friend, I hope you know that. And you are on at least nodding terms with most of our little band of councillors, who let me assure you, also hold you in high regard. So, you'll be inspector before you know it – as soon as a vacancy arises. It's not as if you're trying to get a commission in the Guards or something. It's just a local police inspector we're talking about, and in my experience they're promoted on merit."

Yes that's it, isn't it? Just a police inspector, one of the hoi polloi. I'm just a servant with a different uniform to them; not good enough to mix with the money, and certainly not their daughters. Ignorant hypocrites. "Do you not know inspector Oakden then?" returned the sergeant, but not without humour.

The doctor laughed. "Ha! You have me. But that just proves a point – it is obvious within seconds of meeting the man that he isn't an inspector by dint of his social connections. No. Merit dear boy, merit."

"God help us then," opined Abe before changing the subject. "So, what's the medical verdict?"

"Eh?"

"Cause of death. I mean, apart from bleeding to death."

"Oh I see. Well, the victim was quite thin and the knife quite long and very sharp. Lots of penetrating power when wielded in anger, which I gather that it was."

"Yes, it was quite a vicious attack."

"Well then, those factors, and the position of the wound, just below the diaphragm, and the amount of blood, and the fact that witnesses agree that he died very quickly, I would guess, although I would have to do a proper examination…"

"What?" prompted the policeman.

"I should think that the knife penetrated deep, probably in a slight upward curve, easily reaching the posterior abdominal wall. I would say that the blade punctured the abdominal aorta, or one of its main offshoots, or both, leading to massive exsanguinating haemorrhage."

"So he bled to death?"

"Essentially, yes," agreed the doctor.

"Well I'm glad we sorted that out," said Abe Lively, his genial nature beginning to reassert itself. "Look, when Josh is back and the body moved, I'm knocking off and going for a drink at the Oak. Would you care to join me?"

"No, thank you. Unfortunately, Mrs Wharton made it clear that she expects me straight back. She no doubt awaits my imminent arrival as does," he said, consulting his watch, "dinner. Good evening sergeant."

"Good evening, doctor. Eat well."

"I always do," said Wharton, tapping his paunch.

#

Abe took the doctor's reassurances at face value. He meant well, he was sure, but that fact hardly moved his new-found cynicism. Once he had started to question the way of things, he had begun to see how the game was rigged. Despite Wharton's protests the sergeant saw clearly now that it had never about how he had performed but who he had benefitted in the performance. It was who you knew, and whom you were known to that counted. And if either you or your friends had no money or influence, then you did not count. Then there was Oakden. Perhaps the doctor was blind, but there was no way on God's earth that that bombastic fool had 'merited' his way up the ranks. No, Abe had decided to modify his theorem of cynicism: perhaps it was in his case not so much who he knew, but more about something he knew – about someone. If rumour could be believed, Abe would not believe Oakden above blackmail. That was it: he obviously had something on somebody; so, not only an incompetent cop, but a dishonest one. His belief in the iniquities of the system reinforced by a dubious logic, he repaired directly to the Royal Oak.

#

Not unusually, it had been a busy evening at the Hailstone. But Sarah was in a good mood. Customers meant money of course, but, also, the sergeant was on an early shift and had promised to come round for a drink and to keep her company as she worked. By closing time her sweet mood had soured. There had been no sign of the handsome police sergeant, just the boring regulars and her estranged ex live-in lover: Charlie Spragg had hung around all night like a lost puppy trying to get her attention and showing himself up. But he had let her down too often and been too free with his favours once too often, which is to say, once. Therefore, she had made sure, as always, that she did not serve him personally, did not make eye contact, and certainly did not deign to smile in his general direction. For his part, it was clear that he was not getting the message, or at least was desperately trying to misunderstand it, for he sank each succeeding pint the more quickly, in the forlorn hope that the purchase of the next would win him some brief contact. As the night wore on though, his ploy did have some effect, for Sarah began to feel sorry for him, and concerned that he would not be in a fit state to walk to wherever he called home at present. And as the night wore on, she became increasingly vexed at the absence of Abraham Lively. In truth, she knew that he could not always just knock off like a factory hand…But if something had come up surely he could have sent word? Yes, of course he could, she reasoned. Which made her suspect that he had stopped off somewhere else. If he had gone home to change, and that sister knew of his plans, she would do her best to delay him, she was sure. And he a willing fool.

Having shooed out the last of the boozy sluggards, including Charlie, she quickly barred the door and resolved to get to bed and extinguish the lights – and 'cock a deaf 'un' to any potential knocking from the feckless Mr Lively. Then he would just have to walk back home.

Her instinct was good. Barely had her head met the pillow and the gas light's afterglow not yet finally faded, when she heard a soft knocking, apologetic. After a while, the knocker's patience wearing thin it seemed, it got a little louder, and she huddled a little deeper. Then, little taps, quieter but closer: something small thrown against her window; was that her name? Barely more than a whisper. She almost relented. But then – what if it's not him? What if it's Charlie? He was drunk enough. She pulled the bedclothes over her head and waited for morning.

The feckless Mr Lively had indeed changed, or at least removed his tunic and replaced it with his new cut away mauve jacket, tight fitting to compliment his shape. Not as eye-catching as brother John's military number perhaps, but a darn sight more sober and respectable. He had planned to be off to the Hailstone later. But in all of the excitement what he had failed to take account of was that owing to the murder and its aftermath, he was already running late: it was 'later' already. Again, the telling of the day's tale to Miriam and then to late arrival Jack Beckett, and then to brother John and his girl, and all with appropriate interludes for lubrication of the old vocal chords, took more time than he could have foretold. John was a familiar presence to whom he could relate the whole thing without having to start and stop as he was obliged to do with the duty-bound licensees. No doubt a similar experience awaited him at the next stop. He had needed to tell the story, to work through his feelings. Fights were commonplace, and he had seen lots of blood. Nothing however to compare to the buckets that had spewed out of Henry Higgins and the apparent savagery meted out by a friend. Arguments did not usually escalate so swiftly to murder; in fact, as far as the recent past went, disagreements never elevated themselves to homicide at any pace. Good policing, tough physical policing, but fair policing, had seen to that. Now this, plus the murder of Phillips. Suicide? Oakden was talking out of his arse, as he would describe it. It wasn't the deaths themselves: the sergeant was used to dealing with all sorts of fatalities, on a regular basis; but these were usually accidents, or at least arising out of circumstances to which the law attached no serious criminal fault; factories, mills, mines, canals all contributed to a steady supply of corpses, and quarries of course; even the roads – horses were dangerous things, especially to inebriated revellers, as the ghost of young John Till would no doubt attest, were it possible to contact him, as spiritualists have it.

So now two murders, and so soon after Abe had wished for just one. Because he had done so, he remembered it. Remembered thinking, 'could do with a good murder.' Had some devil read his thoughts? And what was it whispering back? Something bad was coming it said, and he knew now that he was not imagining it. What if it was already here? What then? What next?

His dark imaginings gave way to levity after a few pints of pale ale with John and Sissy. And when Miriam joined them for a break and a sherry, it was almost like old times. He loved Miriam – he loved all of his family – and the fullness of the mood snuffed out, for the time being, thoughts of that other woman. When he did remember Sarah it was getting on a bit and he realised that it would be closing time before he made it to the Hailstone. Still, she could let him in, she was in charge of the place after all. As for being late, well, police business. Which was not a lie: his brother now worked for an alleged racketeer and he had been gathering useful inside information. The fact that Abe was just as likely to use such intelligence to warn off his uncle as to ensnare and arrest him, was neither here nor there. It all contributed to maintaining peaceful streets – with no murders! The sergeant had persuaded himself that if the criminal status quo were not maintained, if the hierarchy were destroyed, then into the vacuum would be sucked new forces, and there would be war, yes, war and murder, before a new power inevitably arose. Better the devil you know…

He tramped along, weighing black against white, until he reached his lady-friend's pub. He was surprised to find it not only locked up but already in darkness. A few tentative attempts to make contact, and he concluded that she must be asleep. Apparently. Well, it had been his choice to delay and he shouldn't complain. He had had a good walk and now he would have a good one back.

He had cleared the crest of the hill at St. Giles' when, out of thin air, a voice mocked him.

"Thrown you out, has she?"

Abe was getting used to hearing voices, which he fancied were his own thoughts, as if they were leaking out of his head but finding their way home through his ears. Or at least he hoped that it was only that. Whichever, he ignored the question and carried on. But it spoke again.

"Cat got your tongue?"

Again, he ignored it. It was only a voice; a voice can't harm you. Why should he heed it?

But then it was incarnate. A shadow disengaging from shadow. And it tried again.

"Sergeant Lively." Not a question.

This was more solid than a bird in the periphery of perception. This was right in front of him, big as a man.

Abraham Lively froze, but just for an instant. Pent up anger and frustration kept fear at bay. This was something real, it was here now, supernatural or not. So he could lay his hands on it. But he could not bring himself to approach; although he would not run, he would face it; fight it if necessary; have his answer. He felt his stomach tighten, and there came a growl which turned into a shout, unintelligible. It had come from his own throat.

This exhalation of fighting spirit only provoked the thing. It moved forward into a paler patch of night. It was then that he saw it for what it was, synchronous with the introduction.

"It's me, Charlie Spragg. Remember? We met in the 'Ailstone a coupla wiks agoo. Bit jumpy ay ya? Sid a blue devil? Or a green mon?"

"I know who you are," said a relieved sergeant Lively, who had learned more of this man from Sarah: the two had been close, living together even. The way Abe chose to see it, Spragg had taken advantage of a vulnerable woman struggling to run a business after the death of her husband. For that and the past attachment, Abe resented the man. And all the more now that he had frightened him like that, and seen it.

"And yes," replied the policeman, "I might be jumpy as you say, but so might anybody confronted in the dark by who knows who armed with who knows what, with designs unknown. But, I will tell you what I do know, which is that it's a good job for you that I do know you, that I recognised you in time, otherwise you may have got a thrashing."

A pause. "Ah see what yoh mean, sorry," said Charlie slowly and in apparent conciliation, "yoh'm a big 'un all right. Mind yoh, yer look a bit werse for wear to me. Or drink."

"You think?" returned Abe, challenging.

Now the skulker decided to back down. "No. Not really. Ah'm sure a mon of yower calibre con 'andle it."

"I don't need to handle it. I've not drunk much at all. I could handle you though."

"Blimey. Sorry, calm dahn. Ah bay lookin' for no trouble," promised Spragg.

The police brain reasserted itself. "What are you doing skulking in the shadows around here?" asked Abe, remembering too late to look around for accomplices.

"Nothin' untoward. Yoh con see Netherton church from up 'ere, but only if ya goo dahn this alley and stond on the wall…"

"Of course, that explains everything. Tell me, why shouldn't I run you in as a burglar?"

"Because I ay one. Ah've on'y just left the pub."

Abe knew it was the truth. Including the fact that he had been at the pub, with her, till closing. And she had locked Abe out! That raised his ire now.

"Stay out of that pub!"

"Jealous bin ya? It's a free country chap – yoh should know that. An' ah'll tell ya summat else," he continued with a deliberate stare, "yoh woh last long!"

"What?"

"Her'll soon get bored o' yoh."

"You're drunk. Go home."

"Ohm," wailed Spragg, "ohm! I ay gorra nohm. Nor eny more. Nora proper 'un. Cuz o' yoh!"

Abe had heard enough of the drunkard's self-pity. "Well, good night then. Mind how you go." He was walking away.

"That's it, fuck off. Ah'll soon be back in there, doh yoh worry."

Blood rising, Abe strode straight back and grabbed him by the lapels. That got his attention and shut him up. But before the copper could say anything Charles Spragg's right fist struck him a mean blow in the stomach. It would have taken the wind out of the sails of most men, but Abraham Lively was not most men. He shook the man like a whippet with a rabbit. When he loosed, he thought he had shaken the tomfoolery out of him. He was wrong. The smaller man swung again, this time to the head. Something of a haymaker, the lawman had plenty of time to see it coming, even within this night's

264

plummy blackness. Raising both arms for protection, he stepped in with his right leg, torso turning off-square so that his shoulders were at right angles to the attacker's front. Now, the more Spragg put into the punch, the harder he would be rebuffed, and Abe was confident that he meant to hit hard. As the policeman's arms met the swing, blocking its path, so his advancing right shoulder met the approaching body and struck it in the face and chest. As expected, not by Spragg of course, the manoeuvre took the would-be assailant off his feet and deposited him on his backside.

"Stay down," warned Abe. "Now, I could call this assaulting a police officer. The justices take a dim view of that. Shall I be arresting you then? Or are you going to be a nice chap and take yourself home – wherever it may be."

"Mar nowse is bleeding," was the reply.

"It's a mere scratch. Are you going to behave? Because, if you don't, I'll arrest you, and that will be it."

Silence. "Do you hear?" Abe was raising his voice now. It seemed to work.

"Ahr."

"Ahr? Hardly the queen's English is it my man? Say yes if that's what you mean. Yes? Yes what? Speak up. Because if you don't, I'll arrest you."

"Ah mean yes, all right then."

"No. I want to hear you say it. I want you to say 'I'll behave sergeant.' You need to say because if you don't…"

"Ah know, yoh'll run me in. Ahr, ah got the message. Yes. Yes, I'll be'erve."

"Sergeant," prompted the sergeant.

"Sergeant," repeated Spragg. He was beaten now. For the time being.

"Now get up and make yourself scarce."

Chapter 21

Classroom and Cell

Monday morning and it was a piece of chalk. Lying in the dark corner where it must have rolled when it was discarded. Not a proper piece of chalk made for blackboards, but a rough piece of chalky stone. Or perhaps a battered and worn fragment of a shattered chalk ornament. Joshua Lively was not about to pick it up to make sure. He would leave it in place until his brother had seen it. He looked across the floor of the cell, to the relatively clear patch where the bed had traditionally stood. It looked like a hurried hand had brushed away the surface dust and scrawled its cryptic last message:

"If you do what I told you you would not lose your life."

Still crouching, the constable relayed information over his shoulder:

"There's a piece of chalk here; wonder where that came from? I don't think he brought it in with him."

"Well, we can hardly ask him," came back the voice of P.C. Payne.

"If you do what I told you you would not lose your life," repeated P.C. Lively, "what do you think he meant?"

"Who cares?"

"Perhaps he was talking to his friend, the one he killed. Perhaps he had crossed him in some way? Not done 'what I told you?'"

"Who knows? He was obviously a nutter. Who cares?" repeated Payne, but in spite of himself added, "perhaps they were God's last words to him, or the Devil's – he hadn't been a good boy so was about to pay for it. Or not. Like I said, we can hardly ask him can we? Are you going to help me get him down?"

Payne was right. The Irishman would not be answering any questions any more. That was the norm for a dead man. Josh stood up and turned and forced himself to face the scene. On the opposite wall, suspended from the bar of the tiny window, hung the deceased person of Michael Hickey, one time murder suspect and prisoner, who had successfully eluded the reach of English jurisprudence and mere human justice. His soul would be weighed by a different judge in an altogether different court now…

The man was dead without a doubt: having quite obviously choked to death he was – still – staring back across the cell with one round and glassy eye; the other closed in an obscene wink as if he was trying to let them in on some joke of the dead; his tongue tip, black and dry, poked between his teeth as if he were trying to hiss their attention from the beyond; but his hands hung limp and mute in defeat, blue blotched. The bootless stockinged feet, one plain and one striped but both holed and thin, had apparently kicked away the bedstead to give just enough drop for a strangulation, probably a slow one. And he had done it stripped to the waist. It was not a pretty sight, and Josh could swear that he could smell decomposition, even over the usual odours. He had no wish to get close, let alone touch it.

"Come on then," persisted Payne, "we need to get him down."

"I don't think that's a good idea. The sergeant ought to see first. He might want the scene photographed."

"What? Why? It's not like it's any great mystery is it? The man clearly took his own life. There's no murderer to track down, no clever sleuthing to be done. It's just routine, as is moving bodies. Besides, it's the right thing to do. Can't just leave him there like that, poor sod."

"That poor sod butchered his friend the day before yesterday," countered Josh, "literally: he stole a butcher's knife to do it."

"The other one was no angel. We found a nasty looking knife on him as well."

"Look," continued Lively, "just because it's an obvious suicide, it doesn't mean there will be no investigation."

"Investigation?" repeated Payne, the light dawning.

"Yes. That's right. We're expected to keep prisoners safe. Only her majesty's judges can order hangings. They're not keen on competition from the likes of us."

"What do you mean?" said a rattled Payne, now stepping away from the corpse as if he expected it to reach out and revenge itself on him, "surely nobody would think that we murdered a prisoner?"

"No. Don't be daft. No – of course not, John. Not deliberately. But questions will be asked about how we let it happen. Obviously. Death in police custody, there's procedures. It will mean an inquest."

"Let's wait in the office," suggested Payne, being anxious now to put some distance between himself and the ill-fated detainee, and worrying himself over the fact that it was he who was in charge of custody last night.

"Suits me," replied constable Lively.

#

Friday morning, and at the ringing of the bell, the thirty odd assorted pupils had begun to line themselves up at the door. First the girls, brisk and dutiful as always; then the boys, not all of whom joined as briskly as they might but all, in the end, dutifully. Out of respect for the institution and what it had inculcated in terms of obedience and

267

expected standards of behaviour, and also out of respect – a liking – for their teacher. Frank Lively was a welcome change from the usual strict and severe, prim and very proper mistresses that the older children remembered. So, he had the advantage there – he was not a woman. And although he taught at a Methodist school, in Hackett Street, opposite the chapel, neither was he a cleric. And for both of these reasons, as well as on account of his usually friendly and non-condescending manner, he was popular with his charges. At least for the moment. Not of course that some did not chance their arm with various infractions of classroom etiquette: some children were simply cheekier than others, and their misbehaviour, as any school teacher would tell you, had to be controlled for the general good. Better to instil discipline now than to allow the recalcitrant child to become a rebellious and anti-social adult. Better to suffer the fleeting discomfort of a few judicious strokes of the cane. The pain soon passes but instructive memory abides. Better that than end up uneducated and a criminal incarcerated on hard labour, or worse. But it was rare that corporal punishment was called for in Frank's class, and he did his best to remain scrupulously fair in its application: always he gave the boys a chance to explain themselves before making his final decision, and he believed that they respected him for that. Of course, he never disciplined the girls that way, nor for that matter would he allow the girls to witness the boys being caned. No, the girls in the class were all very well behaved as a rule; and if there were a small infringement, a short spell of standing in the corner made the point amply. He preferred to teach the girls: they made better students, he thought. His favourite was a girl by the name of Rose Adams, one of the older ones. She was just gone eleven and had already gained her elementary certificate. Frank had ambitions to keep her to thirteen as she was a good girl, a clever girl and a good classroom monitor; a shining example to the young ones.

The line was taking its time to form today.

"All right. Settle down then. Straight line please, two abreast…George, what are you doing?"

"I've lost a marlie sir."

"Can you see it?"

"No sir, that's why it's lost."

"Well, you haven't got time to look for it now. Perhaps your friends can help you find it at play time. All right."

"But…" began the sour-faced little boy.

"But nothing my lad. You're holding everybody else up. To your place now."

At a snail's pace the boy did as he was told.

"Now, all standing straight please. Shoulders back. Ready…quick march."

The uncoordinated millipede trudged past him. He counted them in. Thirty-five. Some missing today. Including Rose, he noticed; and her brother Billie; for a second day.

They found their usual places on the benches. Boys to the right, girls to the left. Oldest at the back, youngest at the front.

"Good morning class," said the teacher.

"Good morning Mr Lively," came the well-drilled sing-song back.

"Please be seated."

Being seated involved a lot of shuffling and a little elbowing and the sound of various objects scraping against wood.

To the well-rehearsed script, Frank Lively took out the attendance register, opened it, dipped his pen; and began.

"Rose Adams." He expected no formal response. He had already noted her absence mentally, and was loathe to mark the absence of both brother and sister in ink…

"Does anybody know what's wrong with Rose?" he asked.

"Please, sir," came back a very small but clear voice, "the men from the workhouse took her. And Billie."

"What?" None of his pupils were from above average income homes, just the opposite in most cases in fact, the exception being Arthur Barnett. But he could not believe that two of 'his' children had been taken into the tender care of the workhouse. Not without him being aware.

"What men? Where did they go?"

"Not supposed to say, sir," replied seven-year-old Gracie Tibbetts, now noticeably less confident. The Tibbets were neighbours to the Adams, and Gracie was a particular friend of Rose at school: she looked up to Rose and the older girl had taken her under her wing. Gracie's cheeks were reddening now in discomfort, nevertheless the school master persisted.

"What about her mother and the baby? Have they gone too?"

"No sir, nor Lizzie, nor Mr Adams…"

"That doesn't sound right."

"Oh it is, sir, honest. It's all all right 'cos they'll be back today. That's what Rose said."

"What else did Rose say?"

"Nothing, sir."

"But her mom and dad know all about it do they?"

"Please, sir, I'm not supposed to say nothing sir." The voice was pleading now, scared.

"It's all right Gracie, you don't have to say anything. Perhaps we will talk later."

Maybe he would question her again later, maybe not. He didn't want to get into a crying match. What should he do, if anything? He thought about as he continued with registration.

"William…" *no not here.*

"Alice Arnold."

"Present sir."

"Arthur Barnett."

"Yes, sir, present sir."

"Samuel Blakeway."

"Present sir."

"Ruth Cooper."

"Present, Mr Lively." And so it went on.

#

As predicted by the sergeant, Old Hill were not slow in coming forward when it came to 'his' murder. And so it happened that the sergeant's arrival that Monday morning was followed almost immediately by that of inspector Millership from headquarters, and a stout old constable by the name of Wothers, in a cab, no doubt to take credit for the arrest.

The tragedy that had been the ending of Michael Hickey's life, and the sheer damn mess of it all, had only just registered for Abe. He was standing at the cell door, not sure whether to blame one of his men, or just chalk it up to the devil's work and the dead man richly deserving of it, when he became aware of unfamiliar voices in the office. The lead was brisk, confident, authoritative, and he knew what it meant, and he opened the connecting door to almost walk into the inspector. Abe edged into the room and pulled the door to behind him.

"Ah, sergeant Lively. Good morning to you. Where's our murderer then?" said Millership. The inspector was not an outwardly obviously imposing figure; rather ordinary looking, slim, about five nine, crow's feet crammed with experience and his once glossy black hair now grizzling into permanent grey, cut very short. It was the voice more than anything: the voice had power; it was soft but clear; it was accustomed to command and it commanded compliance. Thus it was that the sergeant decided to take the bull by the horns straight away.

"Good morning inspector. It's bad news I'm afraid."

"What is?" queried his superior, sharing a glance with his constable.

"It's the prisoner, sir. Somehow he has contrived to hang himself. He's dead, sir."

There was a long pause before the inspector responded.

"Dead is it? I suppose it saves the cost of a trial. What happened exactly?" He seemed to be taking it all very calmly.

"Well, sir, I've not had the opportunity to put it all together…"

"So you don't know what happened then?"

"No, sir. Not exactly. Not yet."

"And what time did it occur? This thing that you don't know how it happened?"

"Not sure, sir. Sometime during the night."

"I see. And do you have any theory as to why the man should hang himself? I mean apart from the obvious. Or, let me put it another way. Should you have foreseen this and

270

prevented it?"

"Well, sir, he seemed of sound mind, once he sobered up. Very quiet, but that's understandable."

"So we must conclude then that he killed himself out of remorse – is it?"

"Best guess, sir."

"Is that how you operate, sergeant, on guesswork?"

Abe felt obliged to defend himself, "Got to start somewhere, sir. I've come across some inspired and rewarding guesswork doing this job. However, in this particular case, the deceased left a message. We were trying to decide what it meant, but yes, remorse for killing a friend probably covers it."

"Well why didn't you say so? What form did this message take? What did it say?"

"He scrawled it on the floor of the cell."

"And it said?"

"Er, I was just about to write it down…"

"Just about to write it down," echoed Millership. "Well sergeant, I am just about to lose my temper," he said, clipping his words slightly and raising his voice a touch – his equivalent of barking. "I mean, I come here to congratulate you and your men on the apprehension of a violent murderer and to examine his statement before – you did get his statement? A confession?"

"No sir…"

"Lord give me strength!" expostulated the inspector.

"…too drunk, sir, then…"

"Drunk is it? What, you lot or the prisoner!"

This last produced the rudiments of an unguarded titter from the Old Hill constable: the inspector rounded on him.

"And it's no laughing matter Wothers!" he warned. He stopped then and looked through the ceiling skyward, as if seeking divine aid. Perhaps he got it, for he then took a deep breath, sighed, and continued calmly.

"All right then. Lead on MacDuff. Let's see what we can piece together between us."

#

Morning had been devoted to reading, spelling and then the writing of letters in copperplate, scratched into thirty odd slates. Now they were on arithmetic, and long division to be exact, and Frank was missing Rose. At going on twelve, she was one of the oldest and cleverest in the class, one big class that encompassed ages from five to almost thirteen. They were a diverse bunch and all from poorer backgrounds with the exception of Arthur, son of the up-and-coming councillor Samuel Barnett. Even though the councillor had chosen this school out of principle, being himself a staunch Methodist

271

– Frank doubted, in his modesty, that he had undertaken a serious comparison of available educational establishments – Arthur's membership of the class had been taken by some as an endorsement of Frank's teaching ability. Which was not to be sneezed at. Arthur was of above average ability, as you might expect given his social advantages, and way out in front as far as turnout was concerned. Also understandable. But some were visibly poorer than others, as their clothing, and in particular their footwear told. And some were bright as a button, and others were slow; some shy and well-behaved; some outgoing and confident; a few bore watching. He endeavoured to treat them all the same, but he had to admit that Rose Adams was his favourite. She and her ten-year-old brother Billie were from a very humble mining family. They had not had the best of starts in life – but that's what the school, and Frank Lively, were there to remedy. Rose was one of three class monitors, students who could be entrusted with imparting their own knowledge to the younger ones. Frank had planned to split the afternoon into three groups, of a dozen or so, under the monitors, with himself having a roving role, smoothing out any particular issues, explaining one to one as required. As it happened, he didn't bother to divide the class up today...

The day ended as it began, with half an hour's bible reading from the teacher and half a dozen of the older pupils in turn. The bible was not Frank's forte, although he was careful never to reveal his shortcomings to his employers. Fortunately, the Church laid down set readings, rather like his mother's Sunday Missal. Also fortunately, questions on the readings were discouraged, lest the school leave itself open to the charge, in defiance of statute, of providing religious instruction.

At 2:50 p.m. the monitors were sent round to collect the slates and pencils and rubbers. At 2:55 p.m. the final ritual, Frank's own contribution to clear thinking and productive reflection, began.

"Right then class, before you leave, sitting straight please."

The prospect of getting out prompted swift compliance.

"Good. Now, arms folded, and eyes closed. Good. And, deep calm breaths now – mouths closed Eileen Sharp; And, think about what you have learned today. Think about your letters, and your spelling, and your sums. Good. Now – no fidgeting please – two minutes silence." Frank began to count down the two minutes on his watch. He had picked up this little trick from big brother Abe: he swore by it; always stopped to, well, stop – and breathe deeply – before his wrestling bouts back home; certainly seemed to work for him, most of the time. These kids were still getting used to it though and to some two minutes must have seemed an eternity. But by and large they gave it a go, and Frank watched them as they struggled with restless feet and against intolerable itches, against impatient eyelids and with incessantly runny noses: like little Alfie Woodall valiantly ignoring the slow green line advancing incrementally towards his lips despite judiciously timed sniffs; like Jimmy Riley, dutifully trying to observe the folded arms mandate whilst also trying to scratch his itching scalp, extending two fingers to meet his now bowed head. Frank would have to check for nits again…

Almost time and the feet really began to shuffle. The kids' shoes all told their own stories: most were well worn, soles were often holed; some were tight, lace-less even, because the owners had simply outgrown them, but had nothing to replace them; others, just as old, but newly handed down, were extremely loose, and children clawed at them with their toes to avoid losing them. It was always the shoes that touched Frank the most. He hoped that their obvious and unfulfilled physical needs were made up for by the love of their families; but he knew better than to count on that. Time was up.

"Eyes open. Thank you class."

"Thank you, Mr Lively."

"I'll see you all on Monday. Be good and take care. Christopher, would you do the honours, please?"

"Yes, sir," replied the monitor, relishing this morsel of power. "Class, stand to attention." Anxious to be away now they stood as one.

"Left turn," squeaked the monitor, and they all turned left, "front row, file out."

The front row's tail was extended by the second row, then came the third and fourth rows, with master Arthur Wilday bringing up the rear. They made their way out of the classroom to form what was supposed to be an orderly queue in the corridor. The teacher locked the classroom door, walked past the restless youngsters, and opened the door to the yard.

Upon the words 'class dismissed' a quick and disorderly escape was effected. Outside, the bunched collection of juveniles fractured into dozens of erratic trajectories as the liberated youngsters went their separate ways at their chosen speeds.

The school building was bereft of human life now. Frank locked up and headed off in an unfamiliar direction.

#

Whether or not Josh Lively had correctly conjectured that his brother would be requiring that the body remain in place for forensic examination, the sergeant as it turned out would have no say in the matter: as soon as the inspector entered the cell he ordered, "For God's sake take him down. And get some windows and doors open, it stinks in here."

And so it was that the reluctant constable, on his brother's order, did in fact have to manhandle the corpse, although, as he was less particular in such matters, the closest contact was made by P.C. Payne.

They laid him out on the bed and the inspector cast his eyes over the ex-human dollop of flesh-wrapped scrap.

"Right, what's this?" queried Millership taking out a pencil and inserting it under a tight wound green cloth clinging to the deceased's neck. He wiggled the pencil around. There was not much give in it, the prisoner in preparation having tied it as tightly as consciousness had allowed. Before the inspector could continue his peregrinations, Josh felt obliged to comment.

"That's his handkerchief, sir."

"And he's hung himself with it," returned inspector Millership, "with something you were aware was in his possession?"

"I can't deny that sir," admitted the constable, "but it was just a handkerchief and not suitable for hanging oneself, you wouldn't have thought."

"No, you wouldn't have thought. And neither would I have to be fair to you. Constable?"

"It's P.C. Lively, sir."

The inspector looked from Josh to Abe and back. "Of course you are. I can see that you confiscated his boot laces and belt, unless he never possessed such items – which I doubt."

"That's right inspector," pitched in Payne, "I've got them in the office…"

"And I take it that you were in charge of the prisoner's custody then?"

"Yes sir," confessed a red-faced constable Payne, "Josh –that is to say P.C. Lively, sir – went off duty at eight, and P.C. Stride…"

The inspector forestalled with a gesture.

"So you were manning the station alone. Yes?"

"Yes," conceded Payne unwillingly, feeling that he was walking into some kind of trap.

"And I'm very glad to hear it," continued the inspector. "We can't be wasting valuable resources; can't have constables sitting around idling away the time sipping tea and chin-wagging like there's no criminals to catch; can't have 'em getting away with murder while we sit on our fat behinds. Can we?"

"No sir," agreed Payne readily.

"Anyway, this one didn't did he?"

"Didn't what, sir?"

"Didn't get away with murder. Now if you want my opinion – and you're going to get it – this," he nodded to the bed, "this is saving us all the time and expense – don't forget the expense – of putting him on trial and hanging him. Assuming that he would have been found guilty that is. So, we just have the little matter of the inquest to get through, and we don't want any dirt thrown our way."

He looked pointedly at Payne. "The coroner might have some awkward questions for you, son. Depends on the coroner. Mentioning no names, but one in particular is a right bleeding-heart radical who has no idea of what the real world is like. If he had his way he'd send robbers to Sunday School and rapists to the Salvation Army – see how they'd get on helping out with those fallen women, eh?"

The turn of events, or rather of pronouncements, had rather taken everyone, with the possible exception of P.C. Wothers, by surprise. Accordingly, there was a short and stunted silence which Millership broke in friendly tone.

"Now sergeant, what's your verdict?" he asked, nodding again toward the bed.

Abe took the cue. "Well, sir, death by asphyxiation, I'd hazard a guess. He must have been very determined: he's ripped his shirt into strips, twisted them and tied them together to make a rope, to go with his handkerchief noose."

"Yes," agreed the inspector, "he used the bedstead to reach up to the window bar…"

"It seems likely sir," rejoined the sergeant. "You can see where it scraped the floor as he kicked it away. Irony is, if it was the other cell, the bed's bolted down…" As nobody seemed inclined to comment upon the ramifications of that last admission, the sergeant hurriedly continued… "After that, there was no getting it back, and no turning back. He probably struggled against it in the end, instinctively, and lost his boots as result."

The sorry-looking scuffed boots lay lonely against the foot of the uncaring brick wall, beneath the grim window, one toppled on its side, tongue stuck out as if it had been in the process of offering some excuse, or prayer…

"And," the inspector continued, "if he was that determined, he would probably know to time his act for an interval between the checks carried out by constable – what is it?"

"It's Payne, sir, constable Payne," said Abe Lively.

The inspector turned to that constable and prompted, "I take it that you did check on the prisoner at intervals?"

"That's the usual practice, sir," replied the constable, somewhat cryptically.

"There we are then," said Millership. "Nothing to be done then. Nobody could have foreseen it; nobody to blame. Do you agree sergeant?"

"There was nothing to be done, sir."

"Good. That's how we'll all present it to the coroner. Anything else?"

"There is that message inspector. What do you make of it? Any ideas?" asked the sergeant.

The inspector read the deceased's written ramblings again. "Not a one," he replied. "You?"

"Not a one," admitted the sergeant.

"That's it for now then. Thank you sergeant Lively. Keep up the good work, and remember, you don't have to around arresting folk willy nilly to get the job done. Sometimes a good bit of physical policing does the trick, and from what I hear you're just the man to administer it."

"But, I thought…" began Abe.

"What?"

"The arrests record, the conviction rates…"

"Are not the be all and end all. There are other ways to measure success – except for certain persons who, shall we say, might have their own not exactly unbiased agendas. And you know who I mean. Just rely on your own judgement, son, and your colleagues here, and that bit of timber at your hip. Now, I must be off. Good to see you again. Come on Wothers man, cap on."

Abe escorted the pair to the street.

"I'll say good day then sergeant. Bear in mind what I said, won't you?"

#

The school master was stepping out and had loosened his collar to facilitate the release of the excess heat generated by the unaccustomed exertion. In comparison to the majority of the working population, and to his two policeman brothers, his was a sedentary lifestyle; bookish even, when he could get his hands on decent printed material; to be expected of a teacher. Not for the first time, he promised himself that he would get round to exercising more: the brisk walk from Hackett Street to the miners' houses at the other side of St. Giles had taxed him more than it should have for a man of his age; perhaps he would join a football club, or get one of those safety bicycles. Football would be cheaper.

The rows of miners' houses were not very old but already they had taken on an old and careworn appearance, borrowed quite possibly from their well-used inhabitants. Some looked like they were sinking already. The people living in them were poor, he knew, little better than slaves in his opinion. Their status of thralldom to the owners was underlined for him by the fact that these houses were not identified by family name, but by a number allocated to each. Each family of human beings reduced to a number. And so he counted – number 35, no number (removed as a small act of defiance perhaps?), no number, number 38, number 39, 40, nothing, nothing, 42 – that was it, 42, that was the one, and it was confirmed by the small white painted affirmation of freedom: 'Adams Cottage.'

It stood in a row typical of the area, and of miners' dwellings in particular, concertina'd tight together as if under the gargantuan pressure of the hands of some giant and macabre musician, but in actual fact merely designed like that, or at least built that way, in order to cram as much life – fodder for the mines – into as little living space as economically possible. Once, before he had left country life behind, as a child, he and a village friend had sneaked into what they had thought was a grain warehouse, only to find it populated by a hundred sows with a hundred litters, but all confined to their own small crates, doing nothing but eating and defecating and growing the next crop of bacon. He didn't understand. Their own pigs were free to roam, at least most of the time. His father had said that pigs in sheds was the future and it was a way of making more money,

276

but that he would never make that kind of money. The people who had created that pig shed could well have been consulted over these sad terraces. Similar logic no doubt applied.

Like the rest of them, the Adams' house had a miniscule front garden, fenced off and gated. The gate was padlocked, and from the look of the lock and chain, and the rusty hinges, it was evident that that entrance to the property did not get much use. That was not unusual: in common with all of the other dwellings, from the gate to the front door there was no path. Instead, the earth had been put to more productive use. Frank could see cabbages and potatoes and strings and canes encouraging the skyward stretch of some kind of legume. He would have to go round the back.

The back was accessed via a dark brick passageway, an 'entry' which he had passed three or four doors ago. So what was it? Four. He made a note of that. Retracing his steps, he made his way down the entry, which would also serve as his exit later. At the end, clearing the line of the houses above, it emptied him into a narrow brick paved pathway, upon which he turned right. To his left now there was a high brick wall, blocking out whatever the view might have been, and on the right lay the small brick and cobble yards of the cottages, bounded by low brick walls with round brick whitewashed cappings. Glancing into the first, in passing, he saw through the open door of a brewhouse an old green mangle with rusting feet highlighted against the flaky white wall, and in the yard a washing line was having an easy time of it, propped at half mast, strung between a drainpipe and the remains of what could have been an old damson tree, drying just a pair of still dripping socks. All typical of such back yards. But the most interesting features of these 'fodes' to the ex-country boy were the tiny square enclosures, each of which looked to be shared between two houses: they were pigsties; and judging by the smells and by occasional snuffling, and one glimpse of pink bristled flesh, at least some were tenanted. And he guessed that some of the human tenants of the properties ahead had been swilling out. He could see where water had been swept through open gateways out onto the path and down the slope towards what looked like a couple of privies. He trod cautiously, but not cautiously enough, for stepping on one particular paviour, it turned out to be loose in its hole, and the hole a natural receptacle for some of the unwanted liquid from the yards. The pressure of his weight on one edge caused the brick to tilt and to squeeze out the formerly trapped fluid. It squirted up his calf; he didn't swear, but he nearly did, and he hoped that it had been mostly water.

He was level with number 42 now, so he turned in and approached the back door. Unlike the front one, this one looked used, a little worse for wear in comparison – naturally enough. The step had been indented by regular traffic and also, he knew, by the daily application of a stiff brush, soap and water – and elbow grease: an indispensible ritual for the women of these households.

He knocked; a dog yapped; the door handle turned, almost immediately, with a loose rattle; and the door was pulled open, slowly. He looked down, and gradually there appeared around the line of wood a little girl. A very dirty little girl, with a streaky face and a sooty dress. She was brushing herself down, briefly, and he waited briefly until she stopped and looked up at him through the palest blue eyes under fair hair swept back and tied with a blue ribbon as pale as her eyes. She was all of seven.

"Hello, is your mother in?"

"Yes, walk forward," she replied…

After the daylight, the room – the kitchen – was noticeably dark despite the tremendous fire stoked in the stove. It kept the room at fever heat, pots hissing, and drenched the air with a strong onion odour. A little multi toned dog was still yapping an excitable yap, from the refuge of the ragged little hearth rug which was evidently its accustomed place, oblivious to the young girl's admonishments. He had just enough time to take in the fact that the mother was in the process of preparing the family tea, when Mrs Adams herself appeared from the pantry with half a loaf in one hand and a well-grown baby on the other arm.

This was the third time he had met Rose's mother, and each time he saw her she looked more tired and less robust. But her eyes lit up when she saw him, and he saw in them her daughter. Before the shutters came down.

"Mr Lively. This is a pleasure. Can I do you a cup of tea?"

"Good day to you Mrs Adams. Have I come at an inconvenient time?"

She looked around her and shook her head with good humour. "Is there ever a convenient time? If you mean am I busy, then, yes, I'm busy. But when is a woman not?"

She went over to the stove and adjusted the position of the pots. "Lizzie, get the best cups out and pour us some tea with milk. We'll be in the front. Come this way Mr Lively."

She led the way into the 'best room.' Frank's extra mural duties had taken him into several of his pupils' homes. Inevitably, the school teacher was shown into the best room, invariably the front room, or the parlour as they sometimes had it. Also inevitably, it was the lady of the house that he met with; the men seemed uncomfortable around a teacher. Although Frank was earning not a lot more than the miners and factory hands whose children he taught, and despite his friendly and out-going nature, the men, even if not working or sleeping, made themselves scarce. Perhaps as a teacher, as a man who used his mind to earn a living they saw him as a challenge to their manhood, a reminder of their own shortcomings and inadequacies; possibly just the opposite. Or was it just self-protective indifference? An engrained version of what a man should be? They were the breadwinners, toiling most of the hours that God sends to house and feed and clothe their families. And perhaps that was enough; perhaps it took everything that they had. To change might take an energy they simply did not have and could not afford; an understanding they could never allow themselves. For they were the breadwinners. Work was work and for the men; home and family was women's work. And rarely could the twain meet.

And so today, it was to the lady of the household that Frank Lively was to address his questions.

"Please sit down," she said, motioning to a chair standing to one side of a two-pound-ten mahogany table pushed up against one wall. As she settled herself on a matching chair on the other side, his eyes briefly took in the contents of the room: there was a little used easy chair and a cheap stand-up piano, upon which, perched in pride of place, was a little glass case containing the stuffed remains of some small animal; a dog it seemed, but of what breed he could not have said; the earthly remains of some much-loved family pet no doubt. Amongst the various framed documents, he was pleased to note a certificate from the Blackheath Methodist Association For The Promotion Of Spiritual Education and made out to Rose Adams, set amongst the faded funeral cards of previous generations and washed-out embroidery samples, possibly those of the elder daughter that Frank knew was in service in Birmingham. An impossible collection of mismatched crockery crowded the mantelpiece, beneath which lay a made up but unlit fire.

Mrs Adams forestalled his opening question with one of her own.

"I suppose you've come to ask why our Rose and Bill weren't at school?" She spoke as a local, 'wor at skewel' was more like the actual sound of those last words, but Frank was used to it now, was even starting to pick it up himself.

"Well, I wouldn't normally be so forward, Mrs Adams..." returned the teacher.

"But what?"

"Are they ill?" he asked looking straight at her.

And she knew that he knew; knew something any road.

"No Mr Lively, they're not ill, thank the Lord. And neither are they here," she said, anticipating his next question.

"Where are they?" he asked.

"Well then, that's my husband's business, and I don't care to poke my nose in his business; neither should you," she replied. Although she half hoped he would, as long as she was left out of it of course.

"Has it got something to do with the workhouse?" He saw her stiffen, and added, "I've been told that your children have been taken off to the workhouse. So you can imagine that I am concerned."

"Can I?"

"Yes, of course. I care about Rose and Billie. Are things so bad then?"

She laughed then, short and sardonic. "Good Lord no. They'll be back tomorrow, Sunday latest."

"So you know where they are then?"

"Of course I do. They're visiting. That's all you need to know. They're perfectly well and safe."

"You'll tell that to the School Board man will you?"

"Doesn't cover your school though does it, the School Board?"

279

"No. No it doesn't to tell true. So, who are they visiting then?"

Nothing.

"Mrs Adams, I just want to know what's going on. I have a responsibility, for their education."

"Like I said. It's my husband's business."

"And he's working, is he?"

"No. He's here, upstairs. I thought you knew…the accident. We're on the parish."

"I did hear, but thought he would have gone back by now."

"Well, so did we all," she retorted sharply before continuing, "but no, he's not fit yet, and it's not just his body…no, we're dependent on the parish," she said and paused before adding cryptically, "and the goodwill of certain friends."

Frank guessed that the family was struggling. If the oldest son hadn't succumbed to pneumonia last year, there would still be a wage coming in. He felt sorry for Mrs Adams, but he was concerned for his pupils.

"I was told that Rose and Billie were picked up by men from the workhouse. Is that right?"

"If you like."

"Why?"

"It's our business."

"Your husband's you mean?"

"Yes – you're catching on. My husband's business, and I'm a good wife. All I can tell you is that no harm will come to the kids; we've done it before. It helps us out a bit…"

At this moment, the door swung open and the little girl came in bearing an unfeasibly large tray upon which were balanced two cups filled almost to the brims with tea. Frank helped her set them down on the table. She stood with the tray in her hand and looked at him.

"Yoh'm our Billie's teacher am ya?"

"That's right."

"Ah'm gonna cum an' all when we con 'ford et. But we gorra save fust."

"Well, I look forward to seeing you then…" began the teacher.

"Right then, get on Lizzie, we're talking. Watch the taters don't boil dry."

"Shall I 'ave Edward?" she asked looking at the baby, which was still perched apparently content and quiet in the crook of his mother's left arm.

"No, he's asleep. Go on now. Go and play with Nipper."

The little girl turned to Frank, curtsied, and left without another word.

Mrs Adams rearranged the baby to take a sip of tea. Frank took the opportunity to have his say.

"I must say, Mrs Adams, that this is a rum do. As you know, I'm particularly fond of Rose. She has a lot of potential. Billie too. It's a shame to pull them out of school for no reason…"

"Not to worry, they'll be back."

"That's not entirely the point though is it? As their teacher, I do have some responsibility for their welfare. I mean, it's my duty to look into anything that might expose them to any physical or moral hazard, I think."

"No, your duty as you call it ends when they come out of school."

"But that's just it. They weren't in school, when they should have been."

"They don't miss very often."

"Granted. But it's still not good for them. And then, there's this other business."

"Which is not your business. You're not their father."

"No. Perhaps I should speak to him."

"No!" It came out too loud, edged with panic. The baby opened his eyes, gurgled a little, and shut them again. Frank was not sure that it was entirely normal. She kissed it on the forehead and continued, "No. If you care for Rose as you say, and her family, it will cause more trouble than it's worth. More than you know."

"You're worrying me now," admitted the teacher.

"It's Frank isn't it?"

"Yes."

"Can I be straight with you Frank?"

"Of course you can. I hope you have been."

"I just mean…look, laying my cards on the table, I'm not very happy about the arrangement."

"Arrangement?"

"They've done it before, borrowed the kids. Nothing bad happens to them, I know that; trust me on that. A man comes, or two men. They say they've come to give them a day out, and they do. Last time it was to somewhere in Tipton –and yes, the workhouse I think. They even enjoy it; get to play with other kids. Then they come back."

"But there's more to it? A purpose?"

"I would imagine so, but I'm not about to pry. And neither should you; let sleeping dogs lie. Unless you like being bitten."

"What do you mean?"

"Nothing. All I'm saying is that if my husband knows that you've been poking around in private family business, he won't be pleased. He'll blame me and I'll suffer for it. I'm sure you wouldn't want that."

"All right. I see. But who are these men?"

"I can't say."

"But you're not happy about this, are you?"

"No! I said didn't I?"

"So, who are they?"

"I'm not sure. Not from around here, not born and bred."

"That doesn't help much."

"Help with what?"

"Getting to the bottom of it."

"Why don't you just leave it? There's no harm done."

"Because something's not right. I don't like it and you don't like it. Maybe I will have to ask Mr Adams. Who knows, he—"

"I said no! Don't do that. I'll tell you what – the answers are at the workhouse. I've heard the name Gross, Mr Gross. If you really must get involved, start with him."

As she closed the door on him she told herself that he had only himself to blame, pushy little sod. Hopefully the people at the workhouse would fob him off with some story or other, if he was lucky. She had not been frank with Frank: she had not warned him about Cutler's men. But how could she have?

#

With all the fuss about the suicide, the little lad in the back cell had all but been forgotten. He was just gone thirteen and small with it, and when constable Lively had taken him his breakfast the streaky face told him that he had been crying. He tore through the chunk of bread and dripping as if he had not eaten for days, which, given his circumstances and reason for his arrest, was quite possible.

He clanged down the enamel mug, now drained of its hot contents, and from his position on a tiny stool looked up at the tall symbol of authority with foreboding.

"Are you going to let me go?"

"It's not as simple as that son. A man has been hurt."

"It was an accident. He did it to himself. He was going to hurt me. It wasn't my fault…"

"And it wasn't your fault that you stole an apple from his barrow. A pocketful of apples in fact. Stealing is a crime."

"I was hungry."

"I'm sure you were," said the P.C. And looking at him in his ripped clothing, at the dishevelled greasy hair and the scrawny carcass, he really was. He was a handsome young lad, or would have been if he had not been painfully thin. But it had become plain to the constable that he was by no means quick-witted. Had he been, he may not have been in a cell.

"So what's going to happen to me then?"

The policeman had skimmed through the report on the lad. He had had a hard time of it, by the sound of it. He deserved a bit of luck.

"It depends," replied Josh.

"Depends? What on?"

"Different things. Do you want another cup?"

"Yes please."

After dealing with the refill, Josh sat down with the report, penned in the unmistakable hand of P.C. Clarke (the poor man did try, but he had not been blessed with the best of educations, and was shabby by nature, as his script reflected.) Josh knew that the young detainee had been seen stealing and that he had been chased by the stall owner, one Matthew Haywood, an old wheezy costermonger with sagging jowls to match his sagging appetite for the life, and a gammy leg. The indignant old stall holder was not about to catch the young chap, of course, not without raising a hue and cry, which, breathless, he had tried to do. But pride and an Englishman's proclivity to defend property rights overruled good sense. So, bent on catching the boy, he ran heedless into the horse road and caught a horse's shoulder right in the face. It was a glancing blow, but the impact bowled him over at some velocity, and he ended up in the gutter nursing at some volume a damaged wrist which was broken according to the statement given to Clark. Clark was dubious about the claim: "Sprained more like," he had noted.

Now, instead of making good his escape after this little diversion, this thirteen-year-old hardened criminal – Jake Collins was his name – had stopped to look back, which was a profound mistake, as it led to him being apprehended by a posse of public-minded boozers between pubs.

Mr Haywood had been insistent that they charge the boy, on behalf of both his apples and his wrist. But the police officers in Rowley village had as yet done nothing of the sort. It was Josh's case and in his opinion it would take witness statements to get a case to stick. And that meant work, and for what? Josh had begun to think that maybe he would have a word with Haywood. A plan was hatching in his mind. The boy had no work; formerly he had been employed fetching water and tea and small beer for the salt-cake pot men and the black ash men at Oldbury Alkali Works; but his short career had offered but poor prospects for a boy whose mother had wilfully kept him out of school; further, had it continued, his health, already compromised by a combination of noxious fumes, sweating heat and chilling draughts, would soon have been irretrievably damaged. Out of the fire and into the frying pan, in Josh's estimation. In the end it had been the boy's lack of education that had precipitated his dismissal, when, an inspection being imminent, the foreman suddenly remembered that the boy had never presented a certificate confirming the minimum elementary educational standard – as required by the Education Act – despite the fact that when that very same foreman had taken on the very same lad, as a ten-year-old what's more, he had very deliberately not asked about one…

Clark had clearly been bored, or lonely, for he had taken down more than usual. As he read, Josh noticed that the grammar was particularly poor, even by Clark's standards, and so he was inclined to believe that he had taken it down verbatim:

"I live at home with me mom. The parish have stopped her allowance now and my oldest sister has got a very bad foot. One Sunday her was drunk and her kicked up a racket and fell off the step and her ankle fell out. Her used to bring men home with her. Me next sister is about fifteen. Hers awful. Her swears awful at me mom and mom don't like to here it and she says one night the devil will come to the house to get her. I bet he wouldn't dare. Her learns it off some of the bad girls. Her goes to clean the bad girls house every day apart from Sunday and has done for years."

At this point it appears that Clark had asked about his education, or lack of it, for it continued:

"I have never been to Sunday school or to any other kind of school except a long time ago. They put me right through my ABC. I could do them now if they would tell me the next letters, not without though. I was never in a church or chapel, nor heard anybody pray. Mom don't talk about God or anything. We had a bible but it had to be sold. A great big thing with lots of writing. No pictures. The track woman come round once and said it was a good un."

And now, the conversation having turned to religion, Josh began to understand that Clark had not in fact been lonely, or at least had not been alone, although he might still have been bored. Clark would have kept the questions to a minimum, less work, but somebody else had been there prompting more, and it took no great leap of faith on Josh's part to know that it was Miss Ricketts. Miss Ricketts was a soldier for Christ in the Salvation Army of General Booth, with ambitions to become a cadet and be ordained. A worthy ambition perhaps, although like many locals Josh found the Army's in your face, blood and fire, singing in the streets approach off-putting, if not to say disturbing. What was more disturbing though was the fact that this lady's proselytising went beyond the general, and was very definitely focussed on Joshua Lively in particular. Josh had no doubt that she regarded him as a future husband, and had made up his mind long since to avoid her as much as possible, thus removing temptation from her. But she had been here recently, he knew:

"I don't know who Christ was," continued the statement, "or if he was a person or a man, or who made the world. After people die they go to heaven, everybody the same, the good people and the bad uns. Nobody told me about heaven except when me Dad died, a long time ago. My Mom said he was in heaven. The devil is a good person. He puts the bad people in a great big fire. I don't know where he lives."

At this point Clark had managed to get the boy talking about more recent history, and how he had come to be stealing apples. Stolen apples, that's what Josh had joined the police for, he didn't think. He did not want to read on. He didn't know whether to laugh or cry at the boy's pathetic inflicted ignorance. No, he was not going to hang criminal charges on this poor unfortunate: he could be saved yet. So, first thing he had to do was confront Matthew Haywood, and put a proposition to him. Matt was not getting any younger and was finding it hard to manage; the boy needed honest work; problem solved. Possibly. But first he must get the boy out of that cell. He couldn't be left indefinitely, nor could he be released scot-free, nor could he go home. No doubt Miss Ricketts ('do call me Geraldine') would jump at the chance to help, but, personal issues aside, how could he release a prisoner into the care of a private individual? Equally to the point, what if the lad ran away? So what to do?

#

Until the post-mortem and the inquest, now a double inquest, there was not much to be done with Michael Hickey but move him and free up his cell. So they moved him to the cellar to lie with his dead friend. With no choice now, Josh had to help manoeuvre the corpse's legs down the cold steps, followed by Payne with the ugly end. There was only one table in the small musty chamber which was the usual repository for any corpses in custody, at least during the summer months. When not used as a staging post for the departed, it was generally empty, but sometimes it was used to house particularly rowdy or violent inmates: a 'naughty cell.' Today, there was no room for any naughty prisoners, unless the dead could still be called naughty, for there were two bodies to be secreted away. The first to arrive had been Henry Higgins, and he occupied prime spot on the little table; Hickey had to make do with the floor, where he was duly deposited and covered with an old sheet, which proved too flimsy a deterrent to stop rodents nibbling off his nose. But noseless or not, another lucrative opportunity for Doctor Wharton.

Outside the station the sergeant sent P.C. Payne off on his rounds and headed for the Royal Oak to catch up with Miriam. It was a quiet Monday morning, and after the inspector's visit, he felt like a drink. Just one. He was on duty, but what the hell? He deserved one. Blow the rules. Who made them anyway? Did they know him? Did they know what kind of man he was? Of course not. Just one, blow the rules.

The pub was quiet, day shift was working, night shift sleeping it off, females young and old preoccupied with the wash. A few old timers dotted about; nobody behind the bar. Where was she?

She was sitting at a small table, strategically placed near to the open counter top of the bar, and she was facing the doors, to get a view of approaching customers. But she didn't see him, not straight away. Because she was leaning in to engage with a man with his back to the entrance. Not Jack Beckett, he could tell that. The sight went in at his eyes and straight to his belly and triggered a surge of chemicals. What was it? Anger. Yes, anger, for he now recognised the man. He had warned her. Why didn't she listen? Didn't she trust him?

She saw him then and flushed, and rose.

"Abe, this is a surprise." She rushed to him and hugged him; felt his coldness. Retreating behind the bar without acknowledgement of her seated guest she asked, "Do you want a drink?"

"In due course. I want a word with you first. If you're not too busy that is," the last added with a theatrical look around the room ending with a pointed stare in the direction of her still seated companion.

Francis Thompson felt it and turned abruptly as if stung. Standing and turning he said, "I don't believe that we have been properly introduced…"

Before he could continue the policeman said, "No, we haven't." And walked past him to the bar.

Awkwardly, Miriam intervened. "Abraham (not Abe), this is Mr Smith, Francis Smith. From London. He's a poet."

Abe half turned so that he could see both of them. "Charmed, I'm sure. How much does that pay then? Poetry."

"Well," began 'Smith.'

"Because," continued the copper, "I've never heard of a poet of that name. Not a famous one anyway. Not a published one. Are you published?"

"Not yet," stated the poet.

"So, what do you live on then? What do you pay for your beer with? Got a job have you?" queried the police sergeant.

"If you must know, I live on a small allowance from my father."

"That must be nice for you."

"It is. It beats working for a living. Anyway, do excuse me, I have an appointment with my muse."

"Your what?"

"I've got some poems to write."

"I know what you meant."

"Well, good day then sergeant, I must take my leave," said Thompson, and added on his way out and whilst looking straight at the policeman, "and adieu Miriam."

Abe could only shout after a shadow. "It's Mrs Lively to you."

His sister came out from behind the bar, sat down and looked up at him. "Don't you mean Mrs Beckett?" she asked quietly. "I'm Mrs Beckett now, not Mrs Lively. Never have been."

"Sorry, I forgot," replied her brother as he sat, "but you are always a Lively to me; always will be, my Miriam."

"And I'll always be a Lively first, and your sister. To the world I'm Mrs Beckett, to the world I was Mrs Hughes. But those names are just labels, worn on the outside, aren't they? It's like you in that uniform. You're not the big tough sergeant to me, although you may be big and tough, but that's not what I see. I still see my brother, the boy who loved the fields and woods, who loved his horses and won the May crown. Remember that little Rabbit?"

"Yes," he said, "always will. I know you love me sis, but do you trust me?"

"Of course I do. I couldn't trust anybody more. But…I don't believe you trust me, do you?"

"You mean that character?" he replied nodding to the doorway.

"Exactly. The way you behave anybody would think I'm about to run away with him or something. All I'm doing is passing the time with someone who has something different to say, that's all. Makes a change from the usual drone about who's been married or maimed this week, or whose pigeons have won a prize, or whippets."

"And you've just said it. There's something different about him, and it's not good. I might trust you, I do trust you, but I do not trust him. There's something wrong."

"Yes, well I'm a big girl now. But I promise to be careful."

"All right," said Abe grudgingly, "but make sure you're never alone with him."

"Good God, whatever are you insinuating, sergeant," replied she, but teasingly.

"You know what I mean…"

"Yes, I do know what you mean. Thank you for caring." And she leant over and kissed his cheek. "Anyway," she continued, "I'm sure you didn't come here to discuss Mr Smith. To what do I owe the pleasure?"

But her brother did not seem to be hearing. Her lips had seemed unnaturally hot. The heat pricked at his scalp, and then there was an insistent fluttering in his head, in his brain and in his ear, and he froze for what may have been a minute, or only a split second, as the fluttering, the fluttering of wings, turned into a soft voice, whispering, tickling, whispering:

"Get up, get up. Get him, get him. Get up, get him. Go!"

Abe was getting used to the voice, the noises that had become words. He did not like it, its demands, but it no longer scared him like it did. And he no longer thought he was going mad, it was just that he heard where others could not. He was special.

Suddenly he was back. "Sorry sis, got to go." He took her head in his hands and gently kissed it and went, abruptly.

But there was no sign of the putative poet now. He stopped to think, because he had been acting on emotion. With a clearer head the policeman in him surfaced and asked what the hell he would do with Mr Smith if he caught up with him. He had committed no crime; and what right did he have to hound somebody based on a feeling? He should forget him: he knew that the voice would not like that, but he was in charge. Nevertheless, perhaps he would get somebody to check on this Mr Smith, when time allowed. Better safe than sorry.

#

Joshua Lively's public duties as a servant of the law left him limited time for personal recreation. When he wasn't on a ten or twelve hour stint, he was mostly engaged in catching up on sleep. And whilst most of the male population enjoyed regular Saturday

287

afternoons off – and Sundays – the police constables were obliged to work them, in shifts, for that very same reason.

So it was that he had been very pleased on that Sunday afternoon to see his brother Frank walk into the office.

The policeman stood with a smile.

"Good grief, look what the cat's dragged in!"

"Nice to see you an' all," replied the twin with a grin.

"It's great to see you," said the older brother, taking the proffered hand and clasping it in both of his own. "It's been a long time," he observed.

"Yes," agreed Frank, "we must try and arrange a drink together."

"That would be good," Josh acknowledged, "are you seeing anybody at the moment?"

"A woman, you mean?"

"A woman, yes," prompted Josh again.

"Well, yes, there is a new one. A tobacconist's daughter, Vera."

"And?"

"Oh, it's early days yet, but we're getting on well so far. She's into her books, like me. How about you?"

"I don't get the time to read. I started to read Karl Marx but…"

"I meant women, you fool, not books. How's your love life?"

"Haven't got one."

"Why?"

"I don't know. Haven't found the right one for me."

"I know, but you can have fun looking."

"Not my style, Frank, you know that. And this job makes it difficult."

"But, I'll bet you meet all kinds of women though?"

"Yeah, loose ones with loose legs," said the copper ruefully.

"Eh?"

"Not what you're thinking young Frank. I meant it more literally."

"I don't understand," said Frank.

"Private joke. Do you remember that big girl you were with at Miriam's wedding?"

"Yes, they were sisters. Sissy and something. Me and Wilf only went out with them once before that. Nothing serious, just a drink and a laff. Why?"

"Well, Sissy, that's the big strapping one, she's going out with our John now."

"I heard something of the sort. He's always been one for the women."

"This seems serious though."

"Really? Fair play to her. Perhaps she'll calm him down a bit. She looks a bit of a handful."

"She's a feisty one; threatening to clobber some bloke who hit John yesterday."

"What, and this bloke was still conscious was he?"

"Like I said, it's serious. And you're right, she seems to have cooled his temper."

"Well, fair play, fair play."

"Seen much of Wilf?" asked Josh.

"Hardly anything. He's too busy making money these days."

"Well, fair play to him, to coin a phrase," said the constable with a smirk, "and how are you enjoying school teaching?"

"It's great. Pay leaves something to be desired, at the moment, but money isn't everything, and at least it's clean. What about you? Enjoying policing are you?"

"It has its moments."

"I know," agreed Frank, "I heard about the stabbing yesterday."

"Bad news travels fast," opined the policeman, "yes, we've got the killer and the body out the back."

"Really. Rather you than me brother."

"You get used to it. Can I offer you a brew?"

"No thanks," said Frank with a vague shake of the head, "but can I ask you something?"

"Of course."

"Well, it's about a couple of my pupils. The parents have taken them out of school, a couple of times, for no good reason."

"Hardly a police matter," asserted Josh, "why don't you report it to the school board?"

"Complicated; a few reasons. The girl's very bright – there's a younger brother too – and I would really like to keep her at the school till she's thirteen, if not with me then with Miss Girdlestone, but I really need the co-operation of the parents for that."

"So, why are you telling me?"

"There's something strange going on. When they don't come to school it's because they've been taken away somewhere. Men just turn up and borrow them, in the mother's words."

"You don't mean…" began Josh.

"God no, I don't think so; I hope not. No, nothing like that I'm sure. But there's money involved."

"Perhaps the kids are working. It happens, and it's not something the police are usually called in for. Or do you think there's something more serious going on, like burglary or something? Because if you do, I suggest that you take it to Abe."

"No, I don't want that," Frank was quick to say, "I think that the mother's afraid of something, probably her husband, and I wouldn't want to bring down trouble on her, she has enough to contend with already. Abe would insist on making everything official. He wouldn't be able to be discrete, even if he wanted to."

"He might surprise you," advised Josh, "but, saying you're right, what option do you have but to walk away? Until you know something definite."

"I don't want to do that. I was hoping that you could make some off the record enquiries for me. The uniform will help, and I'll owe you a pint. What do you think? If only to put my mind at rest…What do you say?"

Josh sighed. "What I say is that I can't promise anything, but that I'll have words in ears and see what comes back. Now, give me as much detail as you can."

Chapter 22

Interlude for an Inquest

The likes of Higgins and Hickey did not get fancy undertaker services, regardless of guilt or innocence, because money, not criminal culpability, or lack of it, was the biased arbiter in such matters. And there was no appeal.

Thus, as there was little profit to be made out of an elaborate funeral for either of the corpses formerly detained at the station, and anything but the most rudimentary and straightforward attempts at preserving them from the encroaching rot of time's carrion-cart would inevitably entail needless and irrecoverable pecuniary outlay, the inquest for these souls in limbo, as customary for their ilk, and also on account of the violence and place of their respective demises, followed expeditiously.

On this occasion, a double occasion, the appointment with the dead's last impediment to a rude, but lawful, Christian burial was set for 2 p.m. on the Tuesday afternoon following the fatal weekend before. The cadavers were wrapped and ready, the holes had been dug and the parish gravediggers were just awaiting the final rubber-stamping before throwing them in and filling them up.

The venue for their rite of passage to the peace of the beyond was the Pear Tree public house, in Bell End, overshadowed by piles of slack from the adjacent pit, and where their earthly remains lay, awaiting viewing by the coroner and inquest jury, as laid down by statute. Had they been looking down, the two inveterate boozers would have almost certainly have approved the choice. Any friends, or acquaintances, attending would certainly have no excuse not to raise a final glass in memory of the pair, or two...

#

But it was early yet and Josh Lively had persuaded Sam Salt to take a little detour with him, as far as Tippity Green that is, and the workhouse, on an errand of mercy. Handwriting notwithstanding, P.C. Clark was left behind to write up reports. Now, although Salt professed to himself that he was not as soft-hearted as his colleague, and indeed that was true, he did not consider himself an unfeeling man; that was also true. But whereas Josh looked for the best in everybody and did his best to find it, and was

291

quick to sympathise with the less fortunate, like the young lad in the cell, Sam looked at things differently. That is to say, he was the same as Josh in looking for worthy traits in others, but was unlike Josh in that he rarely found them. His opinion of Josh? He instinctively liked the man, admired his compassion almost, but could not say that he respected him, and he lamented his lack of discernment. Didn't he realise that some people brought things on themselves, that they were responsible for their hardships, by choice or weakness; that some people didn't deserve sympathy? He understood Josh too well: understood that his uncritical concern for the weak was in itself a weakness. Yes, he liked the man, but he was not what he would call a strong one, not in body of course but mentally; in his head he was compromised by that indiscriminate kind-heartedness which seemed to be an acceptable substitute for real integrity these days. He wasn't like those wealthy types, fat red faced port and cigar types who had made their money from the blood of the workers, and felt guilty about it and made charitable gestures solely to salve their consciences. No, Josh was just naturally soft-hearted, and that made him vulnerable, as Salt saw it. But Salt felt an obligation to protect him: it stemmed from his own obligation to the man's brother, his superior, the sergeant. Now, Abraham Lively was a man to be respected; a strong-willed no-nonsense character, brave and loyal to his family and his subordinates, attributes which Salt shared; and Salt's loyalty meant that he must look after Josh. One day his naivety could put him in danger.

And so it was that it was P.C. Salt in particular who noticed the physical characteristics and the generally toxic feel of the man working in the gatehouse. And it was Salt who decided to overcome the man's objections to their entry by emphasising official police business, his confidence in his own physical prowess boosted by the uniform. And then it was Salt who announced to the shocked and bunned matronly lady who was the master's last bastion of defence against the uninvited,

"Police. To see Mr Gideon Gross."

The lady retreated part way down a corridor, knocked softly on a door, disappeared and conducted a brief conversation indecipherable from outside, returned and announced that the master would see them.

As they entered Gideon Gross rose, but remained behind his desk, allowing them to approach him. To the cynically perceptive eyes of Salt, it was clear that the man was less than one hundred per cent sober. Probably, he needed the security of having the desk under his ample barrel belly in case his balance should fail before his head registered it. He wondered if Josh had come to the same conclusion – probably not. Also, thought Salt, the fat blob of blubber was probably too lazy to walk a few steps: he was in his bad books already. Was he being unfair on the man? He looked again. No, he had been right: nobody worth their salt got into that state. It was like looking at a walking talking pig bladder, a very full one, except that pigs didn't drink beer or whisky, and this one didn't look like it could actually walk very far. Hardly a fit person to run a home for the unfortunate and needy, he would have thought; probably got the job on the back of a few backhanders;

either that or the job's harder than you might think. But no, he didn't think. Anyway, none of his business and why should he really care? He was just here with Josh, so he let Josh open.

"Mr Gross?"

"That's right, Gideon Gross," came the reply. "How can I be of service constable? Please, do sit down."

Two chairs were in convenient positions near the front two corners of the desk, and they all sat. Not too close. Within hearing distance but, fortunately for the visitors, beyond the average smelling distance. Fortunate (also) for the master himself, as he thought. The interval pleased him. Not having expected anyone, at least nobody with the power to barge their way in, he was now anxious that the smell of scotch did not give him away. Unhappily for him, one of the policemen had seen through him and into him instantaneously, and the other would have guessed his secret before he left the place.

Seated, Josh continued, "I'm constable Lively, Rowley police, and this is my colleague constable Salt."

"Pleased to meet you," said Gross as they shook hands, acknowledging Salt with a nod. "Lively? Not the Lively that took care of the Scarrets in Terrace Street?"

"No, that would be sergeant Lively, my brother."

"Yes of course," agreed the master, "yes, you're a little young, I dare say. I mean, it's a few years ago…"

"Yes, I've heard the stories," said Josh.

"Yes, a hard man your brother, to be sure," opined Gross.

"But a fair one," Salt pointed out.

"I've no doubt of it," Gross assured them, "but?"

He left the question hanging between raised eyebrows.

"Right. Now I'm sorry to trouble you sir," began Josh, "but, there's something you may be able to help me with. A favour if you like."

"By all means," gushed the master, happy for confirmation that they were not there to take him in, "do go on."

"Well then. There's a young man of my acquaintance, a boy really, who has fallen on hard times. I think I can help him, get him a job and a place to rest his head hopefully. To put it bluntly, he's destitute and needs a place to stay; a safe place, and a secure one. A temporary measure, you understand."

"Indeed I do. That's precisely what we're here for," replied the master, relieved that the favour required appeared innocuous enough, "I'm sure that we can arrange for an admission for you. No one would ever know."

"We would," interjected Salt with suspicion.

"Of course, of course, I only meant…he is of this parish, is he not?"

"Yes," replied Josh. *Near enough.*

"No problem then. We'll arrange for an appointment for the relieving officer to pop round and visit in the next day or so. I'll need an address for that."

"I was hoping that you could expedite something yourself, today. Personally. You are the master after all," cajoled Josh, whilst Salt sat staring like steel, "and it's only temporary of course; very much so, one or two nights at most, I imagine. And we wouldn't want to create all that paperwork for nothing, would you? It means a lot to me."

"That's as may be, but there are rules," said Gross (and he was thinking in particular about Jack Cutler's rules; wanted to keep his nose clean, as ordered, but knew he would not be thanked for getting on the wrong side of the local law. He was sure that Jack would not want that, he hoped. *Damned if I do, dead if I don't* he found himself thinking, and wondering how easily he had conflated real death and metaphorical damnation.)

As he was pondering, the policeman's voice was going on, "...so if you could bring yourself to be just a little flexible in this case, which is a special case, I would be obliged to you."

Gross had missed the first part of the sentence, but no harm done: "Where is the boy now?"

"To be honest with you, he's in a cell. It's imperative that I move him, but I would also want to be sure that he could not merely abscond. As I said, it's just a temporary measure. So?"

"Well, I don't know," began Gross whilst trying to hold his flying thoughts together. A voice cut through them, swift and straight as an arrow. Salt's arrow, steel tipped.

"Mr Gross," and the appellation alone somehow transmitted the copper's disdain for the man, "do you really want to make an enemy of us?"

The threat brought back a degree of focus, "If you put it like that then," said the master, surrendering more or less gracefully.

"I do put it like that," continued the constable.

"Er, well, er...right. I can fill in the paperwork myself, at a pinch. Just in case..." he said. The two visitors could not have appreciated the irony of the words, coming as they did from the mendacious mouth of that well practised forger.

"Good. Thank You. When can I bring him round?" asked Josh Lively.

"Well, er, I might need to have a word with the matron about a bed..."

"Very well. Good. But before we go, there's something else I'd like to ask."

#

In the dead waiting time before the inquest, in the hiatus between routine and routine, sergeant Abraham Lively decided to repair some fences. Well, one fence at least, that being the one that his casual weekend attitude to their relationship had caused to be erected between himself and the landlady of the Hailstone, by the good lady herself, following his disappointing no-show.

He was in a good mood as he approached the pub, stopping outside to pet the pub's shaggy black and white pony, which he had met for the first time when Sarah had taken him home dazed and bandaged in her little cart. Miriam had not been pleased that night he remembered with a grin. Still, two women arguing over him! Can't be a bad thing. He had seen more of Sarah since then, in more ways than one, and he was really getting very fond of her; her girlish charm housed in the body of a mature woman – older than him at any rate. But what did that matter? She was good company and that was all that Abe cared about at the moment. He thought he must be growing up himself, or something had changed at any rate: his job was not the be all and end all he had decided. It was just a job; a job enforcing laws made by and for the benefit of the privileged classes, a member of which, it had been made clear to him, he would never be. Policing was not the ennobling occupation he had once thought it could be; still, there was satisfaction to be had from doing any job well, and good people were needed to control the bad. But perhaps the law was not the best arbiter of good and bad. A good copper knew when to bend the rules, hadn't inspector Millership said as much?

"Good boy, see you later," he said giving the pony a last pat on the neck. Then he turned away, stepped lightly up to the back door, tapped softly, and entered.

It was dull in the kitchen compared to outside, with just some coals glowing weakly. But it was enough for Abe to see the two figures seated at the table, and it took the wind out of his sails and the smile off his face. It was Charlie Spragg. Spragg and Sarah sitting enjoying a cosy little chat by the looks of it. They looked up surprised, then Spragg looked scared, melodramatically so as a matter of fact.

Abe took a couple of steps, heavy steps now as he planted his boot nails on the tiles, emphasising his weight and power, a tacit threat. He said nothing till he was standing at the table, closer to Sarah than to Spragg.

"What's he doing here?" He had tried to keep his voice calm and neutral, but he heard a hard edge in it.

Apparently, so did Spragg, for he leapt up like a silly mare bitten by a horsefly and retreated to the furthest corner of the little room.

"Leave me alone you," he hollered, one eye on Abe and the other on Sarah.

"I'll leave you alone when you get out of my sight," growled the sergeant.

This precipitated a pathetically tremulous appeal to the lady of the house, "See, see, I told you. Stop him Sarah."

This is crazy talk, Abe was thinking, and then he smelt a rat. Spragg was sporting a real shiner of a black eye, possibly a memento of his brush with his rival on Saturday night. And he was also cradling his left arm with exaggerated care as if it might fall off, an arm splinted and bandaged, not particularly neatly, from wrist to elbow.

"What are you playing at?" he said and made to advance toward the cowering figure. But at that Spragg, with a whimper, shot off and made good his escape through a door which connected with the public rooms.

"Let him go Abe." Sarah was standing now and she hadn't said it kindly.

"Sarah, what's going on? You said you didn't want any more to do with him."

"Did I?" It was not a response fit to pacify her indignant lover.

"Yes you did! You said you couldn't trust him; you said he was deceitful."

She did not reply immediately and so he continued, "You know you bloody well did. So what's he doing here?"

"Not that it's any of your business…"

"You what?"

"…not that it's any of your business, because this is my place, my home, but he came to see me because he's scared – for himself and for me."

"Oh, he's scared is he? I'll give him scared. What's he scared of?"

"You of course, after what you did."

"What I did? I don't know what he told you but you can't believe a word he says. You told me that yourself. Come on, think about it."

"All right then, yes, I'm sorry. But he looked scared to me just, when you came in."

"It's an act! It's a bloody act! Crafty little swine, you wait…"

"It didn't look like an act…"

"For God's sake, it's a bloody…"

"All right! All right Abe. Calm down. Stop swearing. Calm down, please. Right. Now, tell me something if you will."

"What?"

"You know on Saturday, Saturday night, when you were supposed to come and see me?"

"God Sarah, I know, I'm sorry. I came to explain."

"There's no need, I can guess," her finger stifled his nascent protest, "let me finish my question: on Saturday, did you come to see me, but late, after I had locked up and locked you out?"

"It wasn't that late…"

"It was too late. But you came?"

"Yes, that's right! I threw some gravel at your windows, but you didn't hear."

"I did hear."

"Oh, it's like that is it?"

"Yes it is; or was. Or is…I don't know."

"What's that got to do with you having him here?"

"I wasn't having him here as you put it. I told you, he turned up because he was worried about me…"

"Or so he says."

"…because he was worried, or scared. But look, you've just said that you were outside here on Saturday, after closing. He says he was here and he saw you, and he saw you throwing at the windows."

"So?"

"So that proves to me – suggests to me – that you and him probably ran into each other, between here and Blackheath, like he says."

"There's no probably about it. I saw him all right. And he was playing his face, to put it mildly."

"That's what he said: that he was pushing his luck, but that you overreacted and beat him up."

"And you believed him of course!" retorted Abe, his voice and blood pressure rising.

"So do you deny coming to blows?"

"I wouldn't call it that. He tried to hit me so I pushed him onto his arse. Nothing more."

"He tried to hit you? He might be a lot of things, but he's not that mad. And he wasn't that drunk either."

"You noticed, did you? Like you care?"

"It goes with the job. Look, calm down. All right, let's say he was drunk enough. Drunk enough to think he could get one in on you. But what you did to him was a bit excessive though, wasn't it?"

"Look, I told you, I just dodged a punch and pushed him over."

"Well perhaps you don't know your own strength. Because to me a push over doesn't mean blacking his eye and breaking his arm," she began, and seeing Abe's reaction, "but perhaps it was just an accident."

"Look, if his arm really is broken, which I doubt, I'm telling you that I didn't do it, accidentally or otherwise, and I expect you to believe me. And to suggest that I don't know my own strength is a facile cliché and a bloody insult. He was fine when I left him; perhaps he picked another fight after that."

"So, there was a fight then?"

"Oh, for God's sake!"

"A scuffle then, and an accident?"

"Sarah, I thought you knew me."

"I thought I did. But look at you, now, shouting at me."

Abe stopped to think, and continued more level and quiet, "I'm sorry. But is it any wonder? Finding him here?" To stop his fraught pacing he sat; she put her hand on his.

"Abe, I'm worried too. Worried about you. You've started flying into tempers at the drop of a hat. It's not you."

"This? The drop of a hat?"

"I'm not talking about today, you know that."

"I've got things on my mind."

"I know, the job. But what about the funny turns? I can be speaking to you one minute, the next you're dead to the world, but still breathing."

"I've told you, it will pass. I've had it before. It was that bloody bang on the head that did it, the tile off your roof, that's what brought it back, but it's starting to wear off."

"I don't think it is."

"Well I do, and I should know!"

"There's that temper again. It's not you."

"Temper? I raised my voice that's all. God, I had enough provocation. I wish I had beat the bugger up now."

"What if you did though? What if you did but can't remember? I think you should see a doctor."

"Oh for fuck's sake woman, don't talk piffle."

"And don't you talk to me like that you bastard."

"Suits me. I won't talk to you at all then."

Abe left abruptly via the same door through which he had entered. She followed him to the threshold.

"Don't come back Abe. Not till you're right. Go and talk to that Doc Wharton of yours. Please Abe."

"We'll do nothing of the sort," he shouted back.

We? She thought, and "Don't bother coming round tonight," she called after him, "or ever," she added less confidently.

If Abe had caught sight of Spragg at that moment there might have been another murder. But that was not likely, for Abe was travelling away from the Hailstone whereas, contrary to expectations Spragg had never left it. Instead, he had crept back to listen with puerile satisfaction to the exchange behind the door to the kitchen. He couldn't help but smirk as he clucked his approval. *Wonder how long I should leave* this *silly prop on,* he thought, eyeing his self-applied dressing. *Blimey, I ought to be on the stage.*

#

"Adams you say?" said Gross, still playing for time, until his thoughts stopped spinning around his besozzled brain and evaporating before he could pursue them, marshal them into some kind of logical order. The names Rose and William Adams ought to have shaken him sober but panic had taken away his breath and thoughts and images and memories swirled around like fallen leaves in the autumn winds. And mostly he saw Jack Cutler's coal black eyes, melting him; and mostly he heard the rapping of his stick, that dog headed stick, into his cold unkind hand; and he tried not to see it smashing his own cowardly head like a ripe peach.

"That's right. William and Rose. Like I said," prompted Joshua Lively, "do you know them or not?"

Was it some kind of trap? What did they know? If he lied would he give himself away? But better to lie and tough it out than give Cutler away. Again he thought, *damned if you do, dead if you don't, Gideon lad.* "No, I'm quite certain that we've never taken in children with those names," said the master, and not entirely untruthfully. Then, because an unsolicited embellishment, he always thought, added credence to a lie, or at least added helpful layers of obfuscation rendering giving lie to the lie so much less likely, he heaped ex gratia onto his simple denial, a rambling description of a mad woman by the name of Adams who had been shut away in the premises:

"...but as I said this was sometime in the seventies and I've only been here seven years, so, like I say, it was before my time. Anyway this poor soul, this Mrs Adams, she attacked the master at the time with a kitchen knife, right here in this very room. Took an eye out, so they say. They kept her locked up after that, until she hanged herself that is, in the attic it was. So the story goes. They say her ghost still wanders the upper floors. One of the nurses saw it, couple of years back. Never came back after that. Personally, I just think she was drunk..."

Well, you'd know all about that, thought P.C.Salt.

"...she liked her gin, did Alice. But no, apart from an alleged ghost, we've got no Adams."

His ramble into fiction had bought him time to recover the little courage that was his normal allotment, and he could bring himself to ask, casually, "Why do you ask?"

"I'm following up a complaint about an abduction. Stolen away for illicit purposes."

"Illicit purposes?" repeated Gross, trying not to swallow. But neither copper missed the sudden change in pallor, shifting as it did from a sickly shade of yellow to a suspicious red flush.

"Yes. Illicit; illegal. And they tell me that you might know something about it."

Now, strange to tell, the closer it got to it, to his total undoing, the calmer he became. A desperate calm perhaps, but he knew that he was not going to just roll over and die at the first sign of trouble. Besides, it always came back to the same thing – it was Cutler and his men that he was most afeared of.

"Me? How so? Who's this 'they' that's been whispering sweet nothings in your ear? Because there's such a thing as slander you know. I'm a respected member, nay, a well-respected member..."

You're a member all right.

"...of this community and I demand to know who is at the root of such contemptible calumny. So come on, spill the beans, or by Jove..."

Josh stopped him in conciliatory fashion, "Calm yourself, sir. Please understand, we have to follow up on each complaint received, that's our duty," he said, and added, catching the eye of Salt, "no matter how ridiculous it may sound."

"Oh yes. I understand," replied Gross, wondering if he had over played it.

"So?" queried Josh.

"What? Oh, right. No officer, we don't have two children here by the name of Adams, and I've never heard their names before today. Good enough?"

"Thank you, sir," replied Josh. Putting away his notebook and pencil.

"And don't you worry about that other thing. Just bring the lad around this evening, at, let's say six-thirty. Suit you?"

"Thank you, I'll do that."

"And," intervened constable Salt, "you'd better make sure that he is well taken care of."

"Oh I will, I will. You can rely on me."

But in reality, Josh Lively doubted that he could, rely on or trust. He might have to revisit the Miss Ricketts option. Meantime, somebody really ought to be asking questions about the way this man ran the place, and his drinking habits.

Samuel Salt was way ahead of him. He was positive that Gross was thoroughly untrustworthy and thoroughly rotten, and the anomalous presence of the character in the gatehouse only confirmed it.

That character had not remained in the gatehouse, however. Anthony Duberley watched them go. The door to the master's office was solid and thick, but he had heard enough to know that Jack would not be pleased.

#

Richard Merriss was an enterprising man, not a young man but certainly not old, with a head for business, a ready smile and ready fists. All useful attributes for a publican, which is what he was. Fortunately all round, the smile and a winning personality more often than not abrogated the need for argy-bargy and fisticuffs, making the Pear Tree Inn a not unpleasant place to drink away the cares of the working day. A place of refinement and witty banter it was not, but that suited the unwashed miners, who almost exclusively formed the regular clientele, up to the ground. The Pear Tree was one of the less rowdy drinking establishments in that particular neck of the woods, or that is, the whole area long since having been transformed into a black dusty desert where every tree and shrub had years ago been casually uprooted, inconveniently standing in the way of progress, of a sort, and where even the hardiest of weeds struggled, that neck of the slack heaps. But, as Dick Merriss often told his customers, "It's no use crying over spilt milk – have a beer!" For mining was thirsty work and thirsty miners were his meat and drink, and thus to him those heaps were as welcome a sight as the greenest of pristine green hills and the clink of proffered coins and the rattle of cash in his till was better than the song of birds in spring.

He had inherited the pub from his father, Bill Merriss, last in a line of farmers who, in the face of the kind of progress that caused half a dozen of his last sheep to disappear abruptly and forever down a sudden dark cavern that ate a dozen yards of field, had decided that if he couldn't beat them he must join them. And so he concentrated on making money out of the mines, out of the miners. It had been unexpectedly easy, a licence to print money he always said. Giving over a room for the use of the parish for inquests had proved to be a nice source of alternative income, but since his father's day things had changed. Chief Constables of police called the shots these days, in cahoots no doubt with the county magistrates who seemed to be growing ever more parsimonious where expenses were concerned. Only nominated police officers could call in a coroner, and the circumstances when it was allowed depended on the Chief Constable's 'guidelines,' which had become quite strict. Money talks, it is said, and therefore, to those losing out as a result of the changes, like landlord Merriss, the situation was regrettable, if understandable. And regrettable not merely for selfish reasons: some said that justice was becoming a commodity, fine and dandy if only you could afford it. For although the means and opportunity for violent death in mines and factories and furnaces and quarries had by no means abated, yet the number of investigations into same, the number of inquests, certainly had. The owners were getting away with murder, some said.

Still, there were cases where an inquest certainly could not be avoided, and in such Dick Merriss, in all public-spiritedness, was always ready and willing to donate the use of his premises. And the three and six fee was always very welcome of course. For whatever reason, few other local establishments had ever challenged the de facto inquest monopoly he had in Rowley and Blackheath. He knew that the local police sergeant had tried to persuade his sister to set up in competition, her of the Royal Oak, but that she would have none of it. Too squeamish, no doubt, poor woman.

In contrast, and without feeling at all ghoulish, he was looking forward to today. Two inquests in one, that meant seven shillings, or so he hoped. And a nice gory, blood and guts murder. The details of the process, of dying, fascinated him, and he particularly looked forward to any medical evidence. The violent and bloody cases were his favourites; the last case had only been about a suspected poisoning: interesting in its own way, but no blood. He had seen it all in his time, starting from when he was just a boy, crushing, burning, drowning, impaling, falls from heights, falls of rocks and coal, asphyxiation, strangulation. Death fascinated him; he would have liked to be a doctor, or a soldier.

Yes, he would enjoy today, today would be a good 'un.

#

Abe was not clear on how it had all come together. All he knew was that he was in the Oak enjoying an off-duty pint with Josh and Miriam. Doc Wharton had joined them and he in turn had been joined by another professional man, and old acquaintance, in the form of solicitor Alan Griesbach, apparently at a loose end for once.

The two coppers had only previously come across Griesbach in an official capacity, and he had been a useful ally or an irksome adversary, depending on who was paying.

301

Out of court, officious persona shed with the robes, he was, they were surprised to discover, a witty and warm human being who liked his drink and was easy to talk to. It seemed that he was particularly partial to whisky, but although that potent liquid obviously oiled his tongue, the tongue was nevertheless kept under the prudent control of the lawyer's conditioned intellect to prevent it straying into the cloistered cabinets of client confidentiality. But that was not to say that he did not speak about the job. On the contrary, he had amusing anecdotes aplenty. At the moment, he was holding forth about a particularly heinous crime, being the theft of two shillings worth of best silverside of beef from a butcher's shop in Old Hill:

"I was acting for the Crown in that case. On the facts, open and shut, as they say. The only thing that gave us pause was whether to charge the accused with stealing or with receiving; we couldn't do both. But then we thought, 'larceny it is' – otherwise we foresaw ourselves getting into tricky questions of jurisprudence, not to mention of philosophy. At the heart of our agonising was the query, 'can a dog have a mens rea?'"

Wharton had obviously heard all this before and in the spirit of keeping the pot of jocularity boiling he was quick to chip in with, "Well, being a medical man, I know of several dogs that have had men's rears; I know of one that makes a habit of it, ought to be put down really, but as it only offends on private premises it's got away with it so far; a stitches job sometimes, and I don't just mean the trousers!"

"No, no, no my good doctor," said the lawyer, playing up to it, "I speak not of any portion of the anatomy, but of the criminal law's concept of the guilty mind – really I had expected a better command of Latin from a doctor. Without that guilty mind, that mens rea, there can in law exist no criminal responsibility."

"Oh, I misunderstood," came back the doctor, "I thought you meant…"

"We all know what you thought he meant," interjected Miriam. She was enjoying this unexpected get-together and the fact that for once her husband was on hand to help behind the bar.

"Mens rea and active what's not?" questioned Abe. "Isn't that what that coroner chappie was boring us all to death with this afternoon?"

"Who? Sir high and mighty Madden?" replied Griesbach. "Wouldn't be surprised, he's a frustrated barrister; started out articled to a friend of mine actually, but it didn't work out. Next thing, he's swanning round as a coroner; don't know how he wangled that one; talk about friends in low places. And it's actus reus by the way, not active what-not."

"I stand corrected. So what's all this got to do with the story," asked the sergeant in good humour.

"Well I was coming to that, wasn't I? Before I was interrupted…"

"Beg your pardon, I'm sure," said Abe, enjoying himself.

"Granted. Where was I? Oh yes, well, it was the end of the day and he had set out several pieces of meat on a trestle, that's old man Keeling, the butcher, outside the shop, anxious to get it sold. He didn't keep a close enough eye though, and that was his first mistake."

Josh too had been caught up in the geniality of the occasion and the lawyer's delivery, "Don't tell me someone stole his meat. What, thieving? Not in Old Hill surely? So much posher than Blackheath you know, and," he added, sharing a private joke with his brother, "so much better policed at that. Well, whatever next!"

"Ah," said the old lawyer, bright eyes fixing the young constable, a didactic digit commanding attention, "you may well ask, because it's not what you expect…"

"Well?" prompted Miriam.

"Well," continued the solicitor at law, "the butcher, Keeling, said that he only turned his back for a second, but quicker than that, in a split second, a large brown dog with a curly coat nipped in as if on cue and made off with the cut of beef in question. Of course, he ran after the animal hollering all sorts of threats and abuse, and that was his second mistake, which I'll get back to. Anyway, two legs naturally being inferior to four, the old man had but a slim hope of catching the animal. But Lady Luck took a shine to him that day, because the dog ran straight down an alleyway which the butcher knew to be a dead end. Now, at the end of said dead end the butcher saw a man taking the meat from the dog before shinning smartly up a drainpipe to disappear over a wall. The dog itself turned out to be a most docile and affectionate creature, in fact she was a bitch, and not a dog at all, although her endearing qualities were lost on Keeling who was much more concerned with his lost beef and which grieved him out of all proportion. Being of a trusting disposition she was quite happy to follow him back to the shop when he improvised a lead out of his belt."

Here, the elfin little man stopped to take a sip from his pint, and then one from his whisky.

"So, he kept the dog then did he? In lieu of payment?" asked Miriam.

"Why no, my dear. He did nothing of the sort. If the dog had not been quite so trusting and had been a better judge of human character, she might have put up more of a fight."

"How so?" asked Abe.

"Well, the butcher was not a very forgiving man, and he was of quite a belligerent personality. Have you noticed that with butchers? I think they probably eat too much meat. Added to that he was livid when he got back, because in his absence, half the joints that he had set out on that trestle table had mysteriously vanished. Or, as I would have said, predictably so. That's the aforementioned second mistake, by the way."

"Told you. Bad lot in Old Hill, and that's just the police!" said Josh.

"I couldn't comment," said Griesbach.

"So what happened?" pleaded Miriam.

"What happened? Why the crotchety old sod demanded that the police be called and he demanded justice. 'Send the dog to the pound,' he said. It was partly spite and partly in the hope that if the owner turned up he could be detained and arrested."

"And did he, was he?" asked Miriam.

"You're ahead of me, wait," replied the raconteur, "no she never was sent to the pound: enter then the hero of our story, one police constable Wothers."

"Wothers?" exclaimed Abe Lively, "I know that name."

"The inspector's sidekick, we met him on Sunday," added Josh.

"Shall I continue?" queried Griesbach.

"Sorry, please do," said Josh.

"Right then. Well, where was I? Yes, well Wothers was not as green as he is cabbage-looking. He formulated a plan: he took the dog back to the station and waited till the early hours, when the streets were deserted, and the dog would have no distractions. Then, he tied a long piece of string around her neck and just told her to go home. She soon found her way back and Wothers found himself outside the door of a local character not unknown to the local law – let's just call him Alf, not his real name of course. So, the dog started scratching and whining at the door, and Alf opened it to let her in. He got quite a shock when he saw that the dog was dragging something behind, especially as that thing wore a blue uniform! A quick search revealed the stolen item, in the pantry, where it was no doubt deposited in anticipation of a particularly fine Sunday dinner. The crestfallen crook swore that he had planned to return the meat next day, that he was only keeping it safe till he could ascertain ownership. Then he blamed the dog, calling her a 'bad girl' and aiming several kicks at her. That didn't go down too well with Wothers, who was quite taken with the animal, neither did the hasty excuse. He had had reports of similar incidents with an apparently stray dog of the same description, and he concluded directly that this reprobate had actually trained her to steal. He arrested the man for larceny. In custody, at the nick, the suspect's next ploy was to offer to pay for the meat, but that didn't wash, and to cut a long story short..."

"I wish you would," remarked Wharton under his breath but deliberately loud enough to be heard.

"Yes, I know, you've heard the story, but others haven't, so I'll trouble you to hold your tongue," admonished the lawyer, "as I was saying, to cut a long story short, he went up before the beak."

"And then what happened?" asked the doctor, continuing the double act.

"Glad you asked that! Foolishly, our 'Alf' pleaded not guilty. His story was that he was out for a walk with his dog when, totally unaccountably, she ran off. He was searching for her when she ran up to him with a joint of meat in her jaws. Naturally, he scolded her, which caused her to drop it in the mud, so he decided he must take it home and wash it before returning it to the owner. No sooner had he settled on this plan than he was sorely affrighted by the sight of a large man waving a large knife around and

304

shouting loudly and unintelligibly. Fearing that he was about to be attacked by some escaped lunatic he very sensibly, in his own opinion, immediately scarpered over a wall and ran home for safety."

"A likely story," interjected Josh.

"That's exactly how the magistrates described it. Or was that 'an unlikely story'? Either way, he got short shrift and fourteen days' hard labour."

"What about the dog?" asked Josh.

"Wait a minute," said Wharton, "you've not heard the funny part yet. Go on Alan, tell them…"

"Tell them what?" asked Griesbach, pulling his leg and eliciting a scowl, "Oh yes, just as they were leading him out there came from the back of the court a proper 'working mon' voice, and it said, 'Oy up Alf, if yoh ger enny pups off that dog, ah'll 'ave one off ya!'"

"What did the magistrates say?" queried the sergeant.

"Nothing."

"Nothing?"

"I can vouch for that," said Doc Wharton, "I was on the bench that day, and we were too busy trying not to laugh…"

#

Later, the two professional men having departed, the conversation between the three siblings returned to courtroom experiences.

"Miriam," Josh was saying, "do you remember the two women that came in causing trouble a few weeks back, a little fat one and a hatchet faced one, Tromans I think her name was?"

"I do indeed. Hetty the other one is, Hetty Arblaster. What about her?"

"She brought a complaint about her husband, up before the magistrates, he was. She claimed he assaulted her."

"What? Other way round more like! He wouldn't dare, she'd flatten him."

"I know that, and you know that, and it didn't take long for the magistrate to see it either."

"Good. What is he supposed to have done?"

"Hit her over the head – with a haddock!"

"A haddock?"

"Yes, you heard right, a smelly wet haddock."

The image was too much, and they both burst out laughing, till Miriam said, "No, I think you've made that up – sounds like a load of codswallop to me!"

Which started them falling about again.

But Abe did not feel like laughing. Why were they laughing? It wasn't that funny, though admittedly he didn't know the characters under discussion. But it wasn't that funny, surely? Miriam obviously thought that it was, but that was women for you. He hadn't had much luck with women lately; first Alice then Sarah had shown that they were flawed. Perhaps it was for the best: he was going to be busy, he knew it. Since the warning bad things had indeed happened; two murders for a start, despite what obnoxious Oakden and the pompous coroner said. And he was still uneasy about Jack Cutler, he was sure there was trouble to come from that direction. But most of all, the ostensibly insignificant and harmless, but strangely annoying presence of that so called poet was upsetting him, pricking away at the border of consciousness. He could well believe it, something bad might already have arrived. If he needed a sign that what was coming was evil, he had to look no further than Netherton, where for five days subterranean fires had been burning beneath the graveyard, the smoke escaping smelling suspiciously as if from the sulphurous and tormenting flames of hell, and frightening the locals. Perhaps they had good reason to be frightened. Occasionally and at night, the churchyard could be located from the top of Rowley by an ominous red glow. Rational souls pointed out that the fire was undoubtedly the result of the ignition of gasses in some old abandoned mine, forgotten by the current generation, which no doubt lay beneath the church. But rational souls had not the benefit of Abe's insight, nor of his new companion. Suddenly, Abe realised why Spragg had been acting so suspiciously, 'trying to see Netherton church' he had said, or something like it. But he had no wish to dwell on Spragg, it made him too angry…

Miriam was telling Josh how wonderfully he had handled the situation with a little fat fish wife and her friend, and the sergeant could not help but reflect that that was just about his brother's bottle, handling slightly awkward women. There was a kind of skill in that of course, but it was not a particularly vital one for a copper. A copper needed to be able to handle awkward men too, not to mention extremely violent ones, and to subdue them, whether literally or figuratively, criminal or colleague. And Abe was not sure that his little brother was made of the right stuff. If, no, when, he was promoted to inspector, and if they wanted a new sergeant he would be recommending P.C. Salt, who showed a lot of promise and toughness, and not his brother. The way he saw it, it was protecting Josh from a strain he could not bear.

He had been deep in thought and realised that Miriam was gently pulling his beard. "What?" he said.

"I was just saying how I like your new look."

"What?" he said again.

"The straggly beard look," she replied pinching at the new growth where he was no longer shaving.

"Not a new look," he informed her absently, "just easier."

She changed tone suddenly, "Abe, are you all right?"

"What do you mean?"

"It's like you've been somewhere else all night. Anything wrong?"

"No, not at all. I was just thinking." *And conferring with my friend.*

#

The coroner had arrived on a wave of expectation, puffing furiously between breaths on a large bowled pipe which released discrete billows of smudgy smoke at intervals timed to his respiration, like a little tug boat's emissions, but more aromatic. The assorted assemblage of human accessories: yet to be sworn jurymen, witnesses, police officers et al, parted before him like the Red Sea and closed in his wake. In keeping with his important position, Jacob Madden bore his stoutness, albeit on ludicrously small feet, with a decorum which owed much to his natural proclivity to gravitas, aided and abetted by the continued skill of his tailor to flatter. He was a relatively young man, and still looked it, with still dark hair and full and neatly cut dark beard containing just a sprinkling of grey; his slowly expanding figure and flushed countenance had not yet transported him to that critical tipping point at which such features seemed to add years beyond the wearer's true age. On the contrary, he exuded a youthful energy which would have been beyond many men of his age.

He bounded to his place and arranged his paperwork with a very purposeful bustle and a concentration that brooked no interruption and elicited a respectful pregnant quiet in the room. Safely berthed he unloaded from a green Morocco leather case, made in Walsall, a cargo of papers, pens and ink. Suddenly, as if roused to the moment by the silence in the room and the eyes on him, he looked up.

"Well sergeant? Get them sworn in."

The 'them' was a reference to the knot of locals, standing apart, near the other end of the long beech-wood table at the head of which he himself now sat, and who, to the experienced eye, were obvious jury material. Fifteen of them as it turned out, this case being concerned with homicide and the coroner not wishing his intent be frustrated by one of a mere twelve 'good and lawful men' deciding to be contrary, thus thwarting the prescribed number of votes – twelve of them – required for the clean outcome which he had planned.

"Yes, sir," said the tall Sergeant with the straggly dark beard, and to the further encouragement of 'quick as you like,' began the task of taking the oath from the motley collection there gathered.

Meanwhile the coroner was looking over the pre-submitted police and witness statements. Without looking up. "Witnesses please wait outside to be called," he intoned. "If you are neither juror nor a police officer, please clear the room."

It was quite possible that Jacob Madden had something better to do that day, or at least, given his immediate surroundings and company, probably somewhere better to be.

So it seemed to the casual onlooker. But it was also possible, and those that knew him would have said probable, that his apparent haste was merely a result of the fact that he was a naturally quick operator; and that today in particular, was conscious of the fact that he had two cases to get through and was anxious not to run out of time, for justice's sake.

Whatever the reason, the day's proceedings were conducted at a relentlessly expeditious, but by no means reckless, pace.

There was no shortage of witnesses to the first death, by stabbing, outside the Three Furnaces, but only the butcher and a single fellow drinker of the deceased were required in person; and then Doctor Wharton was called to, as it happened, confirm his initial diagnosis at the scene, i.e. that death was caused by a rapid exsanguination (loss of blood as Madden made him explain) consequent to Hickey's borrowed blade slashing almost in two his friend's abdominal aorta. A clear case of murder then, any juror would have had a right to conclude, but that was before the doctor was asked to give evidence concerning the wounding of the second deceased...

The facts and post mortem findings on Higgins were completed very quickly, because, the coroner warned, he wanted to spend more time on the death of Hickey it being, in his opinion he said, by no means as straightforward. Whether the coroner felt that the hanging was the more important case, for policy reasons, with it being a death whilst in police custody, or whether he had any genuine concerns about dereliction of duty, or even foul play on behalf of the local bobbies, was open to conjecture. Certainly this thought ran not unnaturally through the anxious mind of P.C. John Payne. And in due course that unfortunate soul was made to experience the full force of Lawful Authority by way of a series of uncomfortable and curt questions from the august personage of the coroner: what his sergeant would later describe as a 'right grilling', albeit thankfully a short one. Fortunately, as both sergeant Lively and Inspector Millership were gratified to note, the man had listened to advice, apparently, and had got his story straight and stuck to it, answering 'your honour' (as he would have it) with all of the outward signs of equanimity. But Jacob Madden had fired his questions having read the medical reports, provided by Wharton, on the two men, and those reports guided his opinion; his opinion guided his agenda, and his agenda, he had decided, did not include laying blame on the police, although he could not let them off scot-free: thus he had felt required to put the obviously nervous police constable under pressure, in the process providing himself with some harmless fun. Perhaps it would teach the man to be more careful in the future. Be that as it may, what *was* included on his agenda was to cover all of the evidence as quickly as possible, pushing the jury in the direction he wanted it to go, and quit the place whilst the going and daylight was good...

In the case of Michael Hickey then, it was quickly established that he had hanged himself dead, with no suspicion of connivance or illicit assistance from his brief custodians. Testimony from constables Lively and Payne about the arcane last message scratched on the cell floor, it was suggested, pointed to regret or remorse, perhaps strong

308

enough to procure the impulse to self-despatch. As good a hypothesis as any, you as juror would have been entitled to think, you would have thought. But then the coroner called the doctor.

Under oath, doc Wharton revealed that had he not hanged himself, the deceased might well have died, in a matter of hours or days it was difficult to be exact, in any case, because the post mortem had revealed a comminuted depressed skull fracture causing damage to the brain's pre-frontal lobes, with bone lacerations precipitating a slow, persistent, insidious haemorrhage. Life threatening, yes; treatable, no – in the good doctor's opinion.

Bartholomew Brewer was the foreman of the jury, and he was doing his best to pay attention. Physically, he was a fine specimen of working manhood, his body, at thirty-two years, at the peak of its physical potential, with a sun-tan to boot! Mother nature had blessed him with a naturally athletic frame, and he had suffered no serious injury in his working life so far, which was good going for, contrary to what the surname suggested, Bart Brewer was a quarry hand, always had been, and never anything to do with the brewing or the licensing trade, apart from drinking beer of course. In rare moments of philosophising he had cast his imagination back, back a hundred years, to overlook some dreamt-up ancestor busy with his mashes and vats and barrels; and he reflected that the man must have been very unfortunate, perhaps the business being destroyed in some catastrophic fire, and gone overnight; or, in the alternative, perhaps he had just been rubbish at making beer, leading to a longer slower decline as sales became harder. Whatever had happened, his family had been labourers for three generations now, he knew that much. But such deep thinking was rare indeed, for Bart Brewer's mental gifts in no way matched his physical capabilities. Charitably, you might say that they were at best rude, awaiting development, as you might put it. Or, to use the local vernacular, always, but always, to the point of insensitivity – he was a bit thick. Straight as a die, generous to a fault, well-liked by all – but a bit thick.

Therefore, it really was no surprise that during Wharton's delivery of evidence, evidence replete with complicated terminology straight out of anatomical texts, that the sensory apertures of the jury foreman had become glazed over, ossified by bafflement. Whether the other jury members were at all immune to the same effects was doubtful.

Not that it mattered to coroner Madden. He knew where this case would be going, whether the jury understood the fine details or not. But fine detail, or more precisely, arcane professional phraseology, was grist to the coroner's mill. He loved it. Understanding it helped him in his work. More importantly, it made him look wise and learned in front of colleagues, and he wanted nothing more than to be known as such.

So, unlike the men of the jury who were only trying to look as if paying rapt attention and taking it all in, Jacob Madden, with the benefit of medical reports in front of him, really was taking it all in. Every nuance, he liked to think.

And at the mention of the words 'pre-frontal lobes', like a cat outside a mouse-hole, just waiting, waiting – then pouncing, the coroner pounced.

That pouncing awoke the foreman and the rest of the coven of sworn men, and the scales fell from their eyes and the dross their ears.

"If I can just interrupt you there doctor," began the coroner.

"It's all right, I was finished anyway," replied the medical man.

Something in the doctor's informality; a smugness; perhaps, he hadn't called him sir. It irked him, the nearly chubby man with the petite feet. So:

"You're finished when I dismiss you doctor. And I haven't dismissed you. I have a question for you."

The doctor looked perplexed, embarrassed, and possibly angry. Nevertheless, he merely replied politely, "Certainly. What can I help you with?"

"This damage to the pre-frontal lobes…"

"Yes sir?"

"This presumably took place when, during the altercation with his fellow drinker, he was struck on the head with what witnesses have variously described as the spit-pot or gob-bucket. Would you agree?"

"Yes sir. The wound and the fracture were relatively fresh, and the rate of bleeding would…"

"Thank you doctor. Therefore, we can safely say can we, in your expert opinion, that that blow in the pub did the damage? Good. Now, you have given evidence to the effect that bleeding within the cranial cavity would have been continuing until the moment of death, or shortly thereafter, but the question I put to you now is 'what was the immediate effect of that blow'? That is to say, within the seconds and minutes following it, what would the effect have been on the deceased?"

"Well, he would have been in pain of course, no doubt anaesthetised somewhat by alcohol," opined Wharton, "and he was very angry too, by all accounts."

"Understandable I suppose," rejoined the coroner, "but we do not need to concern ourselves at this point with 'all accounts.' However, what we should be very much concerned with here is your account, your medical opinion as to the psychological and behavioural effects of such a blow, causing deadly damage to the brain as, according to your evidence, it did. Not wishing to prompt you, but could you elaborate on that area? Perhaps it would be instructive for the jury if you began by explaining what the function of that part of the human brain is."

"Yes. Yes I see. Well, the blow to Mr Hickey's head came in at an oblique angle, down and across," explained the doctor, illustrating with a chopping motion of his hand, "he must have been facing his assailant at the time, and the aetiology would suggest, in short, that the assailant stood to deliver it, to the still seated deceased. And indeed witnesses have attested to that scenario. This means that the pot hit him with considerable momentum in this area here," said the doctor describing with his fingers a line over the

310

front of his own skull. "As we have seen the implement in question is fairly heavy, five and a quarter pounds (that's empty weight) and it is hard, being of bronze or a similar alloy, with a ridged bottom. Now, the momentum given by the relatively high position from which the attack was launched, multiplied by the object's weight created considerable force, that is in relation to the amount required to damage human tissue, and this force was concentrated into the small area comprising the ridge which this pot stands on, which you have all seen. And all of this concentrated force landed on Mr Hickey's head. Now in terms of muscle power, the attack may not have been particularly savage, but the effect certainly was, depressing an area of skull beneath the skin and hair and causing splinters of bone on the inside of the cranium to detach and injure the brain. This was obvious from my post mortem examination but," and here he shot a covert glance to the sergeant, "it would by no means have had the appearance of a mortal wound from the other side, as it were, I mean from the outside, as it would initially be hidden under the inevitable blood and later by the scab which formed. Anybody could be forgiven for seeing it as just a nasty gash, not uncommon after Saturday night disturbances."

"You are not being asked to give opinions, doctor, except upon medical matters," warned the coroner, "now get to the point."

"Point?"

"Yes the point. We know the brain was damaged. How might that affect behaviour?"

"Oh yes. Well, we have established that there was in this case significant trauma to the subject's pre-frontal cortex. Now, that part of the brain is pre-eminently responsible for rational thinking; for decision making. If you like, it's what makes us human; makes us different to the animals. It's what makes us civilised."

"So," pursued the man in charge, "let's suppose that a man's frontal lobe were completely destroyed, or nearly so. Or excised by the knife of some magical surgeon, so that the man yet lived. Would a man still be able to function in such circumstances?"

"As an animal perhaps. His heart would still beat, and his lungs would still breathe. His eyes would see and his ears would hear. He would respond to stimulus: hunger, pain, fear. But automatically, as do the lower orders of nature, as would a dog, a sheep, a frog even. But this would be pure instinct, with no rational thought and no higher control."

"You are saying," continued the coroner deliberately, "that such an unfortunate would be a slave to instinct? He would have no choice but to react to those instincts, those impulses, because his mind had lost the power to override them. Would that be fair to say?"

"In essence, yes," agreed the doctor.

"And you mentioned hunger and fear earlier, as examples of these uncontrollable impulses. What of anger, would you count that emotion amongst them?"

"Certainly," confirmed the doctor.

"Precisely," exclaimed the coroner with an evident satisfaction, as of one who has just coaxed a toddler to string his first sentence together, "so that, let's say then that, as in this case, a man with a badly damaged pre-frontal cortex – 'significant damage' I believe you described it as, 'significant' – let's say that a man with this handicap, a man in pain, drunk, and angry; that is, subject to the impulses of pain, alcohol and anger, responds to those impulses by striking back with deadly force. Would he be responsible for his action?"

The doctor saw where this was going, "But we're not talking hypothetically here, we're talking about Hickey's actions. He didn't just strike back, he deliberately ran out to fetch a weapon and then ran back to kill. That's malice aforethought surely?"

"You are advised doctor to keep to your own area of expertise and not stray into mine. Now, whether or not there was a degree of 'forethought', malicious or not, my question to you is, and assuming a significant trauma to the area of the brain in question, would Mr Hickey, in giving in to these stimuli, of anger, of pain, necessarily have had a choice? In the absence of a fully functioning rational brain, the decision-making faculty as you have alluded to, in the absence of such, irrespective of what his actions were, would he necessarily have been able to tell the difference between right and wrong?"

Conceding the point Wharton replied, "Depending on the degree of damage, no."

"And," pursued Madden, "in terms of its effects on the man's behaviour, what was the degree of damage here?"

"It's hard to say."

"Take your best guess."

"Well then, I suppose that the subject may have had the moral maturity of, say, a ten- or twelve-year-old."

"A ten- or twelve-year-old?"

"Yes."

"Thank you doctor, that will be all."

#

After a short break, the coroner began to recap on the witness testimony and the medical opinion in both cases: the death of Higgins at the hands of a putative ten, or twelve, year old, and the death of Hickey, by all the evidence, at his own. Sergeant Lively was hearing none of it. Like the jury foreman he had become distracted, but in his case it was not by the perplexing medical cant and legalistic tautology, but by an increasingly comfortable communion with his invisible companion. When he came back, the coroner was summing up…

"…has been a most interesting and unusual case. I say case, the singular, because it seems to me that the two unfortunate deaths today under investigation, and your verdict upon them, cannot be separated without risking coming to the wrong conclusion.

312

Firstly then, I ask you to consider the fatal stabbing. It is not disputed that death was delivered to Mr Higgins at the hands of his friend Hickey. But it is not the physical act here that raises difficult questions; it is not Hickey's hands that should concern us, rather it is his mental state, governed by his brain. Now, in order for you to deliver a verdict of murder, you must satisfy yourselves of two things: first, that Higgins picked up the knife and with it stabbed Higgins, and that that blow was the immediate cause of death. You may find little difficulty on this point. However, and secondly, you must also satisfy yourselves that Higgins had the requisite 'guilty mind' – or men's rea as the law has it – when he committed the act. The mere fact that he deliberately armed himself with a deadly weapon for this assault appears to show," he shot a glance at Wharton, "'malice aforethought.' Even so, given doctor Wharton's evidence you may conclude that Hickey was not responsible for his actions following the damage to his brain inflicted by Higgins. To remind you, doctor Wharton suggested that Hickey's ability to discriminate between right and wrong might have been reduced to the level of moral discrimination possessed by a ten or twelve-year-old. If you accept this, and the good doctor's estimation is the most accurate we can hope for, then I would also remind you, by way of a reference point, that in law, in this enlightened age, criminal responsibility does not attach to a person of less than thirteen years. Of course the doctor's best guess as to the effect of the blow to Hickey's skull is just that, a guess and you may consider that the age parameters to which he alludes are perhaps borderline or arbitrary. Be that as it may, it is clear that we can say that Hickey's mental powers of discrimination, knowing right from wrong, were significantly degraded by the injury to his brain. Now, unless you firmly disagree with that proposition (and that of course is your prerogative) it seems to me that you cannot in all conscience bring in a verdict of murder, but must return one of manslaughter."

"We now turn to the next day, Mr Hickey, in a police cell, found dead. If you are satisfied that the deceased took his own life, and I would caution you," he said looking first at Wharton then toward Millership, "that there is no evidence to the contrary, then you must return a verdict of suicide – whilst the balance of his mind was disturbed. But first, I must return once again to the deceased – Hickey's – injuries sustained the previous day when the now infamous metal…implement struck him on the head. Now, the doctor says that that injury, without treatment, would have proved fatal within days. If we imagine for a moment that Hickey, having been struck, had never ran out and armed himself, had not killed Higgins, had not been incarcerated for it, and had merely taken himself off to wherever he called home and died quietly, on Tuesday say, then there is no doubt that the police would have been arresting friend Higgins on suspicion of murder. But, as a matter of law, I must caution you that you cannot ascribe, in law, Hickey's death to any action of Higgins. You may feel that friend Hickey hanged himself out of remorse, or guilt, or shame. Or, he may have done it precisely because his normal powers of reason had been robbed from him by that infamous blow. Or both, or neither. But his reasons are immaterial to this enquiry: what you must focus on, even allowing that Hickey may not have been in that cell but for the blow he received at the hands of Higgins, and disregarding the fact that the damage to his brain was going to kill him regardless, is that asphyxiation by one's own hand is a very different outcome than a slow death by bleeding from a wound inflicted by a third party. Do you think that Mr Higgins, in striking his friend in anger, could have possibly foreseen that death would come to him, if at all, not from a cracked skull, but from an intervention on the part of the victim himself, from hanging? No, he could not, and did not. Nor would any man, I submit. And this fact therefore changes the whole course of the investigation, for, self-evidently, the proximate cause of death to Mr Hickey was the action of Mr Hickey itself, and something only indirectly connected to the altercation at the Three Furnaces. In such circumstances, gentlemen of the jury, the law applies the doctrine of Novus Actus Intervenus, a new action intervenes. In this case the new action was the hanging of Hickey, which served to break the chain of causation between the blow struck against him and his death. Therefore, in the case of the death of Hickey, you must confine yourself to the immediate cause of death, which is hanging. Now, it is not for me to put ideas in your heads about the interpretation of facts which have been fully explained in the evidence which you have heard. However, it seems to me that you have two choices. One that the deceased hanged himself. Two, that a person or persons unknown took him and hanged him – but there has been no suggestion and no evidence to support that. If Hickey took his own life, you merely have to decide whether he did it deliberately, in which case it was suicide, or if he did it by accident, which you may feel, given what we have heard, erm, unlikely…"

If the poor gentlemen of the jury had not been confused before the coroner began his summing up, they were after it. Nevertheless, two things had been made clear to them, namely that there had been a suicide and there had not been a murder. Thus, coroner Madden was gratified that in short order the jury retired, considered and delivered. The awkward brown faced man had announced quietly, that in the case of Henry Higgins, the verdict was manslaughter; suicide the verdict for Hickey.

For the coroner, most satisfactory, and, following the, laborious, certification of the inquisition, he lost no time in decamping.

But the landlord was out of luck: Richard Merriss only got paid one three shillings and sixpence fee, not the seven-shilling double upon which he had banked. And he hadn't got his murder either, which may also have disappointed P.C. Salt, in particular, not having one under his belt. Sergeant Lively was, as they say, not fussed either way.

Of all of them, P.C. Payne was most relieved. Truth be told, he had not checked on that prisoner once.

Chapter 23

Mistaken Identity

Moses Munn had not done what sergeant Lively had wanted or expected, not exactly. And he had taken his time about it. Yes, he had fully intended to print the exculpatory article on behalf of and at the firm request of the policeman, and put the current incarnation of Spring Heeled Jack, one at least partially fashioned and given life by the editor himself, to rest. But news of fires burning beneath churchyards, one churchyard at least, naturally took precedence, and persuaded him there was life in the old supernatural angle yet. He foresaw that the unholy tidings would if anything only reinvigorate the existing titillation which the appearance of Jack, and his reporting, had injected into the dull lives of his readers. Jack had been a good seller, and Moses reckoned that he deserved another week at liberty before being chained and tamed by the sergeant's forced 'rational explanation.' Everyone deserved a little excitement, Moses had decided: he had blown some up, and he would decide when to deflate it, within reason of course, which he reckoned would be by the next issue; he couldn't imagine the sergeant letting it lie when he found his own account missing from today's pages. But he knew how far to push it, and when the copper's version did go out, he would take some of the credit for defusing tensions, a good enough reason to be discretely smug. As it happened, his calculation was proved right when a visit from a distinctly aggravated and slightly dangerous looking Abraham Lively confirmed to him that the limit of procrastination had been reached. Consequently, details of the sergeant's proof, the big reveal, appeared in the paper in the very next issue, on Thursday. But even then, it did not quite take the form of the out and out denial, total scotching, complete repudiation, that he knew the copper wanted. Too predictable, too over confident. Instead, the old editor invited readers to make up their own minds, after explaining how the confusion could have occurred, through a haze of over-indulgence, between the myth of the monster leaping trees and spewing fire and terror, and the more prosaic, in the form of 'jumping Joe Darby' and his unusual secretive gymnastic routines. In fact, Mr Munn had decided that there was a continuing commentary available here: weekly instalments, following Darby's career and goals. He could become quite a celebrity, local hero even, if the Advertiser did its job. Moses already had enough material from the police, and from the obliging young man himself, to spin it out over several editions. Of course, Mr Darby would henceforth find it more difficult to practise in peace, but the newspaperman was sure he would rise above that. Case of having to.

As for that copper, he hoped that he appreciated it, when talk of a new local hero supplanted in the fickle indigenous consciousness, all memory of its ephemeral former villain. Because that's what happened, Spring Heeled Jack fizzled out, forgotten by the plebs, as is the way of things. But it was not Abe Lively's way. He didn't forget. How could he? He knew he was real.

#

Young Frederick from the Hailstone had found constable Lively manning the station. The lad was out of puff and obviously upset – no child but he was crying as he spoke. Josh left a hasty note for the imminently expected Salt and set off for the Hailstone. It sounded serious. Somebody had attacked Comanche, a horse apparently; cut him. Blood everywhere. There was certainly plenty on young Fred's hands. The landlady, Abe's friend, was with the animal, shocked no doubt, if not hurt herself: Frederick was not making much sense. They proceeded by way of fast walking paces interspersed with bouts of trotting, and the boy could only communicate in short bursts – he seemed in poor shape for a youngster – once having saved up enough spare puff to expend it on snatches of description and exhortations to hurry. It was only when they were almost there that Josh was clear that the principal victim was of the non-human variety. It was the variety with four hooves employed to pull carts, and a love of carrots which had been his undoing. There was a pathetic lean-to which served as a shelter from the rain, leading onto a thin strip of trampled mud which the boy optimistically referred to as the field. And a couple of yards inside the wire fence, a little crowd of trespassers. Approaching, Josh could see that these onlookers had formed a semicircle, a human amphitheatre focussed on a scene below his sightline, obscured by curiosity. He thought he knew what to expect. He was mistaken.

"Make way, make way. Come on, police. Make way."

The fusty grey curtain of grey people parted, to reveal an explosion of colour to assail his vision. The scene was composed of mainly red; mainly blood. So much blood. The black and white body of the horse was covered in red. Her green dress and her white arms and her white apron were spattered and smeared with bright red, and the ground was sticky with the brown red pudding mixture of congealing mortality and mud. Josh doubted not that the little horse was dead, despatched by a stab in the neck, an obvious gap still oozing a last few droplets, as if the creature had been waiting for him, to demonstrate the cause of death. There was nothing to be done for the horse. But what of the woman? Obscured by the red. Unconscious, perhaps, not dead? Presumably also cut, slumped sideways across the horse's shoulder. But then she sat up. And sobbed softly, and stroked the horse again, sorrow spreading scarlet.

"Madam, are you hurt?" said Josh.

She looked at him. "Hurt?" she repeated.

"Are you wounded? You're covered in blood."

"It's not mine. It's Comanche's," said she looking at her fallen friend.

"Are you sure? What happened?"

"Sure? Yes. I just found him like this – we did, Frederick and I," she corrected as she caught sight of her messenger. He was already gone I think, but I tried, to stop the blood.

"Right lad," began the P.C., "all right people, let's clear the field. Out onto the street – do you have anything to cover him?"

"Yes, some tarpaulins in his stable."

"Good lad, go and fetch one. Can you manage?"

"Yes," nodded Frederick and was gone.

"Now you lot, I won't tell you again, get yourselves off this land. You're most likely trampling over clues. Get yourselves back!"

Slowly, they went. Except for one short woman whom Josh's brother Abe would have recognised as that indomitable defender of young ladies' rights who had seen off the bullies and so impressed the sergeant on his first social visit to the Hailstone.

"I'll take her in and help her to get cleaned up."

"Right, thank you, Mrs….?"

"Eddington."

"Thank you, Mrs Eddington."

"Come on love," said the older woman to the younger, "nothing to be done here."

"No. I expect you're right." With a sharp inhalation of breath the landlady abruptly rose and walked woodenly toward her kitchen door, the little woman hurrying after.

As the door closed P.C. Salt arrived on scene, and he was not alone, the sergeant was with him. The two took in the scene at a glance: Mud, blood and death.

"Where's Sarah, the landlady?" was the first question.

"She's inside. She's all right. Unharmed I mean. She looked upset though, poor thing. Who wouldn't?" said Josh as he looked again at the deceased equine.

"Who indeed?" returned his brother, "how about the tosspot that did this?"

"Well, yes," began Josh.

"It's a bloody mess. What happened?" asked Salt.

"I don't know. Haven't had a chance to ask too many questions. Thought I'd let her get cleaned up first, she's got…"

"Cleaned up? I thought you said she was all right?"

"She is, she is. She just tried to stop the blood and got it all over her."

317

"Some chance. Like trying to hold back the tide. That's a ruddy big wound," commented Salt.

"From what I can make out, she found him just before six and sent the boy – where is he? You know him – she sent him to fetch the police," offered Josh.

Abe had been examining the body. "There's no chance that this is an accident, not that I was thinking that it was. That's a deep stab wound, right into the jugular. Too precise to be accidental, and what's around for the old boy to do it on? Nothing. It's a clean cut, with no jagged edges. Murder."

"Except, he was only a horse of course," added Salt.

"Only a horse? I liked him better than some people I know, old Comanche," returned his sergeant.

"Comanche? They're Indians aren't they?"

"That's right. It was also the name of the only survivor of Custer's last stand, on the white man's side, that is."

"But there weren't any," said Salt, sure of that fact.

"Ah, got you there! A horse, it was a horse. He's famous."

"Is he? I never heard of him," admitted Salt.

"Yes, I think I remember it in the paper, when I was a kid," said Josh, "was he black and white then?"

"I shouldn't have thought so," opined Salt, "not if he was a cowboy horse. It was the Indians that had the mongrel ones. What were they? I'm sure they were called something, but I can't…"

"Have you finished professor?"

"Eh?"

"Much as I was enjoying the fascinating historical detail, do you think we can dispense with it, we're on duty."

"Sorry, Sarge."

"Right, then. I do know this place, but just to be sure, you two have a scout round and see if you can find any sharp object that would account for this. Just in case."

Their exploration revealed no obvious means of self-injury.

"So," said Salt, "looks like we've got some nasty lunatic at large – with a large knife!"

"Looks like it," agreed sergeant Lively, "and a nocturnal lunatic at that. Look at the angle of his neck, it's distorted and stiff. Salt, you're a strong man, see if you can bend one of those legs."

Salt dutifully tried.

"There's no chance," he said, "how long do you reckon he's been dead?"

"I'm not an expert, but I've seen my share of dead animals, and blood. First the blood: look at where it's pooled, it's not just the mud that made it darken; and judging by that stiffness, rigor mortis, I'd say he'd been dead for at least three to four hours, no less."

"But the landlady, Mrs Bates…" intervened Josh.

"She saw what she wanted to see. There's no way that animal was still alive at six this morning. A case of wishful thinking I'm afraid," said the sergeant.

"So," continued P.C. Salt, "we're looking for somebody who skulks around at two or three in the morning. A shift worker, d'you think?"

"Not that it helps, but the attack may even have happened earlier. Depending on the depth of the cut, what vessels were involved and so forth, he might not have died too quickly, poor old blighter," added the sergeant.

"Yes," agreed Salt, "it's not easy to see in this mud, but if you stand back where I am…" and they both stepped back to join him, "you can see where he ran up and down before lying down and kicking around. Wait…"

He went over to a patch of hard-standing to the right and made his way back to the fence, "Yes, there's blood there, and blood here, at the fence."

"But you would have thought that someone would have heard something. Surely he wouldn't have gone down quietly?" said Josh.

"Probably not, and maybe nobody heard over the din of drop hammers, depending on wind direction," offered Abe, at a loss himself. He was thinking how the little chap would come up to the fence to him, for a fuss, or a carrot.

"The bastard lured him here, trusting soul that he was, and then he cut him."

The breach of trust was the last straw for the sergeant, and he suddenly filled with vengeful sorrow. He would not show it in front of the men, he was afraid that it was weakness, both the feeling and the showing of it. Nevertheless, the feeling had a target, this culprit who the sergeant was sure he knew. But his face revealed only that he was not smiling.

"So you say Sarah went inside?" he asked.

"Yes, there was a lot of blood, but only horse blood," Josh assured him, "she's inside getting cleaned up."

"Right then. Let's give her some time. At ease men. Samuel, crash the ash."

#

While the law was indulging in a brief tobacco break over the remains of a horse, Jack Cutler and John Lively had been discussing the new day's business with Cyril Crane. Of his own free will John had decided that it was time and right to step over the line, between honest work and crime. Not too far, yet, and not permanently, probably. Today he was to accompany Cutler as extra security for a high-stakes card game, held at one of several 'secret' locations. Cyril's last words to them were:

"John, remember. Look and listen and learn. Jack, keep him out of trouble. You know where to pick up Dan."

"Yes," replied Cutler, and would have added that he was sure that the big man could look after himself, except that Cyril, Sabre following, was already out of the door. So Jack turned to John.

"So, this is it then. We won't need to move for another three hours. I don't know about you, but I'm going to help myself to a half. You?"

"Not for me," said John, "make sure you put it on the slate."

"Wouldn't dream otherwise," came back from Jack's back as it passed into the next room.

John sat quietly, thinking of what was to come, of what his brother would think. All in all, he was looking forward to getting involved in the shadow side of the business, earning more. Also, it would keep him closer to Jack, as his uncle wanted. And he like Jack was confident that he could handle any 'trouble' the day threw up, barring bobby trouble of course. Had he but known, he could have been even more relaxed, for Cyril Crane, his uncle, had considered this assignment carefully, had considered it low risk for his nephew, both in respect of the propensity of the players to cut up rough (office and trade types, a minimum amount of muscle between them, and even less guts), and in respect of the chances of John's name coming up in the wrong quarters. For the purposes of this, and future operation, as a matter of fact, he was not John but Lawrence, or Larry as Cutler would have it.

On the periphery of his conscious senses John was aware of, but not focussed on various chinks, clunks and clanging, a trail of auditory clues as to the progress of Cutler's mission in the tap room; not that he was that interested. After what seemed a suspiciously long time the little man returned, minus his expected trophy.

"I think the barrel must need changing," he stated.

"There's other pumps," suggested John.

"Naw. I was set on the light mild. Gone off the whole thing now."

"Never mind. Perhaps it's better to keep a clear head."

Jack's natural response would have been to get contrary about such a, to his mind, arguable statement, but on this occasion he elected to just say, "Perhaps you're right."

He sat himself back down and consulted his watch, put it away and looked around, at nothing in particular, drumming his fingers on the table for a while before abruptly desisting, apparently to check the state of his nails. That they didn't come up to scratch was proved to John's idle satisfaction when Cutler reached to the small of his back and pulled out what he called his sheath knife. A pretty bone handled knife it was, well looked after, with a smooth brass cross-guard and a single edged six-inch blade that came to a sharp scalloped point, something like a slimmed down and shortened Bowie knife. It was the point he used to delicately clean his nails. Eventually, when there could not possibly have been a single grain of dirt left under them, Cutler seemed satisfied, though no less bored. He began to dexterously manipulate the knife in his left hand, with little apparent thought or concentration to it, point threatening forward, then with a roll over the fingers, point angled back, positioning the edge for a slash; well-practised and second nature. John had not seen this before; he imagined Cutler a dangerous adversary in a knife fight; in and out, small and quick…

Cutler caught him watching and stilled the knife. "How are you getting on with that girl of yours?" he asked.

"Very well, as it happens. We're very happy."

"Well, just you make sure she knows who's boss," cautioned Cutler, pushing home his point with a wave of his knife.

"It's not like that with us," began Lively.

"No, no. I didn't mean…I expect you're right. None of my business really. It's just…"

"What?"

"It's just that you hear things, don't you?"

"Such as?"

"Nothing. Just things."

"No, come on. What are you getting at?"

"Look, I'm not sure it's my place. But as you're family, and a friend of mine, there's something you, or your brother, might like to know."

Something in his tone. John knew he had to pin him down. "All right, so you've got something to say. Out with it."

"If you say so. Just understand, I'm not trying to cause trouble – for anyone – but like I said I've come to regard you as a mate, and…"

"Stop! Just spit it out will you."

"Right then. It's about your sister. Miriam is it? Mrs Beckett. And this man she's seeing."

Those words sparked the big man's ire. How dare this little fart cast aspersions…He leant close and placed an aggravated fist on the other's collar, oblivious to the still live blade.

"What do you mean, 'seeing'?"

#

The good Mrs Eddington having indicated, the sergeant and constable Salt entered to interview the owner of the victim of the night time slashing. The kitchen was of course familiar to Abe Lively but new territory for Salt. P.C. Lively had elected to mind the crime scene and wait the arrival of the knackers.

For the sergeant the encounter, with the woman he had last parted from on such bad terms, was an awkward one, albeit necessary, in his opinion. To his questions of genuine concern as to her well-being she responded in an aloof, even cold manner; guarded, as a suspect in custody might be. So be it, he would keep it on a professional footing.

"Well, I'm glad to see that you are unharmed, but we still have a particularly nasty criminal on the loose, and it's my job to catch him."

She shot him a sidelong glance with an almost imperceptible shake of her head. And she was frowning. He persevered, "So if you wouldn't mind, my colleague has some questions for you."

His colleague's eyes registered surprise, his brows and tilt of the head flashing a question. You go ahead said the sergeant's nod.

The landlady's cool demeanour was a shallow one. Under it Salt detected a heat, anger he supposed. And there was shock, betrayed in the slight muscle tremors which she thought she was hiding. And something more. Fear? Abe had noticed that.

Salt was asking, "And what time was that?"

"Frederick's always up early, before me. He's not one for lying in. He makes a pot of tea for me to come down to, stacks the pots and glasses washed up the night before and goes out to check on the horse and feed the chickens. I always get up when the alarm goes off, at six…"

"So he was up, when?"

"About five I suppose."

"An hour before you then?"

"No, I couldn't lie in. I awoke early today. I knew there was something. I got up just after him. We went straight out to the animals. Say about half past five."

"So you opened up and went out. What did you see? Anybody skulking about?"

"No, not at that stage. A crowd gathered later of course."

"And you saw your horse lying down, bleeding according to Frederick, and what did you do?"

"He's only a pony really. Was." The façade began to crumble and she failed to hold all the tears back before continuing, "I walked over to him. Then I ran. It was horrible. Really horrible."

Abe thought about the mess lying outside. She was saying, "I had to check. I got down, but he was dead. I think he was dead; I knew he was really. But I put my hand onto that wound and it felt warm to me. I thought it did. But he was dead, I think I knew. But I couldn't believe it. I threw myself on him and shouted at him, to get up…"

"I know, I know. Young Frederick told us as much. Only natural…" said Salt hoping she wouldn't break down, "what about the crowd, later. Anybody stand out? Any strangers?"

"No, just neighbours going about their usual business."

"Was there any trouble last night? Perhaps some drunk you threw out? Somebody else with a grudge?"

"No. It was a perfectly normal night last night. Besides, it's not that kind of pub."

"So you've no idea who might have done this?"

Her silence may have suggested to Salt that she was trawling her memory for some forgotten clue. But Abe had other ideas. That she was thinking something that she didn't want to believe. Who was there close to Sarah harbouring a grudge? Bloody Spragg, that's who. He was a devious character and he could well believe, wanted to believe, that he had done this. No doubt he would reappear soon full of smiles and sympathy, and hopes.

But her response to the next question made him think again, and brought him up dead.

Salt: "Do you have any enemies Mrs Bates? Anybody you've recently had an altercation with? Anybody you've upset?"

And bitter grey eyes stabbed straight at the police sergeant, before they were cast down. Abe didn't know whether it was an admission or an accusation: "You'd need to ask your sergeant about that," she said softly.

#

It had been young Jake Collins' lucky day when his path crossed with that of Joshua Lively. Not only had he avoided an uncomfortable stay in a prison cell whilst awaiting a hearing before the justices, he had avoided that hearing altogether. All thanks to the influence and charm of Joshua Lively, aimed in the right direction: that is, at the devout but pliable Miss Ricketts. And the influence of the uniform had had its effect on the cantankerous but by no means obdurate Mr Haywood. To be fair to the old chap, the constant aggravation of a constantly swollen gammy leg was enough to make the best of men cantankerous. The march of time was slowly crippling him, and there was nothing he could do about it, until now, until he was offered a trade involving vicarious use of a pair of youthful legs. It had been P.C. Lively's idea and when the continuing advantages of it were explained to the old costermonger he wondered why he had never thought of it himself. So the copper and the erstwhile complainant struck a deal, an entirely informal one, for the time being, whereby the boy was taken in, out of Miss Ricketts' temporary care, and given a job; an entirely satisfactory arrangement all around thought Josh. Except that he owed Miss Ricketts a favour. All things considered that was a small price to pay. In fact, he was warming to the notion.

But the fruits of the constable's efforts on behalf of the boy were not universally sweet. On the contrary, the effects on the master, Gideon Gross, had left a distinctly sour taste. Ever since, that is, that a certain constable Samuel Salt had started making 'further enquiries' about him. And the man seemed to have the knack of going to precisely those amongst his 'colleagues' who just happened to have a grudge against the master, or else were simply too honest and law abiding for their own good. On reflection, he realised that the policeman's evidence gathering task had been pretty easy, once the first suspicions had been stirred. If only he could turn the clock back. He had always been fond of the booze, but it hadn't been that long since he had taken to imbibing during the day. Nevertheless, it had been going on for long enough for him to have been if not exactly three sheets in the wind when them two coppers had come calling, then at least a couple of sheets in a stiff breeze. Tipsy. Yes, that was the word. It seemed so innocuous, playful even. He had thought he could hide it, but the rozzers had obviously noticed. Talk about bad luck. Or was it? He blamed Jack Cutler. It was Cutler's fault he was drinking more. He made him nervous, made him look for Dutch courage. But if Cutler got to hear about this he would need more courage than you could find in a bottle. A fast pair of legs might serve better. Fat chance.

#

Sarah had put Abe in the embarrassing position of having to explain himself to a subordinate, revealing details of his private life which he would have preferred remain so. That, and the obvious coolness, not to say suspicion with which his former love now seemed to regard him, had rapidly narrowed down the chances of a reconciliation, and indeed the sergeant's desire for same.

As he was telling the constable as the pair made their way back towards Blackheath, it had been Spragg who had turned Sarah against him, working on her, on her fears and insecurities. More than that, if anyone had a motive for wanting her to believe that the policeman was so upset that he would take it out on Comanche, then it was Spragg again.

"So constable, the first order of business is to locate this tosspot and ask him some choice questions. Easiest thing, you drop in the pub this evening. He's bound to be there."

"You really think he's our man? I'm only asking because the name's not one I've come across. There's plenty of nutters and thugs about who probably wouldn't bat an eyelid at this kind of thing, should the mood take 'em."

"Maybe so. But we've got to start somewhere, and I happen to think that Spragg should be number one on the list. I'm not saying he's guilty, but I'd enjoy putting him through the wringer. Just in case, you see?"

"You're the boss."

"Yes. And I appreciate that you should be off at six, but I would deem it a favour if you would head this up for me. Hopefully, he'll show up early on. I want you to bring him back to the station with one of the crew who are on."

"I'll take Clark. If I'm working over, I can at least entertain myself."

"You love him really."

"As do we all I shouldn't wonder."

"Josh tells me you've been looking into the workhouse; at the master to be precise. What's the issue?"

324

"Well for one thing, Mr Gross, that's what the fat slug's called – have you met him? – yes, well, anyway, he's a real drunkard, and getting worse. Staff there say he's constantly on the bottle. I don't see how, as a public servant, his position can be justified, or his pay. I mean, it comes straight out of ratepayers' pockets, yours and mine; food out of kids' mouths, and that's what he does with it."

"That bad is it?"

"Yes, I've seen it. He can't be looking after his charges at all well. Also, I've heard, he's got wandering hands."

"He's thieving you mean?"

"Probably that as well, but no. A bit too free with some of the young ladies under his care. And I do mean young – by some accounts."

"But that's not on," said the sergeant, now very much more engaged, "that won't do at all. What are you doing about it?"

"It's a bit thin, verging on hearsay…"

"Is it? Well, I suppose, being in a state of intoxication within the confines of one's own, er, establishment, isn't really an arrestable offence. As for his wandering hands, without more than hearsay, that's a difficult one. However…"

"However what?"

"Put all your findings down in a report, all together; informants' names, the lot, and I will see that it reaches members of the council. Get him removed as unfit. There's more than one way to skin a cat."

"Good," said Salt, "he's a slob. Also, I think there's some kind of fiddle going on, I know there is. But I can't put a finger on it. Once he's out of office perhaps folk will be more inclined to come forward and give us something we can use to put him inside."

"First things first," replied the sergeant. "You get me Spragg and I'll push this up the agenda. First things first."

#

Josh hung around at the Hailstone till the knackers cart arrived, then he made his way back to the station. To find that a bad day was getting better.

As he walked in, Payne looked him a question.

"Bad business. Some moron took into his head to sneak into the horse field by the Hailstone and cut a pony's throat. The landlady found it dead, earlier on."

"Blimey. Dissatisfied customer do you think? Or what?"

"Who knows? Who knows the workings of a sick mind?"

"Well, we'll have to find him."

"Obviously, goes without saying."

"No, I meant…What if this is his first time? And what if he liked it? The blood? What's to stop him picking on a person next. A child or a woman probably, he's obviously a coward."

"It's a big leap from killing an animal to killing a person. That's murder. That's the rope!"

"Well, perhaps he values people as little as he values an animal. And, as you say, this is somebody sick in the head, so who knows whether the law and the threat of punishment would put him off."

"I see what you mean. That's a bit depressing."

"No, don't be depressed. It hasn't happened yet. And we'll most likely catch the bugger afore it does. Besides, I've got some good news."

"Oh? What? I could do with some good news."

"You've just missed sergeant Southall from the Nimmings."

"What brings him here?"

"Ah," said Payne, pausing for dramatic effect.

"What?" prompted Josh.

"Well, he's Halesowen police, isn't he?"

"Yes, tell me something I don't know."

"Do you remember that poor old bloke, old Reg, the one found dead on the tracks down by the church?"

"Reg Phillips?"

"That's him. You remember your brother thought it was murder?"

"They haven't got a witness?" blurted out Josh, getting excited.

"That's right – they haven't."

"Then what? Get to the ruddy point!"

"All right, keep your hair on. But I'm disappointed you can't guess."

At this point, Payne might have been tempted to indulge himself with another pregnant pause, but a look from his colleague dissuaded him. "You know what the sergeant had you and Gordon looking for?"

"The medal!" exclaimed Josh, "it's turned up, hasn't it?"

"Got it in one," replied Payne, "well, in half a dozen, at least."

"Where is it? Have they still got it?"

"No, no, they haven't," said Payne, much to Josh's disappointment.

"Then…" began Lively.

"They haven't got it 'cos I've got it!" announced Payne in triumph and whipping open a desk drawer and placing on the top a metallic object attached to a ribbon of pale blue and yellow. Reg's medal, no doubt. He had seen it before, two clasps, for Inkerman and Sebastopol, and the familiar bust of the Queen. He picked it up and squeezed it, closing his eyes and willing the thing to impart its story, as if its recent history was imprinted and trapped in the metal, and concentration and a tight grip might release its

326

secrets to the custody of the holder's consciousness. It did nothing of the sort. Josh looked again, at the obverse, where what looked like a Roman soldier was being crowned with a laurel wreath by some kind of angel. No doubt the angels were looking after old Reg now. He put the medal back down, and in that moment he knew that Abe was right. Reg's death was no accident and no suicide.

"Best keep that under lock and key. How did Halesowen get hold of it? And why bring it here?"

"Ah, that's the thing. It seems that our beloved leader didn't just give up on finding this," said Payne, tracing the outline of her Majesty's head with his middle finger, "and he asked his opposite number in the Nimmings – that's Southall – to broaden the search. Sounds like they're very pally."

"Yes, I knew that."

"Any road, they arrested a pawnbroker last week, for receiving. They took a stack of stuff into custody, and the medal was amongst it. They've made the case against him now, he's remanded, and the medal was surplus to requirements as they say, so…"

"So they brought it here."

"Yep. Got a description of the depositor an' all. Big bloke, about thirty, pronounced limp, mutton chops and wearing a red scarf."

That rang a bell with Josh. He had seen that man, could see him now, but where was it? Then he linked it to another face, a distinctive one, generously freckled with extra-large ears. Yes, that was it. Who was that? Wharton, no, Williams? Woolley. That was it Derek Woolley. And then he knew that this was going to be awkward: Woolley was Cutler's man; and Cutler was Cyril's man. Josh's uncle, Cyril. And Abe's.

#

The once daft and nascent notion that he move around in disguise, with a growing understanding of the growing risk emanating from one source in particular, had now developed into an eminently sensible precaution.

It was therefore a few anxious heartbeats before the master recognised the figure that came a' knocking that afternoon. Beneath a voluminous coat at odds with the time of year and big enough it seemed to house twice the bulk, and a wide brimmed hat sporting crow feathers black as night and black as the eyes the hat concealed, lurked none other than Jack Cutler, and a multitude of sins. It was the presence of the accompanying lump of rock, Anthony Duberley, which paradoxically put Gross' mind at rest, but only briefly. There followed a flash of familiar eyes penetrating the concealing shade. The eyes gave the game away: Cutler's eyes, and they were in shark mode. Black as sin and hard as a hangman's. If Gideon Gross could have run from there, then, and never stopped running, he would have. But he could not. He was trapped, by his own decisions, a weak mind and a fat body. But most of all trapped by these two men. Here. Now.

He managed to stammer, "Jack, this is unexpected…an unexpected pleasure."

Jack Cutler stepped inside, simultaneously shedding his outer layer of deceit. Under it was the same old neat and correct figure which usually presented itself. Complete with that bloody walking stick: Gross had dreams about that (not good ones!) Before he could shut the office door, Duberley also stepped in, and shut it for him, with a click like the set of a gin trap. Duberley's presence was not usual, and Gross was scared, which was.

But as soon as Jack started talking Gideon started to relax, as was Jack's usual effect, when he wished it, as usually he did. Once rid of the sinister hat and coat he addressed his business partner in the most casual and cordial manner. Cordial as a cobra.

"Gideon, me old mate. I was in the area and thought 'why not drop in and see ol' Gideon?' For a catch up. It's been a while."

Has it? thought Gross, *perhaps it had.*

"Yes, yes, of course. What can I do for you Mr Cutler?" The 'Mr Cutler' had been the master's attempt not to sound disrespectful to the man, in front of Duberley.

"Mr Cutler?" queried Cutler, "Mr Cutler? What happened to Jack? Have you fallen out with me Gideon?"

The master almost shouted, "No! no, no, of course not no…perish the thought. I just thought…"

"Come, come Gideon old man. We'm all friends 'ere ain't we?"

Gideon looked across at the large human-looking primate known as Anthony Duberley and wasn't at all sure whether anyone could, or should, ever be friends with it. But as long as Jack said so, he supposed that the Duberley could be counted as a friend, at least for the duration of the meeting and Jack's protection.

"What happened to Jack then Gideon? Call me Jack."

"All right then, Jack…"

"Good. That's better. Now, ain'ya gonna offer your mates a drink?"

"Of course. Certainly, certainly. Of course."

"Gideon mate, I heard you the first time."

"Pardon?"

"You keep repeating yourself mate. Anybody would think you was nervous or summat. About summat."

"Nervous? No, not at all. Erm, tea?" he asked reaching for the bell-pull.

"Tea? I think our friend here could do with something a little stronger. He's had some rather sad personal news today," explained Jack, with a sly wink in the direction of his henchman.

"Oh dear, I'm very sorry to hear that," gushed Gross, "would you care to sit down?"

"No," said the big man flatly, before catching his boss' eye and drift, "no I'm quite comfortable standing. Do enough sitting."

Cutler was still clandestinely egging him on so he added, "But thank you very much for the offer. I could use that drink though, if it's not too much trouble," remembering Cutler's advance instructions, "but not tea though," he added hastily.

"In these circumstances," interposed a most amiable Jack Cutler, "me old Mom always maintained that whisky was called for. Gideon, I'm sure you could rustle some up."

Gross was not so sure that he should be 'rustling up' anything that might speak of a drinking problem. But Cutler was at it again, wasn't he? Challenging him to contradict a truth he already knew. A test. Jack didn't like liars, or, more accurately, didn't like being lied to. Besides, after his experience with the visit of the two coppers, he was not at all confident in his ability to bluff, certainly not with Cutler; not for two seconds with him. In the circumstances he thought it tactically prudent to produce the remains of his current bottle: he was reasonably sure that his visitors, or one of them at any rate, already suspected that the master had had a little tipple already. He was wrong. Mr Cutler did not suspect, he knew. They both knew, could smell the guilt and the alcohol.

"Well, as a matter of fact," began Gross with a commendable attempt at blitheness, "I do keep a bottle handy. In case of visitors, you understand."

"Not for medicinal purposes then?" queried Cutler.

"What? What do you mean?"

"For your nerves. How's your nerves mate? Holding out are they?"

"What? Oh yes, no worries there. No, as I say, I do like the occasional tot…"

"No, you didn't say. Not to me anyway."

"Well no, perhaps not. Not as such. It's for visitors mainly."

"So, you've got visitors. Come on."

"Right you are, Jack."

They watched as the fat man huffed and puffed among the contents of his desk drawers, finally producing, as if it were hard to remember its exact location, from the nether regions, an almost finished bottle of whisky. He then proceeded to clatter around in a small battered cupboard to produce glasses.

"Here you are. Only two glasses I'm afraid," apologised the fat man.

"I thought you said you get visitors."

"What?"

"Visitors. Plural. What do you do, take a sip and pass it on?"

"What do you mean?"

"You said you get visitors, that's what the booze is for. But you've only got two glasses. So?"

"Well, er, they don't all come at once. Never get a lot at once."

"Still pushing it though, eh? Don't make for a good host does it, Anthony, a shortage of glasses?"

"Very, inconvenient," replied the big man proud of the big word.

The master had a bright idea. "Well, o'course, it was a set of six. Silly 'ousekeeper broke four on 'em last wik. I'll send out for more fust thing."

He poured and slid the glasses toward the two men, who had taken the opportunity to sit themselves down. He sat himself, behind the now empty bottle, looking apologetic.

It's served its purpose. Just like I think you have mate. "Not having one yourself?" enquired Jack.

The fat man saw a chance to cover his backside. "No, I won't if you don't mind. I've already had a small one this morning, just to settle my stomach, I've been very bilious lately."

I'd stop looking in the mirror then. "Nothing serious?"

"No, no, not at all. I am prone to it you see, and a few sips of whisky normally sets me right. Just a drop, that's plenty for one day for me. But you go ahead."

"Well, there's not much there is there? I mean, for a man in our friend's condition."

"Condition?" stammered Gross.

"Yes. I said, didn't I? He's had a shock. A terrible shock. He could do with a stiff drink, that's just a dribble. You sure you're not hiding another bottle?"

"Hiding? No, of course not."

Jack stared at him then, for what seemed like an age. All of the master's attention was sucked toward the figure in front of him, everything else in the room blurred out to blank. The master found his voice:

"No, no hiding, no. I was just saving a bottle for a special occasion."

"Special occasion eh? Well then, this is it." The words paralysed the fat one. "Wouldn't you say so Gideon?"

"Yes. Yes of course. Excuse me." He went back to cupboard rummaging. Jack winked at Duberley and Duberley quickly grinned, then Gross was back.

"Here we are," he said flashing them with the label of a new bottle.

"Irish? I thought it was a special occasion. Everybody knows Scotch is best," said Cutler.

Not being any kind of connoisseur and wary of contradicting the little man the master merely confirmed that 'I'm not fussy.'

"Are you not?" returned Cutler, the black glint returning and freezing the master in mid unstoppering. "Just pour," broke the spell.

"Say when," said Gross.

They let him fill one glass, but barely had the first golden drops touched the second and Cutler said, "When." He handed the small measure to Duberley saying, "get that down ya mate," and the big man did.

"Gideon, you may as well have the other one, I've gone off the idea. Never been a big drinker me."

"But I can't drink all that…"

"Why?"

"It's too much. I'll be drunk."

"Drunk, eh? Are you telling me that a big bloke like you can't take his grog? I mean, it's only a glass. I bet you get through more than that when you're entertaining."

"Entertaining?"

"Them visitors you referred to."

"Oh yes, of course."

"Also, I wouldn't want to think that a partner of mine couldn't hold his drink. People like that don't know how to keep their mouths shut. And mouths shut are very much a requirement of the trade, are they not?"

"Yes indeed, couldn't agree more."

"Good. Drink up then. Or were you trying to poison us?"

"Poison? Yes, that's a good one!" exclaimed the man's nerves, the same nerves which them prompted him to laugh as if he had just been let in on the most hilarious joke ever, before downing in one swallow half a glass of his most petrified drink ever. In his heart he knew that the joke, the mean little joke, was on him, but he went to swallow again, looking up first, reddening now, and beaming at his friend Jack Cutler.

"Good Health," he intoned.

"Same to you," said Cutler with an ironic wink.

It was obvious to both visitors that despite the rather artificial circumstances, the presence of alcohol in the man's system had readily relaxed him, and that included his tongue.

"Now," continued Cutler, "while we're here, I've just got to ask you something."

"Fire away dear boy," said the master cheerily.

The false conviviality was severed by shards of ice then.

"What's this I hear about you talking to the coppers?"

#

When the pair left the master was as a battered old sail ship thrown onto the rocks of ruin. He attempted to salvage his senses and refloat his composure with more whisky: the newly opened bottle was not going to last long.

Outside Jack turned to Duberley.

"I think that confirmed our worst fears. Thank you for drawing this to my attention Anthony."

"What we gonna do?"

"From what we just saw, and from what I know of the local law, I think we're a hair's breadth away from somebody putting two and two together. And when they do, and when they start to really question our portly pal – about a few issues I might add – then I think he's gonna spill his guts."

"Same question. What we gonna do?"

331

"What would you do?"

"I'd kill him."

"Hold that thought."

#

On balance, he was, he believed, in a good mood. Yes, the day had started with an unpleasantness, with two in fact, but he knew that when he found the phantom horse slayer, which he knew he would because he knew it was Spragg, then he would be vindicated. As his apparently forlorn search for the medal had been. He hoped that Sarah had a large appetite, because she was going to be eating a lot of humble pie. The sergeant was getting quite agitated just thinking about it, he realised that. Another woman who could not see beyond the end of her nose! It was spoiled now. Even if she wanted him back. Spilt milk under the bridge as old Reg or somebody had once said a propos nothing he could recall. He was beginning to think, to realise, that his sister was the only woman he would ever stay friends with. He was on his way to see her now, just for a chat, get the smell of blood out of his nostrils. Reg Phillips though, he was thinking a lot about him, more particularly about how he was found, Oakden's infuriatingly closed mind, and that damned bird. What did it mean? Well, as soon as they found this Vyle character, perhaps he would find out. Good news at last, apart from the Cyril Crane connection, which was bad. Or was it? He changed his mind: he would see Cyril first, as he was passing. It was late enough for him to be back from whatever errands he may have been on. Yes, he needed to clear the air there; come to an understanding.

As it happened, his uncle was out. So too, to his relief was his big black scary dog. And for that matter so was his little whippet, the two legged one called Jack. To his surprise Abe found that his brother John appeared to be holding the fort, sat in a private corner of a bar rapidly filling with smoke and resonating with the buzz of freshly liberated workers looking to let off some steam.

To outward appearances, John had been shut off from the hubbub, but when the sight of a uniform elicited a momentary hush as it was clocked by the clientele, he looked straight up. Then he grinned. In moments the two men were shaking hands and clapping shoulders.

"Abe! This is a surprise. It's great to see you," said John. And he meant it. His new found stability with Sissy and the independence and sense of responsibility for his own destiny which had come with his move to Cyril Crane's employ had enabled him to see his previous unease, jealousy almost, which he had been prone to in his big brother's presence, for what it was, which was insecurity. Only as an afterthought did it cross his mind that Abe was a copper and that he should exercise a modicum of caution, for both their sakes. But it was still great to see him.

"It's been too long," replied his brother, "I see you're settling in. Cyril looking after you?"

"He's been very good to me. And I'm grateful for it."

"Happy in your work?" asked big brother, a little ambiguously.

John looked straight back and held his brother's eyes.

"Abe, I can't tell you how much better I feel. Remember how depressed I was at Miriam's wedding?"

"Drink does that."

"I know, but only if you're headed in that direction already. But I've very definitely changed course since then."

"Thanks to Cyril?"

"And Sissy of course."

"Of course. Yes. Yes, I like her. Give her my regards when you see her."

He could not help feeling slightly envious of his younger brother. He seemed to have fallen on his feet with that girl, unlike himself with women. But perhaps John deserved some luck…

"'Course I will," replied John, "Can I offer you a drink? I see your armband's off."

"Thanks. A pint of what you're having."

Abe sat and his brother did the honours.

"Is this just a social visit?"

"It is now," confessed the copper, "but I came hoping to see Cyril, not exactly in an official capacity but there was something I was going to ask him."

"About what?"

"About a certain character who might be able to help me with certain enquiries. It's about that old soldier found dead on the tracks by the church a while back. Remember?"

"I heard something. But I thought it was suicide."

"That's not been definitively established. That's why we're looking for this man; possible witness."

"What makes you think Cyril can help?"

"Word is, he's known to associate with one Jack Cutler, who is in turn known to Cyril?"

"That he is, and to me. Who is it you're looking for?"

"Do you know a Derek Woolley? Ginger, freckles, big ears?"

"Him? Yes, I've seen him about. Old friend of Jack's I think, but nothing to do with Cyril." *Except that Cyril wants Jack's 'friends' out of the way.* "Do you want me to ask around?"

"Perhaps, leave it to Cyril. It's not him we want anyway, it's a pal of his we're looking for. Big man with a limp, goes by the name of Steve."

"I wouldn't know where to find him, but I met him once, just visiting I got the impression, but I remember the name because it was vile."

"In what way?"

"That's the name. Vyle. Stephen Vyle."

"Grand, thank you for confirming. So, you know Cutler do you?" asked the sergeant suspiciously.

"He's not as black as he's painted."

"I didn't say anything."

"Maybe not…look, yes, we both work for Cyril. It's complicated."

"I know, and complicated I could do without just at present. I was just on my way to see Miriam, fancy coming?"

"I can't."

"All right. Please ask Cyril to make some enquiries about this Woolley character, better still, find Vyle. And, please let him know that this is just about old Reg, nothing to do with our uncle's wider interests. As a matter of fact, I would owe him a favour if he delivered him to me."

"Leave it to me."

"Thanks John." Abe finished his drink and stood and took John's hand, "there's no need for me to tell you to be careful, is there? No, thought not. Just look after yourself."

"And you." But John seemed reluctant to release his grip.

"What?"

"It might be nothing."

"But?"

"Something I heard. About Miriam."

"You'd better tell me."

#

P.C. Salt was thinking that the landlady of the Hailstone was an attractive woman, albeit of the more mature variety. Sarah Bates had recognised him from that morning and had made a bee line for him. Samuel Salt was not drinking, he was on duty, technically, and even were he inclined to stretch a point, the presence of his partner in crime fighting, constable Gordon Clark, persuaded him otherwise. But drinking or not, the pair were still treated to the flirtatious front which was the landlady's stock in trade, this landlady certainly. However, when Salt began to make gentle enquiry as to Mr Spragg's possible whereabouts and movements, she dropped the act and put up the shutters; still polite enough but cooler and definitely more defensive, to Salt's mind.

For her part, between serving beer and smiles, she quietly tasked Frederick with watching out for Charlie and warning him that the police were in wait. Not that she believed that Spragg had anything to fear from the law, not in particular, but she did feel that he should be kept away from Abraham Lively and any of his men. She was sure that keeping the warring parties apart was the best thing at present. Until tempers cooled. She knew that Abe was angry and she knew that Spragg could not be relied upon not to antagonise him. And she did not want a reason to turn from the handsome police man. She could not believe that, in her hurt, that she had actually suspected Abe of killing Comanche, nor could she imagine Spragg doing it, although her instinct told her that the sergeant was barking up that tree, hence this pair and their questions. Yes, best keep them apart and let things cool down. Perhaps by then the police would have caught the real culprit. And then Abe would come back.

Meantime, the two constables did their best to look inconspicuous.

#

Sergeant Lively could not keep up with the day. He had awoken in good mood, sure that Spring Heeled Jack had been explained away and the dangerous and annoying excitement doused down. But then there was that bloody business at the pub, and that was reflecting the increasing violence which he had been seeing. A symptom of something; something unseen, hidden, and bad. The police had always had their work cut out in this town. Wharton had once likened it to a wild west frontier town, and Abe was beginning to think that the comparison was not as flippant as he had first taken it. Blackheath had always been rough, with the mines and foundries sucking in outsiders, men desperate for work, families often in tow, like the Welsh miners, or the big Derby contingent set up outside Netherton, or for that matter, down at heel country folk from Shropshire, like the Livelys. And that had always called for aggressive and somewhat physical policing. But, for no tangible reason, things were getting worse. Drunks were getting drunker, fights were getting rougher, fists were wearing brass knuckles, robbers were more rapacious, knives were longer and brandished more often. And the coppers had to meet force with force, acting first and asking questions later. The fear of the uniform gave them a brief advantage in their various clashes, and this they did not waste with procrastination; rather the law was delivered summarily at the stroke of a truncheon and the judicious, and injudicious, use of the boot. Less and less was punishment meted out by incarceration in claustrophobic cells and a morning visit to Old Hill and the magistrates, and more by the pain of beatings and broken bones. This was a natural reaction, for the police were people too, and were afraid; they moved only in pairs for the time being, sergeant's orders.

The sergeant felt the situation justified his new approach. Hadn't inspector Millership himself suggested it? They simply didn't have time to pussy-foot around with increasingly violent incidents. He had had two murders in as many weeks, for God's sake. First Reginald Phillips (suicide? Not in a million years), then the Irishman, quickly followed by the inconvenient death of his mate while in custody. Lucky the coroner saw that the fool had brought it on himself...

Not so long ago, his major concern had been to scotch rumours of some evil monster running and leaping about the parish. Well the rumours had been duly scotched, but he couldn't help but feel that the influence of something, a spring heeled something, was still abroad, fomenting trouble, feeding off violence, and bleeding animals to death in the dark now. Something bad, certainly. But where was it coming from? If he knew where it was, he knew he could stop it. Whoever or whatever.

Somehow, the death of Reg was connected. He knew not why, but things started to go pear shaped in Blackheath after that. So, finding the medal had been a big deal, but they had yet to find the seller, a definite thief and possibly a murderer, depending on exact events. It all kept dragging him back to the stretch of railway track, under the bridge. And a little bobbing bird with a blood red breast. And he knew it knew, something bad was coming. It had said so, but not much more, nothing definite, not about the bad thing. And then Abe remembered something Sarah had said, and it sent his mind off elsewhere: what if the bad thing was closer to home? In him? The friend whispering in his ear, something else, not that bird even? Angry now, at his own fearful credulity, he slammed that door shut on that dark room of infectious thoughts. On reflection, he decided that the day had not been mixed at all, utterly bad rather.

And now, he must speak to his sister again, about that bloody man again! Did she not realise that she was being talked about? He hoped it was old news; that, following his warning, she had stopped talking with that so-called poet. On the other hand, if he came in as a customer, what was she supposed to do? Not a conversation for today, he decided. Because what he most needed was a drink. A good drink, out of uniform. Alone, with the voice in his head.

Twenty minutes later, he stood, a civilian, against the bar of the George And Dragon, slowly and surely sinking the pints.

#

The Cock Inn in Springfield had been a popular and regular venue for cock fighting at one time. A man might reasonably suppose that that's why the place was so denominated. A certain kind of man, on the other hand, a man in the know, a man who moved in typically shady circles of rough and ready shady acquaintances, such a man might not have to suppose, might have no truck with such supposing. Such a man would not stop to suppose, and not stop to guess, that's for certain, for a man such as that would know, very well, that enforced gallinaceous combat, although banned by the law of the land, passed down from on high, nevertheless still took place on these very premises at intervals, accompanied by the diverse chicaneries that inevitably accompany illicit activity, and the exchange of hard cash.

But the man standing alone, brooding and drinking at the bar, was not such a man. All that Charles Spragg esquire knew was that he had frequented this place for years, until the object of his affection and the benefit of his custom had switched, nearly two years ago now, to the Hailstone and its recently widowed landlady. Both conveniently situated just down the road.

But he had been warned away from that other place today, so that his presence at the Cock, far from being a pleasant dip into nostalgia, he saw as an unwelcome banishment. And he was not pleased. He thought he had got one up on Lively, pushing him out of the picture. But no. What was the expression? The long arm of the law? Lively had that all right. As well as a swollen head (now, there's an idea.) Charlie Spragg certainly had plenty to be thinking about, and the origin of a pub name was well below the horizon of interest or concern…

#

Another man with plenty on his mind, Francis the poet's current and immediate object of interest just so happened to be the same as Mr Spragg's. Both had had cross words with the same police sergeant, both over a woman. Spragg's plans this night had been disrupted by Abraham Lively's investigation, Thompson's by the sight of him.

Having over stayed his welcome at the Hailstone, at least with that dog which was threatening to give him away, he had been on his way to the Royal Oak, drawn partly by his liking for the sergeant's sister, partly by something else – call it devilment. But in the street some instinct had caused him to turn, to see a figure walking into the street opposite, his back to him. Straight away he knew it was the copper, even out of uniform: he had never seen him minus the blue suit. The same instinct bade him follow the man, albeit cautiously. When Lively entered the 'Dragon' so, at an interval, did Thompson, but via the other door. When the sergeant ordered a drink, so, across the bar in another room, did Thompson. Abe stood at the bar to drink, seated was Thompson; concealed but watching.

At the end of his third pint, the sergeant abruptly left. Head down, Thompson felt him go, then picked him back up outside. It looked like he was heading toward the police station. Nothing unusual in that, but for some reason he followed nonetheless. Lively went into the station, journey's end for the night in all likelihood. If the poet was thinking of giving up and reverting to his original plan, it never came to it, for, not two minutes later, not even one, Lively re-emerged and strode off toward Rowley.

Thompson was a long way from his base here, but that was all to the good; certainly had been last night. Last night, he had challenged the other world to show itself, had approached it in the swift supplication of a thrust of steel and bloody offering; the very life force released, freed from the inertia of matter, to find its home in that other place. That the experience was profound, and thrilling, he could not deny. He still smelled the blood, ejaculate of scarlet, the terror…and knew it could free him of the shackles of the material, he knew it. But, it had not been enough. He had been left behind, had not penetrated the veil, not seen the other world, blocked by…what? Morality? Fear? His religion? Or perhaps his choice of sacrifice had been too random; perhaps an animal's blood could not be expected to carry the weight of a human spirit; perhaps, he would think on it.

For now, he was enjoying himself following this copper, this man that had made himself his enemy. He had no idea he was being followed, stalked as a pig by a tiger. It made him feel powerful, a predator…He smelled the pony's blood again, revelled in the fear in the little animal's cries, and it filled him with a restless energy that wanted to erupt into action, to do violence, destruction. Or death. He had created a hunger for it now, and he must nourish himself or die. He was not sure why he had started down this road, he just knew that he had. What was done was done, and it felt right. Was right. The voice in his head told him so.

#

The sergeant was not in the best of moods. Spragg had not been delivered and it was already way past nine. He was heading toward the Hailstone now, to sort it out himself, whether it upset Sarah or not. All his mind was to the front, rehearsing the journey to his destination. But then, for no good reason, he was apprehensive, as if something were rushing up behind, or about to fall on him. He turned around sharply, but saw nothing but the street stretching away down toward Blackheath, lights in houses and pubs rousing and pushing back weakly against the descending dusk, a few random pedestrians, on their way home or making their weaving way to the next pub on despairing unstable feet. Nothing unusual, just a feeling. He was anxious to put it down to overwork and a bang on the head; it had been a particularly trying day, he was thinking, picturing the morning's carnage – and that brought it back. The voice. It was urging him on. He realised that it did not stop, just that it was sometimes too soft and low to hear. But not at this moment, it was clear now: 'That's just the start. Don't let him get away with it. We've got to stop him. It's a bloody cheek anyway, coming here. He wants to hurt us you know. You do know? So stop it. Find him. Finish it….'

He had not understood before, but he did now. Spragg. Spragg was the enemy and he would put him away, but not before having a more immediate revenge on him.

#

An apparently random ordering of events that night conspired to assure that the two love rivals, the peace keeper and the trouble stirrer, were destined to meet. The policeman's out of kilter consciousness meant that the chance of Spragg surviving a close quarters encounter unscathed was strictly limited. Fortunately, for Spragg perhaps, the Fates deigned to give him a sporting chance. Although he himself was worse for wear,

338

he saw the copper coming, and recognised him. Quick as a flash, he hopped over the wall into the churchyard, resolving to lose himself amongst the dead. But the trouble with flashes is, they attract attention. Had Charlie Spragg took his time, calm and smooth, and casually walked away, or even slipped over the wall slowly, possibly hugging close to it to hide his silhouette, then perhaps attention might not have been attracted. His quick physical reaction, after several jugs of ale, had been commendable, but his panicked thinking had let him down: Abe Lively had seen him. And after having been hardly ever out of Abe Lively's thoughts for quite some time now, there was no chance that that the sergeant would not instantly take the guilty apparition for the man he was seeking. It must be said, of course, that the light was going rapid, and that the copper, in the circumstances and at that location and in his state of mind, would likely have taken any suspiciously moving character for his particular quarry. It was just Spragg's bad luck that he happened to be that very thing.

"Where the bloody hell are you Salt?" was his question to himself as he dashed up to the church. He had taken a split second to react visibly to the sight of Spragg, because he did not want the man to realise that he had been seen; that way, he hoped, he would feel secure and slow down. Spragg's likely line of flight, over the wall and towards the cover of the church itself, was intersected by the path from the main gate, and the sergeant entered holy ground via that portal, just in time to see a shape sliding toward the corner. He ran after it, not knowing whether he had been betrayed by the gravelled path. Abe reasoned Spragg would use the building for cover and circle round to end up somewhere behind him, to watch him till it was safe to slip away. He would catch up with him before that. Senses opened, he made to close with the church wall, speed and stealth in dispute, with speed winning out. Startled like a crouching pheasant, a shadow erupted from a dark patch, and fled, disappeared round the next corner. Abe moved fast, but when he turned that corner, nobody was there. There had been no time for it to reach the next corner, therefore it had left the circle, off at an angle. Off on this path right here, between the graves. Hiding amongst the graves then. He would not have gone far. Would have gone to ground again. Had to have.

"I know you're here Charlie me boy. I don't know how you got away from my constables but you can bet they're on their way. So you may as well come out. It's not as if you're under arrest. We just want to ask you a few questions." He paused. Nothing. Worth a try. Above him a lone tawny owl watched and waited, and wondered how long the big two-legged things were going to be, spoiling her hunting. This place was a good one for rats, nice fat ones that dug down through the earth and cheap coffin wood, and gnawed on wizened remains and sharpened their teeth on dead old bones...

"Look, you may as well come out now. Where are you going to go?"

Too much bother to try elsewhere; the owl opted for a nap.

"Are you listening to me?"

Abe had been edging down the path, quiet as a cat, keeping his eyes peeled. It looked like there was only one place he could be, skulking behind a larger than average slab of useless hubris, this one fenced with iron as if the occupants were planning on escape…

He approached it unblinking, approaching as softly as humanly possible, focussed, blinkered. *If he risks a quick peek, I'll know exactly where he is, and I'll be on him. If he doesn't, and he doesn't hear me, I'll be on him. And I'll have him.*

Trouble was, he wasn't there. He was lying, very still, in the long grass between a couple of smaller stones, and the copper was creeping right by him now. Might have carried on going; might not have seen him; might have reached his chosen spot and pounced on thin air and given up. But Spragg was not taking that chance. In his less than sober state, he had forgotten that this was a policeman, and, that policemen are bound to uphold the law, are constrained by the rules. Aren't they? But he had played the role of innocent victim of a violent aggressor far too well, and now part of him had been persuaded to take the play acting as truth: consequently, he was at that moment very afraid, but not too afraid to do something about it. His monster was now almost upon him, and his heart beat hard, pumping power to his limbs and decision to his brain.

*That's it. When he's mid-step…*He threw his arms around both passing legs, and pulled at them, attempting to lift them clear of the earth. But Lively was a big man, and Spragg only succeeded with dredging the ground with those feet. If Spragg did not come up with more it would go badly for him, for this particular policeman had become disenchanted with 'the rules' of late and saw little wrong in ignoring them when it suited. Even were that not so, he was already facing a night in a cell, court, prison? Assaulting a police officer was taken seriously; the law looked after its own. Failure then not being an option, he found strength and sure footing whilst the sergeant was still mentally and physically off balance. Once kneeling with one foot planted he was able, from a crouch, to lift at the knees whilst rising and simultaneously charging his shoulder into the copper's hip. It was a scrappy move, and but for the element of surprise would not have been effective against an opponent of Lively's size and skill. But it was enough. Enough to move his man, so that the sergeant toppled like a felled tree, pitching point of shoulder onto the ground, the temple following, and sliding along to gash his cheek against a protruding stump, remains of some portion of an old hazel. As for the sergeant, he was still recovering from his head wound, and his body remembering was enough to induce a momentary stupor. Charlie Spragg could have left it at that. Could have got home, got changed, got himself some kind of alibi. After all, the copper had not seen his face; it was dark; it would be difficult to make a case stick, he reasoned. But no, he had a mean streak, and it would not leave be. He aimed a kick with his stout boots, not from in front mind, from behind: couldn't risk him seeing his face close up, give him the chance to swear so on oath. Of course, that would not matter if he killed the man. Who was to know? But he knew the answer to that, someone would know, someone would find out. No he did not have the guts for that, but he still had that mean streak. So from behind he aimed that kick, out of sight, to the small of the back. That would hurt; he wouldn't be walking easy for a bit. He felt like he had kicked an oak tree with a coat on, not very satisfying. So he aimed another one, up the backside too, for good measure, then he was off.

#

"Where the hell is he going?" Thompson asked himself aloud as the sergeant suddenly jinked off and into the church yard. Graveyards had never bothered the poet: he had never seen a ghost and would merely be fascinated should he do so, he liked to believe. So, intrigued, and not at all anxious, leastwise not in anticipation of a supernatural encounter, he swiftly followed. And swiftly it had needed to be, for he could only just make out Lively now, rounding a corner of the church, silhouetted against the sky's last red residue as the descending night was squeezing the last of the living daylights out of the dying sun. He would not follow directly, that might be a mistake, and there was no need to make one: if he walked around the opposite way, widdershins, on a circle of greater radius than anybody would naturally take following the path around the church, keeping to cover, then he would come across him, obliquely, and, expecting him, would see the copper and hide before the copper saw him. He was confident of his ability. In London, in the densely populated East End, often had he had occasion to avoid detection, whether for amusement, as a certain kind of research, or, sometimes, from sheer necessity. Like a shadow, he was. And an inquisitive one: a rum do this was, the town police sergeant sneaking around the church at night, out of uniform.

He made his way carefully, cautiously placing his feet, gliding, almost as silent as the owl's flight. Noises. Something crashing about. That meant something human. Lively. Suddenly, he thought how he hated him. Had he taken time to reflect, he may have thought how irrational that was, him barely knowing the man. But all he felt now crouching in the dusk was a nervous thrill, as last night, when he had used the blade. And there was the voice, *get him, smash him, nobody will know*, and *yes, yes, I know I could; I have my stick and the dark and he has, nothing*. If he had had time he might have reconsidered, in bright of day and sober, realised how serious a thing it would be, different to killing an animal. But he didn't have time. Lively was heading straight toward him now, rushing at him. He stood and swung the heavy stick. He went down without a sound, and then carried on going as the body, rather appropriately Thompson thought, rolled into a recently dug grave. Dead? Or just damaged? Did it matter, he was in the clear? Still, best make sure…But then, somebody else coming, time to leave.

#

341

He could smell the damp earth, possessive mother that created each new life whilst begrudging it, jealous; foreclosing on mortgaged mortality with unavoidable predictability, calling it back to her bosom, her womb of timeless blank. This holy ground was rich with her decay. He lay in it. But he knew that this darkness was anything but timeless. It was temporary. He knew that he was not dead; he doubted that the dead could smell the grave. He just needed time to gather his wits, clear his head – open his eyes. And as he did he felt the pain, in his head and his back, then lesser hurts in various limbs. At the same time he remembered; that Spragg had done this; lain in wait and tripped him up. He suddenly pushed himself up from that cursed earth, as if contact with his flesh would infect him through the concentration of spent mortality lurking below. The effort of sitting up hurt. He winced from the sting of the boot and felt contusions which he knew would soon be ripening to blue and yellow. Blood was on his cheek. Carefully, he retrieved a handkerchief and dabbed at it, turning it pox red, before folding the bloodied portion in on itself, keeping a clean square at the ready. Another moment and he stood, with difficulty, and took stock. Cuts and bruises he concluded as he pieced together his fall. But the back. That was done when he was down. *The little shit kicked me. No excuse. No bloody excuse at all!* Vicious and underhand; the sergeant was now more than ever convinced that it had been Spragg who had paid the Hailstone a nefarious nocturnal visitation. And he was not getting away with it. And then this! He was not getting away with that either, especially that. He would make sure he had his wits about him in future, and his truncheon. And he would not be shy of using it. The little shit!

Unbeknownst to the sergeant, he had gotten off lightly. But for a case of mistaken identity he might have been felled by something more damaging than an inexpert grappling technique, and finished off by the same, more damaging than the boot: the body of Charles Spragg lay where it had fallen, violence to the head evidenced by the bloody misshapen jaw and broken and missing teeth, a bizarre angle of the left arm attesting to some collateral break or dislocation, blood dripping life into the grave.

For Abraham Lively, the trail was obviously cold. His quarry over the hills and far away by now, as he walked, no limped, very gingerly, and in fact within six feet of Spragg, making his way to the boundary of Church Of England property. And straight into the strong arms of P.C. Salt, who with Clark was retracing his steps after a longer than expected, and fruitless, vigil.

"Sarge? Blimey! What happened to you?"

"I fell over. Where have you been?"

"At the Hailstone, like you said. Looking for our man Spragg."

"He never turned up," offered Clark obligingly.

"I know he never turned up," said the sergeant testily and not surprisingly given his discomfort and the circumstances of coming by it, "because I just had a little altercation with him in there," he explained, jabbing his thumb over his shoulder, toward the gloomy shadows of the boneyard.

"What? And he got away?" queried Clark, unsure and wishing the question had not sounded so much like "and you let him get away?"

"No, I let him off with a warning."

"A warning, why?" asked Clark, a picture of gullibility. But not even he could not remain that dopey for long. "You're joking, aren't you Sarge."

"No, I'm bloody well not! Do you see me laughing?"

"Eh?" squeaked constable Clark. "No. I mean…I didn't mean…"

Salt came to the rescue, "I take it you didn't let him off sergeant. What happened?"

"Of course I didn't," replied a calmer sergeant Lively, shooting Clark a sardonic wink. "I was coming to see how you two were doing when I saw Spragg nip into the churchyard. He must have seen me coming and tried to hide. I followed, but I lost him. When I wasn't looking he tripped me over and attacked me. Must have had a stick or something."

Perhaps unwisely Clark asked, "Are you sure it was him?"

But Abe was recovering his composure now, and merely said, "Sure as I can be. But point taken, it was dark…"

"…and if you had seen him clear he would never have escaped," added Salt, trying to be helpful.

"Actually, that's another fair point. Only my word against his that it was him that assaulted me, an officer of the law. Still, any judge would take a copper's word for it, I'm sure."

"But just in case Sarge, I'm sure that if I catch up with him he can be relied on to resist arrest, if you catch my meaning."

"You're a good man Samuel," said the sergeant.

"So what do you want us to do then?" said Clark.

"Why, find him, arrest him," interjected Salt.

"That's right, quick as you like," said Lively.

The owl watched them go. It would be good night after all: the crashing about had stirred up the rodent population.

#

In fact, the dashing young men of the Blackheath constabulary were to be beaten to it. By a man of the cloth, at seven the next morning. But that was a few hours away.

#

"Right Gordon," ordered Salt, "you take his other arm, and you can help me get him home."

"Thank you lads," said the injured man, "I'll be fine in a day or two, but I'm bloody sore at present. He's got it coming he has."

"Don't worry Sarge, we'll have him. And it won't be pleasant. Not for him anyway. An example has got to be made."

No reply. Preoccupied with his thoughts and injuries no doubt. With the support of his two colleagues, the sergeant was getting along at a reasonable pace, but then, with no warning, they had a dead weight on their hands. He was out. Sharply, they sat him in a shop doorway.

"Is he dead?" breathed Clark.

"Dead? Of course he's not dead, he's just passed out," said Salt. Nevertheless, he put his ear to the man's mouth till he could detect an exhalation.

"Oh, yes, that's right…" began Clark, then thought better of it. He was not supposed to know of Abe's 'condition' and doubted whether Salt did.

"Must have had a knock on the head. Wish we'd taken him to the Doc's now. We were right there."

"Well, we're nearly back now. Let's get him home," urged Clark.

"I don't know. I think one of us should fetch Doc Wharton…"

"I don't believe he would want that."

"What do you mean?"

Before Clark was able to dig himself any deeper, their charge was himself again.

"No, I don't need a doctor. Just a rest; get me home. Come on, help me up."

#

Francis Thompson had seen enough. He would have to hit his man harder next time. Or stay out of his way. And there would be no more easy opportunities, therefore staying out of the way it would have to be. He had begun to feel that his days in this place were numbered. He walked quietly away.

#

To the casual observer, two police officers were escorting home, or to less congenial lodgings, just another casualty of some alcohol inspired act of deliberate or accidental violence. Nothing out of the ordinary. Luckily for Salt and Clark, and more particularly for their sergeant, most candidates for the 'casual observer' appellation were either in bed or in the pub. Approaching their destination it was Salt who said,

"There's muck and blood all over you sarge, is your sister in or…"

Abe took his meaning, adding more of his own. Miriam would worry if he limped in like this, dragged through a very thick hedge backwards he looked, more than once. He

344

would get a right earful, and he didn't want that, especially now: he had not tackled her on the other matter yet.

"Wait, cross over here," he ordered.

The resulting manoeuvre brought them directly before the Shoulder Of Mutton.

"Clark, take off that armband and your helmet, Salt will hold it, and go in and make enquiries, polite ones mind, for John Lively. You know John?"

"Yes, I know John," replied the constable.

"Good. Speak only to him and get him to come and fetch me. Got it?"

"Righto sarge, gorrit," said Clark, affecting cheery confidence: this place had become, by unvoiced convention, off limits to ordinary police constables; they all knew that their sergeant had a tricky balance to uphold, between the job and his uncle. It was evident that Abe was never going to pursue his uncle professionally, unless of course, they assumed, he did something beyond the pale, and it had also become evident that Cyril Crane recognised and respected that. Salt for one had said openly that this was a good thing, that Cyril actually kept some of the habitual criminals within check, and made the lives of hard-pressed peace keepers like himself that much easier. But, as Clark had told him, "You fancy yourself as an English Wyatt Earp, you do. If it was up to you you'd shoot 'em with your six gun, rather than arrest 'em." And Salt certainly did not try to persuade him otherwise, "Too true, mate. Unless they were gonna hang o'course. Now, where did I put me trusty oss?"

So, if it had been Salt entering Cyril's domain that night, perhaps the mission might not have been entirely peaceful, for anybody looking for trouble would find in Salt a man not at all nervous about reciprocating. Perhaps that was why the sergeant's request had fallen on Clark.

"Don't forget, only John," said Abe Lively at the disappearing blue shape.

#

John Lively had fallen out of the habit of visiting the Hailstone. Which was a pity, because he had always enjoyed the beer and the atmosphere in the place. So, tonight, as Sissy had never set foot in the place, he had promised to take her. Besides, he liked landlady Sarah and wanted to offer his support, or at least sympathy, following the terrible goings on of the night before, news of which had naturally spread like wildfire. And he might well bump into his big brother, to whom, he felt, he had been getting closer as of late.

It had not gone to plan. Introducing, reintroducing, Sissy to Sarah seemed to stir partisan emotions: they had last met when Miriam, supported by Sissy, had virtually thrown the older woman out of the Royal Oak.

And when John asked, "How's Abe? Are you expecting him in tonight?" he got both barrels:

"How should I know how he is? Apart from touchy and changeable that is. Or worse…and if I never see him again it will be too soon. Here's your change. Next please."

"I see what you mean, she really is the model of hospitality isn't she?" observed Sissy as they made their way to a table.

"She's not usually like that. It's probably the shock; of what happened," said John.

"I don't know, you'd think she would be glad to see you, for the support. And the custom of course. And, all right, I'm a friend of Miriam, granted, and she knows that, and they don't get on, we know that, and you're her brother of course, but she obviously didn't hold that against Abe, by all accounts…"

"But, that might have changed. He didn't seem to be in her good books."

"That's it, then. They've had a row. Split up you think? He's been a bit…"

"A bit what?"

"Nothing, he's a busy man, that's all. Maybe he didn't pay her enough attention."

"Like you said, he's very busy. That's his job. Change the subject."

"All right. You haven't finished telling me about the card game."

"Getting into dangerous waters there Siss."

"Why am I? We love each other, well, I mean, I love you. And you tell me you love me."

"Stop it. I'm just trying to protect you."

"I don't need protecting. I'm not a child, I'm a grown woman: you may have noticed. No, we protect each other, that's the deal. Remember them chaps outside the Dragon?"

An image of an incandescent and beautiful, but controlled, fury confronting the Percival thug burgled in from memory and made him smile; made him relent.

"All right, but no names. And I've told you most of it already, come to think of it."

"What about the outside man. You said he was an agent. An agent for what?"

"If I tell you, and you're questioned at any time, it's best you don't know the details."

"Or," she said coyly, eyes down and soft, "you could marry me."

"What?"

"A married woman can't be forced to testify against her husband…"

"You know I have a problem there…"

"I know love, I was joking. But would you? You know, otherwise?"

"I would love."

"Good enough for me," she said taking his hand and kissing it, "so tell me of this agent chap."

"In actual fact, it's all above board and legal, probably."

"Explain."

"Well, you know how people like to gamble? On games of chance? A game of cards say? Well where there's a need, a demand, there is always going to be somebody to feed that need. For a price of course."

"And that's where your uncle Cyril comes in?"

"And that's where somebody who should not be named comes in," cautioned John.

"Because it's illegal," she stated.

"Basically, yes, but he's in the clear because he is never personally involved, only through a third party."

"Ah! An agent you mean."

"That's one word for it. A buffer if you like, a decoy even."

"But what if somebody was caught, and twitted on him?"

"To the police? Unlikely. More than their life's worth, in a manner of speaking. And then there's a little thing called evidence. How could a magistrate trust the word of what would have to be a known criminal, a cornered criminal, over that of a respected local businessman?"

"But we all know he's not that."

"Of course he is: there's the pub, the haulage business, and the butchery business. That's not to say that he doesn't have other commercial enterprises. I'm just mentioning the obvious ones."

"The legal ones you mean?"

"I didn't say that, and I didn't necessarily mean that…"

"And the 'probably' legal ones?"

"Ah, now. Can I just say that while certain gambling is illegal, and gambling debts unenforceable in the courts, a debt that's incurred outside the, er, illicit premises, is something else; a debt let's say incurred by somebody wanting to get their hands on some ready cash because, say, they lost some on a game of chance, a totally unconnected game of chance…"

"I see! And of course it's up to that person what he does with that cash, might want to take it straight to an illegal card game…"

"And you get the drift."

"I never thought I would ever think like this, but I have to say, it beats slogging your guts out over a hot forge for a living."

"Yes, it's a different way of life, that's all; with its own dangers nonetheless. But the rewards, well, it's a different world."

Sissy took time to think about this, then after a swig of beer, she continued the interrogation, "So, these debts, it's money lent out by this agent person, yes? But it's really owed to…"

John forestalled her with a finger to her lips. "And that's something else that goes with the life, biting your tongue."

"Of course. Sorry."

"But I'll tell you something Siss, these incidental debts as you might call them, they're all looked after personally by the boss, except," and he leaned in and lowered his voice still lower than it had been, "I've been asked if I would consider collecting them."

"John my love, I think you ought to buy yourself a new suit."

"Do you know, I might just do that. Another one?"

"What, here?" she said glancing over to the bar where the landlady was busy selling charm.

"Why not?" returned John, "stuff her," he said laughing.

It was during their second drinks that another reminder of John's new career cropped up, in the shape of Jack Cutler, no less, and a dour looking companion.

#

It was not John Lively who reappeared with P.C. Clark, but it was Cyril Crane. It was uncle Cyril who persuaded the two constables that they could leave, Abe in good hands.

A simple, 'come on Abraham, let's get you looking presentable,' was enough for the battered copper, and he let his uncle take charge, leading him through a private passage to the kitchen. It was a big kitchen with a big solid well-used and well-scrubbed table set in the middle. Cyril set down his nephew and went to a door at back and called:

"Mick. Mick, you there? You there Mick? Mick!"

Some sort of muffled reply.

"What are you doing?" persisted Crane.

More suffocated sound.

"Well leave it. I need you here. Now please."

Cyril returned to the table and sat himself close by his nephew.

"Looks like you've been in the wars, son. No, you don't have say anything. Not unless you want to. Tell me later."

While his uncle was talking, Abe was conscious of vaguely metallic bumps and clangs taking place, suggestive of someone laying aside tools; not particularly gently. A pause, flutter of footsteps, then the door squeaked open and standing there an individual of average build with a very much smaller than average pointed head with a small delicate freckle covered nose above a thin lipped mouth with small neat white teeth; the hair was carrot red curly and there was a hint of a bronze moustache, but the thing that struck Abraham Lively most about Mick O'Rourke was the incredible glitter from the greenest green eyes he had ever seen, like there were distant swarms of glow worms living in their depths, constantly on the move, intermittent flashes continuously escaping as he cast his gaze around the room, settling a while on Abe and then transferring their luminosity to Crane. And it was then, when his intention settled and his eyes stopped moving that the twinkle was doused, and Abe could see that his lids looked tired, red and rheumy. Perhaps, the sparks he had seen were little fires, burning him up, burning him out. That's what he imagined anyway. Perhaps contending with an inner arcane power was what put the 'mad' into 'Mad Mick'; the copper was looking tired himself these days.

He spoke. "What is it then?" he enquired with a distinct Irish accent, a suiting soft but bouncy one. Cyril nodded toward Abe. "Oh I see. I reckon I know who this is all right," continued Mick, and turning to Abe, "your uncle talks about you a lot." At this point powers of concentration seemingly slipped from the Irishman and the eyes lit up again with involuntary movement; symptomatic fiddling with the buttons of his jacket as if for reassurance that they were still there, that he was still there, and walking around the table and back as if unsafe to stay still.

Not knowing why, not really himself, the sergeant's reply was comically starchy: "I'm afraid you have me at a disadvantage, sir." He had been looking at the man as he delivered it but the response came obliquely, beyond his right ear.

"Oh, it's a disadvantage is it? And me being so famous an' all." Now he was back in front and the twisting about was making Abe dizzy again, and his neck ache.

Cyril's eyes were laughing but his voice cut. "Mick, sit down for God's sake. Now!" He pulled out a chair and snared the man into as he passed, "have you been smoking that funny stuff again?"

"No, zir. On my honour zir, not in the last hour."

Cyril gave up on the questions. "Now then Abraham. This is Mick. Mick O'Rourke…"

"And only but slightly mad, zir," in what was probably mock seriousness.

"And," continued Cyril, "as you intimated, you've not had the pleasure. So allow me: Mick, this is my nephew Abraham."

At this the Irishman took Abe's hand and squeezed it with an intensity matching the fire in his eyes, zealously sealing some unfathomable pact, or trying to impress.

"So you do exist then? I was thinking you were made up," said Abe to the now seated but still fidgety figure.

"Oh yes, I do indeed, yes. Last time I looked."

"Right Mick," said Cyril, "my nephew has had a little accident. Now, I don't want him going home in a mess to upset my…his sister. So get some hot water on, get the iodine and clean up his cuts. While you're doing that, I'm going to find him some clean clothes," he looked Abe up and down, "a jacket and trousers – all right? – then you can clean his boots for me. Don't worry Abraham, Mick makes a very good nurse, take my word for it."

And Cyril was as good as that word: Mick's shaking hands became as steady as a rock, but gentle; only the iodine stung. He was about done when Cyril came back.

"Try these," he said, tossing a bundle onto a chair, "they were mine, when I was a lot younger and slimmer, so the trousers should fit, around the waist at least, may be a bit short though. But at least they're clean; if you're wearing dark socks nobody will notice. The jacket should be fine."

It was fine, as long as you did not object to the impregnation of almost a decade of pest repelling naphthalene. Mick was sent off to clean Abe's boots and generally make himself scarce. Cyril produced more gifts. "Here, brush your hair," he said placing one on the table. He also produced a bottle of scotch and two glasses. "What could be better? A good fire, good whisky, and two good friends. Marvellous!"

#

It was not than John disliked Jack, but he couldn't afford to like him either. Not really like him; not considering that he was a potential enemy; not if he had to take Cyril Crane's side against him. But it wasn't even that: he had planned an evening with Sissy, only Sissy. But as soon as Jack saw them he made his way straight over, that is, he made his way straight over after his companion disappeared, and he had disappeared after what looked suspiciously like a dismissal, and it had come right after Jack had noticed John, or so it seemed. He would have to remember that face, it didn't belong to anybody that worked for Cyril, the furtive and swift departure told him that. John pretended not to notice. It was hard to credit Cyril's version of the man, calculating and treacherous, him so affable and straight-talking, on the outside. Perhaps that's what made him so dangerous, he had to believe that his uncle had learned something from his years handling people like this. Whatever, John would maintain his own mime, it was more congenial that way. And he was always glad to see Boadicea – how bad could a man be who loved dogs, at least this dog, so much? And she was always glad to see him.

Boadicea was not, on the other hand, at all pleased to detect the presence of another, one she had met before, one who threatened her master, one she did not at all like. If he came any closer, she would see him off, as she had before. He was bad. The others did not know, could not see him, but she was ready.

By careful choice of location combined with skilful and discrete mannerisms to blend into the general working man melee, Thompson had concealed himself well; willing the light not to travel from him to the eyes, the consciousness of those he watched, bending it away. He had forgotten about a dog's sense of smell, however…He recognised the girl of course, from the Royal Oak, Miriam Beckett's friend, Cutler he had met before, and that had not gone well but he was prepared to overlook that in the right circumstances: it really was a small world, he reflected, especially if you deliberately made it so. Then there was this other character, big and confident he looked, if he wasn't the sergeant's brother then he was a monkey's uncle, even as Mr Darwin had claimed, silly old loon.

"Ado John," said Cutler, not offering a drink as convention might dictate, although to be fair it was quite obvious that the couple's glasses had only just been replenished.

"Hello Miss, I'm Jack. Jack Cutler."

"Yes, I know," she replied sweetly.

Rest and fresh clothing, a fire and warming whisky were relief and relaxant to a bruised and battered Abraham Lively. Soon, the ambiance, the alcohol and the soft persuasion of his uncle's companionable hospitality had him warming to the man as he had not thought possible, not anymore.

Here, now, cloistered in this once familiar kitchen, the ties of kinship and Cyril's unlooked for kindness were breaking down barriers, drawing him in, his soft hypnotic tone conjuring a growing sense of camaraderie, and belonging, pushing back against the years of conditioning which had estranged the two. Now, it may be that the police sergeant was feeling particularly vulnerable after his ordeal, and another knock on the head, albeit a minor one in comparison; and it may be that the whisky made that worse, but the fact is that he liked it. He liked it and he remembered how close they used to be, before he had had to choose between Miriam and his uncle, and for reasons he had never understood, only imagined. He loved Miriam, but had it been fair, what she had done? His brothers? He didn't really talk to them much. Josh maybe, as he saw him most days, but he was still such a child and so naïve sometimes. He worried for him. With Cyril, he felt he was with an equal, someone who understood the burden of responsibility, even if they were on opposite sides of the law. It didn't make them enemies, not really. That part of his life was just him playing a part in a game, he saw that more and more. The whisky was telling him that again now…

They talked of many things, of this and that, of Cyril's brief and disastrous career as a merchant seaman, his love of dogs, of Abe's love of horsemanship, which he greatly missed, his wrestling, past encounters whether flirtatious or violent (both at the same time on occasion!). Anything but 'business.'

Catching up in time Cyril was saying, "I hear you finished with Haden-Best's ward, daughter, whatever she is. Sorry to hear that."

"Don't be. I'm better off away from that lot."

"What happened?"

"Apparently, a lowly police sergeant isn't good enough for her."

"You mean her so called father doesn't think so."

"You got it. Bloody snob."

"A short-sighted snob, if I may say so. I shan't be doing him any favours any time soon."

"The problem is, he's right. He lives in a different world to the likes of me, of us. And so does she now. I could never hope to compete. Still hurts though."

"I know. Didn't he know your background?"

"You mean our former station in life? I hardly think a country squire's living compares to the wealth of men like him. And even if it did, what would be the good of bringing that life up? It's gone, broken. That's the thing about backgrounds, they're always behind you. In the past. Finished."

"But you've done all right for yourself though, haven't you? Next stop inspector, eh?"

"Big deal. It's not as if I actually own anything, property I mean. Not like you. If anybody in the family's done all right for himself, it's you, isn't it?"

Crane had no wish to venture where the conversation seemed to be heading, so he returned to a reliable theme.

"Anyway, I also hear you've been seeing a lot of that handsome woman who runs the Hailstone. Straight up and back in the saddle eh?"

"Except that I fell off again."

"Eh?"

"I've fallen out with her too. It was good while it lasted but it was never going to last. Too much of an age difference."

"Right," reflected Cyril, almost absently, "nothing lasts forever. Like I said, take a tumble, get straight…"

"I know, straight back into the saddle and all that. Bit of a flippant attitude really, isn't it? Come to think of it. Truth is, I don't think I can handle a serious relationship and this job, not both together I mean. Sometimes, I think that I don't understand how women think; then sometimes I do, and despise them for it. Take Sarah – the Hailstone woman. Did you hear what happened to her pony?"

"Yes I did, and if I catch the bastard before you do…" Cyril shook his head.

"I know, nasty business. But the ludicrous thing is, I'm sure she thinks I did it. Out of jealousy."

"Jealousy?"

"We had a row over her previous boyfriend. Now, he's the jealous one. Of me. Tried to hit me so I pushed him over; I was quite civilised about it I thought, could have given him a right clobbering and thrown his worthless carcass in gaol. And what thanks do you think I get?"

"Treachery," suggested his uncle shrewdly.

"Dead right. Next thing he's telling her that I attacked him and broke his arm."

"And she believed him?"

"Yes!"

"Silly mare. Abe, you did the right thing by that one. You're better off without that kind of friend."

"You think so?"

"I do. She's obviously not good enough for you."

"I see that. Trouble is, who is?"

"You'll meet her at the right time. Plenty more fish in the sea."

"I suppose you're right, but who wants to go out with a fish?" replied Abe in all apparent seriousness.

They looked at each other, and both burst out laughing. Cyril poured again.

"You know," confided Abe, "I sometimes wish we were all still together: Miriam, you, me, John…"

The nostalgia, the fire and the whisky had leaked into the very air and shrouded the policeman in an opium cloud of sentimentality.

"…what happened?" he said, almost tearful.

"You mean apart from you becoming a zealous upholder of the law?" returned his uncle, although not unkindly.

"No, it wasn't that. I didn't mean that."

"It didn't help, but no, you're right, it wasn't just that."

"So?"

"So your sister told you what?"

"Nothing. She made it clear it was a taboo subject. The most she would ever say was that you were stifling her."

"But you could have stayed."

"Not if I wanted anything to do with her, she made it clear; battle lines drawn and all that."

"Does she still hate me?"

"Hate? I don't think so. She can be very angry, for a long time, our Miriam, but I don't think she hates you. I hope not, because hate eats you."

"It's been a long time."

"I know…"

They sat quiet then, amidst their own separate thoughts, staring into the fire and the past as they swilled whisky around the mouth. Then Cyril knocked back his dregs and poured himself another. "Abraham?" he offered holding aloft the bottle.

No response. "Abraham."

"Hmm…"

"Are you feeling all right?"

"I don't know. To tell you the truth, I feel a bit queer. What's that smell?"

"Smell?" Cyril sniffed around. "Oh, it's mothballs, the jacket, the fire; you're sitting too close. Blimey, yes, it's very strong over there. Look, come away from the fire now and take off the jacket for a while."

As Abe began to obey Cyril was already divesting him of the offending garment. "Look at this," he said, "the pockets are full of them," and he held out a handful of mouldering and malodorous white spheres and dust, "and they're melting. I'll get Mick to clean them out later," he said as he replaced the debris and wiped his hand down his trouser leg. "Now get this down you."

Abe mechanically took the next glass of scotch.

"Listen to me son, I want to tell you something; get it off my chest. But I'm afraid of your reaction. It's why Miriam won't talk to me. Will you hear him out before you judge me?"

Suddenly his nephew was a little less drunk, more alert. The voice was helping him. It had been getting more talkative since he had arrived. "All right, go ahead uncle."

"Right then, big headline first, I'm Miriam's father."

A dozen flying thoughts were pulling Abe Lively in a dozen ways. Had he heard correctly? Did his uncle just say that, or was it somebody else? Himself, his voice? The feeling in his head might mean it was a dream…

"What?" he heard somebody say, then more urgently, "what did you say?"

"Easy Abe. Yes, you heard right, I'm her father," replied Crane, and, no doubt fearing the reaction, "remember, hear me out," he cautioned.

"My sister's father? Not mine?"

"Good God no. No, I didn't mean…that wasn't my way of telling you something else. It's just that I'm Miriam's father – not yours – and I think you ought to know that."

"My mother? My mother?" He didn't feel angry or outraged, just puzzled.

It's all right. What's the big deal? You're a grown man, things happen, no big deal. Keep calm and listen.

And Abe found that he was calm, detached. He listened to the words and obeyed, but they were not Cyril's words.

"Abe, just listen. Wait. Hear me out remember," his uncle was saying.

"It's not possible."

"It is Abe."

"So you're telling me my sister is not my sister?"

"No, she's always been your sister, in spirit, and I've no doubt, in love. But as far as blood goes, she's your half-sister."

"But you mean, you – and my mother…"

"Things happen."

Didn't I say so? Things happen, yes. Listen to him.

"Are you telling me that that's why Miriam fell out with you, took us all away, and still holds a grudge. Over this? Is it because she doesn't believe you? Knew you were lying? Like you're lying to me?"

"On the contrary. It's because she did believe me. I'm not lying. I think you know that."

No, he's not lying. We know that. Ask him.

"What's wrong with her then?"

"It's complicated…"

"I can handle complicated. I'm a big boy."

"If you say so. I think there are a number of factors."

"Such as?"

"Such as, one, I was stupid. I tried to use my newly revealed status to put her off that match with Hughes."

"Whatever for?"

"Looking back, now, I'm not sure. I'm ashamed to say that I was jealous, envious that is. At the time I told her that there was too much of an age difference."

"Like you and that silly woman," said another voice, clear as day.

"But she really loved him."

"I thought she was doing it to spite me, and that made matters worse between us. But, if what you say is true then I'm doubly a villain."

"If? You didn't see them together."

"No, perhaps I did not. And perhaps you saw only what you were meant to see."

What was uncle Cyril on about? What did he know? The voice considered this: "She's told you so herself, at least with this new one."

"All right uncle, she resented you for trying to stop her getting married. But, as a friend of mine likes to say, 'big deal.' So what? She did marry, and was happy. Why the prolonged separation? Fences can always be mended."

"Don't forget, it must have been a big shock. It destroyed what she thought she knew about herself. I think, in a way, that she felt that she had betrayed your father, just by being born."

"That's ridiculous. If anything, it's our mother she should be angry with, God rest her soul."

"No! Never say that. She loved your mother and your father, and the rest of the family. Look, she didn't blame your mother for falling in love with me. It's me she blames, for…"

"What?"

"Abe, I was already married to your aunt Lucy and your mother was betrothed to your father when…"

"And you're sure he is my father then, are you?"

"Of course. And John's and Josh's and the twins. Just not Miriam's."

"And did he know?"

"Ah. That's what I'm coming to. Just listen."

That's right. Listen. Calm down, just listen. Save it.

"We shouldn't have done, but your mother and I fell in love. At least I did. I was the sophisticated older man who whisked her off her feet: it really was like that, even though there was not half a dozen years between us. Only, she came down to earth first and saw things for what they were. I was a married man, and married to her own sister what's more. She was loved by your father, and due to marry him. In the end, I think, she saw that an infatuation was not worth two broken hearts. She married Gabe and she learned to love him, I think, for a while at least. When the first child was born, Miriam, it was always presumed she was premature. But I knew better."

355

"But she looks like a Lively."

"No, she looks like a Lawley. Think about it. Your mother's features fit as well, better."

"What did my mother say?"

"What could she say. Nothing. She said nothing."

"And they all lived happily ever after."

"Yes, in fact they did. As your childhood memories would confirm, if you care to look them up."

They did confirm it, in so far as the older the memories were, the happier his parents had seemed to be. Coming forward, Abe remembered a souring; uncomfortable silences, raised voices, slamming doors; his father coming home late, after they had gone to bed, his mother sleeping often with the twins...

"But it didn't last, did it?" he said.

"No. And that's what Miriam blames me for. In her heart, she knows that your mother once loved me, that I'm probably her father."

"Probably?"

"In her mind yes, I've no doubt. But that's immaterial. What counts is that at some time after the birth of the twins, a rumour reached your father. An old secret, disgorged on a death bed I shouldn't wonder, by somebody who had been close enough to us, Hannah and I, to guess it. It was only that, could only have been that, a rumour I mean. But it was a seed and eventually it would grow. He must have desperately not wanted to believe it, but he never asked me about it, in fact he avoided me when he could. I don't know what went on between him and Hannah. What I think is that he came to believe that your mother and I had been close at some point. Too close. But he got the time, and the child, completely wrong."

Pieces of an emotional jigsaw began to arrange themselves inside Abe Lively's head; "Josh?"

"Yes. He singled him out because he didn't look like you and the others. Pure coincidence."

"Miriam and I knew something was wrong, but we thought it was just the drink."

"In one way it was. Unfortunately for my brother-in-law he was just one of those individuals who couldn't take their drink, but nevertheless took it in ever increasing quantities. An alcoholic you might say."

"But it was the shock of that rumour that did it, that seed as you said. The booze just made it grow," said Abe.

"It was just one factor Abe. You wouldn't know this, but your father was subject to unaccountable melancholy, it was part of him, had been for a long time. He was already drinking too much when the mood was on him; before all this came out," and forestalling the next question went on, "I know this because, out of the blue, your mother started writing to me again. It was getting worse, and she had nobody else to turn to you see?"

356

"That's why we suddenly started bumping into you is it?" asked Abe, recognising the truth but sarcastically.

Cyril nodded. "I gave what comfort and advice I could, but at a distance, or else under the pretext of some family gathering, as you say. I also tried to keep an eye on your father as one vice affected another: he started to lose money gambling, with so called friends. Not that cards was a new pursuit for him, but now he was not exactly exercising the best of judgement."

"And losing out to people like you?"

"No, not like me. I have standards – you don't shit on a friend. These people were born with silver spoons in their mouths, the so-called cream of society, and so-called friends of your father. No honour amongst those people."

"So, you kept an eye on him while he lost our home did you? Good job."

Wait, wait, wait!

"On the contrary, I made it my business to arrange things so that he could not get into big enough games to do serious damage. I even sat at the same table on occasion, and lost money accordingly."

"Pity you weren't a good enough friend to make you think twice before stealing his fiancée."

"Fool! I wasn't doing it for him, but for your mother, and Miriam. All of you."

Cyril's raised voice brought the big dog to the door, whining and scratching at the wood.

"Look, I've upset the dog now. Down, Sabre, down. Good boy. It's all right. Isn't it Abe? Good boy," said Cyril, nodding to his nephew across the table.

"I'm sorry, m'boy," he continued, "I told you it wasn't straightforward. I'm human. I made a mistake. So did your mother. We both repented of it, and I've been trying to make amends ever since. Will you let me?"

"How?"

"Let me be your friend." Cyril stood and offered his hand. Abe stood and gave his own, and promptly crashed back down again.

"Mick," Mick's boss hollered.

"Here zir," replied mad O'Rourke, appearing suspiciously quickly.

"Coffee," ordered Crane.

#

"So Miriam blames you for everything then?"

"Yes. The way she sees it, my secret started your father drinking, drinking caused a rift between them, drinking and cards and bad company exacerbated it, and your mother, sickened with care, succumbed to the disease which eventually killed her. He saw it

357

coming, and he was grief stricken – he really was – and that set him completely off the rails, and so on and so forth."

"But you're asking me to believe he was already off them?"

"Yes. And if you can trust me I shall prove it to you."

"How?"

"I still have letters from her, your mother."

"Oh," was all that Abe said. But it said everything: it said, 'I know you're not lying. I believe you. My father was not the man we children had thought; our parents kept things from us – we were only children after all, except perhaps Miriam. Miriam had been wrong.'

"There's more," added his uncle, "as far as I can make out, you children were led to believe your father lost everything gambling. Is that not so?"

"It's what I was told."

"But, you're a police officer, you know that gambling debts are unenforceable…"

"There are ways."

"Yes there are ways, but not legal ones. Not if he lost at cards, is that what you thought? That he lost playing cards?"

"Er, yes. What else?"

"There are other types of gamble. And dressed up as 'investment opportunities' they might look perfectly respectable on the surface, and technically having the backing of the legal system behind them, because sometimes the surface is all the law bothers to scratch, if you catch my meaning," said Cyril spreading his hands with a theatrical frown.

"What are you getting at?"

"Ever heard of opals?"

Chapter 24

Gabriel and the Opal

Rupert Gerald Henry Hill was proud of his family connections. Or, at least, he played on them, to augment the appearance, the front, which he showed to the world – a man of influence, of business, wealth, culture, good judgement and most of all of integrity. Wearing that mask however was what the refined classes might call a cad, others of less gentle disposition might call a crook. For in truth, within the social spheres within which he was wont to circulate from time to time, as tonight, he was a relative pauper. And that was not right. What with providing himself with and regularly replenishing his own personal necessities – these inevitably, in his current enterprising lifestyle, of an outwardly luxurious nature – his was a hand to mouth existence, maintained by a combination of wits, flexible morality and debt. And neither was that right. Bad luck, he called it, result of his own poor choices notwithstanding. Thus he was always scheming to change his fortunes for the better; no more than he deserved.

In both coming by ready cash and in stretching the forbearance of his creditors it was essential of course that he look the part. Therefore, he made a point of wearing the latest fashion, sporting expensive looking accessories, and arriving in style in the best conveyance at any venue, even if, and whenever possible, from just around the corner. On the premise that those with money that could be talked out of it did not deserve it, he made it his business to cultivate an upper-class silver tongue, and he employed it readily in embroidering in the minds of lesser men fantasies of easy pickings and easy profit. Himself a dishonest man? He did not subscribe to it. He wasn't a crook, not exactly, it was merely that he had a predilection for speculative get-rich-quick ventures, but saw no reason to risk his own always meagre capital, not when there was always a ready supply of men with more wealth than wits willing to contribute.

With a name affiliating him to the redoubtable Hills of Court Of Hill fame, he had recently inveigled his way into the acquaintance of Miss Arabella Mills, by filial inheritance owner of this very house, the elegant and grand Whitton Court, in the shadow of the Clee hills, where he now sat in the splendid drawing room, planning his next move over brandy and biscuits.

The hour was late and most of the revellers had already departed, bidding the lady of the house a formal good night. Himself and two persons of especial interest remained, bowing to his persuasion. As well they might: hadn't he deliberately lost to them to them at cards? A small sum but a worthwhile investment, experience told him.

One of the men was already in his grasp. In fact he had swallowed the dream hook, line and sinker. On the subject of opals, mining and marketing he was an established expert, having been so for at least a month on the basis of information fed to him by his newest good friend, Rupert Hill: Charles Swinnerton was a local landowner of not insubstantial lands and means. Having two hundred and fifty guineas in cash sitting in a bank account doing nothing in particular had not really bothered him, not until he met Hill, who, as a good friend, pointed out his financial naïveté and the error of his ways.

The other man was almost convinced, but wondering how to broach it with his wife; whether to. Gabriel Lively had been a regular at the same card tables as Hill for a year or more. As far as he knew, Hill was an honourable man who paid his gambling debts. It was thanks to Hill that Gabriel Lively had been invited to this prestigious place, privilege built into the very fabric. He owed him for that, but it was late now, and he should be off.

"Gabriel, how's the brandy? To your liking I trust?"

"It is indeed, Rupert. However, it is late and I have to find my way home, or rather my horse does! I'll make this my last."

"Oh, shame. Look, you promised to think about that little proposition we discussed."

"I did, and I'm still thinking."

"Well, as I said, time is limited. And you have to admit that it's an exciting prospect. A once in a lifetime chance it is. Come on, admit it, you've got to be tempted."

Gabriel looked across into the earnestly enthusiastic eyes of Rupert Hill. Not an old man by any means, he did not look exactly young, and he was certainly not exactly handsome, with a lean cratered face and a high forehead fronting a cap of dry hair already tingeing grey, a pre-geriatric ferret. But, an open face, Lively thought; no guile in it, even if it was not pretty to look at. No reason to distrust his motives, but still, there was always some risk, parting with money…And so he had been stalling, not ready to be pinned down yet. Rather than reply, he glanced toward Swinnerton.

Hill's practised brain recognised the evasion: "Oh, no need to worry about Charles, quite the reverse. He's one of us, a fellow investor."

"Yes indeed, I most certainly am," responded Swinnerton, perceiving a cue, "took the plunge, what is it? Three weeks? Yes, three weeks ago. And I can't thank you enough Rupert for letting me in on the ground floor as they say. My dear Mr Lively…"

"Call me Gabriel."

"Well then, Gabriel it is. I can't tell you how excited I am about this. It's not only a splendid investment opportunity, but it's precious stones: opals, and all the romance that goes with it. And I'm not generally a romantic type, not at all."

Gabriel could believe that. Swinnerton had nothing of the soulful poet about him, nor anything of the dashing warrior in him, nor anything that hinted at fine sensibilities. He had the gift of the gab all right, but the poor man had all the charisma of a bloated sheep floating arse up in a ditch. And he was rather portly, to put it politely, but he would not hold that against him; like Hill, he was not particularly attractive when it came to his face, with a selection of small warts visible from the collar line, one in particular like a small white slug grazing on his eyelashes; Gabriel kept expecting it to crawl further…but, he would not hold that against him. Not his fault. Probably. But what he had already begun to hold against him was his conceit in his own opinion, holding forth upon each and every subject which randomly arose as if he were the very fount of all wisdom and understanding. Horses, politics, shooting, boxing, you would think that he had been expert in all of these pursuits over the years, to hear him talk over the cards tonight. Perhaps it was just his way of distracting opponents? No, he was still at it, on the subject of opals now, if Gabriel's bored and benumbed ears could still be trusted. Rupert seemed to egg him on. Apparently, Mark Antony had stolen a famous opal from Julius Caesar to give to Cleopatra. "And, as we all know from William Shakespeare, it was his undoing. Hers too of course, thanks to that snake. The queen? The queen loves 'em of course. And to me, the quality of the Australian opals is so superior to the Hungarian ones that I can't see that market holding up. That's why I've invested in Wannagulla options…"

Wallangulla corrected Gabriel mentally.

"…and if we can cut out the German connection with on-site cutting and polishing, then I believe the returns will be enormous, and I would like you to follow my lead on this Mr Lively – Gabriel – because…"

Hill gave the conversation a steer, "Perhaps you might mention the experience of our mutual friend?"

"Mutual friend?"

"Sir Mortimer?"

"Oh yes, sir Mortimer, of course, how silly of me. He's a great man Gabriel. I have the honour of counting him amongst my friends, a select company which I very much hope you will join dear sir, by the way. He's high up in the government; knows prime minister Disraeli."

"More to the point," Hill interjected, "he's an astute investor, and that's made him a very rich man."

"Oh yes, yes he is," continued the farmer, "do you know, he made two thousand pounds in a similar venture. Two thousand pounds! And, he's reinvesting some of that in Wannagulla. You can't get a better recommendation than that!"

"Some of it?"

Hill was quick to explain, "We're looking for a good spread of investors. If the equity was in the hands of just a few big shareholders we would be vulnerable to a takeover. I can get my partner to go over the sums I've already showed you, along with the surveyor's report from the bank again, if it's really necessary, but we really only need another ten or fifteen percent of the private capital we've set out to raise, so, time's at a premium here."

"I see," replied Gabriel Lively. He was sure that he did not understand the intricacies of company law, but he trusted that Hill did. And, while Swinnerton was a babbler, he liked the idea of making two thousand pounds. When Hill took out the gems again, set in simple silver clasps on a silver chain, the sight of them removed all doubt. For they caught the light and threw it back at angles revealing a refulgent lustre in which all the colours of the rainbow swirled; ochres and oranges and honeys, the green of a spring forest and summer sky blue. Heart stopping. Life changing.

Gabriel gave his word that night. Only later, much later, did he think to question the facts, the stories, the evidence, produced by Hill, his motives. Only later did he stop to think about what a good card player the man was, for someone with such an open face; with no guile in it.

When Lively had gone and only Hill and an impatient hover of servants remained, a man of average height and build emerged from concealment. His unremarkable looks enabled him to play many parts.

"Another one then?" he asked.

"Yes, he's in the bag. Thanks Alan, or should I say 'partner'?"

"I rather like Sir Mortimer. Has a nice posh ring to it, don't you know. But, you can call me what you like as long as I get paid," replied Bill Arrowsmith with a wink, and a question.

"Don't worry. Another three or four like this and we're done. Be rolling in clover before you know it. Now, here's the copy," said Hill handing Arrowsmith the pendant, "make sure you get it back to the shop first thing."

Arrowsmith took it. "Looks good for a bit of glass."

"It's a work of art in itself, I think. It's just that it's worthless in comparison. Nevertheless, make sure you get it back or he'll have our guts for garters. Are you listening Alan?"

'Alan' had to remind himself that that was his name. As far as this little caper was concerned, as far as Hill was concerned, he was Alan Hale, not William Arrowsmith: why take unnecessary risks?

"I'll make sure of it. Now, I think we had better be leaving before they throw us out."

Chapter 25

The Witch

Through a cracked window pane she had caught movement. Through the window she watched him come. A young man. A strong man. Hesitant though, not exactly striding out, thinking hard no doubt. Typical of most of her visitors. Wanting her help, but arguing with doubt. And fear of course, oftentimes. Many feared her, just a little. After all, was it not well known that she was a witch?

It had not gone away, his little friend. It whispered unabated. Abraham Lively was pretty sure that he was not mad, that he was just different, gifted even. But he needed answers, answers might help him cope with it, before its incessant distraction and the disturbed nights did drive him mad. And it was not just the voice. Hadn't he seen it too? When others could not? At least, most, he corrected, thinking of Jack Cutler and his dog, and wondering whether he was similarly gifted, or afflicted, or mad. But no, this was an occult phenomenon, and who better from whom to seek guidance than a practitioner of the occult? A witch. It made sense, no? Yes. But even so he felt foolish. How many gullible fools made this ascent on some trivial and pathetic private mission? Help with mundane matters of domestic strife, finance, the heart? This was different, but he still felt it, foolish. Also anxious. What if she were just a charlatan, peddler of potions and charms strictly for the credulous? What if she saw nothing? Could see nothing. Only as far as a money-making charade? Was he just deranged after all? But no. No. There was more to it than that. But that was perhaps what he feared most of all.

Powke Hill had a bad reputation. Haunted. Where many criminals had been lain to rest –or not to rest – in the past, graves unmarked. He wondered what kind of woman would live here, alone by all accounts. He had thought to come across a cliché, some kind of rude hovel. But when he rounded the shielding bunch of sooty gnarled hawthorns he was surprised to see a single storey building, of brick no less, not wattle and daub or whitewashed animal dung, and in a good state of repair. Originally a base, come stores come office for some sort of finished and forgotten construction project, he conjectured. But what? And why here? Unexpected, and a bit of a mystery. So what of the witch then? An ugly old hag? Probably some quite ordinary local.

He was wrong, Mollie Mogg was not ordinary. He could tell that immediately: she met him at the door as he was about to knock. And she was certainly not a hag, old or otherwise.

"Good day to you young man," said she, and stopped him dead; speechless.

First thing, her manner of speech, and this also told him that he had been wrong for it was eloquent of exotic parts, that is to say, certainly not around here: confident but gentle and relaxed with not a trace of the black country dialect; genteel, in an unforced and natural way, as tends to attach to those with an above average start in life. But mostly, it was the accent: unfamiliar, strange, mysterious somehow; he could not place it. Had he been a well-travelled man, he might have immediately recognised it as the tongue of an inhabitant of the United States Of America, but he was far from it and so did not; had he been a well-travelled American man, he might also have recognised the accent as belonging to a big city, New York; being however a small-town Englishman, she might as well had been from the moon.

Next thing, her shape. A woman's shape in all the best ways. A fit and an undeniably feminine woman, despite the small detail that, above her long mauve skirt, pinched in at the waist by a broad black leather belt, she wore a working man's shirt, collarless and its too-long sleeves rolled neatly back to the elbow, and a man's waistcoat: a small man's as it fit her well although but five feet tall, admittedly with a shape that helped fill it out, decorated in a grey and pink paisley pattern. The grey caught the grey in her long hair. Still mostly black, but enough of grey to be noticeable, it was all tied back, reaching as far as the small of her own. He thought that she looked unusual, but not particularly 'witchy', except, he saw it now, for her unusual bracelet: affixing itself to her forearm it had a man's head, open mouthed as if shouting some silent sound, and the antlers of a red deer stag. That teetered him off balance; reminder of something else…

She caught him looking, azure blue eyes fixing him, bringing him back. He was about to speak when something black and hairy passed over his feet and on into the house. He was looking at her lips now. He thought them uncommonly red…

"Cat got your tongue?" they asked.

"No," said he, "I've come to see Mollie Mogg."

"Yes, I am she."

"Oh…" he was stammering, "sorry, I expected…"

"A witch?"

"Yes, I thought…"

"You thought you might find some local enfeebled unfortunate reduced to selling potions and reading the cards to make ends meet?"

"Not exactly. I was hoping for…"

"For a proper witch, yes? Well, fear not, you've found one, or as near as dammit. Witch is what everyone chooses to call me, and that's close enough. But pray don't tell the parson or I will only deny it," she laughed.

"And 'Molly Mogg'? 'Old Molly Mogg' I've heard. Somehow, that name isn't you."

"And I'm certainly not old of course, thank you for mentioning it! But no, you are right. Not my real name, but that I keep secret. There was a reputed witch of that name lived hereabouts many years ago, according to the locals, the more imaginative of whom have it that I am her returned in flesh, as she apparently promised. It's not my inclination to dissuade them. So, you had better call me Molly. Not Moll mind! And you are?"

"Sorry, I'm Abraham. Abraham Lively. I would like your help."

"Abraham. A good solid biblical name. Well, come in then, Abraham."

He went to step forward, noticed a niche set in the wall behind the door frame, a squat glass jar within, sealed with wax, or tar, containing a dark liquid and the remains of some twiggy plant.

"What's that?" he asked.

"It's to keep the mice out."

"How does that work? Can they smell it?"

"I'm a witch, remember."

"Mice is it? What does the cat do then?"

"Cat?"

"The one I just saw run in."

"Oh, you saw him did you? Martin. Lots of things."

"Unusual name for a cat."

"After Martin Luther. Look, I'm sure you didn't come here to make small talk."

Are you coming in or what? said the blue eyes. He stepped in.

He was aware of firelight and of its warmth. It was a good-sized room, with an old table and some old stools, and a new dresser. Also, lots of shelves stacked with glass jars and containers of clay, all cork stoppered. The jars he could see contained some liquids, a few powders, but mostly dried herbs. Tools of the trade? Cooking ingredients? Or stage props? He was still not convinced that he should let go of all conventional logic…There was no stove but the large open fireplace had a lively fire going, burning wood, under a suspended cauldron, bubbling away. Very Macbeth he was thinking, before he realised it was onions cooking that he could smell. And lamb – whatever it was she did, it must pay well…

"So, you want help," she said, "the kind that you think a witch can provide."

"Yes. how much…"

She forestalled him. "Later, follow me."

She led him into an adjacent room, if anything an even larger one, longer, he imagined. He only imagined, for a portion of the room was fenced off by what looked like a folding screen of cane and raffia. On this side there was an oblong table and a couple of chairs. On the table was a dark blue cloth and on the cloth nothing but a large wooden box, devoid of any markings, placed to one side. She motioned him to take a seat and then seated herself opposite.

365

"Now, what appears to be the problem?" she asked almost playfully, "because you look a big strong man, and I can't imagine you've come here about a herbal pick-me-up. A love spell is it?" she suggested.

"No, no, of course not, Nothing like that, no."

"I thought not. But something troubles you. Tell me."

Abe dove straight in: "I'm hearing things. And seeing them."

"Have you seen a doctor? I'm sorry, I mean, have you consulted one?"

"No, it's not like that. I know it isn't. And it's happened before."

"Tell me."

He told her. And there was no mischief in her then, no twinkle in her eye.

"I've been expecting something like this, and it calls for more than a quick chat over the cards. Please, wait here while I get ready." She left him and disappeared behind the screen. He could see little beyond bar a moving shadow, but he heard the striking of a flint which preceded three points of yellow light which he knew must be from lit candles; then he smelled the smoke, scented, but not like any church incense; then her, intoning something in a remarkably deep voice for a woman, and so small, and in a language he had no inkling of. He lost time, in the silence. Yes, silence, in his head there was silence…Suddenly, the screen was drawn aside and he saw her. She had changed, her clothes at least, or, that is to say, had donned a robe, presumably over her ordinary clothes; a dark blue one with a hood, like a monk's habit, but with shorter sleeves, and she now wore a necklace threaded alternately with stones of opaque amber and black jet. She signalled him to stay put and, "Don't move," she commanded, and she walked away from him, back to the source of the candle light, and that smell, the odour of some almost familiar herb. It was the candles which made him realise that this was an altar, although, as with the incense-like smoke, not like anything you would experience in any Christian church. He could make out most of it now: candles either side, and one central and higher, a metal goblet, metal cage emanating the smoke, and, alarmingly perhaps, an implement which had the appearance of a knife, the handle being the foot of some ungulate, roe deer from the size of it he calculated. When she picked it up he was sure. It was a knife, with a blade as exotic as the handle, being not straight but undulating, like waves or ripples; like a snake. She proceeded to cut shapes into the smoke and the air, facing each of four walls in turn and all the while voicing that sound so that the whole space seemed to vibrate. Then the power of the sound and the knife were aimed at him, pushing into him, before she turned and gestured to the altar, saying something in a now soft voice, before replacing the knife. After standing in silence for a time she turned and made her way back to the waiting policeman.

Saying nothing, she opened the box and took out some white feathers: a wing, a goose wing, which she used to very deliberately sweep invisible dust, occult debris, off the table. Five passes she made, all South to North, although her visitor would not have known the orientation of the room, not without a certain knowledge, or a compass. She laid the wing to one side, not back in the box, and put a thin wooden roundel, a slice of sapling carved with what looked like a Star of David, directly in front of him.

"We'll start with the scrying glass. I'll need some blood please. Come closer. Give me your hand." She gently took his right hand and then, in hers, there was a small sharp white bone handled knife. He did not flinch and blood dripped onto the piece of recently deceased tree. He trusted her; ever since he had entered the place he had begun to relax; he felt good; and the voice had shut up; he trusted her, and in her protection. She gave him back his hand and he found a handkerchief. Meanwhile she had recovered from the darkness of the box a black looking glass with two small black grips set into the metal surround, and holding with both hands, circled the fresh blood three times. Signalling silence then, she stared into the midnight glass. For ten minutes she stared, occasionally asking a question, of him or of nobody in particular, nobody that he could hear, but mostly she just stared. When she was done she wrapped the mirror in black silk and returned it to its place. The bloody wood, she disposed of on the fire. The goose feathers did their job again, then away they went. She looked at him.

"Well?" he said.

"Well Abraham, a doctor might say that you have brain damage. That that blow to your head did it, that your brain was damaged, blood not getting out. That it's causing you to see things. Normal people, sane people, don't see things that aren't there do they?"

"What? So I'm mad?"

"No, let me answer my own question. The answer is that sane people can indeed see things that are not there, apparently not there. You're not mad Abraham, you're as sane as I am. A doctor might drill a hole in your skull, to relieve the pressure, and an olden days medicine man might have done the same – to let out evil spirits! You shouldn't let the first one near you because you're not mad, you're perfectly normal, and you shouldn't let the other near you because you don't get rid of spirits that way. But that's not to say they don't exist. I've seen them, and heard them."

"But, isn't that to be expected, in your, er…line of work? Why me then?"

"First, it's not a given that we in the craft all have such gifts. Why you? Well, I think that story from your childhood proves that you have a certain, let's say aptitude," *let's not say vulnerability*, "for it. More importantly, this place is a magnet for what, for want of a better term I'll call spirits. There's something in the rocks, in the quarries…"

"Blue Devils!" exclaimed Abe.

"Yes! You've heard of them?"

"Yes. You believe in them then?"

"It's partly what drew me here. A sister on the path discovered this place a dozen years ago. A natural psychic she was, but too open to influence, she couldn't protect herself against them. They invaded her everyday thoughts and she had to leave in quite a hurry in the end. It did the trick though, she left them behind, but she's never chosen to use her gift again."

"So, I'm still not sure, these things, are they real? Or just in the mind?" pursued Abe with an involuntary tap of his head.

"What's real? If something's in your head, it's real, isn't it?"

"Because it's only your brain that lets you see it, feel it, perceive it. Once it's here," she said, aping his tap to the temple, "it has an existence, it's real."

"I don't know…"

"Look, say you are up a ladder, cleaning windows perhaps. You're very near the top. Your friend is holding the bottom for you, steadying you. From where you are you can see into the next street, you see a stranger walking along, going about a stranger's business. You see him, because your perspective, your view into the street, is enhanced by the ladder, artificially enhanced if you like. So, you see him, and therefore you have no doubt that he exists, that he's real. But your friend doesn't see him. Does that make him not real? Or does he take your word for it? Because Abraham, I absolutely take your word for it."

"I still don't see…"

"A step too far? Trust me, they exist, but you have to be careful who you tell. You can't describe a colour to a man born blind; likewise people like us, yes, like you and me, cannot make people believe in what they cannot see. But that's no reason to torture yourself. Once you accept the fact you can begin to deal with it."

"This is making my head spin. Where do they come from?"

"From, 'elsewhere.' Some say they exist here, in exactly the same place as us, except that we can't detect each other, usually; from other worlds if you want to think of it like that, through doors that connect at special places. Like hereabouts. Like I said, accept it. Much less painful."

"If you say so."

"I do. I assure you. Now – your particular problem."

"Is it a problem?"

"Possibly, if you let it be so."

"Tell me."

"It's nothing you don't really know. You have a companion, invisible to others but very real. That's what the mirror's for, to see the unseen things. It's trying to communicate with you, we know that. Don't worry about the 'something bad coming' it may be nothing bad at all, at least not for you."

"What is it? A ghost?"

"No. No such thing as ghosts, although these things, these creatures, these intangible but very perceptible creatures, they do often masquerade as a human spirit. But no, these things are more like angels, very low level and simple angels. Elementals we call them. More like an animal, let's say a pet dog, than a human. But, like big powerful dogs, you have to know how to handle them, keep them in their place, earn their respect. Or they bite."

"Marvellous, nothing to worry about then?"

"Strangely, in your case no. I'm not exactly sure of the shape of this one, but it's not out to do you any harm, not at all, not directly. I get quite the opposite impression. But it wants something, they always do."

"Like what?"

"Who knows? You most likely. Whatever it is you may end up as allies for a while, and it may actually benefit you, but its motives are its own and for its own self. You've no idea what it wants? What all the whispering is about?"

"No. Except that I think he's looking for somebody."

"He's dropped lucky there then."

"What?"

"Nothing. You were about to say?"

"I was about to say, there's something else. A feeling that's all, but I think that if we do find this somebody, it's not going to be pleasant. Can't you tell?"

"No, I don't get that. Only that it means you no harm, I'm pretty sure of that. But remember what I said, these things are single minded and that could change if you get in the way."

"Great. What else do you know? I mean, can it come to life, so to speak, and physically touch you, hurt you, physically, on its own I mean?"

"Unlikely, and it could appear to you as different things."

"What did it appear to you as?"

"It didn't do any appearing, it's not here, but I can get an impression of it."

"And?"

"It's sounds silly, I know, but with all the talk recently, I can only see it as Spring Heeled Jack."

His heart missed a beat, or three, then he breathed again. "I knew it. I bloody well knew it," he whispered, then with hopeful determination said more strongly, "can you help me get rid of it?"

"I could try to, er, expel it, but that's not without its own dangers and I would need help, to conduct the ritual, help which is not exactly to hand. Or, you could let it run its course: it may fade of its own accord, as it did before."

"But if it doesn't?" asked Abe, not unreasonably.

She hesitated.

"All right, if I wait, what will happen? If I just wait?"

She hesitated again. "I don't know…but I could ask the cards."

#

As the king of pentacles Abe was covered and crossed by six more of the pack, strange pictured cards the import of which he could not begin to guess at. And perhaps

369

it was the same for her, for what she told him was disappointingly vague, he thought: a struggle, a decision, success, loss, a separation, a reckoning.

"So, how much…" he began.

"No. I can't take payment. Not for this. But before you go…"

She went to re-draw the screen, disappearing behind it. When she returned it was with a small cloth bag. Carefully, without touching, she emptied the contents onto the table. A stone, it rumbled out softly and came to rest, waiting. It was a dull green, smooth but not spherical, more rhomboid with indistinct edges, about two inches in height by about half that in the other dimensions.

"What's that?" he asked.

"Take it," said she, "it's charged for protection…"

"I thought you said it meant me no harm."

"Yes, but perhaps something else might. If your 'friend' is here, it may not be alone. Why take chances? Take it. It's what we colonists call an Indian gift: use it while you need it, but when you're done I want it back."

"All right, I understand, yes, I'll take it, thank you." She offered him the little bag and he put the stone in, it was heavier than he thought, then slipped it into a trouser pocket.

"That will help, but remember, if it all gets too much, I'm always here. Now, let me show you out."

Outside, he tried once more.

"Are you sure there's no fee, or anything?"

"I told you, no. You can just owe me a favour, although I hope I won't be needing one from the police!"

"How did you know?"

"I'm a witch sergeant!"

He looked only part convinced.

"Not really," she said, "we're not that far off the beaten path! Your fame precedes you Sergeant Lively. Or did you think I would let any strange man in?"

"You all right there, ma'am?" A man built like a buffalo had appeared silent as a mountain lion.

"Yes, thank you, Victor. This is Sergeant Lively. You've heard of him."

"Oh, yeah, you said," responded the big man with the soft tread. He nodded, "Sergeant," and slunk off.

"Well, thank you again," said Lively.

She simply said, "I'm always here," and went inside.

Abe Lively started back down the hill, *looks like rain* he thought.

With uncanny looking intelligent eyes, the cat looked at her intensely.

"Well, what did you think?" she asked but gave no time for a reply, "I think he's basically a good guy. I just hope he can avoid losing himself."

At this point Martin started to vocalise, as if in protest, or disagreement, or perhaps merely because he was getting hungry.

"Yes, yes I know. What was I supposed to do? That's why I gave him the green stone."

The cat had not quit.

"All right, knock it off, I know: swords and the moon; I'll pray for him."

But before she did so she carefully and calmly sealed the house from psychic attack, and checked the chambers in the Colt Navy.

#

Big brother Abraham was not the only Lively going calling. John, in his well-cut new suit, shiny shoes and dapper bowler, was paying a visit of his own. The recipient of the smartly dressed man's attention had been in the wars, as the expression had it. Recently out of the hospital, he was lying in his sister's parlour, bandaged head to foot, or at least around one leg and foot plus around the head, and one arm bound in a sling diagonally across his chest. At his brother in law's insistence this was very much a temporary stop over, just until he was able to get up and about and look for work. For his incapacitation had engendered no sympathy in the heart of his employer's sawmill foreman, seasoned and hardened as it had been by twenty years' worth of hard luck stories. Well, hard luck stories would not 'get the babby washd,' as he would put it – as he did put it, before sacking the man.

Yes, he had had a miserable time of it, and the weather was no help. It was late afternoon and drizzling. Dull. A visitor might cheer him up; the right visitor. Unfortunately for Charlie Spragg, however, John's motivation for coming to see him today had very little to do with friendship or Christian charity.

The sister was just going out, and pleased that her brother would have company. She was gone before Spragg had time to react, and raise the alarm – if he dared. He knew who this was all right, although the fresh and natty look did fool him for an instant. But, yes, he knew who this was all right. And it wasn't all right. Even if he had not been related to the man that Spragg had so recently slyly assaulted, even though he be garbed in a silk and woollen wash wont to indicate respectability in the conventionally minded, and even had Spragg been up to an erstwhile physical very best, he would still have been nervous of an unsolicited call from this character. Understandably then, Charles Spragg felt somewhat perturbed by it. Lively's groomed and respectable appearance only added to the air of menace, as if lending authority to visit violence with impunity. And Spragg saw through the contrivance, and the smiling demeanour. For Lively's eyes did not join in. They reminded him of the stare exchanged by fighting dogs before collars were slipped, his smile a snarl. Spragg was physically helpless. All he could hope was that he could disarm with words. But, he could not think what to say for the best, where to start, without putting his foot in it…

Thus, it was John Lively who spoke first.

"Hello Charlie. Can I call you Charlie?"

"What do you want?" The words distorted by the pain of a recently realigned jaw, lisped between newly broken teeth.

"I'm killing two birds with one stone," came the casual reply.

Spragg did not like the idea that he might be one of two unfortunate avians, marked for death.

"Wha' d'ya mean?" he rasped.

"I'm sorry, let me start again. My name's Lively. No doubt the name's familiar to you? Of course it is. Just call me Mr Lively. My uncle owns some of the properties down here. Crane, Cyril Crane. That's my uncle. No doubt you've also heard that name. Had them built himself. In fact, this is one of them. Nice, isn't it?"

"Uhm…ahr, not bad. It's a good 'ouse."

"Yes, not bad, as you say. I'm thinking of moving into one myself. We could be neighbours; see a lot of each other. But wait. What am I thinking? This is your sister's house isn't it? I mean, she's the tenant, or her husband is. Not you. So, can I take it that you'll not be staying long?"

John had been deliberately baiting. He had a trap to close, but he wanted Spragg to walk into it. That way he would likely take on the message all the better, and remember it longer. His tone and manner had the desired effect. Spragg came back with just a hint of defiance.

"Yoh can tek it any road. None of yower business is it?"

"Oh! Sorry! Of course, I haven't told you have I? I'm the new rent collector. It's my job to collect the rent and generally keep an eye on things: you know, damage caused to the properties, unauthorised lodgers and such like. Members of the extended family say; that's very common, as you can imagine; calls for an increased rent you see."

"Ah bay a lodger, Ah'm just here till ah find me feet," said Spragg with an effort.

"In more ways than one no doubt," observed the rent collector, casting his eye over the rough crutches placed near the make-shift bed, "broken leg is it?"

"No, me ankle."

"Sorry can't make it out."

Spragg indicated his bandaged head and face. "Bost me jaw," John made out, as Spragg proceeded to wipe away the incontrollable dribble before going on to explain that his right arm had also been 'bosted', indicating a point on the humerus just above the elbow. He wouldn't be making mischief for a while, but John guessed that this man had had his share of ups and downs, good times and bad, and of knocks, including literal, bone breaking, flesh punishing ones. He therefore suspected that his spirit was only bruised, not broken, so he would ram home his point,

"Sorry to hear it, Charlie. But perhaps you deserved it. Ever think of that? Which brings me to the point: not to beat about the bush, but there's a nasty little rumour going around that it was my brother did this to you; set about you in the dark and threw you into an open grave. Now, nothing could be further from the truth of course, so I would hate to find out that you had anything to do with such a story. So – can you assure me that you had nothing to do with putting about this foul calumny?"

Spragg was not sure of what a calumny might be, but he got the drift. And, as he well knew that the sergeant was incapacitated when the attack upon his own person was perpetrated, on account of the fact that he had seconds earlier finished giving him a right good kicking, he was content to put John Lively's mind at rest.

"Wor me, ah've sed nuthin. 'Onnist."

"Good. And if questioned you will of course be denying that my brother had anything to do with it. Yes?"

"Yes." repeated the stricken Spragg, as emphatically as he could manage, then added, "Ah know it wor 'im. Somebody else done it."

"Glad of the confirmation Charlie boy. Now, it's been nice chatting with you but I really must fly. Remember what I said, about everything. No, don't get up, I'll let myself out."

He walked into the rain outside and the roar of a passing steam engine, iron pressing on clattering iron, and the jaunty whistle as the train rounded the bend on its happy way out of town. He adjusted his bowler hat and did not feel entirely comfortable. What had he just done? Threats. Blackmail was it? He was used to using force, physical force; when pushed to it. But this was different, subtle, and insidious. He was beginning to appreciate how easily that line could be crossed, moved, obscured, ignored. He had found a new kind of power. Ironic that he had used it, and crossed the line, not in safeguarding Cyril's illegitimate business interests, but to shield an officer of the law – and his brother. On the other hand, he knew enough of the story and of Spragg to know that he had probably deserved what he got, whether from Abe – who denied it – or from whatever other enemy the man had made for himself. And that included what he had just got, in what he must have thought was the safety of his sister's house. And yet, in spite of it all, and in spite of that defiant gleam, John could not help also feeling sorry for the beaten down convalescent: those injuries would take a long time and still not heal properly.

#

Inside, Spragg was also reflecting. In hospital he had had one visitor. Sarah. But his pleasure at seeing her turned sour by the end, when it became clear that she was taking sides in his feud with Lively; and it wasn't his side. As she put it, she felt it best to 'make a complete break' with him, with Spragg. Although she wished him all the best, and all that. That was it. No friends, no colleagues, no drinking pals; nobody bothered. Oh yes, except yesterday, here. A visit from a friend. Trouble is it was not his friend, it was the sergeant's friend, colleague. Constable Salt had made it very clear where he stood in the matter, both on a professional and non-professional basis; what would happen to someone who had assaulted a police officer, before and after arrest – if he did not keep his broken mouth firmly shut. And now this. It was very disheartening. Physically, he knew, he would never be the same. Mentally he was at the lowest ebb of the neap tide of his endurance; haunted by doubts, alone, fearful of the future: recovering, getting a job, somewhere to live, someone to be with. All that effort. For what? Toil and disagreements and disputes broken up by brief interludes of happiness, illusory happiness which disappeared as you sobered up. Then back to reality and staring into the face of your inevitable end. Why bother going on?

Such thoughts were unlike him, but becoming so. And that was unavoidable. For John Lively had been wrong: the spark he had seen in those eyes were just dying embers, gradually being doused, right now, by the thing feeding on his fears, ever greedier, so that fear, his emotions, were but the entrees to the main course of guts, of liver, and of Spragg's very bones. Charles Spragg was not destined to see another Easter. Some would say good riddance.

#

Even as Spragg was receiving his just desserts, a passing housewife on her way back from the butcher's noticed something on the railway track next to St. Paul's. It looked like soil, sticks and stone had slipped down from the embankment. As luck would have it, two police officers were also approaching and she lost no time drawing their attention to the sight, before hurrying home, good mother that she was, good deed as a good citizen done, and unloading her ingredients for faggots.

Perched one-toed on a proud rivet, Gordon Clark leaned over the bridge squinting along the line.

"What do you think?" he said.

"Watch what you're doing Gordon," cautioned Joshua Lively, "you don't want to be taking a tumble, like old Reg."

"God, yes. This is where his body was – where that muck is. Almost exactly."

"So be careful then," advised his colleague, "it wouldn't be any trouble for a train as it is, but if more comes down it might be different, especially if a tree lost its footings. I think that we ought to nip down the line to the station and tell them. They can get some men up here; make up their own…"

"…minds," completed Clark automatically.

But Josh was not listening. He had firstly frozen, then had leaned as far over the tracks as he dared. Amongst the debris he had noticed a large white stone, and amongst the dull coloured bits of twig, an unusually pale looking broken off branch.

"Wait a minute," he commanded, and ran into the churchyard. Clark was too surprised to follow but over the parapet his short-sighted eyes could make out a fuzzy blue figure scouting along the low boundary wall of the churchyard. Once level with the obstruction, it stopped, then all of a sudden started swiftly back. After eight or ten paces, it stopped again and pushed on the wall, from where the copings had long ago disappeared, appeared to consider something briefly, then made its way back to the street.

"Right Gordon, see that white boulder?"

"Yes, I can see something white."

"Well it's not a boulder. It's a skull!"

"A skull? Where's that come from?"

"Er, it's a bloody graveyard Gordon."

"Well, yes, obviously…So, has one been dug up?"

"No, I don't think so. But the ground's very soggy, and it started to feel funny to walk on, like it's sinking down. There's a funny slope I don't remember seeing before, and when I touched the wall, bricks just rolled off it."

"Well it's bound to be a bit boggy. We've had a lot of rain in the last couple of days," observed Clark.

"It's more than that. I think there's been some subsidence, and the grounds shifted, along with some of the graves, and spilled out."

"What, from underneath like?"

"Yes of course from underneath like. Some of the bodies are probably lying very close to the embankment, possibly moving with the ground movements, and the pressures from later burials, to within a few feet of the line."

"Could have been foxes," asserted Clark.

"What?"

"Known for it, digging up bodies. They eat them you know."

"Gordon?"

"Yes Josh?"

"Don't talk such twaddle. You ever see a fox with a crowbar?"

"Eh?"

"How are they supposed to break into the coffin?"

The inanity of Clark's observations made Josh conscious of the dialect which he had fallen into the habit of ignoring, or of filtering it out and translating it to himself.

"Doh 'ave to be a coffin, does there? It might be somebody too poor. Mah granny come 'ere from Cornwall, and ah always remember 'er tellin' me about the rabbits digging up kids' boones in the churchyard. Mind yoh, this was sand dunes o'course, but still. Rabbits ay very big am they? Ah'll always remember that. And that was just rabbits. Wharra bout a fox then, eh? Or a gang on 'em. Eh? And wharr if the coffins had gone rotten? No need for a crowbar then then, eh?"

"All right! Look, all I know is that there's a bloody skull on the chippings down there, and we could have a whole crowd of corpses to complete the set if the embankment does collapse. You get down to the station sharpish and get them to stop the trains till we can investigate. Then get yourself back here as soon as you can. I'm going to fetch Wharton, he's a magistrate and a doctor."

"All right," replied Clark, already on his way, "but Ah doh think he'll let us do 'em for trespassin', 'specially when he realises they'm jed."

"How very droll," commented Josh to himself, and then shouted after him, "you'd better hurry, it looks like…rain," as the first hard splashes struck his face.

They both ran, in opposite directions.

#

Abraham Lively arrived back in Blackheath in a good mood. The meeting with 'Mollie' had been strangely stimulating. Just talking to somebody, somebody with a brain, about his companion had been liberating, a weight off his shoulders. He literally felt lighter, was more nimble, than he had been mere hours earlier. Every so often, he felt for the green stone, took it out, squeezed it. It seemed to him to be sustaining his mood. Or was it all about meeting the witch? The woman was undeniably attractive, in an almost literal sense. Shyly, he admitted to himself that her looks, that accent, the little ritual he had undergone, the feeling of being under her control – all this had aroused him. The more he thought about it, the more erotic it became for him. An older woman. What, again? No, best not go there, he would not go there. No doubt, imagination was better than the real thing – he had always found it so. He would admit to one thing though: she knew her stuff. That is, to judge by the fact that his little friend had been stilled and was still silent. He planned on forty winks before changing for the afternoon shift. As he was about to climb the staircase in the Royal Oak, however, he was accosted by his sister.

"Hello stranger. Nice of you to drop in."

"Miriam. Hello, I was just…"

"Just about to take coffee with your sister?" She looked at him and he looked back, non-committal, "that's right, yes. Thank you for offering…" she continued, "come on, it's just perked."

"I can smell it," he replied. "All right, let's go."

The kitchen was clean and tidied up from breakfast, the table bare.

"You sit yourself down while I pour," said she, "biscuit with it?"

"No thanks. You have one though."

"I won't bother. A girl has to watch her figure, you know."

"Does she?" he asked, just for something to say.

She set the drinks down and sat opposite him, but close.

"So, where have you been today? You were up early. I missed you again. Been for a walk?"

"Yes."

"Anywhere nice?"

"Not especially. Went down the hill as far as Coombes Wood. Just to stretch my legs."

"Oh."

She volunteered nothing else so he thought he had better offer something to fill the gap.

"I'm sorry I've not been around much. I've been busy."

"Not too busy to be getting all pally with your uncle though," she said pointedly.

"Oh, you've heard have you? What can I say? Except that he's been very good to me recently. Got me out of a jam you don't know about and which you don't want to know about," and he raised a hand to forestall her question, "nothing serious, just a little altercation with a local character which I could have done without."

She looked dubious, head cocked, inviting more.

"Look, if you want to know the truth, I got kicked about by somebody through my own stupidity. I fell and hurt myself and got thoroughly filthy – and I didn't want to bring more trouble here again. You gave me enough of a hard time after…after that woman brought me back from the Hailstone."

"Yes, but not for getting hurt. I always look after you when you're hurt. But no, you have to go and cosy up to that man."

"Well, right or wrong, I felt I needed his help."

"You're supposed to come to me for help. That's the way it's always been."

"Like I said, I didn't want to worry you."

"Well, you did. Did you think I'd not notice the cuts and bruises? They don't disappear overnight." She reached out to touch the graze on his cheek. He pulled away.

"Goes with the job," he said.

"Hadn't used to. Not for you."

"Yes, well times are changing out there, believe me. It's getting a lot rougher."

"You must take care of yourself then. Do you carry your pistol?"

"No. That's frowned on. Well, it's not allowed actually. Besides, that would seem like an admission of failure, of inadequacy."

"Well, I think you ought to get some more recruits. You can't be expected to work miracles. Look at you. Have you lost weight? You're certainly tired, your eyes look like grey smudges."

"Well yes, I could do with a kip. I was about to have one when you caught me."

It was not a reproach but she took it as such. He continued.

"But I'm glad of the chance to talk to you. Look, there's some things I've been told…"

377

"What things?"

"Where's Mary?"

"She's out."

"Mary, out? Really?"

"She's getting really good. It's only a little walk, to the bakers, to get some bread. What things?"

"Cyril. He told me about him and Mom."

"Told you what exactly?"

"About their relationship…"

"And you believe him do you?"

"I can't really see why he would lie."

"Can't you?"

"No. Why would he?"

"To push us apart of course. To stir up trouble, break up the family. Like he pushed mom and dad apart. Why do you think dad started drinking? Why did he kill himself? If it wasn't for that man we would all be living happily at home in the green hills, in the clean countryside, not in the, this shit!" She voiced the last word with vehemence, infected with emotion now.

After a pause, he said, "You don't know that."

"Yes I do. Yes I bloody do. So do you."

"No, I don't. You can't know for sure; we can't know it for sure. Remember, Cyril took us in. Remember how grateful we were?"

"That was guilt that was. Rather proves the point don't you think? And I daresay he was glad to get a ready-made family, seeing as he couldn't make one for himself. Then he went and ruined it, spiteful bastard that he is."

"What? By telling you the truth?"

"Truth, lie. Why say anything? Ignorance is bliss, isn't it? But once I knew, how could I forgive him? Live under the same roof? Knowing what he had done to us? To you, to all of us? If we were back home you wouldn't be earning a living by having thugs try to hurt you, and I…and then he has the gall to start planning my life, interfering, as if I was something separate, not part of you and the rest, stealing me for himself, stifling. The man that destroyed our parents! My father he said!"

"But, if you want to look at it like that, you may as well hate our mother too. It's just life Miriam. It's the way of things: people aren't always faithful to each other. It's just life. It happens."

"Yes, and then other things happen. Consequences. In this case his selfishness caused the death of our parents. Can you forgive him for that?"

"Well, if you ask that, you may as well ask whether I can forgive her. It takes two to tango."

"Don't be crude!"

378

"I'm not. You don't blame mom for killing dad, then dying and us having to come here, do you? Of course you don't. So why be so hard on him? It's irrational. I can't understand it."

"You don't know what I've had to put up with. You don't know what I've gone through! You don't know me." She stood and walked away.

"Know you? What are you talking about? I've known you all my life."

"Have you? You've known somebody to run to when you hurt, or get hurt. Like when you nearly killed yourself coming off that horse, or that night when you turned up with that slut from the Hailstone."

"That was nothing – and don't call her that."

"Oh, sorry. Didn't want to hurt your feelings. It's all about you though isn't it? Always you, you, you. What about me, my feelings?"

"What feelings?"

The banal insensitivity of that made her throw the coffee jug at him, or at least in his direction. He stood sharply and shouted, "What the fff…"

She was in tears now, head in her hands; then she tried to run. But he caught her and held her to him and whispered to her, and stroked her hair. "Sorry, sorry, sorry…"

When she was calm he led her back to the table and sat her down, and sat with her.

"Looks like we're all out of coffee," he said. She managed an apologetic little half laugh. "Miriam, now I'm the one that's worried. Where's all this coming from? Please. Please tell me. You know I care, don't you?"

Through red rimmed eyes she looked at him then.

"I'm sorry. Sometimes…this life…"

"What do you mean? Miriam? What do you mean?"

Big sigh. "Abe, little rabbit, I'm as bad as Cyril. You know? I'm living a lie…"

"Of course you're not. I know we all get strange moods, God knows I've had a few of those myself recently. You're young, you wait until you've got young ones of your own to love. You'll have…"

A cry of anguish stopped him.

"Don't you ever listen? Don't you ever bloody listen? First thing – I don't love him…"

"God sis, we've been here before though, haven't we? I'm sure that we children kept our parents together…"

This time it was a slap which pulled him up short.

"I can't listen to that shit, not from you. Listen. No, sit there. Just listen. I'm going to tell you again: life is nothing but a game of charades. If you're lucky, you get to play it with someone you like. But that's rare. Most often you have to pretend, and hope that you'll start to believe one day that the pretence is real. As you say, I'm still young – but I'm on my second husband, with no kids to show for it. Why not? Hasn't the question ever formed itself in that beautiful head of yours? Well? Has it?"

"Well, I just thought, there's a time…"

"Yes, and it's gone. I'll say one thing about Wharton, he knows how to keep a confidence."

"What do you mean?" asked Abe, suddenly queasy.

"The miscarriage. I had a miscarriage Abe, when I was with John Henry. You knew about that."

"Yes, but…"

"But you never thought beyond that."

"What? But, you were fine. You told me, or Wharton. Wharton said you were fine."

"I didn't die he meant. I would recover. But there was more to it."

"I didn't think it was my place…"

"You've just said – we've known each other all our lives, yours at least. Of course it was your place."

"All right, I'm listening. I'm asking: tell me now."

"I can never have children Abe. Or at least it's highly unlikely. If it did happen…"

"What?"

"Nothing. It won't. There won't be any children for me, no consolation there. So enough of the trite platitudes."

"God, I'm sorry. I didn't know," he said. And he picked her up and hugged her, and made up his mind not to berate her about the poet, or even mention him. He still did not like the idea of her being friendly with him, but, he reasoned, she had enough on her plate.

At length she said, "I'd better clean up the mess," indicating the caking brown liquid and the coffee grounds, "before Mary gets back and thinks we've been fighting."

He smoothed down his ruffled thoughts. "Right, if you need me I'll be upstairs. I'll always be here, remember that. I don't care what Cyril says, it makes no difference: you are my sister." He had meant it as a parting reassurance, light-hearted but meaningful. But it elicited only more sighs.

"Bloody Cyril, that was his cruellest piece of work. Half-sister? Yes. Yes, I believe it, I do. Only half related, but half is enough."

"Well then, that's good isn't it?"

"Oh Rabbit, sometimes you can be so stupid."

#

It was only later, lying in his room, that one particular interpretation of what she had said occurred to him. Thinking on it, he knew he was right. And they had a problem.

#

Summer was in dispute with Autumn. It was intolerable to him that she was showing her face now, before her due time; precocious. It was against the natural order, this premature birthing of wind and rain.

But she was following her own imperatives, she had to test, to send out her scouts…

There would be a time when he must cede his temporary fiefdom, but not now; not yet. He had strength yet and would fight hard to expel the impertinent young upstart.

And so they did battle.

#

Although not particularly old, the big elm tree in the churchyard had had decades to establish itself, time to witness the comings and goings of many of the congregation, from baptism, to marriage, to committal of the dregs to the ground. It had an extensive root system, and that should have been enough to withstand any storm – except that it's anchoring to the earth was uneven, being precariously close to the embankment so that it's searching roots found no purchase on that side, or died, or were cut off. Also, unheeded, there had been a gradual settling and moving of soil as gravity and water shifted weight toward the cutting. Now, on top of days of rain, tonight's storm was a good windy one, and the elm held on for dear life.

#

The sergeant finished early, at one a.m., and made his way back towards the Royal Oak. The rain was gone, but he wore his long mackintosh regardless; easier than taking it off and carrying. The streets were not exactly quiet, they never were, but after rain and with everyone either abed or labouring the nightshift out of sight, everything seemed fresh and peaceful.

It was at times like this that he remembered that he could fly. When he remembered, he knew again that he had flown many times. Not so often these days, so that he was having to concentrate on his technique. Also, he knew that whatever happened next, the knowledge and the trick of it, his faith in himself, would be lost to him, perhaps tomorrow, perhaps next week. But soon. He always forgot. In the past he had tried to show others his gift: Miriam, friends in the village. But it was as if some spell attached to him which had rules which he was not allowed to know, for either they forgot too, or else he was prevented from floating as he wished in their presence.

But now, in this moment, he remembered. He knew exactly where he was in the street, and where he had just been and he knew that this was real. The gas lamp was real and solid, the horse dung real and smelly. Real. Right, he knew that if he now took three very deliberate steps, with just the right feeling, he knew that he would be – and there he was! Floating. Three feet off the ground. Levitation, some called it.

He knew that he had to concentrate: he folded his legs under him as if kneeling on a cushion, an invisible one. Four feet now, six. Without thinking about it he rose above the houses, shops and factories. It looked different from here, the wet rooftops with dribbles of sleep-time smoke from soot grimed chimneys and the bigger stacks belching red cindered black clouds, graphite blocks against the darkness; the skeletonised winding gear of the mines; and everywhere, stretching away, conflagration and stabs of molten light. But now, he was getting higher, wafted up, a feather on a breeze. But the higher he got, the more afraid he became, because at that altitude, he knew, a stray thought would propel him at a dizzying, uncontrollable speed. A deathly speed. Beginning to panic, he was gone like a bullet. Butterfly-belly breathless, falling to earth now, he made a grab for a low chimney. Her chimney. The little American witch person. Anchored now, and safe, he pulled himself down and lightly moved toward the front door. Bang! A loud popping bang. It was followed by a whoosh of air and a whirl of projected shards of blue light. It felt like they were cutting his skin. He halted. The lights were coming from the bottle tucked into the niche, a broken bottle. He was pushed back by the force of the whooshing air, a shower of blue sharpness still falling. But now, they bounced off his shoulders and hit the ground where they were transformed into small shrill furry things which scurried away. He went to step forward. The cat ran at him, but it was different. Not a real cat; not an everyday cat. No, it was the size of a large dog, leaping at him with amber-eyed hissing fury and murderous claw. Now he floated again, out of reach. But then, the bull-necked man appeared and threw a stone at him. It caught him in his manhood, and reminded him that he should be embarrassed, that he was naked under his night-shirt. The man picked up a stone as big as a football, and Abe went high and fast, out of control again. He managed to stop somewhere, mid-air, somewhere dark. He heard a sound, another anchor. Miriam's voice. The football stone flew over his head, followed by another, bigger, disappearing into the dark. He heard them, off set, rolling along, rumbling.

"Abe, where are you?" He flew to her.

"Get it off me," she gasped. One of the boulders had her trapped against a green sward. She held up her arms and he pulled at them. She was unhurt but she could not move, would not move despite his strength. As he pulled he noticed her breasts, he was pulling her out of her dress. He had no time to look, but he did look. And then another boulder trundled in. Abe sidestepped but it obscured his sister all the more, making it all the more difficult to budge her – he felt he would pull her arms off. And then another came, and another. Till only her voice remained:

"Get me out Abe. Get me up."

But it was not her now but Jack Beckett intruding, her husband, his voice. And the rumbles were more regular, knockings; a knocking.

"Abraham! Are you awake? You've got to get up."

"Stop. Go away. I'm trying...she's gone."

"Abe. Sergeant, you're wanted."

Knock, knock, knock.

"It's an emergency. Can you hear me?"

Urgent knocks, overlaid with more knocks. No, not knocks, rocks, rumbling. *No, not rocks, that's thunder. A thunderstorm.*

"Abraham?"

"What?"

"It's Jack. You're wanted."

"All right. Give me five minutes."

#

Constable Lively had been in charge of the desk when the summons came. He was the first policeman at the scene, and it was just light enough to make out what was happening on the tracks below. The line having been cleared of the previous day's debris, the authorities had cautiously reopened it with a view to making good in a more permanent fashion today. Unfortunately, today was too late, for yesterday's spilling had been but a precursor, and fair warning: the stray skull whose provenance had been debated by two police constables was but a macabre herald presaging more of the same. The warning had been taken, but action had not. Thus, sometime during the night, it seemed to Josh, probably toward dawn, during the storm which was only just blowing itself out, a goods train travelling out of Langley had ploughed into a much larger stack of mud and rubbish and remains from the graveyard, splitting and scattering coffins and spewing bodies in various states of decay all around the scene, posed as if depicting the suffering of the damned in a tableau of hell. A strange, only half-familiar smell of green mustiness oozed upwards and crept along the tracks.

As for the train, by dint of quick reactions brakes had been applied in time to prevent a derailment, and by dint of the skills of the driver and company banksmen, it was successfully shunted out of the mess. Well trained in emergencies, in no time that section of track had been closed, but commerce being no respecter of the dead and loathe to wait, forthwith a posse was sent to the Council House to request all possible aid in removing this unfortunate impediment to its inexorable march.

With the light had come curious pedestrians; a crowd was gathering. Some individuals tried to get themselves closer, onto the cutting, against the express instructions of the men from the G.W.R. The crowd grew. It is a known phenomenon that the bigger the crowd, the more normally law-abiding and sober folk feel inclined to challenge boundaries, disregard authority, and hide in the herd. Being an observant man, Archibald Plant, a ticket inspector with nothing currently to inspect save the situation, and fearing an altercation, had walked briskly as far as the police station to alert the law, which consisted at that present time of one Joshua Lively.

In turn and having assessed the situation, constable Lively lost no time in sending for reinforcements: Stride and Payne first, who had only finished their shift an hour earlier – a note left at the desk would apprise Salt and Clark when they next checked in, but that could be two hours away. The unlucky Payne and Stride would have to help out till then. And of course, the sergeant would have to be informed.

But for now, Josh was alone and hemmed in, his back against the bridge in the very spot from which old Reg had taken his tumble. Cheeky youngsters, unaccompanied it seems, were sneaking into the churchyard to get a better look. As Josh was pulled away to deal with one such incursion, so the crowd was able to get close to the parapet and, seeing what they saw, some climbed the fence on the other side of the tracks. Josh could only shout at them, clearing the churchyard with generous applications of the traditional and well-deserved clips around the ear. Then, he rushed out and back round to attempt to remove the other trespassers, older transgressors who ought to have known better, by way of threats of dire legal consequences. Then, more kids taking advantage and sneaking into the churchyard…

He felt like a puppet on strings, being yanked this way and that, and the frustration and the sheer physical exertion of it were evaporating his usual cool equanimity. As well as making a mockery of the law.

Fortunately for both Josh, and those that might have come within swiping distance, the cavalry arrived, a detachment of two, having hastily re-donned their uniforms.

"What the bloody 'ell's gooin on?" demanded Stride.

"Bit of an emergency situation, take a look," invited constable Lively, "all right everybody, stay back…"

"Bloody 'eck John, look at this," added Stride.

"Fucking spiders!" exclaimed P.C. Payne, "that cor be right. Is it? Is that? Ah con see coffins!"

"Calm down, and keep your voice down," said Josh. "Look, each of you take one end of the road where it passes over the line. Seal it off."

"Seal it off? What with?" remonstrated Stride.

"Why, with the power of your presence and the authority of the law of course."

"Speaking of which," interjected Payne, "where's the sergeant?"

"Now that you're here, I'll fetch him. He's probably in bed."

"Good for 'im," remarked Stride ruefully.

Josh turned his attention to the swirling body of townsfolk.

"Now, come on now, clear the area, on your way. Come on now, don't want to have to do you for obstruction. Oh, Daisy, not you, wait please," he said.

The assembly began to thin. People had a living to earn, after all. As always, some straggled.

"Come on now. Come on now please! Now move along. Move along! Nothing to see here."

"Except your dead relations maybe," muttered Payne, glad to be a Methodist.

"What if somebody needs to pass through here?" shouted Stride. He was struggling to restrain as tactfully as he knew how, on the one hand a shuffling toothless old man with saggy jowls and a saggy scowl, whilst on the other his left ear was being barraged by an even older and much louder old woman loaded to the armpits with an impossible looking collection of dusty bags no doubt containing bits of coal scavenged from some spoil heap. She looked a tough old bird, and Josh found time to grin at Stride's predicament.

"Tell them to go round. They'll have to go round," replied Josh, "now Daisy, hello."

The one-legged girl had crossed his path a few time since they had met for the first time at the station. They were on good terms, if only passing acquaintances.

"Hello constable. Josh."

"How have you been?"

"Cor grumble. Doh do any good any road."

"Good, good. Now look Daisy, you can do me a favour."

"Anythin' for yoh darlin," she said with a wink.

"Er, it's only a small one. I'd like you to take a message to the Royal Oak."

#

With Payne and Stride forming a rather thin cordon, Josh looked over the bridge and onto the tracks for a longer look. He saw at twenty yards distance the same pile of debris and mortal remains which had so shocked Payne; he saw clearly that the collapse had been greatly aggravated by the toppling of a big tree which had fallen inwards, leveraging out and displacing a surprisingly large wedge of soil together with whatever it had contained. And it had contained, that he could make out, juxtapositioned in the general jumble, nine, possibly ten coffins or parts thereof, spewed out of the rain-soaked ground, claimed by gravity, and deposited at the bottom of the cutting. But then, one in particular; one in particular was not like the rest; not covered at least partially, or almost completely, with soil and stones and gravel; not intact or with but minor holes or cracks so that the contents could be seen so indistinctly that the suggestion of the presence of anything that had once been human could be simply and mercifully attributed to imagination. No, for as he let his eyes wander from the main body of wreckage, onto the bank, halfway down, now he could see another. One of particular garishness: the coffin had come to rest mid-slope, apparently snagged; its lid had become disconnected, lying neatly to one side, as if the occupant had awoken from a slumber and casually opened the door, in sure and certain hope of the resurrection to come – which had indeed come – but then closed his eyes and decided to have a lie in. Or her eyes: Josh thought that the blue-black remnant of what looked like plastered down fabric was probably once a dress. Long hair, or the fine groping roots of some plant searching for nourishment filled the top of the box, so that the face was only to be observed indistinctly. It was sickening, sad, and scary all at the same time.

"Crikey. Looks like all hell's broken loose!"

#

The sergeant's first order was to Payne and Stride: to get down to the Council House and make sure that they understood the scale of the problem and sent as many sappers as possible as soon as possible, and spades and shovels and tarpaulins, and then get themselves back off to bed. The tarps would be needed to cover the modesty of the dead from the gaze of the quick and the curious, once the exterred cubicles, their rotting pieds a terre, had been extricated and placed to one side. They might also be fashioned to screen the scene from the road. In the meantime, Clark and Salt had replaced the two off-duty conscripts at the incident.

"What the bloody 'ell's appnin' rahnd 'ere?" said Clark to himself, but loudly.

The sergeant jumped on it.

"What do you mean?"

"Well, ah mean. It's odd ay it. Spooky even."

"It was the storm. What's spooky about that?"

"Why now? Why now eh? That's whar Ah say. We've 'ad the fuya under the church in Netherton, murders, stabbings. Just in a few wicks. Ah mean, why 'ere an' all? Where old Reg fell – or was pushed. P'raps it was the Devil pushed 'im. Cor all be coincidence connit? Like ah said, spooky."

The sergeant listened to that, and heard something else. The voice was back, prompting him.

"So, you think something bad's come to town do you Gordon?" asked he, "something unnatural."

The manner of asking, as if with a cold certainty of the answer sent a chill through P.C. Clark. Nothing to do with the cool breeze that was chasing away the rain and announcing that it would soon be autumn, when the leaves fall and fruits ripen and decay, and the damp soaks ague into old bones and infuses pneumonia into soot laden old lungs.

More calmly now, Clark replied.

"Summat's cum to tahn, an' wharrever it is, it bay no good. An' it started right 'ere, there, where we fahnd the owd mon."

And I saw that bloody bird.

"Don't blame the bird. It's only a messenger. It was meant to warn you. But you never listen. You do not listen," said the third party, aloud.

Because you talk in riddles.

"No. You do not listen."

Bloody tell me then. "Bloody plain English."

"What?" said Clark.

"Nothing. Go and help Josh with that horse."

#

"Don't give me that Rupert. That's what you said last week. Do I get my money? Or do I have to take my pound of flesh?" William Arrowsmith drew aside his jacket to reveal the rosewood handle of his double-edged knife.

Rupert Hill had seen that blade in action, and it was not for peeling potatoes, he knew that. Apples more like – Adam's apples. Arrowsmith knew enough of Hill's usual tricks not to fall for them, and he, Hill, therefore knew that he could not afford to ignore this threat. But neither could he pay. How to play for time?

"I've told you. I don't keep that sort of money on me. You can hurt me all you like, kill me. But that won't get you into the bank, figuratively or literally."

"I know, but you could pay off some of the interest in blood. I might enjoy that."

"My dear Alan," began Hill, feigning an insouciance which he hoped would reassure 'Hale' rather than provoke him, "are we going to let a little thing like money ruin our relationship?"

"Money is our relationship. Now, what will it be? The knife? A bullet? Bludgeoned to death? If I were an old-fashioned highwayman I might be saying 'your money or your life.' But I'm not, so I'll just say pay up you stinking rat!"

"Keep your voice down. Do you want the whole inn to hear?"

"What? Do you mean the deaf decrepit old landlord or the two feeble-minded yokels pickling themselves in cider? They wouldn't notice if a bomb went off. So I repeat," and he very deliberately raised his voice, "where's my fucking money?"

"All right, keep your voice down," responded Hill nervously, "look, I understand your frustration, I really do…"

"No, you look. I did my job, helping you get those so-called investors on board for your pie in the sky scheme…"

"It's not pie in the sky," protested Hill, "I told you – unexpected survey problems means we have to raise another…"

"You said it was a legal thing."

"Same thing. It's all connected. It's just a question of time. All we need is one more new shareholder. One more small contribution will open the doors for us to make thousands."

"I don't believe it."

"It's true…"

"No, I don't believe it. I don't believe you, your cheek. You've swallowed your own bullshit you have. Regurgitating it doesn't make it any different, it's still the same old bullshit. So don't think I can't see it. A banker might call it 'highly speculative', and a

387

card player might be willing to take a gamble. But remember, I know it for what it is, which is a total humbug."

"No, you're quite wrong there you know…"

"Wait a minute. Are you trying to cozen me now? Because it's the last thing you will do…"

"I assure you."

"Cut it out. Who do you think you are dealing with here? I'll tell you what's going to happen, you and I, being directors of this august company, are going to sign a cheque made out to 'cash' and we are going to empty the account and disappear. Shouldn't be difficult seeing as we didn't use our proper names."

"I told you, that was just insurance; you know, just in case."

"Of course it was. So? How about it?"

"What about Lively?"

"Lively?"

"I told you. He's kicking up. I think he's suspicious."

"Of what? You just intimated that this thing was a legitimate enterprise! You're talking out of your arse you are, believing your own fucking fantasies. Alternatively," he added with a particularly piercing look, "you're thinking that you can pull the wool with me like you have with these other fools."

"No, of course not. It's not that at all," replied Hill in diplomatic tone, "and yes, given the way things have turned out, the things we are still finding out…I think you're right – we should take the money and run. It's just that, if we do it now, the bank won't let us draw down against the agreed advance, not unless…"

"You mean we can't touch the borrowings till the surveyors come back with a glowing report. Yes?" interrupted Arrowsmith.

"You've hit the nail on the head, yes."

"But the funds we raised are still sat there in the account. I hope?"

"Well, yes, of course, less the legal and survey fees and…"

"So why wait? We both know that the odds of that report not advising that that field is economically unworkable are thin as a whisker. Let's face it, the jig's up. And if our investors get wind of it, well, need I say more?"

"If you put it like that, I'll fetch the cheque book."

"Good, now, what about Lively exactly?"

Hill measured his response carefully. He saw a chance to both get rid of the thorn in his side that was Gabriel Lively, and to have some future control over his unpredictable partner.

"Well, for one, he's been looking into your Sir Mortimer alias, and he's finding it wanting. He's talking about lawyers, and the police; writing letters to Parliament for God's sake, he even asked me if I had checked with Burke's Peerage about 'Sir Mortimer.' We've got to shut him up."

"He's your problem. He never met me."

"He wants his money back. Our money."

"Oh…"

"Exactly. Says he's changed his mind. Sounds to me like his wife has changed it for him, moaning about how he's always arguing with her over it."

"It's always a bad idea to let women have a say. Once they get started they never shut up. No, an obdurate woman, that sounds bad."

"That's what I'm trying to tell you. We've got to shut him up."

"You mean I've got to shut him up."

"More your area of expertise than mine…I'll make it worth your while."

"I want double."

"Agreed."

Arrowsmith took his time, gazing off into the distance and the future, weighing risks, considering options. At length:

"Well then. You leave our pal Gabriel up to me. A toast! To green fields and suckers new!"

#

Back in Blackheath, and the 1880s, by dinner time a dozen burly no-nonsense council road diggers had made a start in clearing the track and segregating the dead for later re-interment; a repatriation; an extradition to the jurisdiction of the weigher of souls to await judgement day – the storm had merely been a false alarm, a false hope.

But the clear-up was all proceeding very satisfactorily as far as sergeant Lively was concerned. He needed an excuse to vacate the area: it stank of something that he could not smell; his skin crawled and his ears buzzed to the sound of the voice. With the arrival of help from Worcestershire constabulary, to wit two constables from the Nimmings under the somewhat dubious direction of an erratic Reverend Hodgetts he took his chance. He had intended to go home, to resume his conversation with Miriam. But the more he thought about it the more unsure he was about what he would say, and the nearer to the Oak that he got, the more nervous. He chickened out. He would rather face Spring Heeled Jack. No, not him, not as such. But, yes, it was about time he took control. The witch had proved it was possible. Hadn't his…his what? Companion? Tormentor? Protector? Imp? Hadn't it been stilled by her? Until a couple of hours ago at any rate. And, he now had the stone.

So, no. Not home. Instead, he resolved to get to the top of Portway Hill, where he had first met this thing. Perhaps he could also lose it there, should he wish to.

Passing Portway Hall, the Four Ways, licensee William Rose esq., in front of him. It looked like Rose had stretched a point and opened early, or else the drunk making a nuisance of himself in the street outside had a poor head for last night's drink. The man was obviously the worse for wear, alternately muttering then shouting execrations at some absent third party, lost in his own head, oblivious even of the approaching uniform until the last seconds.

"What appears to be the problem, sir?" asked the policeman in a neutral policeman kind of way.

"Problem? Whad'ya mean? Ay gorra problem."

"No? Well if you don't desist and move on you will have a problem. Am I clear?"

"De-wah'? Cor a mon 'ave a, 'ave a, 'ave a, bir'of a sing? Cor a mon be 'appy? Yoh'm miserable yoh am."

"That's it! Shut up and go home. Now. Or I'll arrest you."

"No, ah'll just rest 'ere," declared the drunk, depositing himself atop a large rock which had no doubt originated in the adjacent quarry.

"No you won't. Get going."

"Ah'm just waitin' for me – hic – mate. Ah'll sit quiet."

"Too late for that, get up!"

"Yoh gonna mek me?"

It might have been comical, but Abe was in no mood for frippery. Or insolence. Forthwith, he grabbed the man by the wrist and elbow and levered him standing, roughly. He tried to wriggle free. Too vigorously for Abe's liking, with no respect for the uniform or the man, and the drink was no excuse. The copper's right fist took the wind out of his sails, and lungs, and Abe took the drunken arm again and pushed it up the offender's back, propelling along in the general direction…

Then, the drunk did what drunks are prone to do, especially after a punch to the solar plexus: he threw up. The copper had been expecting it.

"You pissed up pratt. You've got it all over you now. Well, allow me."

The policeman forced him to the watering trough, pushed him to his knees, and ducked the profane and stinking head. He let the man up, who began to struggle violently, most likely in sheer panic, although the copper could not be sure of that. "Not learned your lesson have you?" he said and ducked him again. And held him down. Next time when he came up the water had dissolved away all his fight. Limp and half drowned he could only cough and wretch. When the sergeant released him, he flopped onto the ground like a badly tossed pancake. He wasn't moving much. Not at all.

"Oy!" The copper booted his backside, "don't come that." No movement. "Get up," growled Lively, and kicked again. From the speed with which the drunken man reacted, he had been shamming. That earned him another kick, and one more for luck. The man began to shamble his way toward Tippity Green.

As the copper began his ascent of the lane sounds from the pub followed him. Nothing to do about it: a pub full of them, half-drunk ne'r do wells; not worth the effort in any case, sad bastards. Besides, as he now deciphered, the rowdy commentary was not all bad. Evidently a bipartisan crowd, the drunkard must have had both friends and

390

enemies, for there were cheers amongst the boos, also whistling and clapping, which he chose to interpret as an endorsement of his policing style.

"Somebody appreciated that." The voice was here. With an explanation under his belt now of what it was, Abe did not feel so silly listening to it, did not feel that letting it in would make him vulnerable, to madness. He now knew that he was not at all mad – asinine idea! It would never have come to him if he hadn't been preoccupied with hen-witted women. It went on.

"And you enjoyed it."

"It's my job," he replied as naturally as if he was talking to a real person. Not that this wasn't real of course, just that it was invisible, and not a person of course…

"Why didn't you arrest him?"

"Better things to do. Immediate punishment for his transgression: you don't train a dog not to foul the house by clouting him half an hour after the deed's done. Best thing for him, not wasting my time or that of my men putting him in a cushy cell. There's too much of this low-level insolence going on. Good bit of physical intervention's the answer. They'll think twice before pushing it again, or promoting themselves in the criminality rankings. No, it's all good."

"But still, you enjoyed it, you followed your instinct. What's wrong with that? It's what men do: if you're thirsty, you don't deny yourself drink when it's there; you take food when you're hungry. It's the way it is. Your instincts are good, you should follow them."

"Except there are rules; laws."

"Rules are just generalisations for ordinary people. Why should they apply to the out of the ordinary?"

"To me you mean?"

"Most certainly I do. You're above the ordinary, surely. That's why I'm talking to you."

"I think, I know that I'm somewhat different, I'll grant you."

"There you are then!"

By now they were back to where Abe had first dozed under the weary old hawthorn, and that bird had found him.

"This is where we met," remarked the creature, "I recognise it through your eyes."

"Where you latched onto me," corrected the man. He had taken the green stone from its wrapping and gripped it tightly.

"You don't mean that. You accepted me. You knew I could help you."

"Help me how?"

"Well, look at yourself. Your eyes are open, your ears are open, your mind is opened. You know more than their narrow little world. Some men would give their all for a mere glimpse of me. A gift to you which they search for in vain in their science and in their churches – but few are worthy. For what is mankind that God should care for them? Has He not made him lower than the angels?"

Those words, Abe knew, he had heard before. But they didn't ring true coming from what he had come to think of his companion.

"You're not an angel."

"Am I not? What's an angel?"

"it's…it's a big thing with wings."

"I've got wings."

"I said a big thing, with big wings. I hardly think a robin's wings count."

"Don't confuse the postman with the letter-writer. You want big wings?"

And suddenly the man was rooted to the spot, and his sight was dimmed and a cold downpour as if of rain, but no rain only cold, drenched his head and percolated down through his every bodily fibre, cooling him and pinning him, freezing him in place, turning him into something that could feel but never move, like the old hawthorn. The creature was behind him; he felt it was behind him. He could not turn toward it, would not turn toward it. But it cast a huge shadow now, it cast a huge shadow like a man, but then, gradually, spreading silent shadow wings ten feet across.

Abe felt like a pigeon, pinned to the ground by a sparrowhawk – he was not about to let her start plucking. The green stone began to warm him. He fought back. "You're not a bloody angel! Let me go!"

"I'm doing nothing, you're doing it yourself. I was merely revealing myself to you. You panicked, that's all. I'm disappointed in you. I only want to help you."

"You said that before," Abe was now, quite suddenly, able to move. He whipped around, but only a voice remained.

"Where are you? Hiding?"

"I'm here, but if looking at me affects you so much, I prefer to remain hidden."

"Do you? What are you really hiding from? If you're an angel?"

"I'm not an angel."

"You just said you were. The witch was right. You're not to be trusted."

"It's your head that you cannot trust. I never said I was an angel, you merely assumed. I would never say that."

"What are you then?"

"A friend. Looking for a friend. For you Abraham. I feel I can call you that. And you, please, call me Jack. That name seems to have stuck."

"What did you just do to me?"

"Nothing, it was your fear. At seeing me. You won't be afraid next time."

"Next time?"

"Yes. I can help you."

"And again I ask, how?"

"What is it that you most want?"

392

Abe was not ready to reveal all. "Promotion would be nice."

The creature, Jack, seemed to ponder a while.

"All right. I can promise you this, that you will be elevated before the year is through. Then perhaps you will trust in me."

"And what do you demand in return?"

"Why nothing. Demand? I demand nothing. But if you accept me, as a friend, then perhaps one day you might be minded to do a friend a favour. No?"

"Have you no other friends?"

"Alas no. Perhaps only enemies I fear. As you may have gathered, I'm not from around here. I'm far from home, not lost exactly, but I cannot go back. One day, maybe, with luck, one day," replied Jack with an air of such pathetic desolation that Abe was tempted to believe it. Then he lost consciousness.

Chapter 26

Dudley Wake and a Fight

Miriam had decided to keep herself busy. Custom was not particularly brisk. It never was on a weekday, in the day; not till six, when lots of factory hands traditionally knocked off and miners downed tools and emerged from their subterranean labours. She had Marlene of course, but was making a point of serving herself, perhaps exchanging a few words with regulars across the counter. A few words. That's what had done it, all it took. She couldn't take them back and she dreaded her next encounter with Abe. Had he realised? That what she felt for him was not precisely the love of a sister for a brother? A half-brother. Half-brother? Perhaps that accounted for it. Which half was she attracted to, with an unnatural attraction? Because that's what they call it, your vicars and priests and upright citizens. What did they know? What did they know of the bond she shared with Little Rabbit, since they were small? What did they know?

And what would Abe say? Would he be angry? Indifferent? Judgemental? Or pleased?

And she hated Cyril. Hated him for opening this wound, cutting right across that childhood scar and giving it new meaning. New possibility, new pain. But, it had healed again, as wounds do if life is to go on; if you are alive. And she had learned to accept that this life could never be perfect, and that the world is casually cruel. Jesus knows that this place brought that home to anybody who bothered to open their eyes. Anybody who dared.

So, she had learned to accept her lot with a man whom she had respected, and was learning to love. But gluttonous death had wanted him and felt nothing beyond that appetite. Therefore, she had started again, as needs must, wearing a new mask for the world. She had auditioned for a better part, nevertheless Mrs Beckett it was and she had settled on giving a good performance. Until she had opened her mouth. A few words. They might turn her life upside down. Or not.

Smith, the young poet, self-styled, was diverting a fellow drinker, a visiting man of commerce, to be sure, with some disputatious views wrapped in a softer covering of romanticised language. Today's theme appeared to be on the essence of existence for what he called the 'working classes.' Miriam listened in, although careful to ensure that the garrulous polemicist did not catch her eye. He had been visiting regularly, mostly during daylight, with an uncanny knack of not being about when Abe was – one small mercy. More than gradually, the surface veneer of charm had dulled and worn thin enough to see through, and what she saw she did not like. She had had little truck with poets in her life, not in the flesh, so perhaps, although she doubted it, perhaps his affectation and the offhand, almost contemptuous manner in which he held forth on the most serious of subjects was typical. But if it was, she wanted none of it, just his custom, if she must. So, she exchanged the usual landlord and customer banalities, and took his money if not his compliments. She saw him now as Sissy had first seen him, and was more than happy to follow Abe's prohibitions where this character was concerned. Abe…Not wanting her mind to wander, she was eavesdropping:

The businessman had been staying at the Handel Hotel. She knew that because, for one, she recognised the businessman type, this one having a way of talking that she took for American, and for another, a porter from the Handel had deposited the man's luggage in a corner and had been tipped, evidently from his expression handsomely, for the service. It was not unusual for such travellers to make the Oak their final stop for a drop of what was a superior on account of it being meticulously well-kept ale, and on account that right outside was the regular stop for cabs to the railway station. The conversation had soon established that the businessman – a bespectacled and proud-standing gentleman, handsome in a hawkish and mature kind of way, with neatly trimmed hair and beard, and a pipe from which emanated a most peculiar aroma – not normal tobacco, it reminded her of something, horse liniment, yes – had been on a tour of various factories, potential business partners, suppliers or buyers, in Birmingham and Tipton and most recently, completing his peregrinations, of the premises of Messrs. Albright and Wilson, in Oldbury. He did not volunteer the nature of his business. Why should he? He was merely killing time with a stranger, after all. But the stranger…his story was not in tune with the one he had told when he had first arrived in these parts, which made the landlady distrust him the more…

They seemed to have drifted into choppy waters on the subject of religion:

"Don't talk to me about the Church. All your priests and vicars, they're well-educated men, in the main – ought to know better. What sane, civilised, educated man believes in all that hocus-pocus, eh? I mean, it's a heck of a lot to swallow, an invisible, 'supernatural' being that listens to you, your prayers, and looks after you. Looks after? Cares? Take a look around. If I were the all-mighty father of these poor folk, I'd damn well make sure life was a lot better. What father wouldn't? So, all the poverty, suffering, what's the big idea? I'll tell you, it's not a big idea, it's not an idea at all, nobody's big idea, certainly not the part of a plan of any omnipotent and caring father that makes any sense to me. Because he does not exist. But no, don't face up to logic, do what the Church does, and bury your head in the sand like one of those ostrich critters. What's their answer, the clergy, what's their response to suffering? I'll tell you: jam, that's what, jam tomorrow. Fiddlesticks. There is no tomorrow. When you're dead, you're dead. And the dead don't eat any damn jam."

Like a well fed and content carp, the poet did not rise to the bait. "I take it that you're a rationalist then?"

"You might say that. I'm a scientist my boy, and proud of the fact. And of course, it doesn't end with this omnipotent God, then they've invented the devil and all his works – good excuse that one – and all his demons, and don't forget angels. And all flitting around completely unseen and unheard, undetectable except by the insane, and getting the credit for all manner of circumstantial good fortune, or the blame for some harmful happen-chance. It's all hokum of course, but men are cowards. They shy away from responsibility for their own actions; the Church encourages it, and knows it's going to get away with it – and why slaughter the goose that lays the golden egg, eh? Hypocrites, the lot of them."

"Surely you can't tar them all with the same brush?"

"Yes I can. Or perhaps, no, you're right. I'll have two brushes, one for hypocrites and one for the terminally stupid."

Not forgetting cowards of course, thought Thompson.

"No, make that three, I forgot the cowards," corrected the American.

"I was brought up as a Catholic," confessed Thompson at this point.

"Well, I can't blame you for that my boy. Can't visit the sins of the fathers, or however that goes. As long as you've seen the light since."

"Oh, I'm getting there, believe me. But tell me, you being a scientist, can't science admit to powers, forces of nature if you like, that exist but which science has not yet found a way of detecting, let alone explain."

"Ah, I see what you're up to. Very crafty. Still a streak of Christian in you is there? You're obviously not a man of science, otherwise you would realise how fully science has mapped our world, and why it's technology that dominates it. Technology and commerce of course. No, unfortunately, the more we discover, the more we must come to admit that there is no proof for the existence of God, simply because God is an illusion. Haven't you heard? God is dead."

"The majority of people would disagree with you."

"The majority of people are wishful thinkers."

"Doesn't wishful thinking have a force? Doesn't all thought, and emotion, have a power?"

"That's a different thing," the American pointed out.

"Yes. And no. Let me give you an example. I have the mind and inclination of a poet," and Thompson delicately indicated his person with a graceful gesture designed to somehow illuminate the refined sensibilities within, "intuitive, artistic rather than scientific, although I feel I should mention in passing that scientific enquiry is not alien to me, having once trained as a surgeon. But that's in the past, I mention it only to illustrate the point that I have been a scientist, but still admit of the possibility of things which you say science denies. I have been on both sides of the fence, as it were. Now, when you think of poets, you may think of some fuzzy headed dreamer going on about seasons of mists and mellow fruitfulness, of clouds wandering aimlessly and pissing on daffodils, or of some love-struck fool extolling the beauty of his mistress' eyebrow, or of some other insignificant part of some insignificant woman's anatomy. I'm not in that mould. I have deeper insight, and I happen to express it in poetry. Currently, as I said, I am contemplating the purpose and power of life and death: death in particular; its allure, the urge to understand it. And, forgive me if I disagree with you, but I think religion helps with that quest, till science catches up at least."

The businessman was about to object but Thompson was in full spate.

"The idea of death, the fear and the fascination, the urge to get close, to understand, but not too close, is buried in all of us. In my work I aim to bring it all to the surface, to trap it in words, in imagery. I myself see Death clearly, I am becoming an intimate acquaintance, you might say. I see him around here, all over, and I know he likes it here…"

"Oh, come now, this is a mere flight of fancy."

"No, bear with me, let me finish. I'm looking through the eyes of a poet remember. It's how I recognise him, imagine him…see him. And guess what? He is like me, an artist. He is an artist. The modern world has enabled him to find new modes of expression for his art."

"I think I know what you're getting at. You're giving him some kind of allegorical role. Like in Pilgrim's Progress?"

"Well, yes, and no. I mean, not exactly…But yes, of course, yes, an allegory, as you say. An unfolding story, of discovery."

"So what have you got so far?"

"Oh, I'm still doing some, er, research. But everything leads back to the inevitable, to death. What happens thereafter…"

"Which is nothing. Nothing happens thereafter."

"Shall we just agree to say that it's a mystery at present…"

"Not in my book," muttered the American.

"…but that one day a mortal may pierce the veil – by employing just the empirical method you advocate."

"Who are you, Victor Frankenstein? That's not real science. It's fiction. An impossibility."

"As far as we know in our imperfect knowledge, but we don't know everything do we? Not everything, surely?"

"I would have to concede that. But if we did, how did you put it? Penetrate the veil, it would be the end of your religion. Blind faith religion at any rate."

"Oh I dare say blind faith in the God of priests would merely be replaced by blind faith in the God of science. But death remains the great mystery, and I want to get closer. I am befriending Death, in my own way; growing closer to him."

"As are we all. So how do you picture this phantom, in your piece?"

"Exactly as that. A phantom, like smoke, hiding in it, changing shape and form, but able to move things, people, and disappear. This place gives him the best possible opportunities to practise his art."

"His art?"

"That's killing of course, the art of despatch in all its possible forms."

"Ah," said the American, "an inevitable human vice, and a wasteful one. And yet, I guess, there is an art in it, or a skill, or at least there can be. The art of a swordsman for instance, of the duellist. I would even grant you that there can be a kind of honour, nobility even, in personal combat. But we don't fight with horse and lance these days, and killing, or should I say the ability to kill, has now become much more efficient, a purely functional instrument of state policy, and it's based on technology, on the bomb and the artillery shell and the gun. So, you see, your Death is rather a scientist than an artist. A craftsman at best."

"You're confusing the artist with his instruments. Men are the just the instruments. My point is that an artist, such as myself, can appreciate that witnessing death or destruction, and the result, can affect the soul, touch another layer of consciousness. That's art to me. I know what you mean about modern warfare, but surely the greatest shock, stimulus to the mind, accompanies the greatest destruction. Do you know, there's all sorts of weapons today for killing on a mass scale, cannon, mortars and stuff? They've even got guns that shoot out bullets at the rate of hundreds in a minute."

The businessman chuckled, "Terrible, terrible. It's six hundred by the way. Six hundred rounds per minute."

"You're very well informed."

"I read a lot."

"Yes, well, six hundred. I'd like to see that."

"What? Fired in anger? Mass slaughter? Really? No, it will never happen, and I will tell you why: with all of these frighteningly efficient weapons, with which all civilised nations are equipping themselves by the way, you can virtually guarantee that all of them will be too scared, mutually terrified, to go to war."

"What about the uncivilised nations?"

"What?"

"The ones that can't afford these weapons?"

The American could only shrug, and swiftly move on, "they have nothing to worry about. I repeat, these new weapons are going to prevent wars, at least serious ones."

"Mutual fear guaranteeing peace is it?"

"Exactly."

"Like threatening a dog with a stick. A fearful dog will just as often bite out of fear than cower."

"Men are not dogs."

"Maybe so, maybe Man is another kind of cur…but Death will have his way. You give him the tools, these guns —yes, machine guns is it? – these machine guns and artillery, and men of course, and he will find a way to use them. To kill, to add to his flock. Humans are his pawns."

"You're back to your poetic fancy now I hope, otherwise it's just rubbish you're talking." The American seemed to be losing his patience with the other's ramblings.

"You're probably right. War would be insane, given the consequences, and I'm never likely to experience it. But, I'll tell you what, there's no shortage of inspiration around here."

"I can imagine."

"Ah, but can you though? Death. I have seen him stalking the streets and the factories and towing paths, day and night, great claws and crocodile headed; always looking to punish a man's mistakes, human imperfections, remorseless agent of the fall; he turns the wheels of mighty machines, machines for crushing stones, for rolling with titanic power vast chunks of obdurate iron and steel, and feeds them, by way of a change, the bodies of men, mashing up human flesh and blood and bones, transformed into something unrecognisable, hideous; and he pours out amber molten metal, fatally dashing it over those attempting its mastery; then again like a will o' the wisp, he will settle deftly on a man's shoulder, overbalancing him into a tumble and a fiery furnace, as a second Nebuchadnezzer; or he mangles under railway waggon wheels; as miners ascend and descend into pits, to earn their daily bread, he snips the ropes and breaks the chains; and every once in a while, he lets fall a few tons of iron or coal on some unhappy band of labourers – or any other material as might suit his fancy; he blows up his victims down dark mines, or traps them there to drown, squeezing out the air and life, as a fearful gargantuan anaconda; job done, he surfaces, and slithers to the misty banks of tortuous canals and streams, and on dark nights, in the sad small hours, when a man has had a drop too much, wending his unsteady way back to hearth and home, he drags him in and smothers him in four feet of muddy water; as a blood-sucking leach, or a dreadful spider, he slowly slurps the life from women and children, and smears on them a variety of poxes, or consumes them with consumption. His methods are eclectic, his choice diverse. Our constant companion. Death."

"You've been practising that, haven't you?"

"Just a little, yes."

"Have you always been so cheerful?"

"I do have my moments."

"Well, you have quite an imagination there, son," said the businessman, puffing a cloud toward the poet with what might have been growing distaste.

"I wouldn't disagree with you," replied Thompson modestly, "what's that you're smoking anyway? It's not tobacco, is it?" His curiosity was piqued by the prospect of some fresh narcotic.

"No, not entirely. My own concoction. I find that it helps keep my chest loose."

"Nothing else?" enquired the other hopefully.

The American took his meaning immediately. *It's little wonder your capacity for logical thought is compromised.*

"No, no," he replied aloud, "nothing like that. Herbs you know. Medicinal."

"Oh."

"You seem to care a lot for the local working folk. Yet, you're not one of them…"

"What? Care? No, not in particular."

"But you seem so attuned to their suffering."

"I am, I suppose, but in a detached way – in a scientific way if you like! They're just objects of study. That's not what you would think of as caring. Do you care for the sheep that died to give you your mutton broth? Not at all, I'll wager, because I don't. And yet such an animal has done more for me, to sustain me, than these human creatures all around me. You accuse me of caring? I don't. Why should I?"

"You're a Christian."

"And they are all sinners."

"And there we have it, another Christian hypocrite. Sir, I no longer care to engage in this conversation."

"I would remind you sir, that mortality itself is sinful. But you wouldn't understand that. Good day." *Small minded bastard.*

As the businessman rose the indelicate question of where to now put himself whilst awaiting his cab was forestalled by the cabbie himself, who stepped in and announced:

"Cab for Mr Maxim."

"Here," volunteered the American, hurriedly gathering his things.

"Thanks for the drink," remarked the poet sourly, raising his almost empty glass to the receding figure.

The American nodded to the landlady on the way out, "Ma'am."

No, Abe had been right. There was something not right about this one. Something off. If not something outlandish. If not something dangerous. Miriam would avoid him in future, perhaps even bar him? Or Marlene would have to serve him.

#

The little retainer wearing the smart black and grey livery seemed to have lost somebody in the larger crowd that was flocking into the grounds of Dudley castle on that Bank Holiday Monday. Somebody named Jack. "Jack," he would cry, for the call to be taken up by another of the regular adherents – "Jack. Where's Jack?" And then by several

400

and diverse individuals at once, losing patience now it seemed, but not their good temper; a gentle chiding, almost wistful.

"Jack? Jack! Jack, Jack, Jack."

Then more voices, fresh voices, mocking, throwing caution to the winds, singing out now with an irrepressible, unabashed joie de vivre, "Jack! Jack! Yack-Yack!"

Miss Ricketts laughed out loud, "I've told you! I haven't seen your Jack. Have you seen Jack, Jack?" she asked of one of the swirling Jackdaws, whose individuality was immediately absorbed by the flock as he, as they, climbed and swooped and swirled in the clattering of indistinguishable corvids, teasing each other now, it seemed:

"Jack!" one would announce.

"Jack?" asked another, "no, I'm Jack..."

"No, Jack, that's me," cried yet another. It was a joke the birds shared. They all laughed,

"Jack, Jack, ja ja jack, ack ack ack," they went.

"No," shouted Miss Ricketts after them, "this is Josh, not Jack. Say it! Say Josh, Josh, Josh," she repeated in a commendable approximation of the call of Corvus Monedula.

Joshua Lively was laughing too. "They'll be throwing you into a home for the feeble minded if you carry on talking to birds. Anyway, it was Jake they were calling after, they told me."

"You may be right there. But don't they just lift your heart? I swear it's worth coming to the wake just to see these little characters again."

The little characters agreed. "Jac, Jac, Jac," they all shouted down.

Come on you two, urged Frank Lively, you're blocking the gangway.

There were five of them: Josh Lively and Miss Ricketts with young Jake Collins, and Frank Lively with his latest female acquaintance, a raven-haired beauty of all of four feet ten by the name of Jean Murphy. It was Bank Holiday Monday 1887 and the day of the annual and eagerly awaited Dudley Wake.

The old castle hosted the proceedings. Founded on a high defensive position by a follower of the Conqueror, it had been added to over the warring generations so that by the time of the Civil War it was a very imposing statement of power in stone, although already becoming archaic even then in terms of modern warfare. The parliamentarians and then a fire in 1750 transformed the castle into what it was today: an uninhabited ruin. But a grand one, with its formidable keep a landmark for miles around, and dominating the old bailey yard, the focus of the celebrations today. The edifice stood in its own grounds largely uncontaminated by the industrialised ugly architecture that was crammed and wedged into every available space in the vicinity. Although the smoke and smut and noxious emissions did not respect boundaries, even of rich men, in the grounds and the castle courtyard, elevated as was necessitated by ancient considerations of defence, the air was cleaner and the atmosphere happy. And the respite purchased by the property

401

boundaries meant that, unlike in the town, wildlife, like the jackdaws, had retained a footing, had held on for Nature against the tyranny of Man's rape and torture of their mother. Nevertheless, it had never been an easy life. Nature herself was callous, had to be callous: a mother's heart can only stand so much. The happy cries which gave Miss Ricketts so much pleasure were perhaps a measure more of her perception of happiness in a sound than a measure of that emotion within the birds themselves, for, some would say, how can such a thing ever be measured? What the birds were actually thinking and communicating must surely be known only to themselves. That said, however, and it having to be admitted that these little corvids were by no means unintelligent creatures, would it not be reasonable to assume that they had understood full well that this particular gathering of humans meant food, easy pickings? And if their concomitant excitement at the prospect was not the equivalent of happiness, if those little things were not in fact happy, then might not pigs fly?

So, with one imagines a kind of wary anticipation, and yes, today at least, of happiness, they sat on battlements, and glided and whirled and vocalised – and kept their little eyes open!

Below, the Livelys, their consorts, and Jake Collins had passed through the old gate house, through the double wall and passed unscathed under the antique murder holes. Behind them, a relentless pressure as precipitate day-trippers, determined to enjoy themselves, were disgorged from assorted modes of carriage: gigs, waggonettes, carts, cabs for posh folk, or arrived on foot, making their way perhaps from the canal and a boat awaiting their return; the wake sucked them in from miles around. These regiments of one day conscripts were even now surging upwards, a latter-day New Model Army assaulting the faithful old walls. On this occasion, of course, the old timer had surrendered without a qualm, and opened the bailey gates…

Where their capacity for adventure was challenged and assailed with invitations to try their hands at various games of chance or skill or strength: shooting little tin plate ducks, bruising little brown heads with frizzy hair at the coco nut shies, throwing darts at cards for a lucky dip, clubbing wooden rats as they hurtled down a chute, pitting their muscles against man or machine in various unfairly weighted trials. For the less energetic there were side shows where allegedly the rarest of biological freaks could be observed for coppers, from stuffed unicorns and skeletons of antediluvian giants with curiously domed heads and six fingers, to preserved sea serpents and Siamese twins in jars. For the children, there were donkey rides around the grounds, and a petting zoo. Ladies might enter a competition for Best Holiday Hat or Best Bouncing Baby. A particular draw for the black country men, who always took care to show the world that they were men, was the boxing tent, offering no less than five shillings to any man who could go five rounds with any of the three picked ruffians – highly trained ruffians with the benefit of fighting in gloves with far less padding than those of the hapless hopeful contenders. There were many takers that day – mostly from those that had visited the beer tent previously – but few winners, apart from the organisers that is. But for sheer good fun nothing could beat the thrills of the steam driven roundabouts, some hurtling around at an incredibly irresponsible rate, or then, there was the more sedate pleasures of the swing boats.

Shouting each other out, vying for attention for their own individual variations of the same ephemeral tat, noisy hawkers were abroad. And where there were so many forgetting themselves, so were there pickpockets, seeking to part the merry makers illegally from their money, just as others tried to strike a more or less honest bargain. Chief amongst these latter were of course the purveyors of refreshment; it gave one an appetite, enjoying oneself. Bodily refreshment was very well catered for by the hordes of street vendors which had converged on this spot, on this day, like kites on carrion, flies on a carcass. Given the right breezes, and an ability to filter out the smell of the unwashed, a good nose could detect a myriad tempting odours. There was an overriding impression of satisfying warm greasiness, of baked spuds and pigs' trotters and sheep's feet, and faggots and grey 'payse' and bacon, and fried fish and black pudding. And cutting through it all, the sweetness of sticky toffee apples, on sticks, and then there was plum duff, and assorted cakes and tarts. If fresh food and pastries did not appeal, one could always avail oneself of the art and science of the pickler, to choose from oysters, whelks and mussels, and periwinkles or duck eggs, amongst more exotic treats.

Of course, whilst stomachs distracted, pockets were invariably picked, purses purloined. The wake was well known for attracting this variety of petty thief and the Dudley division of Worcestershire police patrolled conspicuously. Despite that, Josh Lively reflected with a certain professional interest, there would be tears enough today for the many who would not be paying close enough attention to their valuables.

"Make sure you keep your bag close, next to me," he advised.

"Don't worry, I will," Miss Ricketts replied, clutching it to her.

Jake appeared in front of her. "Geraldine, Frank said he'll take me to the shooting gallery, can I go?"

"Of course you may. We'll all come."

Frank led the way with Jean Murphy – his Irish leprechaun he liked to call her, he told his brother – and young Jake Collins hanging onto his coat tails. Josh and Miss Ricketts were content to saunter easily behind.

"You shouldn't let him call you that," he cautioned.

"What? Geraldine? It is my name you know."

"I know. It just seems…I don't know, he's only a lad. Doesn't seem right."

"I dare say I've been called worse. No, he means no harm by it. I think he sees me as his big sister."

"Oh dear, I've heard about his sister!"

She flushed. "You know what I mean – the sister he never had. The good one."

"I know, just teasing. You're good for him."

I could be good for you too, "He does look a lot happier, not to say healthier. It's amazing what a little tender loving care can achieve. I've grown quite attached to him."

"Not too attached, I hope, because…" he began.

"Yes, yes I know. I know all that. I'm a single woman, there's no chance they will allow me to hang onto him, not indefinitely; not permanently." *Now if I were to get married, to an eligible young and very handsome policeman…*

"You won't need to. He's not an infant exactly. How's he getting on with old Haywood?"

"Remarkably well, that was a marvellous idea of yours. I think our boy's broken down that hard-baked exterior of his."

"To discover a hard-baked interior no doubt."

She laughed at that, and he noticed again her small neat teeth and the little wrinkles that appeared in the corners of her eyes, the dimpling of her smooth cheeks. He had been seeing a lot of Geraldine Ricketts, more than he had thought he would want, but he had to admit that she was growing on him. He felt comfortable with her, and when she laughed, as she would given the smallest excuse, it was a real laugh. Not loud and demonstrative, not coarse; but refined and quite in keeping with her sex and moral sensibilities. And she laughed from the soul, he could tell. Could tell by the way it overflowed through her eyes and infected him with the same adorable malady and made him smile. He had begun to wonder if this was what they called love.

"Penny for them," came the sweet voice.

"Oh, I was just thinking about Jake," he evaded, "he deserves to be part of a proper family."

This was opening the door onto the secret room where she kept her most precious wishes. He was about to walk in – she felt like yanking open that door and dragging him in, confronting him with her feelings, and his own, and with that all-consuming, deliciously delicate, question. But no: he must enter voluntarily, of his own free will; lest he take fright and run. So she changed the subject.

"I'm surprised your brother could spare you today. It must be a busy time in your line of work."

"Yes. He was strangely insistent that I come though; pointed out that most of our rabble rousers would be here today anyway." Also, Josh suspected, Abe, and the rest of his colleagues, were indulging in a spot of match-making.

"So, you're secretly on duty?" she joked.

"Not on your nelly!" he said.

#

He had been partially right about Abe's motives. It was obvious to all that the young police constable had the respect and admiration, the love, of a good woman. Such women

404

were hard to come by, and Abe was going to help his brother see what he might be missing, and not miss out on what might prove to be a golden opportunity, naïve boy that he was. He had always been backwards in coming forwards.

Also, and in any case, he had a good feeling: he could do without that extra constable. Yes, strange things had been happening, but now that he understood more, from his peculiar companion, from Jack, he was realising that there was no cause to fear him, and with him nothing to worry about. All these unusual events, like the fire under the church, graves spilling, and the unbridling of violent tendencies in some individuals, all these were merely symptoms of something. Something that had come to Blackheath recently, something special, and one such something had picked out the police sergeant as something special. Now, it was connected to him, part of him, for how long he could not know. But it was beginning to feel perfectly normal for him, to be talking to this thing, to be relying on it, guided by it; a willing partner. He believed also that something bad had arrived, he had long thought so and Jack confirmed as much, and therefore he knew that he needed Jack, to fight fire with fire, he knew it. And Jack would protect him, because Abe was part of Jack's plan, and he saw things before they happened, and told him. They were a team; it made the sergeant feel invulnerable, almost invincible. His was now a charmed life, and it would keep his family safe, Miriam and Josh, John and the twins, even uncle Cyril.

Now, one would have thought that advance warning of a band of known trouble-makers would have been both worth having and possible, seeing that Abe Lively was responsible for law and order, and his friend Jack claimed the power of precognition. And perhaps it should have been, on both counts. However, the sergeant's self-styled oracle's gift was presumably on the blink today, or he did not deem the threat worthy of mention, or had some other nefarious reason for non-disclosure...

The threat, in the form of the group loosely banding together under the Smethwick sloggers flag, or scarf, was sitting raising spirits – their own at least – and sinking pints in the Builder's Arms where the eight or nine of them had taken over the place. Proprietor Bill Wilson was torn between thoughts of his takings and thoughts of how much the damage would cost if the mood changed. But he needn't have worried, they were having a good time at the moment and that was all that they were concerned with. Besides, they were on a pub crawl, and a pub crawl was not a pub crawl unless you moved swiftly on, pub to pub (only in the latter stages could such excursions fairly be described as crawls). In the Builder's Arms they were getting their second wind, two pints, not one, but they would soon be ready to move on. Not coincidentally, all the time they were heading closer to the town centre, and the Royal Oak.

It was the Percivals who had cooked up this stunt, one more foray for the sloggers, although, it must be said, but a pale and tame imitation of the original: men were just not as hard these days. For the Percivals, and one Roger Butler, it was a chance to flaunt their presence in the place from which the sloggers had so ignominiously been booted out; Kevin's forearm was still sore and still splinted. Then again, there was still a chance of seeing Spring Heeled Jack wasn't there? Wouldn't that be something? If some of the others thought that, Paul Percival did not, was not interested. He wanted to get back at that sergeant, and he knew Kevin did, neither his arm nor his pride had mended. They had a plan, and it involved the Royal Oak, run by the bastard's sister and where he lived. The plan was affray, and as much damage as possible, then scarper, just the two of them, before the law arrived, in the chaos. They knew where they were going to hide because an old mate had got word to them, just as he had got word out that the copper and his sister owned that pub; and that old mate had been passed that word from a local with a lot of influence and manpower, an impeccable source he had said (that meant very good), that that person was planning something to keep the coppers busy. In actual fact, the impeccable Jack Cutler was planning nothing of the sort, but, if these morons took the bait, then at least Lively would have at least one distraction to keep him and his nosey plods from poking around disrupting his business. It had cost him virtually nothing to set things in motion, so no skin off his nose either way.

#

Cyril Crane was out of town. He had been out of town several times lately, on some mysterious errand or other that John Lively was not particularly curious about. It meant that John was once again in stewardship of The Shoulder Of Mutton, a responsibility which sent a clear signal that John was effectively second in command of Cyril's operation, or at least of the more transparent aspects of it. And although the man took pains not to show it, John knew that Jack Cutler was not overjoyed at this turn of events. Despite his apparently outgoing and frank manner, John had been around him enough to know that our Jack was playing his cards close to his chest, that he undoubtedly distrusted John and his brothers, him being a rival and them being police – and the enemy – in his mind at least. Particularly Abe, he got the impression, probably because of his rank. And by now he must certainly suspect Cyril's allegiance to his old captain, and Cyril certainly suspected Jack's agenda.

#

The sergeant was lazing at the desk at the station. As predicted, it had been quiet, so far, and if there were to be any trouble, he was quite sanguine about his ability to handle it: it would likely be the typical drink-fuelled fracas involving ineffectual fisticuffs between feeble drunks. He reasoned that the majority of serious potential offenders had taken their worthless carcasses off to Dudley for the day…Perhaps he would take a stroll up to the Oak in a while, and Miriam. They hadn't cleared the air yet, not broached the subject; he did not know what to say about it, to her. Nor she to him. So, they had carried

406

on as if nothing had happened, except that Abe knew that he just wanted to be near her today, familiarity and proximity might rub away some of the aggregated awkwardness. Meantimes, P.C.s Salt and Stride were roving to the boundaries of the regular beats, whilst Clark and Payne were off duty and about their own Bank Holiday affairs.

#

The sloggers, including the Percivals, Roger Butler and one Charlie Kelly had moved on to the California. Their retinue consisted of a further three individuals enamoured of the slogging legends, sworn in as 'apprentices,' plus, uncertain satellites, two Wellings brothers. Bored, in need of a change of scene, Jonathan Wellings had allowed himself to tag along, and he took Douglas of the withered arm for company.

The Wellings' constitution, inherited from their father, plus a dose of common sense, had dictated that the two slow down, substituting here and there halves for pints in order to keep up with the rest. It was this that enabled Jon Wellings to avoid a potential family tragedy, for, being less intoxicated than some, he had begun to detect a furtive undercurrent, soft guarded words between the Percivals, followed by exhortations to increasing boisterousness, if not outright aggression. Not what he had signed on for; it had started to smell fishy. He switched from swigs to sips, signalling Dougie to do the same. Five minutes later, and a fiery haired and fiery headed Roger Butler was urging both Wellings boys to knock it back.

"Come on you laggards. You'm mekkin us all wait, 'urry up."

"I'm pacing myself. Don't wanna be too groggy to get 'ome. Me and Doug can't drink like you lot, not as fast anyhow."

"Well we ain't gooin without ya s'urry up."

"We like it 'ere and we don't wanna rush," replied the older Wellings carefully, "we can catch you up. Give us ten minutes."

"Ten minutes? You'm wastin' my valuable drinking time, you are," complained jolly Roger.

"Leave 'em Roj. They'll catch up. Let's get gooin shall we?" interjected Paul P, "we'll be over the road Jon, the Royal Oak. You comin' Doug?"

Dougie took the meaning of his brother's boot under the table.

"No, I'll stay with Jon. Catch up with ya in a bit."

"Suit youselves, see ya later, come on then lads," said Percival.

"Yeah, come on lads," repeated Butler, "let's get out o' this dump," sealing his verdict by directing a gob of spittle between his chipped front teeth and, with practised precision, into an empty glass.

"You're a dirty bugger Butler," reprimanded a curly haired man with a wide grin and a broken nose.

"You'm only jealous Kelly, cos you can't spit for shit."

"Roj, what meks you think I'd want to? Watch what you two get up to on your own," advised the curly head.

"We will, see you in a bit Charlie," said Jon.

And in good spirits, they left.

"What's up then?" asked Dougie when they were out of earshot, "what's gooin on?"

"I don't know, but I've got a bad feeling. I think they'm out for trouble."

"Ain't that the general idea? They have got a reputation to live up to."

"No, I don't mean the usual mucking about and bravado. I think Percival's up to something else. It's got something to do with that copper, that sergeant, getting back at him, I'll bet it is."

"But, I thought he was away today, out of town…"

"That's what we were told. But, now I don't know so much. If they're planning somethin' to get his back up, to get back at 'im, I'm steering clear. And so are you."

"Why did you come then?"

"You may well ask. Same reason as you I expect. To show I could, that I wasn't scared to come; because Gus said not to."

"Well, for myself, I must say I expected a bit of argy-bargy with the locals, it's all part of the fun."

"Not if it gets out of hand. And I think it will. They're blind drunk already. A woman could duff 'em over, and you…" he stopped, embarrassed by his drink loosened tongue, then, "I didn't mean…"

"Yes you did. And you're right, I wouldn't be any good in a serious scrap, I know that. But, it's all right, you're just looking after me, I know that. I understand."

"Well, all right then, I'm sorry. But the Percivals were too anxious to get over there, after getting everybody drunk that is. We'll keep our distance."

"Whatever you say big brother."

#

It was early October, and a decade earlier, and at Brockton the reverend More was hosting a pheasant shoot, a 20-mile drive for Gabriel Lively and Flash, his effervescent springer spaniel. All at the request, indeed the insistence, of Rupert Hill, who had once again contrived to procure for him an invite to a prestigious social occasion, with the opportunity to stay over no less (in consideration of the distances involved). Lively had not had to think hard about whether to accept: even if he might be out of his depth with some of the guests, he was also keen to get Hill face to face and ask some bloody serious questions. Also, he needed an excuse to get away from the house, from her. He needed a break from it all: her accusing him of not caring for his family, of gambling away their money, squandering their savings on an impossible dream, if not a shady scheme in her opinion. Her opinion. What made her so perfect? Because she wasn't, he knew she wasn't, but he would not accuse her, could not, not openly, though sometimes he was tempted to throw it all in her face, have it out. But then what? Once it was out of his mouth, he couldn't take it back. Adultery? He couldn't believe it. Such an ugly word, poisonous. He could not believe it, but neither could he forget what he had heard. A casual remark had stitched together all sorts of incongruous events, and seemed to answer a buried question. Things long forgotten now came back, and would not be dismissed. And yet he could not believe it. But neither could he bring himself to challenge her. Because that would be the end. Of everything. So, he did not ask, did not push, although something in him said he must. But still he did not, and it was corroding his sanity. He could not bear to be alone with her, in case he threw his suspicion at her, and in case he then did something else, something final. Sometimes, like now, he thought that he would learn to forget it, to bury it, to forget if not forgive. But then he remembered his son, Joshua Lively. The Lively who did not look like a Lively.

By ten in the morning, as they were being served drinks with the reverend's impressive residence a haughty backdrop, it had become obvious to Gabriel Lively that Rupert Hill had cried off. To say the least a disappointment, it was also a distinct worry: a change of luck at the card tables meant that Lively was now desperate to retrieve his stake in Hill's adventure; jam tomorrow was no good if you could not feed yourself today. His share certificates were worthless until production was in full swing, he knew that. And he knew that he had entered into a contractual arrangement which by no means obliged Hill and the rest to just refund him at the drop of a hat. Therefore, he had decided to try to incentivise him, using a carrot and stick approach. The carrot would be that Gabriel would offer to sell his shares back at a discount. If they were really as valuable as Hill said, surely he would jump at the chance? Yes, but what if he didn't have cash available? Cash flow was everything, Hill had said. And it wasn't just that which made Gabe Lively nervous: he was beginning to believe there was something in what Hannah was saying. What if it was shady, so highly speculative that it almost amounted to fraud? Then, it would not be a case of jam tomorrow, but of no jam at all, never. The recent treatment he had received from the company, from Hill, had been suspicious, he saw that, with no response to his letters to the registered office, in London. He suspected, with a growing feeling of panic and dread, that he had been duped. So, the stick. Tricksters, like bullies, did not like it if you called them out, fought back. No, once he could just get his hands on Hill, weasel Hill as he was coming to think of him, he would have his money back, if it meant roughing him up, trussing him up, and carting him to the bank, God help him.

His agitated mental manoeuvres were interrupted by an unfamiliar voice.

"Hello there. Would you be Gabriel Lively?"

"That I would be. And who wants to know?"

A neat looking precise sounding gentleman of a rather paler complexion and shorter and slighter than Gabriel, being of only average height, thrust out an unhesitant hand.

"James Gordon, at your service sir. Friends call me Jimmy," he said with an undeniable Scots accent, and such an air of enthusiasm and geniality that Gabe Lively found himself shaking that hand warmly, a smile lighting his dark features.

"Well sir, I am at your service. And you can call me Gabriel. You're down here for the shoot, are you?"

"Down here? No, no, I'm not a sporting man, not really, not sporting at all. No, I'm visiting my sister. She married a Sassenach and lives in Shrewsbury of all places, foolish wee lassie. And the reason I'm visiting her is to do with a certain Mr Hill."

"Rupert Hill, you mean?" asked Gabriel, suddenly more attentive.

"That's the laddie."

"Well, you're out of luck. He's not here."

"Yes, I've established that. I imagine that you're as disappointed as I am."

Caught by surprise all that Gabe could say was, "What?"

"No, please don't be alarmed. And please, just keep on smiling and nodding while I explain myself. Hill might not be here but who knows what confederates, or spies, he might have amongst this lot."

"All right, carry on," agreed Lively through a fixed and affected smile.

"I said smile, not grimace," said Gordon playfully, "and nod occasionally. So, look, I know about Hill's new mining company, the reason being that my sister, or rather her avaricious spouse, has invested a not inconsequential amount of money in it. Now, I say invested, but that presupposes that the business is going to flourish. If it never gets off the ground, then investors, like my sister, will stand to lose their stakes…"

"What's that to do with me, here and now?" interposed Lively.

"Wait, let me finish. I've been attempting to contact other small shareholders – matter of public record before you ask – like yourself to see if we can band together to force a meeting, an extraordinary meeting it's called, a meeting to thrash things out. I was after Hill today, but by a stroke of incredibly good fortune, I found that you were in attendance."

Gabe was willing to grasp at any straw, particularly if it cost nothing. He did not understand how all this meeting stuff worked, but it sounded a good idea.

"Well, if we can do anything, as you say, by banding together, I'm all for it. You'll certainly get my support."

"That's much appreciated and as I say that was the plan – until recently that is. Until I found out something more."

"What?"

"Have you ever heard the name Sir Mortimer Manners?"

"I certainly have!" returned Lively enthusiastically, "and I'm beginning to think that he's a fabrication, an invention of Hill's."

"Och, no laddie. You're barking up the wrong tree there. He exists all right. Still, you're on the right track. I believe the 'Sir' is a mere sobriquet, an affectation. But, as I say this man, this very wealthy man, does exist. He's very rich, but extremely ruthless, that's how he got that way. And he's had companies that have collapsed before…"

"I checked…"

"No, I don't mean as a director or shareholder, not necessarily, but he does provide finance, and a certain kind of business advice…" When Lively did not bite on that Gordon continued, "now, I'm not so sure that our Mr Hill himself hasn't been taken in by this character, in which case I would go far as to say that his game plan, Manners', might be to let this company go bankrupt before it even got off the ground."

"But, he'd lose his money too."

"What money? A backer is not the same as a shareholder. It's the shareholders that would lose out, people like you, and my sister Heather. But, and here's the rub of it, what happens to the funds, those shareholders' funds that have been drawn down, seemingly as legitimate business expenses? Because opening up a mine can be very expensive, what with lawyers and surveyors fees, deposits on equipment, licence applications, etc. What about those expenses?"

"Well, they're lost of course. Expended."

"Or are they? What if the work was never done, equipment never ordered?"

"But why?"

The Scotsman sighed indulgently. "What if, say, what if this Sir Mortimer had actually been here before, with this mine I mean, this particular mine. What if he knew that the survey report would be bad, because he was already privy to an earlier one? What if he knew from the start that the mine was, if to outward appearances a legal venture, nevertheless an uneconomical one? The bank would withdraw their conditional support and the whole scheme would collapse. And all those fake expenses would be forgotten about, normal casualties of speculation, never investigated. But what's the betting that a good chunk of all that 'expended' money would be sitting in this Sir Mortimer's private bank account?"

Gabriel Lively suddenly saw it all: his savings, his home, his wife, all gone. With a desperate foreboding he said through clenched teeth, "But that's outrageous; bastards, it's filthy; the filthy bastards. It's illegal, they ought to be charged over it. What can we do? Bloody crooks!"

"Calm yourself. Calm yourself, please," the Scot's words were smooth and measured and untroubled. Gabriel did not feel calm, but people were watching.

Swallowing back the heart in his mouth he asked, "What do we do about it?"

"First, we don't panic, we keep a clear head. Second, we've got to get the court to order that all company funds be frozen, pending an application for that meeting. After that, we may indeed find that it's a criminal matter."

"But we'll need some kind of proof, surely?"

"We surely will, at least if my brother's any judge. He's a notary."

"But we don't have any do we?"

411

"Yes we do. Now, mark me, I know you said that you would support me, but just think about it a minute. We're up against powerful men with influence, even possibly amongst magistrates, or judges. So I don't expect you to commit to the cause until you see what I've got. Also, we might have to find some small amount of cash for a fighting fund…"

"Yes, yes. What have you got?"

"What if I can prove that mine is worthless? Worthless now, always has been and always will be?"

"I don't know, what would it mean?" The unexpected answer to a rhetorical question gave the Scot pause.

"Er, well, at least we know that our suspicions are well founded, right? And so we can plan accordingly."

"So show me."

James Gordon made much of looking around shiftily. "I do have it on me, but here's not the place, or time. Too many prying eyes. But, tell you what, I've been here before. After they all set off, they'll be heading that way," he gestured with his right arm, "wait ten minutes then take that track," he pointed with his left. "It leads down to an old watermill. We can talk in private there, I'll meet you."

"You're on. I'll just find someone to look after my dog." As he walked away, James Gordon was gone.

#

The Royal Oak was Bank Holiday full, full to bursting, standing room only and precious little of that. Behind the bar Miriam, Jack and Marlene were rushed off their feet. Jack had been up and down, cellar to bar, bar to cellar, changing barrels like there was no tomorrow. They might even run dry, he calculated, and thought of the money that represented. Old Mary was doing all of her very and inadequate best to cope with the house empties, which meant no more than a quick swill under the kitchen tap, and left to drain.

On the floor, if the sheer press of people did not leave you feeling you couldn't breathe, then the smoke pall, brown and grey strands weaving themselves into a thick tapestry of toxicity, should have. But no, this was just the atmosphere that the holiday crowd loved. It meant that they were out, free, having a good time.

In terms of good times, one particular group of young men were having a good day, flaunting their youth and strength in foreign territory, they had arrived like interloping stags on someone else's rut. Confident in their drunkenness, in control, untouchable, it seemed to them. Indeed there was something about them, the way they moved together, predator-like now, a wolf pack, that made other drinkers wary. The respect was duly noted, and the Smethwick sloggers duly commandeered a couple of large square tables near one wall, pushing them together to form their own private sanger. From here, they smoked and drank and looked out imperiously, in petulant and childish sort of way, and waited for trouble to find them.

#

The man with the shotgun, a lost straggler from the shooting party to all appearances, was approaching the old mill. Before the days of steam it had been a substantial structure. Still was in fact, but not a working structure, just a shell; a bit of a ruin, but a substantial ruin. The brick walls still stood, the full three storeys for the most part; but the roof had long ago been stripped of tiles, and the elements and the earthly agents of decay had had their inevitable way: fungus, moulds and wood boring insects had accepted the invitation and commenced their work, top down. The mill's innards had been exposed to the sky, the second-floor planking had gone, floor beams tumbled onto the level below, where in parts they had penetrated weakened timber and appeared as hefty interlopers in the lowermost rooms, near to the now idle hard and heavy hornbeam cogs. From outside and from a distance the water wheel itself seemed intact, its oaken spokes as yet untouched by time, and many of its elm paddles in place and in one piece. But the robust iron work that had once connected the power of the wheel to the big cogs had not seen a lick of grease for decades now and had rusted and snapped, useless. And were it not for the fact that the neglected mill race had over the years been reduced to a stagnant slime populated by a few clumps of scruffy wispy headed old reed mace, and various sedges at the margins, fading as the wetland gave way to invading scrub, then the wheel itself might already have tumbled under the force of water, and the pair of moorhen which called the old mill race and pond their home would never have raised any chicks, for their nest of the last two years sat on its clogged up bottom paddles…

Gabriel Lively had been unable to wait the prescribed ten minutes. He had allowed possibly two, and then headed straight here. He entered through a door-less doorway. There was no Jimmy Gordon. A couple of frameless window openings, now like jagged wounds in a wall, and holes in the planking above, allowed beams of sunlight to play across the dusty darkness of the interior. Eyes adjusting, he noticed a table and chair, not covered in dust like the rest of the place; perhaps a traveller had sheltered here recently. But there was nobody here now. He stood at a hole in the brickwork and looked out over fields. It was a lovely warm and sunny day: a kestrel hovered, a robin sang, and bees buzzed contentedly as they did their chores.

Gordon walked in. Assuming the ten-minute injunction had applied to himself too, he had evidently broken it. In truth, he had wanted be there first, waiting for his guest. But no, Lively was already here, there, shotgun in hand. Making light of it he said:

"You got here quick. Good." And he made a show of breaking his own firearm and ejecting and pocketing the cartridges before standing it innocuous in a dry corner, and moving away. Following his lead Gabriel Lively carefully stood his own gun.

"I know, I was impatient. Nobody was taking any notice of me in any case," he replied.

"Good, good," returned the Scot, "now I suppose you're anxious to see what I was blathering on about earlier."

"I am indeed."

"Right then," he said looking around, eyes alighting on the table, "er, sit yourself down."

Gabriel went and sat at the only chair at the lone table. Whoever had once lived or worked here must have been very short, for both items of furniture were quite low. Sitting not so comfortably, he waited as Gordon spread out an old faded map.

"Here, it's best you see the map first."

In the murk of the mill, especially where the table had been positioned, it was difficult to make out any detail.

"I can't see a thing here," said Lively.

"Oh, hold on, I'll fetch a candle."

With elevated heartbeat, James Gordon esquire, whose gullible sister had been persuaded to invest in the same risky venture that Gabriel had, who had a helpful brother who was a notary, who had just happened to have laid his hands on some conveniently incriminating documentation, who was visiting from Scotland but had apparently visited this self-same spot before, who knew the location of a lonely and deserted water mill, which few ever passed, and who knew where there was a candle to be had in this off the beaten track ruin…Yes, with racing heart now, William Arrowsmith went as far as a little ledge and retrieved, not from the ledge but from his person, not a candle but a piece of lead pipe.

Had Gabriel Lively settled for that ten minutes, to order his thoughts, think, weigh the facts, and had he been able to gain his feet quickly when a sluggard sixth sense prodded him of danger approaching from behind, had he held onto his shotgun, or brought his faithful spaniel, then he may have lived.

But he had not, and did not. It was too late: Arrowsmith hit him without hesitation and with force. It made a mess of the skull, but that did not matter.

"That'll teach you to ask awkward bloody questions. Why couldn't you just keep your mouth shut? Thought you were clever, did you? Not clever enough – laddie."

As he spoke, lapsing into his Jimmy Gordon for the last, almost contrite, irony, he sat the body back up: Lively was slouched dead, or possibly unconscious, over the table. The chair was a low one, but had a good high back, perfect for his purposes. He pushed the table back somewhat then fetched the victim's gun. He took a couple of 16 bore cartridges from Lively's pockets, loaded up, knelt down, at just the right angle, and fired.

In his time with the Lancers in India he had seen plenty of heads lopped or mangled by blade and bullet and shot, so he knew what to expect. He let the gun drop, as a suicide would have. The gun. Dare he make a swap? No. Pity, it was a rather nice Williams and Powell with an exquisite hand-engraved stock. But no: he had set the scene, and it really was an essential prop. As an additional touch, he placed paper and a pencil on the table, to tell of the poor troubled man wanting to say something at the last, but of the words just not coming...

Right. Time to get out. Cautiously, he peered out; just in case. Good. No bugger about. The sound of a discharging firearm would hardly be expected to elicit unnatural curiosity anyway, not today, not in these parts. Arrowsmith stepped into the sunlight and sucked in lungfuls of fresh air, ripe with the smell of hay. He practised a few phrases, to exorcise the Scotsman.

"O'roit mate? 'Ow yer doin' me old cock sparra?"

"I'm doing spiffingly well, thank you so much for arsking."

"Blimey, you're a toff ain't ya?"

"Indubitably, my dear boy."

That was some performance, he mused. Not bad for a disgraced cavalry lieutenant turned out of work actor from Warwick. So much for those clueless impresarios. They knew jack shit. And how did he feel? Excited, and nervous, or was it scared? No not scared: he was too good to get caught. If anything, if some bright copper suspected foul play, and if anybody had overheard the earlier conversation with Lively, then they would be scouring North of the border for somebody named Jimmy. Good luck with that. But what about shame? Was he ashamed of himself? There was something there: it's no small thing, killing a man. And for money? Shouldn't he call that shameful? Perhaps it was, but, it had had to be done, for the purposes of self-protection. Everyone for himself; survival of the fittest.

A splash of blood on his sleeve:

"I told you. I told you I was no sporting man. Why didn't you listen? Why doesn't anybody bloody well listen?"

He breathed deep again. It really was a lovely day. It felt good to be alive – and he felt so alive. Unbidden, a tune came into his head – Cock O' The North – and he began to whistle.

#

It was the sound of someone having drunk enough, or of trouble, or of both. Those in the thick of the crowd awaited further auditory signals. Then, it was confirmed: raised voices and a press of bodies as folk removed themselves from the conflict zone. It was trouble.

It had been a glass breaking, not necessarily in anger; perhaps an accident taken as a slight. An excuse for a scrap. Whatever, it meant trouble. Those with an unimpeded line of sight saw a flat faced fair headed man, an overgrown boy really but one with an air of confident power and in pugnacious stance, facing off against two local miners, not particularly soft men themselves. One of them had a split lip from a fist he had not seen coming, a lightning blow which had quite taken away his own confidence.

"You better get me another drink," the ugly young man was saying.

"It was empty," protested the miner with the bleeding mouth, but sheepishly.

Kevin Percival looked down at the broken glass and a small smattering of liquid trying to soak in.

"What's that then?" he demanded, pointing.

"What? There's nothing there," opined the miner.

"Oh. I'm lying, am I?"

All of this time the rest of the Smethwick contingent had remained seated, a unanimous declaration to the rest of the pub that their standing comrade was a real tough nut, easily a match for these two, even with a poorly arm.

The other miner was anxious to be gone, but would not leave his mate; but he could see this getting out of hand. If he pushed his luck, they would all be up, and it would be a free for all – with him and his unfortunate friend first in the firing line. Would other locals pitch in to help? He had no way of knowing; wasn't as if they were all miners and all out of the same pit – it was very much a mixed bag. Still, he hated to back down, completely, so he feigned casualness and suggested a compromise.

"Look, it was only dregs. Why don't you have my drink? I haven't touched it."

"That's only a half," began the lone agent provocateur.

"Kev, take the drink and thank the man," instructed his brother, "take it I said, then come and sit down with it."

"Thank you – mate," said Percival the younger, dismissively and taking the man's drink. The two miners slipped out with alacrity: they had been hoping for a nice peaceable drink – hence the Oak; they got enough grief from the foreman.

As Kevin Percival sat the other announced, "Right lads, it's time. Your glasses please – or tankard, Charlie." They all took their drinks and held them aloft. In a loud voice Paul took up the agreed toast. "All for one," he said, and the others came back with, "and spare none!" (It had been Kevin's idea, something he had done at school.) They all drained their glasses. Then, also as agreed, they all very deliberately and obviously turned them over.

Those that witnessed it and knew what it meant made sure that they did not lock eyes with the gang of belligerent young strangers, and edged away. Others took their cue from this; the visitors found themselves with plenty of space now, as the more sensible drinkers hurriedly finished and dissolved away. So they stood there, challenging.

"What? Nobody up for a friendly fight then?" enquired Charlie Kelly cheerfully over the hush. People turned their backs, but kept one eye, and both ears, on what was happening: would it die down? Would it kick off? What was the landlord playing at?

The landlord was only just emerging from the cellar, and only just catching on. He heard his wife raise her voice.

"Right, come on you lads, settle down. We don't like trouble here, we don't stand for it. You've finished your drinks, it's time to move on. You'll not be served any more here. Come on now, on your way."

"Who are you?" asked Paul Percival.

"I'm the landlady. This is my place. And I'm asking you to leave please."

"All right then. Give us a kiss and we'll go."

"You watch your dirty mouth boy." Jack Beckett had entered, collecting an emergency pick-axe handle as he rounded the bar. Neither Jack nor his piece of ash had seen much action of the sort that threatened, and it showed. Percival, backed by the rest, calmly picked up a weapon of his own – some old person's walking stick purloined no doubt on some previous stop – and pointed it at arm's length straight at Beckett's face. Now Miriam and Jack stood together, facing the gang.

Percival verbalised the threat. "Look, you, if you don't put that down I'll come over there and ram it down your throat."

"Yeah," said Butler, "you can't take on all of us," and he shot a sudden glance over the shrinking and shrinking away would-be clientele, "unless somebody wants to give you hand?"

That was enough to complete the exodus.

"Thank you, Roger, but I don't think I need any help dealing with this bag of wind – do you?"

"On reflection, no," admitted Butler.

"You cheeky young pups! If you don't leave now…"

"What? What will you do? You, or you, the pair of ya?" Kevin Percival was joining in now, relishing it.

Most probably, what would have happened is that the gang would have faced them off for a while, taunting, hoping to scare. But they would not have acted directly against a woman, unwritten rule that. And Miriam would probably have done nothing, other than swallow her ire as they broke a few glasses, kicked over a few chairs, threw them more than a few curses…Before exiting in triumph, and in one piece.

But, apparently, Spring Heeled Jack – just Jack to his friends, that is, police sergeant Abraham Lively – had another agenda, for it appeared that he had persuaded his human host to visit the Oak, contriving, Abe later saw, to bring him onto the premises at just this precise moment.

"She'll get her brother to deal with you. Just like I did before."

417

They all looked to the door where the light framed the upright and imposing figure of the brother sergeant, all the taller for his helmet. He wasn't supposed to be here, but here he was. And he was looking directly at Kevin Percival, whose pale moon face blanched whiter with the shock of the memory of this man and that day; and then he remembered his brother and his comrades, so that desire for revenge could be allowed to overrule fear, and now the sight of that man, this day, right here, caused anger to wax and his cheeks to redden.

The sergeant did not hold that stare: he knew when a bomb was about to run out of fuse. So he looked to the man he remembered as the brother.

"I thought I told you not to come back."

"Did you?"

"Yes. You know I did."

"Well, you might have. No – yes, you're probably right. I thought you meant not to come back that day. It was weeks ago."

Percival knew what the copper had meant. And he knew why he had led the gang here today. Be away would he? Impeccable source? My aunt Ada! Still, this was an opportunity to make the point, hurt him if they could. But where were the other coppers? If they were with him, he wouldn't be just standing there talking; he would want to be arresting them, for something. To prove a point.

"Don't come it. You know what I meant. Now, are you going to leave quietly, as the lady asked?"

Leave quietly? He was on his own then, surely?

Bloody fool. Truncheon's no good at the station. You're getting careless Abe.

The pub was clear of customers, although many peered in through the windows, comparatively safe, they calculated. Percival was pretty sure that the sergeant was alone, for now. That emboldened him:

"Are you going to make us?"

"That's right, him and me both."

A surprise to all, John Lively had learned of some kind of disturbance via the dispossessed miners who had continued their drinking at the Shoulder, and now he stood shoulder to shoulder with his big brother.

"Make that the three of us," added Jack Beckett, the only one of the home team with the benefit of a weapon.

"Four," corrected Miriam. Marlene had disappeared much earlier.

"All right then, let's think about this," said Paul Percival. All the time he was talking he, with the others following, was advancing into the middle of the room, as if to further the parley, which indeed may well have been his intention, in part. But he was a great believer in keeping his options open, was Percival, and his movement had not merely by coincidence served to drive a wedge between the dangerous looking brothers and the ineffectual looking man with the useful weapon. Good. So far so good. If they could pick off the bar-keeper quickly, and nick that pick-axe handle, he reckoned the seven of them could rough up the two big men and make a run for it, never to be seen again; job done, point proven. They wouldn't be caught. Nobody knew their full names, and Smethwick was a big place, with lots of their friends living in it. He continued:

"Look, there's seven of us and only two of you. No, I can count: only two worth counting, no offence," he nodded wryly to Jack, "so I reckon, if you try anything you're going to regret it, more than we might."

"Jack, if he gets any closer to you, dot him on the head with your stick," advised John Lively.

Found out, Percival raised his hands and backed off, but not much. He looked back towards the policeman but was somewhat perturbed to find that the sergeant, seeming implacable, was holding a conversation with himself.

"If you say that's the way, then I'll do it. But you had better be right. Yes, yes I know. I know I said…" and mid-sentence he stopped and held the entire space in a cold stare.

"All right you, all of you. Wait there, I've got a proposition for you."

Wait there?

Quickly retreating a few paces, the copper slammed shut the doors to the street, barred them, and turned the key, which then went into his tunic pocket. Then, he walked slowly back to them, aware of everything, that was apparent; not a chink in his armour. John was as amazed as all of them, but was glad when Abe was back at his side. He felt like they were crusader knights, brothers in battle and he knew that whatever happened, whatever the cost, he would stand by his brother, faithful unto death.

When Abe started talking now, it was still Abe, but it was not. Not a trace of anxiety, no morsel of emotion, deadpan delivery, like a clever lawyer laying a trap.

"So, pay attention. Here's the proposition: I now intend to stop you leaving; physically stop you. Unless you would care to surrender of course, in which case I will tie you up, and arrest you and you will spend the night in a cell. If you choose to fight and I – and we – win I will tie you up, and arrest you, and you will spend the night in a cell, and then I'll charge you with everything in the book that I can think of; and of course at that point you will have committed an assault with intent to resist your lawful apprehension. That's two years penal servitude for a start – two years hard labour to you. So either way, you are in trouble. But you should have thought of that before you came here of course."

John thought that some were having second thoughts now, but Abe hadn't finished yet.

"However, and listen carefully now, because I'm going to give you a way out; a sporting chance. What I propose is that if you can knock me down, it's over, you've won. Once I'm down, on my back, we stop, immediately. And we let you out, off scot free.

Two conditions. First, no blades. If you're carrying one it goes behind the bar. Two, anybody hurts my sister, even accidentally, then I'll kill them. Clear?"

Paul Percival thought that he could live with that. The man by the bar had his pick-axe handle but looked as if he didn't have a clue how to use it. He himself had this borrowed walking stick, a short one, good for close quarter jabbing, with a sturdy polished bone or antler handle shaped like a large crow's bill, ending in a useful spike. He also knew that at least three of them were equipped with knuckle dusters.

"All right then," he agreed, thinking all the time, "if that's what your conditions are, we've got a deal. Do I have your word?"

"Yes, you have my word." *Yes I give you my word that you're going to regret coming into my home and doing this.*

"Abe, are you sure about this? Let me send for some help from the Shoulder," suggested John.

"No. It's too late. And this is a police matter. Can't invite in a rabble to start a riot. It's my job to keep order. I'm going to do that – with your help."

"You've got it, I'm with you."

"Right then. Knives?"

"We don't carry them. Too easy for things to get out of control," said Percival.

"Good. Sensible."

A nervous voice: "Miriam, get back behind the bar."

"No Jack. It's my pub and I'll fight these people if I have to."

"But you don't have to, big sister," said Abe, "remember, trust me."

She bit her lip and went.

"Remember, you gave your word," cautioned the Percival.

"I know."

"Right lads, get him!"

To his credit, Paul Percival didn't hide behind his gang, he led from the front, heading straight for Abraham Lively, stick raised, threatening a vicious peck to the cranium with that crow beak. Not inexperienced in a ruckus of this kind, Roger Butler stepped out and past, to Percival's right, so that the copper was outflanked and vulnerable to an attack from the red-headed one as he met the Percival attack. And if Abe were able to hold his own against these two, there was another of their number, a fat bloke, used to intimidating smaller fry with his bulk, to lend a hand. Butler and Percival had slipped brass knuckles on their right hands…

Abe was getting no immediate help from John: the other Percival had pushed a bald headed, cauliflower eared recruit at him. From his stance he fancied himself a boxer – he may not have been a good one, but John could not be sure of that and thus gave most of his attention to this frontal threat. Thankfully, this one appeared to be weapon-less, hence, perhaps, his caginess. But again, another of the gang, Kevin Percival, was sneaking around, to the left this time, splitting his focus…

Meantime, poor Jack Beckett was already in trouble, for at Percival's first shout Charlie Kelly had feigned a lunge at him, shouting, "Boo!" and getting exactly the response he was hoping for: Beckett started, losing valuable reaction time as Kelly was already heading in; then, out of time and rhythm, raising the pick-axe handle in his right hand prior to bringing it diagonally down across Kelly's face. A blow to the jaw, or collar bone, that had been his fuzzy intention, but Kelly's timing was good and he had entered into the gap even as the weapon was rising, so that the down stroke had only just begun when Kelly's left took the sting of the wood and his right grasped Beckett's forearm, finger nails biting. Shoulder charging, he knocked Beckett back and attempted to pull the stick from his stubborn grasp. But Jack was wrestling him now, both hands on the handle, he could not afford to let them have it. Then, a short and skinny individual, whose size and shape, ill-fitting clothes and pock marked face were indicative perhaps of a particularly rough upbringing, dove in. Unable to land a blow whilst the pair were engaged in their desperate dance, he hung onto Jack's legs in the hope of grounding him, at which point he would be easy meat…

The man facing John like a boxer seemed to sway back, not moving his feet, but adjusting his weight. John had seen this trick before, and was ready this time. As the bald one feinted with a half-hearted jab, he swept at John's knee with his lead foot; that knee, and the rest of the leg was duly removed from the target area, and now the bald one was off balance and open: even before the sweeping foot found rest, Lively was stepping outside of it, safe side, avoiding a follow up punch, grasping with his left his assailant's left sleeve. Pulling on the sleeve prevented the man from launching a further attack for a split second whilst giving stability, and power, to John's counter attack: a crashing right fist into that long-suffering cauliflowered ear, then another punch, just forward of it, the big man's big middle knuckle connecting precisely with the join of upper and lower jaw, and stopping his opponent in his tracks; a wobble, and he went down, on his knees. As he fell, a distraction, Kevin P. swung an armoured right. John had been expecting it. Quickly pivoting clockwise Lively batted it away with both arms threshing in an expansive movement, sweeping the arm toward the ground and downing the attacker as February hail on a field of wheat. But, vigorous seedling as he was, from his knees Percival came again, hooking into the floating rib. It hurt, and the big man bent, but was still able to lash out with a kick which caught Percival in the shoulder sending him rolling backwards, avoiding the full force, or any follow up, out of range and out of the immediate combat area. Thus, John Lively now had time to finish the bald man: on all fours a kick to the midriff was invited, and duly delivered, knocking the wind and, hopefully, the last of the fight out of him. Young Kevin was not immediately evident, John had time to aid elsewhere…

Abe had his hands full. He had prepared to dodge the blow from the corvid beak, but Percival was canny, and had never intended to strike home: firstly, he was not about to commit G.B.H. by smashing a head – the sergeant had discarded his helmet to fight; that was their rule of thumb, and common sense – avoid the head. G.B.H. was a serious matter, and this was a copper, remember, and that meant life if he was badly injured and Percival caught. So, he did not really want to hit that head, not hard, not unless he had to. No, the overhead threat and his angle of approach (slightly to the right as the copper looked at him) meant that the sergeant would likely dodge to the left, and that would take him in range of Roger Butler. Abe saw the danger, but was confident that he could meet the swing, take whatever Butler might be able to deliver in a brief interval of opportunity, but dispossess Percival. Then, he would lay it on with the stick, and it would be over. But the blow never came, not that one. But Butler's did. Roger Butler was a hefty individual and there was beef behind the brass, which hammered into Abe's ribs with excruciating venom. Then a sharp stab in the abdomen as Paul Percival jabbed with his walking stick. Fortunately, Abe had seen that one coming and took the sting out of it by shuffling back and grabbing hold. He had his back to the wall now, with a solid table denying Butler access to his flank, for the moment. Fortunately the spare fat bloke had been all podgy belly and no guts, hanging back indecisively. Abe was holding onto the stick, which meant Percival had to, which meant, with Butler temporarily side-lined, that Abe could have a momentary breather. However the stick was a tapering one and Percival had a good grip on the handle. So, a couple of seconds grace, then he must do something…

At that point Jack Beckett went down, and the scruffy little chap began to pummel him while Kelly attempted to rip away the pick-axe handle. Miriam went to intervene.

"Stay put Miriam, John, help Jack," cried the sergeant.

Paul saw the danger, or rather felt it: "Get him, Kev," he shouted. The younger Percival had been torn between helping Charlie and helping his brother. What he did not want to do was 'get him', the unencumbered Lively, not on his own…

John wanted to help his own brother, to finish off the ringleader, but if he did that, while he was doing that, Jack would suffer for it: he was not like them, not used to this; not used to looking after himself, not this way. Besides if he could get his hands on that pick-axe handle he could finish the lot off. So he headed to the other side of the room, to where Jack had been rocked and tumbled off his feet.

Young Kevin raced there too. "Come on Dave, you fat fuck," he ordered the spare one.

Dave Wilcox might have been a waverer, but if there was one thing designed to get his back and at least a temporary courage up, it was that particular appellation. He lumbered to the same spot, three bodies converging. John arrived, then Kevin, who was knocked down when John's fist found his forehead; even as he was struck, fat Dave arrived, belly-barging John Lively and knocking him over, losing his balance and falling on top. For a few moments, most of the bodies in the room were in a writhing, grunting and gouging heap, with the piece of coveted ash at the bottom of it…

"I've had enough of this now, haven't you?" enquired Jack.

Abe nodded in assent and fresh strength infused him. He gave one last pull on the walking stick, then loosed. Paul Percival had to step back a pace to achieve a stable posture, but he had the stick now, and he wouldn't be letting the copper lay hold of it again. There were two of them and a stick against one. He gave it a twirl. Now they would put him down. Quickest way, hit him over the head with the blunt end, just to stun him. Then he would be no trouble.

That was not in the sergeant's plan however. He had created a very brief interval, time enough to take hold of the big table, a heavy wooden one with sharp edges and iron legs, swing it round, and charge at the pair of them with it, scraping it along the floor. As predicted they pushed back, aiming to pin him against the wall. But, smooth and sharply, he flipped it. Percival was fast, Butler not so much. The sharp wooden edge caught at least one of his feet, smashing delicate metatarsals. Abe could have sworn he heard them crunching. In the spirit of Spring Heeled Jack, or possibly with the spirit of that putatively imaginary entity, Abe cleared his upturned shield with a stupendous bound and landed next to Butler before the echoes had vanished his sharp yelp of surprised pain; in the air he had raised his arm, making a hammer of his fist; landing, he had brought down that arm and that hammer and played it with force onto Butler's collar bone, dislocating it. Another cry of pain, deeper this time, and prolonged, and Butler sank to the ground and into merciful unconsciousness. Right, the leader next. The copper ran at him, giving him no time to land a meaningful blow. Once at close quarters and held by those arms the smaller man stood no chance: stepping through with his right leg past Percival's right side the copper planted his foot firmly, his leg and his weight blocking and locking his antagonist's knee, one arm encircling Percival's neck like a ligature, pressing down onto his right shoulder. Now, when Abe pushed and turned the flimsy knee broke and the body pivoted over the big wrestler's leg with the force of an avalanche behind it. Percival hit the ground, crippled and stunned. He was going nowhere.

Dimly, the members of the swirling knot had become aware of the despatch of Butler and the elder Percival, and each reacted accordingly: Kelly was desperate to get the weapon off Jack, Jack was filled with new resolution not only not to let him have it, but to let him have it, the little one and the fat one just knew that they had to get to their feet, John knew that they would and that he would be up with them, to deal with them; and Kevin Percival? He was thinking along different lines.

And so they were up. But as soon as they were, Abe Lively was there again, leaping prodigiously, to his siblings' amazement, like a new Joe Darby, onto an adjacent table where, with impeccable timing, his boot delicately tapped the chin of the fat one as he stood, and knocked him straight back down again, with a dislocated jaw –perhaps that would help him lose some weight. At the same time, John lively knocked down the little scruffy one with what he had meant to be a measured cuff, open handed. As it turned out the diminutive little creature must have had flimsy eardrums, at any rate he ended up with a perforated one.

Alone and surrounded, Charlie Kelly ceased the struggle, dusted himself off, and gave up gracefully.

"Are you all right Jack?" asked John.

"I'm fighting fit John, fighting fit," came the reply as he stood. He was already developing not one but two shiners to go with a gashed lip. Miriam came round from the other side of the bar to support him.

"Right," Abe said, but winced as he took a breath to carry on, held his side.

"Abe, what is it?" Miriam left Jack and ran to him.

"No. No Miriam, it's all right, just a bit bruised. Go to Jack, he's been in the wars." Not entirely convinced, she nevertheless did as she was told.

"As I was saying, I suggest that we get them all together in the middle of the floor, and on their knees if they can still stand."

Just then, at the doors, a rattling and a kind of grunt, or a snarl. The bald man was up, trying to make his escape. He turned, and he had a knife.

"Bastards. You better let me out or I'll gut ya."

He was waving around a blade of certainly more than six inches, made for fighting and killing – why else sharpen two edges?

"That's done it. That's breaking the rules that is. Treachery that is. Treason. We know how to deal with traitors." Jack was egging him on, so loud, but nobody else heard. And then it was drowned out by an all-pervading righteous fury.

While everyone else froze, Abe strode toward the knifeman.

"Come on then. Come on you scum."

He went to make a grab for the knife arm; it was retracted and now perfectly positioned to make a straight thrust. Abe knew that, because Jack told him; Jack talked him through it; Jack made sure he had plenty of time, probably reading the man's mind. As instructed, Abe stood squarely in front of the knife, but not too close. Thus propositioned the desperate bald man lunged: Abe turned clockwise on his left, front, foot; used his forearm, fist clenched to sweep aside the man's arm, but with enough power to knock the weapon from his hand; pivoting back the other way now, the policeman drove the palm of his right hand under the man's nose. Again he went down, immobile now. No, a twitch; then a groan. Apparently a red rag to a bull, this inconsequential action caused the sergeant to suck in his breath in exasperation, stinging his injured chest. Then, almost casually, he lifted a heavy stool – like the table it had metal legs – lifted it above his head, and prepared to drop it on this audacious groaner. It was like they were all mesmerised, fascinated. Then Miriam shouted.

"Abe! No! No!"

He looked at her, as if emerging from a dream. He looked at the man on the floor. And then he looked at the stool as if, despite its weight, he had forgotten it was there. He looked at Jack, at his brother, looked at the broken remains of the sloggers. And he looked into Miriam's eyes, and put the stool down carefully and walked to the doors; unlocked them.

Too late P.C. Salt arrived with his truncheon, bursting in, obviously expecting trouble.

"I've just heard…Oh. Have I missed all the fun?"

"You ay 'arf," confirmed Jack Beckett, "yoh should 'ave sin old Abe. 'E was jumpin' abaht like Spring Heeled Jack!"

"Jack!" Abe said sharply, "that's enough. Did you say you had some rope?"

"Yes. I'll get it."

"Samuel, help us get these people immobilised. Some of them might need bandages rather than rope though. Start with that one," he pointed at Kelly, "he's uninjured. Cuff him and kneel him down. Then it's…wait a minute, bandages," then more loudly, "there's one missing."

"It's that funny looking one, the one with the bandaged arm," said John.

"I didn't see anybody go out, did you Samuel?"

"No Sarge."

"So he must be…"

He didn't finish, because Jack Beckett started shouting.

"Help, Abe. Sergeant. Help, police, come quick."

Abe said, "John, stay and watch this lot, you too Sis." And the two policemen went into the kitchen.

Jack was kneeling over the inert body of old Mary. She hadn't died of natural causes or shock: there was a nasty gash on her forehead. Seemed like she had either fallen or been pushed. The younger brother trying to escape; she must have got in the way.

Salt confirmed it. "She's dead, Sarge."

"Damn it! He'll be long gone by now. But the others will give him up. Have to, if they want to live."

"Hold on," said Jack, "why's he long gone? The outside door, to the back, it's locked. Mary always kept it locked, put the key in the drawer, always scared of burglars she was."

Salt was already in action, sprinting out past Mary's little hidey-hole under the stairs, and up to the first floor. Abe followed after instructing, "Jack, stay here in case he gets past us, and keep an eye on Miriam."

His sister had come in and was kneeling speechless and tearful at Mary's side.

It turned out that the fugitive had not gone far. Perhaps he had reasoned that the nearer he was to the exits, the easier it might be to seize a chance to dash out; or perhaps he just panicked and ran out of time. Whatever, Salt found him straight away, hiding under Miriam's bed.

"I've got him," he shouted.

The sergeant met him on the landing, Salt holding Percival from behind, no fight left in him and one arm shoved a painfully long way up his back. They took him downstairs and confronted him with the deed. Miriam took the opportunity to slap him hard, twice.

"You reptile," she spat, "what have you done? You snake. I hope you rot in hell!" Then she hit him again.

"All right, that's enough, take him out with the rest," commanded the sergeant, and, catching Percival's eye – he was crying now – said, "you'll swing for this."

"It was an accident," began the murderer, tears streaming.

"You'll still swing for it. Get him out."

"Where does this leave the others?" asked Salt. As a police officer he knew something of the legal ramifications.

"They'll be lucky not to hang too."

Chapter 27

Mayhem and Gaol

The showdown at the Oak became a matter of legend within a few days. Despite the tragic death of old Mary, the day's events did neither the Oak nor police sergeant Lively any harm. Quite the opposite, for sightseers and the otherwise bored now flocked to visit the location of such an epic struggle. Indeed, if you were one of the lucky through-the-window eye witnesses, or could cozen the gullible into believing that you were, then it was worth a free pint or two to point out the exact geography and actions of the engagement. As for the sergeant, his professional duties became suddenly lighter, as did his temper in consequence, his reputation for toughness enhanced; and the lives of seven troublemakers, mere drunken bullies, like so many of Blackheath gaol's customers, weighing in the scales of a justice that might whimsically kill them should a random judge get up out of the wrong side of the bed one wrong morning with heartburn and a bad mood; all engendering a general feeling, at least for the time being, that you ought to not misbehave in Blackheath. Safely out of the way in Smethwick, the two Wellings boys reflected on a lucky escape. It could have been so different. They had detached themselves from the war party before the real trouble began, they had seen it coming; that was down to their own perspicacity. Prudence, however, had not allowed them to evade the grasp of diligent police constable Salt, backed by a posse of concerned, and well informed, locals. Not having got as far as the Royal Oak however, they were allowed to leave in peace; that was down to the indulgence, the mercy, of sergeant Lively.

As alluded to, the sudden reluctance of the usual troublemakers to make any made Abraham Lively a happy man, or at least a happier one. Jack had promised that things would get better, and Jack had been vindicated. He was going to get promotion, he knew it; and Jack knew it, might even have arranged for it come to pass. The witch had been right about his friend: he knew things. And now the name of Abraham Lively was on everyone's lips, not to mention the agenda of the council and his police superiors.

But as one career was set to bloom, the balance was dictating that, with the autumn leaves, another must fall. Inspector Thomas Oakden had been living on the edge for a long time, but now he was had scuppered himself in one fell swoop. To describe it briefly, it had happened like this:

Joseph Chivers of Cradley Heath and David Taylor of Rowley Village had been friends for years, brought together by their love of sporting pastimes (which to them meant anything where blood was spilled, excepting their own of course). In particular, they both had a passion for fighting bull terriers.

But bonds of friendship, as well as forged can be corroded, and broken. Friends may drift apart, but in this case it was sudden, the break precipitated by a disagreement over a dog: Taylor's dog dying after a fight, he swore Chivers had poisoned him, and he would not let go of the idea which festered within him. It came to blows even, but the indecisive fist fight which occurred did not clear the air nor the toxin from Taylor's system. He next accosted Chivers at his home, despite the fact that the poor man had recently lost his wife, and accompanied by two drunken accomplices, just in case. Chivers wisely decided not to answer the door, Taylor however, kicked it in. Now, we shall never know for certain who picked up the kitchen knife first, all that was plain to witnesses was that within brief minutes of entering, Taylor staggered back out, mortally wounded.

The intrepid and infallible Inspector Oakden being first on the scene, he took no time in coming to one of his famous adamantine judgements, and, knowing he was right, saw no reason not to speed up the creaking wheels of justice by leading Chivers down the garden path, all the way to the assizes. Never mind old men pushed off bridges by nothing more than the ghost of John Barleycorn, this was the real thing, a proper bloody murder – or should that be a proper, bloody murder? And the murderer apprehended and arrested and convicted by none other than Tommy Oakden. Wouldn't that look good on the record? He would show them. He wasn't finished yet. Unfortunately, and as per usual some would say, in his hasty prejudgement and hasty anticipation of the plaudits, he was definitely not thinking clearly. First of all, Chivers could hardly have been said to have been 'apprehended.' He had just stood there, meek as a lamb, seemingly shocked into senselessness by the sight of blood. Not exactly the picture of a callous killer. Then, the only witnesses having seen but the aftermath, and not the actual deed, it might have been that, had the man had time to think, been given time, the 'apprehendee' might have been able to point out that he had not intended to kill his friend, that Taylor had kicked the door down, was bigger than his friend, that Chivers had picked up the knife only to keep it from the maniacal intruder and use it as a threat to ward him off, that Taylor had nonetheless grabbed at it putting Chivers in fear for his life, had pulled it away, and severed a femoral artery in the process, by his own intervention. But no, he was too full of shock, remorse, and fear. The way Oakden got him to say it was that they had had an argument over a dog, that Taylor had come over to 'sort things out', that Chivers had asked him to leave, and when he did not, picked up a knife, and in the ensuing struggle Taylor was seriously cut.

"And you're willing to make a statement, at the station?"

He was. And Oakden wasted no time getting him there, where, still bewildered and bamboozled he scrawled his name in an infantile hand. Knowing no better, Oakden was

428

proud of his night's work. But pride going before destruction, and he being haughty of spirit, the inspector's downfall should have been expected.

So, although not apprehended exactly, Chivers was processed according to the inspector's plan, that is to say, he was next arrested, then charged with, murder no less. All on the strength of his statement. The next step was conviction. But there was no conviction: for upon arrest the law prescribed that a formal caution be properly given. During committal proceedings, constrained by the testimony of the P.C. who had been in attendance, the good inspector was forced to admit that no such caution had ever been given, that it should have been given, and that it should have been given before a written statement was signed, before detailed questioning even, and that he had wasted the court's time, hadn't he? That a man in his position should know better, shouldn't he?

The magistrates ordered Chivers be released forthwith, and reserved considerable vituperation for the unfortunate, but most deserving, inspector; even going so far as to suggest that he should face disciplinary action.

The justices' opinions on the case were, it must be said, coloured by knowledge of things beyond the scope of that action, things about Oakden's method and manner, things the subject of discussion in council, reported to it by their appointed informant, Inspector Millership. They had been uneasy about Oakden's conduct for some time, and this faux pas gave them a perfect excuse to act. Sanctioned by the Chief Constable, Millership was tasked with removing Oakden from his, abused, position of authority. In consideration of his many years' service, and of his family, which to judge by his general behaviour must have been long-suffering, the inspector was given the option of the sack, or of being reduced in rank to constable. Perhaps surprisingly – but then again what's a man with a family to feed to do? – he chose the latter course. And Sergeant Lively obtained another pair of hands to help take the strain. Also surprisingly, and most of his former subordinates would say very surprisingly, he made a model police constable. Perhaps the self-imposed pressure of his self-imposed importance had been too much for the man, but one thing was for sure, he stopped swearing. Almost totally.

#

Abe Lively saw the downfall of Oakden as an omen, and Jack assured him that it was. He was one step closer to becoming an inspector himself now. But then, would they bother replacing Oakden? It had always been an unusual set-up, two inspectors and this normal-clothes business. No, have faith, it will be all right. You'll see. Just believe.

A week passed and the sergeant was patrolling, alone and with no particular destination in mind, taking time to think. The town had begun to feel the way it used to, suddenly no longer sinister, or threatening, not to him at least. Just ordinary. Abe wondered how much of the new atmosphere was a peace dividend bought by the blood and justice of the sloggers incident, or how much was down to him having a new

429

perspective, now that he had his Jack to back him up, as he had in that fight. That bad thing? Well, if it was still here it had decided to keep its head down, and the sergeant forgot about it, decided that it had just been an uneasy feeling engendered by his previous unfamiliarity with his new friend, before he had learned to trust in him. He had forgotten about the witch, her words at least, even though he still kept the green stone with him religiously, and slept with it under his pillow, but not as protection now, but to keep Jack close; he had forgotten about the strange happenings in churchyards; forgotten about Sarah and her murdered pony; forgotten about the awful Haden-Best people; about the Reg Phillips case, if it had ever been a case, perhaps Oakden had been right about one thing at least. But he had not forgotten Jack; Spring Heeled Jack, or the Blue Devil, or whatever other label. And, strangely, he could not forget about that blasted so-called poet. He never had tracked him down and found out more, and perhaps that was it, what bothered him – unfinished business. But he had been busy dealing with real criminals; that man was just a distraction; he irritated the sergeant, still; irrational really, particularly as he had not even seen him around for, what? Weeks was it? Perhaps he had left.

But, overall, things were undeniably looking up. He was getting on well with John, despite of, perhaps because of his links to uncle Cyril; Josh was seeing a lot of that Miss Ricketts (Abe had high hopes for him there), and he and Miriam were back to how they used to be, and that suited him, for now. Professionally, he had great expectations, which seemed to be confirmed when he received a summons from Old Hill and Millership to visit on Saturday. And with the arrival of a travelling theatre group the whole town was buzzing with an innocent excitement.

In fact, he had been tied up half the morning by a couple of travelling players. At first frustrated by the waste of time, he began to reflect that this was in fact a pleasant change from the constant acts of petty or serious violence which had started to take up all of his time. The fight at the Oak seemed to him like a turning point: if it had allowed him to get something out of his system, it had also had a cathartic effect on the town itself, now returning to something like normality…

They had arrived at the station just as he was preparing to leave it.

The spokesman for the 'Mayhem Players' ("That's what it's like in rehearsals, sheer mayhem. But come the day itself, pure perfection, I assure you – generally.") introduced himself as Montague Moran.

For the third time the sergeant tried to pin the man down.

"Yes, well, what can I do for you, sir?"

Moran, balding, bespectacled, and in an appropriately thespianly foppish green velvet jacket complemented by an orange kerchief and silk neck-tie, setting off his pale blue and bloodshot eyes, produced, like a conjuror from a sleeve, a slightly creased and greasy card.

"My card," he announced, flashing it quickly, and making sure it was withdrawn and re-secreted before the policeman could lay hands on it.

"Yes, but what do you want?" His tone may have got through this time.

"Oh yes, er, may we?" He indicated a chair.

Abe sighed inwardly, this might take longer than he had thought.

"Do please take a seat Miss Saunders. I'll fetch you a stool, Mr Moran was it?"

"Yes, that's right, Montague Moran at your service: actor and impresario extraordinaire!"

Did he mean it, or was it meant to be sarcastically self-deprecating?

The sergeant provided the promised stool, so that Moran could sit – next to his far more attractive companion. Emma Saunders, blonde haired, ruby cheeked and ample of bosom had an attractive face, in a doll-like sort of way, for she kept a poker face, a useful ability in an actress no doubt, and only occasionally flashed a tactical smile. And, smiling or not, she looked ten years younger than Mr Moron. Which probably explained the close attention that he paid to her, accompanying his inconsequential comments with unnecessary physical, if momentary, contact with her hand or forearm, as if to reassure her. Of what? His constancy? His lechery, more like, Abe guessed. He could not believe that such a personable female could be affiliated in any amorous sense to such a patently mediocre gabbler. *No, that was wrong: he's a very good gabbler, patently so; just a mediocre specimen of manhood. Perhaps he had hidden talents?*

"Impresario? Sounds impressive."

"Oh deary me no. It just means that I'm the best organiser and negotiator out of our little band. Best of a bad lot. We actors are notoriously disorganised, you know…"

And annoying if you're anything to go by; and fickle I'll wager.

"…it's the artistic temperament. I'm the only one with my feet on the ground, and then it's only the one, ha, ha, ha. No, I count myself lucky to have been appointed shepherd of our little flock."

What a babbler. No, he did mean it. Hubris in his self-denigration. I'll bet he's the worst actor of the lot of them. Compensating, obviously.

He was still going on whilst the policeman was pretending to be occupied in finishing some notes, whilst surreptitiously taking in the lovely Miss Saunders.

"Wouldn't you sergeant?"

What? What was the question?

"I'm so sorry, I was distracted there for a moment, what did you…"

It was Miss Saunder's turn to lightly reach out and touch an arm. Unfortunately for Moran, it belonged to Abraham Lively.

"What Bryan…what Montague meant was…" she corrected, but got no chance to say any more as the unnaturally animated Moran – where did such a skinny body get the energy? – began spouting again, not necessarily on the same tack:

"Shakespeare. William Shakespeare. Are you familiar with the Bard?"

Abe had had a good education, although this one would never guess it. He knew enough about Shakespeare to hold a civilised conversation.

431

"Shakespeare? Yes. Are you?" he teased.

"Well yes of course, very familiar. His works that is, obviously. Never met him: I know I'm getting on a bit, but I'm not that old, ha, ha, ha."

Miss Saunders rolled her eyes and none too covertly. Moran didn't notice.

"Do go on, Mr Moran."

The man was peering at him over his spectacles, as if he couldn't see if he looked through the actual glass. *What were they, just props or something? He was an actor after all. An actor who appeared to have dried. Too much beer last night. No, he looked more like a wine drinker. Cheap wine, the only kind in demand hereabouts.*

Then, as if prodded by an invisible stick he started, "Oh yes, King Lear. We're putting on King Lear, would you be acquainted therewith?"

"I would indeed."

Abe's old teacher had made sure that Shakespeare was included in his curriculum, concentrating on one history (Richard III), one comedy (Twelfth Night) and one tragedy, King Lear, as it happened. Moran looked slightly crestfallen, then decided he ought to offer more.

"I play Edmund…"

Crikey, I hope you've got someone good doing your make-up.

"I should have been happy to give my Lear of course, but you've got to give others a chance haven't you?"

It seemed that this was too much for the lovely Emma.

"Come on Monty, you're no Henry Irving. Stop showing off. I'm sure the sergeant's not a man to be impressed by such things."

"I'm better than bloody Roger though," he said, heating up.

"I presume Roger's this other actor to whom you are offering a chance, as you say?"

Seeing the trap Moran simply said, "Exactly. Roger Sebright. Nice chap, if a bit old."

"Isn't that the point?" offered Abe.

"What?"

"Lear, he's a bit old, hence the plot."

"Oh, yes. Yes I see. Yes, we needed an older actor…"

"He's younger than you," pointed out Miss Saunders.

"Yes, but he doesn't look it," said Moran spitefully.

"That's a matter of opinion of course."

"Yes, and in my opinion he looks like an old fart, next stop, the graveyard."

"At least he can carry Cordelia, which is more than you were able to."

"Cordelia needs to lose some weight, fat tart…"

It was threatening to get out of hand, but Miss Saunders was obviously used to these flare-ups and broke off the engagement abruptly.

"You must forgive us inspector. We actors will have our artistic differences, as you can see, and sometimes we quite forget our manners. But it's all very light-hearted really. Do please forgive us."

"There's absolutely nothing to forgive. I was quite enjoying the diversion. If your shows are half as entertaining, they will be sell-outs."

"Well that's very sweet of you sergeant," replied the actress, "I do hope you can come to one of the performances…"

"I'm afraid I'm very busy…"

"And perhaps we could meet for a drink afterwards? You could give me your opinion on my Regan."

Before the policeman had chance to say anything, Moran interrupted.

"Oh no, no, no, no, no sergeant. If you thought our gentle fencing just now was entertaining, what until you see King Lear, in all its majesty!"

"King Lear? I'm sure a comedy would have gone down better with the locals. A good laugh as they say, is the best medicine."

"I told you," began Miss Saunders.

"Nonsense, I'm sure that it will go down very well. Besides, I've had enough of comedy."

"Still," pursued the policeman, "King Lear, that must be a taxing one for all concerned."

"Oh, it is, it is my dear sergeant. We do suffer for our art."

Along with everyone else no doubt.

"So why not do something simpler, shorter that is? There's a lot of characters aren't there, how many are you?"

"There's fourteen if you count…" Emma began,

"If you know your Shakespeare sergeant, you will know that in his time actors always doubled up in times like this, each playing two or even three roles for minor parts, and we, Mayhem Players, are proud to keep the tradition alive. Why, last season, I myself…" Abe was not about to give him the chance to self-eulogise:

"Still, must get very confusing."

"Not at all, not at all. We are professionals after all."

"No," interposed Emma Saunders, "you're right sergeant. I wanted to do As You Like It, but no. Too 'facile' apparently," she said nodding in Moran's direction, "so, we've got Lear. It's a big challenge for us. Our biggest yet. A huge undertaking in fact," she pointed out looking pointedly in Moran's direction.

"Or," announced Moran defiantly, "it would have been but for my judicious editing of the script."

"Your editing? Yours?" asked Lively, somewhat incredulous.

"Yes of course, it's down to me, what with we me being the director of the piece. Didn't I say? No? Then, yes, I'm also the director, actually a playwright too, unpublished

433

unfortunately, before you ask; jack of all trades…But you can rest assured that any necessary cuts or amendments are always done with the utmost sensitivity, the utmost respect, and grounded in my fifteen years' experience of the dramatic process. Because short cuts are necessary I'm afraid: after all, we're only a small band of travelling players."

Which was my exact point. The wheel is come full circle, you twit. "Well, I wish you all…"

"And Edmund. Such a complex character, such a test of the actor's skills…"

Unprompted, he launched his own soliloquy:

"Thou nature art my goddess. To thy law, my services, are bound. Wherefore should I stand in a plague of custom to permit the curiosity of nations to deprive me? For that I am some twelve or fourteen moon-shines in lag of my brother? Wherefore bastard? Wherefore base?" (*pause for breath*).

The sergeant was pretty sure that Edmund would not have had a Brummagem accent.

"When my dimensions are as well compact…"

But here he dried up, and the sergeant continued,

"…my mind as generous, and my shape as true, as honest madam's issue?"

"Why brand they us with base? with baseness? bastardy?"

The actor looked like a kid who had had his balloon burst by a bigger kid.

Recovering, he said, "You know your Shakespeare sergeant."

"Well, you do tend to remember the famous bits," conceded a secretly smug Abe Lively.

"One does indeed," agreed Emma Saunders, adding pointedly, "or at least some of us do."

"That's enough of that," replied Moran tetchily, "I've got a whole play to memorise, not just the famous bits. It's not an easy thing."

"I'm sure it's not," conceded Lively. "Just as I'm sure that you did not come here to discuss the intricacies of learning your lines, and as I'm sure that I have another busy day ahead of me. So. The point?"

"Right. Right you are sergeant, sir," ejaculated Moran as he stood suddenly and stiffly to give a rather effete actor's interpretation of a military salute. In an irritating semi-mime he continued, "Two words," (he was careful with his two fingers). "One – posters," and here he pantomimed someone unrolling a sheet of, presumably, paper and affixing it to an invisible wall; "and two," he said pausing his speech whilst he stepped within range of Miss Saunders, "protection," with which he put an ostensibly paternal arm around her shoulders and let it rest there until she pushed it off.

"Right. Right you are my dear Mr Moron," parodied Lively with superfluous gestures, "two answers. One – posters. No," and here he thrust out his arm in a fist, and pointed his thumb down, "at least," he continued more reasonably, "you've come to the wrong place. If you want to go about sticking posters everywhere, as you lot do, then it's a council matter." In actuality, the council was happy to leave such matters at the sergeant's discretion, but this person…

"But I was told…"

"No. Council," came the flat reply.

He saw a look of disappointment, of long-suffering anguish, pass over the actresses doll-like features, "…but I dare say I could put a word in for you. I'm sure we could allow a few."

"Couple of dozen," began Moran, "after all, it's a rare opportunity for the townsfolk to see some real culture."

"I'm sure it is," replied Lively not exactly honestly, "but in my opinion a comedy would go down better."

"Yes, well I'm afraid that life isn't a comedy," observed Moran.

"My point exactly. People need something to make them laugh."

"And yet, dare I say, that nothing moves the soul like tragedy."

"In that case, there are a lot of souls on the move around here."

"What?"

"He means it's a hard life for working people whose lives consist of sorrow, and, dare I say, tragedy. Don't you sergeant?" Emma Saunder's porcelain mask had been in the process of cracking and now was shattered by a beaming smile. She obviously found something funny, as she had almost giggled. It turned the doll into a warm and vibrant woman.

"You've hit the nail on the head Miss."

"Call me Emma," she invited.

"Well yes of course, life has its own minor tragedies," Moran was butting in again, "God knows I've seen a few myself, some of them not that minor, come to mention it. Do you know, I started as…"

It was Emma's turn to butt in.

"Yes, yes Monty, you've had it tough. But I'm sure the sergeant doesn't want to know your life history. I'm sure his time is valuable." She grabbed his arm roughly and pulled him off his seat. She was not a particularly large woman, but she obviously had a strength to her, be it physical or mental. Leastwise, Moran was persuaded to stand.

"Oh, what? Oh yes, of course. Thank you sir for your indulgence," he said with a bow, "parting is such sweet sorrow, and all that. We must take our leave, don't you know. Time and tide wait for no man. I bid you farewell sir, or may I say au revoir?"

"Number two."

"What?"

"Number two. Your number two. Explain."

"Er, pardon?"

Abe mimed. "Number one! Posters! Number two? Protection, you said. What do you want, exactly?"

435

"Oh yes, good gracious me. Number two. All the fun we were having I nearly forgot."

"And?"

"Well sergeant, I don't know how well you know the theatre…"

"The travelling theatre," corrected Miss Saunders.

"Yes, yes, goes without saying…We in the travelling community find that we are often assailed by gangs of locals who demand money in exchange for not disrupting a performance…"

"To be accurate, Sergeant," added Emma Saunders, "these bands of blackmailing thugs are often travellers themselves, following us around like fleas follow a dog…"

"Yes, thank you, Emma. Whatever the class of ruffian, sergeant, the modus operandi is the same. Unless we pay them, in advance, they disrupt our performance by catcalls and whistles, even throwing items onto the stage."

"Such as?" asked Lively idly.

"Old fruit and veg mainly. A cabbage on the bonce can hurt, I'll tell you."

The memory of something had made Emma Saunders start to giggle again.

"It's not a laughing matter!" retorted Moran.

"No, no, it isn't, I'm sorry. No, it's true sergeant, it's quite a problem. And we were wondering…"

"Just a minute, Miss, Emma. I thought you were performing at the Handel Hotel?"

"Oh, we are indeed, sir. Friday night and Saturday night, with a matinee on Saturday afternoon…" advised Moran stridently.

"That will be tight, won't it?"

"Oh no! We can do it. I've edited the matinee down to the potted version. An hour and half, straight through."

Could a Brummie also be a Philistine? Abe saw no reason why not.

"Look, I don't know where you've performed before, but the Handel's not that kind of place," began the policeman.

"Still," wheedled Moran.

"All right. I tell you what. You let me have, what? Half a dozen complimentary tickets, and I'll make sure that troublemakers don't bother you, or anyone else for that matter. Deal?"

"Thank you – yes, it certainly is."

Money for old rope.

"Yes, thank you sergeant," added Emma.

Moran extended a hand. Abe took it, relatively gently, as the man did not strike him as being in the best of health; a trifle delicate. As predicted, a weak and shaky hand gamely attempted to squeeze back, without much success.

Miss Saunders, still obviously amused at something, then took Abe's hand and shook it as a man would, with more vigour than the other man in the room, and, of all things, a cheerful, if not to say saucy, wink. Well, she was an actress, after all.

"Thank you again, sergeant," she said. "I do hope we shall meet again – the offer stands."

Obviously in a hurry now to remove his companion from temptation, Moran put on his hat with, "And now, my law enforcing friend, we really must bid you adieu. Come on Emma."

He turned and made for the door, but, unaccountably, chose a route which took him close to the fireplace, where he went flying over an unfortunately positioned coal scuttle with a clang of metal and a ripple of small thuds as pieces of coals rolled and spilled. He skidded across the floor, trousers now blackened by coal dust; his hat had been the first thing to part company with its owner, closely followed by his suspect lenses. For a moment it was unclear whether he had done himself an injury, but then it became apparent that he had not. As he rose, rubbing gingerly his left knee and dusting himself down he exclaimed, "Bloody hell, who bloody well left that there. Bloody hell," he repeated to take his mind off the smarting.

Handing him his hat his lady companion enquired, "Are you all right?"

"Do I look it? Look at my trousers!"

"But you're not hurt?"

"Not seriously, no. But I mean, what a daft place to put something like that."

"What?" she asked, "a coal scuttle, next to a fireplace? Who would have thought it?"

"It pays to keep your eyes open," offered the sergeant.

"They were," he pointed out querulously, and he bent down and picked up his spectacles, "it's this useless pair of glasses, they've never been any bloody good."

"Then why wear them?" asked Lively.

"Well, they were a bargain, you see; and I do need something; these are better than nothing."

"I'd ask for my money back."

"I have, but it's my cousin. He won't do it."

"Yes, skinflints run in the family apparently," added Emma Saunders over her shoulder. "Come on Monty old fruit, we're going."

#

As soon as he had cleared the impressive gatehouse, leaking from the oppressive grimness of the red brick prison facades, a miasma of helplessness and hopelessness buffeted him, again. The autumn sunshine did not help: he knew where his journey lay, plunging into a confusing labyrinth of dark corridors and anonymous rooms, where daylight was strictly rationed, filtered dimly through distant inaccessible windows.

437

Shrewsbury gaol; his second visit. Pity the more permanent residents. But for a little luck, and his own wits, guts, and instinct for self-preservation, but for the grace of God in other words, went Cyril Crane.

The guards all seemed pleasant enough, cheerful even. But then, Mr Chambers, as they knew their guest, was not a convict, nor any kind of malefactor. He was on the right side of the law as far as they were concerned; an ally in righteousness. What with him being a solicitor, and all.

Today's guard and guide, the same as his last visit, was a man with a thick-set physique (useful attribute for the job) and a rugged face that told its own stories of past confrontation (common consequence of taking it.) He was very much like Cyril Crane himself in fact, except twenty years younger, and more talkative. Crane did not mind the talking, he let the guard do most of it, grunting a few banal replies to the usual inconsequential enquiries about the journey, and obvious observations on the weather which such brief interactions between strangers always elicited. Being under false colours, Cyril was careful not to give encouragement to questions which might lead to a more awkward conversation, hence, in part, his own verbal economy. But there was also the fact that he was trying not to breathe it in, the odour of incarceration – it reeked of rot. In through the nose, shallow breaths, and out through gritted teeth, so that it would not penetrate, poison him, and mark him out for one of its own. Getting closer now, closer to the cell blocks, and it was trying to overwhelm him with cabbage and suds and stale urine peppered with lunatic shouts and desperate cries and the clang of confining metal. It was his will against the prison's, and he was losing. And the guard noticed.

"Yes, it can get very stuffy in these corridors. We're over a boiler room here."

Cyril was sweating and puffing with the effort to keep his Satan at bay: the guard saw an old man affected by a lack of fresh air. Cyril was momentarily lost for words, but the guard came to his rescue.

"Here we are then."

They had arrived at the room, same guard, same room, where Cyril had been taken first time, to see the same doomed prisoner. Not a cell as such, not given its present function at any rate, although the small high slit of a window and heavy bemetalled door said it may be. Here it was separated from the main body of cells.

William Arrowsmith had already arrived. He was standing, arms shackled, in front of the bolted down iron topped table. At his side, another prison guard. Tall and thin, hard eyes and one hand on his 'peg', not that Arrowsmith looked like any kind of threat.

"You took your time," he accused Cyril's guide.

"I've got further than you to come Jethro."

Jethro nodded an unwilling acknowledgement of the fact.

"Right, Mr Chambers, my colleague will just…"

The 'just' consisted of Jethro the tall sitting his charge and running his shackles through a couple of iron brackets affixed to the table top, and securing the prisoner to it by lock and key.

"No funny stuff you. Just behave," was his warning to Arrowsmith. Then, just for the hell of it, he offered his own opinion on the consultation which had so put him out.

"Fat lot of good a lawyer's going to do you now. Talk about bolting the stable door after the horse has...bolted," he pontificated, but taking care that the remark could not be construed as being aimed at the solicitor, his better.

The 'lawyer' had by now recovered his composure and his cover.

"Yes, well I'm not here to save his skin, my esteemed confederates at law have already botched that job, wouldn't you say? I'm here to put his affairs in order, which, from the provision of the pen and ink there and the fact that the rope awaits my client, perhaps you may have intuited had you half the sense of your co-worker here. Now, can I have some privacy to draw up a will?"

"Right you are, sir," said the guard with more than twice the sense, "come on Jethro."

Jethro complied with a scowl, as soon as he was behind the lawyer's back. Luckily, the man really was not over-endowed with brains, neither of them really, not like a good copper; somebody like Abraham or that Salt, they would probably have smelled a rat by now. Still, too risky, he vowed never to try this foolhardy trick ever again.

He sat down and looked at Arrowsmith. Prison definitely did not suit the man. He looked ten years older than his forty-five years, if not more. Shaved almost bald, and his eyes looked like two dirty holes into a derelict mine, or into hell, where he would likely be soon. He had lost weight since their last meeting, deteriorated. But who wouldn't? What would be the point of eating, when your days were measured and few? Only the worms would notice.

Arrowsmith had been staring at him intently, but was careful to say nothing, nor to move a muscle until the screws had vacated the room and slammed and locked the door. "So, what news?" he enquired.

#

There were two men, acquaintances, an observer might pronounce them friends, at a push. They had not arrived together, rather had apparently bumped into each other fortuitously, completely by accident. Not a planned meeting, of course not. Or was it?

Keeping themselves to themselves, heads together, two mates, having a quiet pint and a casual chat, Jack Cutler and Anthony Duberley were in fact meeting on business, their kind of business, the to be kept secret kind, in the saloon bar of the Bell, on Gosty Hill.

"I see you made the front page," commented Cutler, tapping a folded copy of the 'Advertiser.'

439

"I really don't know what you're talking about inspector," replied Duberley, winking.

"Sorry. Slip of the tongue. I meant to say, I see that our old mate...no that's not right either is it? No, I was just saying, in passing, have you seen the paper? Apparently, the local workhouse master passed away in his sleep: faulty gas lamp they think. Just goes to show doesn't it?"

"What?"

"How fickle fate can be. I mean, here's a fine upstanding citizen; a godly man, no doubt, helping all those poor people, what do they call 'em? Indigents, that's it, or is it indolents? Dunno. Anyway, this goodly, nay godly man goes to bed one night and, bang! Wakes up next morning dead! Don't seem fair does it? I mean, I don't know the man myself you understand, never met him: for all I know he might have been a really evil fat bastard. And what of his poor wife?" A pause.

"Oh. His wife, yes. What about her?"

"Says here," he tapped, "that she's gone missing. I do hope nothing untoward's happened to her. I mean, that would be just too cruel, wouldn't it?"

"Yes it would," Duberley assured, "but don't worry, I've got a feeling that she's safe and well. Just doesn't want to be found; too frightened to be found, for a few reasons."

"You're sure of that?"

"Yes, there was no love between them, a marriage of convenience so I am reliably informed."

"Good, good. All right, I'm trusting you in this."

Duberley nodded acceptance of the implications.

"I'll tell you what though," he confided, lowering his voice, "he dain 'alf put up a struggle for a tub o' lard; took ages for him to pass out..."

#

"Well, I've checked on a few things, and it seems that the information you gave me is good," said Cyril Crane.

"Of course, it is. I was with Hill long enough, the treacherous rat. I know exactly how he works and," Arrowsmith added more pointedly, "who he uses for what. Did you find Davenport?"

"Unfortunately, deceased."

Arrowsmith had been expecting that answer. Davenport, dirty deeds for a price, murder included, had had his head smashed in in a pointless tavern brawl, five years ago.

"Oh. But that's good isn't it?" he asked disingenuously.

"Well it's bad in so far as, if, as you suspect, my brother-in-law may not have killed himself, but was murdered by this Davenport, then I should have liked the opportunity to kill him myself and take that piece from the board. But yes, as far as our plan goes, as far as your own 'confession' goes, it's good."

Cyril was quite sure that Arrowsmith's talk of murder had been a mere fiction to get Cyril to notice him, but he was not about to let on. The more ammo he had against Hill, the better. He continued:

"I've got a list of a dozen enemies of Hills, a list which as you know I have been compiling for some time. You were on it yourself, of course, in the guise of your alter ego, although I would never have found all of them, including yourself, had you not reached out. As I said before, we've got mainly innocent victims of fraud. But the hurt, and the anger, runs deep with some, as with our Mr Swinnerton."

"Told you so."

"So, you did. So, here's the offer. I promise to make sure that your wife and kids are properly cared for after your…after you're gone. All as agreed. The paperwork's being drawn up now, but, essentially, this is a secret deal and ultimately you are relying on my word. Which is partly why I've taken the trouble to visit you like this, in person. Can you trust me?"

"Cyril, what choice do I have? I already tried throwing myself on the mercy of our Mr Hill, for old times' sake and whatever fear he had of me talking. He just laughed in my face, in writing at least. Denied everything. Never heard of me apparently, Alan Hale that is. Threatened to have the law on me. He was right though. Who would believe me over one of the gentry? Especially when it came out that the 'me' was somebody I had made up. Shot myself in the foot there, I think. That's why I thought of you. And then I got myself into this scrape. Come to think of it I wouldn't be in said scrape if he'd been fair and helped out an old colleague, with a bit of cash. It was arguing over a bit of cash got me here. It's worse now, who'd even listen?"

"I told you, that depends on who you tell. I listened…"

"Too high and mighty he is, the snake. He thinks he's untouchable."

Oh, I'll touch him all right: "He has done rather well for himself," observed Crane.

"Yes, on the backs of other people. People like me. I should have been sharing in the money he's rolling in, not…not this," he complained, raising his chained arms the couple of feet they would go and his eyes to look around the whitewashed walls.

"But your uncle," began Crane.

"Cyril, I know all convicts say it, but I didn't do it, not on purpose; not how they say."

Cyril was not sure whether to believe him. But why lie now? Down on his luck, desperate for money, so it went, he had battered his uncle George to death in a dispute about the whereabouts of a bag of cash. Booze and the cards had done for him, just like they had conspired to end Gabriel. Wouldn't be the first time a jury got it wrong, though…

"It doesn't matter now Bill."

"But it does," insisted Arrowsmith, "and that's the tragedy. But every cloud as they say…I'm already a convicted felon, a murderer no less, and they can't hang me twice. So, my reputation can't be harmed – and that makes it a saleable commodity."

"Yes, about that. You're sure?"

"Cyril, look, I'll be honest with you: I've done a lot in my life I'm not proud of; I bamboozled all those people, on your list and more of them, stole from them basically. I justified it by telling myself that they could afford it, that they were too stupid to have it, that I was more deserving. I told myself that nobody was being harmed, not really. But it was sheer delusion. Sheer self-temptation. I know now where such beginnings can lead and, in a way, I think that perhaps I do deserve to be here now, awaiting my date with God. But let me tell you this: I've never been a murderer. Yes, I've killed, I served in India with the lancers, and we killed in battle. Duty it's called, and that's different. But murder, no. I am not a murderer, and yet am now branded so, and condemned. I mean to do some good with that brand."

"Your family?"

"Yes, so come on, let's pile ignominy upon ignominy, shame on shame, for a kind of honour. It will be our secret." And pausing to breathe deep, he continued:

"Let the record show that, on or about the date which you, Cyril, will provide, I William Arrowsmith took instruction from Rupert Hill, and, with malice aforethought or whatever it takes, on – ditto with the date – did slay your brother-in-law Gabriel, what?"

"Lively."

"Yes, Gabriel Lively, that's it. Shotgun in an old barn you say?"

"Mill."

"Mill?"

"Yes, yes, it will all be drawn up for you to sign – and memorise."

"Good."

"The other witnesses will swear, amongst other things, that they overheard Hill clearly telling you to kill the fallen angel."

"Which I kindly explain was our way of referring to your brother-in-law."

"Yes, can't have it too neat. Might look manufactured," replied Crane, Arrowsmith snorted.

"If you say so."

"I do. Do we have a deal?"

"We do. And yes Cyril, I do trust you. It's taken me all of my life, but, eventually, I've come to be able to recognise an honourable man when he sits in front of me," *which is more than you can old pal, I'm sorry but needs must,* "I know we were never close, but I saw what you did, tried to help your brother-in-law when he was too drunk and reckless with his cash. I only wish that I had had a friend like that."

"You have now."

Unexpectedly, and despite himself, William Arrowsmith began to cry.

"Now look, before I go then, I've taken the liberty to draw up some extra documentation which I want you to sign as Hale, including another begging letter to our mutual friend which I want you to copy out and sign, in the hand that you used previously. Don't worry about witnesses, I'm going to falsify that."

"All right, but why? I'm already going to give you a formal sworn statement."

"Bill Arrowsmith's confession will see daylight only as a last resort. I've been thinking, and I believe that there's life in old Alan Hale yet! Here you are." And he retrieved a bundle of papers from his case. "I'll get pen and ink."

Twenty minutes later, and it was done.

"You won't see me again. I'll send somebody else next time, a minister. Be ready."

"I will."

Crane got up and went and rapped on the door.

"Guard, all done now," he shouted.

#

Suddenly alerted, sitting up, Duberley said, "What's that?"

Nearby, out on the highway, somebody was clanging a large bell.

"It's nothing. Didn't you see it when you came in?" replied Cutler.

"Yes, I saw a bell, but what's happening? Is there a fire?"

"No, no. It's a steep hill outside. Osses pulling waggons get tired. Some of 'em can't go any further."

"So?"

"So the bell's there to let the pub know a waggon's arrived, so they can provide a service," he said cryptically.

"Oh," said Duberley, seeing the light. Or thinking he had:

"So they tek 'em some beer while the osses 'ave a rest, do they?"

"Not quite. It's the beasts that need the refreshment, so they get water, from the trough. But a lot also need help."

"Help?"

"The landlord keeps a couple of draught horses. When they ain't working for him, hauling barrels, they hitch one of 'em – one's normally enough – they hitch one up front in line, an extra set of feet to get to the top. All for the price of a couple of pints."

"That's clever," pronounced Duberley.

"Yes," said Jack, thinking that it wasn't in particular, "now Tony, I met you here for two reasons: one, the usual Blackheath crowd tend to stop down there, and there's a completely different crowd uses this place, none of whom should be familiar with our faces. You can't be too careful…"

"I know…"

"But there's another reason I'm showing you this place, so you know it."

443

"Why's that?"

"I may need you here, but you don't need to know any detail yet. I'm still largely in the dark myself. But, just look out the back there. Them two big sheds; one's apparently a smithy come cart shed the other's for storing feed, except they only use this one 'ere." He gestured with his thumb over his right shoulder at a building behind him and built on a level slightly lower than the pub, "That's the feed store. That other one," he pointed to another, obliquely in front, and set slightly lower down the slope again, "used to be a wheelwright's, but it's empty. That's the one we're interested in."

"Why?"

Cutler put a finger to his lips.

"Shush, that's all I can say for now. Recognise where you are?"

"What do you mean?"

"If you go on past the building we have been talking about, you're in the wood yards down by the cut. The wood shops are set out on levelled ground, like you see there, all the way down to the water. Terracing it's called."

"Is it? I know where you are, by the tunnel, by the Navigation. If you keep going you get to the train station," said Duberley.

"Good, glad you know that. Might be important."

"Why?"

"It's always as well to have an escape route."

"Tell you what," said Duberley, "if I was here and the coppers was coming for me, I'd goo straight down the main road, quick as me legs could carry me. Couple of 'undred yards and you'm out of Blackheath police area and into 'alesowen, which is a totally different force. Or is that what the coppers would expect?"

"Depends on the copper. Right, I'm gooin'," announced Cutler. "Give it five minutes, and you can be on your way, I'll leave the paper," and Cutler whispered in his ear, "be careful how you pick it up, your money's in it," before straightening up, "see ya."

"Yeah. Ta-rah."

Sitting in another corner, blending in but seeing all, as usual, sat Francis Thompson. He hadn't wandered into Blackheath recently, had been warned off, that's why Abe Lively hadn't seen him. Instead, he had been striking off in a new direction, and had found this place, amongst others. There was something living with him, or in him, he knew that now, ever since Birmingham. Since Birmingham he had started to sicken, and it wasn't just the cough, he knew: his mind, his old way of thinking was being appropriated by whatever had moved in. Trouble was, he couldn't decide if he should fight it, or revel in it. He had tried fighting, once he had finally concluded that he was not imagining it. But by then the thing, whatever it was, demon or angel or ghost, he knew not, was well established, and fighting it just made him ill, more ill. "Just accept it," a voice said, "it will be all right, you will see." It was only a whisper, but he could

444

hear distinct words now, not just fuzzy sound, and he waited with, what? Dread? Or was it anticipation? Because he knew what it wanted, it had already tricked him into spilling blood. Although, hadn't he liked it?

Cutler, he knew Cutler. What was he doing here? *It's a pub, why shouldn't he be here?* But his friend was also interested. He could feel it. He knew he would be seeing Jack Cutler again. His new muse, she told him. Fertile ground she said.

#

It was a rare event that got three of the Lively boys out together doing nothing but socialising. But that night's production of King Lear, albeit Mr Moran's own abbreviated version, was sufficiently singular to qualify. In one sense then, they owed the night to Moran, but the more proximate cause was their brother Abraham, and his hard-won free tickets. As Moran had always maintained, a stage production in Blackheath had been sufficiently uncommon for it to have been a virtual sell-out. All it had needed was the advertising. Worth their weight in gold those posters, he always said it, particularly when the posters seemed to promise something exotic, even lurid…

During the half time break, the three brothers: teacher, constable, and big John Lively were lucky enough to get a table. Well, perhaps there was little luck involved. Everybody knew big John – and his uncle – and the popular P.C., and many the teacher. All were figures of authority of one kind or another, and each had earned his own measure of respect in his own field.

As was their wont, John was with Sissy. They took every opportunity to be together. And Josh was nurturing his blossoming relationship with Geraldine Ricketts, his partner this evening. The third of the Lively trio was Frank, who had his latest temporary conquest in tow: a young woman with straw-coloured tresses and the smooth and pretty face of a mere girl, named Betty. Betty seemed shy amongst such exalted company.

"Here we are then," Frank and a tray of drinks were approaching the table, having successfully negotiated their way through the crowd thanks to such exhortations as "mind your backs, coming through; excuse me folks, make way; don't want to spill it on your nice dress Miss; ta very much; thank you! Mind your backs, please! Drinks coming through," together with the deftness of movement that came naturally to a young man.

At the table the refreshments were distributed by Josh Lively. Frank sat and raised his glass.

"Good Health," he toasted.

They all repeated the mundane mantra and chinked glass on glass. It was Josh's turn.

"To Happiness and Long Life."

"A long and prosperous life," appended big brother John.

"Yes indeed," agreed Josh.

445

They all drank, the lads supping in a manly but not uncouth manner, ladies sipping more or less demurely.

"So, what do you think of it so far?" asked John of Josh and Geraldine.

"Well, I'm enjoying it. The bloke playing King Lear's good isn't he?" opined Josh.

"You don't think he's overdoing it, the raging mad thing? I mean, come on a bit sudden don't you think?" enquired Frank.

"No, if that's the way it was written…no, I think he's good."

"Well," interjected Miss Ricketts somewhat protectively, "it is a very fine balance. He's got to show us how angry he is at all this. He's mad, in both senses of the word, I think. And a king's madness has got to be seen as worse than other mortals', hasn't it?"

"Well," Frank conceded, "he's certainly putting a lot into it, I'll give him that. He wants to watch he doesn't have a seizure, silly old duffer," he continued, winking at his lady friend.

"Don't be so cruel Frank," said Sissy, but laughing herself nonetheless, "we all have to get old," and more seriously, "I suppose that's his real problem. He's powerless against time, like all of us…"

"Blimey, you'll have me cutting my throat by the end. Anyway speak for yourself. I for one never intend to get old…" announced Frank.

John gave the conversation a new steer:

"So, which is your favourite character then, Siss?"

"I'll tell you who it's not! It's that sneaky little Edmund. Ungrateful little rat. The women are cruel, but he's worse, the little stirrer. Wouldn't trust him."

"You're not supposed to like him," said Josh, "Which just goes to show that he's a good actor."

"Not necessarily – he might just be sneaky in real life. Then it's not acting is it? Then, it's just down to the script, the script makes you think he's acting well," countered Sissy.

"Well, I suppose that applies to lots of actors. How do you know if they're acting or just playing themselves, unless you know them personally?"

"Damned if I know. Who cares?" interposed a slightly inebriated Frank.

"No, I think you may have something there Sissy," said Geraldine Ricketts, "I mean, without spoiling it too much, in the play he's supposed to have the two sisters falling over each other to get with him, he's that handsome and charming, if evil. But really, is that believable, tonight I mean? He might be a perfectly nice chap off stage, but he's hardly the best advertisement for handsome manhood is he? On or off."

"Yes, but you've fallen into a trap there," said John, "you're relating this performance to your own life, real life. But this is not real life, it's theatre, and theatre is not real, it's make-believe. You have to use your imagination."

"Them two sisters will certainly have to then," exclaimed Frank, "poor darlings."

The way Frank delivered it, it produced fits of giggles among the girls.

Out of the blue Betty announced, "Well, I can't follow it. The same people come on talking different, like they don't remember what they said before."

"It is confusing," Geraldine hastened to reassure her, "but it's because there aren't enough actors for all the parts, so if you see someone like that, he's doubling up, playing two parts."

"Oh, you mean like his old mate?"

"What? Whose old mate? What are you on about?" fired Frank.

"The king's, the one he banished. He's playing that other one then, as well?"

"What other one?"

"The one they put in the stocks."

"No, no, no," remonstrated Frank, "that's Kent, that is."

"Yeah, I know that, but he's doubling up then isn't he? 'cos the chap in the stocks was called something different wasn't he? Can't remember what…"

Frank sighed. "No, no, you've not got it at all…"

John didn't like where this was going. "Which one was your favourite then Betty?"

"Well, like I was saying," she darted a hard look at Frank, "I like that one, that Kent. I think he's handsome, for an old man."

"Handsome?" retorted Frank, "he's as old as the hills. And he's stupid, sticking with that mad old bug…sausage," he corrected.

"There is such a thing as loyalty you know, Frank," John declared sharply.

"Yes, there is," agreed Josh.

"Oooh, pardon me for breathing," replied the teacher, hiding behind a quaff.

The conversation missed a beat. Then:

"How's the world of teaching then Frank? How's your band of little rascals?" enquired Josh.

"The world of teaching as you put it is great, wouldn't trade places with you. And the kids are doing very well, thank you for asking."

"And that, er, what was it? Mary? Mary and her brother? Attending regular are they?"

"Yes, thanks to you and Salt."

"What's this then?" said John, pricking up his ears.

"Oh, it's nothing. Police business," said Josh, "…routine," he added hastily before carrying straight on, "has Frank told you about his little poet?"

"No. Who's that?" asked John.

"His name's Walter, and he's not a poet, he's a little terror, to put it politely," explained the teacher, "funny with it though, I must admit."

"How do you mean?"

"Limericks. He keeps coming out with rude limericks."

"Really?" interjected Sissy, "do tell!"

"Not in mixed company," cautioned Josh.

447

"Oh, so you've heard 'em then. Go on Frank, give us one," urged John.

Amazingly, Frank looked embarrassed.

Miss Ricketts finished her drink and saved him, "Come on ladies, just time to get some fresh air before the second half."

But there wasn't. The three of them got as far as the other side of the room when the bell went.

"Go on then, quick," pressed John.

"All right, this is his latest:

There was an old man from Leeds,

Who swallowed a packet of seeds,

In half an hour…"

Sissy interrupted, "Come on you two," she admonished.

"Tell you later…"

Chapter 28

Dogfight at Fanny's

A desultory drizzle blew against the front windows of the Bell. When enough moisture had accumulated tiny rivulets framed between banks of encrusted soot cried their way downwards. On the same wavy panes orange smudges reflected from glowing coals within; to a fellow of an artistic or imaginative disposition, the smudges might be taken as miniature volcanoes spewing tracks of lava rather than water. To a more earthy character, as were many in those parts, and particularly to one without a good coat, the panes merely confirmed that is was bloody raining and that there was a cosy fire inside.

The interior however, heated by a smoky pot-bellied stove, was stuffy rather than cosy, although it must be conceded that, individuals being individuals, opinions did differ. One particularly averse to the damp and unusually sensitive to the cold would perhaps hardly notice that a whimsical wind at intervals kept wafting the coal smoke in billows backwards down the flue back into the room, might perhaps accept the puffs as nothing more than comradely reciprocation, one pot belly to the rest of the gang of pot-bellied puffers, for almost without exception the fireplace huddlers had either a clay pipe hanging from their lower lips as if glued, or smoked incessant cigarettes whilst all drank incessant beers; whereas, another might curse the eye-stinging, tubes-cutting incursions. As usual however, a bit of smoke was not enough to persuade anyone of either denomination to shift from their favoured positions, after all they were used to it, and coping consisted of nothing more strenuous than knocking back another pint. Which suited the 'gaffer.' Said worthy did offer to prop open the doors, but people had got used to summer weather and the transition, for today at least, to cool and damp, persuaded the regulars that the wood should remain in the 'oles, despite the back draught, not to mention the ejecta from the tens of pipes and fags. Thus did warm but stuffy triumph over ventilated and cold.

The pub itself was half way down the hill and set back from the road down in a little depression, anchored firmly to the hillside, clinging on as surely as a sheep tick on its unknowing host, as it had for going on for three hundred years. Originally a farmhouse, the building had converted to tavern as the bourgeoning industries of the age of coal and steel destroyed the pastures and made that new utilisation economically worth-while.

The present owner, Mrs Fanny Wright Fereday, was wealthy enough, in her own right, to be able to let the pub, and too old to be running it personally in any case. At present, the licensee was Jim Lowe. At fifty he had 'been around' and was sufficiently confident in his position to sanction illicit activity on the premises, so long as it benefitted his pocket. So it was that on that particular Saturday, as observed by a patient watcher opposite, an unusually large number of customers were seen entering, and an unusually large proportion of same accompanied by dogs of the same general type. Had that watcher been entirely impartial, had merely been looking on out of boredom or curiosity, had he not have been briefed about what to expect and ordered to remain unseen, and had he with nothing to fear and in a spirit of general nosiness walked right up to the windows to peer in, it would have seemed to him that he had been imagining the comings – for he had certainly seen no goings – the pub itself being populated by nowhere near the number of bodies that he had counted entering Fanny's (the secreted disguised watcher was a Halesowen police constable and a Halesowen local, and locals always called the place Fanny's, although the eponymous owner was very rarely seen on site these days.)

By 3.00 the comings seem to have dried up; at around 3.10 a knot of men, also locals, emerged, in various states of inebriation. They looked like little kids lost at the fair. A short discussion, and the breakaway itinerants toddled off downhill, toward the next democratically appointed boozer no doubt, the nearest probably, which meant the Dun Cow, a five minute 'kaylied' meander away...

It was quiet now, but the yard was not completely deserted: in the lean-to attached to the stable where two hard working dray horses were looking forward to their Sunday off, there sat upon a bale of straw a man with a newspaper, keeping a watchful eye upon nothing much...

"Right, that's me lot," said the policeman to himself. As arranged, he would now confirm that suspects were indeed in place, so set off first uphill to pass word to one P.C. Payne of Blackheath police then back down to report to his own superiors.

He found Payne stationed as ordered at the Big Beech, where the beer was as ropey as the sparse patronage, and the dead and dying flies crowded out the sticky strips suspended from the cracked and smoke-stained ceiling, and he doing his own piss-poor impression of a bar fly, sat there sipping, ostensibly enjoying, a reluctant off-duty pint (of shandy, by special dispensation)...

The plan was, allow the targets to settle and relax before Blackheath broke in on them. Escapees would no doubt make a bee line down the road, at least most of them, that being the quickest way out of South Staffs jurisdiction, as these characters would well know. Also, information received said many of them would be Cradley Heathens, and down the road was the obvious way home. But they would not get that far, would be scooped up by Worcestershire...

Five minutes after the look-out had released constable Payne from his sham shandy and had passed the Bell, going down, a group of apparently four friends strolled past, walking a dog. But the stroll was not a stroll, not really, not in the usual sense, more of a device to disguise a more fixed intent than stroll usually connoted; Jack Cutler tasked with keeping an eye on the gathering by Cyril Crane, unenthusiastically, there with the others. It was an illegal gathering; dogfighting was illegal. More to the point, Jack hated the so-called sport, as, which rankled, he knew Cyril did. But, so the tale told, Crane was beholding to this Solomon Mallen, to the extent of reluctantly agreeing to allow this day's event, here on his doorstep. Because Mallen, whose reputation as a tough breeder of the toughest fighting dogs he proudly wore in plain sight, was the organiser and leader of this band of bloodthirsty weaklings. For Jack was sure of one thing: men who got their pleasures second hand from forced violence of beast against beast were nothing but cowards; cowards putting on a brave show through their dogs; chickens afraid to confront their own kind or spill their own blood, but just hard enough to exert their human power over animals whose nature was for loyalty and obedience, as for betrayal theirs.

Jack did wonder what kind of debt Crane owed to Mallen but he was not interested to the extent that he could persuade himself to spend too much time around Mallen and his cronies, not today thank you very much, not here. No, his eyes and ears in this, expert ones, were worn by Major Challoner, local dog breeding enthusiast, certainly not of the Mallen camp albeit of the same ilk, and an officer in the Salvation Army. Not that that was his rank in that holy militia, Major. No, that was just his Christian name, baptised in it, although, to Jack's mind it was a funny name for a man, more suitable for one of his dogs perhaps.

Along with Jack and his precious Boadicea then, there came strong man Duberley and Duberley's young nephew, Roland, plus the aforementioned Major Challoner. They all stopped outside the pub for an innocent chat. The man in the lean-to pretended to read his paper.

"Now Major," began Cutler, "you're sure about this?"

"Yes, yes, don't worry about me. These things are all very civilised, I assure you."

"I wasn't thinking of your well-being. I meant can you guarantee if I'm not in there personally, I'm not going to be cheated."

"Oh that! Yes, I told you, it's foolproof. Don't worry. Remember what I said, for every fight there's an independent stakeholder, and the stakeholder is obliged to keep a record of the total stakes held and, thereafter, a note of the split, in case of query. All this is entered in a sort of ledger and three or four trusted people, umpires if you like, can check it at any time. It works. At the end of the day, if there are no disputes, the record is burned, at least the bit to do with money. Now, as you know, with me being chairman of the Rowley breeders' club, I'm one of those umpires today. You tell me you want a note of the value of all stakes placed today, I'm the man can get it for you. Although I'm sure you can trust Solomon Mallen in this. What percentage is your cut then?"

"Mind your own business, you just let me know that figure and I'll see to the rest. Oh, and I'll need a count of the number of dogs booked in to fight today."

"But why do you…"

Jack aimed his palm at Challoner, "Just do it."

"Whatever you say."

"I hope I can trust you Major, because if I find out you've lied to me, in anything, if I find you've misled me, in anything, or if there's anything said to make me even ever so slightly suspicious, expect a midnight visit from my large friend here, and a few more like him, but bigger."

"That hurts, Mr Cutler. I wouldn't dream of cheating you, or anybody else for that matter, I'm a man of the Church you know."

"Yes, I did know," *doesn't seem to stop you torturing animals though, does it?* "But I've found that's no guarantee of anything. So don't come whingeing to me that it wasn't you if something don't add up. Right?"

"I won't. I know these people, we're a close lot in this game. And Mallen, he's the man to beat because he expects to win, and we don't want him to. And, yes, he can cut up rough when provoked, people don't mess with him, but as far as I know he's always been scrupulous honest in settling his debts. Scrupulous. In fact that's why he's feared, because it cuts both ways – you welch on a debt to him you better make yourself invisible or book yourself a bed in hospital."

"There's worse than him and there's worse outcomes than hospital. You bear that in mind. Right? You better be off."

#

She was hearing muffled sounds. Indistinct words. Bouncing around in the void below her feet. What was he doing? Talking to himself. She went up to the bar and leant over. Just as half a torso floated up through the floor, like a shade from Hades, or a man who had been inspecting a cellar.

"We've still got that leak," her husband announced, poised on the steps half way through the trap-door.

She looked hard at him.

"A leak? Beer do you mean?"

"No, just water. I told you."

"You didn't say it was water."

"It's coming through the roof-light when it rains, what else would it be? I told you."

His full materialisation was her cue to turn away and busy herself with the strategic distribution of ash trays. She spoke as she moved.

"When did you tell me? Last week do you mean?"

452

"Yes," he said, over-doing the indulgence, "like I said last week. And I've just checked and there's some water come in again."

"Well, didn't you repair it?"

"Not yet."

"Then it's no wonder it's still leaking. It won't mend by magic or wishful thinking will it?"

"I've just got to have a good look and decide what's the best…"

"For heaven's sake. You said that you would deal with it last week. Right, leave it to me, I've got a dozen pairs of hands as you know. I'll mop it up."

"I've already done that! What do you think I've been doing?"

"I don't know. Procrastinating?"

"What do you mean?"

"You said that you would sort that leak last week."

"No, I think you'll find I said I'll find out exactly where it's coming from, which I did. It's only a dribble…"

"As yet," she added.

"…it's not a lot and I know where it's coming in. It's only when it rains; just need to reseal it."

"Why don't you then? Why spoil the whole cellar for a ha'penny of tar? A stitch in time, et cetera?"

"Well I don't know whether tar will do the trick, not on its own. It might need tekkin out and re-seating and concreting first, to do a proper job…"

She sighed very deliberately audibly. He decided he hadn't heard, or hadn't understood.

"It's not got any wuss," he assured, "I just need to find a bit of time…"

"Ye gods! Forget it. I will have to get a man in!"

A pause. He lowered his voice and spoke slowly.

"What's that supposed to mean?"

"What do you think it means?" she said tartly.

"No, what do you think it means?" he responded angrily.

"Just what I said. If you don't have time, I will get a builder in, or an odd-job man."

"But that's just a waste of money!"

"It's my money to waste."

A pause again. Of taking stock; of keeping control.

"It's our money I thought," he said, "money from the pub and money from my job: our money; all one kitty. As agreed. Isn't it? It's our money."

She relented, a little.

"Yes, of course. That's what we agreed. A joint venture."

"Joint venture. Strange name for a marriage. It's a marriage, isn't it?"

She didn't hear, it seemed, so he continued.

"Any other husband would have taken ownership of the marital home, or at least half a share. I should have insisted," he said, casting his eyes around said property.

She turned abruptly, half perched herself on a table, hands gripping it. A goshawk sizing up a leveret.

"Yes well you didn't. And for good reason as you must recall," she started, almost reasonably, but the tide of resentment, at his presumption, was welling.

"We've been here," she almost growled, "and we made our agreement, set our bounds. Now, I don't know about 'any other husband' but I do know that I'm not 'any other wife.' And so do you!"

He wanted to say something, she did not let him:

"Yes, it's an arrangement, this marriage, but you knew that when you got into it. And, yes, we pool our income, that works for both of us. But this pub is my inheritance, mortgage notwithstanding. This place belongs to me. That's not changing. It's mine, nothing to do with you, and you were quite happy to have me on that basis."

"Except that I don't," he said into his hand.

"What? What was that?"

"Nothing…I'm beginning to think it was a bad deal."

"Are you indeed?"

"I am. And if this place is nothing to do with me, why do you expect me to help you run it?"

"Because that's…" she began impatiently.

"Because I don't see you down the brickyard helping me."

"Don't be facetious."

"Oooh, facetious is it? Another one of your big words. The trouble with you, you think you're better than the likes of mere grafters like me."

"Don't be silly."

"Yeah, that's me, silly. Not like you and your big-headed brothers. They've all got a bob on 'em."

Slow and cold she moved closer, "You would be well advised to give my family some respect."

"Respect? They're all up their own arses. The only one who isn't is Wilf, and he probably is an' all, except we never see him. I mean, what have we got? A criminal, a saft P.C. who's gonna get himself hurt one day, a sergeant who's going to rack and ruin and who talks to the fairies, and you! Oh sorry, I forgot the womaniser."

"You better shut your gob now!" She spat the vehemence of the vernacular, "my brother is very protective of his family, so, actually is my uncle Cyril, and so am I. So just watch it!"

It gave Jack Beckett pause. If he wasn't careful, he might find himself out on his ear. And he was not ready for that. The local law could of course be relied upon not to give him a hearing.

454

He took a few deep breaths, pretended to be checking glasses for smears, whilst she didn't pretend to do anything. She waited for him to back down.

"Sorry," he said, then quietly, "but it's not easy. I know what we said, you know, the pros and cons of living under the same roof, for reasons other than…well, you know…"

She did not bite.

"…but even so, it's hard, the day job and working here…"

"Wait a minute. You talk as if you're working all hours God sends at that works. But I know you're not. I smell the beer on you when you get in, a couple of hours late as like as not. While I'm here struggling with that moron Marlene trying to keep the place running. While you're out boozing!"

"Is that what you think? That I've been knocking off and going round the pub with me mates? For hours on end?"

"Haven't you?"

"No. I mean yes. And no. No because I haven't got any mates, not proper ones. I'm a foreman remember, we don't have 'mates.' By the time I've seen off the day shift and handed over it's gone seven easy. I think I deserve a swift one on the way home. Don't I?"

"You could have one here, and I could see that you're properly fed: you're looking thin."

"But I can't relax here, can I? Once I step through the doors I feel as if I should be rolling me sleeves up again. It's no wonder I'm thin."

"All right, if you say so. I'm sorry for doubting you. I thought you might be seeing a woman."

"Me? Chance would be a fine thing."

"Would it?"

He seized the nettle.

"Yes. Look, I'll tell you. A marriage means sharing. Not just the money, but each other. You know what I mean?"

"Do elaborate…go on."

"All right then. What about my conjugal rights? See? I know big words an' all."

"Conjugal rights? You've had them, remember? And if I'm not very much mistaken, you rather enjoyed them."

"What do you mean had them? A man's entitled to his dues, whenever he wants them. And if that's every night, it's every night. Instead of which all you can do is say you're tired, you've got a headache, it's late, you're not in the mood – or, you're worried about that mad brother of yours. What's wrong with you? A man's entitled."

"And a bloody woman's entitled. To say no. Wrong with me? What's wrong with you? I don't know where you're getting your common ways, but you had better mend them. You were so nice before we got married…"

"Yeah, I didn't know what I was in for though did I?"

"Yes you bloody well did. Have I been wasting my breath? A business arrangement, we said, primarily…"

"Only because you can't…I didn't think you meant…"

"It makes no difference what you thought. If I don't happen to be in the mood for sex…"

"Which you never are…"

"…if I am not in the mood, if I do not feel the need for such needless sweaty exertion, then that's my business and my choice. Understood?"

"Bloody hell, if other men knew what I had to put up with…"

"What?" she challenged.

"I'm just saying. If I told folk they'd ask what was wrong with you."

"Fuck. Off. If anybody's wrong, it's you. No, no – on second thoughts perhaps you are right, I'm wrong, wrong for you, too good for you, yes, that's what people would say, don't blame her for not wanting him in her bed. So go on, tell them all your troubles. You'll be a laughing stock!"

"You cow!" He strode over to her. "I ought to tan your hide for that woman," and he mimed a back-handed slap.

But the gos-eyed stare faced him down. Then she spoke, deliberate and threatening.

"If you ever touched me that would be it. You know that don't you? And if I didn't tear you limb from limb myself, Abe would probably break your neck. You've seen what he can do."

"Oh, big Abraham Lively, I forgot about him. No, wait a minute, I haven't! How could I, seeing as you're always going on about your overgrown little fucking rabbit. Big Abe, big deal!"

"That's right, he is," she replied evenly, apparently calm.

"Well, he's not going to be around for ever is he? If he gets promoted he'll be moving out. Then you'll have no back up, and…" and a dim light came on somewhere in his head; and a mutant inkling scuttled back into the dark "…and then maybe you'll want to get closer to me, and my bed."

She did not want to think about any of that. It threatened panic.

"Well then, you'll have to answer to John instead, won't you? Shall I tell him what you've been saying?"

#

Cutler, Duberley, and nephew had ensconced themselves in a quiet corner of the bar, quieted since they had arrived, since on replenishing drinks quickly finished the previous occupants of the immediately adjacent perches moved their bums further off. They knew better than to be appearing to eavesdrop on this lot, today of all days. Boadicea was lying

456

content at Roland's feet; she liked him. Duberley for one was looking for a refill, or two. Not today.

"All right, Tony, let's go."

"What? Where?"

"In there," Jack indicated the old cart shed, "before they start proper."

"But, I thought you told the carcass…"

'The carcass,' obviously meant Challoner who was one of the gauntest men Jack had ever come across. He grinned.

"Yeah, he is a bit on the meagre side ain't 'e?"

"Meagre y'say? I tell ya, if 'e was caught out in the rain 'e could pick 'is way 'ome between the drops and stay bone dry!"

"Thin as a rake," offered young Roland.

"Anyway," interjected Jack, closing down the anatomising. "I don't care what I said, or what he might have thought I meant, but I am going to show my face in there, just so he knows I'm watching and not sitting here getting sozzled. Besides, Mallen's expecting me. Nobody else mind, just me. That was the agreement."

"I'm coming with you," declared Duberley.

"That's dead right. You are. I told Crane I'd come alone, but he doesn't know about you. You're my secret insurance policy. But you can only come as far as the door."

"What if there's trouble?"

"Why should there be? It's all arranged, Mallen's expecting me, as Crane's representative. By all accounts, if you keep your word, he keeps his. An honourable man they say. You heard what Challoner said."

"And what about him? Do you trust him?"

"Of course! He's in the Sally Army. Saves fallen women an' everything."

"Hmmh. So how come Crane's not here himself, if there's not going to be any trouble?" questioned Duberley.

"Because they only just tolerate being in each other's presence, and Cyril doesn't like this kind of do, and that's probably the reason they don't like each other."

"Then why…" protested Duberley.

"Don't ask. I mean no, really, don't ask."

"All right. But why you? You don't like this kind of do either, do you?"

"Like I told you, I still work for Cyril Crane, for now, and I must be seen to be doing as I'm told, also for now. He trusts me to be here because I've got more brains than any of the others. Good blokes, but not so gifted in the brains department, you know? And I'm supposed to be here alone, remember. But, like I said, he doesn't know about you…"

"The insurance?"

"Exactly. If anything does kick off, I'll shout you and you can charge to the rescue. I presume you've come prepared?"

Duberley indicated the canvas sea-bag he was just hitching over his shoulder.

457

"I've got my trusty cudgel in here, and, if it gets really desperate," he slid the butt of a revolver half out of a pocket, "there's this."

"God blimey, Tony! Put that away, and for Christ's sake don't let them search you. They'll think we've come to rob the place."

"I just thought…"

"I know. Just make sure you don't look as if you have any intention of following me in. Don't want them going through your pockets. Keep that," he nodded down to the pocket, and the concealed firearm, "for an emergency. Right? Only a dire emergency."

"Got it. That was the plan anyway."

"Yeah, I thought so, just making sure. Ready then?"

"What about Bo?"

"That's where your Roland comes in."

"What?" said the boy, catching his name.

"I was wondering why you brought her…" continued Duberley.

"I couldn't leave her. She's been acting strange of late. Scared like. Been wrecking the place if I leave her, and the landlady's none too pleased."

"Oh," said Duberley, beginning to see. He had met Jack's landlady, and as big and tough as he was, amongst men, he was not inclined to repeat the experience.

"So," Jack explained, "Roland is going to sit with her and finish his drink, and then take her for a little walk. Ain't ya, Roly?"

"What?" he repeated.

#

It was an ad hoc meeting of community leaders, to wit, three councillors and the eminent and very rich George Alfred Haden Haden-Best, a man with a long name but a short title, for, remarkably, he was only a 'Mister.' Which was no doubt a testament to his aspiration to live a modest and moral life. But that modesty was certainly not displayed in the way he dressed. If the man himself thought his dress modest, it was only in relative terms: even a modest diamond cannot hide its lustre. His wealth and its in-bred good taste was obvious at a glance to those with very little knowledge of fashion: he was turned out so much better than anybody else in this room. In that regard though, it must be admitted, the competition was not exactly what might be called intense. George, as they were close enough to call him, was a handsome man in his prime with vibrant well-cared for thick hair and moustache – black, not dark brown, but proper black, with just a touch of grey at the temples. A youthful-looking and fit figure he had still, a prerogative of being rich, and his excellent clothes moved with him synergistic and elegant and announced his dominance to all the world. In contrast, the three councillors in attendance were handicapped by either age or social standing or both. Old Azariah Parkes was long past caring about fashion, or so it seemed, for he wore an old

458

old-fashioned serge suit which might have been of good quality once, and might have been composed of vibrant colours once, and might once have hung from his frame to give the impression of something other than an old blanket thrown over a talking coat-stand. It was true, Azariah had always been thin, but in old age his ability to put flesh on his bones had deserted him entirely; perhaps his appetite or digestive tract had been permanently stunted by his incessant smoking: he was even now sending up congenial clouds from his over-sized pipe bowl and creating a haze through which they all had to think and peer at each other; perhaps he had a secret plan to preserve his body much in the way that a kipper is smoked, for his flesh, whether from the smoke or from the consumption of too much jaundice inducing brandy was wrinkled and dried out and sepia-washed. Doctor Wharton had the benefit of twenty years over Parkes, and cut an altogether different figure. If herrings were still the model, he was certainly no smoked kipper, more on the road to bloater, it must be admitted, and a fact that the medical man was well aware of and sensitive about. He was not in the same class as the deceased object of present discussion though, and he had no wish ever to become so. Nevertheless his generous outline did little to flatter well tailored clothes, and he was thus no threat to Haden-Best's sartorial crown. The final member of their quartet was councillor Samuel Barnett, at thirty the youngest of them. Being young and reasonably well off, he could afford to dress well and wanted to. But he did not of course have the resources of a Haden-Best, nor the height, being several inches shorter than the great man although sporting the same hairstyle and moustache albeit in brown rather than Best's trademark black. He looked like a cut-price reproduction.

They had been trying to decide what to do about the unfortunate Gideon Gross incident. Not the fact of the fat man's death – untimely or exactly the opposite depending on your point of view – but the fact that since he had been hammered into his large wooden box, another one, a Pandora's box, had been opened to disgorge torments for the assembled worthies. First of all, since the man's draconian reign had been cut short, emboldened workhouse employees had come forward to report shocking stories: all manner of stories, complaints and allegations ranging from excessive drinking to improper advances made, to suspicious dealings within the precincts with outsiders who had no legitimate business there. All duly noted by a conscientious constable Salt. And there were odd entries in the records, brought to the police's attention by the Relieving Officer. All in all there was the distinct probability that something very unsavoury indeed had been going on, right under their blocked noses.

Azariah Parkes repeated again:

"A proper shambles, proper shambles."

"Yes well I think that we can all agree on that," retorted councillor Barnett, "the question is, what are we going to do about it?"

"It is indeed a sad state of affairs. A sad reflection upon the weakness of the human condition. Flesh is heir to a thousand temptations, a good man must armour himself in the strength of the Holy Spirit and be guided by the Lord Jesus. I'll wager this Gross person was not a religious man, except in sham perhaps. He was obviously ungodly…So…" and Haden-Best stopped mid-flow as if in contemplation of higher matters.

"So what's your point, George," pursued Barnett.

"The point my dear Barnett, is that I'm not at all sure that the laid down religious observances and moral precepts were being followed in that establishment."

You don't say! "I think you may have something there," replied Barnett, with just a hint of irony.

But even that faint whiff was not lost on Haden-Best.

"No, of course, you're right, the situation speaks for itself. It's all most upsetting. Horrible. Let us hope at least that we can all learn from it."

"And that hits the nail on the head," responded Barnett, appealing to them all, "what exactly have we learned, and what are we going to do with that knowledge?"

"For a start, the next man in the role must be a man of impeccable character; goes without saying. I propose he be a man of the cloth," suggested Haden-Best, predictably.

"You put too much faith in the cloth," remarked Parkes, apparently to his pipe.

"There is something in that George.," Barnett concurred, "I dare say you know better than I do that there's bad apples in the churches, like everywhere else…"

More, thought Parkes.

"…and I dare say that Gross was deemed to be of good character at the time, otherwise he would never have been engaged," he pointed out.

"Well I had nothing to do with it," rejoined Parkes. "If I had, we wouldn't be in this pickle. I mean, you could tell by looking at him."

"Could you?" challenged Haden-Best.

"O'course. An absurdly fat man, obviously weakened by self-indulgence – and obviously venal." He had been toying with that word ever since he had been invited to this gathering.

"To use a cliché, you cannot judge a book by its cover," sermonised Haden-Best, "are you saying Azariah that you can look beyond the flesh and into a man's soul?"

"Not exactly. But a rotten soul casts a rotten shadow. Stands to reason doesn't it?"

Barnett laughed. Parkes took it the wrong way.

"Don't you snigger. If you can't see it now, you will when you're carrying a few more years on your back."

"No Azariah, I wasn't laughing at you, but only at the image you painted. In fact, I wouldn't disagree with you. I'm already old enough to have become something of a cynic, and if you ask me our Mr Gross' appointment probably had less to do with merit than palm-greasing."

"And sadly, in turn, I have to agree with you Samuel," said Haden-Best.

"Particularly," added Barnett, "in the light of the diverse nature of his offences. And let's be frank gentlemen, if the evidence is to be believed, and I think that we do all believe it, they clearly went beyond minor indiscretion or petty misappropriation. We're not talking about nicking a bag of spuds from the cookhouse, or stolen kisses with the housekeeper under the stairs, but sordid immorality. Beyond immoral, beyond criminal, his actions toward some of the most vulnerable inmates were so obnoxious that I think the man must have had a devil in him. Far beyond the pale – pure evil."

"And we don't yet know how much hard cash was diverted into his nefarious pockets. It must have been going on for years," added Haden-Best.

At this point the doctor, who, although not in the same class of flabbiness as the workhouse master, had been unnerved by their equating corpulence with immorality, felt obliged to contribute, in consideration of all the poor and unfortunate victims.

"Were he alive today, I'd gladly see him incarcerated in a dark dank cell forever, stewing in his own juice. What he did to those poor girls…the thought of it makes my skin creep. I'm glad he's dead."

"So am I, Lord forgive me," Haden-Best assured him, "heaven only knows how much he's swindled the parish out of over the years. There's nothing more infamous than the abuse of a solemn trust."

"I could think of a few things worse," pronounced the doctor softly and to nobody in particular.

"Well, he's gone," said Parkes, "and I for one regret not being able to look him in the eye and spit in it as they take him down. I suppose I shall just have to spit on his grave instead, lying fat toad."

"Hold on. Aren't we drifting away from the point?" objected Barnett.

"That being?" asked Haden-Best.

"That being, how to handle this unfortunate affair. All right, the man's dead, so justice is served, some might say. And, they might say, that's enough. But you're not going to get the money back, probably, although we can have a damn good look for it; and you're not going to help his young victims by splashing their names all over the papers; yes, look after them if you will, give them something to take their minds off it, and to stop them talking. The staff shouldn't be a problem, got jobs to think about…But the man's dead. So why publicise the affair? Why make ourselves look foolish? Why not just sweep it under the carpet – then glue it down? Or do we own up and air our dirty washing for the whole world to see?"

"Not likely," retorted Parkes, "they'll have our guts for garters."

"I'm not on the council…" began Haden-Best.

"Who will?" interjected the doctor.

"Them! The people. You know, the good people who vote for us. And the press o'course. And it won't be just good old Moses Munn, who no doubt we could persuade to at least tone it down, and keep names out of it. Nah, this is too juicy, it'll make it as far as Wolverhampton or Brum. They'll have a field day, I tell you."

"Well, let's not get carried away, shall we?" came back the soothing voice of Haden-Best, "because we're not going to let the cat out of the bag, are we? We can all agree that letting this get out will do nobody any good. On the contrary, for the reputations of certain of the parish dignitaries, we can foresee it having completely the opposite effect. To speak plain, you all have your positions to protect. As Azariah has pointed out, it's the voters, the fickle voters, from whom you need to protect yourselves. For my part, as a well-publicised donor to this corrupt establishment, as we now know it, I have no wish to become known as a benevolent idiot."

"In short, we're going to keep this quiet at all costs," affirmed Barnett.

"Exactly so," continued Haden-Best. "The argument being that we've all learned a lesson from this: why risk a change of the guard now, and risk the new lot repeating the same mistakes? That won't serve the interests of the parish."

"Makes sense, but can we get away with it?" said Parkes.

"It shouldn't be beyond the wit and means of us four," Barnett assured him, "and if the worst did come to the worst I'm sure our friendly local newspaper editor would prefer to print facts rather than rumour – and we would control the facts remember. After all, it's Gross that did wrong, not us. Some might say that we should have known, but, really, I ask you, how? When he was being manipulated by a master criminal, a master of disguise and illusion…"

"Eh? I thought it was just one or two opportunistic locals…"

"No, no, a master criminal, from London."

"What? Who? Nobody told me…"

"Azariah, calm down. I just made that bit up. To illustrate."

"Oh. And we don't think we could catch this person…as he's back in London?"

"You're catching on."

"What about his wife? Anybody seen her? She must have known something."

"I'm sure she did, but she's disappeared."

"That may well be a blessing," said Haden-Best, "now, may I suggest that, whatever else, we keep an eye on the running of the workhouse in future? Never again must one man have such autonomy."

"Yes, and may I suggest," added the doctor, "that that includes a committee with the inmates represented thereon, to highlight any welfare issues?"

"Excellent idea," agreed Haden-Best, "and while you're at it, we need a financial expert on it. I'm not going to feel half as charitable if I'm not convinced my money's going where it should."

"Goes without saying," said Barnett.

"It does half," agreed Parkes.

"Er, before we get carried away about future plans," ventured the doctor, "there's a rather more obvious issue to deal with in the present."

"Could you be a little more vague?" asked Haden-Best.

"What I mean is, what about the police?"

It all went quiet. Then,

"What about 'em?" Parkes fished.

"What about them? Who was it brought all this to our attention, eh? The police of course…"

"I know, it was a certain sergeant to be precise, was it not doctor? Your protégé is he not?" accused the old man.

"Well, yes, I'm close to him. He considers me a friend. That may help us."

"So what does he intend to do about it?" added Barnett, more animatedly, "because if he does do something, and that something entails the whole sorry tale seeing daylight, then we're toast. We can hardly gag a police officer can we? Insult to injury, to say the least, if it got out. We can't just order him to keep quiet can we?"

It was a rhetorical question, and Parkes gave a rhetorical, if opaque, answer:

"More than one way of skinning a cat."

"Who is the officer of whom we speak?" enquired Haden-Best, but suspecting that he already knew.

"It's a chap named Lively. Sergeant Lively," confirmed Wharton.

"Ah. In that case Samuel, I strongly suspect that the answer to your question is no, we cannot just order him to keep quiet."

"You know him do you?"

"Yes, I've had the pleasure. And no, that's not sarcasm. I happen to think that he's a fine upstanding young man and a conscientious public servant. What you would call a good man." *Just not good enough for a daughter of mine.*

"But that's bad isn't it? The last thing we need is a straight copper," opined Barnett.

"There's more than one path to public service," replied Haden-Best somewhat enigmatically. It was necessarily enigmatic as the man himself was not entirely clear on what his instinct was telling him. Barnett was not at all clear:

"Couldn't we twist his arm a bit, to look the other way," he persisted.

"He's not like that…" began the doctor.

"Proper bloody shambles."

"What is he like doctor? What is he like then?" Barnett pursued.

"What's he like? Ask me if he is a good policeman, then I will tell you yes he is; ask me if he lives by the rules, then I will tell you yes, he lives by the rules, his own rules; ask me if he is a man of honour, then I will tell you yes, he is certainly a man of honour, his own honour, bounded by his own rules."

"Well that's clear as mud doc, ay it? Bloody shambles…"

"Wait Azariah," cautioned Haden-Best. "Explain doctor."

"What I'm trying to say is that the man is no mere automaton, slavishly following rules. Within his own code he is willing to bend them if it gets the job done; that being to stop crime and apprehend, or punish, malefactors; after all that is the object of those rules. You yourself alluded to this George. More than one way to serve I think you said. If we approach the sergeant properly, if a person he trusts approaches him properly, then I think he could be persuaded to see the bigger picture as it were."

"And he'd do that out of the goodness of his heart would he?" interposed Barnett.

"Not at all, out of common-sense and pragmatism. His heart is reserved for his family."

"So, he wouldn't be expecting anything in return? You know, on the quiet?"

"My dear Samuel, if you wanted to upset the whole apple-cart and find yourself in gaol for attempting to bribe a police officer, you just try it."

"He wouldn't dare."

"He would indeed, trust me, and leave this to me. It was one of his subordinates who did the donkey work – under orders from Lively of course – and the sergeant was not personally involved. Having received a report, passed on to me as you know, I'm confident that he considers the matter closed, that we, the council, will do the right thing. He's handed all the evidence over and as long as I reassure him, he won't want it back. If Gross were still alive of course, that would have been different."

"Why didn't you say that in the first place!" retorted Parkes.

"I'm telling you all now."

"So it's all all right then?" said Parkes, calming down.

"Like I said, he's his own man. But I know him well enough to say, yes, I think it will all be right."

"Hope so. Wouldn't want to get on the wrong side of a man like that – and end up like that gang that upset him in the Royal Oak."

"Oh yes, of course, that was him wasn't it?" said Barnett.

"It was indeed. They made the mistake of threatening his family and he dealt with them; in a violent sort of way but that was what they deserved and what the situation demanded –he did arrest them all at the end," Wharton pointed out, "and some of you will remember him as a young constable, making his mark…"

"Taking down the Scarrets, yes!" enthused Barnett.

"There's no doubt that the sergeant is a versatile and talented young man," said Haden-Best, "as you say, we know he can keep order, with his fists if he has to, but I know that there's much more to him than that. His men seem respectful of him, and that's not always a given, and he obviously knows how to be discrete – we owe him for drawing this unfortunate workhouse situation to our attention and for the way he's handled it."

"So far," added Parkes grumpily.

"Don't be so negative!" urged Barnett.

"Day 'andle findin' mar sheep very well," commented Parkes, unheeded.

464

"Now, listen to me," continued Haden-Best, "I believe that things happen for a reason, and I believe that the Lord is asking me to intervene on Mr Lively's behalf right now."

"How so?" queried the doctor.

"Well, here we are extolling the virtues of this man, this police sergeant, this policeman who has become central to this discussion, when only last night, for the first time in months, I happened to dine with the Chief Constable."

"Don't understand, what's your dinner arrangements got to do with it?" queried Parkes querulously.

"And it just so happens," continued Haden-Best, ignoring him, "that he will shortly be announcing that he is looking for a new inspector, to replace Millership. And I think our sergeant Lively more than fits the bill, don't you?"

"I would endorse that whole-heartedly," said Wharton, "but what about Millership, he's a good man, why..."

"Good man," agreed Barnett.

"I agree. I like the bloke. Been through some interesting times, the pair of us. Why change him? What's he done?" asked Parkes.

"He's done nothing. Rather, it's been done to him," announced Haden-Best sadly, "he's very poorly, like to die soon."

"But I only saw him last month..." began Parkes.

"And I've seen him much more recently," interjected Barnett. "I must admit, he did seem out of sorts, a bit breathless, taking to sitting where he would have stood."

"Heart?" guessed Wharton.

"That's certainly a big part of it," confirmed Haden-Best.

"Why didn't he come to me?" wondered the doctor. "Come to think of it, it seems like he's been avoiding me."

"Wanted to keep it quiet, I suppose. But, it's out now, and he wants to go just as soon as they get a replacement. Wants to spend more time with his wife. Time, as the lawyers say, is of the essence," said Haden-Best.

"Don't blame him," mused Barnett.

"And that gentleman presents both ourselves and the good sergeant with an opportunity. This is no mere coincidence. Now, I have the Chief Constable's ear, and I also happen to know that as of last night, he had no obvious candidate in mind. Well, there is now. I take it you all agree."

"Hear-hear," said Wharton.

"Certainly. Excellent idea," said Barnett.

Azariah Parkes though always had to be contrary, it was his nature.

"Wait a minute, what about his violent nature? What about them people he beat up?"

"What? Are you joking Azariah? Those were violent criminals, and not even local ones. They're in gaol for God's sake – beg your pardon George – and one of them at least will probably hang. What's a black eye compared to the rope? That was a fine job of policing in my opinion. And when I see our Mr Lively, I for one will take his hand, clap him on the back, and tell him so. Rough times call for rough measures, don't you know," concluded Barnett.

"Bah."

"He's right Azariah," said the doctor, "you must be living in an ivory tower."

"Bah. I remember when this was a peaceful little town."

"That's progress for you," remarked Haden-Best.

"Bah."

"Look, Azariah, tell me this," cajoled Barnett, "put yourself in his shoes. Let's say that, when you were a young man…"

"When Adam was a lad," pointed out the doctor, rewarded with a scowl.

"…when you were younger, what would you have done if a group of toughs had broken into your home and laid hands on your good lady wife, God rest her soul. What would you…"

"Ah'd 'ave slit the bastard throats!"

"And on that gentlemen, as they say in court, I rest my case."

"Bah!"

#

Duberley sentried at the door, Cutler entered into his nightmare. But, as nightmares go, turning out to be not so forbidding after all. He was in a deceptively large building of good height, but his eye latched onto nothing in particular straight away, a blur of unfocussed human figures swirling. A low reverberation filled the place and his ears, forty or so Black Country voices in anticipatory murmur, but quite calm, sounding politely. The temperature changed as he stepped in and the outside was shut out, warmed by the enclosed bodies. The predominant odour, over even that of reheated stale sweat, was a pleasant one of sawdust and fresh straw, and a steamy soapy smell. That latter now directed his gaze and fixed it on a small forge where a very large copper of water was being heated, early steam wisping like tenuous spectral elvers heading upstream to a watery heaven. From the surface men with towels slung over their shoulders dipped buckets and pails and disappeared behind a wall of bales.

But he saw no dogs, realising only later that they were being kept out of the way by their handlers in the bale-segregated area, where even now they were getting their first wash-downs under the supervision of the day's appointed referees. He took time now to look round, taking in individuals and groups and assessing. More or less as he had expected: working men dusted down and scrubbed up. One was in shirtsleeves and specs. busily scribbling on a blackboard and intermittently peering at a stub of paper, from a collection of same in his left hand. As he completed a line of boxes, Jack saw money changing hands…

And there, in the middle of the space, was the ring: a circle of eight feet diameter bounded by a palisade of blue painted boards no more than a yard high, high enough to keep the dogs in and focussed, low enough for men to step over and intervene, strictly in accordance with the rules of course. He found himself staring into the fighting space, imagining it filled with slobbering and snarls, biting and blood.

A heavy hand on the shoulder, like an arresting copper's, brought him back.

"Yoh gorr 'ere then Jack. Bit late bist tha? Yoher mert's bin in erges. Any rowd, ow bist?"

Solomon Mallen had only met Jack Cutler once, but seemed genuinely pleased to see him. He was getting on now, but still gave an impression of strength. Reputed to have been handsome in his youth, he was no longer so, his face having taken on the consistency and colour of left-over porridge. And whilst his youthful stature had been compared to the proverbial barn door, it was apparent from the way the man moved these days that the hinges needed oiling: you could almost hear the creaks. But his eyes, sparrow-breast grey with blue flecks, were full of life still, repositories of a reputation which issued forth to communicate, inform, intimidate. Jack felt the charisma and wanted to respond to it. But he could not. Would not. He wouldn't let himself go, let himself forget what Mallen was doing here.

"Not to worry, Om 'ere now Mr Mallen."

"Solomon. It's Solomon to frens."

"Yes, well Om 'ere, Solomon. Just checking in. Not checking up y'understand, just need to mek sure our Mr Challoner's all right. I gather he's introduced 'imself then?"

"Oh, ahr, e tode me e's elpin' yoh wi the sums. Ah doh blerm ya, yoh doh know me very well yet. No offence took. An' 'e day 'ave to introduce hisself, we know each otha well enough. Knows is stuff 'e does. Knows 'is dogs. Mind yoh 'e outta kep movin' abaht: one o' the wammels 'll mistek 'im fer a boon. Thin? Ah've sid moher mate unna butcher's pencil."

Jack was not entirely clear on what Mallen had said. Cradley Heath was only just down the road, but Mallen's pronunciation made it sound like a secret language.

"I'll be leaving Challoner to look after things f'me. Ov got an errand in the meantime, be back later."

"But yoh'm sposed to stop. Yoh'll miss the fahts…"

Jack had every intention of missing the fights. He shrugged a fake apology.

"Yoh'm sposed to be Cyril Crerne's aihse, bay yha?"

"Yeah, well – Cyril can close 'is eyes now and then. Let's just call it a nap, eh? Challoner can look after things for me, till I get back."

Mallen looked first perplexed, then displeased. Jack needed to give him something.

"Look, Mr…Solomon. Let me be frank w' ya. Truth is, it's blood. I don't know what it is, but the sight of it…and the smell, it just meks me feel like throwing up. Silly, ain't it? But there it is. So, I don't intend to be stickin' around for the, er, actual action. I'll drop by again later. To settle up. All right?"

Mallen just stared at him, down from his superior height. Jack did not like the way big men looked down, assuming in their ignorance that size gave them some sort of authority over him; and this one with his dodgy knees and his arrogance. *If I wanted to put him down, he wouldn't even see it coming.* Jack felt the weight, the balance, of his wolf-headed stick and was sure of that…

The stare said disappointment, and he dismissed the little man with an inconsequential gesture as if brushing off biscuit crumbs.

"Yoh best mek yom sel scarce then. Ah'm a gooin' t'get summat t'ate in the pub – ahm's fair clemm'd."

With that, he strode off. After a brief consultation with Challoner, Cutler also excused himself.

#

It looked like John's tip-off had been worth it. This would be another feather in his cap, another reason for them to promote him. Abe had been obliged to postpone his meeting with inspector Millership, but that was no skin off his nose, quite the contrary, this operation obviously took precedence, and it would do him no harm at all, as long as it was not messed up, and he had no intention of it coming to that.

With the rest of his Blackheath contingent, he was hanging around just out of sight up the road. At the agreed time, simultaneously with their Halesowen counterparts, they would make their move. Worcestershire had mustered seven men and a sergeant, Abe Lively's friend Southall. They would be spreading out, working in pairs to block escape routes down the road or down the 'bonk' to the cut.

Sergeant Lively had the loan of a couple of police waggons and the blessing of Old Hill, but no extra men. Thus, having left the demoted, and sluggish, Oakden in charge of the prisoner transport and a civilian driver, he was planning to advance with all of his forces: Salt, Stride, Payne, Clark, and his own brother Josh, in that order of resilience in the face of hard knocks. When they broke in there would be inevitably escapees, Halesowen's job, but the diehards, those with dogs and cash to retrieve, they might decide to fight their way out. He was quite excited by that possibility, although he did plan to conduct the operation as smoothly as possible, if only for the sake of the animals. Besides, he was enjoying the period of calm and had no wish to stoke things up into the way they had been, although Jack was quick to point out that into every criminal's life a little pain must fall – to instill a healthy fear. Fear was the best deterrent.

He checked his watch again. Ten minutes – still. His feet ached. Why did he feel so tired? What had she done to him? Nothing, of course, nothing bad anyway. If anything last night had given him a much-needed boost. A proper woman she was, pity he wouldn't be seeing her again, but perhaps that was how it should be…But no, it wasn't her, had started before; he had been feeling a bit drained lately, more than a bit actually, and pale. Perhaps he had been working too hard? Perhaps it was his age…

He shuffled from leg to leg. Don't worry, you'll be above all this street pounding soon his friend assured him.

#

The post knocking-off Saturday rush was just subsiding at the Royal Oak. When Sissy arrived, Miriam and Marlene were catching a breather at opposite ends of the bar, catching back their breaths, like two pugilists between rounds.

Sissy noticed that her friend was not smiling. Not unsurprising it might be said, considering the effort required to man the place. Yet Miriam had always been a smiler, work or no, since Sissy had known her at any rate. She had a dazzling smile, the reason the place had more than its fair share of custom in the saturated beer-flogging market, favoured by some resident males who could have got drunk perfectly conveniently closer to home. Plus, the beer was good, Miriam did not take custom for granted. A well-kept cellar and a handsome, unattainable aristocrat of a landlady: a winning combination. Except that she was not flashing that smile now, not genuinely, not in the old unforced and not exclusively professional kind of way. In fact, she looked decidedly vinegary. A trending demeanour which her friend had noticed.

"Oy up luv. What's up? Yoh look as if yoh've lost a tanner un fahnd a farthin.'"

Her voice penetrated; a flicker.

"Oh, Siss. Hello. Nice to see you. What are you having?"

The chain-maker slammed down copper, "the usual…"

"Cheers," she said.

"Are we expecting John?" asked the landlady.

"No, he's busy. We're meeting later. I just needed a pint. Thirsty work boshing hot metal. I came straight here."

"You don't say," said Miriam, a grin crow-barring into her sour mood, "I thought you might have dropped in on the way to the opera. I like the outfit."

Said outfit was sooty and fire damaged and honest, a series of little spark holes as character witnesses.

"My dear, it's the latest thing. All the rage as they say," she said in her poor posh voice take-off, and she gave a little twirl, and they laughed.

"Ar, all the goo ahy eet," replied Miriam in her poor parody of the local dialect, something which something in her would not allow her to fall into. As if assimilation destroyed hope. She knew that John could drop in and out of it as the mood took him, a chameleon that one, a survivor; strong. But not her. Nor Abe. Abe was like her. He hadn't forgotten where they had come from…

But she was smiling now:

"It's good to see you Siss. I needed a bit of cheering up…Marlene! Leave that alone and go and serve Mr Gethin please."

She poured herself a whisky and water. Why not?

"Why? What's the matter," replied Sissy, picking back up, "you haven't been yourself lately."

"You noticed?"

"O' course I did. What is it? Is it Jack?"

"How did you guess?" came the ironic reply.

"What's he done?"

"I don't know. He's just…annoying. So annoying. I just get annoyed looking at him…he dithers about, he doesn't pull his weight, and he's getting cheeky about it."

"Cheeky? How?"

"Well, you remember I told you that when we married I got Alan Griesbach to make sure that all my property – the pub that is – was kept out of joint ownership, or whatever the legal terminology is, so it remained mine, and he had no claim on it? You remember."

"Yes. Quite right too. I mean, why should a man get you body and soul, and pub, when he's contributed nothing towards it in the first place?"

"Exactly. Thank you. And then there's the body and soul bit as well. Particularly the body."

"Oh," said Sissy, leaning in, "what about it?"

"Well, he's making certain demands…"

"Oh, like that is it. What's he wanting, the filthy beast?"

"No, stop. Stop Siss. It's not like that; not like you think. That is to say it's nothing what you might call unnatural. No, it's just that he's a man basically, a certain kind of man at any rate. His view of marriage is that it gives him a right to what he's calling his conjugal rights –he's been talking to somebody – whenever he wants them."

"Oh, I see. Er, yes I suppose everyone deserves a break don't they? If you don't fancy it, you just don't fancy it, do you?"

"And that's the thing exactly. I don't fancy it ever. I don't fancy him, not a jot. I don't know that I ever did."

Sissy did not know what to say. Eventually she merely said, "Oh…"

"Oh indeed."

"What are you going to do?"

"I don't know. Live with it? Until something better presents itself at least."

"Better? How? What?" *Who?*

"I don't know. I don't know yet. You never know, I might even sell up, leave him to it. Get away from bad memories."

"But, did you ever care for him then? You must have, just a bit."

"Care? Yes, I suppose that I did. But care's not love. I could never love him, and I thought he accepted that. I couldn't love him, I shall only love once."

"John Henry?"

"Something like that," said the landlady before changing the subject:

"You haven't told me about King Lear. How was it?"

Sissy was happy to switch topics.

"Oh, it was really good. I enjoyed it anyway. We all did, except Frank possibly."

"That's Frank, has to be the contrary one. Not unaccompanied I don't imagine?"

"No. He was with a new one on me. A young girl name of Betty, or Annie. No it was Betty."

"That's a new one on me too."

"She didn't look much older than one of his pupils! Oh, it's a pity you couldn't come. It was a real loff. The get together I mean, not the play. Even Abe popped in."

"Abe? What, on duty?"

"No, not on duty, definitely not I'd say. Unless that actress was helping him with his enquiries!"

"Actress," repeated Miriam sharply, "what actress?"

"One of those out of the play."

"Out of the play," intoned his sister, "and did he introduce her?"

"No, he didn't really speak. We only saw him to wave to on our way out."

"Oh, it was late then?"

"Getting on, yeah. Why?"

"Well, he was out early this morning. He needs his rest. He's been overdoing it – working too hard I mean. He holds this town together you know, it's a big responsibility."

"In that case, perhaps he needed a bit of a distraction. A bit of fun."

"A bit of fun? Is that what she is? A distraction?"

"I should think so yes. Or was. The whole troupe has gone now, the lot of 'em. On to the next stop on the tour I suppose."

"That's just as well. My Abe's not very good around women. They lead him on and end up taking advantage of his good nature."

"Surely not. He's such a confident bloke, as well as handsome. Like my John."

"Ah now, that's where you're wrong. Abe's big and strong on the outside, and when he's dealing with men, but he's soft on the inside, and blind, where women are concerned. I do have to keep an eye on him, always have…how friendly did they look?"

"What do you mean?"

"You know what I mean. It's a hotel after all."

471

"No, I'm sure it was a bit of harmless flirting, on both sides. Abe and Miss Saunders had an early morning, the both of them."

"Miss Saunders?"

"That was the actress' name."

"Actresses now. He never learns."

"Oh, I wouldn't worry too much love, he'll meet a good woman he can settle down with when the time's right, you'll see. In the meantime…"

"Change the subject Siss, Jack's coming."

#

The sergeant was passing the time re-running the night before, the time spent with Emma. Already, he was struggling to remember the details of her face, but he yet remembered how she had felt when he put his arm around her – her waist he could almost encompass in his hands, although she was by no means a frail little thing, quite the contrary…And her voice, silky smooth with a refined accent, had stirred him strangely: even though he knew it was a manufactured play-actor's voice, it was a breath of fresh air in this place of man-made miasmas and alien dialect. Mostly though, he remembered the smell of her, like birdsong on May Day morning…May Day, he was back in Nash now…

"All right everybody, wim on!" announced P.C. Clark loud enough to wake the dead.

And indeed, it was time. Time to move at last. The men in blue out of Blackheath made their way swiftly downhill, confident that both jaws of the trap were closing. Followed by his men, sergeant Lively entered the Bell and advanced to secure the rear exit whilst Clark barred egress from the front.

"Right," he announced loudly, "police business. Nobody move or you'll get what for."

The dazed and drink befuddled clientele, mostly old men apparently minding their own business, just looked up, for all the world bewildered innocents.

"My colleague will take your names and then you will be free to go, or stay if you will. Clark, take particulars please."

The gatehouse breached, the police force was ready to storm the main fortress in a surprise attack – when the alarm was raised behind them. The Halesowen spy had either not spotted the enemy lookout with the newspaper, or had neglected to pass the word. Anyhow, he had started on his bell for all he was worth.

"Clark, get him," ordered Abe, "the rest of you come on, quick!"

They raced out the back surprising half a dozen unsure individuals who had only half believed the bell, silenced now by Clark's valiant intervention: the bell-ringer had seen a uniform approaching at a decent speed, and scarpered at an even more commendable velocity. Precisely similarly, the half dozen scattered in six directions as soon as they saw a flash of blue.

"Leave them for Southall, come on block the door," ordered the sergeant.

The big man allotted to control egress and exit also bolted. Nothing to be done about that one. The top of a torso leaned around the door, others appeared behind, a diminishing concertina, blinking in the scene then rabbiting back inside in what would prove to be a fruitless attempt to find another way out. One little fellow, relying on his dodging skills, attempted to penetrate the now tight cordon. He was netted effortlessly by Salt who propelled him forward with his own right arm bent forcefully up his back, which was becoming his signature move.

Inside, people were running around like headless chickens. Someone had, evidently upon hearing the bell, begun to dismantle the panelling and the ring with the result that two erstwhile canine adversaries, in doggy truce, were allied in barking at all and sundry, losing themselves in the melee.

Abe and his five constables barred the exit with their bodies. Having nowhere to go, the panic turned into a kind of resigned curiosity, combined with an unconscious group calculation of the chances of rushing the police and legging it. But nobody wanted to make that first move.

"Right! Everybody calm down," commanded Salt, with only slight effect. "Simmer down," he was warning now, "nobody's going anywhere, not till we say. Let's keep things peaceable and civil shall we? You wouldn't want it any other way, would you?"

They wouldn't. Not at the moment anyway.

"Thank you gentlemen. Sergeant?"

"Thank you constable. Good afternoon all. I'm police sergeant Lively and you've all been caught indulging in illegal activities. Now, whether we charge each and every one of you, and what we might charge you with, is very much an open question, as I speak. But before we get onto all that please be aware that if there's any misbehaviour from any of your number, then it will go bad for the rest of you. And, by the way, if you're thinking of breaking out and taking your chances, this area is surrounded by our colleagues from Halesowen police. Now, they're a fine body of men, the men from Halesowen police, but they do tend to rely on brute force rather than brains, a bit over-enthusiastic with it, if you know what I mean. Batter you first and ask questions later, after you've come round that is. Oh, as well as arresting you and locking you up of course. Take my meaning?"

They did.

"Now, first things first. Hands up those that own any of these dogs. Come on, I'm thinking of the welfare of the animals now, not about who's done what. Good, better. Go and get your dogs, get them on leads and stand over in that corner away from the fire. Go now."

Thompson was doing nothing in particular, just sitting on the canalside, chucking in the occasional piece of clinker, watching the ripples spread and die. But they didn't really die did they? They went on forever, just getting too small to see…we could probably measure them, still spreading, with some new scientific invention, if we wanted, still living on long after we could no longer see or feel them…and then, as our science improved, even further…Yes, potentially, his throwing this rubble could reverberate forever. Like, a life could never really be over…it just depended on how sensitive the instrument of perception. He was one such instrument…that's why he could feel ghosts, or whatever the spirit was which had latched onto him. But he wasn't scared, he was special. He knew it, and she told him so.

Then, some kind of commotion behind him, around the pub on the hill. Nothing unusual about that, it was Saturday after all. Still, she seemed interested, and that transferred to him, uncomfortable and agitated over nothing now. He stood up and dusted himself down and headed for the bridge. Before he got there a pair of cloth capped characters issued out of the scattered accoutrements of industry as if pursued by hell hounds, taking the bridge before him, but abandoning it instantaneously, disappearing almost literally in a cloud of dust.

She stood him on the bridge to wait. He knew not for what, but he waited.

The police operation had been a great success, he thought. In little more than an hour names and addresses had been taken, cautions given, and arrests made. The bag destined for the cells of Blackheath and Old Hill was a baker's dozen. Eleven of these most culpable, as far as mouldy wheat could be separated from mouldy chaff, had already been stuffed into waggons and carted off.

The last two desperate criminals had been sat outside on a bale of straw awaiting the return of the transport. Both were young, with the hard hands and raw knuckles and weather-lashed faces of men who laboured in the elements. Navvies of a kind, Abe guessed, but the notes would confirm.

It so happened that, at that precise moment, only the sergeant and a wounded P.C. Clark – he had been bitten on the calf by a dog – watched over the prisoners. The two were not cuffed, the supply of these restraints having already been exhausted, the sergeant ordering that they be left attached to the prisoners in the waggons – he had had no desire to be told that in his absence they had started trouble at the station, or even absconded. That's what he told himself anyway.

Precautions had been taken, however: the prisoners' shoes had been removed, parked at a distance on the yard. That should stop them: if they ran they wouldn't go too fast or get too far, and if they kicked it wouldn't hurt anyone except themselves.

It had gone so smooth and well, and yet the sergeant was half disappointed that somebody had not 'had a go.'

Thus, his motive for sending Clark off into the pub on some trivial errand could have been interpreted as questionable. Indeed the sergeant questioned it himself, almost immediately, but Jack said to leave it be, to just wait and see, and be ready.

And ready he was when after a brief furtive whisper behind his conveniently turned back, the pair made a break for it, heading first for the shoes.

Abe cut across and tripped one of them up just as he got to the footwear. The other grabbed a pair and kept going. He didn't look like much of a runner, Abe had targeted the more athletic one first. But now a dilemma: he wanted neither to escape. What to do? To the downed man he shouted,

"Stay there, if I have to find you, you'll get worse than this." With which he very deliberately stamped on the man's instep, sock little protection against studded leather. To be fair to the policeman, he could have mangled that foot good and proper, but he was proud of his control, that was the name of the game, he was a police officer after all, and so the fugitive was lucky to escape with a trauma which prevented him from walking only temporarily, probably; no broken bones, or at least only one or two little ones, hairline fractures at most, or so Lively reasoned. That was enough, the instep can be extremely sensitive.

Decision and action having been concurrent, the second runner had got as far only as an adjacent alleyway, nipping in quickly with his shoes hoping that the copper hadn't seen where he went, and buying time to get shod.

But the copper had seen, and was right on his tail. And it was a dead end. The navvie mustered a hasty alternative plan, sounds of police boots already close. The runaway had slipped on one heavy shoe but with no time for the other he resolved to take the copper on a rush, brushing him aside as he rounded the corner...

The timing was right, both parties reaching the entrance to the street together.

"Gotcha!" relished Lively.

The poor refugee was in a panic and picking up speed. In his agitation, he tried to shove the copper away. Mistake. Two reasons: one, the magistrates took a dim view of violence committed against the constabulary, and, two, it was Abe Lively. The unfocussed push hardly moved the big man. The copper pushed back, battering the man's chest with the knife-edges of both hands. The runaway stepped back to regain balance, dropping the useless shoe, his arms naturally starting to rise; stepping in smartly the copper grasped his victim's right wrist with his left hand, encouraging it up and back, while his own right grasped the man's throat like an implacable bull dog and forced his back to the wall, pinning him there. The would-be escapee had a free hand yet, but it was neutralised by the sergeant's superior reach, and he was short of air to boot.

Abe Lively squeezed and the smaller man flailed, frightened eyes bulging. The copper looked into those bulging eyes as panic turned to terror, disbelief to a kind of certainty, as his tissues glutted on carbon dioxide, slow poison which a simple breath would eliminate but to which the iron grip would not consent. This was power, life and death, and it would be so easy to be seduced by it…But Abe Lively was not going to be trapped, not seduced by it. He was a man with a responsibility, a duty to the uniform, and more, to himself – he allowed the escapee to collapse onto his knees.

"Now let that be a lesson to you."

"He deserves more than that, kick him down," urged Jack.

"No, that's not necessary."

"So was letting him run."

Lively merely shrugged.

"I don't know what I'm going to do with you. You're no fun anymore."

#

It was only a nip, she thought it was in any case. A gentle warning. Perhaps, she had bitten deeper than intended, the sudden sound had startled her. Still, she could have bitten harder; he didn't have to shout so, fuss about nothing. She could have pulled out a chunk of skin and muscle had she chosen. But she had not, and it had been enough: he loosed hold of her.

And young Roland had to make a decision. Boadicea had bitten a policeman. It was the pound for her, or worse, if they got her. He slipped her off her lead.

"Go on girl, run."

She did. Through the pub and out the other side. She knew that her master had gone that way, but, outside, there were lots of confusing smells and sounds, coming from behind closed doors; and then lots of men came running out of the pub. Home was straight ahead, somewhere down the bank. He must have gone home. She followed.

#

Cutler had already left the cart shed when he heard the bell. He assumed the worst and decided to make himself scarce. If he could clear the immediate vicinity, get to the road, he could saunter by all innocence, a nosey passer-by, and look for his girl and Roland.

"It's a raid," asserted Duberley and ran over the gulley and cleared a low wall, heading down hill.

"Tony, not that way…" but he was gone.

Jack had guessed, rightly, that police would be coming through that way as well as through the pub. Best to slip past the ones you could actually see, the ones with other things on their minds, like bottling everybody up in that shed. Tony would have to take pot-luck.

Jack reasoned that he stood more chance of getting past the police at the front, and out onto the road, the which he would be able to assess more clearly from roof height. Clambering onto a wall, then via a window ledge he edged sideways till he could hug the brickwork round onto a low roof with a low pitch next door to the Bell, but nearer the road. Flattening, he saw the coppers, the last one at a limp, coming out and heading for the cart shed; in the nick of time saved by the bell. Yes, they were all too busy to notice him. He made his way to the front of the building and found what he was looking for, a rainwater downpipe. It was rusty but Jack was fit and light and he scampered down like a squirrel.

Quickly but seemingly unhurried, he walked to the other side of the road. No sign of Roland and Bo. Which way then? He decided to walk downhill. When he got to the cut he would follow it back toward Old Hill and home. Perhaps Roland had taken her back.

#

Sergeant Lively had fully expected to be rounding up Jack Cutler in the raid. When he had first heard about the illegal gathering, and especially as the warning came from John, Jack's was one of the first names and faces that he imagined. No, he had fully expected to be not at all surprised if Mr Cutler were caught bang to rights with the rest of the criminal congregation. But that was before said Mr Cutler had turned up unsolicited on the sergeant's doorstep in the week. Since then Abe had only half expected to see him there....

It had been a quiet Tuesday evening and Lively had stoked up the stove, poured himself a brew, and was poring over a week's worth of incident and arrest reports: compared to a few weeks ago, things seemed tame, or perhaps it was all down to an altered perception now that Abe's mind had had chance to sift through things, categorise his thoughts and feelings; and file them appropriately, in good order, like the records kept here at the station. The operation could not function without good records and filing – but it was nice to be able to finish a shift and close the desk drawers and lock away your cares...

To Abe's mind, the reports confirmed his walking the streets impressions: drunks were still getting drunk, but with a new found good grace, it appeared, and the sense to move on when requested – rather than coming back with the verbals; and those on night duty counted themselves lucky that those inebriates who had incautiously crossed the line, those who found themselves locked up, that these apparently wanted nothing more than to sing and sleep themselves into sunlight and sobriety, rather than bounce discordant invective off cell walls, and the insalubrious contents of waste pails. And fights. Fights were as wont to break out as they ever did, and ever would; but even here, to Abe Lively it seemed, things had calmed down. Weapons of choice were fists rather than sticks and bars, and combat was carried out with a sense of fair play, and like as not a ceremonious ending marked by the shaking of hands. Back to how things once were. Before the madness of the summer. Other than that, thieves were still thieving and itinerants were still tramping in and out, nothing much changing. But if the sergeant were constructing a mental jig-saw of law breakers, he knew he would have trouble affixing some pieces, although they were close to home...

For the most part, the job had reverted to routine. He had liked routine once, gave him a sense of control, order maintained. But now, he was more concerned with getting bored. Perhaps if he made inspector? Perhaps he would welcome another dangerous gang to deal with? As it was, he had dull routine to look forward to.

Or not. In the quiet of the station on that quiet Tuesday evening, Jack spoke to him.

"No fear of that. Make the most of it. Things never stay the same. You'll see. There's big change coming. You wait and see."

With that, there was a knock on the door. And nothing. Another knock. Whoever was there was obviously waiting for an invitation.

"Come in," the policeman duly invited.

For some reason the sight of the little man with the round dark eyes and the fluid movement and soft footfall of a feline caused him to physically start. The visitor saw it but his face said not.

"Sergeant Lively. I don't know if you remember me it's..."

"Mr Cutler. Jack Cutler. I know."

"Ah, good. But you can call me Jack," said Cutler, offering his hand.

Abe had no real reason to refuse it: masculine mores dictated in fact that he must accept the gesture at face value and respond in kind. Neither was surprised to recognise a certain kind of strength in the other, a feeling of the other extended and communicated through the grip. It confirmed to the policeman that the man was confident and controlled, as if holding some power, or secret, in reserve; the kind of man who would perhaps make a good friend, but a dangerous enemy definitely. A little like himself, he thought. He knew that Cutler worked for Cyril, so what did that make him? Friend, or foe? Let's find out.

"I'm surprised to see you without your dog. I heard you were inseparable," he was saying, but then something cruel made him add, in all apparent solicitude, "he's not died as he?"

"She's a she!" came the hot response, before cooling to "and no, she's very well thank you. I just thought you'd appreciate not being growled at – she's very protective of me where strangers are concerned, as you've witnessed."

"Indeed I have, and thank you for that," conceded the policeman, "so what can I do for you Mr Cutler?"

"I'm taking her for a drink later, she likes a drop of beer; your brother's looking after her for me actually," persisted Cutler, and point made, corrected the copper, "and it's Jack, remember. Mr Cutler sounds so formal." *Like you're arresting me!*

"So, how can I help?"

"May I sit?" said Cutler indicating a well-worn wooden chair, the seat eroded glassy smooth by decades of rear ends of reporting P.C.s and squirming interviewees.

"Of course, please do. How can I be of assistance?"

"Do I need your assistance? No, I don't think I do. Not at present, thanks for asking," responded Cutler jovially, "it's more a question of how I can help you, isn't it?"

"Is it?"

"I would have thought so. Don't you have some questions for me?"

The copper did have questions to ask, of him and about him. About his comings and goings at the workhouse, which he had no doubt believed to have been clandestine, and of his relationship with that dead and disgraced fat bloke. But surely he had not come here voluntarily to confess…confess what? Abe needed to be cautious, not show his hand too early.

"Questions about what?"

"Sergeant, cards on the table. When you get to know me you will know that I like to keep my ear to the ground. I have friends. I get to know things."

"Like what?"

"Like the fact that your constable's zealous enquiries about the goings on at a certain public establishment and the avaricious, if not to say the downright thieving antics of its former head have revealed an apparent connection between that establishment and or person, and myself. Am I right?"

"Did you ever train as a lawyer Mr Cutler?"

"Please, it's Jack, or I cannot guarantee prolonging this conversation. And no, I've not trained as a lawyer, chance would've been a fine thing. Why?"

"Because you're stringing words together like one."

"Oh, I do like to talk proper sometimes. Nothing wrong in that is there?"

Depends on what it's hiding.

"Let's talk plainly – Jack. You're talking about the workhouse, Gross, and your connection to both. Yes?"

"Yes."

"So you admit it then?"

"Of course, no sense in denying it is there? I know for a fact that my name appears in your report on this unfortunate affair…no, no," he added with a forestalling gesture, "I have friends, remember, friends all over. I get to know things."

"All right. So you've come here of your own free will to tell me about your links with the workhouse, with Gross, and the goings on."

"That's right. Not the behaviour of a man with something to hide, nothing bad anyway, as I'm sure you will agree…"

Abe was sure of one thing, his experience as a copper was telling him firmly that he did not agree: this could all be some elaborate bluff. Nevertheless he would hear the man out.

"…so fire away," urged the little man, "ask your questions."

At this stage the sergeant saw no reason not to dive straight in.

"Right then. What do you know about the fraudulent and larcenous activities that have been perpetrated by Gross under the aegis of his position, and how did they involve you, Mr Cutler?"

"Hold on! Hold on. Hold onto your 'orses there. With all due respect and all that, don't you think you've jumped the gun there sergeant? And it's Jack remember, as well, please."

"All right. If you say so – Jack. Jumped the gun? How so?"

"Well, I'm no expert in these things but it seems to me that you should have started with something like 'we believe you recently paid a visit to the workhouse'…"

"Or visits," corrected Abe instinctively.

Thanks for that.

"…'where you met with a Mr Gideon Gross. Would you care to confirm that, and, if so, relate the purpose of said visit – or visits?' To which I would have made reply, 'yes, I did visit him, in fact two or three times, but for totally innocent reasons.' How about something like that?"

"I stand corrected. Please explain – Jack."

"Cards on the table? I was there making donations, anonymously I had thought, for the benefit of the poor inmates. Cash donations."

The copper pursed his lips and let out a long breath of air.

"Oh come on! Do you expect me to believe that? A man with your reputation?"

"Oh! My reputation is it? My reputation!" exclaimed the little man, almost exploding, it seemed, before bridling his anger and tongue. "What is that thing 'reputation'? What is it? Nothing more than rumour spread by lesser men; fishwives and cowards. You ought to know that. You ought to know better. You have a certain reputation of your own, don't you? But it's not who you are, it's not who I am: it's a mere caricature of a man. The reputation distorts the man like a fun-fair mirror. And that's all some people can see, common folk. A man like you is surely above that, as am I. Can we not talk frankly, each to the other? Forget the preconceptions?"

If it was an act, it was a good one. At any rate, Lively took the point.

"All right, I apologise – for not starting at the beginning. So tell me Mr Cutler – Jack – tell me Jack why you were visiting Gross."

"Before I do, let me tell you something else. About me. I don't remember my mother. She died, giving birth to my sister. She died too. I was not even four yet. And I never knew my father, not my real father, he left before I was born. But I remember the man who called himself my father, the one who was…he had been living with her. Uncle Will is all I knew him as, that and bastard, as soon as I learned the word – from him; nasty piece of work. I don't know why he kept me, unless it was to vent his spleen on something, or he had plans to use me like some latter-day Bill Stokes – like the one in Oliver Twist. But he would have ended up killing me first, I know. I still hate him. I hope he's rotting in hell."

"What's this got to do…"

"Coming to it. No, it was Sykes not Stokes…I think. No, fortunately, I never found out what his plans were, because there were other people around, good people, who recognised him for the dirty bag of washing he was. Anyway, cutting a long story short, they rescued me. I am the man I am today thanks to them. I grew up, till I was twelve at least, in a workhouse, much like the one we have been talking about, but with a kind, and honest, master; nothing like Gross. You may think that being brought up on the parish like that is nothing to be thankful for but believe me, when you have started from where I did, it most certainly is."

"So, what, you were visiting to relive old times? Soaking up the atmosphere?"

"What? Tripe and onions and damp and the kid in the next bed getting a thrashing for pissing the bed? Hardly. No. My time as a kid was spent looking forward to getting out of the place, despite what I just said. I knew there must be something better out there for me, you see. I just had to bide my time, but I do look back on it fondly now, I must admit, because as I said, it made me: it fed my growing body and gave me an education of sorts."

"What kind of education was this?"

"Oh, the kind you would expect. But we're straying from the point, which is that yes, I did have reason – I do have reason – to be grateful to the people and the organisation that saved me, basically. I'm just a redeemed orphan wanting to give something back. Money that is."

The policeman had to check that he understood.

"You mean to tell me that you were there to physically hand over cash? To Gross?"

"That's about the size of it, yes," replied Cutler, round brown eyes projecting nothing but candour toward the copper.

"But why?"

"I told you."

"I mean why go to him, to Gross. Why not to the trustees?"

"Ah, well, you see, we're back to reputation, aren't we? Can I be frank?"

Not sure, can you? "Of course. Cards on the table, as you might say."

"As I do say." *Sarky bugger.*

481

"Yes, go on."

"In this life there's different ways of making your way in the world; of earning a living. Right? I mean, there's them that are fortunate to own businesses that make things or sell things, and there's them that are content to work for them, in shops, factories or mines. All earning their daily bread, and the rest, legitimately, as far as respectability and the law is concerned at least. I hear that there are others, political thinkers you'd call 'em, that think differently, who even advocate revolution, but I don't understand all that: I'm just a simple man who wants to be left alone. I suppose my motto might be live and let live – as long as nobody is trying to shit on you! What do you think?"

"I'm not sure an officer of the law could live by that code."

"I can see that it might be problematic. Because there's the others aren't there? The ones that aren't rich, don't own businesses but also cannot bring themselves to work for a living. To earn an honest day's pay as you might say. Your stock in trade."

"Criminals, yes."

"Yes, there's respectable folk at one end of the scale, but at the other there's bad 'uns. Robbers and thieves and burglars – out and out criminals who just take other people's hard-earned cash by force. And it's down to pure laziness and moral weakness in my opinion. They find it easier to prey on the weak than to work. Work scares 'em, and that's why they're cowards in my book. So you've got good and bad, light and shade, black and white. But what about grey?"

Abraham Lively was starting to get a little uncomfortable with this, he could see where it was going.

"To a policeman, it's very straightforward: you're either breaking the law of the land, or you're not."

"What if a particular law is not a fair law?"

"I'm a policeman not a philosopher."

"Take the police out of the man and you've still got a man, haven't you? You weren't always a policeman, just as I am no longer a poor orphan. We are all made up of many parts."

"Well, that's a statement of the obvious. And all this has been very interesting and I would be happy to continue in the same vein if we were two mates passing the time together over a pint in the pub. But we're not in a pub. Let's get back to you and Gross."

"All right, but before I do can I just finish my train of thought? There's that grey area I mentioned."

He looked at Lively. If he pushed much further he would lose the man, and only be left with the copper…

"The point is sergeant, as your mention of 'reputation' made clear, you suspect that I earn my living in ways that according to the strict definition of things might be labelled 'illegal.' I may not be able to part you from that belief, and all I can say to you, here and now, is that I will always deny it. What I would say to you, on a hypothetical basis, is

482

that should I ever have been persuaded in the past, or were I to be in the future, to cross that often arbitrary line that you call 'the law of the land' then you can rest assured that Jack Cutler has never, and never will stray so far into the dark as to become one of those cowards I was talking about. I would never harm anyone, unless in self-defence and I would not take money from anybody that did not agree to part with it. But a man could hold to such a code and still find himself in that grey I mentioned. There's many a respected citizen gone that far, as I'm sure you would agree."

"A rogue with a heart of gold is it?" said the sergeant sounding deliberately sceptical. But he knew what Cutler was asking him to reconcile, and he didn't like it. So he changed tack.

"If you were concerned about questions being raised as to the source of your funds, you could have sent money anonymously."

"That's what I thought I was doing! Through Gross. Turns out he was one of the worst of the bad 'uns: a thief and a coward. I can't believe he took me in. I hate him for that."

"Well, he got his just desserts."

Didn't he just? "I know. And there's nobody more pleased than me that the old git's dead." And he meant that part at least.

"And you're willing to make a statement to that effect are you?"

"If I have to. But I'd rather not. And I'd deem it a favour if we could just keep this between us. Fact is sergeant, I'd rather not let it get out that Jack Cutler made a fool of himself – think of my reputation!" he said with a wink.

"I can understand that."

"Thank you. I'm not proud of it. Also, there's something else. And I don't even know whether to mention it now, with him being out of the way; let dead dogs lie so to speak."

"I would advise you not to keep anything back."

"Very well. It's just that last time I was there, I saw something. And it made me start to think. Now, I can't be sure – and if I was I would have got word to you sooner believe me – but I did come to suspect that Gross might be abusing the youngsters in his care. Physically abusing I mean; and when I say physically abusing and tell you it's young girls I was thinking of, you will know what I mean."

"Sexual exploitation? Yes, we know. But we only found out once he was gone. You should have come to us earlier, Mr Cutler."

"So I was right? Oh my God. Bastard! Oh God, I wish I'd done something now. God forgive me, because I can't forgive myself."

Cutler's tone and demeanour had so changed, his confidence and strength so retreated, he had seemed so moved, revolted, that Abe Lively felt he understood the man a little better now. But, at any rate, that would teach him to sneak around the fringes of the law. Justice served, he reckoned (and he couldn't prove anything anyway.) He had so skilfully been led to that conclusion that he forgot, for the moment, to delve deeper into Jack's excuse for consorting with Gross, for there were further questions to be asked there, to be sure.

But if Cutler felt like he was getting the upper hand, the copper's next question came like a left hook out of nowhere:

"On another matter, I believe you are acquainted with a certain character by the name of Vyle. Is that true?"

Jack's mouth was moving and he set his mind racing to overtake it:

"Well I've come across a few vile characters in my time, like the one we've just been talking about!" And his mouth laughed. What was Lively getting at? What did he already know? Jack would bet his last penny that this was to do with that old tramp that Vyle and Woolley had contrived to allow to fall in front of a train. Idiots! But Lively seems to have made the link, at least between himself and Vyle, may as well admit to knowing him at least. The copper was elaborating.

"The man's name is Stephen Vyle, and he's wanted for questioning about some stolen property which he pawned."

Stolen property? What's he been up to? Nothing to do with me.

"Yes, sorry sergeant. I do know him. Not well. He ran a couple of errands for me once, for me and your uncle Cyril. Nothing dodgy, collecting rents as it happens. But then he just disappeared."

"Disappeared where?"

"I don't know. Back to where he came from I suppose."

"Which is where?"

"No idea."

"Isn't he from Smethwick, like you?"

"Well, you know more than me sergeant. Except that I don't come from Smethwick, I'm from Harborne originally," he lied.

"So you have no idea of his present whereabouts?"

"None at all. If I did, I would tell you."

"Why?"

"Why would I tell you?"

"Yes. Why?"

"Because, he's nobody to me, and I would rather not make myself more unpopular with you and your colleagues than I already am. An easy choice really. So, if I do see him, I'll let you know. That's all I can say. Fair enough?"

"Fair enough," agreed the copper.

The two parted on good terms, considering. Like other men before him, Abe Lively had been diverted by Jack Cutler's distinctive brand of charm. Not as black as he had been painted he thought; a bit of a wheeler dealer perhaps, but amiable enough once you got to know him. The archetypal likeable rogue.

Jack left the station in mixed mood. He had cleared the air with Lively – if misdirection and obfuscation could count as clearing the air – and thereby bought himself some time, to settle his affairs and move on. That was all to the good, but then there was this thing with Vyle. If the law caught up with the imbecile and started to push him, who knows what else would be exposed? He knew that Lively would be a problem the first day he clapped eyes on him. And Vyle? He might need to stay disappeared. In the meantime he had given the copper plenty to think about. Cards on the table? That's a laugh. Jack Cutler had laid out precious few, and those not even from the real deck! Lively would be after him in due course, but for now he was off balance and Jack was off to the pub.

Back inside, a debate was taking place.

"You let him off far too easily. You cannot trust that man. Surely you see that?"

"Why, what do you know? Can you read minds?"

"No, not his. But I feel him. Don't trust him."

"Who said I trust him? It's not all black and white."

"Oh but it is. It all is. You have friends and you have enemies, whatever side of your law they lie. Enemies must be dealt with, like that gang we got rid of."

"I don't agree. I think, you just like me to hurt people. That's your nature."

"No, it's coming from you, that violence. I'm only telling you who you should be siding with, or against."

"And I don't agree. I think you feed off it."

No, it's more basic than that. "Agree or disagree, you need me now. I'm here to help you. Haven't I helped you already, warned you, guided your hand?"

"If you say so. Look, you're right. I don't completely trust him, but I can't believe that he's all bad. Nobody is. And, really, as a copper, I don't have anything on him."

"You mark this: he's dangerous, and you'll regret not dealing with him, one way or another. I really do not like him."

"Oh, that's all right then. I can see it now – 'I'm arresting you on the grounds that a voice in my head doesn't like you.' They'll think I'm completely deranged."

"What do people know? Forget their law then, we could just kill him. I'm telling you…"

"No, I'm telling you. I won't have you pushing me down that road. You want me to lose control, so that you can take over. The way I've been behaving…it's got to stop."

"Hasn't done you any harm."

"Yet."

"Nonsense. I'm not trying to control you, I'm just advising you. A counsellor, if you like. And you'll see I'm right, stick with it."

"I don't think I need a counsellor."

"A protector then. I've been useful to you. And will be again: you need me."

"No, I think it's time you left."

"Left? What does that mean? I can't just 'leave.' It's not that simple," warned Jack.

Abe was too afraid to ask why, and settled for, "You've got to behave."

"If you say so. So, I'll warn you one last time. Listen to me, and get rid of that man, or you'll come to regret it, I promise you."

"We'll see." Abe was inclined to say more but as on previous occasions when he had prolonged the conversation with his 'friend' he became listless, then fell into a torpor. The last thing he heard before his eyelids and an oblivion descended was:

"You're making a rod for your own back. You'll regret this when I'm gone."

#

Jack's assumption was wrong: Roland had taken her nowhere, although she had taken herself, somewhere. And Clark, bitten by what he assumed was the young man's dog, had ordered him to stay put, under the supervision of the landlord, who was understandably eager to please. Having been brought up half decent and honest, the young man was doing as he was told. Had the back door to the pub been properly closed, Boadicea would be in custody herself right now and Roland having to explain that they had been innocent bystanders, that she had only snapped out of fear. And Jack Cutler might have been reunited with her that very evening.

#

Still standing on the bridge, Thompson heard someone else approaching. No, not a someone, an animal; a dog, definitely a dog. Also in a hurry.

Bo knew where she was heading. She knew she had to cross the water and she knew where. But there was something wrong. That smell. Not a natural smell. Something unfamiliar. But not completely unfamiliar. She remembered that man. The man that did not smell right, did not smell quite like any other man, except perhaps one…It had disturbed her, that strangeness, and when the man had wanted to touch her master, she would not let him. Now she wanted to cross, but the smell was hanging on the bridge. She had to know for sure, and edged closer. Now she saw too. It certainly appeared to be the same thing, and when it spoke she knew.

"Hello. I know you, don't I? What are you doing out on your own?"

This time Boadicea did not bark. No need, she was protecting nothing. And besides, she had a feeling that the other men, behind her, would be looking for her, and not friendly. She was torn between growling frustration and puppy whimpering in despair: her master was over there but this was in the way. She started to cry, and ran back and forth along the water's edge.

Thompson saw that she was in a state and felt for her. He watched her run up to a tethered narrow boat and jump up onto it. Running across, she was again blocked by water and again ran indecisively hither and thither. The water was narrower here and she looked like she was weighing the chances of clearing it. But really, it was still far too wide for a little dog, but she was not giving up yet, testing how close to the edge she could position her feet before making the leap. And that's how she slipped in.

"Now look what you've done. I suppose I shall have to drag you out. Don't go biting me for it."

Thompson knew where there was a rusted old boat hook on a broken and mossed green shaft. He could hook it under her collar.

Hook in hand he ran to where she was trying in vain to scrabble out. She was frightened of him and the water both, but her exhaustion and his encouragement decided her. She went to him.

"Now look young lady, when I pull you out remember your manners. Come on."

At that he managed to hook her. *Good girl* formed in his head but another voice overruled.

"What do you think you are doing? This dog is no friend to us. It's vicious; it doesn't like us."

Thompson remembered her growling in the Royal Oak – she had meant it – and at the Hailstone, he had had to leave because of her.

"What are you saying?"

"Finish her. This is Cutler's dog. I have a use for that one. He is my balance. This dog is my weapon."

"Weapon? How, if she's dead?"

"You wouldn't understand, not yet. Do what I say, finish her. Kill it."

And so the poet held the frightened animal under until all life had fled. Nothing to it, after all death was merely a transition.

#

"Quickly," she commanded, "back on the bridge now."

"Why?"

"You'll see."

Thompson did as he was told. It was not that he was under her control, not at all. He did not believe that at all. What he was was curious. This friend, companion…Diana, yes, he would call her Diana, his teacher, his muse, she seemed to know things, hinted at knowledge he would give his life to possess, the answer to all his questions. So, in anticipation, he co-operated.

Some time later, walking purposefully along the towpath to his left, he saw Jack Cutler. He was obviously looking for something, and Thompson knew what. He would not find it. The body was weighted with scrap. Oh, it would be found all right, one day, but not today or right now. And when it was found it would be just another unrecognisable unwanted mutt drowned by an owner too mean to pay for its meagre keep.

She told him what to say.

"Good evening to you. The night's are drawing in now, aren't they?"

Cutler fastened onto him immediately.

"Have you seen a dog come this way?"

"As a matter of fact I have. You've lost one I take it?"

"Yes, what can you tell me?" said Cutler desperately.

"A policeman went by with one, oh, 10 or 15 minutes ago, bull terrier type…"

In that, Thompson was not lying. A policeman had caught up what looked like a stray, but the poet knew that was not the animal that this man sought.

"…wait a minute, don't I? Yes, I do know you. We've met, well almost. I remember your dog. Yes of course, that's the one the policeman had."

"Oh, where did they go?"

Thompson used the interval to get closer to Cutler.

"That direction," he said, nodding vaguely behind. "Most likely heading for the road."

"Thanks," said Cutler, making to move past.

Thompson stopped him in his tracks.

"You know that police sergeant, lives in the pub?"

"Lively? It was him, was it?"

"No, but he's got a younger brother, also a copper. It was him." Pure invention, but's that what she said.

"I'm obliged to you."

"Anything I can do, I'm at your service. It's Mr Cutler isn't it? I'm Smith, Francis Smith," he said, offering his hand.

"Got him," she said.

That same flaccid handshake – that normally meant somebody you couldn't trust. But this man was helping him, so perhaps it was not an infallible rule. And again Jack felt uneasy, but put that down to worry.

He walked on into the descending night. Ahead, the sunset was red with promise, it would be a good day tomorrow. Behind him the blood red was already bruising to black.

Chapter 29

Home to Roost

The years had been kind to Rupert Hill. His physical condition was hardly much changed from the man's of ten years ago. An impartial witness might well equivocate along the lines of 'that's not saying much' but Rupert Hill, judge in his own cause, would have none of it. No, he looked as good as he ever did ten years ago, and ten years ago he looked good. That's the way he saw it. Of course, his head was now covered exclusively in grey, but a grey head of hair only served to make him look the more distinguished, his wife affirmed as much. The hair was an anomaly though: as far as Hill was concerned, he was still young.

In terms of mental well-being, things couldn't be better: he had not looked back since his extremely advantageous match to a distant relative seven years hence; not looked back, and not thought back. His murky past stayed where it was, in the murky past, and he seldom allowed it to trouble him. Not now, not while he was enjoying life so much, at last.

Obsessed with what should have been, he had clung for years to the old family motto, Spero Meliora. Yes indeed, he had 'hoped for better things' every waking minute, and some of the others. Well, if the power of thought, concentrated hope, were ever doubted, then Mr Hill, now the proud occupier of a fine manor house near Bromsgrove, would never be amongst the doubters. From the comfortable vantage point of his providential present he reckoned that he had not merely hoped but had always known, for certain, that he would amount to something; a conviction far beyond that flaccid 'hope' of the old motto, he now saw. And, his perspicacity had gone far beyond even that, he assured himself, for he had always held not just a general sort of conviction, not an everyday sort of conviction little better, again, than 'hope', not a mere conviction that good fortune would somehow find him, but a genuine and specific conviction that his own brains, hard work and his own pedigree as a scion, if a previously obscure one, of the Court Of Hill, would deliver him from obscurity. His faith had been in himself, not in fate. And his faith had not been misplaced. He was proud of himself, rightly in his view. Now, he moved, and was accepted, in exalted circles, mixing with the cream of local society. He was no different to them now, never had been really, one of the pack. In brief, Mr Hill had a high opinion of himself.

The past? Say, nine or ten years ago? He had persuaded himself to reimagine it. Reinterpretation had always been his gift to himself: there never had been any such man as Hill the fraudster, the forger, the conspirator. No, it was business acumen, and breeding, which had made him the man he was today, a self-made man – certainly if marrying a rather plain and portly woman counted. That was a kind of business acumen in itself, wasn't it? Yes. Yes it was. For he was conveniently and selectively forgetful. He forgot that his rise had begun at the expense, the breaking, of others; or that his marriage proposal was pressed home riding upon professions of affection, of love, which he did not feel, albeit, he would come to love her (or so he preferred to fondly fool himself). In fact, there had ever only been one love in Rupert Hill's life, and that person he kept in secret contact with – via the medium of the nearest mirror. Pangs of troublesome conscience were rare in that looking-glass couple, but when on occasion they were felt, they told themselves that it had just been business, that they had had a run of bad luck, those others. In truth, their bad luck had started on the day they had met Hill, and not run a mile…

Yes, today's Mr Hill had much to be thankful for, including an imposing residence. He was master of some fine horses and sporting dogs; also, two lovely daughters upon whom all and sundry knew that he doted. And his wife of course. Life could not get much better for the self-deluding snob that Hill had become.

It did, however, take a turn for the worse, when in the autumn of 1887 he received a letter which essayed to dredge up a muck encrusted shell of a man, a prisoner, from the dark sediment of the past and the flooded dungeons of Hill's mind. It was the second such letter, but not the same. This one was more urgent, more threatening, in so far as it spoke of detail to which the writer should not have had access. No, he could never rest easy now till the affair was dealt with; till Alan Hale was dealt with.

#

Stephen Vyle had drifted back into Blackheath on the lookout for Woolley and the off-chance of work. But Woolley's instincts had been better than Vyle's. When he left he covered his tracks: they were looking for Stevie, and if they were looking for Stevie they would soon be looking for him; and if they were looking for him, Jack Cutler would be doing the same. Not necessarily in a good way. So, in order to avoid embarrassing his former employer, but in the interests of self-preservation more importantly, Woolley disappeared.

Oblivious, Vyle came back and moved around in plain sight; plain as day. It was Josh Lively who got to him first and persuaded him to come in for a chat, all innocent like, about some lost property they had in custody. They were trying to trace owners;

somebody had suggested a big man with a limp; couldn't be too specific because, well, people had been known to lay false claims to property, you know; would count it as a favour if he could help out, and so on and so forth…

If it had been Samuel Salt, he would have just bundled the man into custody. But Josh was not as muscular as Salt, nor as big as Vyle, so…

You would think that Stephen Vyle would have been suspicious, would have thought of the medal. But no, his mind did not work like that. The medal was not lost property, so this man, a rather likeable bloke for a copper, must be talking about something else, and if it wasn't his old jacket with his dad's old watch inside, which he had left at the playing fields after an impromptu game of cricket with some school-kids, then perhaps it was something else he could lay claim to. It shouldn't be difficult to fool this softie…

He gave no thought to the medal, no thought to poor dead Reg Phillips. He had got used to that, giving them no thought. That was just a bad dream, and he had lost his jacket since. No, if anything was going to be said about that – the other thing – it would have been said long ago. No, there had been no witnesses that night – to the accident – otherwise he would be on every good citizen's wanted list by now, and he knew that he wasn't, because nobody had batted an eyelid over him. Nobody was looking for him, and he had nothing to hide.

But contrary to Vyle's deduction, somebody was looking for him. More than one somebody. Not advertising the fact, but looking none the less. Amongst others, the police were looking, and Daisy Hackett knew that the police were looking. And Daisy needed no description, because she knew Vyle well enough. She had nothing against him, did not dislike him, but knew enough to suspect that the coppers thought that he knew something about Reg. And Daisy had definitely liked old Reg. She also liked constable Joshua Lively. It was she who tipped him off, who now led the lamb to slaughter.

#

At almost the exact same time as Mr Vyle was accompanying the policeman to the station, Francis Thompson, face muffled as if presenting a barrier to the smog, or as if a respectable man presenting a barrier to recognition by his peers (accompanied as he was by a lady of dubious virtue) was engaged upon his next experiment in metaphysics. She was leading him toward one of her trusted trysting spots, a lamb leading itself.

It was the three-sided ruin of a burnt-out workshop off the canal towpath, not a million miles away from the Navigation. Although assailed from all sides by the clitter-clatter and the banging and stamping of industry, the noise itself only served to confirm their privacy, signifying a working population otherwise engaged. There would be plenty of time for the usual quick knee-trembler. But a quick one of those was not what her client had in mind. He had started out with some such intention, sure enough, but the more he thought about it, the more thought how boring, sad, and tawdry it was. How

491

demeaning. How animal-ordinary. Besides, she probably had the clap, or worse, and he had enough to contend with with his chest, thank you very much.

As they walked, she pretended to be engaged in trivial conversation, and, he not listening anyway, had revised his plans.

And as they walked, as they passed, their shadows invaded the already dark and miserable kitchen of Betsy Colman, widowed mother of seven surviving children. Three of these were on permanent loan to relatives, two, twin boys, were at school, soon to complete their education. She couldn't afford to send their young brother, although he was of an age to attend now – he would need to be clothed and shod, you see – and two were therefore at home that day. She was losing the will to struggle. There were two of them at home that day, two under her care. The flickering black against the light made her start in her despair. Upstairs a sickly little girl lay in bed, not yet three. She had always been delicate, having been born five weeks premature, and she was prone to any illness doing the rounds. And then there was Edward, apple of his father's eye, stick thin and finishing off a crust of bread thinly smeared with the scraped out remains of a jar of jam. That was his dinner poor soul. Mrs Colman was not one for favourites, but if she were, young Edward would have been the one. And so there were two of them under her care; two of them home that day…

"Mom, that was nice. Can I have another piece?"

Betsy Colman wept. When she was young she had been all innocent, could not wait to leave home and get married, become an adult. Then things would be different. Her own man and her own home, then they would be happy, then they could do anything they liked. Except that she found out very soon that they could not. That marriage was a trap, children were a trap, and only money, lots of money could unlock it. Girls like her and men like her husband would never have that kind of money. Without money, the first blush of love soon withered. They ran out of money and her husband ran out of luck…

No. There was no more. No more jam. Or bread. They had been living on despair and bread and jam. Now only the despair was left. If she broke into the rent money, again, they would be thrown out into the street, to survive like stray dogs, as others had been, and would again. She couldn't have that, and she couldn't have her babies sent to the workhouse. It was an evil place, the papers said so. But they had no food in the house! She was losing the will to struggle. There were the two of them at home, two in her care. They could not possibly know what life had in store for them. And they had no food in the house, and she their mother! She was losing the will to struggle. The shadows had passed but something lingered: a blackness; a parasite looking for its next feed. There were the two of them. She knew what to do. She would care for them, she would stop them suffering. She reached again for the bread knife: she had lost the will to struggle.

#

Inspector Abraham Lively had been appointed such for just about a week when he received word that Stephen Vyle had been located and was being held by Sergeant Salt in Blackheath. He sent word that he should be brought to Old Hill.

Meanwhile, the newly appointed sergeant lost no time in questioning the detainee. Poor Stevie Vyle, he had been looking forward to getting his property back, or at least coming away with someone else's unclaimed items. No such luck. Instead of the soft-spoken, obviously green, young constable – nice bloke but a bit thick he thought – an immaculately turned-out sergeant, authority oozing from every blue stitch of the Queen's uniform, stared him hard in the eye. Before placing an object on the desk in front of him.

"Recognise this?"

"No, what is it?"

"It's a medal. They give 'em to heroes. This one belonged to a chap named Reg Phillips. Ring any bells?"

Vyle was not naturally a quick thinker. Also, he didn't like lying, he wasn't very good at it, because he didn't like to do it, unless he had to. It dawned on him that he could not be sure how much the copper knew, so, honesty would have to be his policy. Up to a point.

"Yes, I think I have heard the name. Ain't he the bloke that got himself killed on the railway line?" he said with an unconvincing air of only the mildest curiosity. "By a train," he added hastily.

"He is indeed. Or was," confirmed Salt, "fancy you remembering that, you being a stranger in these parts."

"I'm not a stranger," Vyle stammered.

"You're certainly not a local though, are you? You know, I'll bet you, I could ask a dozen local folk if they recognise that name and I bet that half of them wouldn't. Only the people that actually met him. His friends. Close acquaintances like. Was he a friend of yours? Were you close?"

"Oh, no, I hardly knew…"

"Oh, so you did know him?"

"Well, I've seen him about."

"Really? And did you see him about on the night of eleventh of July?"

Vyle knew that he had indeed 'seen him about' on that date, if it was the night he was thinking of, which no doubt it was. In fact he had been one of the last people to 'see him about.' Not to mention seeing him off. He was sweating buckets now. He looked from the dour sergeant to the soft-spoken constable who had brought him in. But there was no comfort there, and the softness had gone: Josh Lively had liked the old man even if he had been a bit of a bore with his limited repertoire of tales of past glories.

"Can we have a window open?" asked Vyle.

"No. I'm cold," lied the sergeant.

You are that, thought the constable.

"So, Mr Vyle," continued Salt, "did you see the deceased that night? Because, our informants saw you, speaking to him." It was a reasonable guess. The medal had changed hands almost certainly on the night that Phillips had died, and there was no reason to assume that that had been after death.

Vyle could feel the walls closing in. *So, there were witnesses! What did I bloody well tell you Woolley!* "Well, erm, I was around on that date, I think, thereabouts. Probably. I only remember the night because of the news the next day, about him being dead and that."

"So what were you talking about," prompted Salt, who had picked up the scent now.

"Talking? No. Nothing…I might have said hello or good night, you do don't you?"

"So you saw him to say hello?"

"Yes, that's right. We were going the other way."

"We?"

Oh shit. "Me and a friend. We had a drink in the Handel Hotel…"

"The Handel? That's a bit posh for the likes of you, isn't it?"

Embarrassed, the unfortunate Vyle had to admit that it was, but that he just went there to meet a friend before (and he remembered the story) returning to that friend's house where they both got blind drunk and fell asleep.

"And the name of this friend?"

"What's that got to do with anything?"

"Could be everything. I'll be the judge of it. Now. The name. Or do we need to march you around to this house where you claim you spent the night and find out for ourselves?"

"It was Derek."

"Second name?"

"I, I don't know."

"Come now Mr Vyle. I think you know perfectly well what this character's second name is. As a matter of fact, we have a very good idea already. In fact, we know who he is."

"So why ask me?"

"Because, my vile Mr Vyle, Stephen, if you hadn't already guessed, we're just testing you, assaying your veracity. Before we charge you with obstructing the police."

There were at least two words there that Vyle could not handle. And now they were talking of charging him.

"What?"

"I mean, that if we find that you're not telling us the truth, or holding something back, we'll have you locked up for a long time. When you go up before the beak you'll have to tell the truth, the whole truth, and nothing but – otherwise you'll be done for perjury. And that's very serious of course. Lock you away at her Majesty's pleasure I'll be bound. Except it certainly won't be a pleasure will it? Ever been to prison?"

Vyle was white. "No."

"Glad to hear it. Want to keep it that way do you? I would if I were you. So, I'll ask again, for confirmation. What's the name you're holding back?"

It seemed to Vyle, in the light of what had been said, that there was no real harm in mentioning the name. Not if they knew it anyway, more or less. Not if it would get them off his back.

"All right then. It's Woolley, Derek Woolley," I think.

"How do you spell it?" asked Josh, taking notes.

"I don't; I can't."

Josh could believe that.

"Which is the correct answer," continued Salt, making a play of consulting with his own pocket book, "see, not so bad, was it?"

At this point the constable leaned over and whispered something in the sergeant's ear. The sergeant nodded in apparent agreement.

"Now," he continued, "our sources tell us that Woolley worked for a man named Crane, Cyril Crane. You can confirm that can you?"

But Vyle had been kept at arm's length. He knew Woolley, had heard of Mr Cutler, but that was it. So he replied quite truthfully, which suited his inclination.

"No, Derek never mentioned anybody of that name."

"What name did he mention then?"

"Nobody, what do you mean? Why should he? We'm just mates, that's all. Sometimes he might have an odd-job and I help out. If it's shifting heavy stuff like, and that."

"Look Stevie, we're testing you, remember?"

But there was no way that Vyle was going to mention that one name that he knew they wanted. No way.

It was like his brain had produced the sound itself:

"What about Jack Cutler?"

Vyle jumped. Visibly. But he was not going to confirm it, not in words. Not that.

"No. I've never heard of him," he said, palpably untruthfully.

"Sure about that?"

"Yes."

"All right. Back to this. Where did you get it?" pursued Salt, tapping his side of the desk where sat the recovered campaign medal.

"What? What do you mean? You just…" He was so obviously jolted that he was struggling to get words out.

"Look chap, we know you pawned this medal. We know it. That's why you're here. We just need to ascertain how you came by it. Right? Because we believe the old man was murdered you know. No, he didn't fall. Murdered he was. And if you had that medal…well you don't have to be a genius to see where this is going."

The puzzled, if scared, look on Vyle's face persuaded Salt to spell it out.

"Look Stevie, that medal was taken from the old man the night of his murder, taken we can only assume by the bastard who murdered him. And as you were the one who pawned it, that means you must be the murderer!"

"No!" shouted Vyle, and went to stand but was forestalled by Josh Lively's firm hand on his shoulder.

"What do you mean no," asked the sergeant.

"I dain't kill 'im," blurted Vyle.

"Who did then?"

"I …I don't know. I thought he fell."

"Did you? You 'thought.' Why?"

"I, er, I…I thought…" Vyle was stammering again.

"All right. Again. Where did you get the medal?"

"I found it."

"So you're a thief then."

"No, I found it."

"Ever heard of stealing by finding?"

"That's not…" *or was it?* "It was Derek."

"Ah, now we're getting somewhere."

"It was Derek that found it. He gave it to me."

"Did he? And where did he find it? In the old man's pocket?"

"No, he, he, he…" came back on shallow breaths.

"Look Stevie, just calm down and tell us the truth. You'll feel better for it."

But at this point, some of Woolley's impromptu training surfaced.

"Am I under arrest?"

"Arrest no, possibly not, depends how it goes. You're just helping us with our investigation, aren't you?"

"Can I go then?"

"Could do. But think on this: what happens when we find Woolley? Will he confirm your story? Or make up something totally different. Because if he doesn't, confirm your version of events that is, if he says that he never clapped his eyes on the old man, never laid his hands on this, we'll know you've been lying and if we can't trust you, and we've no reason to distrust Woolley, well then, you must be the murderer, mustn't you? Ever seen anybody hang? I have. It's not very nice, they…"

"So Stevie," interposed the constable soothingly, "would you like to have another think. Start again; get your head straight?"

All that Stephen Vyle knew was that there had been somebody out and about that night, somebody they had not noticed, but who had certainly noticed them, together with the old soldier; had probably seen them march him off toward the bridge; and that they didn't hang you for larceny.

"Look, I didn't know anything was going to happen; I didn't want it. But it was Derek. I don't know why, but Derek killed him."

#

As requested, instructed, by the fresh Hale missive, Rupert Hill had made his way to this particularly dingy black-country town and, at precisely 2 p.m. had called a pint at the bar at some dive called the Shoulder Of Mutton, and asked for 'Billie.' An odd-looking Irishman serving said that he would pass it on, and that he was to take a seat.

He sat at a small table with only his anxious pint for company. He didn't like beer, much preferring gin or port these days, but had wits enough to realise that he should blend in: he couldn't do much about his clothes; but he could pretend to be a beer drinker. Was this a typical pub hereabouts he wondered, because there seemed to be a fair sprinkling of able-bodied young men who were obviously not short of cash, but neither were they out earning it. One in particular, a big fellow sporting a flamboyant military tunic of some kind seemed to be taking a particular interest. A colleague of Hale's perhaps? He had been a military man. But, no, this man was far too young…try to avoid looking at him.

What the hell was Alan Hale doing here of all places? There again, it was perhaps unsurprising given his past proclivities. He realised that he had made a mistake. What if the help that Hale had requested, in the form of the cash that he was carrying concealed, was just an excuse to get him here? What if he wanted more than just the money? He wished now that he hadn't been so stubborn at the first time of asking. But it was too late to back out, there were gang members watching him; he had no doubt that that's what it was, a gang. Probably run by Hale himself.

Hill's conclusions were right in some respects, wrong in some others. Yes, there was a gang, and although its loyalty was somewhat fluid these days there was no question of any of it ever having belonged to any Alan Hale, and no question of the man who had once used that moniker ever laying claim to any, him being dead by now. And yes, he had been lured there, but again, it had been nothing to do with Hale, not directly in any case. And the 'help' that had been requested, 'Hale' had not needed. He was beyond help now. Unknown to Hill.

At length the big man with the black hair in the incongruous jacket scraped back his chair and stood and walked over. He looked familiar somehow…

"Mr Hill." It was not a question.

"Yes, hello." He would have offered his hand, even in this situation, to this one, but he knew it would be ignored, so he refrained.

"Are you alone?"

He thought of lying, just in case. Just as he had thought of bringing some 'back-up', some burly henchman. But of this he had decided against, had thought better of

497

introducing any loose-lipped third party to this aspect of his past. It was too risky, and anyway Hale had always been far too devious for him. Besides, in his current social circle there was little contact with the elements which could furnish such manpower. In point of fact, in the old days Alan had always been his back-up, and now that looked like it was backfiring. These days his first recourse would be to use the police to come down on any shady characters which the family felt undesirable; move them on; warn them off; but he could hardly enlist P.C. Plod on matters of such delicacy. And so here he was. Alone.

So, "Yes," he said, "as requested."

John Lively knew that he was. He had been tracked from the moment he had caught his train.

"Come with me."

He followed the man around the bar and into a corridor where the man turned on him.

"Do you have any weapons on you?"

"What? No, of course not."

"Then would you mind?"

"Oh yes, of course."

Quick as a flash, the Irishman was there, patting through his pockets.

"What's this?" he asked removing a large wallet.

"It's just my wallet," said Hill redundantly, and desperately.

"All right." It was handed back and they advanced to a door. The Irishman knocked it.

"Come in," somebody commanded.

All three entered: Mad Mick, Hill, and John Lively last, locking the door.

There was a long table with six chairs to one side. There was one sitter at the table. He looked like an accountant, except that he was not working on any books but riffling through packs of cards.

There was a fire, around which sat an old man with steel grey hair and a flattened face with a broken nose, like he had had an argument with a steam engine, and won. An unsettling face. When Hill could take his eyes off that face, he saw that there was a good-looking dark-haired woman standing behind it, handsome but unsmiling; and there was a big black dog lying at the scary man's feet. Three pairs of eyes, two brown and one grey, one animal and two human, stared straight at him. Whatever lay behind those eyes, it was certainly not friendship.

Nothing happened for…what seemed a very long time. The eyes burned and stabbed. They were going to kill him, he knew it. He suddenly needed a privy. Could he make a dash for it?

But then, a surprisingly soft, and lisping, voice spoke, and the lips smiled at least, and it said, "Hello Rupert. Long-time no see. How the devil are you?"

And the years fell away, and he knew what it was about.

"Cyril," he said, "Cyril Crane."

#

It hadn't taken that long to strangle her. Too quick really. As soon as they were hidden, the urge came, sudden and uncontrollable. To kill. He used his gloveless hands and he could feel the life draining away, fading into dusk; but he could not tell where it was going and it would not tell him. And when it was all gone, she was just an empty shell; a piece of meat.

The overwhelming compulsion, the rage, the passion was gone with her breath, together with the other, the voice in his head which, having urged him on, had now lost interest it seemed. Francis Thompson was just a man on his own now, with a corpse on his hands. He looked at it and felt pity, and hate. *Why? Why tempt me so? Now what have I got to show for it? For murder? I got more out of the horse. Was a human, this human, so unworthy then? But wait. Blood. It must be the blood. Cut her.* But he did not have his bag of surgeon's steel with him – that would have been a dead give-away. What he did have was a small lock-knife in his back pocket; not as sharp as he would have liked, blunt in fact, but needs must…

He ripped and tore her clothing and set about her abdomen. But it was hard work and he had to make several ripping and raking cuts. The skin and subcutaneous tissue he gouged away but he was having trouble getting through muscle. And there was not much blood. Her heart had stopped, hadn't it? He thought about putting her on her side and puncturing her, or cutting her throat to let the blood out. But, no, the moment had gone; the knife was dull and the blood was dead too, by now. No magic left. He would do better next time, she told him, perhaps just strangle them into unconsciousness, without killing the blood. Or take out vital organs while they were still warm, he knew how to do that. What else?

He would have to think on it anon. Right now, he had to slip away from this, this failure.

Bloody whore. Yes you were. He would label her as such, Jezebel. Taking the knife he carved into its forehead, starting with 'J.' But it was too much of an effort and he decided that just an initial would do. The silly coppers would probably think it a cryptic clue.

#

"You want me to what?"

"I want you to sell me the farm that you bought – for a steal – from my sister-in-law, Hannah Lively. You remember it don't you? You remember her?"

"Yes, yes, of course I do. Is that what all this is about? And what's Alan Hale got to do with it? Where is he?" Rupert Hill checked around the room, in case the man he had known as Hale had been there all along, hiding.

"Let's leave our old friend out of this for now, shall we," ordered Crane sweetly, "more of him later. But to answer your question, yes, that's why you're here. We want the farm back, oh, and the fields behind the old smithy, down to the mill pond, and the smithy too while we're at it, all of which I am given to understand you are now the proud owner of."

"Well, yes, that's perfectly correct. But why all this cloak and dagger..." Hill regretted the unfortunate use of that phrase, the connotations, as soon as he had uttered it, but his nerves gave his mouth a life of its own, "that is to say, why not simply arrange for an appointment to see me for discussions? If your offer were successful, we could leave it to the lawyers..." in truth he had a shrewd suspicion about why they had done it like this: He was about to be fleeced, but his mouth, as has been said, had a life of its own, "I mean why..."

"Oh, we don't want to involve any lawyers," interposed Cyril Crane, "and in particular I don't believe that you, Rupert, will want to be running up against the kind of lawyers that might take an interest, given what I have in my possession. So let's just leave lawyers out of it, shall we? This meeting does not concern lawyers. It's between us. It's about justice."

"I, er, what do you mean?" The eyes again. "I don't understand."

Crane suddenly seemed to change tack, and tone. "Oh, I am sorry. Where are my manners? I haven't done the introductions: Mr Hill, may I present Mrs Miriam Beckett, my niece, formerly Miss Lively, and her brother John, my nephew and a close friend I may add, John Lively. You might remember their poor departed father. Gabriel by name. I'm sure you remember...Miriam, John, this is Mr Rupert Hill, of Bromsgrove these days but formerly much closer to home, the home you lost that is. Oh, and he's the man responsible for the death of your parents."

Hill had already worked out who the young man and woman were, as soon as the farm had been mentioned he had been sure. The boy looked a lot like his father. He had wondered, briefly, what had happened to those farm kids. What they were doing here was anyone's guess, but that was hardly important right now. He had to get out of here in one piece. Fight and flight were both out of the question, so he was left with bluff and bluster. He had his indignation ready.

"What? What did you say? That's an outrageous accusation. Outrageous and slanderous sir. I demand that you apologise, or you will be facing legal action."

"Lawyers, back to that are we?" remarked Cyril in conversational style, before growling, "and what makes you think that you will be walking out of here alive?"

Hill was scared now. But he had been scared in the past and talked himself out of it and out of trouble.

"You don't think that I came here without telling anybody where I was going and why, do you?" said Hill, hopefully.

The woman was about to say something, nothing pleasant, but Cyril saw it coming.

"Miriam, let me handle it please. As we agreed."

She stopped, decided and gestured assent.

"Rupert, if I was a gambling man, which I'm not, I would bet that you hadn't. But, I've never been that successful at games of chance, and I might be wrong. So let's say that you did tell somebody where you were going. What of it? You were meeting a man called Hale, or whatever other alias you may have chosen for him, and you were to meet him here, in this pub. So? So you met him, as our observant barman, Mr O'Rourke here, would be only too willing to testify, and then you left, together. Never to be seen again. And that would be it, because you and I both know very well that the reason for your little foray, the real reason, you would have kept strictly to yourself. Neither of course could you have had any inkling of meeting me again. So, if you do disappear, the trail goes cold from the moment you leave with Mr Hale, or a man fitting that description, all as sworn to by my good friend over there. I take it you wouldn't disagree?"

Hill had nothing to say, there must be a flaw in the argument somewhere. If only he could think.

"Ah, I see that you doubt my logic. Let me put you straight: you don't think old Alan brought us into this without revealing the contents of the letter that brought you scuttling here, do you? John, hold him."

Two strong arms pinned his ineffectual limbs behind him. Cyril casually searched Hill's pockets. He found what he was looking for.

"Oh dear, oh dear. You kept the letter. Another bit of incriminating evidence."

"How so? It's just a letter from an old friend wanting help."

"Help which you previously denied. But the mention of other names from the past, like Swinnerton, and that reference to the fallen angel, they obviously changed your mind; not to mention the survey. You changed your mind, I wonder why?"

"Look, if it's money, I brought some. You can have it."

"Why did you bring it?"

"To help an old friend, as you know."

"You mean to buy him off. To shut him up."

"No."

"Yes. Oh yes. But I have to tell you Rupert – to cut to Hecuba – that there's no shutting him up; that he's provided us with a signed and duly witnessed declaration, which to say the least is very incriminating for you."

"Rubbish! What's he saying? No, it doesn't matter, because who is he? He's a nobody! On the run no doubt, a wanted man, that's why he's not here, isn't it? Too afraid to show his face. On the other hand, look at me, a highly respected member of society."

"But isn't that exactly the point dear Rupert?" enquired Cyril.

Before he could reply the woman retorted, "Respected? That's a laugh. Not around here you're not. And especially not in this room."

And around that room, at the faces, Hill dared not look.

"And," continued Crane, "let me assure you, upon my word, that Mr Hale is certainly not afraid, not of you, not at all. And he is most certainly not as you put it a wanted man." *Quite the opposite.*

"So what's the point? To blackmail me out of land is it, on his say so?"

"Now, now Rupert. That's not a nice thing to say to someone trying to help you."

"What do you mean, help? You just threatened to kill me."

"What? No. Did anybody else hear that? There you are you see, you imagined it. You probably just misunderstood a bit of playful banter, between old friends. That's right isn't it?"

"I suppose," Hill agreed.

"No Rupert, it's Hale who has decided to blackmail you. As I said, there's no shutting him up, not till I can find him anyway. And I could find him, for you. That's what friends do. Of course, I would expect you to reciprocate the favour."

"How?"

"I've already said, the farm."

"I don't know…"

"Before you decide, let me explain what evidence old Al has managed to muster."

"Go on then. Baseless allegations no doubt."

"Well, I'll let you be the judge of that. The document contains several allegations, as you say. The first concerns your allegedly crooked opal mining scheme."

"Oh, that. Sour grapes is it? Look, it was a perfectly legitimate business venture. All such schemes have an element of risk. Unfortunately, this one just didn't work out," came back the well-worn patter.

"That's not how our friend has it."

"Of course not. He's already tried to extort money from me with these wild tales. I told him where to go."

"You certainly did. Denied even knowing him I understand. Yet you're here now. Why respond to this letter? Is it because he mentions something else? Something more than fraud. Something far more serious?"

"I don't know what you mean."

"What's the reference to the fallen angel?"

"I don't know. He's a little mad that one, morally insane, in my opinion."

"Why did you come then?"

"Well, I got sick and tired of him pestering me. I thought I would pay him off, once and for all. I'm a respected man you know, can't afford even a whiff of scandal, calumny though it may be."

Thanks for confirming that.

502

The woman almost spat, "He's lying!"

"No I'm not!"

"All right, Miriam, let's calm down. Let me handle it, eh?"

"Yes Miriam, we agreed," said John.

Hill stood. "Nobody's handling it. This is a wild goose chase. I'm leaving," asserted Hill as confidently as he could.

Crane's manner changed, thunderclouds blotting out the sun.

"Look Rupert, you'll bloody well sit back down if you know what's good for you. Sit down and be quiet, you're upsetting Sabre here and if he flies at you I may not be able to stop him; and that will trim your feathers good and proper. Now sit down and listen!"

The dog picked up on the mood and played along perfectly, stood itself, hackles raised, teeth bared. Cyril had a half-hearted grip on his collar. Hill sat down.

"It's all right, boy," cooed a newly serene Cyril Crane, "now Rupert, where were we? Oh yes, the allegations. Now, first of all, please be aware that it's Alan Hale making these allegations, not me, not anybody else here present. And I'm going to make you aware of what he has against you, but know that he has kept copies of everything. He's a careful man, as I'm sure you know."

"But why…"

"Just hear me out. This declaration," and he picked up and waved around a piece of legal-looking documentation, "clearly states that you started this whole opal mining scheme knowing that it would fail, which it did, and in the process ruined your so-called investors, like my brother-in-law. You didn't give a shit about them, that's what Hale said."

"No! It's lies! All lies!" protested Hill, and, before a different audience, he would have been very convincing, hardly surprising when he had been fooling himself about his motives for years now.

"And what would you say if I told you that Al and I had taken the trouble to track down something more persuasive?"

"What? There's nothing."

"Ah, but there is. Hale mentioned it, and when I get something in my head, I'm like a dog with a bone. It's taken a while, but do you recognise this?" He held up another document.

Hill knew exactly what it was. Had been half-expecting it.

"It looks like the bank's survey report on the Wallangulla claim. It's why the bank pulled out. Like I said, a normal business risk. Just unfortunate, that's all."

"I see. And what about this?" This time it was obvious to all that Hill recognised the document in Cyril's hand. The pause, the pallor, and the squirming told them that.

"I…no, what is it? It looks…" words failed him.

"It looks like another report on the exact same subject matter as the one you just admitted to knowing. And it reaches the exact same conclusion. Only it's dated three years earlier."

"But how? I mean, I've never seen it before, obviously. I didn't know."

"Oh, but our Mr Hale says that you did know. You knew, that was the whole point wasn't it? He says."

"That's preposterous! There's no proof. You can't prove it."

"Well Rupert, my old friend, you may have a point there. There is only Hale's word as yet, and this paperwork of course. But I know for a fact that he will keep going now, keep on digging. As a matter of fact, it's quite piqued my curiosity too, and, while I don't want to believe it, if something is turned up, well…"

"Well what?"

"Rupert, I'll be honest with you. When Alan Hale came to me with these stories I did not want to believe them. But, as other things turned up in, what is it they say? Corroboration. In corroboration, then I must admit that I was quite willing to fall in with him. I know his plan was to extort cash, but mine was quite simply to obtain justice for my family, by handing all the evidence over to the police. But it strikes me now that justice can come in a variety of forms, restitution for instance."

"The farm you mean?"

"The farm."

Hill had been gaining confidence. It looked like Crane was not a killer after all. Just a publican trying to help his family. Just a common publican. "I don't think I'm going to be able to accommodate you there."

"Come now Rupert. Be fair. What if I were to tell you that Hale and I have had a bit of a falling out? In fact, a serious one. And what if I told you that I could guarantee that he would never trouble you, or anyone, again?"

Had he heard right? Perhaps he should recalculate on the publican. But, no, he was talking too much, bluffing. He was going to get out of here, he knew it now.

"That would be most convenient."

"And in return, no doubt, you would be willing to grant me just one small favour."

"I still have no intention of selling."

Cyril forestalled Miriam again.

"Like I said Rupert, be fair. A debt is owed and you well know it. All right, as you say, there is no incontrovertible proof against you, not yet anyway. But, there's no smoke without fire, is there? If this got out, how many of your posh friends would stick by you? You've married well I'm informed, the Lowes is it? Very genteel. You've risen high, but that just means that you've got further to fall."

"My friends are all people of commerce. They understand business risks. Rather than castigate me, they would applaud me for taking those risks. That's the only way business is done and the only way the world progresses."

"What would your wife say, or your father-in-law?"

"I'll take that chance."

"You're a brave man."

But Hill did not feel brave, he was bluffing.

This left Cyril to play his trump card:

"And what do you think they would say if you were party to murder?"

#

Jack Cutler had been beaten to the punch by the longer arm of the law. Which for Stephen Vyle was debatably the least toxic outcome. But not for Cutler. For him it was just another worry. What had Woolley told him? Because Woolley had had the sense to go missing and stay missing, Cutler could not ask him. Whatever he knew, would he keep his mouth shut?

It really was getting time to move on. But how could he go? Without his beloved Bo. It had been three days. Three days of him worrying himself sick. That man on the canal, he had said a copper had taken her. But Jack had spoken to the copper in question, the young Lively bloke, and he had denied seeing her; had been busy rounding up dogfighters and dogs, from the raid; had seen no bitch, only dogs; hadn't seen her, so he claimed. He had seemed quite genuine, concerned; promised to keep an eye out; but no, no unclaimed dogs had been handed in; had he tried the pound? Yes he had; same answer, less of the concern. So, that Francis character, had he been lying? But why? Mistaken then? He couldn't be found to be interrogated further. Or was Lively lying? But he had seemed so plausible; still, we can all dissemble. Put up to it by his brother perhaps. So they had something over him? Unlikely. Or was it? What had he said about that man? A fly in the ointment he had once called him; more like an annoying wasp – swat it before it stings. Or had somebody merely taken her in? Taken her for a stray? What if...

All he knew was that he would not be able to think straight nor sleep sound till she was found.

#

That word had sharpened Hill's attention. He listened as Crane continued. As soon as murder had been mentioned the remains of his resolve had evaporated: out of his heart, out of his guts and through his very pores, flavouring the thick sweat which competed for egress. Like a pig, so the saying goes. If they thought that he had had anything to do with the murder of their father, the big man and the vicious woman, then he was not getting out of here after all. He was dead.

But what did they know? He knew himself that he had paid Hale to 'get rid' of Gabriel Lively (or at least the problem he represented – which was it?) And yes, they did refer to him as the fallen angel, certainly at the end, in case of eavesdroppers. All right, he had not specifically used the word kill (had he?) but Lively had wound up dead and Hale took Hill's cash. He knew that much. But did they? Because, and this gave him reason to hope, if they knew as much as him, they wouldn't be working with Hale in the first place, the man who pulled the trigger. They would have killed him! My God! What if they did? Beat a confession out of him, and I'm next?

Cyril's voice. "Are you listening to me?"

"What? No, I'm sorry. I've not been well. It's hot."

"Pay attention!" A soft hand cuffed him around the back of the head, the blow hardened by anger and the edge of a large silver ring.

"Sorry," was all that he said. The woman remained unrebuked.

"As I was saying," continued Crane, "not only do we have the testimony of our friend Hale, and several others, as to their suspicions as to the fraudulent nature of your opal adventure but we also have the far more serious matter of you – allegedly – ordering the murder of my brother-in-law…"

"Oh come on. That's ludicrous and you know it. I'm just a businessman for God's sake."

"I think you had better leave God out of this…As I was saying, not only does Hale's declaration accuse you, it's backed up by the statement of one of your local worthies, a Mr Charles Swinnerton, who heard you issue the instruction."

"It's a lie! It's a bloody lie! What are you trying to do? The…bleeding bloody bastards. It's not true! It's a bloody lie."

Cyril grinned to himself, *that shook him up all right.*

"Language please, ladies present."

Hill realised he was wet with sweat. His mind was racing; something not adding up; something wrong; same again, why would Hale incriminate himself? Why?

"When was this supposed to have taken place," he eventually asked.

"We don't have an exact date…"

"I'll bet."

"No, that would be too convenient, wouldn't it? But both agree on the month and year, September 1878, the month before my brother in law's death. According to the story, there were four of you drinking, not to excess, but together, drinking: you, Hale, Swinnerton, and a chap by the name of Arrowsmith. So the story goes, you took this Arrowsmith to one side and propositioned him, to kill my brother-in-law. The other two overheard but agreed to keep quiet for fear of their part in the fraud coming out."

"And that's all nonsense isn't it? I never heard of this Arrowsmith."

"You said that about Hale."

"That was different. It's a conspiracy, sour grapes like I said. And how could Swinnerton know anything, he was never party…"

"To what?"

"To our conversations of course. Look, I don't know what Hale's game is, besides the obvious, but it's all made up. I swear to you. I swear to you that I didn't ask this Arrowsmith to do anything to your brother, on my children's lives." And that was a safe bet because he really hadn't met any Arrowsmith, as far as he knew, and had not told him, not that individual, to do away with Gabriel Lively. And this was a trap, a clever one, because he could hardly tell them why he knew that it was Hale that had done the deed, now could he?

"Let me see those documents."

And there it was. In black and white. Statements from Hale, Swinnerton and this Arrowsmith character. He sat still and tried not to shake. If he couldn't persuade them that it was all a lie, a plot, then he was done for. Eventually:

"Astounding. The audacity of it. I mean, it's ridiculous. Ludicrous. Mad! Cyril, you know me I'm a man of commerce, a tough negotiator when I have to be, but certainly no murderer. Surely you can see this is all a plot? After all, I'm a man of considerable wealth, is it surprising that someone might be looking to relieve me of some of it?"

"If it's a plot, Rupert, they've certainly gone to town. Take a look at that," he said tossing another document. Under the eye-catching if legally impotent title of 'Dying Declaration', it was Arrowsmith's 'confession', in chilling detail. Hill was about to throw up. And he screamed now.

"No! No! Please! I didn't do it. I don't even know any Arrowsmith. Cyril, you know me surely…" and then his rational mind kicked in. "Hold on. Why would anybody admit to a murder they didn't commit? Dying or not? It makes no sense. There's got to be an ulterior motive. It's all false, can't you see it?"

"Relax Rupert. I agree with you, on the murder part at least, otherwise you would be dead already. But would an overenthusiastic copper? Out to make a name for himself? Agree with you I mean; believe you? Just a thought."

"But you believe me?"

"As it stands, yes I'm inclined to believe you. I've always known you were an entrepreneur, a bit of a wheeler-dealer, bending the law a bit. I recognise that, because I'm the same: and, as I know, you make enemies like that, men who are prepared to do anything, say anything, to get you. But, I don't think you have it in you to kill, and so I believe you. Me? I don't share your scruples, and, in exceptional circumstances…well, you get the drift; and I'm thinking that our Mr Hale might be an exceptional circumstance. Eh? My offer still stands. I can make Alan Hale disappear for you, all the allegations, all the evidence. But it's tit for tat."

"The farm?"

"Yes. And if you can't accommodate me, do an old friend a favour, then not only are you on your own against the machinations of Hale, then I shall keep digging. And once I find enough to get you arrested, you'll be sitting in a prison cell before you can blink. Because, make no bones about it, whilst I believe you on the murder part of this mess, I'm damn sure that you're guilty of the other stuff."

"All right, I give up. What's your offer?"

"So, just for my personal curiosity, you do admit to the fraud?"

"Let's just call it sharp practice. It's not that unusual. If you want to know, the way it worked was…"

"Just spare me the sordid detail. I've learned enough from Hale."

"As you please, but just know this – I never intended to hurt anybody. I was just greedy I'm afraid; didn't think it through."

"Yes, yes, I'm sure."

"What are you going to do?"

"There's been an injustice done," he heard John Lively's voice behind him.

"Don't worry Rupert, we're not going to harm you," Cyril reassured him, "where would that get us? No profit in beating you, or cutting bits off you, or anything. Only fun, some might say. Me? I prefer money in the bank, and that's why I've decided that your offence, which you have admitted, should be punishable only by way of a fine. Compensation for a wrong done. Sound fair?"

Relieved, and only too keen to extricate himself from the cess pit he had stepped into, Hill was glad to say that it did.

"Yes, I'm sure that we could come to some kind of accommodation."

"I know we can. Now, you've admitted swindling – no let's not make any bones about it, the word is swindling – swindling our family. All right, it's your bad luck that your actions have finally caught up with you, but given that they have, you surely must agree, on moral grounds, that some sort of recompense is due. Not just because we have you here, under our power, as it were, but on universal principles: ethics, justice and fair-play. Well, would you?"

Truth be told, Hill's conscience did sometimes prick, albeit but rarely, because as soon as it showed itself it was invariably whipped back into its hole. But the occasion gave it courage to emerge and demand to be heard. Hill wanted to fight it, but it had allies in the room now. Recompense? Well perhaps that was something he could concede, if it wasn't too much. But just remember, his conscience reminded him, *they are only talking about the lying and stealing; it looks like you are getting off light with the killing part of it, the murder. Because there was a murder, you know that, and it would not do for anybody to start digging into that dark deed, not do at all. You can prevent that, thank the grace of God for that – and don't quibble with Him!*

"Would I agree? Well, yes, I would have to wouldn't I?" he said looking around, before adding hastily, "on moral grounds if nothing else, given the premise."

"Good, that's settled. Now as to the Wergeld."

"The what?"

"Wergeld. It's Saxon. From a time when justice under the law was more immediately accessible to the people. Like the people in this room, men like John here."

John Lively moved closer and then moved out of sight behind him. But still close, Hill could feel it.

Cyril continued, studying his face for any sign of protest.

"Wergeld is the price you pay. The price of the injury you have caused."

"All right. I understand. It's fair in a way…no, I mean, yes I see, fair's fair. I can live with that." *I hope to live with it*, "how much are we talking? I have monies on me…"

"Stop. Money is not enough. My niece and nephew lost their home as a result of what you did. We want it back, remember?"

Hill's conscience was having a temporary breather.

"What? Are you mad?"

"No, are you?"

Hill certainly wasn't, just prone to hanging onto possessions which in his view had been hard won, and shocked by the idea of losing one. But his sense for self-preservation told his avarice and pride that he must button his lip now.

John Lively again, a voice from over his shoulder, breathing down his neck.

"Have you forgotten what I said about justice? Are you going to prove to us, villain that you are, that there is not a shred of decency in you?"

It was not a question that required an answer, but it was succour to Hill's hard-pressed good angel.

Cyril now. "Look Rupert, I've been doing some checking. You wouldn't miss the farm, not too much. You are a very wealthy man, even if it is through your wife. In fact, that's why you will sign it over. Because if you don't, I will let Mr Hale continue on his merry way, continue with laying his plans against you, including informing on you for conspiracy to murder and, as I said before, if I keep looking and find just one more piece of the puzzle, I'll set the law on you myself, and give them this to boot," he said tapping the confession. "That could ruin your life, one way or another. I can see that high-born wife of yours throwing you out; might even come to divorce. That would be a turn up wouldn't it? So, come on, do the right thing for old time's sake. Let us buy the farm; let us take care of Hale. Salve your conscience now, or keep looking over your shoulder. Choose."

But there really was no choice to make. And particularly as they were talking about buying, so it would not be a total loss, whined his obsequious avarice. What his avarice did not bank on however, what it did not know, was the fact that the buying price would be heavily discounted, as would be what was left to him after he had lost a chunk, all fair and square of course, in the game of cards which would be the price of exit today. As it was though, that misapprehension was enough of a chink in the armour to let in the darts of his newly invigorated conscience and convince him that in fact Mr Hill was doing a noble and righteous thing, righting a wrong, putting a dark past to rest. Besides,

509

something told him, if he did not agree, there was still a chance that they would pay themselves in blood. He started pulling down his defensive ramparts. Yes, he saw it now. Hadn't he always been secretly ashamed of it, his past? Yes, this could be a kind of redemption for him. And then he could close the book forever. But what about Hale?

"What about Hale?" he asked, "if I do a deal with you, will he, er, go away?" *Along with anything linking me to that killing?*

"Oh yes, completely. I can guarantee that you will never hear from him again. I give you my word. Come now, I've taken the liberty of having all the necessary paperwork prepared. Oh, and before you go, as you are here, how about a friendly game of cards? For old time's sake."

#

It took Inspector Abraham Lively just ten minutes, over a cup of tea, in an interview room (they had all the best of facilities at Old Hill), to decide that Stephen Vyle was basically a simple soul with by no means a black heart, not by any stretch of the imagination. Josh's verdict had been similar, not a bad bone in his body, he had said. And perhaps Josh had been fortunate in that, him being the one who had brought him in, for they were large and strong bones, damaged knee not excepted, supported by strong muscles. The man must have stood six feet three, as tall as Abe himself, but seemed to perceive the world and its works with child-like innocence, a trait which had immediately endeared him to Abe Lively, although the policeman in him knew well enough how dangerous men like that could be when they came under the wrong influence. Some people, soulless, unprincipled people would have no hesitation in using such a simple heart as a living weapon, like a guard dog, or, yes, like a war elephant sweeping aside opposition. He wondered how far they had corrupted him. According to Salt he had tried to remain loyal to his friend, this Derek Woolley, although it was a certain bet that that character did not deserve it. Salt had done a good job again, he was making a good sergeant; and once more Abe was grateful, for it was certain that it would be Abe who got the credit for uncovering a murderer, even if they had not found him yet! He had been right all along: murder it was. Had Salt let Oakden know? Had he rubbed it in? If so, it would probably have been taken in good spirit: Oakden was doing a solid job himself, and was actually becoming popular with his work-mates, a sought-after drinking companion even. How things change: you had Oakden, working out of Blackheath and a mere constable, and apparently so much happier for it; and here he was himself, now an inspector, inspector Lively sitting pretty in Old Hill. And was he happier for it? He had always thought he had deserved promotion, so he should be, happy that is. But in reality he felt no different, apart from being a little home sick. Content, that was the word, he felt content. Yes, that would cover it for now.

510

But back to business. Woolley had dragged Vyle into an awful mess, and Vyle did not realise the half of it.

"Stephen, are you ready to carry on?"

"Yes, sir, ready when you are, ready when you are constable." This last to P.C. Wothers, taking notes, who was proving to Abe why Millership kept him close: a more conscientious and discrete individual you would be hard pressed to find.

"Right, Stephen, you've told us that your associate Woolley tipped the deceased – that's the old man – over the bridge into the path of a train. Now to me that looks like a deliberate attempt to kill him, to murder him, which of course is what he did. Now the problem…"

"But it might have been accidental," interrupted Vyle, perhaps not having been entirely sure, perhaps having second thoughts about being a 'grass', or perhaps he just did not want to believe it of his friend.

"An accidental murder? No such thing," said the inspector. "No, seriously Stephen, we've already covered that ground haven't we? Think again, think back, think about poor old Reg falling and what Woolley was doing, what his face said. No, look at me, look at me and tell me you think it was an accident."

A silence, Vyle was expressionless. Then, "No it was on purpose. It was on purpose! But I don't know why. Why? What for? He didn't tell me, we weren't supposed to…" And the big man was getting worked up and that could be dangerous, like being knocked over by a runaway horse.

"Mr Vyle, you will calm yourself please. Now please, or you will have to sit through this interview in restraints!" Abe knew that some nervous horses required a firm hand, and so it was with this big beast. "Good. Are you sure you are going to keep calm now?"

"Yes. Sorry. I'm all right."

"Now look Stephen, as far as the unfortunate incident itself, the old man's death and its aftermath, I think we've got that straight now, so I'll just recap: you and Woolley had the old man on the bridge. Now, for whatever reason, Woolley pushed him over. He killed him Yes?"

"Yes, I've said. But I didn't know. I wouldn't…"

"Shush, it's all right, we know that. Let me continue. After the train was gone, Woolley sent you to check on the body…"

"Yes, but I wanted to help as well, but he was dead when I got down."

"And that's when you decided to take the medal?"

A grunt.

"I'm sorry I can't hear you. That's when you took the medal. Is that right?"

"Yeah. He didn't need it anymore, and I was saving up…"

"It doesn't matter why you took it. You took it. That makes you a thief – that's a long stretch in gaol. But it could be a lot worse."

"What do you mean?"

"You may not have heard of it Stephen, but there's a thing the law calls joint enterprise. Ever heard of it?"

"No."

"Well you may come to wish you hadn't. To put it simply, in your case, the fact that you both in effect abducted this man and one of you killed him means, or could mean, that both of you, that's you and Woolley, could be found guilty of murder. And hanged."

"But I didn't. I never meant to hurt him. It was just supposed to be a chat. To find out what he knew."

"About what? About the thing you would not tell the sergeant about? Let me explain things very carefully again. You both walked with this man as far as that fateful bridge. That in itself could be construed as abduction, kidnapping. That's a felony right there. But then, there's the joint enterprise question, and I must say, on the facts it looks bad: two men engaged in a felony killing another. As I said this could, could, open you to a conviction for murder."

"What do you mean could?" said Vyle hardly daring to breathe.

"Sorry? Speak up."

"You said could leave me open, do you mean it might not?"

"Glad you asked. Because it all depends on how events are interpreted. Between you and me, the way I suspect it happened, you had no idea what would happen when you picked the old man up. But a clever prosecutor could easily make a jury see it differently. That's why context is all important. So, look, you tell me everything and I promise you that I will do my best to help you. I might even make the larceny charge go away. After all, we're trying to catch a murderer, pilferers are two a penny. So, is it a deal?"

"Yes, yes, thank you."

"Right then, where's Woolley?"

"Oh God, I really don't know. All I can say is that I would have thought he had gone home, to Smethwick."

"Good, we're getting somewhere. Whereabouts does he live in Smethwick?"

"I don't really know. We met here. He mentioned Windmill Lane once, but that was just where he was born, I think…"

"That's not a lot to go on Stephen. Is there nothing else?"

"No, sorry. Oh, we were talking about pubs. He knew the Blue Gates. That's on the High Street, by Rolfe Street station. He might go there for a drink I suppose."

"Good. That's a bit more, but nothing very definite is it? All right, what did you and he want with Reg Phillips that night?"

Vyle did not have to think about it. He just took a deep breath and said, "Ah, now there I can help you. It was to do with the workhouse, and somebody called Jack Cutler."

Cutler again. Abe made his mind up to pull him in, for a far less civil talk this time. According to John, Cyril had fallen out with him too, so no worries about stepping on his uncle's toes. In fact, their relationship had soured so much that, as he now knew, that it had been Cyril's fervent hope that Cutler had been arrested at that dog-fight; indeed Cyril Crane had arranged things so. However Cutler, John assured him, was as slippery as an eel. Whatever racket Cutler may have had going at the workhouse, Cyril obviously disapproved, and good for him. But Cyril's plan had gone awry; if in consequence Cutler was now aware of it, that possibly put not only Cyril, but also John – family the both of them – in jeopardy. He was beginning to suspect that Mr Cutler, not to mention his silver tongue, was far more dangerous than he had hitherto imagined. He would make him a priority.

"Thank you Stephen, that's what we wanted. Like I said, I'll do what I can for you. Now go with the constable please. Take him away Wothers."

#

Not wanting to voice his concerns in front of his sister, John caught up with his uncle in the pub's privy. It had been an hour since Rupert Hill had been escorted back to the railway station, and they had been celebrating their apparent victory with port and whisky, the uncle and two siblings.

"Do you think he's going to leave it like that Cyril? A man like that. Will he swallow his pride, as well as let us fleece him? And do nothing?"

"It's because he's a proud man, proud of his so-called standing in society, that I think that we are safe. He would be stupid to uncork this lot again, I think."

"You think?"

"Remember, I do know the man of old, and if there's one thing that might rival his hubris, it's cowardice. He wouldn't want to start a feud with people who have cause enough to hate him already, with people who might decide that enough's enough and publish everything that they know about his past; but more than that, they might decide to kill him, for all he knows. He wouldn't want to live with that worry. What he might want to do is try to track down Alan Hale himself, but as there's no such person, he won't get very far of course. Plus, like I say, he hasn't got the guts. So, we're safe, I'd say."

"You're sure about that? What if he tracks down Arrowsmith?"

"How? He won't. Where would he start looking? For a person he thinks is made up? And even if he did, there's no way he could make the connection with 'Hale'"

"Again, are you sure about that?"

"90 percent."

"What if I were to say that ten percent's too high a risk?"

"I would say that we've already been sailing close to the wind, but that we've got away with it, in my opinion, and let's not push our luck. The bluff worked perfectly, and there's enough distractions, also witnesses of course, to make even the best lawyers in the world despair. He's got nothing on us, don't worry. If he tries to contest this," and

Cyril tapped his pocket where lay the newly signed bill of sale, "let's say that I will be most surprised."

"What if he does?"

"He won't."

"But what if he does?"

"Then we will release all the information we have about his shady dealings, including the confession from the real Alan Hale, from Bill Arrowsmith. See how he likes that."

"If he got away with blocking the sale, Miriam would kill him!"

"Yes, well, I'm sure she wouldn't be best pleased, but let's have no talk of killing, or even of roughing him up. If that came about hot on the heels of alleging that we coerced him into a bad deal, who do you think the coppers would be arresting first?"

"All right, let's say you're right. We've got the farm, great, though what we do with it isn't straightforward. Strictly speaking it should go to Miriam, being the eldest, I suppose…"

"We don't have to discuss that now."

"Yes I know. What I meant to say was, he stole the farm, and we've got it back. But what about our father? What if it really was murder, not a suicide? And even if it wasn't then he's still the one responsible, isn't he? What do you think? What do we do about that debt?"

"We've been through this. I told you, Arrowsmith had it in for Hill –couldn't blame him – and he wanted me, us, to kill him, I think. Hence the story about this murderer for hire, Davenport. Getting our friend Hill locked up for fraud or whatever wasn't enough for him, so he embroidered a bit: worth a try I suppose. But I can tell when a man is lying to my face, and Arrowsmith was definitely dissembling about something. So, as I've already said, I had his story checked, at some personal expense I might add, and I repeat, it turns out that this Davenport was not at liberty to murder anybody at the time, because he was in nick himself, for assault. And when he did get out he didn't last long, killed in a revenge attack it seems. Look, I've already told you both all this – Arrowsmith thought he could get one over on your uncle Cyril, but you would have to get up early in the morning to do that."

"Like they do in prison, you mean?"

"Eh?"

"I've been thinking about this. Yes, Arrowsmith lied to you. And no doubt your instinct was good: you knew he was lying. But instinct is nebulous by nature – I mean it's real but not precise…"

"What are you getting at?"

"Hate to say this, but did you consider that he was lying not about the murder, but only as to the perpetrator?"

"But why…"

"Why d'you think?"

Cyril thought it through in an instant. He blanched, recovered immediately and convinced himself that he could not possibly have been wrong.

"No," he said firmly, "I think we're letting our imaginations get the better of our common sense now. No, nothing's changed, and we've achieved what we set out to do. It's all good. Miriam's waiting. Come on, it stinks in here."

#

There was nobody standing outside Inspector Lively's office door that afternoon. Had there been, it is very doubtful whether any but the sharpest of ears could have picked up the sound of the human voice from the other side of the thick door. The sharpest of ears, however, might have been confused to hear the occupant apparently holding a conversation on the telephone, because telephone technology was still several years away from Old Hill nick…

"Yes, all right, yes. You were right, I was too soft on him. I'll bring him in again, and this time I damn well won't be being half as friendly. Quite the opposite. But I certainly won't be setting out to kill the man, I'm an inspector now thank you very much. Yes, I know, I just said thank you. What? Well that's what I meant. Yes I know you promised. Although, come to think of it, I don't think you ever said it in so many words, did you? What? No, no I don't think so. When? I don't remember. Yes, well I don't remember. What? Take your word for it? I suppose I must. What do you mean? No, I was just saying…Yes, of course I'm grateful, and all that…This one? What this one in the cells? I don't think he's a bad man. He's just been led astray. No I'm not going soft, there's worse than him about. Or don't you care? Would you have preferred I beat it out of him? No? You don't care either way? That's new. Bigger fish? Yes I know, our Mr Cutler. What? No? Who else?"

I told you, something bad is coming. She's here. Help me get her…

#

Sergeant Samuel Salt was enjoying his new position. Barely a week into it, and he had solved his first murder. Following the capture and successful questioning of Vyle he had rounded off a perfect day with four or five well-deserved pints. But he was a young man and keen, and after a good night's sleep he was back at the station ahead of time next day wearing his well-pressed uniform and duty arm-band and his enthusiasm – he couldn't get enough of this! He was planning the day's duties (having decided that a change would be good for the troops, shake them out of any complacency) and enjoying one of Oakden's strong and sweet coffees when the door was yanked open violently and

515

a red-faced little man with steamed up spectacles, two side patches of short dark hair separated by an expanse of bald pate, regulation rolled up sleeves, and the smell of greasy metal about him, catapulted himself in.

"Oh, thank God yo'hm 'ere. It's murdah, an 'orrable murdah. Thank God yoh'm 'ere. You gorra cum. Cum quick."

Even Salt had trouble calming the agitated visitor, but ascertained between outbursts that he was a foreman from a metal-bashing shop on the other side of town, down by the canal running under Waterfall Lane. And that he had discovered a dead body, a woman it seemed, who in his opinion had been done in, 'an 'orrable murdah' apparently. Well, he would be the judge of that, bodies did turn up for all sorts of reasons, and murder was not at all a common one. As to 'orrable, the man was obviously excitable and prone to exaggeration. Still a body was a body and Salt was not going to waste any time before investigating.

But the agitated man would brook no delay. "Yoh gorra com quick, yoh woh believe this constable, ah tell ya."

All right, all right, for heaven's sake. She's not going anywhere is she? Salt took up his note book and his kepi (it seemed so much smarter than the helmet, for a sergeant that is.)

No rest for the wicked. And it's sergeant by the way.

Chapter 30

A Loss

They had come to an understanding, Cyril and his niece. And part of that understanding referred to just that nomenclature. No matter what he may be biologically, he would only ever refer to her as niece, not anything else. That's the way she preferred to think of things: Cyril was her uncle, and her father was her father. Her ingrained emotions were stronger than a mere accident of conception, discovered years later. Whether within his own private thoughts uncle Cyril saw her as anything other than a dear niece, then that was a matter for him and his own psychological needs. Just as long as outwardly, to her and to the rest of the world, he described himself and acted as an uncle. Just as long as he stuck to the arrangement, she could live with it, and with him.

The impetus for her conversion as far as Cyril Crane was concerned had of course come from Abe. Cyril had become close to her brother, two of her brothers in fact. If they, knowing the truth about…about that relationship, if they had accepted Cyril, accepted him back into the fold as family, then she had had to question her antagonism. What had they seen that she was missing? And whatever it was, did she want them, want Abe, to feel uncomfortable with her, have divided loyalties, drift away from her? No of course not, that would be cutting off one's nose to spite one's face, wouldn't it?

Besides, although the eldest of the children, she realised now, a battle-scarred survivor of two marriages, that she was still a child when their parents' marriage apparently ran aground, and that that could have happened for diverse reasons, not necessarily involving Mr Crane. God knows she understood that now, especially, stuck in a loveless marriage and still having to show a smiling, gormless face to the world, because that's apparently what the world expected. Well, stuff the world. The Livelys were not meant for a normal life, they were better than that, Beckett was right about that at least. Look at her brothers: John on his way up and looking to rent a much larger house in Whiteheath; and Abe. Little Rabbit was an inspector now! Unfortunately for her, that had meant that he had left his room at the Oak for more suitable, and convenient, lodgings in Old Hill. But she would not begrudge him that. On the contrary, his former occupancy, though welcome in one sense, had been for her just one more tie to the Oak. That tie had been severed. Next for one of a completely different hue, that being her union with that tiresome dullard that in a moment of miscalculated madness she had married.

And then there was Cyril Crane of course, he was a Lively too, by adoption at least. Family it seemed, that she in particular must now allow. And no matter whatever else you thought of him, you had to admire the way he had come to this benighted midden and took it by the scruff of the neck and shook and shook till it disgorged for him both cash and also respect, of a kind; a respect it seems which was even shared by our newly appointed inspector of police!

And, crucially, her new found cordiality with Cyril Crane was the key to changing her life, for change it she was now determined to do. The discomfitting of that man Hill and the consequent restitution, rightful restitution, of Lively property was her way out.

The dog came in first, headed straight for her, tail wagging, pushing against her legs.

"Hello Sabre, how are you boy. Yes I know, you're a good boy aren't you?"

Sabre knew that he was. He was followed by his master.

"Hello, uncle," she said.

"Hello, niece," he said very deliberately and smiled affectionately, "it's nice to see you again so soon. Making up for lost time?"

She could have been offended, but she wasn't. Now that she had let him in again, she knew that she quite liked the man, especially since his masterful performance with that Hill person.

"Well, you could say that, but I do have another motive."

"Yes, I knew you would have. And I suspect I know what it is."

"Do you? You who have been cut off from me for so long? You're a mind reader then?" He had pushed a little too far, but again, she found herself not as upset as she might have been.

"I'm sorry. That sounded a bit forward didn't it? I only meant that since it was this business with the farm that brought us back together, I am guessing that you want to discuss it. What I intend to do with it."

"And you would be guessing absolutely correctly. I want it," she replied.

"And you shall have it. Why do you think I went to all that trouble? Stuck my neck out. It was for you. You are the rightful owner, in my book at least."

"What do you mean? You'll give it to me?"

"Of course."

"What about Abe?"

"I haven't consulted him."

"But, he's the oldest male heir…"

"But he's not an heir though, is he? Because your mother didn't leave it to anybody, she had to sell it before the bailiffs…well, you know what I'm saying. There's nothing stopping you sharing with your brother of course."

"I know that. I also know that I didn't come here to throw myself on your charity, your pity, or anything else. I came here with a business proposition."

"I'm all ears."

"All right. The farm belongs to us, and when the paperwork goes through – which it will – I'd like to go back. Make a go of it…"

"It's a bit run down, I'm afraid…"

"I'm not. Not afraid of hard work. I, we, get the farm back, and you, being a publican, get the chance to expand your holdings here. I'll give you the Royal Oak in exchange. And I'll even leave you with a manager, should you wish."

"Beckett you mean?"

"The very same. When I go, he stays."

"You've discussed it with him?"

"No, not yet. Not told him. And it will be a telling. There will be no discussion."

"I don't suppose he would be pleased."

"You never know. And quite frankly, I don't care what he thinks. I've had enough of being miserable, unfulfilled. I've had enough of him. I need this."

"Miriam, if it's what it takes to make you happy, I think we have the beginnings of a deal."

#

He had been wrong. It was quite obviously a murder, and even a man of Salt's ingrained grit had to admit that it could, in all fairness to the little foreman, be described as ''orrable.' The young woman, a local prostitute, he knew, had obviously picked upon the wrong customer. For he had killed her brutally and treated her disgracefully – her post-mortem shame had been covered at the crime scene by an old blanket that the little bald man had sourced from somewhere, since he had returned with Salt. To his credit, he had held up well, considering what he had found, considering that he had merely been expecting to find an absent barrelling shop employee whom he suspected had sneaked off for a quiet fag and to chew the fat with passing bargees, female ones that is. Salt awaited the arrival of the inspector. Before that Lively arrived, however, another one did, in the form of Josh, in company with Clark.

"What is it Sarge? Murder we heard," asked constable Clark, not quite as quiet as the sergeant would wish.

More professionally, P.C. Lively merely enquired, "Anything we can do?"

"Yes, as it happens, there is. Get that lot back into their place of work and make sure nobody else comes gawping. And yes, there's been a murder, a young lady known to us, a woman of the streets. It's Charlie."

"Oh, no," said Josh, moved, but not that much: he only knew her to move her on. Still, it was a shame. And murder? Who would do that to her? Clark may have been reading his thoughts:

"Occupational hazard," he opined.

"Just get on and move those people. No not that one, he found the body, let him sit there, your brother may want to speak to him."

Abe would indeed be speaking to the man, but briefly because Salt had had ample time to take a very detailed statement by the time he arrived, Wothers in tow. First order of business was to look at the body. Although no less hard-boiled than Salt, as soon as the blanket was lifted a shock hit the inspector like a prize-fighter's fist connecting with his forehead, a black film swirled and his stomach turned…

"Are you all right, sir?"

A firm hand was supporting him, a firm friend to rely on. Shortly:

"Whew, yes. Sorry about that, I think I had some dodgy eggs at breakfast. But thank you Samuel, good morning Josh," this latter to his brother who had made his way across when he saw Salt lending the new inspector his arm, "and yes, I'm all right, bit light headed for a moment that's all."

"I don't blame you," said Josh, who had clocked the still uncovered corpse.

"Cover her up sergeant," ordered the inspector, "do we know who she is?"

"Local prostitute. That would explain what she was doing here…"

"Do we know that for sure?" asked a voice as if from nowhere. Wothers entered from the periphery, "or is it an assumption?"

As if there weren't enough in on the act, Clark contributed with one of his famous misplaced comments:

"Well, they doh call 'er Charlotte the 'arlot for nothin.'"

Abe rounded on him. "That's enough of that Clark. There's a woman dead here, and a murderer loose. Make yourself useful and move that bloke on before I lose my temper."

'That bloke' was walking his lurcher up the cut, but had stopped walking. Clark went off to tackle him, sharpish.

"Now what do we know about her?" asked the inspector.

"I do recognise her as a street-woman," confirmed Salt, "and I know she's called Charlotte, Charlie to most, but she behaves herself and doesn't push her luck…"

Except she has now, more than one thought.

"…so I've never charged her. You?" The last was directed at Josh, who had never arrested or charged her.

"No, and I'm like you. I only know her as Charlie. No second name. But I know her friend's name, she has been in the cells. Maybe she might know."

"Good Josh," said inspector Lively, "you follow up on that. Now, while you're all here, and I expect you to make this point to Clark, Josh, I want no details of this getting out. All we can say is that we have found a woman, dead, and investigations are continuing. I don't want the word murder mentioned, and if anybody does use the word, without my say so then you see this?" He indicated a foot, encased in a large black shiny boot, "Then expect to find it so far up your arse you'll think it's coming out the other end." The huddled coppers looked at the boot, at the way the laces pulled into little slits, grinning with anticipation. They got the message. The inspector continued.

"Right, first thing, let's get hold of whoever was with her last, aside from her killer that is. These girls look out for each other and there's every chance that somebody saw this nutter pick her up. We want a description at least, or a name ideally. Josh, see what that friend knows. Sergeant, see if anybody around here saw anything useful, but be careful, I don't want to stir up too much talk, I've got a bad feeling about this. And make sure that foreman chappie keeps his mouth firmly shut."

"You can rely on me, sir," replied Salt. Abe knew that he could.

"And if you've got time after that, or during, I want you to find somebody else for me. You know this Jack Cutler character, mixed up in that workhouse business?"

"Cutler, yes, what of him?"

"Do you know him to look at? Could you find him for me? Just find him, then you and I can take it from there? Could you do that?"

"Yes, I could do that. I do know him."

"Good, keep me apprised on that."

"Will do."

"I'll make enquiries myself," offered Josh, only to receive an unexpected sharp response.

"No, you will not. You will make no enquiries about, not ask after, not mention the name of Cutler. Is that understood?"

"But…"

"Look, I've asked the sergeant to do this. I have business to conclude with Cutler, and I have had past dealings with Cutler, and those dealings persuade me that the further business I have with him is not going to be appreciated, in fact it's going to anger him. A lot. And he's no pussycat, he's dangerous. So please do as I ask and leave it to the sergeant."

That hit a nerve. That word. Sergeant. Josh had longer service than Salt, and he was Abe's brother after all, and he knew for a fact that Abe's word, his recommendation, meant a lot with the powers that be. So why had it been Salt? Salt was big and tough, and yes, people did seem to like him. But people liked Josh too, responded to his less confrontational approach. Because policing wasn't just about twisting arms was it? Anyway, Josh could be as tough as the next, if push came to shove, he thought; but policing sometimes required gentle persuasion, he also thought, which in turn required a certain amount of empathy, a different way of perceiving, which often could prevent trouble before it even got the chance to turn into a crime. He had proven that to himself many times. A quick tongue could be as useful as a brawny arm, although Josh just happened to have both. As much as he liked the man, Josh could not say the same thing about the new boy. In short, Josh thought that Salt should not have been promoted over him.

"Right-ho, I'll leave that to the sergeant," he said, almost sarcastically, "I'll be off then."

"Leave Clark here, I'll send him to find you after the doc's been. Wothers, give Clark a hand please."

Alone with Salt Abe asked him, "Do you remember that pony, throat cut at the Hailstone?"

"Yes, of course I do. What are you thinking? Same nutter?"

"Yes…I don't know. It's different, but the same."

"The same? How do you mean?"

"I'm not sure. It's just the obvious cruelty. Why do that, why mutilate the body? Why slit a horse's throat and let it bleed to death? Both killings involved blades of some sort. I'm just…it just smells sick, this does, like the pony. It's the work of somebody sick. Sick to the soul."

"Well, yes, we never did catch the nutter at the Hailstone. And I think everybody agreed, he was a nutter. A nutter at work here as well, of course. But is it the same one? How many lunatics of this ilk do you get per square mile? In the same year? One is too many, and that argues for this being the same bloke, upping his game to humans. And yes, both incidents involved knives, or blades. But that actually argues the other way, because whoever killed that poor animal had a very sharp blade and knew how to use it, like a butcher, or a surgeon. In contrast, whoever did this," he said nodding behind him, "looks like an amateur, scraping away with something about as sharp as a rusty nail by the looks of it. Where's his sharp knife gone?"

"I don't know. Perhaps he lost it. Perhaps it was not a knife at all, perhaps something bigger, something that he couldn't carry around in broad daylight when picking up a prostitute. I don't know. All I know is that this kind of savagery is too much of a coincidence. If it is the same man, then it looks like he has a compulsion to kill, which means that he will kill again, which means that we must catch him before he does. And in the meantime, I don't want details of this barbarism to get out. I'll let my superiors know, and the council leaders, but, even if we have to own up to murder, we don't want folk to get the idea that there's a random bloodthirsty predator out there, looking to strike again. I had enough of mass hysteria in the summer."

"So it's a cover up then?"

"Yes, at least for now. Just make sure that foreman understands he can't talk about it. Something tells me we haven't heard the last of this maniac."

"Right. Oh, look, here comes the doc with the cavalry."

"Thank the Lord for that."

Geraldine Ricketts was a religious woman. A religious woman with a sound mind; and a mind which had had an above average education, considering her sex and social standing. And so, she was telling herself for the, hopefully not the thirteenth, time that this was silly. It was not logical, she knew. But what power had logic over a woman in love? On the other hand, if she believed in God and His angels, who was to say that those angels…

But no, stop. "What do you think you're doing?" she said out loud, to her reflection, but softly in case of waking her father. *You ought to be tucked up in bed, not messing with the supernatural, and on a Sunday too.* And she looked at the sensible-seeming and rational looking woman sitting across the dresser from her. *Oh, get on with you,* came her twin's reply, *are you afraid or something? Afraid that the old lad's going to get you? Silly, it's just a bit of fun; and look, it's nearly midnight now anyway, so you may as well carry on. Or don't you want to see who your husband will be?*

Geraldine was quite sure who her husband was going to be. She didn't need this, waiting up when she needed her beauty sleep, sitting in front of the looking glass in the sombre glimmering of a single short wicked flame, moonlight pressing through thin curtains…

She jumped, a sound. It was the mantle-piece clock downstairs, not loud, not loud at all, but her nerves had been waiting for it, expecting it, yet half dreading it. She could imagine the workings taking a deep breath to tackle the big job ahead: counting out the quarters, and then the long slow slog of twelve strokes. As the second chime sounded, she took a breath herself, and began.

It was Halloween, and she was following the advice of folk lore, the dubious wisdom of our less enlightened forbears, which assured, according to the local paper at least:

'If at Midnight with a pumpkin light

You steal to your room unseen,

In the mirror appears the face

Of your husband to be on Halloween.'

The present supplicant was making do with a candle, but she expected that that would do the trick just as well.

So, as the strikes traversed the clock face in sound, she placed the candle to her left, so that that eye was if anything overburdened with light, whilst the other looked into the reflected darkness, made blacker by the contrast. No doubt there was some kind of conjuration expected now, some form of words, like a prayer – or a spell. But Miss Ricketts had not had the confidence, the nerve, to ask around on the subject: after all she was a religious woman, known for it. And sensible.

Twelve chimed and the house fell strangely silent; not even the usual sounds of snoring from her father's room. All right, what now? She stared a while. Nothing, except a dimming and a lightening, in barely perceptible degrees, as her eyes struggled to adjust.

"Who will I marry?" she asked the air.

"Who will I marry?" she asked the walls.

"Who will I marry?" she asked the dark.

"Who will I marry?" she asked the candle light.

"Who will it be?"

But the mirror showed her nothing, and she was starting to feel that she might get a migraine, with that candle so close and off-centre. She blew it out. A relief. After a while she realised that it was by no means dark, the moon was lending her her light. She opened the curtains and saw that she was sitting behind some thin cloud, or smog. It looked like a full moon, and moonlight now imbued the room with an altogether different atmosphere. *Best go to bed now, I'm being silly. Silly to believe in it; that I would see something. It's just a silly superstition, like when Josh told me that a sparrow had flown into the station this morning:* immediately she had warned him to be careful, that it was bad luck, and immediately after marvelled at what rot stays with you, educated or not. It had been her mother speaking she recognised afterwards; she remembered a sparrow incident from her childhood, the dire warnings…

It's just silly!

But silly as it may have been, she was on that track now and decided that she would try once more, just once, quickly by moonlight, say her prayers, and get into bed. She was getting cold.

She went back to her seat at the dresser. She sat a while, gathered her thoughts, thinking of Josh, and asked no question this time, but commanded, "Show me my future husband."

This time it was instant; indistinct but instantaneous. She saw a definite darkening in the mirror; something moving as if pushing against it, the darkening, like kittens in a bag. This continued even though she blinked, several times. She was frightened now, could not turn round, could not stop looking, wishing she hadn't started with it, meddling with the unknown…Then a flash, or a glimmer, as of a fire, oceans away. Gradually, she imagined that the darkening formed a man shape, and it wasn't black, it was dark blue. A police uniform! Must be. Josh? And she could make out the uniform now, but not the face. Light was glinting from the buttons, but then there was just a big hole, a hole in the blue, and a smokiness ran out of it, fell to the ground – and the man shape was gone, only the head remained. It was a blond head and it smiled at her, but then the smile became the grimace of a bleached white skull, with perfect white teeth and black empty sockets, which looked right at her before evaporating. She had been unable to move, but now she screamed, before scrabbling for the matches. She lit the candle, and the lamp. There was nothing there, she had imagined it, of course she had, she was overtired. The familiar sound, for once not annoying, of incredibly loud snoring was coming from her father's room. Her scream had not awakened him: he could sleep through an earthquake, in fact his snoring must have been just as loud – loud enough to wake the dead, she used to say. She shivered, wondered if she should wake him, thought better of it, and buried herself beneath the bed clothes.

That would teach her. Even if she had only imagined it. So much for the comfort of seeing your future spouse: she felt not in the least comforted.

Silly, silly woman! Just a bit of fun indeed! For the rest of her life, she would never forget that night.

#

Joshua Lively knew nothing of his paramour's midnight adventure with the spirit realm, why would he? And Geraldine Ricketts would never tell him. At the time that she was scaring herself silly, he had been soundly asleep for some time, looking forward to another day, having decided upon a plan of action: he would find one legged Daisy Hackett, break the news about her friend Charlotte, as gently as he could and letting her in on as little as possible, and get some useful information back to his brother, show him how police work was done. Also, he had a shrewd idea that Daisy could tell him where our Mr Cutler might be found. She had told him in the past that he was friendly with 'the girls', in a strictly non-professional kind of way. He was it seemed just an acquaintance who genuinely cared about what happened to them, about whether anybody was mistreating them, and how they were doing; generally keeping an eye on them, but only when he was actually around himself of course. He hoped Daisy could steer him right. And then? Well, and then he would march into the station in company of the said Mr Cutler. And prove that constable Joshua Lively was a peace-keeping force to be reckoned with. He was sure that there would be no need for Salt's strong-arm tactics, if only he could find Cutler and talk to him, persuade him. That's what Josh Lively did. It worked. And the man himself had always shown himself to Josh to be courteous and polite at least, even if he did have criminal leanings. Daisy seemed to care for him, or at least respect him, so Josh reckoned he couldn't be as bad as Abe had suggested – his brother probably had his own reasons for that. No, he didn't seem like the violent type to Josh, more of a talker, like himself, although Jack Cutler's talk would almost certainly be directed to ends completely antagonistic to those of most policeman.

Yes, he had come up with a plan; roll on tomorrow.

#

Sleep hadn't come easily that night to inspector Lively, as might have been expected. Murder was bad enough, but this was worse: this was the work of someone deranged, somebody who might well strike again, no, someone who would strike again. And then it would all come out, they couldn't hush up things again, or indefinitely. And there would be panic from the citizenry, and questions asked by their leaders; questions asked of him. And very soon the newly lauded and appointed inspector could find himself their whipping boy. Got to catch him. Got to. And soon. Despite Salt's doubts, Abe Lively knew that this was the same killer that had killed that pony, Sarah's pony. He got the same uneasy feeling, as if the killer had killed just for him, to get to him as much as for the fun of killing, like he was trying to communicate. He was controlling the thing inside him, had found that concentrating on the green stone, squeezing it, would hush it, but he wanted to hear it now because he wanted confirmation. Not disappointing, it said to him, just once, "I told you, something bad is coming." That was all the confirmation he needed and he allowed himself to fall asleep, entering a haunted dream state where night devils flew on leathery wings and eviscerated human prey with talons of sharpened steel before fleeing, and hiding in the form of a man as the rising sun's rays burnt off the night's shadow. He awoke to those rays, and shivered.

#

If the inspector had slept less than soundly, he had at least done better than Cutler. Jack had not slept at all, at least by his own subjective rendering, although it is possible that he had cat-napped without knowing it. But mostly, he lay awake worrying about his lost dog, about Bo. He had gone back and forth over the same routes calling for her for over a week, and he was losing hope that he would ever see her again. He had got to the stage where he just wanted to know either way – alive or dead. It would be better than this not knowing. Perhaps then he could sleep. But he was coming to dread sleep, because his dreams were beginning to worry him. They were nightmares really, he knew, and he knew they had been disturbing, because he had been finding himself waking sweating and shouting. But he could not remember, not much. He knew that a voice was calling to him, as he was calling to Bo, but it was not a friendly voice, it was the voice of cannibal bidding his dinner jump in the pot. Sometimes, when he awoke, he still heard its echoes. It was no wonder he had taken to drinking more...

#

Morning broke. A new day. If inspector Lively had thought that things could not have got any worse, not yet at least, he was proved wrong before that morning was over. The news had skewed sergeant Salt's plans for the day: he had fully intended to occupy himself with his orders of yesterday, to wit questioning locals in the vicinity of the murder, and making enquiries concerning one J. Cutler, esquire. But that was put on hold when the message came through that three bodies had been found in a house not so far away from where they had found the ill-used corpse not twenty-four hours earlier. Another three? And kids amongst them? Stabbed. Their fears had been realised, the killer had done it again, in spades! In fact he had probably done them all on the same day. First order of business was to get down there with a constable, Stride drew the short straw today, secure the area (because he knew that Moses Munn, for one, was already there, asking questions), and at the same time send for Doc Wharton and the inspector.

This was getting out of hand, they needed to find this bastard, quickly.

#

After yesterday, Josh Lively reckoned that the last place that he would be needed, or welcomed, would be this new crime scene. Abe and Salt would no doubt be tied up all day with the doctor, gawpers and the press, and undertakers probably. This gave him a head start. He would find Daisy Hackett and see if she knew who Charlie had gone off with; and he would hopefully locate Jack Cutler. Two feathers in his cap.

He had a pretty good idea where to find her today, and he did: hanging around outside The Portway Tavern. He took her in and bought her whisky and water. He told her merely that Charlie had met with an accident and that they wanted to speak to the last person she was with, to see if that person could explain what had happened.

"Why doh yoh ask 'er?" she asked, knowing that she would not like the answer, "ow bad is 'er?"

"It's very bad, I'm afraid, Daisy. She's dead."

Daisy said nothing else. She sat for a full minute and then tears fell, silent, unaccompanied by even the softest of sobs. Suddenly, she wiped her eyes.

"Can I 'ave another drink?" she said.

Josh left her to her thoughts and fetched a large one.

"Yoh know it 'appens. Ah know it 'appens. Ah've bin on the bad end o' sum beatings, believe yoh me. Is tharrit? Did sumbody goo t' far?"

Josh hated himself. "We're working on the theory that there was an accident, that she fell and hit her head, and that her, er, client, ran away. Scared to report it."

"Bastard," she said, and knocked back the spirit, minus the water. Then, "'Er was a bostin wench…" she began but continued as if for his benefit, "a really lovely wench, she was, a good girl, very polite not like some of the rough buggers we get round 'ere, pardon my French. Oh well, looks like I'll 'ave to find another friend."

"I'm sorry, Daisy."

"S'oright. 'Appens. Not your fault."

"You can help us by telling who she went off with yesterday, before…Did you see?"

"O'course. That's what frens am fower. Ah knows ooh it was."

"That's good Daisy. What's his name?"

"Oh, ah doh know 'is nerm, but ah could descrarb 'im. Y'know Mr Cutla?"

"Jack Cutler? Him? It was him!" exclaimed the copper, incredulous.

"No, it wor 'im, no. Ah just meant to say, 'e looked like 'im. Not very tall, slim, dark, with big rownd dark ahyes an'dark skin. Swarthy they call it, y'know? An' e was dressed smart lark mister Cutla, but diffren' smart."

"How do you mean?"

"Yoh'd call it mower formal. Ar that's it, formal. Lahke, Jack wears a cap – a nice 'un – or a bowler, 'op an' a catch, but this bloke 'ad a topper. An' 'e always wears this westcoat – ah've sid 'im afower – diamond pattern it is, black an'wharte, ah think."

"And you've no idea of his name?"

"Towd ya, no, ah doh. Ah wish ah did."

"Any idea where he lives?"

"Ah doh, 'e just pops up. But 'e bay from rowend these parts; doh spake like one of us, more like yoh, or yower sista. Posh."

"Thanks Daisy. That's helpful. How are you keeping anyway, you look like you've lost weight. Are you all right?"

"Oh ahr, ah'm alwys all right. Ah'm just on one o' them diets that's all. Gorra be able to get into me ball gowns ay I?"

"Well, just you take care, and get yourself something to eat," said the copper, sliding a sixpence over the table.

That turned on the waterworks again. Finally she said, "Yoh'm a good bloke yoh am. I sid it the fust time ah met yah. Thank you."

"Daisy, there is one more thing. I need to speak to Jack, to Mr Cutler. Nothing serious, but I would like to talk with him before the sergeant, who's also looking for him. You wouldn't happen to know where I could find him these days, would you?"

"Yeah, o'course. 'Es started using The Fower Ways of an evening. Try there."

#

As it turned out, Charlotte's killer had not been on a multiple murder spree, not yet anyway. It turned out, as verified by the medical opinion of Doctor Wharton, that the two dead children and their mother had been killed by poverty and the hopelessness spawned by it. The way it had happened was that she had put both the kids to bed, stabbed the boy in the heart, then suffocated the girl (there was her brother's blood on the pillow). Then she had laid down in the scullery and slit her wrists. Bad way to go. She was found by a neighbour who had picked up more of her kids from school. Bad thing to come back to.

There had been murder, yes, two counts of it, but the murderer was dead too. It had been a long day for inspector Lively, but it was case closed as far as the police were concerned. It was a tragedy which would be the topic of gossip for a long while to come and would perhaps divert attention from the incident at the canal, which as far as the average Joe was concerned had been an accident of some sort. That's how it was being sold, giving the police time to investigate free from interference from an over-excited populace.

Leaving Salt to mop up details and liaise with the authorities reference the murder suicide, inspector Lively put the day behind him and returned to Old Hill where he sequestered himself in his office with a bottle. Tomorrow he would start the hunt for the killer. First order of business would be to find out what Blackheath had discovered so far: as Salt had been otherwise engaged this meant asking Josh to report on what he had got from his chat with the victim's friend. Abe assumed that meant a colleague engaged in the same profession…

After a couple of small glasses he was about to stow the whisky when the desk sergeant announced that he had a visitor – his brother.

Josh, out of uniform, was shown in.

"Josh, this is a pleasant surprise! Come in, come in. Take a seat."

"Not disturbing you am I?"

"Not at all. I was just relaxing after a hard day. Want one?" He gestured to the bottle which he had been about to cork.

"Yes I heard about some of it. And no, I wouldn't say no," said his brother, "just a small one thanks."

"There you go, cheers."

"Good Health," responded Josh, as the glasses chinked.

"Where have you been then?" enquired Abe, noting the civvies.

"Just for a couple with Geraldine, just left her."

"You seem to have hit it off with her."

"Fingers crossed, but yes. We like each other very much, she's fun to be with."

"Serious is it then?"

"I don't want to tempt fate, but yes, I think it is. On both sides."

"Josh, that's marvellous. I'm very happy for you. This calls for a refill…"

"The reason I came Abe, inspector, was to report on this person who was last seen with Charlie, Charlotte. And it's Bailey by the way, Charlotte Bailey."

"Family?"

"None that I know of."

"This friend then?"

"Daisy Hackett…"

"False leg Daisy?"

"That's her."

"She doesn't know anything about the girl's family I presume."

"No."

"No enemies, that kind of thing, I suppose?"

"You suppose right."

529

"No, whoever did this didn't need an excuse. Tell me you've got a description, and a name."

"No luck I'm afraid – on the name that is! But, I do have a good description."

And it was a good description. Abe recognized the slimy poet straight away. And if he wasn't the prime candidate to indulge in this kind of deranged and gruesome activity, then he would hate to bump into the real killer on a foggy night. He had known there was something off about him. And the way he was hanging around Miriam – and she letting him! It didn't bear thinking about. If he was still around Abe would deal with the bastard personally. If not, he would release the name and description to the entire force. Francis Smith, so-called poet, fop and overall smart-Alec; and insane and vicious killer. The thought of him sent the blood rushing now, and the sight of that face in his mind's eye made him feel sick. *I owe Spragg an apology,* he reflected, *at least for that.* He despatched Josh with an instruction to keep his information to himself till he sent him word.

"Have another drink," the voice said.

"I don't want any more."

"Up to you. But I've got something to tell you."

"What is it?"

"There's another. Here. Like me. Stuck here like me, but she likes it."

"She?"

"I don't know how else to describe. It's part of me, sometimes, but opposite. Bad, sometimes."

"Something bad is coming?"

"Yes. Here now, and now it's time. We must be together now, or we will both die. It's time. I see her clearly now, and she sees me; sees you. She wants me, and you. But if you help me, we can leave. I will make her although she does not want it. If we are together, the door will open."

"What door?"

"The door to somewhere else. It's not good for us here, we shouldn't be here. It will kill us. In time, in a long time, it will kill us. I just want to go home now. It's time, I see her. Will you help?"

"You know you're just something I imagined don't you?"

"Yes. Or did I imagine you? What did that woman tell you?"

"Which woman?"

"The one that gave you the weapon."

"Weapon?"

"The thing you keep in your pocket; the thing you put under your pillow."

"The stone?"

"The stone, yes."

"This is madness."

"This is but part of life that you, your people, cannot understand. Not yet. One day."

"It's madness."

"Yes it is. I've tried to help you. And you've seen things that men would give their souls for. You should be grateful for such a madness. But, if you want me gone, there is a way. You must help me."

"You promise? You'll go?"

"If it is the will of God, as you might say."

"All right, I'm mad. Let's say I'm mad. Talking to myself – again. So let me try and talk myself out of this affliction. What do you want me to do?"

#

The witch had had vivid dreams. Something was coming to a head, soon; maybe tonight, with the conjunction. Maybe something connected with the quest, maybe not. But something was up. She had asked for guidance, an insight from the earth entities which had proven helpful and trustworthy in the past. But nothing. Nothing tangible. She could feel a build-up of energy, the vibrations changing now, as if two forces were pushing into each other. That's how it felt at least: she was on edge, and that was not like her.

Yet again she had dowsed with her yellow crystal over the map. Yet again no result. She was beginning to feel that their quest had been fruitless, would prove fruitless. Had the calculations been wrong? Had something changed? With the conjunction tonight, time had, really, already run out. What chance of finding the portal in the hours left? She gave up, and made a decision.

"Martin. Martin, come here!"

A small fat hairy man in dungarees sloped around the corner.

"I'm here ma'am. What is it?"

"Get a hold of Victor, and start packing up our things."

"We're going home?"

"Yes, our time here is up. Now I know you'll be sad to leave…"

"What do you mean? I don't like it here, I should have thought…"

"I know! I was joking," she said. Martin had no sense of irony.

"Oh. So, no luck?"

"No, and it's not down to luck. Fate perhaps. We know these entities had to come out somewhere around here, or at least we thought they did. But I'm blowed if I can find any kind of portal."

"I think, the door blew open and then blew shut. I think they're stuck here now."

"That's as good a theory as any, I guess."

"Yeah, and that's why one latched onto that cop, I reckon. Abraham wasn't it?"

"No that was something else. Unless…"

531

"What?"

"He fooled me, that's it. He fooled me."

"Who? The cop, or the thing?"

"Could be both. Change of plan. Are you safe to go into town and find the cop for me, this Abraham Lively?"

"Not really. Don't put your trust in me. Fickle, my kind. Just a fact of life."

"All right, I'll go myself. Carry on packing."

"What's so urgent?"

"I don't know exactly. But something's building up and he's in the middle of it. He could be in danger."

"So? You like him don't you."

"What if I do? That's not important – but he also has the green stone remember. It's time to get it back, before it does any damage. Well, don't just stand there, hitch up the buggy."

#

By the time that the witch reached the police station in Blackheath the day was drawing in, and the daylight was giving up the ghost. The bad news was that Abraham Lively was not there, but the good news was that the sergeant in charge knew where to find him. Inspector Lively now. How had she missed that? Hopefully, the promotion had all been down to merit. Not sure of the road, especially in the fading light, and as she was a lady after all, the sergeant insisted on giving her an escort, in the form of a talkative constable by the name of Clark, though whether this was his first or last name she was not sure. She imagined that if he were a familiar, he would have to be a rabbit, or a squirrel, what with those wonderful teeth: she had never heard of a donkey familiar.

#

But by the time that the lamps had been lit on her buggy, and the horse allowed a drink, inspector Lively, as per his decision of the night before, had left on his own quest. Jack, as still he thought of the voice in his head, was sure now. He took the inspector, out of uniform today, as far as The George And Dragon and bade him enter. Across a crowded bar he saw into the next room – and looked straight into the eyes of that miserable poet. He felt a shock go through him, was momentarily paralysed, within which interval his quarry made good his escape, barging through the crowd and out into the gathering gloom. Quick as the copper was, there was no sign of the poet when he got outside. He knew they were onto him now; Jack said that so did she, and she was hiding now. Jack was not making much sense and seemed obsessed with coming to grips, not with the poet necessarily, but this 'she' that he spoke of. But the copper in him was still

532

thinking clearly, and he retraced his steps and re-entered the pub, making a bee-line for the man that Thompson had been speaking to.

"Excuse me, sir, my name's Lively…"

"Yes, I know who you are sergeant."

"It's inspector now."

"Oh, congratulations."

"Never mind that. That man you were talking to, wearing the topper, do you know him?"

"Well, only to speak to. He's a past customer of mine."

"Explain."

"Well, I'm a porter at the railway station in Old Hill," explained Lenny the porter, "I carried his bags and got him a cab when he arrived, and I bump into him occasionally, and we just say hello, talk about the weather, that kind of thing, that's all. Why?"

"A cab you say? So you would know where it went, where he stayed?"

"I most certainly would. As far as I know, he's at the same place."

"Which is where? Quickly lad."

"Well, you know Waterfall Lane?"

Abe grabbed the man's collars and lifted him bodily.

"Spit it out you fool!"

"I was just saying. The Navigation. It's The Navigation, down Waterfall Lane. If you follow the road down as far as…"

But the inspector and his partner were already gone, the rattle of the door punctuating the end of that brief visit. Conversation levels returned to normal and it was forgotten.

Instinctively, whatever that meant, Abe knew that Thompson, Smith as he knew him, would be heading for home, like an animal, to lie up, or lie in wait. He proceeded with both speed and caution.

#

Josh was following through on his plan. The route he had chosen, deliberately, would take him past, if his information was correct, what was Jack Cutler's current watering hole. He crossed the road as he passed the hangman's tree. In the dark the gnarled branches always seemed to him that they were reaching out to hug another victim to its bosom, not discriminating between fair game and an officer of the law such as himself. Halloween was but two nights ago, could be that some spirits still lingered! He quickened his pace until it was safely out of hair-pricking range. A brief climb and then he was on the easy stretch, down Portway Hill on a familiar circuit which took him past the pub at the bottom, the aptly named Four Ways: the sign at the crossroads read Dudley, Oldbury, Blackheath, Rowley. He knew this part of his beat – in fact all of his beat – like the back of his hand. He had been treading it for over twelve months now. After just a few months

533

the new boy had been able to say that he could have found his way around blindfolded. As it happened though, tonight was not a particularly black one. The moon was full, more or less, and it shone bright. He felt it, inside, tingling in his belly, throbbing with an elusive power; like a huge silver machine, defying gravity; close enough to reach up and grab – almost.

It would be a cold one. There were no clouds, and the usual obfuscating smog was by dint of the breeze and the lay of the land, refreshingly absent. From his elevated position he could see the familiar red and orange gashes in the blackness which betrayed the positions of Oldbury and Blackheath; their mines and workshops and the furnaces which blasted and banged and clanged day and night, night and day without end; sucking in the men who slaved there day and night and night and day until their own ends – tending Titans of steel and steam and fire which fed not only on the coal, but the very life forces of the puny men who scuttled around them like ants around a queen.

Despite his recent disappointment, not for the first time did Josh say a private prayer of thanks that Abe had found him a home in the Staffordshire Constabulary, and that he had not ended up with those men down there. Down there in the low blackness; in the noxious pall of smoke and steam and gas which draped itself over the houses. As if to hide their shame…

He looked away and took deep breaths of cold air, and pulled his cape tight to keep out the wind. A sound, and he felt for his ironwood truncheon. It had got him out of a few scrapes before now. It's all right – just a wandering sheep in the farmer's field. Not a spook out of the quarry then…

By now through the pub windows he could make out figures: gas lit shadows of unnatural shapes, and impossible dimensions, playing on the wavy lines of old glass. And voices, muffled and conspiratorial. And drunken shrieks. And laughter. Ramparts of sound.

For a second, he thought again. He was known at the Four Ways, yes; not a complete outsider. But more as policeman than ought else. The working men inside – and the women, of no doubt questionable morality – had been drinking for some time by now. He could come back tomorrow with Abe. In the day. But there was no guarantee that Jack Cutler would be there tomorrow, day or night. No, he was an officer of the law and a grown man. He didn't need the back up of a big brother. Besides, he only wanted a few words, no fuss.

#

The inspector had expected the poet to make good his get-away, but was surprised to make him out, courtesy of the shape of his topper, not running but walking, albeit briskly, at the bottom of 'Heartfail Hill' approaching the canal. Did he think he had made it? Did he think that running would only draw attention? His quarry glanced around as if nervous, and swiftly, as if he did not want to be seen looking. He may have made out the shape of the copper, and may not: there had been a good moon till now, but clouds had come from nowhere, almost blacked it out; it felt like rain…

Or perhaps he was just checking, to make sure his enemy was coming on, as intended. Abe was not going to give him chance to secrete himself and lie in ambush, and so he ran for him. The move was immediately detected, and now Thompson really did run. He dashed across the road and darted into a narrow gap between a couple of rancid workshops whose grimy windows at the frontages leaked a diffused dirty light, testament to the presence of other human beings, at least on the street side. But the rat hole that Thompson had headed for was dark, there were no windows in its weathered brick walls, and it opened out, eventually, into a deserted chaos of discarded rusting machinery, spools of wire, dilapidated masonry, holed and rotten barrels, all set upon a foundation of polluted mud, gravel, broken glass and broken bricks. And he was nowhere to be seen. He had managed to secrete himself after all. But to what purpose? Would he attempt to sneak away in the dark? Or was he lying in ambush? But why? Why would he wait? It made sense for him, now that he knew the police were on to him, to leave here. Didn't it? But, he knew that the poet was waiting for him, of course he was. He just knew it. And he didn't need the whispering voice to tell him so. To wait for a bigger and stronger man, to attack him and risk retaliation, for no apparent reason, was folly – and it made no sense! That's how he knew that the poet was doing exactly that – because it made no sense! Just as it made no sense for him to be listening to something in his head; just as it made no sense that such a thing actually existed and that it was in fact the fabled Spring Heeled Jack, in hiding now it seemed; and just as, preposterously, it made no sense that Inspector Abraham Lively, pillar of the community and scourge of the criminal classes, was chasing this character about the place, not because he was a suspected felon, a murderer, but because, truth be told, Spring Heeled Jack was after him, but not him. So who? What? A sister? Daughter, mother? Lover?

This madness had to stop. Abe had been getting the upper hand with the voice, the thing – whatever it was. After this, after he had brought in this murderer, he would do his very best to rid himself of it. Unguarded thought: it heard.

"I've told you, you can't get rid of me. Especially not now. We have her. One last effort and we'll have her. Then we will be strong."

"No, I'm here for the man, that's all."

"All right then. So, good. He's close, when you get him you should kill him, he's an evil thing now. Bad things will happen if you don't do it."

"Enough! Enough of this rubbish. I'm not listening to your bluster any more. You're just making things up, just trying to get me to behave, to let you stay. I'll not have it. You should go now."

"If I go there's nothing to stop it."

"No, I'm not going to ask. You're trying to lead me by the nose…"

535

And it was his nose that felt the first shock as a piece of mildewed and worm-eaten floorboard hit him full face.

It could have been worse. The weakened weapon had a slightly spongy texture which cushioned the blow. Nevertheless it bloodied and floored the copper and just as he was hitting the ground the force was magnified by a body which sprung on top of him, all scrawny sharp elbows and knees. One pointy projection projected into his solar plexus with some velocity and Abe felt a familiar sick and winded sensation: he needed to breathe. But that was not on his attacker's agenda. So, he was lain there in the muck, half a house-brick, or something equally uncomfortable and painful, jabbing into the small of his back, straddled by a raging fury, a madman's hands around his throat, fingers given strength by passion digging in, probing around his windpipe, in preparation of ripping it out, like a mad dog in the fold. He needed to breathe; time to recover. The thing inside him was willing him on, telling him to get up; to kill him. But there was something else now. It was afraid. He knew it was. And this made him fear too. He looked into the man's eyes. But they were not his eyes, he knew it. They were not his eyes! They were like two blazing mirrors where things danced darkly. The face they were in was rasping, coughing and drooling; the face of a weak man; a sick man. But something was giving him strength, Abe felt it. And Abe feared it. And he knew that it was the same as the thing in him, and that he should fear that too. And fear paralysed him. They were going to win.

#

He lifted the latch and stepped through into a different dimension: a warm brown-grey fug of smoke and conversation interspersed with shouted orders and yellow blobs where the spheres of gas lamp floated as beacons in the gaseous shroud. More than the murk and the thrum though, it was the smell. The smell always hit you. Smoke of course – sweet pipe tobacco and the cutting odour of Turkish cigarettes – and stale beer, competing in the nostrils with a claustrophobic stench of greasy clothing and dried sweat and the impetuous vomit that had not brooked the journey to the street.

He was familiar with the smells in such places, but they still registered. It was the smell of the life of working men. Their homes offered no comforts and little solace and so, knocking off, they universally packed out the many pubs on offer, just as on shift they were packed together in drudgery and danger: like sardines shoaling for protection, except they knew that they would not escape the sharks, not forever. Sudden death, mayhem, starvation and disease, or a painful wearing out – more than a match for a temporary redemption bought by the death of John Barleycorn, esq. Respite nevertheless. These were stoics by day, desperate epicures by night. It was almost noble…

Young constable Lively took all of it in in a second. Then, sozzled heads began to turn as voices were lowered. But the herd continued with its boozy business whilst keeping a curious eye on the outsider. Josh went to one end of the bar and waited. The

536

proprietor's niece, a stiff wench with a no-nonsense look about her, was busy handing over a tray of sloshing black beers to a couple of quarrymen who looked like they had already had enough, and they spilled a good deal as they made their way back into the recesses of the crowd. The proprietor himself replaced a beer glass he had been wiping amongst its none too clean fellows and made his way down.

"What can I get you sir? Or is this an official visit?"

As far as Josh knew, Bill Rose ran an honest business. Well, relatively. It was perhaps a rougher than average pub, but that was down to its strategic location: the catchment area ensured a variety of clientele. Looking round, Josh could see coal-blackened miners, furnace men with leathery brown skin, and dusty grey quarrymen mingling like ghosts. Then, a small group in the far corner whose means of support was not immediately obvious. He could not see Cutler and turned to Rose, indicating his armband.

"I've not dropped in for a pint. I'm looking for Jack Cutler. Told I could find him here. Just want to ask him a few questions. That's all."

The landlord said nothing and stared back. Was he trying to recall whether Cutler had been in? Or did he know very well and didn't want to say? Josh couldn't read him. He gave the impression of being shifty, but perhaps that was just the way he looked at you: he was obliged to look up and at an angle to make eye contact owing to his formative years being spent as a lock-maker's apprentice and foreman in Willenhall, or somewhere like that…

"He's right there." Rose nodded to the 'no visible means of support' corner.

"Jack? Mr Cutler!" He obviously got a response invisible to the copper.

"There's a visitor for you."

A few low words and the shuffling of leather on sawdust, and the corner party unfurled to reveal a short figure that Josh recognised as Jack Cutler, although not exactly the dapper man that Josh had expected. A wiry man with that extra indefinable something about him: the way he carried himself, the way he moved; there was a certain spark of life about him. Had been. But not tonight. Tonight there was something different, something tired, no spring in his step, and he looked more thin than wiry. Something had dampened down that spark and it made him look quite ordinary; it made him look like what he was, a man small of stature. Perhaps it was down to him having had a drink, reasoned the copper: he was holding a pint pot. Tonight he was dressed much like his companions: in corduroys, thick dark jacket and cap. His were noticeably newer and of better quality than theirs, even including a white kerchief which looked suspiciously like silk, but nothing seemed to be hanging at all well on him; his shirt was un-pressed and he had not shaved. But he was not drunk: he spoke clearly enough.

"Looking for me constable?"

"Good evening, Mr Cutler. How are you?"

"Not exactly up to scratch. Can't deny it."

Cutler was looking at him those big round brown eyes. He reminded Josh of a whippet, but not an exactly docile one, "What do you want?" he continued.

"Well, it's not what I want. I'm here on behalf of the inspector."

"Your brother you mean? I've been expecting him."

"Have you?"

"I've been awaiting a summons, yes. Is this it then?"

"In a manner of speaking."

"Well in a manner of speaking constable, you can tell your brother that if he wants me he can come and bloody well get me himself, instead of sending his minions."

"I'm not a minion," retorted Josh, barely holding back his resentment, both of Cutler's remark and of Abe's apparent opinion of him, "and he didn't send me. As a matter of fact it was my idea to come and talk to you, seeing as he couldn't find you himself."

That brought a twinkle to Cutler's eye. "Oh, it's like that is it? Big brother all high and mighty now is he? I hear he's moved to Old Hill. Blackheath not good enough for him no doubt. Well, I'm sorry to disappoint but the answer's the same. If he wants me he'll have to fetch me – and he'll have to bring help."

So what to do? What could Josh do? Manhandle him? But that would mean an arrest. On what charge? And, really, he might have to fight half the pub just to get out. That was not up his street, not at all. As it stood, he at least had half a victory, in that he knew where to find Cutler. But he had come here knowing full well that he was never going to use force. Persuasion he had decided. Persuasion. He tried a different tack.

"So, did you find that dog of yours? How is she?"

Unknown to Josh, for a change immediately came over Cutler, suddenly all smiles, the little man took this as a deliberate taunt. Two could play at this game.

"Constable Lively, Josh. I'll tell you what. Your brother has obviously been giving you a hard time. He has me an' all. I know I've got to say something, eventually, about some things as went on at the workhouse. Not the things I've already talked about mind, told your brother about, but other things. Things he knows bugger all about. Well, I'm not going to tell him. I'm going to tell you instead. What do you think of that? I was finished here anyway. Have you got a spare half hour to hear me out? If I accompanied you to the station, as they say?"

Josh could not believe the turnaround in his luck. First, he had the description of the man that killed that poor girl, then he had found Cutler, and now Cutler was offering to spill the beans about something that had obviously become a bone of contention between him and Abe. So, "Yes. Yes of course I have. That would be splendid. Shall we go now?"

"Why not? Saves getting bored."

"Good, can we…"

"Just a minute. I've got to go out the back for a piss first."

Giving himself too much credit, perhaps, Josh thought he caught the whiff of one particular kind of rat, the kind that makes a run for it.

"I'll come with you."

"No you won't! I'm not having you watching me!" Cutler was getting excited: "Look, you stay here and I'll be back in two shakes. Honest," he continued more reasonably. "I'm a man of my word. Ask anyone."

Josh was getting out of his depth. It had looked like it was going to be easy a second or two ago. Now it was getting complicated.

"Look," continued the whippet "that's my coat on the wall over there." He gestured toward a canvas duster draped over some iron hooks. "I'm not leaving without that. All right?"

Makes sense I suppose thought Josh.

"All right." And Josh sat on a stool near the front door, and watched as Cutler disappeared out the back with a couple of mates. "Can't be that shy then." This last under his breath – he realised the pub was now very much quieter. The crowd had been thinning as folk drifted away. Ever since the word 'Cutler' had been mentioned as it happened. Couldn't blame them. Law abiding chaps – and wenches – had a right to a bit of fun without the law poking its nose in. He had intended to be in and out quicker than this. Oh well, there were plenty of other drinking establishments within staggering distance for them to choose from. Bet Bill Rose is none too happy about the loss of custom though. Verifying that assumption from his demeanour proved difficult however, for Rose had disappeared.

Josh was still wearing his cape, though he had removed his helmet on entry as a partial concession to trust. But the room was already hot, and Josh was twitchy. He became aware of a thick cloying sweat prickling in his armpits. How long had it been now? Had he been duped after all? Cutler's coat was still on its hook. Or was it? Who said the coat belonged to the whippet? It looked a bit long, thinking about it. He was beginning to regret coming. But what choice had he had? Abe had put him in this position. Abe had had him passed over. He would prove him wrong. But still. At night and alone? Rash to say the least. Stupid Abe would tell him. 'Course, Abe was never wrong was he? Well, I can bring home the bacon this time, if it hasn't scarpered already...

#

It was afraid. The thing was afraid. Of what? The other? Or were they afraid of each other? Was the thing behind the poet's eyes just as afraid? Lashing out? And then Abe realised, knew it, felt it. And it gave him strength, like the strength he used to have before...*No, it's afraid of me, it's a weak thing, here, in my world. That's why you talk so much, to disguise it. I know, and now, you're going to go.*

539

"And so are you!" he shouted to the pathetic thing on top of him. "Bloody well hit me would you! Hit me! Swine!"

Easily now he removed the murderous hands from his throat, and thrust them back into the poet's own face with such force that he fell backward and off the policeman.

"Now you're for it," roared Abe, although the effort caused a singing in his ears.

The poet still had some wits about him however, for he rolled as he fell, regained his feet quickly, distanced himself by a few paces and tried to decide what to do. Whatever had been the conversation going on in his head, the man won out over the other it would seem, as he scooped up his hat and made to run as the copper began to rise.

"Come here you!" was the shout. But the poet had no intention of obeying. He was going, threading himself as adroitly as possible between the obstacles that barred his path to freedom.

There was no way, however, that Abe Lively was going to let him slip away – or so he thought: as soon as he stood and started to run the singing in his head got worse, symptom of a knock to the back of the head when he went down, or the effort to banish his squatter. Because it was banished, all but. Abe realised he had the green stone in his hand, had been clutching it. He felt free, and strong again, although temporarily giddy. But that meant the poet, murderer and madman, was getting away.

"Stop," he shouted in frustration, and then to the stone, "go and get him if you want him." And he thought he could make out the shadow of a retreating figure, could see it in his mind's eye, and he threw the stone with all the force at his disposal.

Against the odds, he thought that he had hit him. Had he though? He had thought that he heard a satisfying thud, but whether this meant a strike against bone, or merely against a random piece of wooden debris, he could not of course be sure. What he was sure of however was the next sound, because it was most definitely a splash. Something big had gone into deep water, something as heavy as a man, he would have said. Then he remembered. The build-up of rubbish just here had made the place less than familiar, but if he was where he thought he was, and he was sure now that he was, then he knew that not far ahead there was a very deep hole, a disused excavation, a marl hole long since abandoned to nature, or at least to the elements. It had been flooded for years, and when Abe Lively had been a constable it had been his unpleasant duty to pull out the body of a ten-year-old boy whom it had enticed in and killed. Yes, he knew where he was. Presumably his attacker hadn't; and if he was heading 'home' toward The Navigation he would probably have stepped right in, dark as it had become. He hadn't heard any sign of struggle after the first splash though. Had it been a ruse? A boulder? Or had he really hit him? There was something about that stone…

When he was rested he went to see what he could see. The fence that had been erected around the deep water had rotted and been pulled down by adventurous children and there would have been little warning of danger for someone unfamiliar with the terrain and travelling at night, especially someone more concerned with what might be behind him than in front. Then, upturned, in the mud at the crater's very edge he found that topper. Gone in had he? If he was alive and in there, Abe would be hearing something. If dead and floating he would be found in daylight. If dead and sunk – for they said that the hole sucked victims down and that the bottom was littered with skeletons – then perhaps that was an end to it; he was not going to kill anybody else.

But what if he had not really gone in? What then? Well then, by tomorrow every copper in the county would have his description, Abe would see to that. But that was for tomorrow, *right now I need to get out of these clothes and into bed.*

#

His blood was flowing thick and tacky now, his breathing shallow…He hadn't paid attention to the time when Cutler had gone out, but the clock behind the bar now said five and twenty past. He stared at it, and, straining his ears, heard it clunking away. A sinister beat, Josh always thought, each swing of the pendulum counting down the days of life: Tick-Tock, Tick-Tock. A beat that could never be slowed or stopped even if you smashed the clock. That clock served as a reminder to get your drinks in before last orders was called for the last time…

The heat left him drowsing. Come on. Another ten seconds…Tick-Tock. Nearly half past. Come on!

Come on now. Tick-Tock…another ten and he would go and find him…Ten. As the copper stood up the whippet sauntered back in, with his overcoat over his shoulder. But – his coat was still on the hook?

"Told you I'm a man of my word," said Jack cheerfully.

With that the whippet covered the space between them like he was after a rabbit. Smoothly, he discarded the coat from his right shoulder, revealing a cane, and drew a slim shiny blade of Birmingham steel all in one expertly flowing motion. A sting.

"I won't be accompanying you to the station after all."

#

The inspector was a little battered, a lump on the head, a sore and probably broken nose, small glass cuts on his hands and a large scratch on his right calf where something had torn at his trousers; and his back felt bruised. But he felt good! These were just bodily hurts, he had received worse. Such punishment really did make you stronger.

On the downside, he had a long walk back. To Blackheath. He wanted to go to Blackheath. But as luck would have it, he heard a cart of some kind approaching. Perhaps he could persuade the driver to give him a ride. He turned to hail them.

"Inspector? Is that you? Do you need a lift?"

"My God, Clark, you're a welcome sight."

541

"Aren't I always?" asked P.C. Clark, always ready to push his luck.

More perceptively, another voice asked, "are you all right inspector Lively. What's happened?"

Because of the lamps he could not make out her features, but he knew the voice well enough. It was the witch.

"What are you doing here?" he asked. Given what had just occurred, this seemed like a tremendous coincidence.

"Looking for you as it happens. And it's nice to see you too."

"Sorry. I've just been involved in a slight altercation, and I'm a little bit shook up."

The little cart was level with him now, and she had a good look.

"Looks like you've been in the wars," she said, "but Abraham, tell me, are you all right now?"

He knew what she meant.

"Actually, I'm very well, thank you."

"That's good to know. Kindly help him in constable."

"I'm afraid I've lost your stone," he said.

"That's all right, it wasn't really mine. I'm sure it will turn up. Always does."

"Where to inspector?" interposed Clark.

"To Blackheath. The Royal Oak, if you please." *I want to see Miriam.*

#

Josh opened his eyes and made out the cracked smoke-stained ceiling of the bar of the Four Ways. Lying on his back, he must have passed out. Disembodied heads converged in his field of vision. But he recognised none. They blurred and merged as red blotches on a greyish background. Like on a pretty bird's egg, a robin's…He heard sounds, but they were fading, going away, though the blotches remained. Then a woman's voice – definitely a woman's voice – cutting through.

"Stand back. Give him some air for God's sake."

It was Lily Maddock, the publican's niece. She had seen blood before and this looked bad. The man was bleeding like a slaughtered pig. That's why she had already sent for the doctor – but he didn't live close-by.

Josh felt a welcome rush of cool air from the open door to the street. And he remembered: the rushing in, the draw – he saw himself standing paralysed, fascinated by the unreal timing and only able to think, uselessly, that Cutler was left-handed – then the whippet was turning and Josh was falling.

"The bastard stabbed me!"

Lily's uncle appeared with some fusty pillows. One went under the policeman's head and another she held against the hole in his uniform where blood was gushing like flood water pumped from a mine. A constable though! This meant serious trouble for the whole

542

family. She cursed Cutler, prayed for the doctor and prayed again. The ruddy face of the copper of five minutes ago was now as white as the face of the clock. The copper was beginning to panic now.

Josh just knew he had to get up. But the woman said, "Hold him still." And he felt hands on his shoulders heavy and cold as anvils. And the cold spread through him – somebody shut that door. The clock beat out its steady rhythm unperturbed, never slowing, never stopping, while his heart was banging on faster and faster, weaker and weaker, repeating an urgent message…

And the message went unanswered. Because Josh was alone in a cold room where the gaslight was failing and silence and the night were stealing in.

Chapter 31

Unfamiliar Territory

He had dozed off. He had not wanted to, sitting at his old desk in Blackheath, Abe had dozed off. And the dream-world had been waiting, welcoming him back with apparent friendliness at first. But familiar images and sounds mutated again into confusing offspring, disturbed and disturbing, as now: right now he was walking along an unfamiliar waterway. It was a canal; a cut. The light was going and he had to strain to see. A dead pig floated by, yet not dead because although the head was submerged the little wriggle of tail was spinning like a top; it was pursued by a dog, like the ones, the ones...where? He couldn't remember, but the dog did not care; seemingly intent on catching the pig it winked at Abe as it swam past. "Is it here?" he asked, but the dog had disappeared into blackness with the dead swine. Abe could only see light when he looked the opposite way, up the canal toward a tunnel which was in the process of disgorging a narrow boat. He was shouting to the bargees now.

"Is it here? Did he come here?"

He was looking for somebody. Yes, Josh. Looking for Josh, but he couldn't remember what he looked like, or why he was looking in this place. But the boat people could not hear. The boat had turned and was heading back, and they could not hear, or were ignoring him, running away. He started to jog to catch them up, but the boat got no closer and now it began to drift sidelong away on a wide lake. They couldn't see him now...

Abe began to run hard now. He ran and ran. He ran past the blue brick wall with the white painted invitation: 'Spend Eternity Here', it said. *Who was offering?* "That's stupid," he managed to think between breaths, "who the hell would want to?"

He pushed on through a black hole, a tunnel, and under a bridge, very high above, seeming to span the clouds. Was that someone standing there? Or just a shadow? If he could fly, he could get up there, but he couldn't, it didn't work: that told him that he was not dreaming, or that he was. Which was it? He turned, running back now...

There was somebody coming. Along the towpath. Ask him. Look at him; it's somebody you ought to know. Jack, little Jack. It was Cutler, but not Cutler. He looked

544

a hundred years old and shrunken to dwarf-like proportions. He came straight up to Lively and stopped, sniffing at him like a nervous mutt.

"You shouldn't be here. You don't belong. Leave me alone. There's nothing for you here. Go away."

"Where's my brother? Have you seen him?"

"He's all right. He's up there," said Cutler pointing up an embankment. "He's on the other line. It's the old one." With that he took off like a hare, on all fours, up and up he went at an incredible rate. Abe blundered after him on leaden feet. His legs had never felt so heavy. In fact his whole body was stiff, cramping up. Like an old man.

The old man persevered, climbing on, up into the Shropshire Hills now, up and up till he was at the top of Brown Clee, respite earned. And here was that thing that had been Jack Cutler, crawling over a rock like a black beetle, a black beetle with rabbit ears. It was not right, it should not exist. Abe crushed it under his boot, pretending not to hear the pathetic high-pitched whine of pain and terror. Wiping his sole on the green sward he looked around. *I can see for miles. But this is not home, there's no green to be seen.* No green, no vitality. Instead stretched a man-made landscape of brick and concrete and steel and debris. All was shades of grey, no colour allowed, no life allowed. But something else was amiss: *I'm sure it's not any kind of holiday, but where's the smoke? Where's the banging and clanging?* No ribbons of yellow, brown, black wormed skyward; of the myriads of stacks not one exhaled, all held their breath, smoke-stopped, waiting, or dead. Gone was the incessant percussion of human progress; of the myriads of forges, no sound drifted on the air, the beat was stretched to infinity, silent. There was no sound, was no smoke. No people.

Then, ants, they began to emerge. From their factories and furnaces and mines, their dark hovels, scurrying aimlessly, lost. Next, as under some hellish compulsion, or at the whim of a minor god of retribution or revenge, they moved as one, a rodent horde now, spilling into the great water filled abyss which had been a canal, and sinking and disappearing till there were none left. There was only Abe. No. A voice, "Come on!"

He looked around. It was Josh, or what Josh had been at ten. He disappeared into some bushes.

"Wait!" shouted Abe, as he ran to catch up. But every time he gained on the boy he would step into cover and reappear a distance off. So Abe stopped and waited and said, "What are you doing?"

The boy came then. "I'm looking for nests," he said, before starting off again.

"Stop. Josh." No reappearance, no reply. "Josh just you be careful."

He was there then. "Why?" he asked. "Don't worry, I won't get lost. Five minutes."

Abe knew it was a mistake to take his eye off him, but there was another movement which caught his eye, another life up here. He turned. A robin. It had been a robin. Still was a robin, and it too winked. Abe recognised it of course.

"Oh it's you is it? What do you want?"

"Do you know me?" enquired the bird courteously.

"You know I do."

"In that case, what's my name?"

"It's…"

"What was it?"

"It's Seth isn't it? No, Jack."

"Nope! Wrong," said the bird that was not a bird, "you're wrong Abraham."

"See, you know me. I know you."

"Perhaps you thought you did once."

"So it is you! Whoever you are. Who are you? What's your name?"

"You won't see me again."

"Your name. You must tell me your name!"

"If I must, why then it's Sbarionat."

"What?"

"Goodbye. We could have been friends. But you shouldn't have come this far; not your place. Go back. Goodbye." And with a flutter the redbreast was gone.

Abe turned. So was Josh. He had expected it. It was green up here. He missed it, missed the green days of his youth. He didn't want to go back down, wanted to stay here, with Josh. "Josh! Josh! Josh!"

"I'm here, I'm here, it's me. Wake up Abe, you're dreaming, wake up!"

And he did. He opened his eyes and Josh really was there, there with him in the station, shaking him to his senses, looking handsome in his uniform.

"You were dreaming," he said, "and shouting out."

"Oh, sorry, it's just…"

"I know, imagine how I felt!" he laughed heartily.

But it wasn't that funny.

Miriam said, "Josh, just you be careful, you'll start bleeding again."

"Don't worry, I won't. I'm all healed up now."

"You're not, look," said his sister.

A suspiciously scarlet stain had appeared on Josh's tunic.

"Oh no, I'm bleeding again," said Josh, matter of factly.

"Do something Rabbit," ordered Miriam, "it's up to you."

Josh was lying on his back and Abe took out an extraordinarily large white handkerchief which he proceeded to struggle with folding into a square. Every time he folded it seemed to get bigger, till it threatened to engulf him. So he gave up folding and pushed it into the hole in his brother's torso, plugging it up.

"That's it," he pronounced, "call for the doctor."

But before either could move the plug was ejected and blood flooded out copiously, more blood than Abe had ever seen. He put his hands over the wound, but it was bigger than the span of his hands. And as he pushed, he fell, fell right in…

The nightmare, that particular nightmare, ended when he hit the floor. He had fallen out of bed; it was light, and his candle had long since expired. He had taken to letting one burn all night as a precaution against bed bugs, he told himself; although he knew, really, that his night time terrors had nothing to do with those little blood-suckers.

He could hear piercing screams and laughter from outside. Children playing. He checked himself. He was sore, but nothing new sore; *perhaps, being lighter than I used to be it makes it easier to take a fall, like a mouse that would not even notice a drop that would kill an elephant, but not as extreme as that obviously; still, the principle is the same surely? On the other hand...*

A polite knocking at his door, but authoritative. Miss Orton was what people would call a 'a nice lady.' Not the most attractive of women, even for one in her late forties, she made up for it with an open heart and a generally sunny disposition. And although she seemed to love children, had never married, a fact that she had not been reluctant to reveal to her new lodger. Instead her life was devoted to her business which she had built from a modest bequest from her father, one time licensee of the Boatman, a public house situated in this very street. Yes, this street. Great Arthur Street. He was still in Smethwick, and he knew that he was awake now.

"Mr Jones, are you all right?"

"Yes, I'm fine Miss Orton."

"Only I heard a bang. Did you fall over?"

"No, it's all right. I fell out of bed, that's all."

"It's not like you to sleep so late. You're not ill are you?"

"No, no, nothing like that. Tiring day yesterday."

"It's no wonder you're tired, you're not eating properly at all. You can't live on bread an' dripping snatched off the table on your way out, because I'll bet you don't bother getting a proper sit-down meal when you're out all day, looking for your brother..."

That particular brother, a prodigal but loved one, was another invention of 'Mr Jones', a necessary one. After all, Miss Orton was a respectable woman running a reputable business: she could not afford to let her rooms to just any old itinerant and Abe needed an excuse to be setting out each day, because he was obviously not working. He could hardly tell her that he was conducting a private vendetta, that he was looking for a man, that when he found him...what? *Kill him of course. An eye for an eye – that's what you call justice.*

"...look, do me a favour, and yourself, and join me in the kitchen for some breakfast and tea. There's ham and eggs and pig's pudding and bread and butter and tea, with sugar. I'm sure you'll feel the benefit. Agreed? Mr Jones? I said are we agreed."

Abe gave up, it was easy. A fried breakfast suddenly seemed immensely appealing. Perhaps his appetite was coming back at last. He knew it would eventually.

"Thank you, Miss Orton. You're right. Yes, I would like to accept your kind offer. Shall we say a quarter of an hour? I need to get dressed."

"That's lovely. And you're sure you haven't hurt yourself, falling?"

"No, like I said, I'm fine. Fresh as a daisy."

"Good, I'm glad. See you in a bit."

"Yes, I'll see you later."

"All right, 15 minutes."

She seemed to be waiting for more, but then he heard her bustle off.

He checked the mirror. A very light stubble, but it would have to do. Just a quick piss and a swill…But as he turned to his rudimentary ablutions, the fuzzy one in the mirror called him back. He stared out at him, a gaunt face now, dark circles around the eyes, tired looking you might say. Perhaps his landlady had something there, he must try to eat better…

No, haunted. That's the word. It was indeed. Abe Lively was haunted by what used to be, and what could have been, by the loss of a brother and by the hunt for that man, that most of all: the hunt for Jack Cutler. Cutler the murderer.

#

Abe had been very careful not to let on exactly what he intended to do and where he was going. Yes, as far as his superiors were concerned, as far as Miriam and John and Frank and Wilf were concerned, he was having some time off to get over the shock of losing Josh, and yes he might check in with the police in Smethwick to see if they had heard anything of their fugitive. But John had made a point of keeping close to his big brother during the days and weeks following the killing, and he saw him both going downhill and keeping himself going by brooding on getting Cutler, by himself, and not necessarily with the object of arresting the man. Eventually it had become obvious that the inspector was becoming a hindrance to his colleagues and so a period of respite had been agreed, to give his wits chance to recover and return.

It came as no surprise to John Lively that the first thing that his newly excused from duty brother did was announce his intention to visit Smethwick police and register his interest in their own hunt, they having been informed that the wanted man might head for their jurisdiction. As it had turned out, the off-chance that a miscreant from outside their area might possibly stray into their territory rather than prudently getting himself many more miles away was not exactly a priority for them. And that suited Abraham Lively, for although Smethwick's manpower would have been useful, they would just arrest him, if they got to him before Abe. And he was not sure he wanted that. In fact he was pretty sure he did not. Neither did he want Cutler affrighted and flown. Thus, the inspector from Old Hill chose not to provide them with information which would enable them to concentrate the search as he himself since had, that is to say, in the vicinity of the High Street, and the Blue Gates Hotel in particular, although it happened to be right on their doorstep. And therefore he had also neglected to tell them that he had found the very same narrow boat that had carried the little rat from Netherton as far as Smethwick Junction, and dropped him off at the loading station for Sandwell Park Colliery, from where, as he discovered, it was but a short walk to the road, Brasshouse Lane as he now knew it, knew it very well, and over the railway line to the very pub that Stephen Vyle had connected Cutler with – the Blue Gates. *Not a coincidence, surely? Thank You.*

The locals were distrustful of him though, a stranger asking questions; a stranger with a hint of the law about him. One tiny man, engrained with grease and toil-worn to the core, did admit, in drink addled state, to knowing Cutler, but only as far as he knew him as a user of the Gates. On the other hand, in his strained squeaky voice he did reveal that the man had been in no more than two nights ago. But where he lived and who were his acquaintances, the midget had had no clue, indeed it was eminently possible that his informant had falsely owned up to knowing Cutler just to get a free drink. Yes, that was quite possible, but Abe took some comfort from the fact that the man had seemed a permanent fixture, in an apparently regular spot, but since having spoken to the copper, to the apparent disapproval of other denizens, judging by the glances and mutterings, he had never reappeared. Warned off probably; hopefully because somebody else knew exactly whom the stranger had been enquiring of. It was a crumb, and his only one.

Since then, progress there had been none. Abe reckoned his best hope would be to catch Cutler at the Blue Gates, follow him, and deal with him. He had exhausted any goodwill that buying other folk drinks might have bought him, and he was at the point where further questions, or even a too regular frequentation of the place was likely to get him into trouble. So, he waited and watched, and he patrolled the area, and gradually widened it, spoking out in different directions, downing innumerable half-pints at diverse locations, ears open, mouth mostly shut, eyes peeled. But always the Blue Gates was at the hub of the wheel. Had he been his proper self, he would have told himself that it was a desperate plan, a forlorn hope, and a waste of precious time. But he was not his proper self, Cutler had seen to that. So, on it went. He had found himself using the canal on his rounds, after all that's how Cutler had got here. The water, the bridges, the embankments, Galton Bridge in particular which spanned the canal majestically one hundred and fifty feet above it, were becoming carved into his brain, so much so that he was dreaming about them, he knew; even the wall with the white-painted proselytising proposition, "Where Will You Spend Eternity?" daubed by some over-enthusiastic, and over-confident, congregant of the chapel that no doubt reposed on the other side. And each time he saw it, Abe Lively became more annoyed at it; at the cheek, the presumption, the downright bloody ignorance of it. A symptom of frustration perhaps…

But he could not stop, would not rest. His days were made up of spells of observation in and outside the Blue Gates, followed by walking and watching, but always he was watching. Twice, he had called in at the police station, to see what they knew, but they knew nothing, and he did not want to remind them too often, or tell them too much.

Thus obsessed, he might forget to even eat: sometimes he bought food from a street vendor, sometimes he did not. At night, after chucking out, he slept; but never well, always dreaming…

And so inspector Abraham Lively had disappeared and was shrinking away. But John Lively knew why, and John Lively had been close enough to his brother to know that he wanted Cutler, and close enough to have worked out where his brother was likely to look.

Thus it came to pass that a smartly but not ostentatiously-dressed young man, a well built and healthy-looking man, had stepped off a train at Rolfe Street station, with no luggage but a well-stocked wallet and a determined expression, and knew exactly where he was heading. Which was down toward the High Street, toward the old turnpike.

Smethwick! Abe had spoken of nothing else, except Cutler of course. This is where he would find him, and he would take him home. Abe had to forget Jack Cutler, he was long gone, like Josh.

John remembered the week when they had all first arrived in Blackheath, a waggon-load of lost kids. That place had been a shock: the noise, the smell, the black. They had become used to it, immune to it, but this place jolted him back. Already he felt he was getting a headache with the great smashing of the drop hammers and the clatter of metal, as smut essayed to fly into his nose and mouth, like the minions of Beelzebub, lives of their own…

As he walked further away from Rolfe Street and turned the corner, he found that the noise was thankfully a little abated. Rounding the bend, he did not see the Blue Gates immediately, despite its large size, for it was nestled amongst even larger, or projecting, structures: corporation buildings, a fire station, an iron works. But he had been informed of where it lay, standing opposite the railway line and the toll house. Abe had told nobody else about this place, this Blue Gates. Not police colleagues, not the rest of the family, only John. John was the only one that understood. With luck, he would be there right now.

But it was not to be. John's luck was not in, Abe was not in. But somebody recognised him. An old acquaintance, you might say, in the form of one Augustus Wellings. Gus Wellings was in, knew the stranger immediately, although he chose not to show himself at first.

#

"Take a seat Jack. Can I offer you a drink?" enquired Cyril Crane.

"No thank-you," replied Beckett, on his guard. Things had gone from bad to worse with his wife, speaking seldom, communicating only the necessary and the mundane.

550

Miriam had had her way: their relationship was now nothing more than the convenient business arrangement upon which she had lately insisted, not that it had ever been anything else if his wife were to be believed. But admitting to it, and giving in to the fact had not been easy for him, and he had fought it, and her, and in the process had irrevocably burned any bridges to her affection, or even to friendship. And the convenient arrangement was rapidly becoming decidedly inconvenient for her, he could tell. And he was at a loss as to what to do. The Oak was his home now, and he did not wish to leave; in any case that would mean finding somewhere else, and that would be an extra expense…

But in his pushing he had made an enemy of her, and therefore of her entire family. Including this man.

Melodramatically, as was his wont, Cyril continued.

"I expect that you are wondering why I asked you here?"

Why indeed. Is it to warn me off, tell me to get out of the Oak? The town? Her life?

"I've got an idea, but you tell me."

"All right. It concerns you and Miriam, and her pub."

"With respect, Mr Crane, what goes on between a man and his wife is private. It's their business, and theirs alone."

"Well, normally I would be inclined to agree with you," began Crane equably, "but this particular case is an exception, because not only is our family extremely close knit, as you will know, but, as it happens, I am talking to you today with the full knowledge and approval of my niece."

"Oh," was all that Jack Beckett could say. *Here it comes then, make yourself scarce or else.* How he hated them all. They were all bloody snobs really, looking down their noses at ordinary people; and what were they, really? Fucking jumped up country yokels, nothing but criminals and bullies. He looked at Crane, sizing him up. He had a reputation as a hard man, but how tough could he be, silly old bugger? Because he was old, he was just an old man. *I could take him, jump on him quick…But then what? I would have to kill him. But then what?* And what about the dog in the corner? Beckett clenched his fists till the nails drew blood. He was beat, whichever way you looked at it. *Spoiled my life, them bloody Livelys.*

He was swallowing his spleen, trying to stop himself screaming at the man, and something must have showed, for something brought a twinkle to Crane's eye and distorted his poker face with the hint of a smile.

"Now Jack, don't go assuming the worst. I've brought you here to make you a proposition."

"What kind of proposition?" asked Beckett, still suspicious.

"A business proposition of course. Look Jack, you and Miriam haven't been getting on…"

Jack went to protest but Cyril waved him down.

"…you haven't been seeing eye to eye, and that's putting it mildly. Look, don't deny it, she's told me. You're not an idiot Jack, you can see the writing on the wall. You've been drifting apart, to coin a phrase. And that situation is not going to somehow reverse itself. You know that don't you? Go on, be honest."

"Well, I have been thinking that. But where's all this leading?"

"Where indeed? I can't see into the future, but I can tell you this, Miriam is planning on leaving, and she's not planning on taking you with her. But you saw that coming didn't you?"

"I suppose I did. I had hoped…"

"Ah, if only hopes were prayers, and if only God made all our prayers come true. But he doesn't. Probably not even listening most of the time. So it's up to us to sort our own affairs out; make the best of things. I can help with that."

In spite of what Cyril had just said about hopes, Beckett began to hope. Not for a miracle, but that there would be something at least to salvage out of the wreck of his life.

"Tell me about this proposition."

"Well," began Cyril, "I don't know whether you know this yet, But Miriam is going to sell the Oak to me…"

#

As the Fates would have it, John had not found his brother that afternoon; had supped a languid pint and took a gentle stroll, to think, and to get the lay of the land. Somehow, impetuous and expectant, he had imagined he would find Abe sitting there, drinking and chewing the fat, surprised but pleased to see him, amenable to persuasion, to come back. But he was stumped. Abe was not there, and nobody admitted to knowing him. But no, of course: if Abe were lying in wait for Cutler, he wouldn't very well be advertising the fact would he? Sitting round in plain sight? Like a gamekeeper sat on his own pole-trap and expecting the crows to introduce themselves before offering themselves to the jaws of death. Of course not. He might visit, probably when the place was busier, and he might be keeping watch in the vicinity. *Right then, I'll come back later and look again, and ask around. Perhaps I ought to give it a couple of days?*

John came to the conclusion that, as Nash was to Blackheath, so was Blackheath to Smethwick. Nowhere had he seen industry concentrated so tightly, to the utter exclusion of all that natural world that God had fashioned – he must have been a naïve god, a thoughtless one, for was it not he who had created Man and all His works? The creature that was intent on destroying them? This land must once have been pleasant and fruitful, and not long ago, but the only fruit of a man's labour here now was money, cold hard cash. It was metal that ruled here: everybody sweated over it, its melting and moulding and cutting, and stamping and spitting out; likewise the men, all had the same stamp to them; and they too had been spat out, for the machines had relented, consented to a change of shift. Discharged, the lucky ones hit the pubs to wash away the day.

The afternoon wore into evening, and John returned to the Gates. It was payday and the place was well crammed; beer transported overhead, hand to trusted hand, from the bar to the back, and the places between, it worked like a well-oiled machine.

So this is the Blue Gates is it?

John paused awhile to just observe. There was something about these men; like the place they were brash and brazen faced; like the iron and the tin and the brass. Hard, sharp-edged, he would say, but not big of stature, not like him anyway. Not big men at all in the main, but there was a vigour there, a certain pace of life. Somehow, he thought, they do not have patience. Not the patience, nor the dignity, of what he thought of now, as his own piece of the black country.

They all seemed in so much of a hurry. The way they drank and counted their money. And most of all in the way they spoke: quick and nasal, like Cutler, little weasel.

He thought of pushing into the free for all at the bar. He was big enough to force his way, but that would earn him no friends, he knew. He might not need new friends, but he would avoid making enemies, well remembering the Percivals. He wondered if they had allies here.

Whatever the case, odd man out as he was, he was uneasy in the crush, too easy for pickpockets, or worse. It did not look like Abe was here anyway, and there was another room of boozers to try.

The Blue Gates Hotel had been an old coaching inn, its heyday the age of horse drawn travel and the turnpike. But progress and the railways had put an end to regular and lucrative stop-overs by one-night travellers on their way to who knows where. They could get to who knows where in half the time and double the comfort on a train nowadays. So now, many an old guest chamber grew fusty and lonely as, moth-ball secured and curtained, under lock and key they pined for a dead era. But on the brighter side, the Gates was still an extremely popular pub, full of life. Especially on pay-day.

And there was more than one room available for drinkers, there were two in fact. John walked into one labelled 'smoke.' Why so, this room in particular, was a mystery to him as it was no more and no less wreathed in the familiar blue-grey tobacco fug as the main bar, which he had just now vacated, although to be fair to the designation, it was, whilst still achieving the same density of reeking vapours, noticeably less compactly populated than the bar. It was smaller than the bar too, but not by much: both were very large examples of their ilk; and it boasted a separate bar of its own. It was easily large enough, and contained enough bodies, to conceal that of his brother unless he checked properly. That meant a drink!

In contrast to the previous, this room appeared to cater for the old and infirm; the retired and the misfits. It seemed to him that like lepers these people had exiled themselves, presumably voluntarily, from the society of the others, those next door, the young, the healthy, the workers: those contributing still to the common good, or to the profit of their masters at any rate.

The denizens here looked ancient and wizened; calloused hands, arthritic. And rough faces grooved by care and corrosion, as if miniscule railways had plied their way, invisible, back and forth, cutting hard over the decades, leaving their mark. Their brand. We Own You, it said.

And out of cloudy memories they told coarse jokes; and hauled along anecdotes of prolific prowess, long lost. Desperate nostalgia of old men. But still there was that edge, a simmering urgency, even here. Aggressive, John called it.

He headed for the bar: get a drink and make a few tactful enquiries. But something pulled him up: he had only ever seen one black man before, and then at a distance. But here were two, just drinking, just like everyone else. Looking right at them he could do little else but nod. They nodded back from their own little patch: he noticed that there was a distinct interval, a space, between them and the rest of the pub, a unique one, not repeated between other groups of drinkers. In fact the others in the room, the white locals, seemed to be doing their best to ignore them, making it obvious that they were not welcome. But nevertheless, there they were, doggedly standing their ground, albeit conveniently close to an exit. John would have liked to talk to them. Talk to a black man! That would be an experience worth having surely? What tales might they have to tell of the Dark Continent, eh? Assuming they spoke English of course…

But, no. He was a stranger here himself, and he deemed it prudent to take his cue from the majority.

#

Abe had indeed made a late start that morning. But what the hell? He wasn't exactly on the clock. He could dictate his own pace. And, as he absorbed the warmth of the kitchen and a cooked breakfast, much needed sustenance, he found that he was not in the usual hurry to move off. The food seemed to fill a space within him entirely unconnected with the digestive system, and he passed a good hour distracted in trivial conversation with Miss Orton, who had also seemed to be in no rush that day. He was not sure what had brought about the change. Perhaps some human contact, some consideration from another human being, or perhaps the food, or both, had come at just the right time, just when the tide of his mood was turning.

When duty called away his landlady, he wandered outside, into the large yard, the communal focal point of the three houses owned by Miss Orton, where tenants hung their washing and, in the case of two of the houses, for only the one occupied by the landlady had internal plumbing, collected their water from the standpipe. There was no washing hanging today, but Abe had to be careful not to throttle himself on the un-propped lengths of line. He hurriedly passed the two privies – with water closets! – which made up the fourth section of the rough enclosure and looked down toward the canal. There was a scrap of land where the children congregated, an assortment of crusty kids with snotty noses and holey knees and dresses with the pattern washed out. Evidently, school was closed today, or else there were parents here who cared nothing about their offspring's education. Because he counted eight of them, boys and girls, all engaged in a single game of football, four a side, littlest relegated to goalies and to fetching the ball when it was booted past them, as it frequently was, for there were no nets of course, and goalposts were nothing more than single house-bricks. Again, he paused. He stood and watched their antics for quite some time, till at least a score of goals had been claimed. Full of life they were, making the most of this time of innocence, relative innocence. No thought for the future, not at this moment at least, and full of life. He could have hated them, begrudged them that life that Josh did not have, that innocence that he himself had lost, since he had become a copper, since he had moved to Blackheath, since he had had to grow up. But he did not begrudge them a thing, in fact he realised that he should be grateful to them: for the first time in weeks he found himself smiling. The ball came his way. He picked it up and held it aloft like a trophy. Could they have their ball back, please mister? Of course they could.

Abe threw it to them and carried on walking. When he got to the canal he sat on the bank and spent an hour gazing feckless into the water, watching the boats coming and going, and coming to terms. Coming to terms with the fact that he was on a fool's errand. Really, what was the chances of finding Cutler now, at this stage? If he had been here at all, and he was no longer at all sure of that, he must be long gone now. Really, why had he come? Expecting to find Cutler? Or needing an excuse to disappear? To avoid the pain of carrying on as normal, as if nothing had happened, behaving as if there had been nothing he could have done? Because there was something he should have done, wasn't there? And that was to pay more attention to the activities of Mr Cutler and lock him up for them. But no, he was too wrapped up in other things, not least getting that inspector job and listening to…that thing. It was gone now though, or was it just that he was sane again? He hoped he was sane…

But what sane man would do this? Run away and pretend he's looking for something he knows is not there, and neglect his family, his sister? Miriam was probably worried sick. And, really, what would he do if he found Cutler? Would he kill him? A policeman? Kill him in cold blood? Without getting caught and letting his family down again?

No, he spat out the tobacco he had been chewing – a recent bad habit to rid himself of – and he decided that enough was enough. Leave it to the law, let the police do their job. He must get himself back home, and to himself. He could get a train or he could cadge a ride on a boat, in the morning, after he had settled up with Miss Orton. Despite his overcoat and muffler, he was cold, and he got up stiff, not like the old Abe Lively at all, not like the young Abe Lively. He decided to treat himself to a pie and a pint, and give the Gates a miss. Perhaps he would give it one more parting look later. That decision was the reason that he missed his brother that afternoon.

#

John was sitting alone in the smoke when a figure approached. Nothing remarkable about it, a man of average height and build, but yet there was something familiar about him, he was trying not to spill his beer and he was wearing a red scarf. John knew him. The man was smiling, and, taking the liberty of depositing his precious pint at John's table, said:

"I thought it was you, mind if I siddown?" Which he did anyway, "remember me?"

"Yes. Yes I do. You're Gus. That's right isn't it?"

"That's dead right yes," he confirmed, offering his hand, "so tell me, what brings you to these parts?"

"Oh, I heard that the beer was really good, so I thought I would try it."

"And?"

"And what?"

"And is it?"

"I've had better to be honest."

Gus laughed. Then: "Don't get me wrong, it's nice to see you again. But I know you'm not 'ere for the beer, and I'd like to forestall any trouble."

"There's no trouble. I'm just looking for my brother, you know, the sergeant."

"Shush, keep your voice down. Don't mention the P word in 'ere, not in a good way anyway."

"Why? It doesn't exactly look like a den of iniquity," replied John, looking round at the assortment of old timers, the enfeebled and the lame that occupied the space.

"It's not. Most are just ordinary people out for a drink, but there is an element of a different sort that uses the place, especially in the other room, and it's not easy to tell 'em from the rest. So, it's best for strangers to tread carefully."

"Got you. Thanks."

"So, looking for your brother are ya? Why?"

"I want to take him home. He's...I don't think he's been well. Did you hear what happened to our other brother?"

"No. Tell me."

"A man called Cutler..."

"Keep your voice down, remember."

"Sorry. Well, there's this man called Jack Cutler. My young brother, the young constable, you know the one, was just having a conversation with him, in a pub, when, without warning and for no reason, he came at him with this bloody long sword and ran him through, right into the vitals. He died on the floor right there."

"I'm sorry for that. I dain't know that. And your brother's after this Cutler is 'e? And he thinks 'e's 'ere?"

"That's it."

"That explains it. Your brother was 'ere."

"What? When?"

"Been in a few times, asking questions. Too many. People think he's the law, which it so happens 'e is, and that's potentially dangerous, for 'im. And possibly for anybody who 'elps 'im."

"You've spoken to him then?"

"No, I've seen 'im, but I didn't let 'im see me. I'm afraid that wasn't difficult, 'e does seem a bit distracted."

"Is he all right though? What did he look like?"

"Truthfully, 'e looked like a dying duck in a thunderstorm."

"What's that mean?"

"It means what it sounds like – tired if you like, worn-out, exhausted. And thinner than 'e was. As you say, 'e may not be well."

"But, why didn't you talk to him? What did he want?"

"It was obvious what 'e wanted, 'e wanted to find somebody, as a policeman so I 'ad to presume. I couldn't be part of that, not if I wanted to carry on drinking 'ere. Like I said, most people 'ere are just ordinary, law abiding; but still, nobody likes an informer, makes everybody nervous…of course, this was before I knew what you just told me. On top of that," he said, lowering his voice still further, "the Percivals, the ones your brother put away, they've got brothers, and some people who sometimes drink 'ere know them brothers, and think the Percivals were some kind of heroes. I know different, and I have no sympathy with 'em for what they did, dragging me own brothers into their mess as they did. Anyway, your brother was fair with me the day you and me met, and after that, 'e was fair to me brothers, when 'e could have lumped 'em in with the Percivals and the rest. So, rather than admit to knowin' 'im, and therefore inadvertently identifyin' 'im, I chose to keep an eye on things, made sure they didn't decide to set about 'im. This old thing still commands some respect," he concluded, fingering the red scarf.

"So I suppose I have to thank you."

"If you like."

"Thank you then," said John, giving his hand. "Now, what can you tell me about his whereabouts."

"Your brother?"

"Yes – why, do you know where Cutler is?"

"No, no, I don't."

"But you've heard of him? You know him."

"Heard of him, perhaps, but that's more to do with the fact that the rozzers have been bandying the name around. But I certainly wouldn't know him to look at. And if I did I don't think I'd tell you. I'd prefer it if you took your brother and left."

"Well, that's my intention. Any idea where I can find him?"

"No. If 'e comes in 'ere, people know that I've said, basically, that 'e's 'armless and that I would prefer it if 'e's left alone, and that nobody talk to 'im. But that's it. I've 'eard 'e's been in a couple o' times. All I can suggest is that you 'ang round till 'e turns up. He may not o' course. Might 'ave decided to goo um."

"Well, he wasn't there this morning."

Wellings merely shrugged. Then there was another voice.

"Gus! What you doing in 'ere?"

John recognised the Wellings with the withered arm.

"Dougie, sit down, I'm talking to my mate here. You remember him don't ya?"

Douglas Wellings cast a guarded look around before joining them.

"Course I do. Blackheath warn't it? Where's that feisty woman o' yours?"

"She's back home, making chains."

"No, y'not joking am ya?" decided Doug Wellings.

"No, I'm not Dougie. It's John. Remember?" John was not sure that Gus had remembered the name, so he introduced himself.

"You pair am tekkin' a bit of a chance coming round 'ere ain't ya? What if you was recognised?"

"I'm just here to take him home. Have you seen him?"

"Yeah, but you'm too late. 'E just left."

#

What had happened was that those vexatious Fates had not yet finished playing with Abraham Lively. His mind had settled by now. He was leaving: not giving up, more like facing up to facts; he had begun to relax, strolled all the way down to where they were working on a new park. It was going to have a proper boating pool and a bandstand and everything, so an enthusiastic local girl and the signs told him. The people of Smethwick were not so hard done by after all, he decided.

After treating himself to a proper afternoon meal in a very reasonable chop house he returned to his lodgings to get what little there was of his things together and to settle up. Then, the evening stretched ahead. A dark December evening. With nothing in particular to do, something told him to make good on his earlier thought, to make one more stop at the Blue Gates. And, bugger it, he would stop and have a drink, a parting defiance.

But he never did have that drink. At first, he thought that he must be dreaming again. He arrived at the Gates just as the knocking-off rush was dissipating, as drinkers headed home for their teas, appetites sharpened by alcohol, leaving only late-comers and the more dissolute hardy perennials. Still a good crowd, but not as dense as it had been. He called in his pint and unbuttoned his coat. But as he was tugging at his scarf and his pint was being pulled, he felt someone watching him. Someone in the room was watching him. He looked around, expecting to meet a definite gaze, someone looking right at him. But there was nothing, then a sinuous and suspicious movement as a body moved off through the crowd. From the moving and swaying of bodies he could tell where the bashful watcher was heading, and he followed, as the men on elephants followed the tiger through the grass in India. The crowd was the grass, but harder to move through than grass, and his quarry was gone when he got to where he thought it was; and then he picked up the trail again. He was getting hot and agitated now and was buffeting people around in his haste. That was not appreciated, and as of in telepathic agreement they would all close ranks whenever he approached, slowing him down, frustrating him all the more. Whoever it had been looking at him was gone now, he had lost him. Then he heard someone say, as if in surprise, as if trying to keep it in – 'Lively!'

He looked. There was someone, skulking still, but still showing an interest in him, not trying to leave. Abe's heart was pounding, sweat ran down his face and neck, mopped up by his collar. He had not imagined it had he? It was not just the name, it was the voice – it was Cutler's. But Abe knew that he had 'not been right' since Josh. Could his mind be playing tricks? He just needed to see, just a little more, just a glimpse. And the man leading him that merry dance obliged him. Just for an instant. But there it was. It was Jack Cutler. Hiding behind a beard now, but he knew him. Quickly, what to do? Abe had not planned to have it out with Cutler in public, but as it had fallen he had Cutler trapped now. The door was behind the policeman and he was closing in. He was not about to let Cutler escape. He would grab him here and take him outside. But what if the pub turned on him? *Let them, it's do or die now.*

Abe moved closer, inexorably closer to the point where Cutler had disappeared behind a knot of baggy overalls. The knot parted – and nobody was there! Was he going mad? All over again? A ruckus by the door. And there was the beast of his quest, there he was, no question at all, looking straight back at him, like he couldn't help it, taunting him. Before slipping swiftly out.

By the time Abe reached the door and stepped out, Cutler had been swallowed by the night. But that did not mean that he could not be seen! The street lighting was good enough for Abe to pick him out, a slight figure moving toward the footbridge. No other would have been able to swear it was Cutler at that distance, but Abe knew, and he followed, and Cutler, who had not even bothered to turn, who in his arrogance thought that the dark had hidden him from his pursuer's eyes, carried on, oblivious.

\#

But Jack Cutler had not really been oblivious to Lively's trailing presence, and contrary to the copper's impression, had not been taunting him. In fact he had been luring him. He had him exactly where he wanted him.

Jack had thought that a change of appearance and a change of name might be sufficient to allow him to lie low till wanted Jack Cutler had been forgotten about. Yes, the police had been making enquiries of him, and that was probably down to that Vyle not keeping his trap shut, but they were only going through the motions, he could tell. Still, that should have been a lesson to him: if the coppers could home in on him because of someone like that, there was always the chance that there were more of them, people round here with runny mouths who knew who he was. He had made up his mind that Vyle would become a lesson for him, and much as it pained him to totally up-sticks and start again far away, it was better than ending up at the end of a rope. And when Lively started poking about, well that was the clincher.

Talk about rotten timing! Jack was all set to depart, very much for far-off pastures new. All he was waiting on was the repayment of a loan, an investment he had made to someone who should have known better than to 'reinvest' it where it could not readily be liquidated. Well, that was someone else who had learned a valuable lesson, and Jack had charged him interest on it. And then Lively turns up again, tonight!

Jack had nothing against Abraham Lively or his clan. Not anymore. That slate had been wiped more than clean. But Lively was persistent, and he was a copper, and he was out for blood. Had to be. The faithful Duberley had spotted him coming tonight. Tonight of all nights, when they were ready to go. So, forewarned, why not do just that, go? Just avoid him, once more was all it would take, then disappear? That was Jack's inclination. But Anthony counselled differently. He thought that Lively would not stop, that they could never be sure of their backs, that he would keep looking no matter how far they ran and no matter how long it took. There was something in that, but violence had always been his preferred way of solving things, his only way, and he did not stop to weigh up the risks, of solving one problem and replacing it with a bigger one. Subtlety and subterfuge were in deficit with him.

On the other hand, Jack had always been a student of alternative strategies, feint and deception: he had not grown up with the physical attributes to attack every foe full on and frontal. And he was toying with another idea, to throw Lively of the scent, send him forever searching in the wrong place. He had assumed an Irish accent and name to avoid the local cops, and he was of a mind to persuade Lively that he was on his way to Ireland, to make a fresh start. It would be risky though. But he had Duberley and Lively was all alone. So, he would give it a try, best of both worlds. Because he didn't want to hurt the man. He had only been doing his job, and he had been through enough because of Jack Cutler. Had not wanted to hurt that one either. He couldn't explain it, but he wanted to explain it, to Lively. He wouldn't listen, he knew, but he just wanted to say something.

Of course, if it all went to shit, they still had Duberley's plan, and he had Duberley's gun in his pocket.

#

John rushed outside, not pausing long enough even to put on his hat. It was dark, but the street lighting here was not bad, and unless Abe had been in a hurry there was a good chance he could pick out his distinctive figure. Or not. There were a handful of pedestrians ambulating up and down, all men between pubs or between home and pub, a couple of cabs clip clopping along, but no big brother. Looking up and down the High Street and there was no sign of his brother, no clue. Bad timing? Or was Abe trying to avoid him? Where else? He could have crossed the road, and then gone either right or left; but he might have carried on across, toward the canals, over the railway line. Cutler had apparently escaped by boat, and Smethwick had been his destination, according to Abe. Was he living on a boat? If so what were the chances it was moored around here, right now? He couldn't shout, for fear that Abe might disappear – if he was trying to hide from him; worse, he could give him away: somehow John doubted that he was here as Inspector Abraham Lively; not as a copper, not as an ex-copper, not from Blackheath, not on the track of one of their own, these people, and probably not even as a man called Lively at all. So, what? A group of half a dozen men approached from the footbridge and stepped off the kerb opposite, heading for the Gates. From their dress he imagined that they were bargees, on a night out. Dare he enquire of them, of a little man with dark round eyes, by the name of Jack? Of a big man, a stranger with a way of talking like, like what? His own? With the same dark looks? No, too many imponderables. So he watched as they passed, flowed around him as if he were an obstruction in the water. Had he, in fact, posed the question, he might well have been rewarded, for the men had not two minutes before passed first the aforesaid little man and then the big man on the footbridge. They may have not only remembered that, but may have had the time and the inclination to confirm as much to him. That was water under the bridge now however...

But John's luck had not entirely deserted him, and the Fates decided to give him a second bite of the cherry. The cherry was represented by a hat and a pair of trousers. They were a distinctive combination: plaid trousers and an outmoded felt hat, banded with two ribbons, or strings, hanging down at the back, and beaded. He recognised them, but not from around here; and the general configuration of their wearer – large – accorded with his memory. The man was wearing a topcoat which John did not recall, but there again, the weather had not been particularly cold up until now, and he was recalling a sighting of some weeks ago. But he was sure now. He had seen that character in Blackheath, somewhere, sometime, but definitely in that town and no other. And now here? Not a coincidence. Possibly some confederate of Cutler, moved here with him, watching his back...?

Duberley had indeed been watching Cutler's back, as arranged; but more particularly, and more literally, he had been watching Abraham Lively's back. Lively had only just disappeared over the footbridge and Duberley was just giving him a few seconds before following, leaning with ill-studied indifference against a lamppost, smoking. But the lamppost took it ill, that familiarity, and it sought to repay the affront, drizzling him in lemon light, highlighting him for the world, and John Lively.

John himself was stood, prominent, at the roadside, outside the pub. He knew that figure, would that figure know him? Did it see him? He took a step back and stooped, as if to attend to an unruly shoe lace, just in time to see the man throw down his fag and step briskly toward the footbridge. It was virtually a certainty now that Abe had gone that way, and that this man was following, and not for any innocuous reason. On inspection, John found that the burning cigarette was less than half-smoked, which only strengthened his conviction. He joined the procession.

#

Jack Cutler was leading them on a merry dance; a not so merry dance; and he had not reckoned with the fourth participant. He had made sure Lively was following, knew that Duberley would not be far behind, and headed for the new main line, the cut.

Lively was conscious that Cutler might be aware of him, but if he was, he was not trying to get away. So that left the possibility of some kind of ploy, some kind of trap. But, he could not worry about that. He had his revolver in his pocket, and that would be his insurance. He was counting on the fact that Cutler was not armed, not with a firearm at any rate, and according to John, who had got to know the man quite well after all, he shunned the use of guns, preferring a knife, or blade, as Josh had found out. In his single-mindedness, and albeit a copper, who was supposed to know the ropes, he neglected to consider the possibility that he himself might be followed, and did not bother to check.

And Anthony Duberley had not been as inattentive as he had let on: he knew that there was somebody on his own tail, clocked him in the street, and he had a pretty good idea who it was. But whoever it may be, it was an obstacle to be dealt with, and that might prove easier than it might have, considering where they were heading: off the road, onto dark towing paths.

Abe had followed Cutler to the water. By the time he reached the towpath his quarry was moving purposefully in the direction of Oldbury. Well over one hundred and fifty yards away, he could be picked out because he was now carrying a lamp, perhaps stashed for regular use, perhaps nicked from one of the narrow boats that were moored here. And it was lights from these clumps of boats that enabled Abe to move surely through this night. That, and the fact that he did know these paths, ought to by now, and knew that the paths themselves, although not necessarily the margins beyond, were kept clear of any objects which could possibly impede or concern a horse, which meant just about anything. On the subject of horses, he could make out a couple, tethered near a boat, feed tins in place, looking deformed in shadow. He guessed that the rest were installed somewhere up the tracks which led to a patch of land between the old and new canal arms, which probably meant that there were some men left behind to keep an eye on things, whilst the rest went to the pub, like the ones he had seen five minutes ago.

He had half expected Cutler to board one of the boats, give him a chance to quietly catch up, but no, on he went. Abe was much closer now, but the last boat had now been passed, and the canal stretched long and dark toward Galton Bridge. If Cutler were going to ambush him, this would be the place to do it. Abe was not prepared to go on benighted whilst Cutler's lamp was apparently still swinging jauntily along. Apparently. Who was to say that was Jack Cutler carrying it anymore? Perhaps an ally was using it as a decoy? Or perhaps Cutler had put out his lamp and Abe was merely following some obscure stranger? *Who knows?* But he would not walk on blind. He retraced his steps, as far as the nearest boats. As things fell, the first one didn't have what he was looking for, but the second one did, an oil lamp hanging at the stern, lighting the way aboard and presumably to deter nefarious night-time prowlers. It didn't deter Abe: it told him that the boat was not likely to be occupied at present, and it wasn't. He borrowed the lamp and got back on track. Edging along now, he drew his gun from his pocket and held it close, ready to go but not obvious. The light ahead appeared to have stopped. He took his time, getting closer and closer to that light…

It turned out that it was not Jack's light, or at least if it was Jack was no longer with it. It was a lamp that had been set on a hook, apparently randomly, by the authorities presumably. Why here and nowhere else was anybody's guess, but all Abe knew was that Jack Cutler was gone. Escaped him. Got away. In all likelihood at any rate. He was approaching Thomas Telford's Galton Bridge, the highest single-span bridge in the world, he had heard, or had been, and an ideal vantage point. For somebody. If Cutler was up there, the lamp would be a give-away, at least as he got close enough for it to reveal enough detail. Abe decided that it was more likely that Cutler had left the cut here, at the bridge – a shortcut for him? – than that he had plodded on in the dark toward Oldbury. At any rate, he determined that this is where he himself would ascend. *Time to dowse this lamp.*

And it was at this point that the Fates, Lady Luck, an Angel Of Fortune, or a Devil, Destiny, or whatever other force was at play, decided that the game was not interesting enough, and intervened. Whether for good or ill depended of course on your point of view.

He would have been better off to just set the lamp down, or throw into the water; but instead he decided to blow it out. Except that it was not as simple as that. It would not blow out; designed for outdoors, lamp housed inside a glass and tin housing. But neither could he find a wick-winder. Inconveniently, it seemed that the whole lamp must be removed from its casing to get to it. No doubt there was some simple way of releasing it, but Abe was unfamiliar and it was dark. Stooping, he fumbled underneath; probably just wound out. But no. He was rushing now, needed to get on. So he tilted the thing, to see underneath. Bit of a mistake. Oil spilled from somewhere and there was a miniature conflagration, sudden light and heat. Instinctively he dropped it, and glass broke and the fire was free. On a reflex he swept the pieces into the cold water. Panic over, he stood; his eyes needed to get used to the dark. He remembered the Enfield as he took a step. Just one step, but it was enough. He knew immediately what he had done and he knew instinctively that there was no way that he would not next hear, above the background noise, the ominous sound of his revolver plopping into the canal. It was dark, it was cold, the water was deep, the gun was gone, lost.

"Fuck! Somebody's having a fucking laugh!"

He had lain it there, handy, ready to protect him. Well, it would not protect him now, it was gone. Nackered anyway – the both of them.

And Cutler was gone. Probably. There was still a chance he was waiting for him out there, or up there, somewhere. So what should he do? *Take the bull by the horns; take the bastard by the balls.*

Even more carefully now, he advanced. It seemed very lonely on this stretch, darker now, no boats, no horses, not much sign of human activity except high above him on the bridge where he was aware of someone either coming or going.

He looked up. Way above, the bridge was artistically painted in soft gaslight of which the excess ricocheted off the ironwork or else spilled over the parapets, down toward the dark depths, called down by the hungry dimness of the water, down toward this hopeful supplicant; but it never reached him; snatched by the cold hard night.

But now, there. The comings and goings had ceased. Now, a solitary figure, a short figure, was loitering under a gas-lamp. A single figure, not tall, waiting it seemed. It seemed to consult a watch, marched to one end of the bridge, then back to his station near the lamp. Loitering, or waiting. For what? His eyes could not be sure, but Abe knew. There stood Jack Cutler.

#

John had always been nervous around horses. Ever since he had seen what one had done to his brother, and perhaps earlier than that. Too flighty they were, unpredictable. Not like dogs. He was coming up to one now, on the towpath. It looked placid enough, munching on the contents of his tin: at least he couldn't bite. And there was plenty of room on the path, though the light was not of the best, and his owner was with him, he could make him out vaguely, on the far side, back to his boat, doing something with the horse's tack – he could have hoped the man had been this side, between John and the big grey beast.

Or not. For in truth a man is more dangerous to Man, or Beast, than any beast: he has only to set his mind to violence and he is the most ruthless of creatures. And this particular man had set his mind to violence, and he intended to direct that violence against one particular man, his on-coming obstacle, imminently. For it was not his boat, and he was not the horse's owner, for he was Anthony Duberley, hatless, head bowed, awaiting the moment. John Lively's mind-set when it came to horses had misled him, to assume that anybody standing so closely, so intimately, must be well acquainted with the animal, must be its owner or keeper, one of the bargees. But Duberley had no such irrational foible and the grey mare represented to him a perfect opportunity to launch an attack. So John had not considered that the man he had been following might be hiding behind this animal, or indeed that the man had detected him in the first place, and he did not think to give it too wide a berth, not wishing to advertise his weakness. And he was concentrating ahead, having lost sight, amongst the shadows, of the man from Blackheath for a moment. That should have put him on the alert, but when the feeling came, that prickly neck, something on the outskirts of vision feeling, he would have been too slow to heed and react. Were it not for the horse. The horse saved him.

Like the lamppost the tow-horse took Duberley's trespass, his presumption, poorly. A forbearing and forgiving soul, as these always were, as they had to be, she was nevertheless peeved, trying to eat in peace as she had been. At the crucial instant she vocalised her displeasure with an impatient snort and stamp of a hefty hoof. It caused John Lively to start and step quickly away…

Quickly enough to avoid getting his head splattered: Anthony Duberley was caught cold, slungshot in hand, but out of range now for that contraption – it was a weapon of lead and leather, surprise and stealth, and Duberley needed to get closer if he was going to use it. Both of them had been surprised, but Lively now reacted faster, throwing up both arms and shouting; "Haah!"

Whether it made Duberley miss a beat is unimportant. Because what it most certainly did do was cause the mare to react, shying away from the loud man, turning on her tether – and nudging Anthony Duberley in the back with her quarters. He staggered forward, unbalanced and unable to strike. But John was ready. He could strike. Duberley had meant to settle things with one sly blow, Lively did it in two: an honest fist to the face, and a concluding kick to the chin. Ever since the trouble with the sloggers, John had taken self-defence more seriously. He had not had chance to reach his knuckle dusters on this occasion (a lesson in itself) but he had been conditioning his hands for striking, aware of each knuckle. It was the point of one large knuckle that had caught his attacker, very deliberately, just in front of his left ear and it would probably have been enough to knock him out, just as it had that lout in the Oak, without the added assurance of a kick. But the man had deserved it, his weapon could easily have killed.

Now, there were footsteps, shuffling along quickly. A man and a woman and a young boy, obviously from one of the boats. Before they could say anything John said:

"It's all right, I'm a policeman. This man is a wanted felon. I'm going to leave him here and send colleagues to escort him to the station."

So saying he added credence to the lie by handcuffing the still immobile Duberley. The cuffs had belonged to a real policeman, to Josh. In fact though, he himself looked every inch a typical copper, and Duberley every inch a villain. At the policeman's insistence the bargees headed back. And just in time, the unconscious man was stirring now. *Good, you've got some questions to answer, and quick, otherwise we'll see how well you swim wearing hand-cuffs.*

#

Abe had taken his time walking up the embankment to the bridge, too many shadowy places hiding who knows what, ears straining over the background clash and clatter of nocturnal manufacture, eyes straining into the obscurity of the night. But eventually he reached Roebuck Lane, and the bridge. Now it was the light that seemed an enemy: he stood looking down the span, exposed for all to see. But there was nobody to see up here, not a soul about. Unless of course somebody hiding, out of sight but seeing.

Where was Jack Cutler? He knew it had been him. He had been waiting for someone, or something. Had he got fed up with waiting? Had he gone? Or had he been waiting for him? Like Cutler before him he paced the bridge, down as far as the crossroads. There was a lull at this time of night which made everything seem unnaturally still, even there. He walked back, looked down, far down toward the canal. A figure with a lamp would be seen coming the figurative mile off. There was no movement detectable now, on either side. He started to walk back again, toward the Oldbury road, just as a goods train was passing through, brief red cinders sparking into the air. For a moment, its sound blotted everything else out, and then it began to fade. And in the fading, a voice, behind him.

"Be careful what you do. I've got a gun."

Abe turned. It was Cutler. Cutler with a neatly cut beard, and a bowler rather than any kind of cap, but Cutler all right. And he did have a gun, at his waist and pointed straight at Abraham Lively.

"You should have run further."

"Oh, I will sir, so I will." He was affecting an Irish accent now.

"But there's nowhere I won't find you."

"Maybe. Unless you die tonight."

"If I die tonight it will be at the hand of a miserable coward." Abe was talking and all the time getting closer…

"That's close enough. You're pushing your luck. Now, you were saying?"

"I was saying that you're a miserable coward. What you did to my brother, it was pure evil. You're not going to get away with that. I'm going to get you, you little shit."

"Not if a bullet gets you first! Watch your tone!"

"Watch my tone? You're the murderer, you're the one with a gun on an unarmed man. I'm entitled to take what tone I wish."

"And I'm entitled to shoot you, so shut up and listen."

"I suppose you think you're hard, don't you, holding a gun? Do you want to try putting it down, sort things out man to man?"

"No, I don't think I'm hard, that's why I've got it. And you must think I'm soft in the head if you think I'd fall for that claptrap. Let me ask you something. Do you feel tough, do you feel hard, you know, when there's all that six feet odd of you plus a truncheon beating up some little dwarf of a petty thief? Do you? You got your advantage, I got mine," concluded Cutler tilting his revolver as illustration.

"It's not the same."

"Of course it is. We were given brains to fight, not just fists."

"No, it's not the same, because I uphold the law, and you break it."

"Don't make me laugh! Anyway, as I recall, we've had this conversation already. So, what to do with you, eh?"

"I've told you, throw the gun and we can have it out, just the two of us. Thanks to you, I'm not the man I was. I've been told I've not been looking after myself. You might have a fighting chance."

"What, a fighting chance to get murdered? Don't talk rubbish. I'll keep the gun thanks…no you don't," this last to forestall Lively's manoeuvring into lunging distance. Cutler stepped two paces back. "Like I said, don't push it. I didn't bring you here to kill you. If I did you would be lying bleeding right there, or floating in the cut. So, there you are, you owe me."

It was too much.

"I owe you nothing!" spat Lively and advanced with his fist raised. A bullet on the cobbles at his feet stopped him.

"Now, now, I said I did not want to kill you. That doesn't mean I won't."

It would have done Abraham Lively and the quest for justice no good to have got shot that night in that place. He backed down.

"So, why? Why this silly charade? You obviously wanted me to find you. What's the point? If it's forgiveness you want, you don't have a cat in hell's chance. That is to say, none at all – you can check on that when you get there."

"I know what I've done. There will come a day when I will answer for it, there will come a day when I get my just desserts, and yes, there may come a day, when I die, that my soul is consigned to damnation, if you believe in that kind of thing. But that day is long off, and if it comes you will certainly not be my judge."

"It sounds to me that you're not very bothered at all, by what you have done. That's the mark of real evil."

"Oh please! Give it a rest. Good, evil, what does it matter? They're just inventions of the human mind, to try to give meaning to the brutality of the world. What I did to your brother, I regret, but in the vast sordid and bloody history of humanity, I dare say that it barely elicited a raised eyebrow from that bloke up there."

"So, before you kill me, or I kill you, tell me. Tell me why."

"That's what I've been wanting to do. I don't want you dead, not unless my own survival depends on it…"

"Then…"

"No, let me finish. You see, you owe me…"

"Yes, you said…"

"No, I didn't. Let me explain. When I say you owe me, the sum is paltry compared to what I can never repay. But I have been trying. Do you know, the very first day that you turned up at the Gates, word got back to me?"

"I'm not surprised."

"No, but the trouble is, that word got as far as other ears. These people, I wouldn't say they are as formidable as me, all things considered, but they are set in their ways, and opinions, anything but subtle, and with a propensity to violence. That can make them very dangerous if you cross them and don't have the wherewithal to defend yourself."

"What's the point?" Abe had now reconciled himself to the fact that he was the underdog, for the moment, and that he would play along, to live to fight another day. His head ruled. Much as his heart and his gut wanted to rush in and crush the little insect.

"The point is that they don't like informers, and they don't like, so it seems, nosey parker ex coppers poking around on what they consider their territory, like in the Blue Gates."

"You mean me I suppose?"

"I mean you. Tell me, how well do you know our area?"

"Why?"

At this point voices were heard. A couple strolling arm in arm, crossing the road.

"Keep talking like we was two mates, having a chat. I'll put the gun in my pocket but it's still pointing at you, remember. I hope you won't try anything which puts these two in danger."

Abe nodded understanding. Cutler continued.

"Well, did you come across the glassworks, just down the line there?"

"Yes, I think I did. Chance Brothers or something."

"That's right…Good evening," he bade the passing couple.

"Evening," said they, and passed on.

"Yes," continued Cutler, "very proud of their glassworks they are, round here. Did you know that they provided all the glass for the Crystal Palace? Big Ben an' all."

"Really? What's that got to do with anything?"

"Right, well you might not have noticed, but there's usually some big metal tubs knocking about, full of broken waste glass, crushed down a bit. Cullet, they call it."

"So?"

"So, getting back to informers, you've no doubt heard of the practice of tarring and feathering?"

"And?"

"Well, there's some round here like to go one better. They replace feathers with cullet."

"Well that's barbaric, but I'm not surprised. Humanity seems to be a rare commodity hereabouts."

"I wouldn't disagree with you. I don't like culletting, especially for so trivial an offence. Like you say, barbaric. The latest victim was a little midget from the Gates I'm told."

"You swine!"

"Hold on, nothing to do with me. Now, if it wasn't for me stepping in, there may have been another victim by now."

"Me you mean?"

"You I mean."

"So what? You said it yourself, you can never atone for what you did. The rope's waiting for you."

"Well, it'll wait a long time, I hope. And I know I can never atone for what I did, but before I leave these shores forever, I just needed to tell you what happened."

"All right. What happened?"

"I was mad," pronounced Cutler. A simple assertion, but it hit Abe's gut like the kick of a mule. His head began to swim, he held the iron railing for support.

"What's the matter?" asked Jack Cutler suspiciously. He took a pace back, then checked his watch and shook his head, an action which Abe was hardly aware of. Then:

"What? What did you say?"

"I said I was mad. Or thought I was. Something just took me. Only for an instant, but it was enough, too much, for…"

Abe was feeling sick now. Those simple words had reminded him. Of when he walked Blackheath as if on opium, under the influence, of something; something clinging to him like a wet blanket, dragging at him. When he had been mad. That place, it had done bad things, but on the sly, insidious. At least the badness was in the open here. He was still running from it, he knew, that place, that thing; yes indeed, something bad. Was Jack Cutler? Running from the same thing?

"But there must have been more than that. Something sparked it off. Josh was always so…"

"He killed my dog. No, wait. I mean, I thought he had. She disappeared."

"What? So why blame my brother."

"Because somebody told me to; told me it was him."

"Who?" he asked, dreading the reply.

"I don't know whether you ever come across him. Not a local; some self-styled poet."

That did it. Abe really did have to hold onto the rail now, with both hands.

"What's the matter?"

"Nothing."

"I just wanted you to know that, I never intended to kill your brother. Things just got on top of me; I wasn't sleeping; something just got into me. I know it doesn't help you, but I just needed to tell you, because it helps me."

Abe was only half as strong now as when he had walked onto that bridge. Something began tapping at a little door in his brain, wanting to be let in; guilt was getting insistent. He stood silent. Cutler glanced around, checking that the coast was clear Abe thought. And he checked his watch again, and shook his head again.

"Expecting someone else?"

"A colleague."

The copper was on instant alert.

"Nothing to worry about. I told you, we're going overseas, somewhere the law will never find us, even if you did know our new names. We're leaving tonight. I had to see you first, that's all. I hope you enjoyed Smethwick."

"Hardly. You're a rough lot you know, coarse, not like..." he stopped.

"Not like what?"

"Nothing."

"Well, the way I look at it, nice blokes don't get on. And it's all about survival, ain't it? You have to be rough, or at least hard skinned, to survive."

"That's sad."

"Ain't it though?" Cutler checked his watch again, was he getting worried? *Just you let your guard down, and I've got you.*

There really had been no need for Cutler to keep looking at his watch, he didn't need a watch to know that Duberley was way overdue. He had told him to keep close to Lively, give him five minutes, then join them. He needed Duberley to ensure that they could detach themselves from Lively cleanly, tie him up if need be. Jack had no way of knowing that it was his man that had been tied up. *Where the hell are ya?*

Cutler would have to keep the conversation going.

"But you're right, hard lives breed hard folk. Here's a little anecdote for ya. 'Once upon a time, but not long agoo, last month I think it was actually, there was a young unemployed man, sat around doin' nothin' in particular along the canalside, up that way a bit, on the old line, where all the locks am. Anyway, this bloke, let's call 'im Bill, e 'ears a splash an' then a cry, an 'ollering from the cut. Any road, e runs up an' e sees somebody strugglin' in the water. All coughin' an spluttrin', stirrin' up all the muck an' mud. Om drownin', om drownin', shouts the bloke in the water, all panicky. Well why don't ya gerrout? I can't, me leg's stuck on summat. Save me om drownin! What's

570

y'name fust. It's Fred, shouts the bloke in the water. Fred what? Fred 'urley. And where is it you work Fred? At the bloody Evered, now get me out for God's sake, om drownin.' Om sorry, said Bill, it's too late for you Mr 'urley, yawl 'ave to drown. I need your job.

"Next day, bright an' early, our Bill presents 'imself at the gatehouse at the Evered. Does a bloke named Fred 'urley work 'ere? e enquires. Yes, but 'e ain't comin' in today. I know, said Bill, it was me left 'im to drown: can I 'ave 'is job then? You'm too late is the reply, the bloke that pushed 'im in started yestedy.'

"Like I said, it's all about survival. Apologies for slipping into the vernacular, by the way. Gives it more atmosphere I always think…"

But his captive audience was not paying attention to him. His attention was on something else, someone coming. Cutler noticed and glanced over his shoulder. Saw a large figure wearing a distinctive banded felt hat.

"Bloody hell Tony, you took your time. Where have you been?"

When there was no immediate reply Cutler stepped back against the railings, so that he could observe the new arrival out of the corner of his eye, and keep his gun hand, his left, aimed at Abe Lively.

"I don't know where he's been, but I can tell you where he is, and it's not here. How are you Jack?"

He recognised John Lively's voice of course.

"John, stay where you are. I've got a gun on your brother and," he added, cocking the trigger, "it's cocked. The slightest twitch and it will go off. I can hardly miss at this range." He now had both brothers in view, one either side, a tense triangle.

And Cutler was not the only one with a gun. John Lively had one, pointed straight at him.

"I think you had better put your gun down," opened the newcomer.

"Is that that old target pistol you told me about? It is isn't it? Only got one shot hasn't it? I've got six, well, five anyway."

"I only need one shot. Put your gun down."

Abe went to move, Cutler took a step closer to him, away from John.

"No, be careful. Cocked remember," he said to both, and then to John, "percussion cap isn't it? You sure it works?"

"It works all right."

"You don't sound that sure. So, here we are then, a happy little band of warriors. As I was just saying to your brother, John, I don't want to hurt him, or you. I just wanted to talk. I've done that, and I'll leave quietly now, if you allow me. Of course, if you don't, if your gun doesn't work, or if you miss, or only wound me, then I've got enough bullets to finish both of you."

"Assuming your gun works," John pointed out.

"It does, ask your brother. He'll tell you the truth of it. Stop wriggling: you can have your brother back, but you can't have me. And if you insist on having me, you'll end up

571

losing him. It's one or the other, you can't have both. Now, are we agreed? Shall we all exit peacefully?"

As always, Cutler sounded so reasonable, so pragmatic. How could they not agree?

"John, he doesn't intend to kill me, I believe him. But don't push him, not here, not now. There will be other times," cautioned Abe, very conscious now of the close proximity of that cocked revolver.

John however was not finished yet. He was fresh to the fray, and his mind was sharp. He looked hard at his brother, hoping he would get the message.

"Jack, you know me. You know how I must feel about my brother, about Josh. But I'm not about to let that kill my other brother. You're right."

He stopped pointing his weapon and bent his arm so that the muzzle looked up at the sky. That got his attention. The gun pointed at Abe still, but his eyes were on John. All his brother had to do was step out of the line of fire and rush him when – bang! – when he did that. John's was a heavy calibre weapon and Cutler jumped, for a brief instant froze, as was entirely natural. It was only the briefest of intervals and the timing was touch and go: Cutler was turning his attention back towards Abe even as Abe was closing. As he turned his gun hand collided with the approaching body and unsurprisingly, in retrospect, it went off. The unexpected report at close range startled all three of them. For John, that meant that he was slow to run to where his brother was trying to get to grips with Cutler; for Abe it meant that he failed to get an immediate secure grip on the little man; and for Jack Cutler it meant that he dropped the revolver. The revolver with four bullets left, enough to save him if he cared to risk going for it. He did not care to risk, he had another option, which was to flee. He had once or twice been described as whippet like in terms of appearance, he was now set to prove that he could run like one, as he knew he could. He squirmed his way out of the copper's tentative hold and contorted his way past him. Then the whippet was off, jinking like a rabbit, because like a rabbit he was running for his life. Time was short. It was John who picked up the gun, John who took quick aim and fired. A calculated risk, loosing bullets off into the street. He only fired twice. Jack Cutler fell. They had got him! Was he finished though? The world seemed to stop. But then Cutler was up again, running to the street, ducking left, and disappearing.

They waited for the outcry from passers-by, ready to run away, holding their breath. It did not come: no alarm was immediately raised, no hue and cry, not even a mild hubbub. They proceeded to the street. No sign of him. Little did they know that Cutler had arranged this rendezvous, that a cabbie had been paid a lot of money to be ready, come what may, and to keep his trap shut.

"Where did he go?" said John, "I know I got him. He couldn't just disappear. But it's like he's turned into smoke or something, because that's all I'm seeing. Look, there's nowhere he could have gone, not wounded. Because I did hit him. What is he, a magician?"

"No," said Abe sharply, "just a devious bastard. Look there's a blood trail, then it stops, in the road. You got him all right, but there was someone waiting here, to pick him up."

They went back to where he fell, found more blood.

"Look, he was only down a moment, but that's blood there, I mean, considering it had to get through his clothes, it must be bad. I think he's finished," said Abe.

"Or, we could have just hit him in the leg."

"No, he's finished I tell you."

"How do you know?"

"I just do, John."

"You don't want to make sure?"

"As a matter of fact I don't. I've had enough. He'll get what's coming. Now, I suggest we make ourselves scarce, somebody must have seen or heard something. We don't want to be anywhere near here when the police arrive. We'll go back via the towpath. It's damn good to see you, John. Like the hat by the way."

"Likewise, let's go."

They went back over Galton Bridge, intending to make their way back via the canal, where with luck nobody would see them till they were well away from here. Suddenly John stooped, picked something up, examined it under a lamp.

"What have you got there?"

"It was shining, it seemed to wink at me. I thought my luck was in, a florin or something. But it's just a stone. A pretty one though."

"Let me see," said Abe. John handed it over. "Yes it is unusual," said Abe, "but it's just a stone." With which he threw it far away down the canal. There was a faint plop, or had he imagined it? "I suggest you do the same with the gun John."

"Oh, God yes." He threw it in, to keep company with the stone.

"I reckon it's going to snow," remarked Abe.

"Do you? Right then brother, let's go home."

The End

Epilogue

Spring of 1888
Worcestershire

Rupert Hill liked the spring. In fact he liked summer too, and could tolerate autumn, it had its own charms, he would admit. He did not like winter though, and the last one had been particularly bad. Too much snow. He disliked the snow; bad for business.

So he had been glad to see the last of it and was in ebullient mood on that spring morning. Every morning, early and weather permitting, he rode out, as today, on his good looking but safe black gelding, across the Worcestershire countryside. This was a good day, the sun was out and the birds were singing. He liked that, the birdsong, although he could not distinguish that of a blackbird from a blackcap, or very few others for that matter. Butterflies danced by happily, and made him feel the same, albeit he had no idea what kind they were. The various trees and plants were sprouting, he noticed, although what kind of trees they were he would have been hard pressed to tell you, saving the oak and the elm and the silver birch. The plants he knew best were cash crops...

He rode on, following his regular route: he had become a creature of habit. The sky was clear except for a dark cloud hovering ahead, over the woods where he was wont to ride. Change route? No, too much bother, ride on and hope it doesn't rain. At regular intervals there was the sound of a shotgun being fired, a farmer scaring crows, killing rooks, or rabbits? Somebody with nothing better to do? He paid it no heed.

He was thinking of nothing much, except perhaps breakfast, when he rode into a patch of woodland liberally dotted with holly – yes, that was an easy one. He let the horse pick its way, ducking under low branches, till he reached a clearing where he generally trotted. Not today though. There was a body on the track, in a cloak. It looked like a woman. Fallen from her horse perhaps, though there was no sign of a horse.

He dismounted to investigate. Shadow was a good lad, he wouldn't wander. Was she dead? Knocked out? The woman was immobile, right up until the time he touched her, when she rolled away and stood.

"It's all right..." he began.

But stopped. The first thing he had seen, the first thing untoward, and the thing that he could not help but stare at now, was the pistol, aimed right at him.

"What…" he began again.

But stopped. He was being robbed! By a woman.

"Look, I don't carry anything valuable on me, no cash, save a few coppers…" he was explaining.

But stopped. For he had looked away from the gun now, and recognised the face.

"You!"

"Yes, Mr Hill, me. Good morning to you," said Miriam Lively.

He remembered her. The anger. The malice. Not a brave man at the best of times, he was scared now.

"What do you want?" was all that he could think to say.

She ignored that. "John, where are you?" she called.

A man emerged from the bushes. A big one, also with a face he recognised.

"What do you want?" Hill repeated uselessly.

"Why, Mr Hill, we want you of course. And the Devil wants your soul," she said coldly.

"But, we had a deal. I've given you back the farm. We had a deal. I've paid my tithe, I've atoned for what I did."

"For skulduggery and theft maybe. But what about murder?" she asked.

"Murder? I didn't do any murder," he pleaded, "your uncle Cyril said…"

"Cyril's not here," the man pointed out unhelpfully, "we are, and, guess what? We don't believe you. And I'm afraid to say, we don't trust you either."

"Trust me?"

"You're just not a reliable person. You've kept quiet so far, and left my sister and the farm alone. But, knowing you, who knows? You're not a man to rely on, you see."

"I am, I am. You can rely on me, of course you can. I've kept my side of it," he blustered, "you can trust me."

"No. Even if we could, there's still the matter of our father's murder."

"But I told you, I had nothing to do with his death."

"And there you are, you see, we know you did, and that's another lie. Can't trust you, you're not reliable."

The woman was getting impatient, or nervous. She flicked her head and her brother walked away. Now was his chance, while she was alone.

But he soon found that she would not let him get close, not enough to get the gun, so he opened a negotiation.

"Look, I didn't have anything to do with your father's death, but you obviously believe I did. I can't imagine how hard it has been to carry that pain around all these years and, if there's anything I can do…"

"There is."

"Oh, what?"

"Wait."

The brother came back, nodded. She handed the gun to him.

John did not want Hill to move or shout out so he merely said, "Now Mr Hill," and quickly shot him, twice. Quickly, he died.

Over the wood a black cloud of jackdaws billowed in response, before returning, like settling dust.

She was gasping now, supporting herself against a tree. Shadow was seemingly unperturbed, nibbling around.

"It had to be done Sis. We would never have slept soundly in our beds knowing he might set the law on us on a whim."

"I know, and he had to pay for Dad, and Mom."

"Yes, well, there we are then. We need to make this look like a robbery, I'll strip him of any valuables, you check the horse."

Hill had been lying, there was cash on him, and notes, not coppers, and a nice watch. They took those, he would destroy the watch later.

"Right," he said, "we'd better get off before he's missed. Make sure you've not dropped anything."

"I haven't, I was careful. Come on, the horses are waiting. And remember, not a word to Abe," she warned.

"Of course not, never. He's got enough on his mind, without this added burden. Not that I shall be seeing him of course, unless you both come to see us in Blackheath."

"I think we've both seen enough of that place, for the time being at least. The offer's still open you know, for you and Siss. There's a place for you with us. We love you, you know that."

"Of course I do. And I love you. We're family, that's how it works."

#

August 1888

London

Gazing across the broad expanse of Commercial Street toward the magnificent spire of Christ Church, Spitalfields, and watching the dusty comings and goings of countless carts and carriages and cabs and delivery waggons, all busily serving the cause of commerce, all furthering the interests of the rich and successful in society, the gaunt figure in the smart suit, complete with new topper, no longer resented it. Did not, because he had now prised his way into that world, the world of the rich. He had money now, expected more. He was what any man of his ambitions, the earthly ones, would call a success. More importantly his work had been given the attention and the recognition it, and he, deserved, for Francis Thompson had been published.

And his muse had made it possible, his daemon, as he called her. Following that terrible night in the Midlands, he thought that he had lost her. He couldn't remember escaping that peeler, could only remember a desperate struggle, darkness; and he distinctly remembered something hitting him hard, on the back of the head. After that he had wandered, got back to London, God knows how. Strange thoughts had come unbidden, too many, too quick, too loud, drowning each other out. If inspiration there was, it was lost in the melee, and if speaking to him she wanted, something prevented it, a battle of her own: those thoughts had been voices, contending; daemons, fighting.

Later, he realised that his own dark night, losing the Path, it had been a catharsis. Like Jesus Christ his body had suffered, like Him, he had undergone a kind of death. His purgatory had been to return to Whitechapel, to struggle again with obscurity, no roof over his head, sleeping on the embankment, doing the meanest of tasks to earn enough to meet the most basic of needs. He could have been subsumed into the squalor, forever a meaningless morsel of the basest mortality for a careless Providence to chew on. But it was not to be. That he came close to Death had been ordained, part of her plan. But she had not shown herself yet, not until…

It was a woman of the street who had shown him the way, shed light on his darkness, lifted him up. A street woman, a common prostitute. And yet not so, for what was she but his daemon come to him in disguise? A mere vessel, she had been, and a sower of seeds.

And she had returned, his daemon, the voice in his head, constant companion. She gifted him inspiration, she saw to it that that inspiration was rewarded, appreciated by other minds, minds with access to the necessary means of promulgation.

And so he was here. They were here. He looked again at the immense Roman arched portico opposite, gleaming white with spiritual radiance, triumphantly proclaiming its precedence, its sovereignty, over the motley collection of dingy buildings which it dwarfed. It was beautiful, noble. Like his own purged spirit. Across the way lay the Ten Bells, a den of vice and human degradation. He knew it well, had debased himself shining shoes on that very street corner. There it stood, some might call its proximity to the holy precincts of the church an obscene insult to religion. But he called it a living lesson.

Yes, he had come a long way, but there was still a long way to go. Still so much to learn, so many mysteries to penetrate. But she was with him now, guiding him. His other work must continue, and thanks to his recent recuperative sojourn in the hospital, he was ready for it. He still had that old leather apron. That might prove useful.

#

577

Autumn 1972

Tividale

The young man had been to a nurses' party in Wolverhampton. He was returning alone because the so-called mate that he had gone there with had got off with a pretty radiologist and was spending the night. Rather than hang round like the spare proverbial, and despite exhortations that he should sober up a bit, his pride dictated that he should leave immediately, after all it was getting on, and all the pairing up that was going to take place already had, and he had only had three cans of Banks's, hadn't he? So he had left. He had failed to 'score' despite the fact that he was the proud owner of a nearly new Ford Escort 1300 GT in Olympic Blue with the 'go faster' stripes and extra spot-lamps and everything. It had been his 21st. birthday present. But even a flash car had not done enough to magic away his awkwardness around women.

Travelling down the Wolverhampton road heading toward Oldbury now, he decided to put his foot down a bit – it must have been getting on for half one and there was nobody else on the road.

Suddenly, there was somebody else. Somebody standing in the road, the spot-lamps lighting him up with a blue glow. Somebody? It looked twice the size of a man. A way off yet, he began to brake. But then the thing came at the car! It seemed to jump. What? Somebody on stilts?

He was going to hit it, he couldn't stop. He was still going too fast, pushing hard on the brake pedal. Just as he thought he would have to swerve into the middle of the road it was gone, jumped over the car! He checked the mirror, straining to catch sight...

And in doing so allowed the car to hit the kerb, pitch up, and leave the road. Before dipping back down and hitting a lamp post full on. It did considerable damage to his precious car, but he would never know that.

The ambulance crew didn't need to examine him very closely to see that he was dead.

"I hate this part of the job, Frank. You know, when there's nothing you can do for 'em. He's only a young lad, I'll bet his mom and dad are waiting up for him. Nice car, or was. Bet they're not short of a bob or two."

"Probably been boozing," opined his partner. "When will they learn to wear seat belts eh? It's a nasty bit of road here, we've had 'em here before, John. It's a killer this road."

"I know. But what beats me is why. It's a straight bit of road, well lit. There's no reason for it. There was that couple last year, over the other side there..."

"I remember. He died, drove straight off the road for no reason, she said. You know what I think? I think it's haunted."

"That's not as far-fetched as you might think. Why do you think that's called Bury Hill?" said John, nodding to the park.

"What? Do you mean?"

"I don't know, but it's a bit of a coincidence isn't it? So, yes, haunted, cursed, I can well believe it. Don't tell anybody at the station though, they'll think we're mad."

"Don't worry, I won't. Right, let's get him to the morgue."